UNDER AN EVER-
SETTING SUN

The Ever-Setting Sun – Book 1

to Dean,
thank you for supporting
Indie authors!

Mdphillips

MATTHEW PHILLIPS

⊞⊞ Northwood Press

Special thanks to:

Kevin, Dario, Laura, Cristian, Mark, Adam, and JJ

~ THE TWILIGHT CITY OF ~
LA CROSSE

Isla Fuego

Isla Hovella

Isla Festa

Isla Punta

Isla Leonora

Isla Hannah

Isla Puntina

Isla Okinawo

Isla Antonia

Isla Sierra
Maestra

Isla Manza

Isla Fosch

Isla Clara

Isla De Zan

Isla Roble

Isla Pasifina

Isla Montana

Isla Don-Croix

Isla Euchara

Isla Muerto

Isla Verdinho

Isla A'Vellio

Isla Caracas

Isla De Castro

Lac Castration

Isla Rasta

Isla Nouveax Croix

Isla Dijon

Isla Vecta

Isla Arkaya

Isla Rosa

Islas Hermos

Isla
Roja

Isla Verdé

Isla Virga

Ponté L'Emilia

Flotsam

Prologue

The great tapestry hung infinite on one wall of the weaver's mind, its ethereal strands glowing with a beguiling rainbow radiance, each thread a life. The past stretched out above her; the unbroken weave of generations of her forebears disappearing into the gloom of distant antiquity. But below her – where the tapestry should stretch eternal into a peaceful, nurtured future – it instead ended abruptly in fire and death. Sundered and smouldering, every last thread would soon be cut and cauterised and, in the destruction of the tapestry, the weaver foresaw the destruction of the world. There would be no future past that point.

Carefully, she traced the malignant thread back from where it would cause the rupture. It was as beautiful as it was familiar, so innocent yet so destructive. Her forebears had looped and twisted the thread; had bought the world more time – a full century – but now their time was running out.

Smiling, she reassured herself that it was not yet too late, that the future might yet be saved. Her younger self had been anxious and in need of such reassurance, but the weaver had grown much in confidence since she set out on this path, scared but determined to succeed even where all other weavers had failed. It had taken fifteen years, but she had taught herself how to read the warp and weft of fate; how to weave the threads that might avert the coming cataclysm.

With the disembodied hands of her mind, she grasped the malignant thread and the six others that she'd patiently woven around it, casting her mind's eyes over her work with grim satisfaction. She was nearly done with her part – with weaving the strangers together – but she knew the rest was beyond the grasp of fate. Her success would depend on the choices those strangers made.

She opened her eyes – her real eyes – and beheld the city that sprawled across the twilight horizon in front of her; acid green, dark and drear. She nodded her thanks to the ferryman, feeling its cold dead gaze bore into her from beneath its tattered hood. It reached out a skeletal hand, its ancient blackened bones draped in ragged scraps of parchment skin, and she clasped it, steadying herself as she stepped up from the dismal little river-raft onto the dilapidated jetty.

She kept the seven threads with her as she set off to complete her weave. Her anxious younger self followed her into the city.

CHAPTER 1

A strong wet wind filled the sails of the triple-masted clipper Volant as she cut through the cresting waves, shearing sprays of salty water into the evening air. The ever-setting sun sat low on the western horizon – as it always did – casting its ever-waning light across the twilight realm, and silvering the wave-tips of the ocean with its pale argent glow. Long shadows tottered drunkenly across the Volant's deck as the ship pitched up and down on inky waves, her bow rising and falling with the easy rhythm of the sea.

The Volant was a good ship, one of many fast clippers that plied the trade routes around the twin continents of the known world, and across the Gulf of Mezarcana that separated them. Having been at sea for several months, she was finally on her way home; profitably laden with ice and grain and paying passengers for the last leg of her voyage.

Expectant faces broadened into beaming smiles as the Volant's destination came into view ahead; first as an eerie lime-green halo just over the horizon, then soon after as a dense green glow uplighting the twilight sky. The dense green glow of thousands of viridian lamps; the dense green glow of La Crosse.

Thessu watched on as the other passengers clamoured to see the city; to be the first to make out the core islands, or perhaps the famous bridges or the Ziggurat. Smiling inwardly at their giddiness, he resisted the temptation to join the press of eager people. In truth, he was just as excited as they, but giddiness had been frowned upon at the monastery.

Years of strict discipline had taught him patience; there would be plenty of time in the coming weeks and months of his posting to see the city from every conceivable angle. Years of strict discipline had taught Thessu not to clamour.

Continuing its approach towards La Crosse – the city of a thousand isles – the Volant soon skirted past the farthest outcropping of land that guarded the city's south-eastern approach; a slender spit of rock thrusting sheer out of the waves, topped by a soaring lighthouse that shone with emerald light at its summit. Beyond, the massed green glow of the city soon resolved into several distinct clumps of chartreuse light – those being the many teeming islands of La Crosse – while smaller twinkling pin-pricks were no doubt the viridian lamps of the many boats in constant transit around the city.

The Volant passed a larger island next; a sprawling low-lying morass which had the press of passengers squawking delightedly in recognition. They had spotted that this was no island at all, but instead a ramshackle floating platform formed of hundreds of wrecked and salvaged hulks, an impossible wooden raft structure supporting a vast jerry-rigged shanty town; the infamous pirate outpost of Flotsam.

A flicker of trepidation touched Thessu's eyes beneath his mask at the sight of that outpost of villainy, and he turned to check the presence of the Volant's escort ship astern. It was still there, a sleek pirate galley with the red sails of the Scarlet Fist; paid protection for this final leg of the journey.

The Volant soon passed the artificial island, unmolested by its attendant fleet of scavenger ships, and her shadowy escort then peeled away towards the outpost, slowing to dock alongside an outlying pontoon. The Volant continued towards the city unaccompanied, and Thessu saw the relief on the faces of the two marines charged with security aboard the ship as they safed and shouldered their muskets.

The vista ahead opened up as the ship cleared the outlying islands, and Thessu finally got his first proper look at La Crosse. The city was the largest in the northern continent, and patience be damned if he didn't press forward through the crowd, craning his neck to take more in. The throng of passengers parted, unnerved by his presence as they had been for the entire voyage, and Thessu soaked in his first sight of the city.

The ancient city state of La Crosse was the gateway to the interior of the northern continent, sitting as it did astride the Poconovo Delta, where the great Poconovo river emptied into the Gulf of Mezarcana. The land here, such as it was, was low-lying and swampy; most of the islands of the city having been reclaimed from the surrounding mangrove swamp over many hundreds of years. Regular dredging of the channels kept them navigable – indeed the mighty Poconovo was navigable for hundreds of miles into the interior of the continent – but the treacherous shallows and strong currents of the river delta kept Flotsam well supplied with wrecks.

It was easy now to pick out the large central islands of the city from the many dozens of smaller isles and islets ahead, all sprawling with buildings and teeming with life, and all twinkling with acid green light. Isla Roja – the administrative heart of the city – was particularly hard to miss, dominated as it was by the enormous Ziggurat of the Basilica Grandé and the many grand palazzos that surrounded it. An adjacent island was connected to Isla Roja by three bridges which spanned the narrow river channel that separated them. Overcrowded and overflowing, Thessu recognised that larger island as Isla Verdé – the city's commercial centre – and he smiled, for the end of his journey was in sight.

Shouts went up from the first mate, and the crew of the Volant got to work reeling in the sails in a practiced, disciplined manner. The ship momentarily slowed as it lost the wind, then, from below deck, came the click-thunk of two dozen galley ports snapping open. Moments later, long powerful oars were thrust into the water and the ship's galley corpses – the Risen dead that manned the oars – powered the ship towards its final destination, a trade berth in the dock quarter of Isla Verdé.

The vast ocean docks of the island soon loomed close; a wide vista of piers and jetties filled with sailing ships, junks and galleys of all shapes and sizes. Large ocean-going trading vessels and clippers like the Volant moored alongside smaller coastal ships and cutters, as well as ferries and steam barges that plied the waterways of the city and the inland settlements and plantations upriver. The docks were a bustle of activity as ships loaded and unloaded cargo and passengers.

Thessu watched – fascinated – as teams of porter corpses carried huge loads on their skeletal shoulders, moving goods from the docked vessels to the dock-front warehouses, or to waiting wagons hitched to skeletal horses. What had at first seemed like a chaotic hubbub was actually an efficient and orderly ballet of goods and people. "Order appears from chaos," he muttered under his breath. That was one of the mantras of his order.

Remaining on deck to watch the Volant approach and join the ballet of the dock, Thessu was unmoved by the crew attempting to clear the deck for docking. The pilot expertly guided the ship towards a vacant berth, the deck crew signalling instructions by whistle to the galleymaster and crew below deck. Two pips signalled the galley corpses to pause after the next stroke, then two longer toots signalled a rapid backstroke to slow the ship to a stop. Other signals had the Risen corpses ease forward on one side and backwards on the other to turn the ship in place, manoeuvring it slowly into position alongside a wooden jetty.

The other passengers had been hustled to their cabins below deck by the ship's steward to collect their belongings and prepare to disembark, but Thessu had nothing to collect; he was already wearing everything he owned. Besides the dark green hooded robes knotted at the waist and the beaked leather medical mask that were a symbol of his order, he had a brown leather satchel slung over one shoulder and a pair of tan leather gloves. He fiddled idly with his gloves while he watched the docking manoeuvre, pulling his fingertips back and forth inside the supple leather. Catching himself fidgeting, he tutted, imagining Brother Superior's disapproving look. Brother Superior always wore a disapproving look.

Instead, Thessu reached into a pocket and withdrew once more the dog-eared scrap of parchment he'd been staring at for the entire voyage, and once again tried to make sense of it. It was a cryptic vision from Mother Oracle, the ancient seer at the heart of his order. He knew the words by heart of course, but still he read them again, searching for new insight.

'The southern queen arrived at last, a century deserted. Thessu finds the witch was cast, a doom may be averted.'

The first line was obvious, and had brought him on this voyage to the far-off northern continent and its capital city of La Crosse. Everyone in the twin continents had heard the story of the Queen of the South, a paddle steamer that had disappeared a hundred years ago on its maiden voyage down the Poconovo. However that wasn't what made the Queen famous, for ships vanished all the time; sunk by treacherous waters or storms or captured by pirates.

The famous part was that the ship had finally arrived a year ago, intact and undamaged, with its crew and passengers seemingly unaware that a century had passed since they set off. Nobody knew why. Or rather, the retelling of the story that had spread to all corners of the realm had not included a consistent cause; there were too many explanations, not too few. Thessu would seek out the truth. "Truth wins out from lies," he muttered. That was another of the mantras.

No, it was the second line of Mother Oracle's vision that perplexed him. *'Thessu finds the witch was cast, a doom may be averted.'*

What witch was the vision referring to? What did it mean that she was cast? Cast overboard perhaps? Did the witch have something to do with the ship's disappearance? And what was the doom that may be averted? Most intriguing was that he'd been named personally in the vision, which was unheard of; he hadn't even known that Mother Oracle knew his name. Maybe she didn't. She knew things she didn't know when she was struck by her visions.

He knew he would never have been selected for anything as important as a vision quest across the ocean if Mother Oracle hadn't foreseen his involvement. Even Brother Superior couldn't object to his assignment of this mission. He had frowned deeply though; Brother Superior always frowned deeply.

Thessu's contemplation was interrupted by the clunking of galley ports as the ship's Risen withdrew their oars in response to a final trill of the whistle. The pilot and galleymaster had manoeuvred them perfectly alongside the jetty; no mean feat in the swirling eddies of the delta and the mischievous half-light of the ever-setting sun. Crewmen threw mooring ropes to waiting corpses on the dockside, and the ship was soon tied off and the gangplank lowered. They had arrived.

Thessu folded the slip of parchment in half and returned it to his pocket, then adjusted his mask to ensure a snug fit around his nose and mouth. Walking over to the gangplank, he offered his hand to the crewman standing nearby. The man reacted instinctively, grasping Thessu's hand in a firm grip, before realising whose hand he was shaking. His grip loosened as he tried to take back his hand, aghast. Thessu placed his other hand over the man's, holding him in the grip and shaking vigorously to the man's immense discomfort.

"Thank you so much for a wonderful voyage, I have enjoyed my time aboard the Volant immensely," Thessu exulted loudly, his words emerging slightly muffled by his mask.

Looking extremely uncomfortable, the man stammered a polite "y...you're welcome," and Thessu considered embracing him in a hug; the man's mortification was very amusing. He decided against it, and instead held the man's grip for a long moment beyond what was necessary for a handshake. The man blinked, a pleading look in his eyes, and Thessu relented with a sigh.

Releasing him, Thessu stepped gingerly down the gangplank, and set off into the city to find the Queen of the South.

***

De Ville Manor was once a grand brick-built mansion in an overly-ornamental gothic style, built over three stories with a steep mansard roof of grey slate, and an ornate double-height wrought iron portico flanked by asymmetrical square pitched-roof turrets. Some three hundred years ago, the third Baron De Ville had built the manor on a small islet that he'd won at cards – or so the family history maintained – and it had been the family home of the De Villes until the fourteenth and final Baron De Ville had died childless and without heirs thirty years ago. Since then the house had fallen almost to ruin.

The islet – Isla Festa – sat on the very outskirts of La Crosse, in the thick of the impenetrable swamp at the far fringe of the Poconovo Delta. Abandoned after the death of the last Baron, its shoreline had since been consumed by mangroves, sealing it off from the surrounding swamp. The mangroves, revelling in their victory in that battle over this far-flung outpost of the city, had been tightening the noose on the islet's interior ever since.

However, Isla Festa – uninhabited for three decades – had for the past year been home to precisely one inhabitant, who had taken up residence in the derelict and overgrown manor. He had spent the past year working tirelessly to clear thirty years of overgrowth from the islet, cut back thirty years of mangrove growth from its shore, dredge thirty years of swamp from its shallows, and patch up thirty years of neglect around the house. He had boarded up windows, patched holes in the walls and roof, replaced shutters and stairs and doors, unblocked chimneys and gutters and gargoyles and fixed up much more besides. He had to; he was lord of this manor.

After a century lost aboard the Queen of the South, the eleventh Baron De Ville had returned to his family home to find it overcome by the swamp and abandoned, his family line ended three generations after he was lost, and all his relatives deceased.

When he had first returned, he had come triumphant in his finest white pinstripe suit, worn over a collared black shirt and white silk cravat and accessorised with a matching top-hat, cape and cane. Anticipating his return to first shock and scandalise the present Baron and his family, he had expected to then be warmly welcomed as a treasured ancestor... after all, he had also brought Belle home.

There was to be no triumphant return. Nor was there a delicious scandal or anything like a warm welcome. Instead, he had had to hack through the swamp to reach the islet, and had found the front door ajar, rotting on its hinges, and with an alligator nesting in the parlour.

It was not the return he had hoped for, but at least the house was largely intact, and most of its contents – the priceless heirlooms of his family – seemed to be untouched except by time and neglect. He had felt the reassuring weight of history and the stirring of his ancestors as he stepped inside, and had resolved to restore his family's manor and their prestige.

He had hung his hat and cape on a coat hook by the door, under the suspicious glare of the alligator. Regretting his choice of clothing, he had frowned at the trouser legs of his white pinstripe suit, which had been soaked brown with muddy water to the knee while the jacket had been splattered with more mud and filth.

He had looked warily at the alligator and the alligator had looked warily back. The Baron was pale and slight of build, with jet-black hair oiled smooth. He had sunken hollows under his dark eyes and a pencil moustache over a perpetual crooked smile; for despite his sallow features, his face was more often joyful than not. In the top pocket of his suit jacket where the handkerchief should have been, there instead had been tucked a whimsical knitted doll with brown button eyes.

The alligator had snorted as the coat hook fell, dumping the Baron's hat and coat into the puddle of mud and detritus in the doorway. "I am glad I amuse you," he had said to the alligator while smiling his crooked smile, before picking the garments up and dusting them off with a glint in his eye.

"Shall we show him a trick, my dear?" he had asked, winking to the doll in his pocket as he peeled off his immaculate white gloves. He had then flicked his hands over the sodden coat and hat, and the wet mud powdered into fine dust which trickled onto the floor to leave the garments looking pristine. He had then flicked his hands down his trouser legs and the mud and filth trickled dry from those as well, leaving them clean and pressed.

The alligator had snorted again – perhaps unimpressed by parlour tricks – and the Baron had admonished him with a wagging finger, while moving confidently into the room. "You might think I am an unwelcome guest in your house, but in fact you are an unwelcome guest in mine! Do you have a name?" The alligator had made no answer. "Then I shall call you… Rufus."

"Belle my dear, this is Rufus," he had said, then indicated to the lifeless doll in his pocket. "Rufus, this is Belle. And I am Baron De Ville, lord of this manor." Neither Belle nor Rufus had acknowledged the other.

The Baron next found the butler. At first he had thought it was a cadaver, propped up on the stool by the pianoforte. A cadaver with paper-thin skin pulled tight across its skull, blackened by age and decay and covered in cobwebs. The Baron had wiped and lit the dented brass lamp that sat on top of the pianoforte cabinet and the lamp had spluttered to life, uplighting the dark, shuttered chamber with eerie green light. The corpse had reacted by moving creakily on its stool, its skin cracking and splintering like crusty bread as it twisted to regard the Baron with dead eyes drawn wide by the rictus of desiccated skin.

The Baron hadn't missed a beat. "Pardon me! I didn't mean to disturb you. I am the Baron De Ville, lord of this manor, and this is Belle."

The corpse had rattled its jaw – as the Risen do – in mimicry of speech. The Baron had then leaned in towards the mummified corpse, pushing its lank locks of hair aside almost tenderly to examine the blackened copper disc that was hammered into the centre of its forehead; its marque of ownership. Rubbing aside the dirt, he had squinted at the tarnished symbols hammer-stamped into the marque. "It seems your designation is 'corpse J' and you belong to the estate. So I guess, to me."

The Baron had then released the Risen corpse's head, and they had continued to stare at each other for a long moment while he considered it. "I'm fond of naming things, J. How do you like 'Jeff'?"

The corpse had clacked its jaw in response, the taut skin of its cheek almost tearing. "Jeff it is," the Baron had declared, smiling broadly before gesturing to the pianoforte. "Do you play?"

Shaking off dust and debris, Jeff had then turned back to the pianoforte, his arms crackling and flaking as he stretched out to reach the keyboard. He had tried to play, his worn and brittle fingers tapping mechanically on worn and brittle keys, producing flat discordant notes. The Baron had winced, then spent the rest of that first eve cleaning and retuning the pianoforte while his unspeaking companions looked on. He had spent every eve since in their silent company, as he cleaned and renovated the manor.

A year had passed, and De Ville manor was still a cantankerous old derelict that stubbornly refused to be clean or fixed up. The old house seemed to enjoy its air of damp and disrepair, relishing every opportunity to leak on the Baron's head when it rained. Whole rooms were still sealed off and given over to dust and decay, but, like a stray dog begrudgingly domesticated, De Ville manor was slowly made habitable once again.

The renovations had stalled recently however, as the Baron kept losing his consciousness and blacking out. At first he found himself sleeping far longer and deeper than he ever had, and chalked his dreamless slumber up to tiredness from his labouring around the house. Then it started happening during his waking hours as well, usually whilst right in the middle of something.

His eyes would roll back in his head while hammering a nail or chopping a mangrove root, and he would be gone, his vacant husk left looking very much like a soulless corpse himself. He would just stand there stupidly holding an axe or hammer mid-swing for hours unless he was moved inside and made to sit on a chaise longue and then he would come back to his senses sometime later, usually resulting in him falling off his chaise as he continued his phantom hammer or axe swing.

For hours, sometimes whole eves at a time he would be completely gone from his body, then return just as suddenly as he had left, having no idea where he had been in the meantime. For that was what it felt like; like suddenly leaving his body and going elsewhere for a time, and then returning to it later. Not only was it very frustrating, but also he had no idea why it was happening. He resolved to find out.

***

The outer island of Isla Hovella was a dense shanty town of overcrowded multi-storey wooden lean-tos, which overspilled the narrow sandbar of the island proper, and into the dismal everglade swamp beyond. Each of the rickety interconnected structures of the shanty was built on thick wooden stilts driven deep into the sand of the island and the pungent muddy swamp that surrounded it.

The poorest and most dispossessed of La Crosse made their homes in the outer island slums, far from the heart of the city. Here on the outskirts, the city still had to fight the swamp for dominance, the swamp claiming victories where shanty neighbourhoods became overgrown and abandoned, or sank outright into the soft silt. Isla Hovella was typical of the outer islands on the front line of this battle; densely packed and squalid, its urban environment in constant flux as shanties were built and extended around and on top of existing structures, or left to ruin and swallowed by the swamp.

Thousands of people called Isla Hovella their home. Many of them commuted by river bus to jobs on more central islands or else scraped a living in the slum, doing menial work ordinarily done elsewhere by Risen corpses. The Risen were not a common sight on Isla Hovella; few could afford them.

Epifani picked her way back to her hideout, where she had been enjoying the wonderful anonymity that came from lying low in a place like this, among the dregs of society where nobody cared who she was or what she'd done. Just another faceless nameless nobody, carrying in her arms a basket of supplies.

She wasn't supposed to leave the safehouse. She was supposed to wait with the haul of stolen antiques while her associate found buyers, but he had never returned, and she had run out of food. So she had left the loot and gone out for some supplies, and now – having bought some – she made her way back to her hideout through narrow enclosed alleys and across precarious walkways, keeping her face hidden and avoiding other people as much as possible.

Enjoying being out of the hideout for the first time in several weeks, she took a deep breath of the pungent air. She smelled the rancid sulphurous smell of the swamp, mingled with the sweat and shit and damp of the shanty. She took a moment to savour it, and breathed deeply again; her face crinkling into a half smile. She had never thought she would appreciate the smell of poverty – indeed she didn't, it was rank – she was savouring the lack of Risen.

The Risen didn't just smell of death, they also had an all-pervading aura of darkness around them; a baleful aura that chilled the soul. The people of Twilight had largely grown accustomed to the discomforting presence of their Risen servants and no longer noticed it, but Epifani had always been sensitive to it; always despised it. She felt the presence of the Risen like a cancer gnawing at the edges of her mind.

As a child, her sensitivity to the Risen had been seen by her family as a gift, and when she was of age, enquiries had been made of the guild as to whether she might be accepted for training as a necromancer; an honourable and lucrative profession well suited to a younger daughter of a minor noble house. But the house of Pye was not to gain a necromancer, for Epifani loathed the Risen, and that childhood trip to the guild had forever marked her an outcast.

She absently touched the scars on her cheeks that she'd gotten that eve at the guild; the eve her path became clear to her... the eve she had dedicated her life to ending the practice of universal undeath. For millennia, the dead had served the living, but she would do whatever it took to end that disgusting practice.

She sighed wistfully at what she had given up to take a stand against the Risen, and where that stand had gotten her, as she trudged alone across the shit-sodden alleys of the shanty carrying her meagre basket of flatbreads and charred fish.

She found herself wondering again why her associate hadn't returned. He'd always been reliable in the past; always professional. She knew little about him of course, not even his name, and she had never entirely trusted him – he was a thief after all – but she had trusted he would return for the loot if nothing else.

They had planned the heist together; had worked for weeks to get into the Ziggurat, and out again with the relics. It was an audacious plan, executed flawlessly and they had struck the death cult a heavy blow; had stolen valuable artifacts used in their most important rituals. Her associate didn't hate the Risen like she did of course, didn't care about striking the death cult a heavy blow like she did; he was in it for the money. So where was he?

She had just bought enough bread and fish to last another week, and she resolved to stay put in the hideout until her new supplies ran out, and then she would return to the core islands to find him. He had given her the name of an emergency contact in case anything went wrong; a fixer on Isla Verdé who dealt in favours. If her associate didn't return, she would start the search for him there.

As she approached the alleyway that led to the safehouse, the hairs on her neck stood up. Her subconscious was telling her that something wasn't right, and she puzzled for a moment to account for her disquiet.

Then she realised. The alleyway was too quiet; the upstairs neighbours weren't yelling at each other, the leering youths who fancied themselves gangsters had cleared off, and gone too was the scrawny couple who plied their trade as hookers on the corner. Only the old vagrant sailor who lived in the hovel at the end of the alley and spent all eve drinking rum and shouting obscenities was still there, and he too was oddly silent.

Epifani took all this in as she approached the alley, and made the snap decision not to enter and to instead keep walking past. She was sensitive to more than just Risen, and had learnt to trust her senses, especially when they told her something was wrong.

Pulling the hood of her cloak down further to better cover her face, she continued past the alley and on towards the nearest main thoroughfare, hastily forming a plan in her mind to head for the river dock and pay a local youth to scout her alleyway and report back.

She made her way up a flight of wooden steps and onto the thoroughfare. The rickety wooden-decked catwalks of the thoroughfares were raised above the swampy ground, criss-crossing the island as they passed over, under and through the shanty dwellings. This was one of the busier routes across Isla Hovella, and led down to the larger of the two river docks that served the island.

Makeshift structures pressed against the thoroughfare from all sides or were built haphazardly above and below it, fully enclosing the catwalks and blocking sight of the twilight sky. She strode on through the dusky yellow-green light of the lamps that hung above the catwalks or that seeped out through cracks in the walls and shuttered windows of the shanty buildings either side, the green glow mingling with snatches of twilight in those rare gaps where the ever-setting sun could be seen to the west.

It was clear that the river bus had just arrived and disgorged its passengers, as the walkway ahead was busy with people heading up from the dock. Hesitating, Epifani wondered if she shouldn't just go back to her hideout, but she decided to follow her instinct and press on down the thoroughfare.

As she walked, she was assailed by the many sights and sounds and smells of slum life happening around her, but she focused her senses to try and pick out any more signs of things being amiss. She heard her boots clacking on the weathered boards of the catwalk, and smelled the familiar salt and sulphur of the swamp and the stale faecal timber of the slum. She realised she was being followed. She could see it in the faces of the people she passed; someone was following her. Someone unwelcome and unfamiliar and unsubtle; in fact a few someones.

Epifani quickened her pace to try and lose her pursuers, whoever they were, and moved nimbly through the oncoming crowd of workers heading up from the dock. Sidestepping to avoid an old man pulling a covered handcart, she took the opportunity to glance back along the thoroughfare behind her. Her breath caught as she saw them; two hooded figures in black robes edged in gold thread and golden faceless masks. Their vestments identified them as zealots from the Ziggurat; priests of the nasty death cult that venerated and regulated the practice of raising the dead here in the northern continent.

As soon as she saw them, she knew that her instincts had been right, and she pressed on towards the dock. Her hideout was lost to her. Dammit, her haul was lost to her! How the hell had they found her? She couldn't think about it; she had to get off the island.

The catwalk sloped down towards the dock, and the shanty thinned out to reveal patches of twilight sky between the buildings, and patches of foetid swamp between the rickety planks underfoot. Hastening past the last of the crowd of commuters, Epifani risked another glance over her shoulder and saw the hooded zealots pushing people aside not thirty yards behind. The reflection of dusky twilight glinted off the faceless golden masks of the zealots as their eyes met hers, then they broke into a run, and Epifani threw back her hood and did the same.

She tossed aside her basket of bread and fish, which upended onto the catwalk, spilling its contents and sending one of the flatbreads cartwheeling downhill after her. The downward slope of the catwalk was steep enough to make sprinting risky, and Epifani very nearly lost her footing as she dodged around a mother and children, but managed to stay upright.

Stumbling past the last of the shanty structures, she finally emerged from the slum and onto the waterfront, where the wide vista of the city and the Poconovo Delta opened up before her as a vast rippling riverscape. The familiar miasma of viridian light from the teeming islands of La Crosse lent a green tinge to the pale dusk light of the ever-setting sun, low on the horizon behind the city to the west.

Epifani sensed the Risen before she saw them, an ominous unnatural shadow scratching at her mind, along the waterfront dock to her left. So she bolted to the right, where she saw the wooden jetty where the river bus docked a hundred yards along the waterfront; the crew of that craft pushing off with a long pole. Risking a glance back along the path not taken to see what she had sensed, she saw two more zealots heading her way along the waterfront, with a cohort of ghoulish Risen spearmen loping along behind them. The departing river bus was her only chance …but she wasn't going to make it!

With reckless haste, Epifani ran as fast as she could towards the departing vessel. Behind her, she heard the clatter of someone tripping and the yelp of children being clattered into. A woman let loose a string of curses and Epifani didn't need to look back to see her pursuers had bowled through the mother and children she had just passed. They were close. She kept her focus on the departing bus.

The bus was a rickety steam barge with a shallow draft and a coal-fired boiler amidships, belching smoke from a tall brass chimney pipe, as large steam-powered paddle wheels either side of the hull churned the water, spinning rapidly to gain traction to pull the barge forward and away from the jetty. The bus had an open deck fore and aft of the boiler, both decks full of passengers holding the wooden gunwale that ran the perimeter of the deck, as barge corpses shovelled coal into the boiler.

Ignoring the burn in her muscles, Epifani summoned a last burst of speed, accelerating towards the end of the jetty. She launched herself into a head-first dive towards the stern of the river bus, her arms and legs spinning for purchase in the air to try and gain her the extra few feet she needed to reach the boat. It wasn't enough; it couldn't be enough. She wasn't going to make it. She sucked in a deep breath and held it as, looking down, she saw the foetid water of the swamp rushing up to meet her belly flop.

When her palms slammed onto something hard, she was so surprised that she almost let the gunwale of the boat slip through her fingers. Almost. Her hands clamped on instinctively, her fingernails gouging across the grain of the coal-blackened wood before she found purchase. She held her grip as the rest of her body swung into the stern of the barge with a slam that winded her and left her feet and calves dragging through the boat's churning wake.

Passengers on deck hauled her up and helped her in, crowing and laughing about her jump, but she could barely hear them, her heartbeat was so loud. One beat. Two beats. Three.

Looking behind, she saw both pairs of zealots reach the end of the jetty and stop, with their ghoulish cohort close behind. One of them gestured to the next jetty over, where some other boats were moored up, and they all hastened in that direction. They disappeared from view as the bus turned towards the south-west. Towards the core islands. Good.

CHAPTER 2

Thessu screeched to a halt at the far side of the northern jetty of the Isla Doblé river dock, alongside the harbourmaster's cabin. The Risen were usually ponderous and slow, but they could move quickly when properly motivated, and he'd paid the fat-faced man at the rickshaw stand extra to ensure his rickshaw corpse was properly motivated.

He hadn't actually been in any great hurry – indeed Thessu hadn't meant to hire a rickshaw at all – but flicking open the filter slits on his mask to get a sense of the city, he had caught a whiff of the fat-faced man's illness. He hadn't noticed him there at all, else he would have kept his mask tightly sealed and filtered, and simply walked to Isla Doblé.

Instead, he had sucked in the shit and rot of La Crosse – unpleasant but not unexpected – and had gotten a side order of gout and gonorrhoea. He couldn't help the man; or perhaps he could, but didn't want to be waylaid so close to the end of his long journey. He had felt sympathetic enough to want to give the man something though, so he gave him a silver coin of the southern continent. Once he realised he'd inadvertently rented a rickshaw from the man, he gave him extra to spur it faster. He was glad he did when the corpse took off at speed; the journey through the busy streets of Isla Verdé and across the pier bridge to Isla Doblé was made much more fun that way.

He had relaxed in the wheeled chair and taken in the sights of the city as the corpse sprinted him through the bustling streets of Isla Verdé, sending other people and Risen workers flying out of the way. The maritime district – with its squat, functional warehouses and workshops – had quickly given way to the elaborate multi-storey balconied boulevards and bordellos of the commercial centre, where the lights shone brighter and the curses flung at him were more imaginative. The rickshaw had then dashed across the densely packed Piazza Grandé that separated the city's two arenas – which smelled vile – and on through the quieter back streets of the northern quarter, then on to Isla Doblé.

He had also managed to avoid paying a toll on the Doblé bridge – the long wooden piered bridge that connected Doblé to Verdé – as his rickshaw had pelted past the toll-booth midway across, even as the Risen corpse manning it had rattled both its jaw and its collection box in his direction. His rickshaw had then continued on round the esplanade of Isla Doblé to the river dock from where the Poconovo passenger ferries launched.

Risen don't breathe or perspire, so it was no surprise that his rickshaw corpse wasn't panting or sweating after the exertion of the sprint. They show their fatigue in other ways though, and this one was definitely showing signs; swaying side to side with its jaw lolling open and its shoulders drooping. It had done well to skip the toll – Thessu hadn't thought it would – and enough people had had to duck out of his way while cursing him and calling him a menace for it to have been pretty good fun.

Stepping down from the chair of the rickshaw, he placed some extra coins in the tip box that swung on a chain around the corpse's neck. The corpse rattled its jaw at him in thanks, then it turned to wheel its rickshaw back in the direction from whence they had come, slowly this time and still noticeably fatigued.

A group of dock workers were congregated outside the harbourmaster's cabin, sipping hot sweet-smelling drinks from ceramic mugs. Whatever they had been talking about had been interrupted by Thessu's arrival, and they looked over suspiciously. One of them made a mocking remark to the others, whilst holding his empty mug over his nose like a beak, and they all stifled a laugh, their suspicion turning to amusement.

Thessu adjusted his beaked mask and strode over. "Lady and Gentlemen, I'm wondering if you can help me. I'm looking for a particular paddle steamer; the Queen of the South. I was told it was moored at this dock?"

The dock workers – three men and a woman – stifled further laughter. "You a lil' early, friend," said the largest of the four, an imposing man with a bald head, speaking in the deep south accent of the Poconovo bayou.

"Early?" Queried Thessu.

"I'll show ya, hon," said the woman of the group, pressing her hand on the arm of the bald man as she stepped past him. Draining her drink, she handed her empty mug to one of the other men – the one who'd made the mocking remark – and walked over to Thessu.

"This way," she said, gesturing towards the far end of the jetty, and set off in that direction. Steam barges and cargo ferries were moored up at intervals along the jetty, but there was no sign of any larger passenger steamers.

The woman walked at a brisk pace, which Thessu matched, and she eyed him curiously as they walked. "Y'aint from here are ya?" she asked, and Thessu shrugged noncommittally.

She pressed further, "Southern continent?" and Thessu shrugged again. "Ain'tcha goin' talk? What's with the beak?"

Stopping abruptly, Thessu turned towards her. The woman took another pace, then stopped as well, a quizzical look on her face. Thessu flicked open the filter slits of his mask and took in the air, then closed them again. She was healthy at least. "You're ovulating," he said dispassionately. "And you are aroused in the presence of the large bald man back there. Those facts are probably related." The woman's quizzical look became an affronted glare.

"Also, you have a dog which you let lick your face. You shouldn't; your dog has worms." They walked on in silence.

At the end of the jetty, they turned a corner, and the woman gestured to a row of three huge wooden structures that stood nearby, fronting directly onto the water.

"There," she said tersely. "The Queen is bein' refurbished in the first dock. It's bein' modernised. Won't be no more sailin's for a couple months," and she turned abruptly and strode back towards the harbourmaster's hut.

Thessu looked up at the structures. What he had taken for warehouses were actually three covered docks, sealed off from the river by huge wooden river doors. They were certainly big enough to house a paddle steamer, he thought, and it would make sense that refurbishments would happen under cover. He saw printed posters had been plastered on the side of the structure, and walked closer to read them.

The posters were newly printed, all identical. *'Coming Soon,'* they announced in bold writing, *'The River of Destiny!'*

That text was overlayed over a picture of a paddle steamer – presumably the Queen of the South – being attacked by a medley of monsters including giant alligators and a kraken. Below that was more text.

'The amazing true story of one man's hundred year struggle to return home, retold by the realm's most renowned mystery writer, the one and only Sofokles of Halla!'

Thessu snorted derisively at the last exclamation. Sofokles of Halla was a renowned hack. He guessed that any novelisation by that man would be a complete work of fiction.

'The illustrious author will be reading from his ouvre,' the poster continued, *'and signing copies of his work at the following time and place...'*

A space had been left for a time and place to be added, which had been filled in by hand; overmorrow's-eve at ninebells at an auditorium in the necromancers' guild. The hand-written entry concluded with an announcement.

'Special guests in attendance: Gerard Malblanq and Joanna Pianna!' Thessu had no idea who they were.

Ultimately, he knew he would find no truths in any book by Sofokles of Halla, but he decided to go, if only to tell the man that 'oeuvre' had two 'e's. He peeled one of the posters off the wall, noting the glue was still tacky; it must have only been hung recently. He folded it neatly in half and half again, then slipped it into the front pocket of his satchel.

Putting that out of his mind, he looked for a way into the covered dock structure. He was interested in facts not fiction, and so he was eager to examine the Queen of the South to try and uncover some clues about its disappearance.

He repeated the words from Mother Oracle's vision; *'The southern queen arrived at last, a century deserted. Thessu finds the witch was cast, a doom may be averted.'*

He hoped he could learn something from the vessel about the witch and the doom. First though, he had to get in, and he was very much hoping to find a nice doorway so he wouldn't have to swim in under the river door.

He found an entrance on the other side of the covered dock, a pair of wooden double doors fronting onto a path between the structure and the neighbouring one. Having heard no sounds of refurbishment happening within – or indeed any noises from within – he was saddened but unsurprised to find the doors locked shut. Sighing again, he rattled the padlock, muttering under his breath. "Purity of purpose demands..." but he had forgotten the end of the tenth mantra. "...sausages?" It definitely wasn't sausages. Sacrifices, maybe? He walked over to the water's edge and started stripping.

He removed his boots and gloves, placing them beside his satchel with his green robe neatly folded on top. Bracing for the overwhelming stench of the city, he removed his mask last of all. His eyes watered as the foul humours all but overwhelmed his senses, and he tried not to focus on the scent.

Sitting down on the dockside, he focussed instead on his shrivelled reflection in the rippling water below. Long years of wearing the mask as an initiate and then a novice of his order had left a deep oval rut around the features of his face; an airless seal within which his skin had grown pallid and wrinkled and inhuman.

Resisting the urge to scratch the scales of itchy flaky skin on his cheeks and jowls, he lowered himself slowly into the water, which was cold and oily with a surface film of scum. Edging along the side of the dock to the structure, he kept his head above the water as long as he could. Then, with no further handholds, he took a deep breath and submerged himself.

The water was dark and cloudy with silt and sand, and tasted brackish from where the swirling eddies of the delta carried salt upstream from the south. He swam down, feeling with one hand for the bottom of the door, and upon finding it, pulled himself under and began to swim back up inside the covered dock.

He broke the surface and cursed. The covered dock was empty. The Queen of the South was missing.

***

The Baron returned to his body with a start, and fell off his chaise longue. How long had he been gone? A moment before, he had been scraping bat guano from the floor of the attic room of the north turret, when rain had started pattering on the window shutter and he had reached for his umbrella, expecting the roof to spring a leak above his head at any moment. Had he managed to raise the umbrella in time? Pushing himself up off the floor, he felt his head. Damp. That answered both questions; he hadn't managed to raise his umbrella in time, and he'd been gone no more than an hour or two.

He became aware of a commotion outside; the muffled sounds of thrashing around and splashing. It sounded like someone had tried to approach the house, and had fallen into the alligator pit.

He looked over at Jeff, perched as ever at the pianoforte across the room. Jeff looked back, making no attempt to rise. Sighing, the Baron brushed the guano off the knees of his trousers and strode to the front door, his suit once more pristine.

Outside, the rain had stopped, but the front lawn and gravel paths were slick with dirty brown puddles. Three men in brown donkey jackets and flat caps were the cause of the commotion. One of them – a lanky young man whose jacket was at once too loose in the chest and too short in the arms – had indeed fallen into the alligator pit, and was splashing around trying to fend off an irate alligator.

Rufus, the alligator, was in no mood for uninvited guests in ill-fitting jackets, and was snapping angrily at the man, while the man's colleagues – one a squat, portly man, whose jacket was too tight; the other an older gentleman with a bushy white beard whose jacket was inside out – both peered down at him from the far bank.

The lanky man in the pit yelled up, "Dal! you gotta get me outta here, that bloody crocodile is gonna eat me!"

The portly man on the bank yelled back, "I fink it's an alligator not a crocodile." Rufus snapped angrily at the man in the pit. "See, look, I fink you 'urt its feelings, Rud!"

"I'm not worried about 'urting its feelings!" the lanky man replied. "I'm worried about givin' it bloody indigestion!"

The Baron watched on, amused, as the lanky man in the pit grabbed a long branch and waved it furiously at Rufus the alligator while the other two men offered unhelpful advice. Rufus snapped at the branch, and finally grasped the end of it in his powerful jaws, then angrily shook it side to side, shaking the man with it. The lanky man wrenched it back, pulling so hard he fell backwards when the branch came free. He landed on his backside in the foetid mud, to sniggering from the other men and a snort of derision from Rufus. The portly man shouted down, "Come on, Rud, that's enough flirting with the wildlife. We got a job to do."

The Baron cleared his throat and they all of them looked up as one towards the house, to see the lord of the manor had emerged from within.

The portly man looked surprised to see anyone else there, his look of surprise giving way to a grimace of dissatisfaction. "Is this your crocodile sir?" he asked finally.

"Alligator, Dal!" corrected the older man beside him.

"Well I don't claim to own him," replied the Baron, "But yes it's probably fair to say he's my alligator; and also fair to say that I'm his human." To the alligator, he said, "be a good chap, Rufus old boy, and let the young man climb out. It won't do to be eating them until we've at least found out what they're here for."

The alligator begrudgingly backed away from the lanky man – whose name was evidently Rud – who scrambled back to his feet and out of the pit, with a little bit of help from the older man and none from the man whose name was Dal. It took them several minutes of squelching through the mud before Rud was safely out of the pit, though he'd had to abandon his footwear to the sucking mud; he'd tried to wade clear, and had waded right out of his boots.

Rufus got on with straightening up his nest – which had been much disturbed by the encounter – though he seemed quite happy to have been gifted a sturdy pair of boots. The alligator placed them reverently with the others in his collection in pride of place at the back of his nest on a wooden crate that served as a display stand for his treasures. Rufus did have a thing for footwear, the Baron mused. Most of his treasures were shoes that he'd acquired from who-knows-where.

Once the three men had gotten clear of the mud and walked round to the entrance portico – Rud grumbling all the while as his socks slapped wetly on the gravel path – the Baron halted them. "Now, what is your business here on my property?"

Pulling a ream of documents out of a folio he was holding, Dal stepped forward and made to square up to the Baron, straightening his shoulders and rising imperceptibly onto his tip toes. "Well sir, it's exactly this 'ere property we 'ave come to discuss." The Baron noticed he said 'this property' not 'your property'.

"We 'ave come to take possession of this 'ere property sir," Dal continued, "on behalf of its rightful owner, er..." he checked his papers, and frowned, "...which is information that is not recorded on this lawfully acquired writ of possession." He flashed the writ under the Baron's nose and the Baron had a glimpse of an official-looking printed document, stamped with a signet seal.

"The rightful owner – whoever 'e is – 'as employed us properly licensed and accredited bailiffs to take stock of the 'ouse and its contents, removin' anythin' of value, prior to demolition."

The Baron grew in his boots and loomed over the man, his jaunty smile disappearing as his face stretched and contorted with barely-restrained anger. As his mood darkened, the house darkened with it, and even the ever-waning light of dusk thinned and grew darker around him, as when the ever-setting sun disappears behind clouds. His voice deepened as the shadows around him grew, gaining more than a touch of menace in its tone and timbre. "This is De Ville Manor and I am the Baron De Ville. By what authority does another man stake a claim on my home?"

Dal physically shrank away from the Baron, looking around for support and, getting none, looked down at his papers again as he stepped back. The bailiff, clearly not expecting trouble on an uninhabited island, stuttered as he once again flashed the papers at the Baron. "The wr...wr...writ of possess-"

The Baron snatched the document from the man's hand. "I don't care about your damn writ! This is my house and my island! Get off my island before I do something you'll regret!"

The bailiff staggered backwards before recovering as the Baron's darkness ebbed away. The man looked like he might issue an ultimatum of his own, then he saw Rufus had climbed out from the pit and was waddling over to stand at the Baron's side, and seemed to think better of it. "I can see we've erm... caught you at a bad time, sir. Perhaps we should come back er... at a more convenient time?"

He reached out towards the writ, but the Baron made no move to return it, and Rufus growled a low, dangerous rumble. Withdrawing his hand with a defeated look, the bailiff backed away, gesturing for his colleagues to follow. Once safely clear, they turned and jogged quickly away down the path towards the little jetty, where they had presumably moored their boat.

The Baron watched them go, then patted Rufus gratefully and returned to the house. His darkness had now fully faded and his crooked smile had returned. "Well that was a little bit of excitement, wasn't it, my dear?" He spoke of course to Belle, the knitted doll in his pocket. He walked through to the study and placed the document down on the large leather-topped desk that dominated the room, and studied it.

It was indeed a legal writ of possession granting unfettered access to the islet for clearance and demolition work, signed and stamped by a functionary of the Cabal Court, the highest authority of La Crosse. It seemed the men had been truthful; Isla Festa and De Ville manor had a legal owner that was not him, and the owner had contracted bailiffs to carry out the work. The document didn't list the name of the legal owner, but it did give the name and address of the man who held the contract for clearance and demolition.

The Baron sighed and imagined Belle looking at him quizzically. "Yes, a big problem, my dear." He rubbed his eyes with balled fists and emerged looking grave. "We have to find out who this so-called owner is, and reclaim our home from them." Belle said nothing, her button eyes unseeing as her knitted head lay slumped against his lapel.

"I know, my dear. So first of all, you and I are going to take a little trip into town. We have to go and see the man who sent those Bailiffs. He'll be able to tell us who contracted him and issued this writ." He read the document again. The contract for clearance was held by someone called Don Gusteau, and gave an address for him on Isla Verdé. The Baron recognised the name, and frowned.

The three bailiffs, the men he just chased off, worked for a gangster.

***

The Madrigal Saloon was a tall wood-framed building that enjoyed a prime spot on the corner of a row of commercial properties fronting onto the southern esplanade of Isla Doblé, near where the Doblé bridge connected the island to Isla Verdé.

The row of buildings all had matching facades of wraparound galleried balconies, which was an architectural feature peculiar to La Crosse. The Saloon had a large downstairs bar which served a local clientele of workers and residents of Isla Doblé, and benefitted from a good deal of passing trade across the pier bridge. Above the saloon bar were three galleried stories of accommodation which was let out on a weekly basis, and rooms were also available by the hour for discerning patrons with money to spend.

The nicest of the rooms were tastefully furnished, and benefitted from private gallery balconies and river views of the Poconovo Delta looking south across Isla Verdé and Isla Roja, and to the Gulf of Mezarcana beyond. The attic room had no such luxury. In fact, it was the worst room in the place.

Sparsely furnished with just one small roof window that faced away from the ever-setting sun and therefore never let in any natural light whatsoever, it was uncomfortable, draughty and threadbare. It had a shabby wooden bed, a small table and chair and two wall-mounted viridian lamps that gave off a miserly green light, barely strong enough for reading by. The most remarkable thing about the room was the two-person rope swing that hung from the rafters above.

The solitary figure of Remy Du Rosier sat hunched over the table surrounded by the few meagre possessions he had left, staring at a *'final notice to vacate'* letter laid out on the table. He was two weeks overdue on his rent and, despite pawning everything he had left of value, he had still come up short.

Years back, when he had first arrived in La Crosse, he had been sure to meet the right people and gain the necessary introductions to become a regular fixture of the social scene. He had stayed in the Madrigal's nicest apartment, funded by one of his rich gentleman friends. He had become friends with a lot of rich, generous ladies and gentlemen and had enjoyed a privileged bohemian lifestyle of high-society parties and masked balls and cotillions. They all just adored his fiery eyes and his horns.

No longer. He was part of that scene no longer. He was their exotic plaything no longer. Also, he could put off his humiliation no longer. With no other options available to him, he would have to do the unthinkable and ask his father for money. He was regretting it already, and he hadn't even done it yet.

Remy's pre-emptive regret was interrupted by footsteps climbing up the rickety staircase that led to the attic room, and he looked up as the door swung abruptly open without so much as a knock. An amorous couple stumbled in, him kissing her neck as she fumbled with his belt buckle. Remy recognised Isabela, one of the girls who earned an hourly rate there at the Madrigal Saloon. She was a pretty girl, tall and thin with a pale complexion and strawberry blonde shoulder-length ringlets. Remy didn't recognise the man she was with. She finally triumphed over the man's buckle and looked up, startling as she noticed the room was occupied. The man's trousers slipped down, bunching about his knees, and he continued to kiss her neck.

To Remy, she said, "Oh sorry honey, I didn' see ya there, I was told this room was available …Remy? Remy is that you? I didn' know you was still here baby!"

Remy rose to his feet and bowed graciously, "Good evenin' Miss Isabela. I'm happy to say I'm here at least another eve. Madame Cass ain't cast me out jus' yet."

Brushing the amorous man off a second – he had still not looked up, or rescued his trousers – she looked almost wistfully at Remy, and asked in a low drawl, "Remy, how come you don't party any more?"

Remy looked away sadly. He didn't reply, and there was an awkward silence until Isabela continued. "Well, Madame Cass asked me to entertain Mister… er…" She scrambled to remember the man's name.

"Leroy," the man supplied, between kisses.

"…Mister Leroy," she pressed on, "and I thought we might have a go on the swing since Madame Cass tol' me the room was available… I don't want to upset Madame Cass now do I?" Remy guessed where the conversation was headed and reached for his tunic, cape and sword belt.

"Do you think y'all can take a walk for a lil' while, Remy?" Isabela urged. "I should only need an hour."

"Two hours," the man – Leroy – said without looking up. Isabela brightened.

"Two hours? Please Remy? …Unlessin' maybe you wan' stay and watch?" she continued coyly, "…or maybe join us for a bit?"

The man finally looked up at that suggestion, and gave Remy an appraising look. Remy's long twisted horns were his most distinctive feature, but he was also lean and muscular and handsome with glossy copper skin and jet black hair. Leroy actually didn't seem too averse to the idea, and he smiled winsomely. Sighing, Remy gathered the rest of his things, and went for a walk.

***

Remy had intended to go straight across the bridge to Isla Verdé, the long walk of shame to his father's place; there to eat humble pie and macarons, and scrounge enough money to stay a little longer at the Madrigal while he figured out how to fix his big mistake. He had fallen at the first hurdle, unable to take even that first step towards his father, and had walked right past the bridge and kept going, lost in dark thoughts of betrayal and guilt and vengeance.

His walk along the waterfront had taken him right round Isla Doblé on a circuit of the esplanade, and he was almost back where he started at the Madrigal. The leisurely walk had afforded him a good look at the comings and goings of the many ships docking and launching from the islands; steam barges plying the river routes, ocean-going corpse galleys and cutters coming and going from all over the twin continents, as well as flotillas of smaller craft – river busses, punts and skiffs – that threaded their way around the islands of La Crosse.

He stared for a time at the lights of the city. The many islands of La Crosse shone their green hazy glow into the silver twilight sky, to be reflected twinkling in the inky water. He marvelled – as he often had since he first came to the city – at the sheer number of people that called this place home. He had grown up in a small village deep in the swamp; it was rough and rustic and parochial, and he could never go back.

Resignedly, Remy continued along the esplanade, knowing he would have to cross the bridge and go see his father, or else keep walking laps of the island forever. Just ahead, a group of Risen porters were loading barrels onto a wagon at the side of the esplanade. The wagon was too small for the weight of all the barrels the corpses were loading, and was creaking under their weight, but Risen being Risen, they lacked the sense to stop piling more barrels on.

The inevitable happened and, with a crunch of wooden splinters, the rear axle of the wagon collapsed, dropping the wagon to the ground and scattering its load in all directions. The corpses rushed to the crippled wagon, throwing themselves in front of the heavy barrels to stop them escaping, but they weren't quick enough to stop them all. One barrel rolled clear across the esplanade, gaining speed as it careened down the slope towards the edge of the quay, where a wooden bench faced away, overlooking the steep drop to the foreshore below.

Someone was sat on the bench; a woman perhaps, though it was hard to tell with the ever-setting sun behind her. She turned at the sound of the wagon spilling its load, but either hadn't spotted the barrel racing towards her, or was frozen in place; stupéfied by indecision. She wasn't going to move in time.

Spotting the danger, Remy reacted instantly and sprinted forward to intervene. Another passer-by reacted just as quickly and also set off to stop the barrel; a teenage boy from the look of him. The kid was closer.

The kid reached the barrel a split second later and Remy, still closing the distance, realised the well-meaning youth had no idea what he was doing or how he might stop the runaway barrel from striking the woman on the bench. Flailing at it with both arms, the kid succeeded only in bowling himself over, and he tumbled clear having singularly failed to stop it. His intervention had marginally slowed the rolling barrel though, which maybe bought Remy the heartbeat he needed to get ahead of it, and bundle the woman off the bench and out of danger.

The woman shrieked as he pushed her clear just as the barrel smashed into the back of the bench. Luckily, the bench was sturdier than it had seemed and, though it jolted forward under the impact, it didn't break and wasn't sent crashing down over the edge of the quay; which was a good thing, because Remy had put himself right in harm's way if it had. The barrel was not so sturdy, and cracked open on impact, showering Remy in shards of wood and drenching him in dark, viscous liquid that reeked of yeast and bad decisions.

The woman mumbled a terse 'thank you' and Remy waved her away angrily. Why hadn't the damned woman moved? He pulled out a handkerchief and wiped the frothy muck off his face and horns. It had gone in his hair and his eyes and up his nose and in his mouth, and he cleared his throat and spat out what he could, finally recognising the liquid from its warm earthy taste. Stout. He had drenched himself in dark beer. He turned to speak to the woman, and see if perhaps she would pay to have his clothes cleaned since he had saved her, but she was gone.

Sighing, and ready for this awful eve to just be over, he wrung out his sodden handkerchief, and went over to check on the kid who had tried to help. He was still lying on the floor, dazed, and Remy reached out a hand to help him up. He looked about fourteen or fifteen, tall for his age and skinny, with a smooth, youthful face and piercing green eyes. He wore a tired and grubby blue tunic which nevertheless was of extremely good quality tailoring, with slashed sleeves revealing a white satin lining, with matching breeches, cap and cape. They were nicer clothes than Remy's were, even before the beer.

The kid had a mop of unruly blonde hair under his cap, which he wore forward in a bushy fringe. The fringe was completely failing to hide the protruding red nubs of bone at his temples; he had recently sprouted horns.

Standing up, the kid self-consciously patted his fringe down to cover his horns, then looked up at Remy, and his eyes widened. "You're... you're just like me!" he said, incredulous.

"Well I ain't quite jus' like you," Remy replied, reaching out a sticky hand for the kid to shake. "I'm covered in beer for one thing, an' for another, I don't hide my horns. I'm Remy Du Rosier."

The kid – still stunned and still staring – left Remy's hand hanging awkwardly for a few seconds, before repeating his name back to him slowly, as if captivated. "Remy... Du... Rosier..."

Seeming to wake up, he continued rapidly. "My name is Salvatoré Col Haolim Primo Martelaar Delmond Du Laurentin... but everyone just calls me Colin." The kid's name was a garbled mouthful of words, delivered staccato, but his accent was upper class. Remy's interest was piqued; perhaps the kid had money.

"It's a pleasure to meet you Colin. Are you goin' shake my hand?" Colin shook his hand. "There ya go. Nice... Let go now. Nice. I'm guessin' you ain't met many of our kind?"

"Remy you have horns!"

"Mm-hmm"

"Big ones!"

"Mm-hmm. I can see you a smart kid."

"Remy are you human? What even are you?" and then the kid finally looked down, blinking away tears and shame before meeting Remy's gaze again and asking what he really wanted to ask, in barely a whisper. "Remy, what am I?"

CHAPTER 3

Epifani stood at the back of the river bus, keeping the press of commuters between her and the filthy corpses that stoked the boiler amidships. Risen put her on edge; she felt their presence like an ominous shadow in her mind, which she forced herself to ignore. A barge corpse had approached her soon after they had set off from Isla Hovella, rattling its collection bucket at her presumptuously. "I have no money for you!" she had said angrily, then admonished herself for even speaking to the abomination like it was a person. It had persisted in rattling its collection box, and clicking its jaw together in a facsimile of speech, and other passengers had looked back at her like she was deranged.

Deciding not to make any more of a scene – her panicked late arrival on the boat had already drawn too much attention – she had reached into a pocket and tossed some copper deniers at the corpse to make it go away. Some of the coins even went into the bucket, and the corpse had scrambled to collect the rest, which had clattered onto the deck and rolled away.

It had left her alone after that, which was good, because she had more important things to worry about. She glanced behind again. The silhouette of the unlit boat was still there, following in the wake of the bus as it had done since shortly after they departed Isla Hovella, and still gaining. She had guessed it was a river galley from the outline of it and the churn it seemed to be producing, and now it had drawn closer she could make out the four hooded figures on the deck of the galley, silhouetted in black against the twilight sky. It was definitely still gaining, but her river bus would be arriving at Isla Doblé shortly, and they wouldn't catch her in time.

She turned back, and startled. A skeletal hand was right up in her face, its nauseating aura filling her throat with bile. Alarmed, she recoiled, gagging, and shrank back hard against the stern gunwale. The barge corpse was back; it was presenting her with the ticket she'd paid for! Snatching it, she bolted forward before it tried to give her change, pushing through the crowd to get to the front of the boat and be first to disembark.

Isla Doblé wasn't ideal, it was a little too quiet to lose herself in the crowds, but her emergency contact was just a quick dash across the pier bridge, on Isla Verdé.

***

Remy looked incredulously at the teenage boy; Colin. How could he not know what he was? The team of Risen porters were scrambling around noisily stacking the runaway barrels they had recovered, so Remy guided the kid over to the quayside out of the way. He wiped his sticky beer-covered hands on his sodden handkerchief as he walked, then discarded it over the edge where it fluttered limply down onto the slick stones of the foreshore and was lapped up by the swirling river.

Remy turned to face the kid. "You a fiendlin', Colin."

"A fiendling?" the kid replied, trying the word out for the first time.

"Mm-hmm. How come you don't know that? Your parents must ha' been fiendlin's too. Didn' they have horns like mine?" Well, not exactly like mine, Remy thought. His horns were particularly impressive. No other fiendling had horns as imposing as his.

Colin shook his head. "No. My parents are the Marquis and Marchioness Du Laurentin. They don't have horns, they're normal. I was adopted." He looked away bitterly, staring out across the twilight river delta.

Remy smiled to himself. A Marquis? The kid definitely had money. Then he frowned, registering what else he had said. "You normal too, Colin!" He reached out and pushed Colin's fringe aside, which made the kid flinch away, his eyes still overcast with tears.

"These horns, they normal for us," Remy continued, "though you a lil' old to be jus' gettin' them in… Damn, Colin! Did you try an' cut these?" The nubs of bone at the kid's temples had jagged half-healed gouges like a saw might have made.

"I tried, but it hurt so bad, I could not do it," Colin replied, his voice cracking. Here the tears that had been threatening to fall finally did, rolling down the kid's rosy cheeks. He wiped them with a sleeve, and looked away again, downcast.

Remy placed his hands on the kid's shoulders, turning him back to face him. "You a fiendlin', Colin. And I'm a fiendlin' as well. That means I know a lil' about it. Bein' a fiendlin' means you special. It means you got devil blood. It means you got super powers."

"I h…have devil blood?" the kid stammered, aghast.

Remy chuckled. "Yeah, so the stories go; thousands o' years back, a mummy Colin or a daddy Colin got jiggy with a devil, an the first lil' baby Colin came out lookin' like us." He could tell he'd only alarmed the kid further, so he gave him a reassuring smile. "It don't mean you evil or nothin'! Hell, most devils ain't evil… They kinky though, an' maybe that's why there so many fiendlin's."

Colin now looked both alarmed and confused, so Remy tried again. "Fiendlin' is just a name that human folk gave our kind. There ain't a lot o' truth to the tall tales folk tell about us; an' layin' with a devil ain't exactly a common occurrence." Though it did happen, Remy thought to himself… he would know.

"My family, my community, are all fiendlin's. They good, wholesome, generous god-fearin' people, full o' love an' kindness. An' now they your people too."

This seemed to reassure him. "And… I have super powers?"

Remy chuckled again. "Not yet. But you will once you older. How come you only findin' out about this now? Didn't your adopted parents tell you nothin'? What they think would happen when your horns came in?"

Here the kid saddened again. "I did not know I was adopted until these things – these horns – sprouted from my head. Before that I thought my father was my father and my mother was my mother. And I thought I was human.

"My parents threw me out of their house when they saw them and realised what I was. They told me I was adopted; that I was an abomination, and they disowned me." Here Colin seemed to wince at the memory.

Remy winced too. The kid had tried to mutilate himself in order to fit in, and had been treated appallingly by his parents. Worse still, the Marquis had disowned him; Colin definitely didn't have any money.

***

The De Ville family once owned a plethora of watercraft including several river barges and sailing yachts. When Isla Festa had fallen to disrepair, most of the family fleet had been abandoned in the islet's boat house, which had suffered far worse in the intervening years than even the main house had. It was in a parlous state of disrepair with a rotten, collapsed roof and walls. The building had essentially folded in on itself, and the Baron had done little in the past year to fix it except replace the old rotten jetty and clear the mangroves from the launching shallows.

The little flotilla of boats that had been moored inside the overgrown building were all sunken wrecks. All except a narrow four-man gondola, which had been stored out of the water and had miraculously survived the building collapse that wrecked the rest, and had remained water-tight. Mostly.

It was a harrowing journey across the delta in the deceptive half-light of the ever-setting sun, and the warped wooden gondola had almost capsized more than once, thanks to the treacherous currents and swirling eddies of the delta. Water had been slowly seeping in for a while, and the Baron was relieved to be finally pulling into the diffuse green glow of a dockside light as the gondola drew up alongside one of Isla Doblé's many jetties.

He stepped out and tied up, then stowed his paddle, and picked Belle up from where she'd been sat facing him in the bow of the gondola. The limp woollen doll was sodden with river water, and he wrung her out and flicked away the excess water before placing her – dry – into the top pocket of his suit. "Thank you my dear, for bailing the water out."

Now disembarked, he could see the gondola was sitting far too low in the water, and getting lower as it gently rocked against the jetty. He would need to patch it up before they risked the journey home. Recovering his cape and cane, he took a moment to thank the little boat for delivering them safely, and the little boat rocked gently in response.

It was a pleasant Twilight evening as the Baron strolled along the jetty and climbed the steps up to the esplanade. It was always evening in the realm of Twilight; but evening wasn't always this pleasant.

Looking round to get his bearings, he saw a steam barge with big side-mounted paddle wheels pull alongside the next jetty over; a river bus from the look of it. A dark-skinned young woman hastily jumped off the bus before it had finished docking, then sprinted along the jetty and up to the esplanade just ahead of him, taking the steps three at a time. She then darted off westwards towards the Doblé bridge. Something about her caught the Baron's eye, and he wondered why she was in such a rush on such a pleasant evening.

Then he noticed a corpse galley row up to the end of the same jetty without slowing, and a trio of figures in gold-trimmed black robes with golden masks leapt off the craft as it careened recklessly past the end of the jetty. The three figures in black and gold ran the full length of the wooden jetty, barging past the crowd of commuters disembarking from the bus. The three figures then set off at speed in the same direction as the woman, while their galley powered on past the jetty, heading westward round the shore, with another of the masked figures visible on deck.

Instinctively, the Baron hoped they didn't catch her, and he quickened his pace to find out.

***

Since he'd been in the water anyway, Thessu had checked the other covered docks for any sign of the paddle steamer 'Queen of the South'. He hadn't found any. The ship was simply gone.

Frustrated, he climbed out of the river and dried himself off, then got dressed again. He took the opportunity to replace the bundle of dried herbs and aromatics from the beak of his mask with a fresh posy from his satchel, before donning the mask once more. He was running low on aromatic bundles; he would need to prepare more.

With no sign of the paddle steamer, he was unsure how to proceed. He would probably need to trace some of the passengers and crew who had arrived with the ship a year ago, a hundred years after setting off. It would take time; he ought to get straight on it.

First things first though, he would need to find some lodgings here in the city. He had passed some lively looking places on his rickshaw ride from the ocean dock, and Isla Doblé was as good a base as anywhere in the city. So he set off back round the esplanade towards the Doblé bridge.

Thessu had almost reached the bridge, when a young woman sprinted past him, in great haste to reach it first. She glanced back over her shoulder as she passed him, and Thessu got a brief look at her face; she had shoulder-length black hair and heavy scars on both cheeks.

Despite the filter slits on his mask being closed, and the beak containing a fresh bundle of lavender-scented posies, he smelled the rage seeping out of her pores. Woe betide anyone who crossed this woman, her fury was magnificent!

He heard the rapid patter of more people running behind him, and turned to see three men in ridiculous black and gold clown suits chasing after the woman. The clowns rushed past him, and Thessu hoped they caught her; the furious woman would make mincemeat out of them. He pressed on after them to watch the show.

***

Remy and Colin looked out across the river delta from the quayside, watching the coming and going of the little boats in companionable silence, the viridian lights of La Crosse twinkling in reflection on the rippling river under a clear twilight sky. Remy figured the kid would ask him to be some sort of mentor, and spent the time thinking of a way to politely refuse; the last thing he needed was a sidekick.

He was right. Colin turned to him abruptly, breaking the silence. "Remy, I have been thinking about what you said and I was wondering…"

Remy cut him off; something else was happening. "Hold that thought, Colin. Somethin's goin' on over there…"

They both looked on as a tall dark-skinned woman with an athletic build was chased along the esplanade by three men in the black and gold of the Ziggurat. She skidded past the broken wagon, pausing to upend one of the newly stacked barrels into the path of her pursuers, though that seemed to delay her more than it delayed the men in black and gold. Two of them vaulted the barrel, while the third clattered past the irate porter corpses without stopping. The woman turned onto the Doblé bridge, with her three pursuers close behind.

"Cultists!" Remy spat, and he strode forward after them, grateful for the distraction. He unclipped the hilt clip on his sword belt as he went, leaving Colin behind at the quayside. "Stay here," he said, without looking back at the young fiendling.

***

Epifani ran along the esplanade just ahead of the three masked men who pursued her. A group of ghastly corpses were stacking barrels beside a broken wagon that was blocking the way, and she slowed just enough to upend a pile of barrels into the zealots' path, hoping that would slow them down. She bolted off again towards the bridge, grinning with satisfaction when she heard the sound of clattering behind her. She was going to get across that bridge. She had to.

Breathing heavily, she turned onto the bridge and started running across, her feet rattling the wooden planks underfoot. Then she skidded to a halt.

"There's nowhere left to run, Epifani," said the man who now blocked the bridge ahead of her. It was the fourth zealot. He must have rowed ahead with the cohort of Risen, and had beaten her to the bridge. He was flanked by half a dozen corpses from his cohort, the rest still clambering up the wooden piles and onto the bridge from the river below.

Epifani turned, looking for a way out, and saw her first three pursuers were also now on the bridge behind her, stalking forwards with weapons drawn, penning her in from behind. "Will you keep your dignity Epifani, and come willingly back to the Ziggurat?" the fourth man said. "Or do we need to beat you and drag you there?" His voice was silky with veiled menace as he spoke from behind his golden mask.

Epifani glanced over the side of the bridge to the roiling river below. It wasn't a long drop, and she was a strong swimmer, but the last thing she wanted was to be hauled bodily out of the water by a galley-full of corpses. She considered surrendering; she didn't think her chances of fighting off a galley-full of corpses were any better on the bridge than in the water, but giving up just wasn't who she was. No, she would go down fighting and take as many of the bastards down with her as she could.

She reached down to her boot and drew her own weapon, a long stiletto knife, which she held reverse grip in her hand. The death priest shrugged, and gestured the corpses forward. "As you wish, Epifani. We don't need you alive to question you."

***

The Baron hurried forward towards the bridge. He bridled at the sight of the woman being rushed by a group of armed corpses, and quickened his pace further. The dead were supposed to serve the living, not assault them. Arming corpses was an offense against all decency, and no matter what the woman had done to upset the men so greatly, attacking her ten on one was patently unfair. "That isn't very sporting is it, my dear?" he asked Belle. "We shall have to even those odds!"

"Yes, I completely agree," came the reply. Not from Belle; the doll in his pocket was mute, instead from a man – a stranger – who had been heading in the same direction. The stranger had stopped by a broken wagon to unburden himself of a cumbersome satchel, handing it to a startled porter corpse without explanation.

The stranger had a long green robe and an odd leather face mask with a long drooping beak. He raced off towards the woman as well, and was incredibly fast on his feet, quickly outpacing the Baron. Further ahead, it looked like some other passers-by were also not going to let this woman be accosted by Risen thugs. Good.

***

"I tol' you to stay there!" Remy barked, when he realised Colin was following behind. He had nearly reached the bridge, just as the woman was facing off with four cultists and a bunch of mean-looking corpses.

"I know Remy," Colin replied. "But I want to help too. We already helped one woman out of danger together, now we are a team! We are the Fearless Fiendlings!"

"This is different, and we ain't no team!" Remy growled, reaching into the basket hilt of his rapier, and drawing the blade smoothly out. He definitely wouldn't be part of any team with such a stupid name. He indicated away from the bridge, "Wait there and don't move!"

"But I have a blade too," Colin pleaded, pulling out a small utility knife from his belt, better suited to tackling apples than cultists.

Remy flared red fire in his eyes and gave the kid a stern look wreathed in flame that brooked no argument. Colin shrank back a step, then trudged over to where Remy had indicated he wait.

Remy stepped forward onto the bridge, just as two strangers did the same. A man in green robes with an odd-looking mask and goggles, and next to him a pale man in a white suit and a tall hat, holding a silver-topped cane, with an incongruous knitted doll in his top pocket. The three of them looked at each other in silent acknowledgement, then strode forward towards the cultists. Beyond them, six Risen corpses were rushing the woman, and more were now clambering up onto the bridge from below to join the fray.

***

Epifani side-stepped the first spear-thrust and jabbed her stiletto backhand into the corpse's chest, where the blade slipped between its ribs and sunk in to the hilt, a vicious thrust through the heart that would have killed a living assailant. The corpse ignored the wound, clacking its jaw at her. It twisted to bring its spear to bear again, and Epifani barely pulled her blade free before the corpse's movement could wrench it from her grasp. She cursed under her breath and gripped the stiletto tighter. Risen wouldn't die that way!

She couldn't hang about for the first corpse to circle round for another thrust, the next two were already on her, one jabbing with its spearpoint while the other scythed its spear downwards in a diagonal sweep. Closing the distance, she parried the jab with her left hand while taking the blow from the wooden shaft of the scything spear on her shoulder, safely inside the range of its blade tip. She pivoted to let the force of the blow continue past her; it would bruise, but no bones would be broken.

Moving fluidly forward along the spear shaft of the jabbing corpse, she stabbed her stiletto hard through its eye socket, deep into its brain, projecting a spurt of foul necrotic juices that spattered up her arm. The corpse spasmed and buckled, its grip on the spear loosening as it disanimated. Epifani let it fall away with her stiletto still embedded in its face; she was wrenching the spear from its grasp.

Hefting the spear, she spun around just in time to block another swing from the first corpse, but the force of the blow against her spear-shaft sent her staggering backwards into the wooden railing of the bridge. Three of the Risen pressed forward, hemming her in. She lashed out at the advancing corpses, swinging her spear in a wide arc, the blade cutting deep into the arm of one assailant.

Unflinching, it lunged forward regardless, aiming a vicious spear thrust at her stomach which she narrowly dodged by jerking aside. Too narrowly; she felt it graze against her flank inside the open flap of her cloak, the spear-tip juddering as it tore through her undershirt and scraped across the side of her abdomen. Continuing its lunge, the corpse bore down on her and pinned her bodily against the railing, trapping her own spear-shaft between them as it leered its foul stink right in her face.

She shrank back, feeling its hideous presence bearing down on her mind as well as her body and, completely pinned by the corpse, she fought it off the only way she could. Ignoring her instinct to mentally recoil in disgust, she instead reached out with her mind, grasping the odious presence tightly where it seemed strongest, and squeezing it as hard as she could. The corpse gnashed its teeth at her, but it was already fading as she suffocated its essence. She gave a final mental squeeze, and the corpse collapsed to the deck, disanimated. The effort made her queasy; in order to suffocate the hideous presence, she had had to embrace it, consume it.

Swallowing down the nausea rising in her stomach and breathing hard from the mental and physical effort, she pushed away from the railing and brought her spear round to bear on the other assailants. They all seemed to be engaged elsewhere; three strangers had come to her aid.

***

Thessu had no doubt the furious woman could fight off three thugs in clown suits, but a fourth clown and a horde of Risen convinced him to intervene rather than simply watch the fracas. It seemed that some of the locals had had the same thought and, after securing his rolled-up sleeves with a knotted cord, he strode forward onto the bridge flanked by two impromptu allies.

To reach the woman – who was now being rushed by the Risen spearmen – they would have to get past the three clowns who had pursued her onto the bridge. Thessu was first to reach them, and the nearest clown turned, swinging a vicious backhand swipe at him with a black hook-bladed knife.

Stepping forward to a position behind the clown's shoulder, Thessu blocked the back of the swinging forearm with his own before sliding his hand down to clamp onto the clown's wrist, pivoting to extend the swing and draw the clown off balance around him. With his other hand he reached over the clown's head and grabbed hold of his golden facemask, pressing his fingers through the eye slits to hook both mask and orbital bones beneath. He yanked backwards and the clown crumpled back, yelping with pain and surprise.

Thessu dropped down to one knee as the clown fell, expertly guiding the clown's head to the deck on one side of his knee, and the clamped knife hand towards the deck on the other side. There was a sickening crack as the clown's arm bones broke across Thessu's knee and the knife skittered away harmlessly. Thessu was up and moving instantly, back on his feet and pressing forward towards the furious woman, and the throng of corpses that surrounded her.

***

The Baron followed behind the unarmed stranger in the green robe, watching with admiration as the stranger raced ahead and quickly dispatched one of the figures in black and gold with a single movement of graceful violence.

A second figure in black and gold stood directly in front of the Baron, blocking the way forward. The figure hefted a heavy wooden bat, which he swung forehand in a wide arc aimed at the Baron's head as he approached. The Baron leant backwards, just enough so that the bat whistled past his face with a whoosh of displaced air, then he stepped forward again, holding his cane in a wide two-handed grip to block the returning backhand swing. The centre of the cane caught the figure's backswing just above the elbow, and the jarring impact caused the figure to release his grip on the bat, which whistled off in an arc that carried it up and over the railing to land in the river below with a plop.

Wheeling around as the figure recoiled in pain, the Baron fetched him such a blow across the head with the cane that his golden mask flew off to land, dented, on the deck of the bridge, and the figure crumpled like a puppet with his strings cut.

Looking back to check on the fiery horned stranger, he saw the third masked figure had a sword in hand, but the fiendling was laying into him ferociously with his own basket-hilted rapier. He was fine. The Baron turned his attention back to where the woman was fending off corpses, and saw they had her pinned against the railing, though the unarmed stranger in green had already dragged one off her.

The Baron clicked down the catch on the silver handle of his cane as he hastened forwards to help, letting the hollow wooden shaft fall away to the deck, to reveal the slender foil blade within.

***

Remy laid into the third cultist, their swords ringing as they fenced. He hadn't expected a priest of the Crosse Cult to be especially proficient with a sword, but he was. In fact, he was very good, and Remy grimaced as he saw his erstwhile allies easily pass the gold-masked men in their path and move on to tackle the corpses beyond.

He had started well against the gold-masked man, who had recoiled from his fiery gaze and vicious assault, but had recovered quickly and pegged him back with a flurry of rapid thrusts and slashes that had him on the back foot, hard pressed to defend against the flickering blade. Remy was left-handed, and that usually gave him an advantage, but this opponent wasn't fazed at all. Why hadn't he picked the big one with the bat? He looked much easier.

A flick of the cultist's blade slashed past his face, and Remy flinched back, parrying the sword down and away and stepping back to give himself a little space.

Suddenly something flew over Remy's shoulder from behind him and skittered across the deck towards the gold-masked man, who neatly side-stepped it. A little utility knife.

"Colin! Did you really jus' throw your knife into a melee?" Remy yelled incredulously over his shoulder, his eyes not leaving the cultist's expressionless mask.

"Yes Remy, I am staying put like you said. But I still want to help!" came the reply from the kid behind him.

"You gots to work on your aim; you shit at knife throwin'! You as like to hit me as help me!"

Remy could see the other two strangers were both now fighting through the corpses and had almost reached the woman. Goddammit, he was being shown up by an unarmed foreigner and an old man! Stalking forward towards the cultist, Remy thought he might circle round him, but his opponent was too wily and he side-stepped neatly to prevent from being circled.

Suddenly, Remy glimpsed a blur of motion in the corner of his eye and, turning, saw a slender figure dashing right past him towards the cultist. It was the kid. "Colin! That ain't stayin' put! What in the hell you doin'?"

Before Remy could stop him, Colin had darted past him towards the man's flank. Wheeling towards this new threat, the cultist slashed his sword at the kid, and it flashed over Colin's head as he dove at the deck towards the man's feet. The man, taken by surprise, stumbled backwards as the kid grabbed at something from the deck. "I'm retrieving my knife so I may throw it again like you suggested!"

The cultist grabbed at the railing to steady himself as he almost tripped, his sword flailing wildly as he teetered off balance. Once again, without knowing what the hell he was doing, Colin had unwittingly given Remy the opportunity he needed, and he sprung forward to catch the man as he stumbled. Their swords clashed as the cultist deflected his thrust with a desperate parry, but Remy swept inside his guard and wrapped his left sword arm over the cultist's right, pinning it, and grabbed him by the throat with his right hand, holding him against the railing.

Remy's eyes flamed red once more as he mentally focused, pouring heat from his molten core down his arm and into the cultist's throat. The skin of the man's neck blistered and smoked, while the chin of the golden mask blackened from the heat, the thin gold-leaf coating flaking away to reveal the heat-tarnished steel beneath. The man screamed, dropping his sword and clawing at Remy's hand to pull it away.

Relenting, Remy withdrew his hand and reached instead down between the mans legs, taking a grip of his backside, then lifted him bodily up and over the railing, letting him fall flailing into the water below.

Colin, who had now retrieved his knife, stared bewildered at Remy. "Super powers…" the kid whispered, awestruck. Remy glared angrily at him, his face incandescent with fiery rage, and pointed back off the bridge. Colin trudged off again. "I know, I know. 'Wait there and don't move.'"

***

Two of the strangers seemed to have knocked down a zealot apiece before Epifani even noticed them, and they were both now each grappling two Risen corpses away from her, while the third stranger – the fiendling – was clashing blades with the third zealot. They seemed capable enough. She focussed her attention on the fourth zealot and the rest of the corpses; two on the bridge and several more still lumbering up the support piles from the river below.

The fourth zealot was stepping back, perhaps fearfully, though it was impossible to tell through his mask. The corpses were showing no such fear or trepidation though; the two already on the bridge rushed forwards, spears outstretched to impale her. Epifani dodged to the outside of the leftmost spear thrust, batting the shaft away with her off-hand, then thrust her own spear forwards and up into the corpse's onrushing face. The thrust caught it under its clacking mandible, the force knocking its head back as the tip powered on up through its brain to lodge on the inside of its skull.

The spear was wrenched out of her hand as the corpse fell, but she wasn't left defenceless. She grasped the shoulder of the other corpse with both hands as its momentum carried it past her, and as she grasped it physically, she reached out with her mind to grasp it mentally. She grasped its noxious presence. She embraced it. She consumed it. It collapsed – disanimated – to the deck on top of its fellow; she was getting the hang of this now.

She spat black bile onto the deck and, concealing her exhaustion, squared up to the fourth zealot, who was still edging away. Behind her, she heard an agonised scream as of someone being burned followed by a big splash. Glancing back, she saw the fiendling stranger had finally disposed of the zealot he was fighting, and he was stalking forward to join the others.

The others were finishing up with their corpses. As she watched, the stranger with the odd-shaped mask had a Risen corpse in a headlock in the crook of his arm, and snapped its neck by falling backwards to the deck and rolling back onto his feet in one fluid movement. Meanwhile the stranger with the top hat and pocket doll skewered two corpses with a single thrust of his cane sword. They fell either side of him as he withdrew his slender blade leaving it covered in black, necrotic ichor. He tapped it with a finger and the ichor smoked and dissipated away from the now spotless blade.

"Don't imagine this is over, Epifani!" the last zealot said. He had continued to back away and, now joined by the remaining corpses from the boat, they were fully retreating across the bridge. "The Faithful will recover the goblet and you will pay for your heresy! I will see to it your corpse becomes my plaything... the dead serve the living, Epifani!"

Epifani spat again. She knew the vile things the death cult liked to do with their Risen slaves, but she had no intention of being raised once she died. She turned away as the man fled and the odious presence of his corpses receded from her mind. It was time to meet the strangers who had helped her.

CHAPTER 4

A nameless small but sturdy longship of single mast and twenty oars made its way northwards through the choppy twilight waters south of La Crosse. It flew the red sail of the Scarlet Fist; the privateer company that protected maritime routes in and out of the city from their base on the floating shanty outpost of Flotsam.

The blood-red sail hung slack and lifeless in the limp wind as the longship eked a slow path northwards towards La Crosse, fighting against the swirling flow of the Poconovo river that emptied here into the Gulf of Mezarcana; the boat powered feebly through the inky water by a mere half dozen especially rotten, stinking corpses.

From her position in the bow of the vessel, Valanthé had watched the core islands creep slowly closer for half an hour, the city twinkling with light as the chartreuse glow of La Crosse silhouetted the grander buildings of the city against the twilight sky.

The short routine journey from the floating pirate outpost of Flotsam to the core islands shouldn't have taken more than twenty minutes, but the longship was under-crewed, and the galley corpses were well past their prime rowing months. In fact this would be their final row.

The corpses were destined for the second-hand auction at the Lesser Pit, where they would no doubt be bought in bulk to work the fields instead. The plantation owners never bought expensive new corpses; not when second hand ones would also toil, but for a fraction of the price and, when they could toil no more, they would fertilise the fields for free.

Valanthé would instead be going to the Greater Pit, to assist Captain Lugwort in the purchase of fresh corpses to crew his galleys and transports.

Valanthé wasn't the slightest bit surprised that Lugwort and the other scarlets sat idle at the stern of the longship. The pirates made no effort to assist the decrepit oarsmen with the rowing, even as the vessel struggled to maintain course and forward momentum as it bimbled through the swells and ebbs of the swirling river current.

She eyed the pirate captain narrowly. The Risen were doing their best but were clearly fatigued and losing steam. Why had that oaf only brought six? At the very least, surely he cared that he would get a better price for the six if he didn't wear them out before they were auctioned?

Lugwort was in charge of provisioning the fleet and, despite not having a ship of his own, he still held a valuable privateer commission from the city, which meant he could lord it over any pirate who didn't. Valanthé didn't like him. She never liked anyone who tried to lord it over her. For the short time she'd been working for the Fist, she had mostly been doing jobs for Captain Crosskeys, who was far more senior and far more likeable.

Lugwort noticed her glancing at him and, with a nudge and wink at one of the leering goons he surrounded himself with, he hefted his bulk up off the coxswain's seat and made his way forward.

He was a very fat man, but he crossed the longship deck with the easy grace of someone who'd spent a lifetime at sea. Valanthé begrudged that he was competent at anything, but there was no denying that Lugwort was an able seaman. He had a bald head which he hid under a tricorn hat, and a thick ginger beard, fading to grey at the roots.

"Somethin' troublin' ye, girly?" he said, giving her a leery look.

She gestured at the corpses. "They're looking tired. They'd fetch a better price if…"

He cut her off. "I ain't payin' ye to eyeball the stiffs, girly!"

She tried again. "Maybe we'd get there quicker if…"

He cut her off again. "I ain't payin' by the hour, neither! Listen, girly, Cap'n Crosskeys reckons you're smart and handy with them blades and you've a good eye for trouble... see that you don't turn your eye for trouble in the wrong direction, got it?"

Valanthé drew herself up to her full height, which only brought her level with his beard, but still he took a half step backwards, her movement so quick and so fluid that it surprised the big man. She wasn't imposing; in fact she had a slender physique and a plain, androgynous face, but she moved with a feline grace and her pale almond eyes shone with a furious intensity. She also carried a lot of weapons.

A long moment passed, then she saluted him grandly, with a loud "Aye, aye skipper." Lugwort grunted in acknowledgement, and withdrew to rejoin the scarlet goons at the stern, while she sat back down, resigned to endure an unnecessarily long and ponderous journey that would knacker their corpses.

Lugwort and his companions seemed to enjoy every excruciating moment of the slow, boring journey after that, and leered at Valanthé from the stern of the longship for the whole rest of the way. The boat eventually pulled up at a wharf on the west coast of Isla Verdé, in the channel that separated it from Isla Roja.

Roused to action, one of the scarlets jumped out as the galley glid in to dock, and tied up in a well-practiced fashion, securing the boat to the wharf. The captain and the rest of the pirates disembarked, followed by the Risen corpses in single file. Risen don't sweat or show their exhaustion in an obvious way, but they had noticeably deteriorated after their punishing row.

One of the scarlet goons reached out to help Valanthé off the boat; a skinny boy with wispy ginger bumfluff on his cheeks. He smiled as he offered her his hand, saying, "You'd be prettier if you smiled more, y'know?"

She ignored him, and stepped gracefully onto the deck without any help from the goon, then adjusted her sword belts. The goon watched her lustily, before continuing. "Not that you're not pretty anyway; you're at least a seven… But you might be an eight if you smiled a bit." He demonstrated a big toothy grin.

Valanthé looked at him darkly. She definitely was not smiling. In fact she was wondering whether the goon would grin so widely after she broke his jaw.

Lugwort spotted the danger. "Bumfluff!"

"Errr. Yes dad?" the goon said.

"Ye just volunteered t'take these stiffs to the Lesser Pit!"

Bumfluff groaned, and the captain beckoned him close for a quiet whisper, their eyes flicking over to Valanthé, who was still nonchalantly checking her blades.

She had excellent hearing though, and heard the fat pirate warn his son, "be careful where you stick it, lad. That one'll bite it orf!"

The group set off through the docks towards the two arenas – Valanthé falling in behind the corpses – as Lugwort and the scarlets led the way to the Greater and Lesser Pits; where the dead were bought and sold.

***

The Pits of Isla Verdé were a central pillar of city commerce, huge oval arenas of granite stone in the centre of the island. Built centuries ago, primarily as gladiatorial arenas, the Pits served many other functions in the city; marketplace, exhibition hall and civic centre, but their primary use now was as a weekly corpse market for Risen slaves, and all other uses had diminished due to their constant overwhelming stench of death.

The Pits straddled two sides of the Piazza Grandé, the vast plaza which was the bustling commercial heart of La Crosse. Bumfluff and another scarlet goon had peeled off towards the Lesser Pit with the six decrepit corpses. Lugwort had handed his son their deeds, and instructed him not to accept less than fifty silver sols apiece – two and a half livres – a price that Valanthé considered obscenely high, though she had no real idea how much Risen were worth.

She and the rest of the pirates pressed on across the Piazza Grandé towards the Greater Pit, pushing past throngs of people all milling around the arenas, here for the corpse market. The smell of the place was almost overwhelming; the charnel stench of cadavers amplified by centuries of service as the largest concentration of the Risen in all the world. Valanthé was glad she remembered to apply a minty balm to her nostrils before entering the plaza.

The Piazza Grandé was filled with businessmen, beggars, and buskers, and hawkers selling all sorts of wares and – for the strong of stomach – street food and snacks.

There were lots of Risen corpses as well – horses as well as people, Valanthé noted – some trooping into the Pits to be sold and some trooping out having been bought. Others still were yet to be raised; fresh cadavers were brought here by the wagon-load to be raised by one of the many necromancers who sold their services here, and cadavers were being traded just as readily as the Risen.

There were corpses working here as well, some swinging censers that pealed out a sweet-scented smoke – a mix of incense and arsenic – that tried and failed to mask the stench and kill the flies, while others swept or scrubbed the cobbles. It was a raucous, cacophonic place and Valanthé clutched her sword hilts tightly, keeping a wary eye out for trouble as they made their way through the press.

Lugwort led them through the arched gate at the entrance to the Greater Pit and on into the crowded stone tunnel that ran under the stands of the arena, to emerge into the maelstrom in the centre.

Dense crowds swarmed everywhere around the inside of the arena; both the living and the dead. The stands of the arena supported hundreds of wooden holding pens arranged in tiers that rose up the stands from the arena floor. Most pens were filled with the dead. Some held fresh cadavers stacked haphazardly, waiting to be raised, while others held fresh Risen waiting to be sold. All the surrounding death seemed to focus the charnel stench towards the centre, and Valanthé covered her nose. If this was where fresh Risen were sold, she didn't envy Bumfluff his trip to the second-hand auction in the Lesser Pit. Served him right.

Stewards quickly spotted Captain Lugwort, and the scarlets were led through the crowd to a roped-off area reserved for big spenders; the Scarlet Fist was one of the biggest consumers of Risen corpses in the city. Pretty girls waited in the roped-off area with trays of drinks and snacks, and the pirates wasted no time in getting stuck in.

Lugwort beckoned Valanthé towards him. "Over here, girly," then when she approached, he continued in hushed tones. "Time to earn yer keep... I spotted me some stiffs I likes the look of. Pen seventeen o'er there... no, don't look!"

He gestured almost imperceptibly with his eyes back towards the entrance. Valanthé casually scanned the whole arena as she applied more minty balm to her nose. The spot Lugwort had indicated was a large pen, two tiers up on the north stand, just to the left of where they'd come in.

"I don't want the seller to know I'm interested, see? It puts the price up when the Fist are buyin'. Go get a good price for me without tellin' 'em it's me payin'."

Valanthé nodded and walked off in the other direction. She took her time circling back to pen seventeen, stopping to examine several other pens first. She had spent enough time around the Risen to be a pretty good judge of quality; she could tell a corpse's freshness and suitability for rowing easily enough, and she could recognise the tell-tale signs of shoddy necromancy. But she had never bought one before; she had no idea what constituted a 'good price'.

She eavesdropped on several conversations between buyers and sellers, and was staggered by the prices being haggled. She had had no idea how expensive Risen were, and perhaps that explained why people universally embraced the trade and sold the bodies of their loved ones into it.

Approaching pen seventeen in a casual manner, she scanned the corpses. Annoyingly, Lugwort had a good eye. These were definitely the highest quality Risen she had yet seen; three dozen freshy-raised corpses, most of which were formerly young men of sturdy build, and most in near perfect condition. They all stood motionless, staring forwards with a soulless gaze.

"Can I help you, miss?" a man said, sidling over. The vendor. He was a pudgy man with oiled black hair. "These a mighty fine batch, ain't they?" They certainly were, but Valanthé would play the game.

"Well that's what I thought, but look here." She indicated towards one of the corpses at the front of the pen, which had some yellowing around the wound that had killed it. A puncture wound of some sort; likely it had been shot.

"That's just minor discolouration. It don't affect its performance." He was right of course; it definitely wouldn't make any difference to the corpse's ability to row or its longevity. But still she grimaced and shook her head, feigning disappointment.

"Mind if I take a closer look?" she asked.

"Go right ahead," the pudgy vendor replied.

Valanthé climbed over the rope barrier into the pen, and walked around, examining each corpse in turn, tutting audibly and shaking her head at every cosmetic issue.

One of the corpses in particular stood out though; where the others were dressed in the usual mix of simple clothes and tunics, this one towards the back of the pen was decked out more richly in a fashionable slashed doublet and matching pantaloons. Filthy of course – they were all filthy – but never-the-less an odd discrepancy in an otherwise uniform batch. It also seemed fresher than even the rest were; there was a pinkness to its cheeks that seemed out of place among the dead, and a crust of dried blood around the copper marque on its forehead. However, it had the same soulless vacant gaze as the rest of the corpses.

She avoided looking at that one too closely, better to focus on more flawed ones to lower the price. Not that there were many flaws; the whole batch were in excellent condition.

Another buyer had approached the vendor in the meantime, and Valanthé caught snatches of their conversation as she inspected the Risen.

"…only need three… price for the two here and the one behind…" the buyer had said.

"…raised altogether… single deed…" the pudgy vendor had replied, and the buyer had walked away.

Valanthé concluded her inspection, and stepped back over the rope, shaking her head with a feigned expression of disappointment. She had worked out from the snatches of conversation that the corpses must all have been bound on a single deed. She would definitely get a good price; the vendor needed a buyer who could buy all at once, they couldn't be sold singly.

The vendor smiled an oily smile as she joined him. "Mighty fine, ain't they?" he asked.

"Some of them are," Valanthé replied, washing her hands in a bowl of lemon water set out for that purpose. "I'm interested in twenty, if you'll give me a decent price and let me choose my favourites?"

The vendor licked his thin lips and shook his head, wincing slightly. Valanthé inferred that twenty was more than anyone had wanted so far, but wasn't enough. Good. She had pitched her opening offer right. "Unfortunately miss, they'll have to go together, they all bound on the same deed."

"I'm not sure I follow," she lied. "Why can't I have twenty?"

The pudgy vendor licked his lips again. "Well miss, part of the necromantic process that raises the dead is a legal one, the Risen are bound on a document called a deed, which sets out their ownership, and they're bound to the owner indicated on the deed. Without that, they'd be bound forever to the necromancer what raised 'em and couldn't ever serve anyone else. But these all was raised an' bound on the same deed which means they all get transferred to a new owner or none of 'em do."

She gave a considering look as she wiped her hands on a white towel that hung by the lemon bowl. "Well, I didn't really want the ones with problems worse than that gunshot," she continued with feigned reluctance, "but if it's all or nothing, how much for all?"

"They fifty livres each," he replied, brightening.

Valanthé frowned, and handed him the crumpled towel in pretend annoyance. "They're not worth fifty," she stated, though in fact she had no idea. Maybe they were. "I wouldn't pay that price for singles, and you can't sell them singly. I'll take them all at twenty-five apiece."

Again the vendor winced. "At twenty-five I'm losin' money. Forty."

Out of the corner of her eye, Valanthé noticed a fat man with a ginger beard stood discreetly a little way off behind the vendor. Lugwort. She didn't make eye contact. The pirate was surreptitiously signalling her to try for thirty.

They haggled some more, and eventually agreed a price of a thousand livres for all thirty six Risen corpses; slightly better than thirty apiece. The vendor looked annoyed but resigned as they shook hands to seal the deal.

Lugwort sidled over then, patting Valanthé on the shoulder in recognition, and the vendor looked stricken as he realised he had been played. "All sales be final," Lugwort oozed, with a wide grin full of gold teeth.

The vendor gave Valanthé an angry look as Lugwort led him over to a little desk to complete the transfer. She watched the fat pirate write out a bank slip for the golden livres with a quill pen, and hand it to the vendor, then they both stamped the corpse deed with blooded signet rings. The transfer was done.

***

Gerard Malblanq came back to his senses with a start, and fell over. He had had another of his blackouts. He had no idea where he was or how long had passed. A moment ago he had been carousing in a waterfront bar in the three bridges entertainment district, But this wasn't the waterfront.

His eyes took a moment to adjust, but meanwhile he was struck by the noise and bustle of a busy crowd, and was assailed by an intense, repugnant stench. Then the pain struck him. A piercing headache and sharp pain in his brow. He rubbed at it, and his hand caught on something metallic.

The jumble of blurry shapes around him coalesced into people. Not people. Risen. He was surrounded by Risen corpses. And also some people. People... buying him. Shit, was he in one of the slave pits?

***

Valanthé, Lugwort and the scarlet goons all turned, startled to see one of their fresh new corpses collapse in a heap. It was the one in the fancy doublet and pantaloons, Valanthé realised. It was muttering and pawing at the marque on its head, which was now streaming with fresh red blood. Was it... alive?

Lugwort turned on the vendor. "What the blazes is this? This ones not a stiff! This bastard deed be worthless!" But the vendor pocketed the bank slip and backed away unapologetically. "All sales be final," he parroted back to the pirate, then turned smartly on his heels and left.

Lugwort cursed at the man, and looked like he might haul him back, but instead he marched over to the crumpled corpse – no; the man – who was struggling to stand. "You! Yer supposed to be a stiff! What in the hell ye doin' coming back to life?"

Lugwort put the boot in, kicking the man hard in the back as he lay groaning on the ground. Unsatisfied, the pirate drew his sword – a heavy-bladed cutlass – and made ready to turn the man into a corpse like he had paid for. Valanthé stepped forward to intervene, but one of the scarlet goons beat her to it, holding the captain's sword arm back, and gestured around. A crowd of onlookers were staring at the commotion; it wouldn't do to commit a murder so publicly.

Lugwort kicked the man one more time, and sheathed his sword, cursing. He marched over to Valanthé. "You! This be your fault!" He leaned in aggressively close to her face, while she lowered her weight ready to spring if necessary, one hand resting ready on the handle of her short sword. "How did ye not know one of the stiffs weren't dead?"

Valanthé responded in calm voice, slowly and clearly. She felt a rising anger, and forced it back down; it wouldn't do to lose control here. "You told me to buy them, so I bought them. If you wanted an expert opinion, why didn't you bring a necromancer?" She already knew the answer; necromancers were expensive. The anger subsided and she continued more pleasantly, "What's the problem?" then added "Skipper?" to try and mollify him. "I got you a good price, less than thirty livres apiece. It's still less than thirty, even if one of them doesn't count!"

Lugwort lowered his voice, but not his anger, leaning in to speak in a gravelly whisper. "The problem, girly, is there's no buyin' the livin'. If he's alive, then this deed be void. An' there's naught compellin' these corpses to follow orders. So I'll have wasted me money."

The man on the ground had sat up now, wiping away the blood that had trickled into his eyes. He was a big man in his late thirties or early forties perhaps – stocky, with a muscular frame, broad shoulders and a square jaw – however, he looked hollow and exhausted, and was clearly dazed and confused by what was happening.

Lugwort leaned in even closer. "Girly… I want ye to take this feller for a walk outside. And see that I didn't waste me money. He's no good to me alive."

Valanthé shook her head. "I'm no murderer. I won't do it."

"Ye'll do it or ye'll not work for the Fist again. And then who'll employ you eh? that feller? Take him for a walk, says I!"

She had killed men before when she had to. Several. But she wouldn't kill an innocent unarmed man just to save Lugwort some money. She felt the rising anger again, and let out a calming breath. She relaxed her grip on the hilts of her swords, stifling her rage, and shook her head again sadly.

"Then you're done with the Fist, girl." Lugwort turned and gestured two of the scarlet goons in close. No doubt he was giving them the same ultimatum as she had been given. The scarlets clearly had no compunction about the order, and nodded agreement. Pirates were mercenary; killing people for money is what they did. Her morals had no place in the Fist, and she would have to discard them if she wanted to be a pirate. Filled with regret, Valanthé knew what she had to do.

She walked over to stand next to the square-jawed man. Lugwort and the other two pirates looked at her questioningly. "I'll do it," she mouthed to them tersely, and reached out a hand to help the man up.

The man took her hand. "Valanthé Luxalim," she said, by way of greeting.

"G...Gerard Malblanq," the man replied. His voice was hoarse and weak like he hadn't used it for weeks. "I... don't know what's happening. I'm not Risen though... I just get blackouts sometimes, that's all."

She nodded curtly and, with an effort, pulled him up to his feet. "Can you walk?"

He straightened up slowly to his full height, his back cracking as he did so. He was frail despite his muscular frame, and leaned heavily on her. "I think so."

"Good," she replied. "I'm going to take you for a walk."

CHAPTER 5

"This place is amazing!" Colin gushed, as the strangers sat down in the booth together. They had retreated to the Isla Doblé side of the bridge and, after waiting to ensure the three injured cultists scarpered after their comrade in the other direction, they had made their introductions and retired to the viridian-lit lounge bar of the Madrigal Saloon before any city deputies came nosing around.

"It's just a bar, kid," Remy said dismissively. He didn't remember being so naïve when he was fourteen. "Ain't you ever been in a bar before?"

Colin shook his head. "My father sometimes entertained guests in the salon of the palazzo, but it was always very formal. This place is relaxed and comfortable and full of interesting people. It's like a community living room!"

"That's exactly what it is." Remy said, drawing the booth's curtain closed behind them. Madame Cass had given him a stern look when he came in, and had frowned at his motley companions, but the presence of a smartly dressed patriarch of a noble house had dispelled most of her misgivings. The Baron had placed an antique silver coin – a quarter livre, Remy noticed – on the bar to ensure good service for the evening, and Madame Cass had sat them in a private booth and opened a tab.

Epifani – the woman they had saved – had been reluctant to join them; she had stopped only to thank them all curtly for their intervention, intending to depart straight away across the bridge to Isla Verdé. She had relented only once Thessu offered to dress her wound, and after the Baron suggested she might want to avoid a possible ambush by the cultists who had run off the same way she intended to go. She relaxed further once they came to the Madrigal, and she noted the *'No Dogs/No Corpses'* sign on the door.

"I hope y'all like bourbon, I've ordered us a round," Remy said, stepping past Colin to take the vacant chair next to the Baron. It was one of the larger booths, with six worn but comfortable armchairs arranged around a low wooden table, with a sputtering lamp hung above that filled the booth with a warm lime glow. Epifani lounged broadly, her boots resting on the low table, while Thessu crouched in front of her with a medical kit open by his feet.

"Let's get this over with," Epifani said, sitting forward and opening her cloak to reveal the shirt beneath soaked with blood from a wound just above her right hip. She pulled her shirt up out of her trousers to reveal a long jagged cut seeping with blood where she had been raked by the speartip.

Thessu nodded, saying, "It doesn't look too deep," his words slightly muffled by his mask and tinged with an unfamiliar accent. "It will need some stitches though."

He retrieved a jar of ointment and a selection of dressings and bandages from his kit, placing them on the table alongside a fine bone needle and a reel of thread. He carefully removed his gloves, and rubbed a dollop of the ointment into his hands. "May I?" he asked, and Epifani waved him forwards. "Do your worst, doc."

He carefully examined the wound, then flipped the filters of his mask open for a moment and then closed again. "It's not infected," he declared, reaching for more of the ointment. Then he gestured at Remy and Colin. "You two have an interesting physiology. You're not entirely human are you?"

"We're the Fearless Fiendlings!" Colin blurted out, before Remy could reply. "We have devil blood and super powers!"

"No, your blood is human enough," Thessu replied without looking up. He carefully rubbed the ointment into Epifani's wound, while she grimaced. "Your hearts beat a little slower than is typical given your ages, and with a most unusual cadence but your blood is rich in iron and oxygen, with broadly the same proteins and sugars as human blood. There are other subtle indicators as well, but the giveaway that you aren't human is actually your sweat glands, which produce a strong note of coal tar which is quite distinctive and extremely unpleasant."

"Yeah, and they also have whopping great big horns!" interjected Epifani.

Thessu looked up from Epifani's wound, as if noticing Remy's horns and Colin's stubs for the first time. "So you do."

"Are there no fiendlings where you're from?" asked the Baron conversationally.

"Yeah, where you from, anyways?" Remy added. "And what's with the beak mask?"

"I'm from a place called Yon-Jin-Hué, which is a high mountain valley near the southern tip of the southern continent," he said as he threaded the bone needle.

The rest of them exchanged shrugs; the southern tip of the southern continent was as far from La Crosse as it was possible to get. None of them had heard of his valley.

"Theres no fiendlings there, no," he continued. To Epifani, he added, "this may hurt a bit."

Epifani grimaced, clenching her teeth together and gripping the arm of the chair tightly as Thessu started stitching the jagged wound closed.

"I grew up in a monastery at the head of the valley," he continued, "where I was trained by the Order of Mercy. I developed my senses as part of my training and I wear the mask because the scent of the city would be overwhelming if I didn't."

"The Order o' Mercy?" Remy queried. He had never heard of it before. "They taught you medicine?"

"Among other things, yes."

"Did they also teach you to fight like you did?" asked the Baron.

"Only the strong can be merciful," Thessu replied without looking up. "That is one of the mantras of my order."

Epifani banged the arm of the chair as Thessu drew another stitch tight. "Where's that damn bourbon?" she demanded.

On cue, there was a knock on the frame of the booth, and Remy gestured for Colin to open the curtain, revealing one of the serving girls bringing a tray of drinks. The kid stared wide-eyed at the scantily-clad girl as she leaned seductively into the booth and laid her tray on the low table, but she only had eyes for Remy. Remy looked away regretfully, and she straightened up with a sigh. "If y'all want anythin' else, jus' holler."

"Thank you Miss Marianne," Remy said, and she blew him a friendly kiss as she left.

"You know her?" Colin asked, sounding impressed.

"I know all the girls here," Remy answered matter-of-factly, then he handed out the drinks.

Epifani downed hers in one, while the Baron took a small sip of his, nodding his approval. Remy swirled his around in his glass, savouring the aroma, which left two on the table. "Is one of those for me?" Colin asked.

Remy shrugged, saying, "I ain't your mom. If you want one, have one."

Colin snatched one up and took a big glug, then tried to hold off a coughing fit, failed, and had another glug. "This is the best evening ever! Remy I am so glad I met you this evening!"

"You two only met this evening?" the Baron asked, sounding incredulous. "Belle and I thought you might be brothers."

"Who's Belle?" Remy and Colin both asked at the same time.

The Baron indicated the woollen doll in the breast pocket of his suit. "I'm sorry I thought I introduced her. Everyone this is Belladonna. Belle my dear, this is Thessu and Epifani, and this is Remy and Colin."

Remy and Colin exchanged a dubious look. Thessu continued sewing, and Epifani helped herself to the spare glass of bourbon.

"No, we ain't related," Remy said, and recounted how he and Colin had met shortly before the fight.

Thessu finished the stitches and set his needle and thread down on the table. He rubbed his hands together in a moment of meditation, then without warning he raised one hand and brought it down hard to slap the wound, and Epifani yelped. Remy and the Baron leapt up from their chairs.

"What in the hell you doin'?" Remy demanded.

Thessu gestured at the wound. "Healing."

They all peered at the wound, Epifani included, and sure enough, the ragged gory edges had softened, and the flesh had knitted together around the row of neat stitches. It wasn't fully healed by any means, but it had the look of a week-old wound not a fresh one.

They all looked at each other, impressed. Thessu placed a dressing over it, and carefully wound a bandage around Epifani's waist to hold it in place, the white linen stark against the taut mahogany skin of her abdomen.

"Thanks," Epifani said, flexing her torso side to side to test it, before letting her ripped and bloody shirt drop back down over it. "Shame about the shirt though."

"I can help with that," the Baron said, leaning forward, and brushed the shirt with stiff flicks of his hand. The blood dried and powdered and trickled onto the floor leaving the shirt clean and, remarkably, repaired.

"Does everyone have goddamn super powers except for me?" Colin demanded angrily.

After that, they got another round of drinks and recounted the fight blow-by-blow, congratulating each other on their exaggerated exploits.

***

Gerard leaned on Valanthé as they made their way out of the pen, with Lugwort and the scarlets watching them dubiously. Gerard grabbed the little bowl of lemon water as they passed it, and drained it greedily, slopping water and chunks of lemon down his doublet as he drank. Valanthé pulled him forward impatiently.

She led him down the tiers of corpse pens that made up the stands of the Greater Pit arena and on through the press of people and corpses into the unlit tunnel that led out to the Piazza Grandé. "Those men wanted to kill me didn't they," he said hoarsely. "Will you tell me why?"

Valanthé didn't reply. She glanced back as they emerged from the darkness of the tunnel into the bright green and twilight glow of the busy plaza, to see Lugwort and two of the scarlets were following casually behind, and she urged Gerard forwards. His strength was slowly returning, and he gestured for her to let him try and walk unaided. He was stiff and wobbly, but he was mobile. Good enough.

"Will you at least tell me where we're going?" he asked. "I'd like to go home." He sounded lost and vulnerable, despite his impressive stature.

"Where's home?" she asked.

"Well, it's not really home, but it's that way," he said, gesturing to the south side of the plaza. "I have rooms in a little place called the Casa del Sol Riz. It's not far."

"I know it," she said, and frowned. "Why do you have rooms there? If you're a gangster, now would be a really good time to tell me." She looked back at the pirates and gestured for them to back off. They didn't. It seemed a lot like Lugwort didn't trust her.

"A gangster? No of course not. I came into a little money recently, and they've been very hospitable there."

Valanthé snorted. "I'll bet they have."

"What is this evening's date?" he asked. She told him the date and he exhaled deeply, whistling.

"Eight eves! I've never blacked out for that long before! No wonder they thought I was dead. No wonder I'm so drained!" He wiped again at the blood that was still dripping down his face from where the copper marque was pinned to his forehead. He needed it removed, and he needed food and water, and he needed rest.

"It's happened before then?" she asked. "Blacking out, I mean?"

He nodded. "None of the docs can explain it. I told them it feels like I was absent; like I left my body and went somewhere else for a time. They told me I needed a priest not a doctor."

"And the priests?"

He smiled ruefully. "They exorcised all the demons out of my wallet."

They made their way through the crowds to the edge of the plaza in the direction Gerard had indicated. Ahead, various side streets and alleys headed south. Valanthé guided him towards a narrow unlit alleyway between two tall stone buildings. "Why this way?" he asked suspiciously, after they'd walked a short way in.

"I'm taking you this way because the fat ginger pirate back there" – here she gestured a thumb over her shoulder – "told me to take you somewhere quiet and cut your throat," she replied, drawing her two swords and rounding on him.

Gerard recoiled from her, and reached instinctively for his own sword, which wasn't there. Instead he squared up, adopting a boxing stance. He was a bear of a man, but frail; weak.

"I'm not going to kill you Gerard. I'm no murderer." She gestured with a sword point back towards the three pirates who were casually walking into the unlit alley behind them. "But they are."

"Why's he still alive girly?" Lugwort called out. "Run 'im through now, that's a good lass."

"He has money," Valanthé ventured.

"That's true, I do! I have money!" Gerard confirmed.

Lugwort shook his head. "Oh aye, maybe you do. But this ain't about you now, lad. This about her. I need t'know when I gives her an order, that she'll obey it. More important, she needs t'know it too."

"I'm done taking orders," Valanthé retorted, adopting a defensive duelling stance. Gerard tried to get her attention. She realised what he wanted, and handed him one of her swords. She preferred to fight with two, but she was committed to saving this man now, she could better keep him safe by arming him than by trying to fight three pirates by herself.

There would not be a fight. Lugwort lifted his flintlock pistol and fired at Gerard.

There was a flash of black powder smoke. Valanthé's roiling emotions bubbled over and she screamed, "No!" in a panicked voice.

No bullet reached him. Half-way along its trajectory between the muzzle of the pistol and Gerard's head, the bullet flapped its wings and fluttered lazily away. It had been turned into a beautiful pink butterfly.

Astonished, Lugwort startled as if in recognition. He seemed to have seen something similar before. "Darkmourn!" he exclaimed breathily – reverentially even – and backed away, drawing the other scarlets back with him.

Gerard had flinched from the gunfire. He emerged from behind his hands, then checked himself for wounds. There weren't any. "What happened?" he asked, surprised to see nobody harmed and the pirates retreating. "Did he miss?"

"Come on. Let's get you home," she said, sheathing her swords and dragging him away.

"I still have questions!" he exclaimed. "What's 'Darkmourn'?"

"I don't know," Valanthé replied. And she really didn't.

***

"Where are we going now?" asked Colin, running to catch up with Remy. The kid was persistent, he had to give him that. Remy maintained his fast walk across the bridge without slowing or pausing, and the kid trotted up beside him, hurrying to keep pace.

Epifani had been the first to leave the saloon. The others had probed but she had been extremely cagey about why she had been being chased by priests of the Crosse Cult. Clearly though, the dark-skinned woman had somewhere important to get to on Isla Verdé, and she had tersely bade them farewell and departed through a back door without giving out any answers, headed to a water taxi so as to avoid taking the bridge. The rest of the group speculated about her motives, but frankly anyone who got on the wrong side of those religious fanatics was okay by Remy.

Thessu had been the next to depart, bidding them good evening and heading upstairs shortly after Epifani left. Madame Cass had agreed to provide him lodging, and took him up to show him to a room.

After they left, the Baron stayed a little longer. He was another very interesting – if eccentric – character, and Remy had been fascinated to discover the Baron had been on the ghost ship that was lost in time for a hundred years. He relayed that from his perspective, he and the rag doll Belle – for the Baron often referred to the doll as if it were a person; which was one of his eccentricities – had embarked on a perfectly normal voyage of a few eve's duration, but somehow a hundred years had passed for the rest of the world. He had returned to his family home to find it abandoned, and he was now embroiled in some sort of legal wrangle to reclaim ownership of the estate, and he had come to the core islands on an errand that might help resolve the matter.

The conversation had turned to Remy and what had brought him to La Crosse. He told them a little about the insular swamp community he grew up in, which fascinated Colin who had never left the city or even seen the outer islands or ever met another fiendling, and couldn't imagine half the things Remy was saying about his home. But Remy sensed the conversation was circling around his mother, and he was not ready to talk about what had happened to her. It was still too fresh a wound; the grief and guilt still too raw.

And so he had wished the Baron good luck in resolving his legal issues, and wished Colin all the best for the future, and bade them good evening. His abrupt departure had the double benefit of ditching the kid without explaining why he would make a terrible mentor, and leaving the Baron to pay the tab at the bar. In any case, he had something important to do that he had put off for too long. He would suck in his pride and go see his father and ask for money.

Which was a great plan, until Colin decided to tag along anyway.

"Listen kid, I got a lot o' shit goin' on in my life right now, an' I ain't exactly what you'd call a decent role model."

"I don't understand Remy, I thought we were a team... you said yourself we work well together..."

Remy quickened his pace. "No Colin, I said you throwin' yourself into harm's way bought me an advantage..."

"Precisely!" Colin interjected. "That is the very definition of teamwork!"

Remy shook his head. The kid was smart; annoying, but smart. "Shit like that will get you killed. It ain't teamwork if you die."

The teenage fiendling jogged ahead of Remy, turning to jog backwards along the bridge in front of him. He had a big grin on his face. "See, you do care. That's why you'll make a great mentor."

Remy sighed, and stopped walking. "Okay Colin, here's how it is." He took a deep breath. "I am broke. I got nothin' but a handful o' deniers to my name. I am goin' to see a man about getting' myself a lil' stipend so I don' end up homeless myself.

"You can come with, an' if he gives me anythin', I'll give you a lil' sum'n, and send you on your way. If you want to learn more about bein' a fiendlin', I'll put you on a boat back to my home village in the swamp, an' I'll write you a letter to give to my sister Elise, an' she'll see you right.

"An' if I don' get any money this evenin', I'll still write you a letter, but how you get there's your own business. I suggest you try your luck with the Baron back there. He seems a decent sort, and it sounds like he could do with some help gettin' his household up an' runnin' again. Now excuse me, you're in my way."

Remy resumed walking, and Colin slunk along in silence, half a pace behind.

After crossing the bridge, they continued south through the quiet residential quarter of Isla Verdé; an area of narrow cobbled streets lined with rows of prim three- or four-story terraces. Many of the terraces had balconies and galleries that overhung the street below, some almost touching the buildings opposite in places. There was no sign of the cultists waiting in ambush for Epifani or anyone else, and they emerged onto the Piazza Grandé.

It must have been the eve of the corpse market, as the plaza was bustling with people and Risen corpses, and the smell was eye-watering. What was it Thessu had said about his senses being overwhelmed by the stink of the city? That guy definitely shouldn't linger in the Piazza Grandé!

Colin must have had a similar thought as he held his nose, saying "Ugh! What died? I could do with a beak mask like Thessu's right about now."

They crossed the plaza, with Remy having to keep Colin from wondering off distracted by the sights and sounds, and continued on to the commercial district on the southern side. Here, the crowds continued in busy boulevards that were lined with stalls selling all manner of things, overlooked by the balconies of bustling bars and bordellos.

"Remy! Remy Du Rosier!" someone called from one of the high balconies, a shrill voice that cut through the bustle and noise. Colin and Remy looked up. A young woman in a black bustier with a pink feather boa was waving frantically. Colin's eyes bulged.

"Evenin' Miss Annabel," Remy replied, just loud enough to be heard. "Can't stop right now. Catch you later," and he kept on walking. "Much later," he added under his breath.

"Remy! How come you don't party any more, Remy?" she called after him, her voice almost drowned by the crowd, but her disappointment clear. Remy mimed that he couldn't hear and led Colin, goggle-eyed, away through the crowd.

They reached the end of the boulevard and pressed on into the maritime quarter that sat between the commercial district and the docks, where the streets were narrower and quieter, and were lined with wide squat warehouses and craftsmen's workshops for the nautical trades; shipwrights, ropers, riggers, blockmakers and the like.

"Why do you have that effect on all the women, Remy?" Colin asked.

"It's the horns, kid," Remy answered, without looking up. "They love the horns."

"No I don't mean that... though that's good to know." He self-consciously touched the nubs of horn emerging from his own temples. "I mean why do you leave them so disappointed? It was the same with the girls at the Madrigal. Seriously, why don't you party any more Remy?"

Remy stopped and gave him a long, searching look. He thought about telling him why, but decided not to. It wasn't like Colin could help fix his mistakes, not like he would even be hanging around much longer anyway. "Come on, it's this way," he said, gesturing towards a short, dimly-lit alleyway between a cooper's workshop and a chandlery. He led, and Colin followed.

The end of the alleyway was shadowed by the wide overhang of the neighbouring building, and at the back of the shadow was a blank unmarked door. A woman remonstrated with the door, or with someone behind it. Someone behind the door who wasn't letting her in.

"Remy... isn't that Epifani?" Colin asked. He was right; it was. What was she doing here?

A rickshaw pulled up to the end of the alleyway behind them then. Turning, they saw a pale man step down from the rickshaw and tip the Risen corpse that had pulled him there. "Excuse me gentlemen," the man said. "Is this the way to the Casa Del Sol Riz?... Oh, hello Remy! Hello Colin my boy!" It was the Baron.

CHAPTER 6

"…I already told you, I'm here to see the Don!" Epifani was getting cross now.

The voice was unmoved. "And I'm sorry miss, but I already told you, I can't let anyone in without the passphrase. Maybe if you could tell me the nature of your business with the Don…?"

There was no chance of that. She was not about to tell this… this… underling about her infiltration of the Ziggurat or her run-in with the zealots. Certainly not when she could sense the presence of the Risen with him behind that door. No. Don Gusteau was her emergency contact; her missing associate had told her to come to him and him alone in an emergency. She would get in some other way and speak to the Don in private. Bitterly, she wondered why her associate hadn't just told her the damn passphrase!

Someone called out behind her. "Can I help you with somethin', Miss Epifani?"

She whirled around. It was the fiendling from the bridge. What was his name? Rambo maybe? No that wasn't it. Remy maybe? He had his sidekick with him as well; Remy and sidekick. She eyed them suspiciously. Had they followed her?

"Did you follow me?" she bristled.

"No, I have business here at the Casa," Remy replied.

Epifani saw Baron De Ville was with them too, and the creepy doll he talked to. "It seems by some happy coincidence, we all have business here at the Casa," the Baron said, smiling. Then he frowned at the door. "Is there some problem? Is the Casa closed for business?"

Epifani couldn't shake the feeling that this was no coincidence, but they'd helped her fight off those zealots on the bridge. "Not closed," she said, booting the door in annoyance. "Just obstinate."

"Might I try?" Remy asked. Epifani waved him forward.

Remy rapped three times on the door. A peephole opened, and he announced, "I live my life in sin and misery." There was a rattle of a chain and a dead-bolt, and the door creaked open, flooding the alleyway with bright light. Remy stood aside to let Epifani enter first.

Epifani pushed the door wide and went through, glowering at the doorman as she strode past him into a plush antechamber, with dark wood-panelled walls and a hardwood floor. The Risen presence she had sensed was a single corpse, stood to one side of the door in a red uniform and hat, standing ready to take coats for the cloakroom. The sound of music and laughter trickled through from a large pair of double doors in the far wall.

The doorman, a burly man in a red uniform that matched that of the corpse, beckoned the rest of them in. "Feel free to check your hats and coats if you wish," he said, gesturing towards the corpse. "But I'll have to insist that all blades and firearms are checked in."

The Baron entered, and removed his hat and cape and handed them to the corpse with a smile, and got given a little ivory token in exchange. Epifani noticed wryly that he kept his cane; and the sword blade concealed inside it. Remy checked his rapier and a dagger, which was very trusting of him, Epifani thought, while the sidekick made a show of handing over a little fruit knife.

"And you, miss?" the doorman asked.

"I'll keep my cloak thanks," Epifani said tersely. She wouldn't hand anything of hers to that noxious thing. She would keep her stiletto too, safely tucked into her boot. What was this place anyway? Why did it need a cloakroom?

The doorman threw open the double doors, to reveal a cavernous space beyond, brightly lit and richly decorated. Epifani's breath caught. It was a vast oval chamber easily two or three hundred feet across at its widest. A mezzanine balcony ran around the perimeter of the chamber, with staircases running between the mezzanine and the chamber floor at regular intervals.

They had entered at the mezzanine level, which was filled with gaming tables, while on the chamber floor below, a runway stage was surrounded by a dining area. Tables were full of people dining as they watched some sort of burlesque show; an attractive young woman in golden body paint, who gyrated lasciviously on the stage to the rhythm of a steel drum band.

The room was filled with people, all richly attired and enjoying the various entertainments. Epifani saw people playing cards, or roulette, or dice in the gaming areas, attended by red-uniformed croupiers and scantily clad young men and women serving drinks. In the restaurant area downstairs, she saw couples and groups dining on sumptuous-looking food, attended by more scantily clad servers.

High above, half a dozen enormous crystal chandeliers hung from the ceiling, filling the place with a decadent golden light, a welcome change from the sickly green of the viridian lamps used everywhere in La Crosse.

"Remy, you bring me to the best places," the sidekick said.

***

"I really am sorry, Valanthé," Gerard said, wiping the last of the gravy from round his mouth with a serviette. "About your job I mean. Do you think you can go back?"

Valanthé shook her head, then looked away pensively. "No. Lugwort is an oaf but he has enough sway on Flotsam that none of the other captains will have me now."

Gerard smiled a half-smile that he hoped was reassuring. "Well I'm sure the Don will take you on. Everyone says he has his fingers in lots of pies in La Crosse and beyond. They say he's got a man in the Cabal, even."

Valanthé nodded weakly – not seeming reassured – then continued staring blankly past him, no doubt lost in dark pangs of regret. In rescuing him from the Greater Pit and defending him from the pirates, the young woman had lost her home and her livelihood, and he owed her for that. He owed her as well for bringing him back to the Casa, and for removing the copper disc from his brow and carefully bandaging the wound. Gerard was unused to such kindness from strangers.

After she had returned him to his rooms and cleaned and dressed his wound, she had made to leave, but he'd insisted she at least stay and join him downstairs for breakfast, and he'd promised to enquire of the

Don if there might be an opening for someone with her particular skill set. She had agreed, but had insisted he bathe and change his clothes before they went anywhere, as he still looked and smelled like a Pit corpse. A short while later they had come downstairs to take breakfast in the salon grand, while they waited for the Don.

In truth, he'd never met the Don before, and he had no idea what Valanthé's particular skill set was; all Gerard really knew about the young woman was that she wore black leather and fought with two swords, and that she protected people she was ordered to kill. All he knew about the Don was that he owned the Casa Del Sol Riz and that everyone said he had his fingers in lots of pies. Asking for a meeting had been simple enough though – Gerard was a long-standing guest in the man's establishment after all – and the maître d'hôtel had assured them they wouldn't be waiting long.

Gerard's head still throbbed from where Valanthé had carefully removed the marque of ownership from his brow. She'd given it to him as a keepsake, and he fidgeted with the copper disc absently while scanning the table for any more morsels of food that he hadn't yet eaten. She pushed her half-eaten grits and eggs over to him, and he tucked into it greedily.

"You seem to have gotten some energy back," she remarked. "How's the head?"

"Still throbbing, and that steel pan band isn't helping," he replied, reaching up instinctively to the bandage still wrapped around the wound on his brow. "But I'll live. Thank you again for bringing me home."

She frowned at that. "This is an odd place to call home. How long have you lived here?"

"Almost a year. It's not so bad; I spent most of my thirties in the wilderness with just myself for company, so it's a nice change to be among so many people."

Her frown deepened, and Gerard wondered if Valanthé didn't see right through him. His friends and family – everyone he had ever known in fact – had all died decades ago, and none of the people he'd surrounded himself with for the past year had cared enough to notice he'd been missing for more than a week. He was more lonely at the Casa than he'd ever been in the wilderness.

"Monsieur Malblanq?" Gerard looked up to see the maître d'hôtel standing beside him looking apologetic. "My sincere apologies monsieur for keeping you waiting. Don Gusteau is a busy man, but he will be happy to meet the young lady in just a short while longer. Perhaps I could get you something else to eat while you wait? The same again perhaps?"

"Just the young lady?" Gerard asked, trying to keep the disappointment from his voice. He was also keen to meet the mysterious Don.

"Yes monsieur, that is what he said," the maître d'hôtel replied, beckoning a waiter to clear their plates and bring more food, then he glid smoothly away.

***

Remy steered the others along the mezzanine and down the polished staircase to the main restaurant area near the stage. "If you wan' talk to the Don, we goin' have to speak to the maître d'," he said, gesturing to a host station, behind which stood a harried-looking man in a black velvet doublet with the Casa's crest embroidered on the breast pocket.

The Baron stood aside, gesturing Remy forward with a crooked smile, but Epifani bristled at his presumption and glared at him. That woman really did not like receiving help.

The four of them walked over, Remy having to steer Colin back in the right direction as the kid veered off towards the stage, spellbound by the dancer in the gold body paint who was now reaching a crescendo.

One hand firmly on Colin's shoulder, Remy approached the maître d'. "Evenin' Jacques," he said, resting an elbow on the lip of the host station and leaning in.

The man looked up, surprised. "Monsieur Du Rosier! What a pleasure to see you again; it has been too long!"

Remy smiled. "He in?"

The maître d's smile faded just a touch before returning. "He is monsieur, but he is very busy this evening."

"Tell him Baron De Ville and Epifani..." he floundered for a moment. He had no idea what the woman's surname was.

"De La Hovella" she supplied. "Epifani De La Hovella." It was an obvious lie.

"Tell him Baron De Ville and Epifani De La Hovella are here to see him," Remy continued unfazed. "And I would like a word wi' him as well o'course."

"Of course monsieur. Would you like some refreshments while you wait?"

"That would be most welcome," Remy replied, and the maître d' gestured for a waiter to seat them at a table, then strode off towards the back of the dining hall.

Remy considered Epifani closely as they were led to a table. Isla Hovella was one of the shanty islands on the outskirts of the city, and there was no way she was from there. He had a carefully honed ability to judge a person's means and background, and from her speech and mannerisms, he had Epifani pegged as a spoilt rich girl. He wondered what her real name was, and why she was so secretive with it. And what was her business with the Don?

"De La Hovella sounds like a made-up name," Colin announced, proving once again that guile was his super power, and earning him a cold glare from their secretive companion.

Someone called out, "Baron? Baron De Ville?"

They all turned to see a tall broad-shouldered man stand up from one of the tables they had passed. He was a bear of a man in a fashionable yellow and white slashed doublet with matching hat and pantaloons, though he looked somewhat pale and gaunt and moved awkwardly like perhaps he was recently recovered from some illness. He was grinning broadly though, and the Baron grinned back.

"Gerard! What a pleasure to see you again my good man!" They shook hands warmly in that way men do when they'd much rather be hugging but are too polite to risk it, then the Baron noticed the man's frailty, and gestured to a bandage on his head. "Are you quite alright?"

"It's been an eventful evening!" the man said, self-consciously adjusting his hat to cover his swollen, bandaged forehead. "Please, won't you join us, and I'll tell you all about it," the man said, gesturing to the empty seats around the table he shared with a slender young woman in black combat leathers.

They were an odd couple, Remy thought. She was much younger than he, and if they were on a date, then judging by the body language it was going badly; for she'd been staring intently at the gold-painted dancer on stage behind him.

Epifani harumphed as the Baron accepted the invitation, and she hovered nearby with her arms crossed in annoyance.

"Allow me to introduce my companions," said the Baron. "You know Belle of course, and this is Remy Du Rosier and Miss Epifani." He didn't bother relaying her false surname, nor did he invite her to make up another.

"Remy this is my friend, Gerard Malblanq," the Baron continued.

"And I," said Colin, sweeping a low bow directed at the young lady, "…am Salvatoré Col Haolim Primo Martelaar Delmond Du Laurentin." He blurted out his full name in a scattergun of syllables mid-bow that was probably meant to impress her. She did not look impressed.

"You can call him Colin," Remy said, shaking the man's hand and nodding genially to the young lady.

"Remy, it's a pleasure," Gerard said. "Any friend of the Baron's is a friend of mine. Colin, Epifani; likewise. May I present Miss Valanthé Luxalim."

"What a beautiful name," Colin oozed towards the young lady – Valanthé – brushing his fringe aside to make sure she saw his magic horns, as he swept into the seat next to her. "I bet you have a lovely smile."

She wasn't smiling. In fact she looked like she might be about to break his jaw. Remy spotted the danger and thought about intervening. Then shrugged it off.

Instead he watched Valanthé lean in to whisper something in Colin's ear. It was likely a warning of some sort, as the kid's smile faded, and he paled and edged away from her discreetly. Remy knew then that he would like Gerard and Valanthé.

"Gerard and I spent a wonderful hundred years together," the Baron said mischievously, taking a seat next to Gerard once it was clear Epifani wouldn't be sitting.

"It flew by," Gerard added, grinning. "I swear it only felt like a few eves. If we hadn't run out of sherry we might have been missing two hundred years!" and they both chuckled.

"Oh, you were on the Queen of the South as well?" Remy asked. "The Baron was tellin' us all about it earlier this evenin'."

"There really isn't much to tell," Gerard shrugged. "It really did feel like just a few eves."

To the Baron he added, "are you going to the book launch?"

"The book launch?" the Baron queried.

"Yes," Gerard replied. "You know the mystery writer Sofokles of Halla?" the Baron didn't. "Well he's written a novel about what might have happened on the Queen. It's all a fabrication of course, since none of us can remember anything happening on the Queen. But anyway, he's launching his book overmorrow's-eve at ninebells at the library of the necromancers' guild and he's invited a couple of us to come and talk about the voyage. You should come."

The Baron smoothed his moustache in consideration. "What do you think, my dear?" he asked the doll. "Should we go along?"

"Joanna will be there… Joanna Pianna," Gerard added with a wry smile.

"Oh yes, the witch!" the Baron exclaimed, and they both laughed uproariously at some inside joke.

**

It was a genuine pleasure for the Baron to reunite with his friend.

He hadn't known Gerard for very long of course; their voyage down the Poconovo river on the Queen of the South had been quite brief – only a few evenings' duration – and they had lost contact in the year since. But they'd shared a genuine connection on that cruise that had only deepened when they learned they had been gone for a century, and now they shared another bond that came from having both lost all their friends and family in the meantime.

Gerard had travelled widely across the northern continent prospecting for gold, and when they'd met on the cruise, he'd confided in the Baron that he was returning to La Crosse to register a large gold claim he'd discovered in the barren hills of the breakspears. It seemed he had been successful in that endeavour; he had made a tidy sum from the look of his fine clothes, though the Baron wondered if his friend would not still rather be ranging in the wilds where he was more at home.

They each recounted the events that brought them to the Casa Del Sol Riz that evening, and it sounded like Gerard and the young lady had had just as eventful an evening as they had. Valanthé blushed as Gerard recounted her brave exploits, while Remy seemed to enjoy the retelling of his. For some reason the young fiendling boy – Colin – was unusually subdued. Epifani continued looking vexed; she really was a very intense young woman. She did eventually join them when waiters brought food and drink.

The Baron soon realised he and Gerard had something else in common when his friend spoke about his lengthy blackouts. That was a revelation.

"My good man, I have been experiencing the exact same thing!" he exclaimed.

"Really?" said Gerard. "Do you have any idea what's causing it?"

"I didn't, but if it's affecting both of us, I wonder if it isn't affecting everyone who was on the Queen of the South?"

"Oh, is Belle affected?" Gerard asked earnestly.

This made Epifani snigger into her biscuits and gravy for some reason, but the Baron ignored her. "Hmmm good point. No, she isn't." He adjusted her in his pocket so her button eyes were angled to glare at Epifani, before continuing. "So it definitely hasn't affected everyone who was on the cruise. Still, it seems like an extraordinary coincidence that both of us are affected!"

The Baron made up his mind then about the book launch. "I think I will come along overmorrow's-eve. We should find out if Joanna is affected; or anyone else who was on the ship."

Further discussion was interrupted by the return of the maître d'hôtel. "Pardon me madames and monsieurs, Don Gusteau is ready for you now." They all rose and made to follow the maître d'hôtel, with the exception of Gerard who remained with the table.

"Not you, Colin. You stay here and don't move." Remy said. Colin looked like he might object, but Valanthé silenced him with a look, and he returned stroppily to the table.

The maître d'hôtel escorted the rest of them towards a swing door at one side of the stage, from which the waiters and waitresses had been serving food. Were they going to the kitchens? That would be unexpected, the Baron thought.

They were indeed heading to the kitchens. They pushed through the door and were hit with a blast of heat and noise. A dozen cooks in white coats and tall chef's hats worked busy stations preparing food, while dozens of Risen corpses cleaned and scrubbed, washed and dried, fetched and carried, and worked the bellows of the massive ovens on the far side. Epifani grimaced for some reason, looking suddenly like she regretted the biscuits and gravy she had eaten. Very odd. Perhaps she had seen something untoward that the Baron hadn't.

The maître d'hôtel led them through the busy kitchen, towards a short corridor off to one side where it was noticeably cooler. At the end of the corridor, away from all the heat and bustle they reached another swing door, and felt the chill emanating from the room. The Baron guessed it was the cooler maybe, or perhaps the dessert kitchen. What an odd place to meet the Casa's notorious owner!

The maître d'hôtel gestured for the group to wait, while he pushed the door open partway and leaned in. "The petitioners, boss."

Beyond the maître d'hôtel, they caught a glimpse of a small dessert kitchen – the Baron's hunch had been right – and a glimpse of a large man in chef's whites working alone at the cook station, carefully piping out purple coloured macarons onto a chilled baking sheet.

No, that wasn't a man; that was a devil. An actual devil! He stood seven feet tall, a horned and tailed silhouette of deepest black. In chef's whites. The Baron saw nothing of his features, none of them did, for he had none. They saw only that he was darkness personified… and he was making desserts.

Remy leaned past the maître d'hôtel and peered round into the room. "Hey, Pop," Remy said to the devil.

"Bonsoir Remy," the devil replied in a rich, thick accent, without looking up from his macarons. "I'll see the scarred young lady first s'il vous plait." Remy nodded and let the door close.

The Baron stared at Remy dumbstruck. They all did.

CHAPTER 7

"The Don wants to see you first" Remy said, gesturing at Epifani, seeming to ignore their bewildered looks.

"Your father is a devil!" Epifani blurted out. The cocky fiendling was Don Gusteau's son, and Don Gusteau – the man she had come to see – wasn't even a man at all! These were important snippets of information that Remy should have shared, and she gave him her death glare.

"He is," Remy confirmed, grinning. "But he makes amazin' patisserie." He waved her towards the door to the dessert kitchen, before darkening as she took a tentative step towards it. "Jus' be warned though…" and here he leaned close, whispering "…he don't give anythin' away for free. Not favours, not advice, and definitely not his chocolate éclairs."

He leant back, eyes twinkling with suppressed amusement. She glared at him, deciding not to trust a word he said. She would make her own mind up about the devil, and she strode past him and through the door as confidently as she could.

She let the door close again behind her and she stood waiting for the devil to look up from his sheet of macarons. He didn't.

"Mademoiselle Epifani I presume?" The devil spoke clearly despite his strong accent, though if he had a face and spoke through a mouth, Epifani couldn't tell. He was a shadow cut out from the world.

He continued piping a violet-scented batter in perfect circles equidistant apart for a long moment then stopped and set down his piping bag and looked at her. He had no eyes, but nevertheless she felt the weight of his gaze as it bore down on her.

She realised then that he'd been waiting for her to respond, but she was so flummoxed that she had just stood there dumbly watching him pipe the purple batter.

"Er… yes. I am Epifani… um… De La Hovella."

She fumbled the lie, but she got no sense from him that he spotted it, although in truth she got no sense of him at all. He had no presence in her mind. She most keenly felt him as an unsettling absence, so perhaps he really was a shadow cut out from the world.

"My name is Auguste Don Gusteau. Zis is my establishment," the devil said. "And you are no De La 'Ovella, though you were on Isla 'Ovella recently, which I suspect is why you said zat. You are Lady Epifani Pye and you are 'ere because your associate is missing and ze priests of ze Crosse Cult found your safehouse, non?"

She was truly flummoxed now. "How did you know that?"

The devil – Don Gusteau – flicked a finger in the air nonchalantly and his tray of macarons lifted up and drifted across the kitchen to the hatch of the patisserie oven as if carried by an invisible hand. Another finger-flick slid the hatch open in the far wall and deposited the tray into it.

"I make it my business to know ze intrigues of ze city." An hourglass on one side of the hatch flipped over at his bidding, while the devil wiped his shadow hands on a hand towel. "And you really stirred ze 'ornet's nest you know!" He sounded amused, though there was no expression on his face. In fact no face at all.

"Perhaps you can fill in some blanks for me zough," he continued, as he wiped down the surface of his cook station with the towel. "Ze cult 'as been going to an awful lot of effort to find you. Ze cardinal of ze Ziggurat 'imself 'as been demanding your 'ead! I'd like to know why... What are zey really looking for, Epifani?"

Epifani shrugged. There was no need to conceal that she'd stolen from the zealots; they must have already recovered the loot when they raided her safehouse. "We took some relics from the Ziggurat, some of the antiques they use in their rituals. We were trying to disrupt their nasty cult."

"Well you certainly did zat!" There was definitely amusement in his voice; the devil was no fan of the zealots. "But yes yes, zat much was obvious. Do you still 'ave any of ze antiques?"

She shook her head. "No, everything I had was in the safehouse. They'll have cleared it out and gotten it all back." She swallowed bitterly that the relics had all been recovered so easily. She should rather have destroyed them.

Don Gusteau rubbed his chin thoughtfully; or that's what she assumed he did. In actuality, the sleeve of his chef's whites waggled under where his chin would have been, and the black silhouette of his hand disappeared into the black silhouette of his head.

"Well ze cult is still blundering around trying to recover something; some missing relic zey did not find in ze 'Ovella 'ouse. Do you know what zat could be?"

A recollection came back to her then; something the zealot on the bridge had said. Without thinking, she blurted out, "the zealot on the bridge said something about a goblet."

"You didn't take a goblet from ze Ziggurat?" he asked.

"No. There was nothing like a goblet in our haul of antiques. Unless…" The awful thought came to her that her associate could have taken it from the Ziggurat without her realising. She looked away, angry with herself. That might explain why he didn't come back for the rest of the loot… or for her. Maybe he already got what he came for. "Do you know what the goblet might be?" Epifani asked, turning the question back on him.

The silhouette shrugged. "A fucking cup; who knows!" He lifted a spoonful of lime-green batter out of a mixing bowl, and spooned it into a fresh piping bag. "But whatever it is, ze Cardinal badly wants it back. Zere is also something else to consider, Epifani. Ze cult found your safehouse because zey were tipped off. Someone told zem exactly where to find you."

"I think I need to find my associate," she said firmly.

"Yes I rather zink you do," he agreed. "Luckily for you I know where 'e is. Also I 'ave a little sway with ze Cardinal… I zink I can get ze cult off your back." He drew her attention to a silver tray of patisserie cakes on a shelf by the door. "Would you like a chocolate éclair?"

***

The Baron had been engaging Remy in quiet conversation while they waited, and they had tried to include the young lady; Valanthé. She was pretty guarded about herself however, though had seemed just as interested as the Baron was to learn more about Remy's unorthodox upbringing with a devil for a father.

For his part, Remy seemed surprisingly open about his early years in a fiendling community in the Poconovo bayou. They had apparently lived as a family along with his mother and a sister, and he told a number of amusing anecdotes about times mayhem had ensued when his father had struggled to adapt to life in the village. Valanthé nodded in recognition at some of the familiar absurdities of village life that Remy described, apparently very similar to the village of her own youth, a small woodland community along the coast; that had been the one snippet of information about herself that she divulged.

Anyway, as Remy told it, in the end his father left and moved to the big city, leaving Remy and his sister Elise to be raised by their mother, and Remy had had a strained relationship with his father ever since. About his mother, Remy was extremely defensive and the Baron got a definite impression that she might recently have died, though Remy never exactly said as much.

After a short wait, the swing door opened and Epifani emerged from the dessert kitchen, clutching a delicious-looking chocolate éclair, but looking troubled. "He's ready for you next, Baron." Epifani said, rather more subdued than she had been beforehand.

The Baron thanked her, and Epifani gave them all a curt nod of farewell, and she left, chomping on her éclair as she walked off.

Remy gave the Baron a winning smile and two thumbs up for encouragement, and he pushed through into the dessert kitchen, letting the door close behind him.

It was a strange thing, looking upon a devil. It wasn't that he was so dark that he appeared black; nothing so mundane as that. It was more that the Baron simply wasn't able to process what his eyes were telling him, so his brain had blanked the devil out.

The devil – Don Gusteau – was now piping buttercream filling onto upturned purple macaron halves. The Baron saw the Don's chef's whites moving and the stark silhouette of his clawed hand emerging from the sleeve clutching and squeezing the piping bag, coating each macaron half in a perfect, even swirl of buttercream that smelled decadently of vanilla.

"Thank you for seeing me this evening," the Baron said, bowing politely. "I am Baron De Ville."

"It is a pleasure to make your acquaintance, Baron. My name is Auguste Don Gusteau…" The devil suddenly seemed to stop what he was doing, and abruptly look up to face the Baron – though of course he had no face – and a trail of buttercream dripped messily across the countertop as his piping was interrupted. "Pardon, Monsieur… did you say your name was 'De Ville'? It was my understanding zat ze De Ville line died out decades ago?"

"You know your history, sir," the Baron replied, inclining his head in acknowledgement. "Yes you are correct the line ended with the death of my great grand-nephew thirty years ago."

"Your great grand-nephew? Surely not. Zat would make you over a 'undred years old, non?"

The Baron smiled. "I was a passenger on the Queen of the South."

"Ah, zat explains it zen. You 'ave my condolences Baron." Don Gusteau tsk-tsked the buttercream mess, and wiped the tip of the piping bag and the counter before continuing. "Zis also explains some odd reports I got from my bailiffs about zeir trip to Isla Festa. I presume zat is why you are 'ere?"

The Baron nodded. "Yes, I came here because the invalid writ of possession listed you as the contract-holder for clearance and demolition. Now obviously I'm not prepared to let my family home be demolished, so I wanted to meet you face-to-face and see if we could come to some arrangement."

Don Gusteau raised a shadow finger in query. "Invalid?" he bristled. "What makes you say ze writ of possession was invalid? It was signed and stamped by ze Cabal Court, non?"

"Indeed it was," replied the Baron matter-of-factly. "But ownership of the islet is now in dispute. Since I never died, my heirs should never have inherited, and they had no right to dispose of the estate."

Don Gusteau had finished piping buttercream, and he paused, seeming to consider what the Baron had said.

"Hmm. You make a good point Baron. And zat leaves me in a delicate position." He started sandwiching the macaron halves together, arranging the finished treats carefully on a pretty silver tray. They looked delicious. "Ze Cabal Court will take months or perhaps a year to 'ear your petition, and meanwhile ze new owner of ze property 'as paid me 'andsomely for demolition. It will cost me a lot of money in penalties if I renege on ze deal, not to mention ze damage to my reputation.

"On ze other 'and, if ze Cabal Court eventually finds in your favour, I am liable to rebuild your family 'ome brick by brick if I am found to 'ave demolished it illegally. Quite a quandary."

Don Gusteau picked up one of the completed purple macarons and bit into it, the buttercream oozing out the sides as half the treat disappeared into the void of his head where his mouth would have been, and his silhouette seemed to chew. The other half followed it into the void. "Of course ze simplest thing to do would be to 'ave you killed."

The devil let the threat hang in the air for a moment, before he offered the silver tray towards the Baron. "Would you like to try one? Ze violet ones are ze most delicious in my 'umble opinion."

The Baron hesitated, then accepted one of the sweet-scented treats from the tray and bit into it. He had to admit they were delicious, and he licked the buttercream from his moustache. The silhouette of the Don looked towards the far side of the kitchen where an hourglass was trickling out its last grains of sand, and flicked a finger in that direction. The hatch of the patisserie oven opened in a billow of steam, and another tray of macaron halves – lime green ones – drifted out, as if carried by an unseen hand, then waited above the countertop for a cooling rack to make its own way over at the Don's bidding.

The devil sighed. "I do not wish to kill you, Baron. It seems my son 'as taken a liking to you, and I know it upsets him when his friends get immolated. Would you like to try one of the lime macarons? They should be cool enough in but a moment." The Baron shook his head, still chewing the violet one.

"It seems in zat case we must find a way for me to get out of zis contract with my reputation untarnished. You spoke of an arrangement, non?" The Baron nodded, gesturing apologetically that his mouth was still full and he couldn't speak.

"Zis is what we must do. I must give you ze name of ze new owner. And you, you must obtain from 'im ze deed of ownership. Now, 'e will not part with it, you must take it from 'im. I will assist you to assemble a team to recover ze deed from 'is property, and also while you are zere, you will recover some other inconsequential things which 'e 'as, zat I want, and which you will get for me."

The Baron gulped, swallowing down the mouthful of sticky violet. "You... you want me to steal the deed from him?"

"Oui... and some other things as well. Ze other things are for me, to make me willing to break my contract. Ze deed is for you, so zat when you present your petition to the Cabal Court, it is iron-clad, and zen my repossession order will be null and void, and I shall wring my 'ands and becry zis unfortunate turn of events zat prevents me from fulfilling my contract with ze legal owner."

The Baron was unconvinced. He was no thief, though the morality of stealing something that was rightfully his could be argued both ways. Stealing some other things 'while he was there' was less arguable. He gave the Don a dubious look.

Don Gusteau shrugged, then continued matter-of-factly. "You must decide before you leave zis room, Baron... Ze alternative is zat I kill you now and demolish your 'ouse."

The Baron gritted his teeth. He had no doubt Don Gusteau would do it without a second thought if he declined the arrangement. "What are these other inconsequential things?"

"'ow about we make it easy. 'e 'as but one thing zat I covet. 'e 'as an egg. Get me ze egg."

"An egg?" That was a very odd thing to covet.

"Oui, an egg. You will know it when you find it."

The Baron looked down to Belle. The doll sat limp in the breast pocket of his suit. He could tell she was disappointed in him. But there really wasn't a choice. He looked back up towards the devil, and nodded almost imperceptibly.

"Bon," said Don Gusteau. "Zen I shall tell you ze name of ze legal owner of De Ville Manor and all De Ville property, is ze Marquis du Laurentin."

***

The Baron emerged from the patisserie kitchen looking just as troubled as Epifani had before him. Remy smiled inwardly. His father did have that effect on people. He wondered what deals they had both struck with him.

"Did you get some resolution to your legal wrangle?" Remy asked. The Baron grimaced, seeming very unsure whether he had got what he wanted or not. His father had that effect on people too.

"I think I need a drink. Would you excuse me Remy, Miss Valanthé, I will head back to the table with Belle." He stepped past the two of them, saying, "Remy, he's ready for you next."

Remy nodded, and Valanthé gave him the same winning smile and double thumbs up that Remy had given to the Baron before his audience. Remy chuckled. As he reached the door, he turned round to her, saying, "I hope you don't mind me askin', Miss Valanthé; what was it you said to Colin?"

She looked unsure for a moment who Colin was, then realised. "The fiendling kid with the baby horns?"

Remy nodded. "Yeah, whatever you said had him spooked."

She stifled a laugh. "I told him I had a bunch of little nubbins I'd taken from horny boys who tried it on, and his would be the smallest in my collection. He asked how many fiendlings had hit on me, I told him he's the first. When I said nubbins, I didn't mean horns."

"Yeah, that'd do it, Remy chuckled. "You was jokin' though right?... You don' actually collect boy's... nubbins?" Her eyes sparkled with amusement, but she didn't answer. Remy went through the door.

His father had two silver platters filled with macarons he had made, and was rummaging below the counter when Remy went in. A cloth was scrubbing the counter by itself, while a pair of nutcrackers hovered over a small bowl, shelling almonds into it. Don Gusteau emerged from his rummaging with a large mortar and pestle which he placed on the counter. "Remy! It is good to see you son."

He strode over to the door, and embraced Remy in manly fashion. Remy returned the embrace. The Don withdrew after a moment and looked Remy up and down. "I 'ave missed you Remy," he said finally. "You don't call, you don't write... Let me get you some food you look like you 'aven't 'ad a good meal in weeks, maybe a pain au chocolat? Or I can whip up a crêpe suzette? 'ave you been eating properly?"

"It's fine, Pop, I got some fixin's in the restaurant."

Returning to the cook station, the Don grabbed a handful of shelled almonds, and placed them into the mortar bowl, then started grinding with the pestle. Remy walked over to the other side of the counter and plucked the nutcrackers out of the air, taking over shelling more almonds. His father nodded appreciatively. "'ow 'ave you been, Remy. It has been a month since your mother…" he trailed off, not finishing the sentence. "You should 'ave gone to 'er memorial service. Your absence was noted."

Remy looked up, surprised, "You went to it, Pop?"

The Don shook his head sadly. "No. I am not welcome zere. Elise told me you didn't go."

Remy continued shelling almonds. "I didn't realise you'd spoken to her."

"Yes she came to see me. She was worried about you."

"She came here, huh?" His sister had been in town and hadn't told him. He couldn't be angry, Elise was right to hate him; to blame him.

"Remy? Why didn't you go to ze memorial?"

Remy plastered an obviously false smile on his face. "You know me Pop, busy makin' ma way in the world, I had a few… pressin' social events I couldn't miss."

"But zat's not true is it, Remy? Not any more. I supported you when you were insinuating your way into 'igh society, scandalizing 'eiresses and sleeping your way round Isla Roja, making a name for yourself; making me proud. Why did you stop?"

Remy sighed, and looked down at the almonds. "You know why, Pop."

The Don placed a fatherly hand on Remy's shoulder. "Remy, you must not blame yourself for what happened. You know it wasn't your fault."

Remy continued staring down. "Remy! Look at me!" his father said. "It wasn't your fault!"

Remy pulled away, still not looking at the devil. "Please don't…"

"Remy I just want to 'elp!"

Remy shrugged him off and returned to shelling almonds while his father returned to grinding them. Remy let his father's offer of help linger in the air awhile as they shelled and ground almonds together. "Pop, if you want to help, I need money. I'm broke."

Don Gusteau nodded. "I see. I can 'elp with zat."

Remy looked up at him and smiled gratefully. Perhaps the old devil would show a generous side after all, and he hadn't even needed to grovel. "Thank you Pop. I just need a lil' stipend to see me through the next few months. Maybe a couple hundred…"

His father cut him off with a laugh. "Tsk tsk tsk, No Remy! You were doing so well, but zat is not 'ow ze game is played! 'Ave you forgotten everything already? No-one gets money for nothing, not even family!"

Don Gusteau set down the pestle, and took the bowl of almonds from Remy's hands. "Ugh and you've got bits of shell in 'ere as well!" Remy sighed. His father hadn't changed.

"A job has recently come up… very recently in fact!" the Don chuckled, picking bits of shell out of the almond bowl and showing them to Remy disapprovingly. "You will earn some money ze old-fashioned way. I need you and your team to rob ze Marquis du Laurentin."

"My… team?" Remy stuttered, unsure who his father meant, when suddenly the door burst open. A young fiendling boy burst through into the kitchen, the door swinging back and forth in his wake. Colin.

Before Remy could stop him, the kid blurted out, "the Marquis du Laurentin! That is my father! That is the man who told me I was adopted and then beat me and kicked me out onto the street like a dog! I will do it! I will rob him! I will rob him and shit in his bed!"

Remy winced and looked anxiously at the Don. His father hated interruptions almost as much as he hated eavesdroppers. The idiot kid didn't know how much danger he was in. Thankfully, his father seemed amused rather than angry.

"Good lad," the Don said. "Zat's ze spirit!" He waggled a finger and the kid's hair ruffled from across the room. "Remy? Surely you will not let your protégé go on 'is own? And maybe get 'imself killed?"

Remy considered it, but he knew his father's question was rhetorical. He sighed. There was no point fighting it; one way or another his father always got what he wanted. "What are we stealin'?"

Don Gusteau held a hand up to indicate Remy wait a moment, then beckoned the swing door wide open with a finger flick. "Miss Valanthé Luxalim, will you come in as well s'il vous plait, zis concerns you too." Valanthé peered in through the open door, and walked tentatively in. The door closed itself firmly behind her.

"You are looking for work, oui?"

Valanthé nodded; she looked totally discombobulated.

"Well, I 'ave a job for you. For all three of you; four if you include ze Baron. I require some items from the Marquis du Laurentin's safe. Inside you will find a small amount of money, which of course you may keep, Some important papers which your friend ze Baron requires, but most of all you must retrieve for me ze egg.

"Recover zese things and you will get your stipend Remy, and you Valanthé will get a lucrative retainer and plenty more work in future if you want it. You will find me more generous zan ze pirates were."

Valanthé nodded her assent while Colin did an enthusiastic fist pump. Remy sighed. He would be stuck with the annoying kid a little longer, though at least Valanthé and the Baron seemed companionable and capable. The matter settled, the Don beckoned the door open once more and waved them out.

As Remy left, Don Gusteau called him back. "Remy, you should go and see Elise. Did you know she 'as taken vows? As a Mama D'Ombre." Remy winced. Their mother had been a Mama D'Ombre.

Chapter 8

Ponté L'Emilia was a tiny outcrop of land, little more than a rock which jutted sheer out of the water a mile and a half into the Gulf of Mezarcana at the far south-west of La Crosse. A narrow ridge of sand just below the surface of the water connected the rock to the swamp of the Poconovo Delta, forming a hidden barrier that was a hazard for shipping. For that reason, the island hosted a lighthouse; one of two along the coast either side of the city, demarcating the furthest extents of its seaward approaches with dark green beams of light.

The skies had been darkening with ominous cloud when Epifani set off towards the rock, and the rain was soon lashing down in sheets. Lightning periodically flashed across the churning sky above, illuminating the city and the bay in brief snatches of violent light as she rowed. The little rowboat she had stolen was pitching dangerously in the stormy water, and she was struggling to keep its bow pointing in the right direction.

It hadn't looked all that far when she set off, and she had dismissed the rain as little more than an inconvenience, but the storm was definitely worsening, and the weather wasn't inconvenient; it was dangerous. Her muscles ached as she propelled the little boat across the treacherous roiling waters of the gulf towards the emerald beacon of the lighthouse, but it seemed to grow no closer. She was out of her depth, and she knew it; there was a real danger her hubris would get her killed.

She continued rhythmically pulling the leaden oars with leaden muscles, her teeth gritted against the lashing rain and rising danger as she focused on each stroke. Catch. Draw. Recover. Catch. Draw. Recover. Breathe out through the draw. Breathe in through the recovery. Count out the strokes until she earned herself a glance towards the lighthouse. One stroke. Two strokes. Three strokes…

With sheer determination she dragged the little boat through the stormy water towards the lighthouse, for that was where Don Gusteau had said her associate had his hide-out. She would find him, confront him, and if he had betrayed her to the zealots, she would kill him. Ninety-eight. Ninety-nine. A hundred strokes. She looked over her shoulder, spitting out a face-full of spray from the choppy water. Now the lighthouse was closer, and she had the measure of this storm. A smile spread across her face as she powered on. One stroke. Two strokes. Three strokes...

She arrived a good while later, pulling up to a small landing jetty in the ever-shadow of the rock, at the base of the sheer cliff up to the lighthouse above. The swells around the rock had been the most dangerous part of the journey, and she counted herself lucky not to have capsized or been dashed against the rock in that last hundred strokes. She needed rest, but her situation was still perilous, so she forced herself to clamber out onto the slick and treacherous jetty. Drenched to the core, and with hands trembling from the exertion of the row, she fumbled the slippery mooring rope and nearly lost the boat to the waves before securing it.

With the boat secured as well as she could manage, she made her way carefully along the jetty to the rocks at the base of the cliff, where she finally caught her breath and looked up at the sheer cliff face above. It was unlit, black and formless. There was no way up. Lightning forked across the sky then, briefly illuminating the crags and cracks of the cliff... and was that?... yes! Just for an instant, the flash of lightning revealed a flight of iron ladder rungs hammered into the rock face a little way off to her right, before they disappeared into the shadows once more. Thunder rolled over as she scrambled across the slippery rocks towards where she had seen the first rung, almost losing her footing as a wave crashed over the rock she was stood on. The first ladder rung was dangerously slick, and she had no doubt they all were. Having no choice but to try and climb them, she set her weary muscles to the task. Reach. Pull. Step. Reach. Pull. Step. One rung. Two rungs. Three rungs...

***

The lighthouse stood alone on the top of the rock, a narrow circular tower rising a hundred feet from the cliff-top, surmounted by an emerald beacon light that flooded the rain-lashed surface of the rock with muddy green light.

Epifani saw the door at the base of the tower hanging broken from its hinges. She hurried over, shielding her face from the driving rain as she headed for the door. She reached it and leaned exhausted onto the doorframe, sheltering in the lee of the tower while she caught her breath once more. Examining the door, there was no doubt it had been broken by forced entry. That wasn't a good sign.

Stepping tentatively through the door with stiletto drawn, she saw the interior of the tower was a spiral staircase running up to the beacon at the top. Here at the base of the tower, the walls were damp and the floor was a puddle of water. She prodded the large section of the broken door that rested on the bottom stair with her foot, and sodden fragments flaked away under her boot. This place had been open to the elements for a while.

She removed her rain-saturated cloak and left it draped over the handrail before climbing the staircase warily. Her clothes beneath were no less waterlogged, but she reasoned that the heavy cloak would restrict her movement, which would be a problem if she needed to use her stiletto.

At the top of the staircase, another broken door rattled against its door-frame. Pushing that aside carefully, she looked through into a small semi-circular chamber, its narrow lattice windows lashed by rain and whistling with wind. Skinny beams of emerald beacon-light filtered down through gaps in the wooden boards of the ceiling above, illuminating swirling motes of dust in the air. The room was a mess. Furniture had been upturned and broken, the contents of the room strewn and scattered across the floor. Someone had likely been looking for something.

Epifani stepped cautiously into the room, where she immediately spotted a trail of dark stains leading from the upturned bed, across the room to a ladder which ran up to a trapdoor in the ceiling; no doubt providing access to the beacon-light on the floor above. Warily, she crouched down to examine the trail. It was unmistakably blood that stained the floor, but long dried. She sheathed her stiletto. Whatever happened here, it happened weeks ago.

Gingerly, she climbed the ladder. There was more of the dried blood on the rungs, and she had to avoid rubbing her wet clothes against it; she hated getting other people's blood on her clothes. The trapdoor was blocked and wouldn't lift. She cursed, guessing what was blocking it. Bracing on a higher rung, she bent her knees and placed her shoulders directly under the trapdoor, then pushed with all her strength. Her guess was right; whoever had crawled up there to die had been inconsiderately blocking the trapdoor with their body, and it rolled off to one side as she heaved the trapdoor open. She averted her eyes quickly enough to avoid burning them on the viridian beacon, but still she grimaced at the brightness of the light.

Clamping her eyes tightly closed and looking away from the centre of the upstairs chamber, she climbed the last few rungs blind, and felt for the body, moving her hands up its torso to its face. The smell was intense, and confirmed her assessment that the body had been there for weeks. She positioned herself with the beacon-light behind her, and risked a quick look through narrowed eyes; she had to know if this was her associate. It was. Shielding her eyes, she risked a narrow look to either side of the beacon, checking to see if there were other bodies. There weren't.

She debated whether to push the man's body down the hatch to the floor below so she could examine him further, but the rotten, charnel stench convinced her not to. There probably wasn't much more she could tell from his body, and the pieces of the puzzle were falling into place regardless. Someone had come here a couple of months ago, killed him, and ransacked his hideout looking for something.

Climbing down, she realised her former associate couldn't have been the one that tipped off the Ziggurat about her safehouse on Isla Hovella, since he'd already been dead for weeks when the zealots turned up there. She still didn't know if he'd secretly taken some extra loot – such as a goblet – from the Ziggurat without telling her, and if he had, who'd killed him for it. She knew it couldn't be the zealots or they wouldn't still be looking for it.

She felt a momentary pang of regret about the nameless man's death, then angrily pushed that thought from her mind; he may not have betrayed her to the zealots but he'd still cheated her out of some valuable artifact worth killing for. He wasn't her ally; she didn't need allies.

Surveying the room again, she considered where to start her search for clues as to who might have killed the man, and what they were looking for. Before she did anything though, she sought out a towel and cleaned the man's nasty blood smears off her hands and clothes.

A careful search of the chamber revealed little to identify the man, and less to identify who had killed him. Interestingly though, only around half of the chamber's contents had been disturbed, implying that whatever the man's killer had been looking for, they had found it. She thought about leaving, but the howling wind and rain that rattled the windows persuaded her to stay and wait out the storm here in the dry of the lighthouse.

Her search had uncovered some clean, dry clothes at least, so she took off her wet ones and hung them up to dry before slipping into an oversized shirt and trousers, and tried to make herself comfortable. She wasn't worried about being disturbed; she knew now that she was alone on the rock, and only an absolute idiot would try and cross the bay to reach this place in this storm. She righted a comfortable-looking arm chair that had been overturned, and slumped into it.

Despite her exhaustion, she couldn't sleep; her mind was still racing from the evening's events. She looked over at a pile of books she had found by the bed and wondered if any of them were worth reading. She had given them a cursory look earlier; they were a mixture of well-thumbed fiction and non-fiction works. She hauled herself up out of the chair and went back to the pile, looking this time not for clues to a murder, but for something entertaining to read. The first one looked like a tedious whodunnit by some foreign mystery writer. The second was a slim nautical text containing tide charts. The third one though…

The third book in the pile was an old textbook with yellowed pages and a tatty black cover so worn that the lettering of the book's title had rubbed away. Flipping it open, she found inside the cover, a stamp from the library of the necromancers' guild. What was this doing here? Intrigued, she flicked through the book.

Written in archaic prose, it seemed like an out-of-date summary of formal necromancy rituals. Such a book had no business leaving the guild library! She shuddered, and almost tossed the vile tome across the room in disgust, but something nagged at her mind. She thumbed further through the ancient book, and found some pages missing; in fact, a whole chapter had been ripped out. She flipped back to the contents and scanned down. She stopped cold in her tracks. The missing chapter concerned some ritual called a 'Rite of the Bloode Goblette'. She checked the missing section again, and found bloody smudges on the surrounding pages. The killer had torn out the missing section.

It had to be beyond all doubt now; her associate had stolen something called the 'Bloode Goblette' from the Ziggurat, and someone had killed him and taken it from him. Worse, it seemed the killer now planned to use it in some archaic blood ritual of the necromancers... If they hadn't already done so.

She would need to look into this ritual; it was the only clue she had that might lead her to the goblet, and she'd promised to find the stupid thing and give it to the Don.

CHAPTER 9

The central tower of the necromancers' guild was an ancient building, much modified and extended over the thousand-plus years since its initial construction. The tower had been built upon the ruins of earlier guild buildings stretching back to antiquity; the guild had had a constant presence on the island of Isla Muerto since the founding of the city. The central tower of the guild was now the heart of a sprawling complex of interconnected structures that served as academy, headquarters and court of the necromancers. By most reckoning, the complex was the oldest continually-habited structure in La Crosse, older than the Corto Dogé; the ancient home of the elected Dogé of La Crosse and the Cabal Court. It was older even than the Ziggurat. It was a seat of learning and centre of commerce, a shining example of La Crosse's supremacy over lesser cities.

Epifani found it a dark and miserable place. As a child, her parents had brought her here to interview for an apprenticeship, and she had been so overwhelmed by dread proximity to so much undeath, that she had screamed and bucked and hadn't made it inside. They had tried to force her into that terrifying place, and she had clawed and gouged chunks out of her own face in her fury. She still bore the scars on her cheeks.

Her sensitivity to the Risen had increased as she'd aged, and while she still felt the Risen as a malevolent presence in her mind, she could now distinguish the sharp sensation of individual Risen from the softer background sadness and emptiness that saturated the places where the raising happened. This time around, she experienced the necromancers' guild not as a place of terror, but as a place of despair. She had felt the same in the Ziggurat.

The guild library was in one of the older buildings that had grown around the central tower over the centuries, a squat stone building with a grandiose entrance portico that gave the otherwise nondescript structure a touch of gravitas. The portico seemed like a newer addition; it had less of the sadness of the old building it fronted.

She had snuck inside through a side door; some function was happening later in another part of the building, and she had swallowed down her disquiet to accompany a group of porter corpses that were bringing in tall stacks of chairs. The storm of yestereve had passed, but the rain persisted, and the corpses were hurrying to carry their loads in without getting them too wet. She picked up a stack of chairs herself and followed behind the group of Risen splashing through the puddles of the service courtyard, then ditched the chairs once she was safely past the glare of the ancient black-enamelled skeleton corpse that held the door.

Inside, the abysmal sadness was all-pervading; the walls wept and the ceiling sobbed and the very air seemed to shudder with grief. Even the dismal light of the viridian lamps seemed to pool sadly in the corners. She struggled not to break down and cry along, and only years of honing her focus kept her moving forwards towards where she hoped the library could be found. She considered slinking in the shadows, but knew it was better to act like she was supposed to be there. She lowered her hood and the neckerchief that had been concealing her face – she was on the run from zealots not necromancers after all – and strode purposefully along the weeping corridors of the guild.

She passed several acolytes and apprentices of the guild, and was relieved when none of them challenged her. She also passed more of the vile skeleton corpses that served the guild; all black-enamelled bones with a hammered golden marque on their brow. They were every bit as menacing a presence in her mind as regular Risen were, but they did at least lack the smell, and Epifani was grateful for that.

She knew the durability of a Risen corpse was dependent on the skill of the necromancer who raised it and of those who sustained it. A truly skilful necromancer could sustain a corpse for decades if so inclined, but it became progressively harder to sustain them the older they got, and it took immense power and skill to sustain a corpse and keep it mobile beyond the wasting of its flesh and muscles. The guild prided itself on its power and skill, and their cohort of skeleton corpses was the envy of La Crosse. Of course other noble houses also employed those most valuable Risen as well; the ones that served in the Corto Dogé had bones tiled in turquoise mosaic. The guild enamelled theirs black.

She again caught a lucky break when a group of young acolytes burst out of a mournful side door into the corridor just ahead of her, and she caught a snatch of their hushed conversation. They were going to the library. Following them, she strode along the morose corridor in their wake. They turned a corner and ducked through an anguished archway. She followed, and found herself in the guild library, a vast double-height chamber with row upon row of bookshelves housing all the accumulated knowledge of the necromancers. She had rarely felt such sadness.

There were several acolytes in the section of the library that interested her, but also two full necromancers; elderly men in the black slashed doublets and capes of their guild. She hid in the shadows a long while until both necromancers had moved safely away.

It didn't take her long to locate a copy of the book of rituals on a high shelf of a secluded aisle in the 'history of necromancy' section; indeed there were several copies co-located on the shelf together. She picked one at random and found a quiet corner to flick through the pages in the sorrowful green light of an old viridian lamp.

It took her a moment to understand what she was seeing. It was astonishing. She had found the chapter that detailed the 'Rite of the Bloode Goblette', the very section that had been torn out of the copy she'd found in the lighthouse. It was written in archaic language which took a little deciphering, but in essence it described a ritual whereby a person's innate power could be transferred at the moment of their death. She knew that rare individuals had innate powers – her sensitivity to the Risen and ability to disanimate them probably counted as such a gift – but that a power could be transferred was new information.

The process required the donor to be exsanguinated – drained of blood – in a precise manner at the moment of death and of course required the Bloode Goblette, which seemed by this account to be an ancient artifact designed specifically for this ritual.

All of this was interesting of course, but not astonishing. The astonishing thing was that someone had scrawled a note in blue ink on top of the printed text. The note was to her.

'There's no more need to look for the cup, Epifani, it's under the bookcase. It was just a means to an end – a truly glorious end that we

both want – a future without the Risen. Together we will end the undead scourge and reclaim the world for the living. I will do my part, you must do yours. Find Joanna Pianna.'

It was unsigned. She went back to the shelf and checked the other copies of the book. There was no note of any kind in any of them. Someone had had the foresight to know that she would come here and pick up that copy of that book. It was astonishing.

Dropping onto hands and knees, she stooped to examine the bottom of the bookcase and found the plinth was loose. She pulled it aside and found behind it a little cloth bundle, which tinkled as she drew it out. Sitting up on her haunches, she carefully opened the bundle, and found inside the broken stem and bowl of a plain terracotta goblet. Well that would never be used again, she mused, placing the bundle of broken pieces in her pocket. Good.

She returned to her quiet corner and considered the message again. End the undead scourge? Whoever had written that note knew exactly how best to motivate her! The name it mentioned – the person she was instructed to find – sounded familiar. Joanna Pianna... she felt as though she had heard that name recently, but she couldn't remember where. She mulled it over while she prised open the old viridian lamp on the table, revealing the cartridge of highly-flammable liquid vitriol within.

* * *

Thessu was surprised by the amount of people who had turned out to hear Sofokles of Halla read passages from his latest work of fiction. The storm that struck yestereve had largely subsided now, but he was surprised that anyone had braved even the tail end of it to come here for this. There wasn't a free buffet or anything, just a boring book reading followed by a question-and-answer session and a chance to have the hack scrawl his name in your copy of his book. Thessu doubted the man could even spell his name right.

Yet when he arrived at the grand entrance to the building, Thessu had found a line of people huddled under the canopy of the portico, sheltering from the last of the rain as they queued to gain entry. A steady stream of well-to-do people were still arriving in liveried carriages and sedan chairs drawn by liveried corpses and corpse horses, and were joining the back of the queue.

Sighing, Thessu opened the filter slits of his mask and breathed deeply. He smelled the nearby Risen, of course, and the rich ochre tang of the guild buildings, steeped as they were in centuries of blood and incense and death. And the petrichor smell of the rain. And he smelled the people. He walked from the front of the queue towards the back, breathing in the people as they shrank away from him. Liquorice… Bowel infection… Brandy and Liver disease… Ambergris… Syphilis… He was scanning for something in particular, and he found it on a well-dressed gentleman near the front. Anxiety. The man's scent contained a whiff of distress that simply hadn't been there until he saw Thessu approach and lock eyes with him. An anxious person couldn't possibly object to Thessu's polite request to join the queue; and nor did he.

Once inside, he found the auditorium already filled with people. More than a hundred had crowded into the tiered seats of the chamber, and more filed in to stand at the back, and the room was abuzz with quiet conversation as the audience waited expectantly for proceedings to begin. Thessu was glad now that he'd paid extra for another speedy rickshaw ride; if he'd arrived any later he might not have gotten in at all. He spotted a place to stand to one side of the seating near the back, and ambled over. Other audience-members made space for him. And then they edged away.

Two men made their way to reserved seats in the front row. Thessu did a double-take when he saw one of them was the nobleman he had met, two eves prior; the one with the dolly. Thessu waved to the Baron, and the Baron waved back, and pointed him out to the man he was with, a tall square-jawed man with a garish multi-coloured slashed doublet and flamboyant wide-brimmed hat. The man looked very silly. Thessu adjusted his beaked mask and gathered his trailing robes, and headed down towards the Baron and his flamboyant friend, who were now beckoning him forward to join them.

"Thessu, old boy! We must stop meeting like this," the Baron said jovially, tucking his cane under one arm and shaking Thessu's hand once he reached the front. "I wouldn't have guessed you were a Sofokles of Halla fan!"

"Yes I think he's amazing," Thessu lied. "And you as well?"

The Baron laughed. "I'm afraid I'm a fraud; I've never read any of his books. I'm here with my friend Gerard." Here the Baron gestured to his companion. "He and I were both aboard the Queen of the South when it disappeared."

Now the Baron and his friend had Thessu's attention. He'd hoped he might meet some of the survivors here at the reading, but hadn't considered he might already have met one. It was a fascinating coincidence. "Order appears from chaos," he muttered under his breath.

"Sofokles interviewed Gerard here as research for his book," the Baron continued.

"I don't know how helpful it was," the Baron's friend – Gerard – said, nodding. "But I told him everything I remembered from the voyage."

Thessu recognised the man's name now from the poster that had brought him here; he was one of the special guests. "Gerard... Malblanq?"

"I am indeed." The flamboyant man bowed a flamboyant greeting, sweeping his wide-brimmed hat in a wide-brimmed arc. "And you must be Mister Thessu. The Baron told me of your escapade the other eve."

"Please, just Thessu. Might I ask you both to also tell me everything about the voyage?" Thessu asked.

"If you like," the Baron shrugged.

Gerard nodded his agreement. "It shouldn't take long."

"Perhaps after the show?" the Baron offered.

"That would be great," Thessu assented with a nod. Waiting until after the 'show' was acceptable, though he might rather have skipped it now that he'd met two first-hand witnesses to events on the Queen of the South.

The viridian lights dimmed over the audience then, as others brightened above the stage. The crowd hushed expectantly, so the only noise was the drumming of raindrops on the lattice windows high up. The Baron and Gerard took their seats, and Thessu took the empty one next to them, brushing its *'Reserved...'* card onto the floor.

Thessu had one burning question that couldn't wait until afterwards. Leaning in towards the Baron and Gerard, he whispered, "was there a witch on-board the Queen of the South?"

"Sort-of," Gerard whispered back. "There was a fortune teller. She entertained the guests with her readings."

"She wasn't a real witch," the Baron added. "She was an actress playing the role of a haggard old crone. It was obvious she was a young woman under the wig and makeup; she was pregnant and hadn't hidden her bump very well."

'... Thessu finds the witch was cast... '

The prophecy! The witch wasn't cast overboard, she was cast in the role!

"Do you know where I can find this witch actress?" Thessu asked eagerly. This was real progress.

"You're in her seat," Gerard replied, and he gestured to the card Thessu had brushed onto the floor. Upturned, it read, 'Reserved for Joanna Pianna'.

***

The Baron's new friend Thessu was a very odd fellow. Gerard had been perturbed by the man's mask, which the Baron had hastily explained away as necessary for his health somehow. But it wasn't just his beak-like mask; he was a little odd. He had claimed to be a huge fan of Sofokles' writing, but had promptly fallen asleep, snoring loudly once the writer had begun his presentation. Gerard on the other hand was enraptured by the reading; Sofokles of Halla was undoubtedly a genius.

Gerard had met Sofokles before of course, a couple of times. He had been interviewed by the man about his voyage on the Queen of the South, and had told him all that had transpired; in short that he had boarded the vessel at a trading post upstream, and had journeyed down the Poconovo river to La Crosse. That was it; there were no interesting occurrences to explain their hundred-year delay. He had told him about the fortune teller of course, and the writer had gone to interview Joanna as well; she had had nothing much more to add to the tale.

Somehow Sofokles had taken the bare-bones of truth and crafted around them a fantastical narrative where the ship was repeatedly attacked by different monsters every eve for a hundred years.

Sofokles read his excerpts in the dulcet tones of a practiced bard, and Gerard pieced together from these snippets that the protagonist of his story – 'Gerald' – kept visiting the fortune teller – 'Joella' – every eve, and each time she revealed to him a different grisly death for him and his shipmates, which then came to pass because she was possessed by a devil.

Each time 'Gerald' would die, he and the rest of the ship's crew and passengers would start the next eve anew with no memory of their many grisly deaths. And it took a hundred years for 'Gerald' to figure out what was happening and trick the devil witch into producing a fortune where nobody died. Fantastical indeed. Nothing at all like the routine voyage it had truly been.

Anyway, it sounded like a jolly good romp and Gerard very much looked forward to getting his hands on the free copy of the book that he'd been promised.

Sofokles finished his reading to tumultuous applause, which Gerard was happy to lead. The thunderous clapping roused Thessu from his slumber, and he stretched awkwardly, asking the Baron – who was sat between them – what he had missed. "Nothing much, old boy," the Baron replied. "Whimsical nonsense."

Thessu stood up, just as the standing ovation was petering out and the rest of the audience – Gerard included – returned to their seats.

"Are there any questions?" asked Sofokles of Halla. "Oh I see our sleeping beauty has awoken!" He gestured to Thessu, getting a titter of laughter from the crowd. "I hope you aren't going to ask me to start again from the beginning!" More titters.

"I have just two questions," Thessu replied, seeming unperturbed by the general mirth aimed at him. "Firstly, where is Joanna Pianna? It is vitally important that I find her and speak to her. Lives may depend on it."

Taking the question in his stride, Sofokles answered smoothly. "Unfortunately, Miss Pianna couldn't join us this evening, though she did send her apologies. What is your second question?"

Thessu looked annoyed by the casual response, but asked his second question anyway. "How do you think 'oeuvre' is spelled?"

This second question seemed to have the writer far more flummoxed than the first had, but he muddled through with some help from the audience, then moved on to answering other more sensible questions.

Gerard wondered what was so important about Joanna Pianna. She was a mediocre actress and a worse witch. Why did Thessu think she was so important? He was going to ask him, but the Baron beat him to it.

"Pardon me old chap, what is your interest in Miss Joanna?"

"I'm not sure yet," Thessu replied. "But I think she might just be the most important person in La Crosse," he said matter-of-factly. "And I need to find her before something truly terrible happens."

Thessu, who hadn't sat back down again after asking his questions, gathered his robes around him, adjusted his mask and strode towards the exit, garnering annoyed looks from Sofokles and many members of the audience, who tutted as he passed them.

He really was quite odd, Gerard thought with a sigh, turning to watch Thessu striding up the steps towards the exit at the back. Sofokles said something amusing, and the auditorium filled with laughter; he had their rapt attention once more. As Gerard watched though, two blonde men in the audience – identical twins from the look of them – were not enraptured by the author, their focus was still entirely on Thessu. They stood up after he passed, and pushed aggressively past other guests to reach the end of their row, and then hastened after him. The men weren't just leaving, they were following.

Gerard tapped the Baron on the shoulder and drew his attention to the men. He understood at once, and they both rose to follow them all out.

"Come along Belle my dear," the Baron said, gathering his hat and cape and cane and patting the lifeless doll in his pocket. "It looks like our new friend Thessu might have found himself some more trouble."

***

Outside, the rain had eased off finally, though the paved area in front of the portico was still puddled with water. The Baron could see no sign of Thessu or the blonde men. Gerard cocked an ear, perhaps listening for them, "This way," he said, heading off at a trot along the frontage of the building towards a brick archway that looked like it might lead onto a service area to the side of the building. The Baron followed closely behind. For such a big man, Gerard was surprisingly nimble, and he turned through the archway well ahead of him.

The Baron hurried and turned through as well and nearly ran into the back of Gerard, who had stopped immediately inside the archway. There was indeed a little cobbled service courtyard beyond the archway, surrounded by the tall buildings of the guild and lit by a pair of wall-mounted lamps on opposite corners. The overlapping pools of green light created a bright spot in the centre of the courtyard where the two blonde men stood, swords drawn. There was no sign of Thessu anywhere.

"What do you suppose they want?" Thessu said. The Baron and Gerard both startled. He must have hidden in the shadows of the portico somehow as they chased past, and now reappeared behind them both.

The two blonde men turned menacingly towards them then, having also seen Thessu appear behind them. Both now released the knots of their over-cloaks and threw the constricting material back to reveal slashed black doublets beneath. The slashed black doublets of the guild; they were necromancers. They adopted aggressive fighting stances.

This was silly, the Baron thought; there was no need for a fight. Gerard was tensing in front of him, clearly ready to pounce, so the Baron placed a calming hand on his friend's shoulder and stepped past him, approaching the two necromancers with his hands open, his cane tucked under one arm. "There's no need for unpleasantness, gentlemen. I'm not sure what the misunderstanding is, but I assure you we have no disagreement with the guild."

"Joanna Pianna is ours," one of them said in a tone of cold menace. "We can't allow anyone else to look for her," said the other with equal hostility.

The Baron kept approaching calmly. He had no idea why a mediocre actress was so important all of a sudden, but the tone of these two men had him concerned for her safety. "Surely we can discuss this like civilised men," the Baron said as soothingly as he could. "Miss Pianna is an acquaintance of ours. Our concern is only for her well-being."

The Baron reached the men's sword-points. He gestured for them to lower their blades. Instead they struck.

The Baron flinched aside, parrying with an open hand as the necromancer on his left lunged forward with a heavy step, simultaneously thrusting the tip of his blade forward towards the Baron's chest. The Baron's parry pushed the blade aside enough to disrupt the thrust, and the blade-tip merely scratched across his suit jacket, catching on the lapel to rip it open, sending poor Belle spinning off to land in a muddy puddle, while the Baron's cane clattered to the cobbles below.

Thessu reacted quickest. He crossed the distance in a blur of movement that left even Gerard – nimble as he was – stood completely still. Before Belle even landed, Thessu had reached the second necromancer and grabbed the wrist of his sword hand as he thrust.

The Baron had no time to study Thessu's technique, he had no time even to pick up the cane at his feet before the first necromancer lunged again. Instead he pivoted, throwing his shoulder back and his trailing arm out so the sword flashed between his body and his arm. His arm snapped back to his body, pinning the blade of the sword firmly in place, as he continued to twist so the slender blade flexed around him, helping secure it in place and drawing the necromancer off balance.

The necromancer pulled hard to retrieve his sword, and the Baron winced as he felt the blade cut through the heavy material of his suit and bite into the back of his tricep. Reaching for the sword's cross-guard with his other hand, the Baron snatched a grip of its quillons. He stepped forward, bulling all his weight into the hilt of the sword perpendicular to the necromancer's thrust, and the necromancer stumbled off balance as the sword ripped out of his grasp.

The necromancer recovered quickly though and grabbed hold of the Baron's wrist to prevent him turning the sword back upon its owner. They locked in place for a second, and then... the Baron felt the life draining out of him. The necromancer had his wrist clamped with both hands and seemed to will his flesh to wither, his bones to crumble and his very essence to wilt away. The Baron buckled, dropping hard to his knees, his vision closing in, as the captured sword clattered to the cobbles below. The necromancer gritted his teeth in concentration, and leaned down on him, adding his physical weight to the crushing force of his necrotic attack. And then Gerard hit him.

Gerard was a big man, tall and powerfully built. Even so, when he slammed into the necromancer, there was no accounting for how far the man flew across the courtyard. The blow lifted the necromancer clear ten feet off the ground, and he skittled back down to the cobbles some thirty feet away, and tumbled on another ten.

***

When Gerard struck the blonde swordsman, the fight was over. Thessu had been just about to intervene to help the Baron, but Gerard got there first and – in an impressive feat of strength – dashed the man in black clear across the courtyard. Thessu had already disarmed the other twin and broken his nose. The one with the broken nose ran over to the one who was prone, and Thessu left them to sort their own wounds while he checked on the Baron.

The Baron was bleeding from what smelled like a nasty gash in his upper tricep, and he had another shallow horizontal cut across his chest. However, his blood smelled rancid; thick and black like corpse-blood. He was clutching his arm where the swordsman had grabbed him, and Thessu knelt to examine it, sucking in a breath. Where the man had grabbed him, the flesh of the Baron's arm was black and necrotic. He had a deathly pallor – more so than usual – and his temperature had dropped by several degrees. Thessu wondered who those men were.

"Who were those men?" he asked.

"Necromancers," Gerard replied.

Thessu nodded. That explained the pallor and the necrotic wound and why the men were such dicks. He reached down to lift the Baron to his feet, beckoning Gerard to help. They needed to leave; alarms were about to start ringing. "We need to leave," he said. "Alarms are about to start ringing."

Gerard looked at him quizzically, but helped lift the Baron up, stooping to collect his cane and hat as well.

"Can't you smell it?" Thessu said, gesturing at the adjacent building. "The guild library is on fire."

The side-door of the building flew open then and someone hurried out in a hooded cloak wreathed in the first faint wisps of smoke. Of all the coincidences, it was the angry woman again; Epifani. What was she doing in there? Didn't she know the library was on fire?

She saw them, and looked indecisive for a second, before barrelling over to join them. "What in the hells are you all doing here?" she said. "We need to go, there's about to be alarms!"

Sure enough, alarm bells started ringing throughout the building, and were joined by other bells from other buildings around the courtyard. Gerard seemed to eye the woman suspiciously for some reason, but she ignored his glare.

They headed to the archway that led out of the courtyard; Epifani following behind Gerard and Thessu who hauled the Baron between them, as palls of smoke started rising above the adjacent building.

"This ain't over!" yelled one of the blonde necromancers from across the courtyard behind them, his voice distorted by the din of alarms and the bloody mess of his nose. "Joanna Pianna is ours!"

Epifani startled at that, seeming surprised at the mention of the witch's name, and turned back to the courtyard.

But Thessu had spotted something else; something bad. "Something is wrong with the Baron. He just went limp, I think he's lost consciousness."

Gerard looked at him as well, lifting the Barons head to check his eyes, which were vacant. "He has, in a manner of speaking," he said, his voice full of sympathy. "His consciousness is certainly lost somewhere. It just vacated his body and went somewhere else. That happens to him sometimes; to both of us. We need to patch him up and get him home."

"Where is his home?" Thessu asked.

"Isla Festa. It's in the swamp," Gerard replied, and they carried the lifeless body of the Baron out through the archway.

Thessu saw Epifani again look indecisively back to where the necromancers were exiting in the other direction at the far side of the courtyard. Acolytes and apprentices were filing out of the buildings now, filling up the courtyard. Epifani snarled in annoyance and followed Gerard, Thessu and the Baron.

None of them thought to pick up Belle.

CHAPTER 10

"How's it goin' kid?" Remy asked, stepping out into the little patch of yard between the kitchen and the scullery. It had stopped raining earlier in the evening, but the yard was damp and overgrown, and almost fully shaded from the light of the ever-setting sun. It might once have been a herb garden for the house, but years of neglect had left it little more than a patch of mud overrun by dusk-weeds.

"I think I'm getting better," Colin replied. He wasn't. He had been throwing that damn knife at that damn stump for hours. He simply could not get the knife to strike the stump point-first and have it stick. The young fiendling stood ten paces from the stump once more, readied his knife, and launched it. The knife sailed through the air and glanced off the hunk of wood, skittering across the ground. "See, Remy, that one almost stuck!"

"Mmm-hmm," Remy said flatly. Perching on the scullery step, he took out a little tin of tobacco and started rolling a cigarette. Even the alligator seemed unconvinced by the throw, and it gave a derisive snort. Colin scowled at the reptile. Rufus had been an unwelcome chaperone for everything they'd done ever since the Baron had brought them to the islet.

"Perhaps if I had a sharper knife I might have more success. Do you have a sharper one I could practice with, Remy? I already asked Valanthé and she laughed at me."

"She laughed at you?" Remy cocked his head.

"Yes I told her my knife had gotten a little blunt and so I needed a brand new one. For some reason she found that hilarious," Colin said bitterly, picking the knife up off the ground once more.

Where to begin? "You… Colin, you know knives can be sharpened, right?"

"They can?" Colin said incredulously.

Remy sighed. He needed to stop being surprised by the things the kid said. He kept forgetting that Colin had grown up in a palazzo; everything was disposable if you were rich.

"Yes Colin, they can. I'll show you once I've had this." Remy finished rolling the skinny cigarette and placed one end loosely in his mouth. He pinched the other end between forefinger and thumb, channelling heat to his fingertips from the molten core that lived within him, and the cigarette flamed to life.

He smoked it languidly as Colin continued throwing the knife near the stump.

"Remy can I ask you something?"

"Go ahead."

"Do you think it is possible that one of my real parents was a devil like your father, and the other was human? Do you think there is even a chance?" Colin stood awkwardly scratching his arm, the knife lying forgotten in a tangle of dusk-weeds near the stump. This was obviously something that had been playing on his mind.

Remy took a long drag of the cigarette. "It's possible, I guess. I doubt it though; devils ain't exactly commonplace. My pops is the only one I ever heard of, an' I'm purty sure you ain't his kid."

"But I could be though, right?" Colin asked, looking hopeful.

Remy sighed. "It's possible. But it's far more likely your parents are fiendlin's. Why you askin'?"

"I've been wondering if my father told me the truth when he said I was adopted. It would be harder to disown me if I was merely illegitimate."

Remy's eyebrows raised. "You think your momma had an affair with a devil?" Colin shrugged hopefully, but Remy shook his head. "Like I said, my pops is the only devil I ever heard of. If he'd had an affair with your momma, he'd have known you was his the instant you burst into his kitchen."

Colin considered this, and nodded, looking a little crestfallen. Remy smiled reassuringly; he knew the kid had only latched onto him because he was looking for somewhere to belong. He would take him to Elise once they'd done this job for the Don; he'd be welcome among his own kind.

A thought occurred to Remy then, and he voiced it as he breathed out a long drag of the cigarette. "I guess either way, your birth certificate or adoption papers would be in the Palazzo Laurentin, perhaps in the Marquis' office with the other things we're goin' take for my pops." He took one last puff, then stubbed out the end of the cigarette on the step. "We'll go over the plan again later, and you can tell us all the places the papers might be. If they there, we'll find 'em. That'll confirm who your real parents are."

Colin brightened at the suggestion, nodding enthusiastically.

"But we got some time," Remy continued. "We ain't goin' anywhere 'til the Baron comes back from his book show. So let's get that knife sharpened, and we can see if a sharp knife helps any."

Remy retrieved oil and a whetstone from the scullery, and Valanthé came out to sit with them as Remy showed Colin how to sharpen the blade of his little knife. She nodded sagely through the demonstration, though Remy could tell she was resisting the urge to take over the instruction. Remy wouldn't have minded; Valanthé had demonstrated she knew her way around blades far better than he.

Nevertheless, it was passably sharp when Colin resumed. He was no better at throwing a sharp knife than a blunt one.

"Ugh, I can't bear it!" Valanthé said despairingly after his fourth attempt had clattered off the brickwork of the kitchen wall. "Colin, come here!"

She unbuckled her sword belts and draped them over the handrail of the steps, then strode towards where the kid had been standing to throw. Colin retrieved the knife from the muddy ground and walked back to give it begrudgingly to her.

"Stand a bit more side-on," she said, demonstrating correct stance. "You're flicking your wrist when you throw and that's why it's over-rotating. Relax your posture a little, but keep your wrist locked through the release. Here, I'll show you."

She demonstrated a perfect throw and the knife slammed into the stump, and stuck in place. Remy had to admit it was a pretty good throw.

Colin was impressed too, and then he frowned, asking, "why did you use your right hand?"

Valanthé looked at him dumbly for a second before answering. "Because... I'm right- handed, Colin."

"But Remy demonstrated it left-handed," he replied. "So that's what I've been doing."

Remy facepalmed. Even the alligator groaned. "Colin are you left- or right-handed?" Valanthé asked, exasperated.

"I'm right-handed of course."

Remy laughed uncontrollably behind his hands. Colin tried it Valanthé's way, and was noticeably better at it.

***

"Are you sure he'll be all right there?" Valanthé asked as they lowered the comatose Baron carefully onto the chaise longue in the parlour.

"Yes, he'll be fine," Gerard replied with a shrug. "He told me whenever he blacked out he woke up here... I guess the house's corpse butler must be bringing him?"

Valanthé looked over to the motionless corpse sat at the pianoforte, 'Jeff', and doubted it could bring the Baron anywhere in this state. In the two full eves she'd been staying at the manor, she hadn't even once seen it leave the pianoforte. She would have thought it disanimated, except its milky eyes followed her each time she entered the room.

It also sometimes played the pianoforte. In fact it was surprisingly competent, though it played slowly and always in a minor key that made everything sound like a dirge, and any music came accompanied by the unpleasant creaking of its joints and the crackling of its skin as it played.

"Well thank you for bringing him, Gerard," Valanthé said, and Gerard bowed graciously. He was looking a lot better than when she'd last seen him three eves prior, though admittedly he couldn't very well look worse; three eves prior he had been mistaken for a Pit corpse.

She noticed the swelling on his forehead was much reduced, though he still wore a dressing over the wound where the copper marque had been removed, the bandage partially covered by a wide-brimmed hat. He caught her looking at it, and self-consciously adjusted his hat to better conceal it.

Valanthé focussed her attention back to the Baron, and positioned a cushion under his head, while saying to Gerard, "it seems like you got your strength back at least?" He had given her a summary of the events at the guild, including his own modest contribution to the fight.

"Yes, it does seem to be coming back slowly," Gerard agreed. "I should probably try and avoid getting into any more fights, though. It's just that the Baron's new friends do seem to attract trouble!"

He frowned slightly before continuing. "Speaking of which, I think Epifani started that fire in the guild library."

Valanthé nodded, unsurprised. She'd gotten the same first impression when she'd met the dark-skinned woman at the Casa; she was a troublemaker. She hadn't met Thessu but he sounded by all accounts to be an oddball. She retrieved a blanket which had been folded neatly on the footstool of an armchair near the fireplace, and handed Gerard one corner. Together they draped it over the Baron.

"So where did they go after the fight?" she asked. "Thessu and Epifani, I mean."

Gerard shrugged, tucking in the blanket by the Baron's feet. "They went to try and find the actress. She seems to be important to them both for some reason, though I get the distinct impression that neither of them really knows why. Very peculiar."

"And the men who attacked you?" Valanthé asked. "The necromancers?"

He shrugged again. "She seems to be important to them too. No idea where they went, they scarpered in the other direction."

"That's odd isn't it?" Valanthé said. Gerard looked at her quizzically. "Why would they run from the scene?" she continued. "Two necromancers got into a confrontation in the grounds of the guild over something important enough that they'd been willing to kill over it, yet they didn't seek help from their guild-mates. Didn't even stick around to report it."

"Hmm you're right, that is odd. I guess that means they aren't working for the guild."

Valanthé nodded gravely. "So who were they working for?" Neither of them could answer that.

Remy came in then, with Colin trailing after him like a puppy. "Why, Mister Malblanq," Remy said. "What a pleasure! How was the book show?"

"Eventful," Gerard said. "I was just telling Valanthé about it, we bumped into some friends of yours, and ended up brawling with necromancers."

"Some friends o' mine?" Remy queried. "Oh! What's happened to the Baron?"

"Epifani and Thessu," Gerard replied. "And the Baron will be fine. He got a little banged up in the brawl, but Thessu patched him up." Here Gerard lifted the blanket so Remy could see the wounds on the Baron's arm, which were neatly bandaged. Valanthé had already checked the dressings after Gerard had arrived carrying him.

The one on his upper arm was a deep cut, which had been expertly stitched closed. The one on his forearm was worse, looking like the skin had been peeled off, and Gerard had explained that that is exactly what happened; Thessu had had to cut dead flesh away so that healthy skin might regrow. Strangely though, both wounds looked like they had happened a week ago, and another cut on the Baron's chest had already scarred over, not even needing dressing.

"He suffered one of his black-outs though," Gerard continued. "So I chartered a boat for the eve and brought him home".

"Well, I thank you for that," Remy said, then he looked thoughtful. "A chartered boat, you say? What happened to the Baron's boat?"

Valanthé hadn't thought of that. The Baron had ferried himself, Valanthé, Colin and Remy to Isla Festa in a leaky old gondola after their visit to Don Gusteau. He had then taken the boat back to the core islands for the book reading. The Baron's boat was a rickety old heirloom of his family that kept taking on water and ought to have been scrapped decades ago – like most of the De Ville family heirlooms – but without it, they were stranded on the islet.

"I'm sorry," Gerard said. "I didn't think about that. Do you have other transportation? I don't want to leave you all stranded here." They all shook their heads. Valanthé and Remy had checked out the boat house when they'd arrived, finding it in a far worse state than even the decrepit manor was; there were no operable boats there. "No we're definitely stuck here," Valanthé said, frowning.

Suddenly there was a boom of discordant noise, followed by another, and they all startled. The corpse had begun another menacing dirge on the pianoforte.

"Might we trouble you for a ride back into town?" Remy asked over the din, pressing his hands over his ears. "We have pressin' business at Palazzo Laurentin, an' once we're done there we can pick up the Baron's boat."

"Of course," said Gerard agreeably. "You have business with the Marquis Du Laurentin?"

"We're going to rob him and shit in his bed!" Colin announced before Remy could answer.

***

Palazzo Laurentin was a grand house in a classical style that boasted a prime position on the Isla Roja waterfront overlooking the channel that separated it from Isla Verdé. It was a six-storey building of pastel stucco, fronted by galleried balconies behind a façade of elaborate stacked white marble arches that rose directly out of the river.

It was by no means the grandest palazzo on Isla Roja, those all being sited in the exclusive enclave that surrounded the Corto Dogé complex on the south side of the Ziggurat. Nevertheless, it was an imposing building befitting the Marquis' wealth and status, and Remy surveyed it discreetly from Gerard's boat as they rowed past.

"The kitchens are this side, with mostly service rooms above," Colin said quietly. "The formal rooms are on the far side of the building, overlooking the gardens,"

Remy nodded. This was to be expected; the river-facing frontage was in constant shade. He'd been in enough palazzos over the past few years to know the formal rooms always faced towards the ever-setting sun to the west; rich folk liked to pretend the sun shined just for them. "And the Marquis' office is on the second floor on the sunward side?" he asked, checking what Colin had already told them about the layout.

"Yes," the kid confirmed. "There's also a guest suite and a billiards room on that floor facing the sun, and on this side there are bathrooms there and there." Here, Colin stood up from his seat in the bow of the boat and pointed out two of the gallery balconies behind the marble arches of the façade.

"What did I say about pointin'?" Remy said, reaching across and slapping the kid's arm down.

"Sorry Remy, I forgot." Remy glowered at him, and Colin sat back down. In truth it was probably fine, nobody was paying them any attention. The river channel was busy with little boats and gondolas coming and going between the jetties and wharfs of the twin islands, and there was no sign of anyone on the river-facing balconies of the palazzo.

This was their second traverse of the channel. The first time they'd rowed past, it had been a hive of frantic activity. This time it was quiet, and only dim light shone out from between the arches of the façade. Hopefully that meant their ruse had worked and the Marquis had departed the Palazzo with the bulk of his entourage.

"Are we good?" Gerard asked from his position at the tiller.

Remy considered. It certainly looked quiet. In any case they would get confirmation soon enough when they picked Valanthé up; they had dropped her at a wharf near the palazzo some time ago, and had completed two leisurely laps of the island while she made her delivery to the Marquis.

"Yes," Remy replied, putting as much certainty into his voice as he could muster. "We're lookin' good from what I can tell." Gerard nodded, and the boat continued steadily on its way northwards along the channel.

The Baron's friend Gerard had not only brought them back to the core islands, he had offered to assist with transportation for the heist, once he learned what they were trying to steal. He was keen to help his friend recover the deed to Isla Festa and De Ville manor, the Baron's ancestral home. There was no guessing when the Baron might awaken, so they had waited the rest of the evening and until fivebells the following eve to see if he woke. He hadn't, so they had set off without him.

Remy sat back in the seat and watched the cityscape pass by. Gerard had extended his charter lease indefinitely, and his chartered boat was comfortable and spacious. It also came with four Risen corpses to do the hard work, the corpse rowers pulling on the oars with sufficient force to overcome the current and keep the boat moving upstream at an even pace. The palazzo soon disappeared behind them and the boat continued on under the last and most northerly of the three stone bridges that spanned the channel.

The three bridges connecting the twin islands of Isla Roja and Isla Verdé were among the busiest thoroughfares in the city, and were each lined with shops and bars and bordellos; they were a famous entertainment district in their own right. Remy had many fond memories of carousing on the three bridges with the rich young elites who made up the bohemian set that he used to party with. But he was no longer part of that world. Not since his mother died. Not since…

Colin must have spotted him looking melancholy. "Is something wrong, Remy?" he asked.

Remy smiled reassuringly at him. "No, I'm fine thank you kindly. Just thought about somethin' that made me sad for a moment."

The kid leaned in to whisper so Gerard couldn't hear. "Are you upset because Valanthé won't have sex with you?"

Remy choked on his cigarette. Gerard looked over, concerned, from the stern of the boat and Remy waved him away as he spat the half-smoked rollup overboard. "No Colin," he coughed, "I'm in no way upset about Valanthé! I respect her as a professional an' I like her as a friend an' nothin' more; I don't know where you got the idea that I want to have sex with her! I don't!"

Colin's eyes narrowed. "You're saying you could have her if you wanted? She's just not attractive enough for you?"

"No, that ain't what I'm sayin'! O' course she's attractive, but I jus' tol' you I respect her an' value her friendship, an'… "

"So you only have sex with people you don't respect?"

"No I ain't sayin' that either! Goddamit Colin you about to get dunked in the river!"

They both looked away angrily and neither said another word as Gerard guided the boat alongside the northern-most wooden wharf on the Isla Roja side of the channel. Valanthé was waiting to board the boat. She stepped aboard, and there followed an awkward silence.

***

Valanthé couldn't believe the crazy scheme was working. Remy had claimed to know his way around high-society, and had alluded to intimate relationships with many of the elite of La Crosse. He certainly seemed familiar with masquerades and society parties, and she believed he probably had attended some. But she had her doubts when he'd suggested they invite the Marquis and his entourage to attend the Dogé at a non-existent masked orgy.

For a start, from what Colin had told them about his adoptive parents – the Marquis and Marchioness Du Laurentin – they were a staid and boring couple with no interest in orgies, masked or otherwise. They were also tremendously unpopular at court, so would never receive a genuine invitation to such a thing. Also, the Dogé was in his eighties and by all accounts in very poor health, so why would he be hosting an orgy? Most of all though, why would an invitation be sent to the Marquis a mere two hours before the function started?

Remy insisted this all made it more likely the Marquis would believe it was genuine and accept it.

Sure enough, she had arrived at the gates of the palazzo in a ceramic mask and blue-green cowl, and had delivered to the gate corpse a hand-written invitation. Nothing fancy or lavish, not even sealed with the stamp of the Corto Dogé, just a simple hand-written note folded in half. Again, Remy was adamant that this would make the invitation seem more authentic, not less.

And somehow it had worked. As soon as she was out of sight of the gate corpse, she had removed the mask and cowl and concealed herself a little way along the street, and watched the palazzo from a distance. The palazzo had been a buzz of frantic activity, and then a little over an hour later, the gate had opened and a convoy of four elaborate palanquins emerged, carried on the shoulders of liveried corpses, and headed south.

She wasn't sure why Colin and Remy were looking awkward when she reboarded the boat, but they asked and she confirmed that the Marquis had taken the bait. "It's an hour round-trip to the Corto Dogé by palanquin," she told them.

Remy nodded. "Add on some time for the Marquis to be politely entertained wi' drinks an' such, so as nobody be losin' face, an' we got maybe an hour and a half. We best get movin'."

Gerard manoeuvred the boat away from the wharf and quickly got it turned around and heading south along the channel, back towards the palazzo.

"How did you know they'd believe such a ludicrous proposition?" Valanthé asked.

Remy's dark eyes twinkled. "They believed it precisely because it was such a ludicrous proposition. I was countin' on 'em readin' between the lines."

Valanthé still didn't understand; and she was sure Colin didn't understand it either, despite how he nodded along sagely with whatever Remy said. She invited the fiendling to elaborate with a dubious look.

"The Dogé ain't a well man," Remy explained. "The nobles all been jostlin' for position, expectin' there's goin' be a vacancy at the top real soon. Now, the Marquis ain't senior enough nor popular enough to ever be in the runnin' to be the next Dogé. An' you right, there's no way was the Dogé goin' invite him to a orgy. I figured he'd guess it was a pretext for sommat else. Sommat like a conversation about him bein' Camerlengo when the Dogé dies."

"Camerlengo?" Valanthé asked. The term was unfamiliar.

Gerard answered. "The Camerlengo oversees the election of the new Dogé during a transition. It's a very prestigious and lucrative role, and it traditionally goes to a noble with no prospect of being elected himself and no ties to the frontrunners."

"Exactly," Remy continued. "The Marquis ain't in the runnin' to be Dogé, but he's for sure in the runnin' for Camerlengo. An' he's gotta think that's the only reason the Corto Dogé would send for him at short notice."

"And you couldn't just say that in the note, because blurting it out upfront would be suspicious," Gerard concluded. "Very clever."

Valanthé was impressed. "You're not just a pretty face after all," she said to Remy.

"I were just sayin' the same about you," he replied, his eyes twinkling again.

Colin pretended to hurl over the side of the boat.

The boat passed under the north bridge once more and, with the current propelling them southwards, they soon came back within sight of the palazzo. Gerard eased the boat closer towards the bank, within half an oar of the façades of the waterfront buildings. They continued slowly, letting the current carry them adjacent to the marble columns of Palazzo Laurentin's façade, which rose sheer out of the water. He then had the four corpse rowers power forward on one side and back on the other to turn the boat perpendicular to the colonnade, then power backwards hard to reverse the boat through one of the gothic arches, into the palazzo's undercroft dock and alongside one of the vacant mooring berths within. They were now beneath the palazzo.

"Are you ready to play your part?" Remy asked the boy as the four of them stepped out of the boat onto the stone jetty of the undercroft dock. A pair of Risen corpses in the yellow and red livery of the Du Laurentins approached the unexpected arrival.

Colin nodded. "I'm ready," and he strode forward to intercept the corpses while Gerard and Remy tied off the mooring ropes, and Valanthé waited, wary for any sign that Colin would be rumbled.

The whole plan hinged on Colin convincing the guard corpses to simply let them in. If the Marquis had already revoked his son's authority with the Risen servants of the house, then they would have to fight their way in, which was a much riskier proposition. They were counting on the Marquis not yet having had the deeds of ownership amended for all his Risen corpses.

Valanthé watched the kid approach the corpses and talk with them quietly. There was a tense moment as the corpses seemed to refuse him, shaking their heads as he pointed back towards her and Remy, but whatever he said seemed to have the desired effect as the corpses stood aside and Colin beckoned them both forward.

"Good luck," Gerard said.

"Thanks," Valanthé replied. She was very grateful to the big man; he had gone out of his way to assist them. She hadn't expected him to bring them into the palazzo nor wait for them while they burgled it.

"We'll be back presently," Remy said, as he and Valanthé strode confidently forward.

The guard corpses eyed the two of them warily as they passed the end of the jetty, and Colin fell in beside them – between them, in fact – and the three of them stepped through the heavy doors at the back of the boatyard, and up the circular staircase to the palazzo above.

"What was the issue with the corpses," Valanthé asked Colin once the door from the undercroft dock had closed behind them.

"Huh?" Colin answered. "There was no problem. I told them I was coming in with two of my guests and they had no objection. I guess my 'father' hasn't bothered updating the deeds to his Risen yet."

Valanthé frowned. "But they shook their heads when you pointed Remy and me out to them?"

Colin hesitated. "Oh um, don't worry about that. That was something else. I was asking their opinion about something. They agreed with me."

That left Valanthé even more confused, but she didn't think she wanted to know what opinion he had sought from the corpses about her and Remy, so she let it go.

The stairwell from the undercroft led up to a small lobby off the back of the grand entrance hall, and they waited in silence in the shadows of the lobby while servants – both living and dead – bustled between the garden-facing reception rooms on either side of the entrance hall.

Once the coast was relatively clear, Remy led them quietly out of the lobby. They slunk across the entrance hall without making a sound, and continued carefully up the grand sweeping staircase that led to the upper floors, where the palazzo seemed much quieter. They made their way up to the second floor and Remy looked back to Colin for directions. The boy pointed along a dimly-lit corridor towards the office. "Second door on the left," he whispered in a low voice.

Remy nodded, and he and Valanthé set off along the corridor. Colin didn't follow. "Ain't you comin', kid?" Remy whispered back to the boy.

Colin shook his head. "I will meet you there. There is something I have to do first."

Valanthé sighed. She knew what Colin was going to do, and the boy loped off up the stairs to an upper floor – where presumably the Marquis' bedchamber was – unbuckling his breeches as he went. Remy obviously knew as well what the boy had gone to do, and they shared a wry look. They were both resigned to Colin's antics now, and neither of them would begrudge him some measure of payback for how the Marquis had treated him.

They passed the billiard room and arrived at the doorway to the Marquis' office. Valanthé carefully tried the door. Locked. They were prepared for this, and Remy knelt down to examine the keyhole, then smiled encouragingly. She watched him unfurl a rolled up canvas pouch, with little pockets for a multitude of steel picks of varying length. He selected two, and got to work picking the lock. In under a minute, the door latch clicked open, and Remy stood triumphant, rolling his bundle back up.

"Ladies first," he said, stepping aside. She turned the handle and the heavy door swung open to reveal a darkened room. She stepped inside, closely followed by Remy. The office was a large rectangular chamber with an oversized heavy leather-topped desk opposite them, in front of a shuttered window, with book shelves lining the side walls. There were no lights in the room; it was illuminated only by the dim green glow from the corridor behind them.

Valanthé crept across the room, and lit the acid green viridian lamp that sat on the desk. Once it had sputtered to life, Remy closed the door. He joined her by the desk, and they both scanned the room looking for the location of the safe they knew to be in there. It wasn't obvious; they would have to search.

Suddenly there was a movement in the shadows behind the desk, and the very darkness seemed to lunge across its surface, dashing the lamp to the floor where it shattered noisily, leaving them in complete darkness.

"Shit," they both said at the same time. There was a dark presence protecting the Marquis' office.

Valanthé drew her swords and heard Remy draw his rapier. She felt his hand on her shoulder, drawing her back towards the door.

"It's a spectre," Remy whispered.

"A what?" she replied. She had never heard of such a thing.

"A Risen shadow. We can't fight it in darkness," Remy continued. "We should get out o' here."

She felt a whoosh of air as something swept past overhead, and she lashed out with the longer of her two swords, but too slow, it had already passed them. A moment later, they both heard the click of the door locking once more; they were trapped. She felt panic surging... She would let it surge.

***

A spectre! How had Colin not thought to mention the Marquis had a goddamn corpse shadow! The Marquis must be richer than Remy thought; spectres were incredibly rare and expensive, the rarest of all the Risen.

Risen all started as simple reanimated corpses reliant on reanimated muscles and brain stem. Increasingly complex necromancy could maintain them as they slowly decayed, and a Risen corpse could be gradually empowered by a gifted necromancer to endure without the need for muscles or brain. They became skeleton corpses. Usually their bones would then be entombed in enamel or pewter or some such thing to preserve them, otherwise even the bones would eventually decay. However, very rarely, a skeleton corpse could be successfully maintained necromantically even as its bones decayed to nothing, and the nothing that was left then had little to anchor it. The Risen corpse would then finally be freed from its cage of flesh and bone, becoming a spectre. Like this one.

Remy was slammed backwards into the bookshelf, cracking his back against one of the uprights and upending several shelves as he flailed, books tumbling down through the darkness to clatter onto the floor of the pitch-black office. Moments later, he heard Valanthé slam into the bookshelf opposite, and he heard a cascade of books fall to the floor in her wake. The spectre had driven between them like a wedge of solid air; it could change its density as it chose, being at once ethereal and impenetrable. It could bludgeon them to death without them ever being able to harm it.

It wasn't entirely formless though. He knew somewhere in this room it did have a physical presence, an anchor. Somewhere in this room was the spectre's marque of ownership. They would never find it in the dark.

A crash of splintering wood high on the opposite bookshelf indicated the spectre had flung something at Valanthé. A side table or a footstool maybe? He heard her gasp, but that was a gasp of surprise, not of pain. The spectre had missed. Had she ducked? There was no way to tell.

Hearing Valanthé by the bookshelf opposite reassured Remy that he wouldn't accidentally hit her if he swung his rapier, and so he lashed out blindly at the space between them where he guessed the spectre was. He slashed nothing but empty air. Had he missed? Or had he hit it and swung right through it without realising? Goddammit he needed to see!

"We need light," Remy said into the blackness.

"No shit, Remy!" Valanthé spat back.

"It'll have a marque somewhere in the room," Remy continued. "If we can find it, we can destroy it." Valanthé didn't answer.

Remy hunkered down in a defensive stance and listened intently. He heard a shuffling movement across the room. Valanthé. She seemed to be edging away from the door. The window! She was going to try and open the heavy shutter and let some light in… which made it Remy's job to distract the spectre. Fine.

He grabbed a book from the floor by his feet and hurled it into space away from Valanthé. It clattered into the shelves opposite. He threw another which struck the door. He reached for a third but was slammed sideways by the spectre. He stumbled and fell to one knee under the blow, then twisted and thrust his rapier at the force that had shoved him. The sword tip seemed to impact something in the darkness, and he felt the blade flex against it, then the something yielded and his blade drove forward unimpeded. He drew back and thrust again, and hit nothing.

He then heard the screech of wood scraping on wood and then a crash, and Valanthé yelped in pain, and he heard her clatter to the floor. The spectre had slammed her into the desk. Or actually no, the spectre had slammed the desk into her. The desk creaked again, a different sort of noise; it wasn't scraping on the floor, it was being lifted. The spectre was toppling the heavy desk onto her.

Then he heard a noise he didn't recognise. A wet, slapping noise. In fact a lot of wet slapping noises, as many wet slapping things cascaded onto the floor and spread out around the room, and he smelled the ocean. What the hell was happening?

"Fuck this," Remy muttered, and he reached up and grabbed the nearest book from the shelf above his shoulder. With a tremendous effort, he channelled heat from his molten core down his arm to the palm of his hand; into the book. It blackened and smouldered at the edges, and the embers glowed like red pinpricks in the darkness, but not enough to see by. He concentrated again and for a moment the book just smouldered a little more intensely. Then it erupted into flames.

Immediately the room was illuminated in the flickering orange light of the flames. Remy barely had time to drop the burning book and throw himself out of the way of the heavy wooden chair that he saw flying towards him. It smashed into the bookshelf where he had been standing an instant earlier, scattering books and wooden chair-parts across the floor. The burning book had landed at the foot of the bookshelf, and its flickering light was now partially obscured by wooden debris and additional books, which had fallen to cover it. The pile smoked furiously.

Remy tried to scramble to his feet, but his hand slipped on something wet and slippery that was flopping on the floor, and he sprawled onto all fours. What had he slipped on? In the dim light of the obscured flames, it looked like... a fish. A wet, flopping fish. What the hell?

The spectre loomed over him, a haze of translucent shadow. With his rapier he slashed at it, and the spectre ebbed away from his slashing blade, unperturbed. He dragged himself up to one knee and looked for Valanthé, expecting to see her crushed under a heavy upturned desk.

The desk – upturned or otherwise – was nowhere to be seen. It had vanished... and where had all these fish come from? Valanthé was crawling out from under a huge wet flapping pile of trout.

Their eyes met as she reached him, and Remy saw she was... embarrassed? Had she... caused this somehow? This deluge of trout? What had she done with the desk?

There was no time to inquire; the spectre was already on him again, and it wrapped its formless hands around Remys throat. And it squeezed. Remy struggled ineffectually against the shadow's grip; there was simply nothing there for him to struggle against. He slashed with his rapier and the spectre ebbed around his sword like liquid smoke, though its grip did not diminish. Valanthé hastened over and tried the same thing, with the same result. She dropped her swords and tried to push the shadow free of him; tried to pull it. Nothing worked. Nothing stopped the spectre from strangling the life out of him.

Remy saw his vision closing, felt blackness encroaching at the corners of his awareness. He smelled the acrid smoke of the burning books and heard the muffled sounds of Valanthé's efforts drowned out by the thumping of his heartbeat, loud as the banging of a drum in his head. Thump... Thump... Thump... Each thump louder than the last, seeming to shake the very room with their ferocity. One of the mysterious trout had flopped onto his lap somehow. With the last of his strength he brushed the damn fish off him; he didn't want to die with a trout on his lap. The thumping continued. Thump... Thump... Thump. And then a pause, and one final thump, and then silence.

CHAPTER 11

CHAPTER 11

Gerard grew increasingly anxious as he waited in the undercroft. The others had been gone a long time and the two guard corpses seemed to be getting more and more agitated at the muffled noises echoing down from the upper floors of the palazzo above. Whatever was happening upstairs, it was extremely noisy.

Gerard detected it before the corpses did; the smell of smoke. It was subtle, but it was there at the edge of his senses, and he knew a fire was spreading nearby. He knew what he had to do; he had to help his new friends.

He stepped out of the boat and walked casually towards the corpses at the end of the jetty. Eying him warily, they tightened their grips on their weapons as he approached. They wore the yellow and red tabards and matching feathered caps of house Laurentin, and each clutched a heavy halberd with a vicious hooked blade and spike.

He was too late. Detecting the smoke before he reached them, the two corpses sparked into life, taking an aggressive stance and levelling their vicious polearms at him. They clattered their jaws angrily, as Risen do, and jostled their weapons in a way that left Gerard in no uncertainty that they wanted him to return to his boat and leave. It was a narrow jetty and he was unarmed, so there was no way past the lethal blades of the halberds if the corpses didn't want him to pass. He really must buy himself a new sword if he was going to keep getting into trouble; otherwise he would keep having to do things the hard way.

He backed away to the boat, which did little to relax the corpses, and he knelt down on the dockside beside the mooring ring. But he wasn't untying; instead, he reached into the boat and stood back up with one of the boat's heavy oars held like a polearm of his own. Turning back towards the Risen corpses, he held it in a low guard, one hand on the butt of the oar and the other in the centre of the shaft, with the wooden paddle blade pointing at the pair of Risen. This enraged the corpses, and they pressed forward with gathering steps to meet him with their own weapons. Thankfully though, the jetty was narrow enough that only one of them could engage him at a time.

The first corpse swept its halberd in a diagonal sweep downwards at the shaft of Gerard's oar, intending to hook and parry it aside. The halberd hooked the paddle blade and swept it down and to Gerard's right. Stepping forward, the corpse continued the circular sweeping motion by rotating the back of its halberd up and forward at Gerard's head, attempting to club him with the back of the halberd shaft.

Gerard was prepared for that though, and stepped forward as well, cycling the butt of his own oar shaft forcefully forward to meet the corpse's arm where it gripped the rising back-end of its halberd. His oar shaft struck the corpse's forearm with a crack, dealing it a heavy blow between elbow and wrist, breaking its arm.

Keeping the haft of his oar moving forwards, Gerard let his right hand slip down from the butt to a lower grip. One-handed, he thrust the shaft forwards at the corpse's head, rocking it backwards. It recoiled, but Gerard kept moving, reaching around the corpse's head with his left hand to grab it and slam it back into place against the butt of his oar.

The corpse was unnaturally strong, and it resisted for a moment while clacking its jaw angrily, but Gerard was stronger and he pressed the corpse's eye socket onto the butt of the oar. It was a tight fit, but great strength was Gerard's gift, and he forced it in. There was a sickening squelch and spurt as the blunt end of the shaft popped the corpse's eyeball, then a splintering sound as the orbital bone of its skull cracked apart, forced open by the widening wooden shaft which continued on to lodge in the corpse's head. The corpse spasmed in Gerard's arms just as its fellow hewed down with its halberd blade in a great diagonal arc aimed at Gerard's neck.

With no time to avoid it, he lifted his oar-shaft high above his head perpendicular to the halberd swing, bracing it with right hand just above the paddle, and left hand propping up the spasming corpse that still held the butt of the oar in its eye socket. The swinging halberd-shaft cracked hard against the shaft of the oar, and Gerard flinched back as the halberd blade was halted just inches from his face.

Yanking the first corpse backwards, Gerard slammed its head down to the deck of the jetty behind him, where he speared the oar-shaft downwards further into its skull, disanimating it. This lunge backwards with the oar also wrenched the hook blade of the second corpse's parried halberd back with it, causing the corpse to step forward, off-balance, as it tried to keep hold of its weapon. Gerard released his grip on the oar and struck the second corpse with a backhand blow across the head as it stumbled towards him. The blow was forceful enough to stun the Risen guard, and it staggered backwards, dropping the halberd, which clattered noisily away.

Gerard left the first corpse on the deck, still impaled through the head by an oar, and grabbed hold of the second corpse. With one hand on the back of its shoulder and the other on its face, he slammed his hands together, breaking its neck and near twisting its head clean off its shoulders. It slumped in his arms, disanimated, and he shoved it off the jetty, where it disappeared into the inky water with a splash.

Straightening up, he dusted himself off. It was time to go help his friends.

There was no need. He turned towards the door at the back of the undercroft dock, just as it flew open and Colin rushed out. But where were Remy and Valanthé? Thin smoke wafted out through the open door. The fire he could smell was definitely upstairs in the palazzo.

Nothing happened for a long moment, and then two figures stumbled out through the smoke-filled doorway. Remy and Valanthé, both looking bruised and battered. They were carrying a metal box about the size of a suitcase, but heavy enough to need both of them to carry it.

"What happened," Gerard asked, rushing over to help them carry whatever it was they were struggling with.

"Tell you later," Remy growled, clearly annoyed by something.

"No Remy, tell him now," Colin said, sounding really pleased with himself. "Tell him how I saved your life!"

"Later," Remy repeated.

Colin ignored him. "So, Remy was getting strangled to death by a spectre and I heroically beat down the door and got it off of him just in time!"

"Colin!" Valanthé interjected, clearly just as annoyed as Remy. "You were heroically taking a shit while we got jumped by a spectre you didn't tell us about!"

"But I still saved you!" Colin protested. "It took me ages to knock down that door but I did it and then I heroically saved you both!"

"We wouldn't ha' needed savin' if you had o' warned us an' stayed with us!" Remy spat back. "An' you burstin' in an' calmly tellin' that thing to stop killin' me an' take a break instead, ain't exactly heroic either!"

Gerard looked confusedly at the three of them. They had fought a spectre? And Colin had ordered it away? Why hadn't the youth simply ordered the spectre away before the fight started?

"Okay, tell me later," Gerard said, taking the metal box from Remy and Valanthé. "What's this?" he asked. It wasn't as heavy as Remy and Valanthé made it look.

"The safe," Valanthé said matter-of-factly. "A fire started somehow – here she looked accusingly at Remy – so we didn't have time to open it. We managed to smash it out of the wall behind one of the bookcases, and brought it with."

Colin had climbed into the boat already, and sat there sulkily. "You never would have even found it, if it weren't for me," he muttered under his breath to no-one in particular.

Gerard secured the safe in the stern of the boat, while Valanthé and Remy untied the mooring ropes. They had just released the boat, when six more corpse guards burst out from the door at the back of the undercroft, and raced towards them. Remy and Valanthé climbed aboard and Gerard pushed off, instructing his corpse rowers to power out at double speed.

The boat leapt away from the dock and out through the marble colonnade of the palazzo's façade, and onward into the river channel.

"Goddammit, why we pullin' to the right?" Remy yelled, looking back from his seat in the bow. "Gerard! Why in the hell is that corpse not rowin'? Where in the hell is its oar?"

Gerard indicated back towards the undercroft where the disanimated body of a guard corpse still lay on its back on the jetty, the oar still protruding ramrod-straight from its skull. Remy saw it and nodded his understanding to Gerard.

"At some point I'm going to need to replace my sword," Gerard said matter-of-factly.

"Someone remind me not to get on the wrong side o' Gerard if he ever does that," Remy said to Valanthé and Colin.

The six fresh guard corpses reached the end of the jetty, and they shook their polearms impotently at the departing boat, which was now well clear of the palazzo and heading downstream.

The corpse rowers powered the boat forwards as best as they could with only three oars. Once they were clear of the channel, Gerard had them ease back, and the boat joined the anonymous traffic around the southern tip of Isla Verdé. Out of danger, Gerard asked the burning question that he had wanted to ask since he saw them emerge from the palazzo. "Valanthé... why do you have a fish in your jacket pocket?"

***

After mooring the boat out of sight on a quiet jetty on the far side of Isla Verdé, they then carried the safe to a secluded rigger's yard nearby in the maritime district. Remy marvelled at Gerard's strength; the big man carried the heavy safe like it was nothing, and set it carefully down on a trestle.

Remy unfurled his pick bag and got to work on the lock. It was far more challenging than he had expected, and it took him half an hour of painstaking work before the last locking pin clicked aside and the door swung open.

Remy looked around to the group triumphantly. "She's open. We in business now!"

They all gathered round. Valanthé and Gerard pressed forward, eager to see what they'd risked their lives to obtain. Colin, who had been brooding since they left the palazzo, hung back, sulkily trying to conceal his curiosity.

Remy reached in and produced first a small suede pouch, which felt weighty in his hand and jingled like money. He tossed it to Valanthé who peered inside.

"Gold coins," she exclaimed. "Looks like about thirty livres," and she piled them up and shared them out. Gerard politely refused, but Valanthé insisted he take a share, and so he did. Colin perked up a little when Valanthé handed him a share as well.

Not a bad start, Remy thought, pocketing his own share. He reached into the safe again and retrieved a large polished ebony box with a hinged lid closed with a brass hook. This he passed carefully to Gerard, who flicked open the hook and lifted the lid. He gasped, and tilted the box so Remy and the others could see. Inside, the box was lined with cushioned black velvet and, nestled in the centre of the protective cushioning, was a huge white egg, perhaps ten inches across.

"Is that an alligator egg?" Valanthé asked dubiously.

Remy immediately shook his head. "No, it's way too big."

"A bear maybe?" Colin guessed, his curiosity piqued.

"No Colin, it ain't a bear egg," Remy said flatly.

Gerard set the box down and lifted the egg carefully out, examining it closely. He exhaled a long whistling breath. "I think it's a dragon egg."

"Dragons aren't real," Colin scoffed.

"Oh, they're real enough, I assure you!" Gerard replied. "Though they don't breathe fire or nest in gold like the story books say. The mountain tribes of the breakspear ridge call them wyverns. I've travelled extensively in that region over many years, and I saw one once, a distant silhouette that swept in and out of the clouds high above. It was majestic. How in darnation did the Marquis get hold of a dragon egg?"

"And what does my pops want with it?" Remy mused.

Colin eyed the egg dubiously as Gerard reverentially placed it back in its box. "Are you going to tell me fairies are real as well?"

"They are," Gerard confirmed, nodding solemnly. "Though I've never seen one."

"I have," Valanthé interjected. "There's one working for the Scarlet Fist. She's the deck chief of a wargalley."

"How gullible do you think I am?" Colin fumed.

Smiling, Remy reached back into the safe once more, producing a thick leather folio case stuffed with papers. He stepped away from the safe, which was now empty, and laid the folio open on the trestle next to it.

Remy skimmed through the papers inside as the others looked on. There were dry legal documents and contracts, bank documents and statements, and deeds. The Marquis was a very rich man indeed. He had large deposits in several of the big banking houses of Isla Verdé, and significant interests in several of the shipping cartels that trafficked goods and corpses around the twin continents. He also owned houses and commercial properties all over the city, plus several plantations inland. He also owned a lot of Risen corpses.

"Perhaps we could transfer some of these over to us?" Colin ventured optimistically, gesturing at the corpse deeds.

Remy shook his head sadly. "No, we would need his blooded signet ring for that. And no transfer would be binding if it was fraudulent. We can't do anything with these."

Colin slunk back again, disappointed.

But Remy soon found what he was looking for among the documents; the deed that granted Isla Festa and De Ville Manor to the Marquis. He handed the document to Gerard triumphantly. "I think the Baron was lookin' for that!"

Gerard took it and scanned the text, frowning. "Well the good news is we don't need the Marquis' blooded signet ring to restore the islet to the Baron."

Remy shrugged. "And the bad news?"

"It looks like the Cabal Court auctioned off all De Ville property when the family died without heirs. The Baron will still have to convince the Cabal Court to rescind the sale."

That was what Remy had expected. Convincing the court would at least be easier if the deed was in the Baron's possession though. He nodded, and Gerard tucked the folded document away inside his doublet.

Remy had found the other document he was looking for as well. Colin's adoption certificate. He beckoned the kid back over, and they read it together.

The document dashed any lingering doubt that Colin might simply be illegitimate. He was definitely adopted fourteen years ago as a baby, just as the Marquis had claimed when he disowned him. The document was signed by the Marquis and Marchioness Du Laurentin as the adoptive parents, but the names of the birth parents were left conspicuously blank, and Colin visibly saddened with even more disappointment at being no closer to finding out who his real parents were.

Remy felt bad for the kid, and very much wanted him to stop sulking. "Colin, once we're done here, you want to come dump these other documents in the river with me?"

Colin looked at him quizzically.

"The Marquis is already havin' a shitty eve," Remy continued. "His office got trashed an' burgled an' set on fire. Some o' his Risen corpses got disanimated and, oh yeah, he turned up at the Corto Dogé expectin' an orgy and surely embarrassed hi'self in front o' the Dogé an' the entire court."

"Plus you left a surprise for him in his bed," Valanthé added.

"Yup, that too," Remy concurred. "Now if we dump all his deeds an' documents, he goin' have a real hard time accessin' or transferrin' his assets. Best of all, he goin' have a real hard time rescindin' your authority wi' his corpses. You can go back any time you like an' leave him some more surprises."

That all seemed to do the trick, and the kid brightened again. "Thank you Remy, yes that would cheer me up I think."

However, Remy wasn't done with the adoption certificate. It also contained a section for the name of the intermediary who arranged the adoption. No name was written there either, but there was the faint red stamp of a blooded signet. He examined it closely, and frowned. The stamp was a series of tribal runes that Remy immediately recognised, and it puzzled him greatly.

"What's that symbol you're looking at?" Colin asked.

"It's the sigil of the Mamas D'Ombre," Remy replied. "They're the midwives, healers, soothsayers an' spiritual leaders that minister to the fiendlin' communities o' the swamp. My mom was a Mama D'Ombre, an my lil' sister just became one too."

Valanthé peered over Remy's shoulder at the stamp on the document. "Why would one of your spiritual leaders foster a fiendling child with a human Marquis who clearly hates fiendlings?" she asked.

Remy didn't have an answer for that, and shook his head in disbelief. "They wouldn't. No way in hell that's legit."

Gerard peered at it as well, and sucked in a breath. They all looked at him quizzically as the big man instinctively touched the half-healed wound on his forehead, still bandaged under the brim of his hat. Then he reached under the collar of his doublet and pulled out a small copper pendant that hung on a slender chain around his neck. No, not a pendant, a marque of ownership like a corpse might have.

"Valanthé removed this from my head the eve she rescued me from the Pit," he said shakily, as he showed it to them. It had the exact same sigil etched onto it.

Remy stared open-mouthed, not knowing what to think. That stamp on the marque implied a Mama D'Ombre had raised the batch of corpses Gerard was part of, which was impossible; the Mamas only ever tended their own communities. What in hell was going on?

***

"Evenin' Jacques," Remy said, resting an elbow once more on the lip of the host station of the salon grand in the Casa Del Sol Riz. "Will you please let Don Gusteau know I got somethin' for him?"

"But of course, Monsieur Du Rosier," the maître d' replied. "Some refreshments while you wait?"

"You know me, Jacques," Remy nodded agreeably, and the maître d' beckoned a waiter to seat them at a table, then strode off towards the kitchens where the Don would be.

The waiter led the four of them to a cozy little table in a private booth at the far side of the restaurant area, a few tables back from the stage. There was no gold-painted dancer gyrating on the stage this time, instead the house band – a pianist and three musicians with brass instruments – were improvising syncopated swing music that didn't seem to follow any of the usual rules that music followed. Remy rather liked it, but could tell that the others found it jarring.

"Are we sure we want to give this to the Don?" Gerard asked, placing the ebony egg-box on the table once the waiter had taken their drinks order.

"No," Remy admitted. He shuddered to think what his father wanted with a dragon egg. "But that's the deal the Baron made wi' him. My pops ain't someone you want to break faith with."

"Was he always a gangster?" Colin asked. "You said he lived with you and your mother and sister in your fiendling village for a time?"

"No he weren't always a gangster," Remy conceded, "but he were always a devil. Folk were always scared o' him, an' he always had a way o' gettin' what he wanted. He were always a master manipulator, but he didn' turn professional until he left the swamp an' moved to the city. I think my mom kept him in check. She were the only one who saw through his bullshit. He could never manipulate her, but she could run rings round him."

"She died recently didn't she?" Valanthé asked tentatively. "Your mom I mean."

Remy nodded sadly.

"I figured," she continued. "You always get this look when she comes up in conversation, like it's painful to talk about her, and you change the subject. My dad died when I was young, and my mum always did the same thing whenever I asked her about him. Sorry. I can change the subject if you like?"

"No, s'okay. We been through some shit together now, an' I don' mind talkin' about it. Yes. She died a couple months ago; she were murdered."

Colin and Valanthé spoke over each other then, Valanthé offering her condolences, while Colin jumped up and demanded to know who did it and how and why. Gerard shushed him.

"Thank you Valanthé, Gerard. It's fine though." His throat felt very dry; hopefully the waiter would be back with their drinks soon. He waved the kid to sit back down.

"Colin, to answer your question, I don't know exactly who did it, though I have a strong suspicion, an' I'm pretty sure it were my fault." The three of them looked quizzically at him. He wasn't sure how best to explain his betrayal. He decided to keep it simple; he would tell them the truth.

"My mom had a gift; a special power. I was supposed to keep it secret, an' so I did. Until one evenin' I was at a party an' I wanted to impress some rich an' powerful people, an' I tol' them her secret. Two eves later she were dead. One o' them tortured her an' killed her because of it."

"I'm so sorry Remy," Colin said. "Do you know who it was?"

Remy shook his head. "No, but I suspect it were the richest an' most powerful o' the men there present; the host o' that particular party, Domenico Dandolo."

Colin let out a long whistling breath and Remy nodded; the kid had heard of him. Domenico Dandolo was the scion of the richest and most powerful family in La Crosse. He was the Dogé's great nephew.

"What was her special power, if you don't mind me asking," asked Gerard.

Remy closed his eyes and let out a long weary breath. There was no need to keep his mother's secret any longer. He'd already betrayed it, and now she was dead.

"She had the gift o' foresight. She knew exactly what was goin' happen before it did. She could read the tapestry o' fate, she said. That's how my pops never fooled her. It's no coincidence she died right after I spilled her secret, I figure whoever killed her – Domenico Dandolo or whoever it was – must o' wanted to know the future real bad, an' tortured an' killed my mom to learn it."

"But if she could see the future…" Gerard began.

"…Then why didn't she act to prevent her own death?" Remy interjected, finishing the question for him. "Those wi' the gift can't see their own future; she didn't know they was comin' for her until they was already there," he continued bitterly. "They strung her up an' drained all the blood out o' her like some kind o' ritual blood-lettin' torture."

They sat in stunned silence for a moment, which made Remy regret having said anything; their sympathy made him uncomfortable. Where were those damn drinks?

Colin broke the silence. "Shit, Remy… remind me not to tell you any of my secrets," which made them all chuckle weakly.

Remy changed the subject. "Since we're tellin' our secrets though…" he said, turning to Valanthé, who was still staring at him with eyes full of sympathy. "I'd like to know yours… You been avoidin' the question all evenin'… What's up wi' all those fish?"

Valanthé buried her head in her hands, then emerged again with a long-suffering look of embarrassment.

"Fine," she said. "I'm sure you've figured it out already anyway; when I'm in situations of extreme stress or danger, weird things happen that I have no control over. The spectre toppled the desk onto me, and I felt a surge of something bubble over, and somehow the desk turned into a shoal of fish before it landed."

"What an astounding gift!" Gerard said.

"That's wild!" Colin exclaimed. "Is it always fish?"

Valanthé shook her head, "No, it's different every time."

Colin looked around at the furniture of the booth. "Can you turn this table into a pile of gold?" he asked.

She shook her head again. "No. Like I said, it's not something I can control, and it only happens when I'm in stressful or dangerous situations. It's saved my life a few times though, so I can put up with the occasional embarrassing shoal of fish."

Remy looked at her in wonder. "Was the fish the most embarrassin' thing you've ever caused to happen?"

Valanthé buried her head in her hands again. "No," she said, her voice muffled from behind her hands. And she hid there for a long moment before telling them about the time she inadvertently made it rain spaghetti during her cousin's wedding vows.

The waiter eventually brought their drinks, and the mood lightened further as they drank, and Valanthé gave them a rundown of more of the embarrassing things that she'd inadvertently caused to happen.

They were laughing happily as they ordered a second round of drinks, when a scandalously-dressed young woman sidled over to their table; one of the hostesses who worked the salon and entertained its patrons privately, for a fee.

"Remy Du Rosier?" she queried. "Why, I haven't seen you in months! Where've you been, sweetness? How come you don't party no more?"

She was pretty, with lustrous ebony skin and full red-painted lips. She wore her hair high in a fashionable bouffant, and her full figure was exaggerated by the tight bustier she was mostly squeezed into. She smiled pleasantly at them, her lips parting to reveal an inviting void of blackened teeth, as was the current fashion for courtly ladies. "Y'all sound like a merry bunch, mind if I join you?"

Remy wasn't interested in partying. He was going to send her politely away, but then saw the pleading look on Colin's face, and relented. "Of course, Miss...?"

Remy couldn't remember her name. That was fine; she was a hostess, she almost certainly used a false name anyway.

"...Bethany," she supplied with a smile, nonplussed that he couldn't remember. She may well have used a different name last time they'd met.

"Miss Bethany, might I present my friends Gerard Malblanq and Miss Valanthé Luxalim. And this is..."

Colin cut him off, having leapt to his feet, and he greeted her with a big sweeping bow. "Salvatoré Col Haolim Primo Martelaar Delmond Du Laurentin." He blurted out his full name in its usual scattergun of syllables. The young lady smiled demurely, seeming impressed. Remy knew better; he had been in her shoes not so long ago, playing this game. She had identified her target now, and sat down next to the naïve but eager young man with the noble title and upper class accent.

"Pleased to meet you Salvatoré. You're a Du Laurentin?" she asked, feigning interest. "Any relation to the Marquis?"

"Yes, I'm his adopted son," Colin replied, sounding as grandiose as he could. Remy could almost hear the hostess' price double.

"He's the Marquis' only son, in fact," Valanthé interjected, feigning earnestness. She must have heard the price doubling as well and thought it would be amusing to ratchet it up further.

"Oh goodness," the hostess exclaimed, fluttering an elegant silk fan. She then leaned in to him conspiratorially to ask, behind the fan, "is it true he's one of the richest men in La Crosse?" She was no doubt entirely aware how much her leaning-in improved his view of her bosom.

"I don't know about that," said Colin, doing his best to maintain gentlemanly eye contact instead of staring at her distracting cleavage. "But I know for a fact he has fifty thousand livres on deposit in the bank of Aldersport. We saw his statements earlier this evening."

The hostess gave Remy a subtle look of amusement that Remy interpreted to mean the price just doubled again. Valanthé saw it too, and struggled to conceal her mirth.

The waiter returned with the second round of drinks, which Colin paid for with a golden livre. "Keep the change," he said grandly, before Remy could stop him. A livre could pay for an expensive round of drinks ten times over. It could fully pay off his debts at the Madrigal. Worse, his generosity doubled the hostess' price once more. Even Gerard was finding it amusing now.

Remy didn't want to embarrass Colin, or cause him to sulk again, but he would have to have a word with him later about hostesses, and also make sure he understood the value of livres and sols and deniers. In fact he would take charge of the kid's remaining money, at least until they got to his village. He had decided to endure the anger and recriminations of the townsfolk, and accompany Colin there rather than just send him to his sister Elise; the stamp of the Mamas D'Ombre on the kid's adoption certificate and Gerard's marque needed looking into. Also he wanted to see Elise and apologise for his mistakes and try and convince her not to hate him.

Colin was still boasting when the maître d' returned to bring them to the Don. The hostess – Bethany – managed to look genuinely disappointed when they left, but she promised to stay put until they came back, and invited Colin to kiss her hand which made him blush.

The maître d' took them once more through the main kitchen with its bustling chefs and corpses, and along the side corridor to the Don's dessert kitchen.

The devil was drizzling lemon jus onto a tray of citron tarts.

***

"Remy, It is good to see you again so soon. Are you well? 'Ave you eaten?"

"I'm good thanks, Pop," Remy replied.

"I must insist you 'ave a tarte au citron; I 'ave just made zem fresh, zey are delicious!"

Remy shook his head, but the Don beckoned one of the tarts onto a gold-rimmed plate which had hovered over to him, then he artfully placed a coil of candied lemon peel beside it on the plate.

"Young Master Du Laurentin, you will of course not refuse me?" the Don insisted, addressing Colin. "And you will no doubt share it with my son?"

The plate drifted over towards the kid, along with two silver dessert forks. Colin looked to Remy uncertainly. Remy indicated he should accept it, and so he did. Colin handed him one of the forks, and he took it resignedly. His father always got what he wanted.

"And one for your other friends as well of course," the Don said, as another tart plated itself and drifted over towards Valanthé and Gerard. Gerard had been staring intently, eyes wide at the devil in chef's whites. Remy realised he hadn't met the Don before, and he looked suitably astonished at the Don's appearance. The plate drifted over to him, and Valanthé accepted it politely on behalf of them both, then she and Gerard self-consciously followed Remy's lead and tucked into the dessert.

"Bon. And I'm told you 'ave something for me as well?" the Don continued as he wiped his hands on a towel.

Remy held out the ebony egg-box, and the devil eyed it greedily. He beckoned it over, and it drifted towards him, opening up as it went. With a silhouette hand, he plucked the huge egg out of the box, and held it up to inspect it, seeming to purr in satisfaction, and as he did so the air around him darkened and hummed with anticipation as before a lightning strike.

The Don's dark aura expanded, dimming the viridian worklights that hung above the counter and all but obscuring him so his chef's whites and hat were but a hint of lightness in the black fog that he had become.

"Finally!" he said triumphantly, in a booming voice a full octave lower than his normal conversational tone. "Finally, I 'ave a dragon egg. Do you know 'ow long I 'ave wanted one of zese? Ze damn wyverns of ze mountains 'ave always eluded me until now!"

Remy's companions looked apprehensively at one another, taking a tentative step back towards the door as the Don darkened ominously, but Remy smiled. Regardless of what horrible thing he had planned for that egg, it was nice seeing his father so joyful.

The dark aura vanished and the Don and his chef's whites were restored to crisp appearance. He lifted the egg high in front of him as if in triumph, then suddenly brought it crashing down, cracking it open into a large mixing bowl on the counter.

Remy and the others watched, transfixed, as the Don pulled out a whisk and started whisking furiously. He next beckoned flour and cream and butter into the bowl to form a paste which he then spooned into a hot pan on the stovetop behind him, and soon produced a big stack of perfect dragon-egg pancakes, which he then proceeded to douse with sugar and lemon. Then he ate them.

Remy and the others were dumbstruck. What had they just witnessed? He ate it! The priceless dragon egg!

"Magnifique!" the Don exclaimed, seeming to lick the last of the lemon syrup from his fingers. "Merci to you all for zis! You will be sure I 'ope, to let me know if you find any more eggs?"

They nodded dumbly.

"Bon. Monsieur Malblanq, Master Du Laurentin, you will convey my best wishes to ze Baron and inform 'im zat I will not act against 'is property until ze Cabal Court 'ave considered 'is deposition. Miss Valanthé, ze maître d'hôtel will 'ave some livres for you at 'is desk, and I will send for you when I 'ave more work for you. Remy you shall 'ave your stipend as agreed."

The door opened, and he gestured for them to leave, and they all turned mutely to do so.

"Not you Remy. I would like it if you stayed behind a moment."

The others looked warily back at him, but Remy gave them a reassuring smile. Once the door had closed behind them, Don Gusteau put a fatherly hand on his shoulder. "I like your friends, Remy."

"Yeah, I like 'em too," Remy replied, and he genuinely did. Even the annoying kid.

The Don frowned. "You still look lost zough, my boy. I know you 'ate to take advice from me, but perhaps I can convince you to go and see Elise?"

"Don't worry Pop, I already decided to go an' see her."

"Good! Zat is good. Bon. I will spare us both ze awkwardness of me giving you advice." He gave Remy's shoulder a squeeze and withdrew his hand. "But still, I 'ate to see you quite so lost, so I shall give you something else instead. Something zat will 'elp you find what you are looking for."

Here, the Don circled a finger in the air between them, where it left a trail of smoking embers in the shape of a circle that hovered unnaturally in the air, like he had scorched a hole in the fabric of the world. Perhaps he had. He reached into the smoke ring, and his hand and chef's white sleeve disappeared into it up to the shoulder as if he were reaching through a porthole.

He pulled his arm back out, and his hand emerged clutching a flat wooden box that might have been a cigar box. He lifted the lid to reveal – not cigars – instead, a row of slender white candles within. He removed one candle, closed the lid and placed the box back inside the smoky porthole, which then disappeared with a wave of his hand. He held out the candle to Remy, who looked at it confusedly.

"As you light it, ask it a question," the Don said in answer to his confused look. "Ze smoke will lead you to ze answer you seek."

"Um. Thanks, Pop," Remy said, unsure what else to say. His father rarely gave unsolicited gifts without wanting something in return.

"Now if you don't mind, I would like to spend some time with my son before 'e disappears into ze city once again. I 'ave booked us a table for dinner. We will 'ave a meal together, yes?"

Remy looked at his father, genuinely touched by his unspoken sentiment, and a lump formed in his throat. "That would be great, Pop."

The Don circled a finger once again, producing a much larger smoke ring, which filled in with a smoky streetscape. "You should tell your friends you will be gone a while, non?"

Remy nodded. He caught up with Gerard, Valanthé and Colin on their way back to the table. They were happy to wait while he had dinner with his father. Gerard decided to take the opportunity of a few hours to freshen up in his rooms and get some sleep. Valanthé accompanied him to do the same. Colin was keen to get back to Bethany. Remy wished him good luck, and embraced him in a hug, which allowed him to discreetly take the kid's coin purse for safe keeping. Colin was too young to be entertained by hostesses anyway.

They agreed to meet back there in the salon grand at twelvebells, when they would head out to pick up the Baron's boat and return to Isla Festa. Remy just had one more errand to run, which he could do on the way to collect the boat.

He returned to the dessert kitchen where the Don stood waiting by the smoke porthole. He stepped through, beckoning Remy to join him. Remy stepped tentatively through, and found himself on a cobbled street outside a busy bistro restaurant. Remy recognised it; it was a rustic dining spot on one of the nicer outer islands, Isla Maria Angelou. His father stood beside him, wearing one of his familiar human forms; the one where he was a kindly middle-aged man with a receding grey hairline and spectacles and a wrinkled suit.

His father nodded pleasantly with his kindly-man face, and pushed the door of the bistro open. "Zis place 'as ze best tartiflette in ze city. Come try it, you'll see I do not lie."

Remy followed him in, and they enjoyed a pleasant meal together where the Don was perfectly charming and convivial and didn't talk business or disparage any of his life choices or offer any unwanted advice at all.

CHAPTER 12

CHAPTER 12

Of all the places Joanna Pianna could have been, it turned out by pure coincidence that she was staying at the Madrigal Saloon, the very same place that Thessu had been lodging since his arrival in La Crosse. He and Epifani had been following her trail together since the fight at the necromancers' guild a couple of eves ago, and astonishingly the trail now led them back to the first place they had encountered each other.

"Excellence comes from repetition," Thessu muttered as they stepped onto the Doblé bridge once again, heading back over to Isla Doblé.

"Is that another damn mantra?" Epifani asked. "How many are there?"

Thessu shrugged. "Wisdom is a limitless resource."

"Yeah, well so is bullshit," she retorted, and quickened her pace across the bridge. Her irritation was understandable, it had been a frustrating search that had ended back where they started.

They had first questioned Sofokles of Halla. The writer had been the last person they knew to have met with the witch actress. He had already been in a foul mood because his reading was interrupted by a fire, and many in the audience – particularly the wealthy literati – hadn't waited in the drizzling rain while the blaze was quenched for an uncertain finale. He was in a worse mood when he left the venue, after Thessu and Epifani had accosted him.

Thessu had asked him again as to Joanna's location, and got a very terse answer from the writer. He was more forthcoming once they'd dunked him in the river. He had given them the address of his publisher, who had apparently been paying for Miss Pianna's lodging in the city, so should know exactly where she was.

So they had gone to see the publisher. He hadn't been at his office so they'd broken in and searched it. There they had found a paper-trail that suggested the publishing house was making payments to several boarding houses around the city.

They had then spent a full eve visiting each of them in turn, looking for the missing actress. It was an exhausting exercise – since the lodgings were scattered all round the city on different islands – and she hadn't been found in any of them.

However, they had found the publisher himself in the last establishment they checked, who it turned out had been using company funds to support a young mistress in luxurious apartments on Isla Roja. There hadn't been a handy river channel nearby to dunk him in, so they had gotten creative with a candelabra instead, and he had quickly given out the Madrigal as Joanna's location.

The bridge was busy with people and Risen as they crossed; workers coming and going between Isla Verdé and Isla Doblé in time for the early evening work shift. Thessu still didn't understand why Epifani hated the Risen as much as she did, but she glared furiously from behind her hood and neckerchief at each one they passed. As usual, she refused to pay the toll corpse, striding past it contemptuously. Thessu at least made a show of gratefully placing coins in its collection bucket; a copper denier for himself and one for the lady.

She scowled back at him, either for paying the corpse or for referring to her as a lady. Maybe both. As a test, he shook the toll corpse's hand warmly – with his gloves on of course – just to see Epifani's reaction. She looked repulsed. He decided to gratuitously shake more corpse hands and then perhaps leave his glove somewhere amusing, like in her hood. Of course, he palmed the coins from the bucket instead of leaving them though; he wasn't going to pay for walking.

The Madrigal Saloon was just along the esplanade from where the bridge landed. It had a prominent corner position at the end of a row of shops and businesses, and the lounge bar was often busy, even raucous on occasion. However, when they arrived it was fairly quiet with only a handful of patrons sat at the bar and a few small groups sat in cosy booths.

Thessu looked around for Madame Cass, but she didn't seem to be present. One of her girls – the one with the unhealthy pallor and unkempt ginger curls – was sat at the end of the bar though, painting her nails daintily. She wore very impractical clothes; Thessu could not see what purpose was served by a corset as tight as that, and her feather boa looked extremely silly. He adjusted his goggled leather beak mask and headed over to join her at the bar. Epifani casually followed and lingered nearby, staying in the shadows between the pools of chartreuse light from the overhead lamps.

"Good evening," Thessu said to the young lady, taking a seat on the bar-stool next to her.

"Hi," she said pleasantly, looking up, then saw him and suddenly seemed uncomfortable. No doubt it was her corset.

"You work here don't you?" Thessu asked.

She looked unsure. Thessu didn't understand her confusion; she either worked there or she didn't, but she answered warily.

"Um... Yessir, but I ain't workin' jus' yet. My colleague Marguerite will be along presently and will be happy to look after you both; Marguerite is more... um... receptive to unusual requests."

For some reason Epifani found this extremely funny; Thessu heard her sniggering into her neckerchief.

"I don't know if I need looking after," Thessu continued, "Or if my requests are that unusual. I have a couple of questions, that's all."

The girl looked dubious, and still quite uncomfortable. Thessu opened the filter slits on his mask, and promptly closed them again after sniffing the air. She had pubic lice and a urinary infection. Maybe that's why she was uncomfortable.

"I'm looking for a young lady called Joanna Pianna. I believe she's staying here; can you tell me what room she's in please?"

The girl considered. "Joanna Pianna? The name sounds familiar... I think there was a girl here called Joanna a while back." She absently scratched her head. Perhaps she had head lice as well.

"Yes, I think I do remember her," she continued. "This would be what, almost a year ago? Quiet girl, kept herself to herself. She seemed short o' funds but didn't want to take any work from Madame Cass." She clicked her fingers then in recognition. "Oh that's right she were pregnant weren't she? I guess she'd have had herself a bonny baby a few months back."

Thessu frowned. Yes, the Baron had said she was noticeably pregnant during the voyage on the Queen of the South; of course she would have a baby by now. "So she's not here any more?"

"No I ain't seen her in months. An' if there was a bawlin' baby here, you'd know it!"

Mercy, she was right! Thessu had heard no babies at the Madrigal. Looking over at Epifani, he saw she was scowling again. She came over to join the conversation, lowering her neckerchief and hood. "Rent is paid here every month in her name. She must still be lodging here!"

The girl shrugged. "I wouldn't know about that. You'd have to ask Madame Cass; ah, here she is now..."

They looked up and saw Madame Cass coming down the staircase from the mezzanine balcony that overlooked the bar. She was a matronly older woman with powdered face and hair, in a too-tight corset under a fur stole. They caught her eye as she descended, and she walked over to join them. She smelled unpleasantly of musk and pomade.

"Why Mister Thessu, I see you've met our lovely Isabela. I sure hope she's bein' accomodatin' to your requests?" She smiled agreeably, though her eyes narrowed when she spotted the girl's – Isabela's – discomfort.

"Actually she isn't," Thessu replied matter-of-factly. "Perhaps you can accomodate my particular request instead?"

Madame Cass's smile slipped an instant, and Epifani stifled another laugh into her neckerchief. What was she finding so funny?

"They're lookin' for someone called Joanna," Isabela interjected. "I think maybe they mean that pregnant girl who was stayin' here las' year. They sayin' her rent is still paid for each month, but I thought she left months ago?"

Now Madame Cass's smile slipped completely, and she frowned at them all. "Isabela dear, can you kindly go an' ask Cook if the gumbo is ready for servin'? I'm feelin' peckish."

The girl smiled sweetly and slipped off the bar-stool, headed away towards the kitchen area. Once she was out of sight, Madame Cass regarded them coolly. "I know you ain't from the publishin' house, so what business is it o' yours if her rent's paid or not?"

"We're not here about the overpaid rent," Epifani said. "We're just trying to find Joanna. Do you know where she is?"

The woman sighed. "Sorry darlin' I ain't got a clue. She left here abruptly what, nine, ten months ago. At first I kept her room for her since it was paid for an' all, but when she never came back, I figured there's no point keepin' the room empty, so I let it out to one o' my girls instead."

"And you never told the publishing house?" Thessu asked.

Madame Cass shook her head. "No. I figured she could have her room back if she ever did return. But I ain't heard a peep from her since she up and walked out."

"She just left? Without saying anything?" Epifani queried.

"Yep. She jus' left without a word in partin'. There was a woman came to see her the eve she left. They drank together here in the bar, some awful peppermint liqueur she brought with, and then they both upped and left together."

"Who was the woman?" Epifani asked.

"No idea. I ain't never seen her before or since. She was old though. An old woman wi' dark skin like yours an' white hair."

"Can you tell us anything else about her?" Thessu asked. "It's a matter of life and death that we find Joanna."

Madame Cass thought for a moment. "Well she was blind, the old woman. Did I say that already?"

Thessu and Epifani looked at each other and shrugged. They didn't know any old blind woman.

"You can take a look through Joanna's things if you like, maybe that'll help you find her?" Madame Cass suggested. "It's all in the back storeroom there." Here she indicated a narrow door behind the bar. "It's a bit of a mess in there though; you'd be surprised how many o' my guests leave things behind. I keep it as collateral in case they want it back and owe me rent."

"Thank you Madame Cass. I just have one more question," Thessu said, as he and Epifani rose to go search the storeroom. "Assuming we don't tell the publishing house about their overpayments, what sort of discount can I expect on my rent?"

***

The storeroom was bigger than it looked, with shelves by the near wall piled high with clutter, while the rest of the room was filled with racks of clothes and piles of boxes and crates and trunks, all stacked higgledy-piggledy and covered in dust and smelling of mould. The room was lit by a single flickering viridian lamp, while the solitary window let in no light, being high on the far wall facing away from the ever-setting sun.

At the back of the room, rifling through boxes in the great pile, was Remy.

"What the hell are you doing here?" Epifani said as she entered. It was getting ridiculous now, how she kept bumping into the same people everywhere she went.

"I'm lookin' for my stuff!" the fiendling said. "It seems my room has been let out to someone else. What in the hell you doin' here?"

"We're looking for a mother and baby," Thessu said, pushing in behind Epifani.

Remy looked around the cluttered storeroom. "I don' think they here."

"Apparently her stuff is here," Epifani said flatly, lifting the lid on the nearest trunk and peering in. Crumpled bedsheets.

"Well you're welcome to look. You know what you're lookin' for?"

"No clue," Epifani replied. This would no doubt be another waste of her time, just like the past few eves had been.

"Actually, she was heavily pregnant when she left here," Thessu said. "And she left everything behind. I'm expecting there'll be some maternity things and baby things in here somewhere. If we can identify which things are hers, we can search them for something that'll tell us where she went."

Epifani shrugged. That was a good idea, but it still sounded like a waste of her time.

"Well I'll keep an eye out," Remy said as he picked through the pile. "An' if you find a lil' wicker case containin' a porcelain teapot, you let me know."

Epifani thought that was an odd thing for Remy to be searching for, and she made no effort to look for it; though in truth she made very little effort to find Joanna's things either. She headed to one of the clothes rails, which was stuffed full of abandoned clothes and jackets, with more draped over the top of it. She wondered if anything there would fit her.

It was mostly men's clothes, which was good, but they were all dirty and crumpled and far too big. She took a cursory look at the few dresses on the rail to check if any might have belonged to Joanna, but there was no way to tell – what did she know about dresses for pregnant ladies? – so she tossed them aside.

She pushed past the rail to a stack of battered-looking cabin trunks. Opening the top one, she peered in. Amongst other things, there was a little wicker case inside.

"Wicker case," she said as she pulled it out. "Might be your one Remy?" Remy looked up from the other side of the storeroom. She tossed the case to him.

He dropped what he was holding in a panic, and lunged frantically to catch the case. He just about snatched it out of the air before it could strike the wall behind him. "Goddamit Epifani!" he yelled, "I tol' you it had porcelain inside!"

He opened it up and pulled out an ugly-looking little blue and white tea pot, and examined it for damage. It looked ancient.

"Remy that teapot is revolting!" she said. "What do you want such an ugly thing for anyway?"

"It were my mother's," he replied, looking at her angrily. Were his eyes always red? He glared at her with eyes the flickering orange-red of firelight.

"Maybe you should buy her a new one, that thing looks ancient," Epifani said, and went back to searching the trunk. No baby things. Possibly more of Remy's stuff though. She held up a man's toiletry bag and he nodded slowly, still glaring at her, eyes still burning. She placed it back and lifted the trunk off the pile, holding it out towards him casually. "Why so angry Remy? You caught it didn't you? It's just an ugly old teapot, why does it matter?"

"My mother died, Epifani," Remy said, picking his way towards her without lowering his intense burning gaze. "Someone strung her up an' killed her with a thousand shallow cuts that drained all the blood out o' her."

He took the trunk from her and leaned close in. There was definitely fire in his eyes. "It ain't just an ugly ol' teapot; it's *her* ugly ol' teapot. Be. More. Careful."

Epifani broke eye contact, looking away. When she looked back, he was already sorting through his other things from the trunk. The fire had faded from his eyes; they weren't red at all, they were the dark blue of the twilight sky.

What he'd said though, about his mother's death; That sounded a lot like what she'd read of the ritual of the Bloode Goblette. She would need to ask him more about his mother's death, and whether she had had any innate power. Epifani would have to think first about how to question the fiendling without making him suspicious about her motive.

If she was right, then here was another astonishing coincidence; the mysterious person who'd set her on the trail of Joanna Pianna – who'd promised to rid the world of Risen – must be the same person who'd killed Remy's mother. She fingered the pieces of the broken goblet in her pocket. Whatever innate power Remy's mother had had, Epifani's mysterious benefactor had used this cup to steal it from her. She wasn't sure how she felt about that.

"Baby things!" Thessu exulted. They both looked at him, and he held up a tin rattle and a fine lace bonnet small enough to fit a newborn. They both peered over, and saw the trunk he was picking through contained a woman's things as well. Rifling through a cosmetics case, he picked out pair of silver hairpins which he passed to Epifani. Turning them over in her hand, she saw they were monogrammed 'JP'. This was Joanna's trunk alright.

Epifani squatted down to join him in picking through the rest of it, looking for clues as to the blind woman's identity, or to where Joanna might have gone. But it was just as she had thought; a waste of her time. There was nothing helpful like a letter from the blind woman with a return address on it. Of course there wasn't; she was blind, she wouldn't be writing letters.

Thessu had opened the filter on his mask and was sniffing Joanna's perfumes. She watched him uncork each one in turn and grimace at the contents. "Sandalwood," he pronounced about one of them. "Ambergris," the next. "This one's mint," he said of the third one.

Epifani snatched it off him. "This one isn't perfume," she said, examining the unusual bottle. It was an almost spherical green glass bottle, almost fully wrapped in knotted rope netting with a knotted rope handle behind a curved spout. It was about two-thirds full of a syrupy clear liquid which did indeed smell of mint. "Didn't the madame out there say the blind woman was drinking a peppermint liqueur she'd brought?"

Before they could examine any of it further, there was a smash as a burning projectile came through the lattice window from the street outside. They all ducked as the projectile – a flask of burning oil perhaps – exploded onto the junk pile, spreading burning liquid fire around the room.

From the sound of smashing windows and screaming elsewhere in the building, that hadn't been the only firebomb launched at the Madrigal Saloon just then.

CHAPTER 13

Valanthé was getting impatient now. She and Colin and Gerard were once again waiting for Remy. He had been late to meet them at the Casa – after disappearing with his father for hours – and he had then begged their indulgence while he ran yet another errand. So they were waiting while he 'quickly' paid his debt at the Madrigal Saloon and collected his things.

She soon realised that 'quickly' must have meant something entirely different to Remy than to everyone else… or perhaps the fiendling just needed a break from Colin's constant whining about losing all his money and having been abandoned by the hostess at the Casa. Valanthé certainly tired of hearing it.

From where they waited just along the esplanade, she had been surprised to see the belligerent woman the Baron had introduced her to – Epifani – enter the Madrigal, and she had subtly pointed it out to Gerard. In return, he had pointed out the oddball in the beaked mask who accompanied her – Thessu – and they had shared a look of dismay at the sight of the two trouble-makers. She hoped they weren't the cause of Remy's delay.

"Hey look, there's Thessu and Epifani," Colin had announced. "We should go and say hello!" Thankfully however, the belligerent woman and the oddball hadn't heard him, so they avoided having to say hello. Instead they had moved further away from the Madrigal, with both Gerard and Valanthé hoping not to get caught up in any more trouble.

Trouble caught up with them anyway.

A pair of galley barges moored up alongside a jetty at the far side of the saloon, and a large cohort of Risen disembarked from each of them and loped up the steps to the esplanade. One cohort lingered by the dockside while the other headed up the side-street that ran past the Madrigal towards the centre of the island. Valanthé kept half an eye on the cohort that remained, wondering what they were up to.

Gerard drew her attention to two men who stepped up onto the esplanade after the Risen. "Those two blonde fellas are the necromancers from the guild," he whispered. "The ones who jumped the Baron and mortified his arm."

Valanthé's hands went to her swords. The corpses were passing something between them; bottles maybe. One of the blonde men – the necromancers – joined the cohort lingering in front of the saloon, while the other disappeared after where the other cohort of Risen had gone.

The necromancer she could see lit a taper, and Valanthé realised too late what those bottles were, when he used the taper to light the bottle that the first corpse was holding. The bottles were incendiary bombs. She realised then as well that the cohort she had lost sight of were probably heading round back to surround the saloon. The necromancers were leading a coordinated attack on the Madrigal for some reason.

"We need to get Remy out," she said hurriedly, drawing her swords. "They're going to torch the building!" and she set off at a run. Gerard followed behind and they ran a short distance, then both turned round and – at the same time – yelled, "Colin, wait there and don't move!"

"Yeah, yeah," the boy replied sulkily.

The corpses loosed their bombs before Valanthé and Gerard could reach them. Windows shattered and fires exploded into life in the ground floor lounge bar and inside the upstairs windows and on all the gallery balconies of the upper floors.

Valanthé cut down the first corpse she reached, hacking into the back of its neck with enough force to sever the spinal cord, if not the head. She continued past, whirling as she wrenched the blade free of the corpse's spine as it fell, then hacked it straight into the face of a second corpse, where it cleaved its marque of ownership in half and shattered the nasal bone between its eyes. Either of those might have done for the corpse, and it crumpled backwards, disanimated. The Risen needed brute force, not finesse.

She caught a glimpse of Gerard behind her, still barrelling towards the corpses. Crap-in-a-clap! He needed a weapon; he was still unarmed! She couldn't focus on him though, another two corpses were bearing down on her, barring her way forward. She would have to trust that the big man knew what he was doing.

The corpses were grabbing at her bodily now. She halted her headlong rush to thrust her slender long sword through the gaping maw of the next one as it lunged at her, trying to grapple her arms. Her sword severed its tongue and drove up through the soft upper palette of its mouth, and on towards its brain. Its tongue fell wetly to the floor – followed out by a dribble of black viscous slime – but it clamped its jaw shut onto the blade and the blade lodged between its teeth.

She felt its grip on the sleeve of her leather jacket tighten as it locked its jaws onto the blade, cracking its teeth but resisting the thrust. She set her weight behind the sword and leant into it – driving the blade deeper – and the corpse's grip loosened as it disanimated. Its jaw remained clamped shut as it fell however, wrenching the sword from her grasp.

She let it go; her heavier short sword was better for hacking at corpses in close quarters anyway, and she used her now-free hand to strike the falling corpse's bony claw from her sleeve. Then she felt cold dead arms wrap around her body from behind, pinning her own arms to her side. She had been too slow.

Suddenly there was an almighty whack, and she staggered off-balance but the arms were gone and she was free to move once more. She caught a glimpse of a Risen corpse flailing as it flew through the air over the side of the esplanade. Gerard had hit it. The big man did know what he was doing!

"Get to the door," he yelled. "Before the fire spreads. I'll hold them off here!"

She nodded, and sidestepped away from another on-rushing corpse. Gerard grabbed it with one sturdy hand and yanked it away from her. Only one Risen corpse now stood between her and the entrance to the saloon, but she could see that the heavy doors were already ablaze, as was the doorframe, and the floor of the lounge bar beyond. She caught a glimpse of people inside, cowering from the flames and unable to get out. She would have to be quick.

Another corpse launched itself at her. So suddenly had it lunged, that she barely had her sword ready and pointed at its face as it rushed forwards onto it. The tip of the blade caught in the hollow of its cheekbone, but it didn't penetrate the thick bones of its face. Instead, the blade-tip skittered across the front of its skull, ripping a great flap of desiccated flesh off its cheek as far back as its ear, which dangled wetly from its skull as the corpse continued its lunge.

She pivoted as its arms wrapped around her midriff, turning her body so her sword-arm wrapped around its head while her off-hand grabbed its opposite arm and pulled it round her. She stuck her trailing leg out behind her to trip it as she pulled it round. It tripped and crashed onto the ground at her feet, its arms flailing to grab hold of her and bring her down with it, but she kept her balance and stayed upright.

She didn't have time to finish it off though; she sensed another corpse had come between her and the saloon, about to grab her. She spun around once more, hacking her sword at head-height. It clashed into another blade, held up by the corpse to deflect her swing. No, not a corpse; a man. One of the blonde necromancers. He stepped back, adopting a low fencing stance. His blade was a slender rapier; longer, lighter and faster than her own short sword.

She raised her sword in a defensive stance and looked past him at the door to the saloon. She wasn't going to get through; two more corpses had taken position in front of it. They held long poles – oars maybe – and as she watched, someone inside tried to barge their way out; one of the patrons, she guessed. The patron had a cloak held over his head to keep the flames away, and would have made it out except the two corpses by the door jabbed at him with their poles to prevent him from leaving. The patron fell just inside the threshold, landing in the flames, and the heavy burning doors swung closed once more.

Valanthé looked around for Gerard and saw him still fighting, but on the verge of being overwhelmed. Corpses had piled into him – he had two on his back he couldn't shake – one of them had sunk its teeth into his neck and clamped on, and his expensive slashed doublet was ripped and soaked with blood. She saw him reach up over his shoulder to grab the one that had bitten him; with one hand he wrenched it off of him, slamming its head into the ground in front of him with a roar and a sickening crunch, but his hand came up bloody from where the shattered shards of its skull had sliced into him.

The necromancer in front of Valanthé flicked his rapier at her face, drawing her attention away from her friend and back towards the imminent danger. She beat the attack away with her own sword, and stepped forward with a riposte, closing the distance in two quick steps.

But the necromancer was too smart to let her close in when he had the advantage of a longer reach, and their swords clashed again as he stepped back nimbly maintaining his advantage. Corpses pressed around her, hemming her in; restricting her ability to manoeuvre, and she couldn't force them back without giving the necromancer an opening for a killing thrust. The necromancer smiled menacingly – he knew he had her beaten.

She felt the familiar rising surge of panic that accompanied whatever wild power she had inside her. She let the surge rise up. It felt like a rising tide of... oh crap!

She opened her mouth and vomited. The necromancer looked startled for an instant before he disappeared under the deluge of dense black thrashing matter she brought forth. Living matter. She had hurled out an unending stream of half-digested toads and toad-parts, slick with digestive enzymes and stomach acid, writhing and smoking with foul humours as they slammed into the necromancer and splashed wetly onto the ground around him. He screamed in pain and terror, and got a mouthful of toad juice before he fell under the bombardment. He dropped his rapier and collapsed to his hands and knees – where he cowered from the foulness that drenched him – then brought forth his own vomit to add to the torrent.

Valanthé turned the spray onto the corpses that surrounded her, who all stopped pressing and stepped back under the foul onslaught. She soaked them until the stream of filth petered out and she could soak them no more. She dry retched twice, and burped out one last half toad which dribbled sloppily to the ground at her feet.

Risen don't feel fear or pain or surprise, but the corpses had no idea how to deal with what just happened, and they stared at her blankly as the smoking soup of toad-slime and stomach acid dribbled down them. The whole cohort had completely stopped what they were doing to stare at her. Gerard pushed through the crowd of motionless corpses to stand by her side, his hat missing and his doublet a ruin of blood, and with one hand pressing a wadded handkerchief to the wound on his neck.

"Well, that was weird," he said calmly as he reached her, picking a steaming toad off her shoulder and dropping it to the ground where it hopped away.

Through the gaps in the corpses, Valanthé saw two more men were watching events from the dockside of the esplanade. She recognised them. One was a fat man with a ginger beard greying at the roots and a tricorn hat. The other a tall, muscular middle-aged man with a scar across his face running under an eye patch. Two pirate captains, Crosskeys and Lugwort. Both of them had their mouths open in astonishment.

Her eyes locked with theirs, and their eyes widened in recognition. Recognition of her, and of the wild surge that she had produced. Crosskeys' bitchy black parrot seemed to recognise it too, and the bird flapped its wings and jumped three feet off of the pirate's shoulder. Across the distance, and over the din of the fire and the noise of the necromancer vomiting, Valanthé heard it squawk, "*Darkmourn!*" …and …was that fear in the pirates' eyes?

The corpses started to come round as the oddness of what had happened subsided, and Gerard grabbed her, pulling her across the slick ground towards the burning building while they still had that option. They shielded their eyes from the smoke and heat and, barging the door corpses out of the way, prepared to dash in. They had friends in there.

Someone shouted "Valanthé!" and she halted at the threshold. It was Captain Crosskeys. The pirate stepped forward from the dockside, and corpses moved out of his way unbidden. She saw it now, this cohort of corpses were galley corpses; his corpses. The blonde necromancers worked for him as well. Worked for the Scarlet Fist.

"We ain't here for you Valanthé," the pirate captain called out. "Come lass, ye don't have to die this evenin'. There be people in there been sniffing 'round things they shouldn't, and they die this eve, but ye ain't one of 'em. Come back to Flotsam and let's figure this out!"

She had always liked Captain Crosskeys. The gruff old pirate had taken her under his wing and looked after her ever since she had first arrived in La Crosse. "Fuck you!" she shouted at him, then she headed inside with Gerard.

***

As soon as the flaming oil exploded into the storeroom, Epifani bolted for the door. Glancing towards the lounge bar, she saw it was ablaze as well, with more burning flasks pitching in through the big lattice windows to smash around the room, setting more of the floor and furniture and bar alight. She turned instead towards the kitchen, figuring that the service areas of the Madrigal likely had fewer windows for flaming oil to pitch through, and likely also had less flammable furniture.

"Drop the damn box, Remy!" she screamed at the fiendling, who had followed her out clutching the stupid wicker case with his mother's ugly teapot in. Ignoring her, he thrust his arm through its handles, hoisting it onto his shoulder, then he headed for the lounge bar. "Damn it Remy, the lounge is on fire, we have to get out through the kitchen!"

"You and Thessu clear the kitchen, I'll get those people out," he replied, gesturing at the lounge bar, where a handful of patrons had been sat, along with the madame and the tart.

Nodding curtly, Epifani pushed the door to the kitchen open, and saw that too was ablaze, but not nearly so fiercely. The cook and his assistant were trying to douse the fires with heavy blankets. As she watched though, burning oil from the worktops cascaded down onto the floor, setting that alight as well. The two men weren't going to be able to douse it all and, seeming to realise this as well, they bolted for the back door.

She looked around for Thessu, and saw that he had gone with Remy. Well, she wasn't going to put herself in danger to help total strangers too stupid to save themselves, so she followed the cook and his assistant towards the exit.

She felt the Risen before she saw them; their odious presence pressed on the boundaries of her mind like a malevolent shadow, and as the cook opened the door to the corpses, so her mind opened the door to their presence. Two by the door and dozens more behind. The two Risen corpses by the door immediately struck the cook with heavy cudgels, but he was a big man and fended off the blows, still trying to push clear of the building. His way was blocked by a man in a black slashed doublet and cape. The man in black ran the cook through with a rapier blade, then shoved him back in through the burning door.

A spurt of blood sprayed from the wound as the cook fell; covering his assistant who had been following him out, and who caught him as he fell. The assistant stared dumbfounded at the bloody body in his arms, and the man beyond the door who had killed him. Epifani stared at him too, a blonde necromancer, and she recognised him from the confrontation outside the guild. He still had a swollen, misaligned nose from where Thessu had broken it.

The murderer smiled, and another volley of burning oil flasks was thrown through the open doorway to smash against the worktops and walls of the kitchen. One struck the fallen cook and his assistant, dousing them in burning oil. Then the necromancer kicked shut the burning door.

Having been shielded behind the cook's body, the assistant avoided most of the incendiary liquid, but the sleeves of his white coat were on fire. Epifani shoved the burning body of the cook away from the young man and helped him remove his coat. She looked once more at the burning door, and turned away from it; she wasn't getting out that way. The assistant followed her back out of the kitchen.

As she reached the bar at the back of the lounge, she saw one of the patrons was making a dash for the flaming exit onto the esplanade. She saw Remy try to stop him, but the man held a cloak over his head and ran towards the heavy flaming door at pace. He managed to force it open with his momentum, but then staggered backwards, falling sideways into the flames. The tart screamed as the man writhed in the flames, and then stilled.

Epifani peered through the smoke that cloyed the burning door to the esplanade, but she already knew what she would see there. Risen. A pair of them had forced the man back into the burning building with long poles, and she could feel dozens more of the foul creatures beyond them on the esplanade. She wasn't getting out that way either.

She watched Remy and Thessu both dash to the man, shielding their faces from the heat and flames, then grab his arms to drag his still-burning body away from the worst of the conflagration. Remy doused the man's flaming clothes with his bare hands, while Thessu checked the man over. He shook his head, and they both left him.

The smoke was stinging Epifani's eyes now. She wiped them on the side of her hood and, when she looked back, the lounge was completely obscured by smoke and she could no longer see Remy or Thessu. She pulled up her neckerchief as the acrid fumes started burning her throat while, close by, the madame and the tart had already succumbed to coughing fits. The cook's assistant too.

Remy strode out of the smoke and flames then, and grabbed the two Madrigal women. "Hold hands and follow me, y'all," he yelled over the din of the blaze, seemingly unaffected by the fumes. "This way!"

They all allowed him to lead them through the burning lounge, where he skirted round to the far side of the bar. He headed for the stairs up to the mezzanine floor that overlooked the lounge, and led up to the upper floors. Hells! He couldn't really be thinking their best way out of the burning building was upstairs, could he?

He could. They found Thessu and the other patrons already on the staircase, struggling to see the safe path through the smoke and flames. The mezzanine was also burning, as was the staircase and the banister. Remy moved to the front of the little group, and led them carefully up through the smoke and fire and along the mezzanine towards the back of the building.

There was a crash then, as part of the burning floor of the mezzanine ahead of them collapsed onto the bar below, and Remy slowed, picking his way even more carefully.

Then there was another crash as the saloon door burst open and two figures burst into the burning building from the esplanade. Epifani couldn't see who it was through the obscuring smoke, but they didn't feel like corpses. One of them yelled "Remy!" then succumbed to coughing. It was the Baron's big friend again; Gerard. What in the hell was he doing here? There was a woman with him as well.

"Up here," Remy shouted down at them. Whether they heard him or not, or saw him on the mezzanine or not, she couldn't tell. A third figure burst through the door after them, and then Epifani lost sight of them all through the smoke, and she started coughing as well, despite her neckerchief.

Epifani reached the section of burning mezzanine that had crashed into the flames below. Thessu had crossed to the other side with some of the bar patrons, and Remy was helping others across the burning gap to join them. Thessu's mask seemed to be protecting him from the effects of the smoke, while Remy seemed to be simply unaffected.

Between the two of them, they guided the rest of the patrons across safely, then the madame, and then the tart. Then it was the turn of the cook's assistant. He slipped while crossing and Remy lunged to grab him, but to no avail; the man slipped through his fingers and fell through the gap, disappearing into the burning ruin of the bar. Was that one person the fiendling had dropped, or two?

Remy turned to Epifani with a grim expression. It was her turn. She hoped he would make more of an effort to stop her from falling than he had for those strangers, but she remembered the angry blaze in his eyes from earlier. She was sure that if she slipped, he wouldn't save her. That was fine; she wouldn't save him either if their situations were reversed. She blinked the acrid smoke out of her eyes and grabbed Remy's proffered hand. She would have to squeeze past him then stretch across the gap to take Thessu's waiting hand on the far side, then release Remy and allow Thessu to pull her across, while flames lapped up through the gap at them the whole time.

She stepped as close to the edge as she dared, then leaned out towards Thessu. Suddenly the floor buckled below her feet as another board collapsed into the flames below. She dropped down through the gap, with only Remy's arm to hold on to. She grabbed it with both hands, as the flames licked around her. The heat of the blaze was intense.

"Don't let me drop!" she screamed at Remy, and she saw his eyes aflame once more. This time though, they blazed with determination, and she realised that he wasn't going to let her fall. He couldn't haul her up with one arm though, he needed two; but his other arm seemed to be snagged on something.

She saw him struggle to free the arm from whatever was restraining it, and he finally reached down with it as well, grabbing her and letting whatever the obstacle had been fall through the gap into the fire. Epifani watched it fall. It was the wicker teapot case; he had sacrificed his dead mother's heirloom to save her. She wasn't sure how she felt about that.

Remy hauled her up. She tried to cross to Thessu once more, and this time made it across successfully.

More boards fell away though, and the burning gap widened, now looking impassable, with Remy trapped on the wrong side of it. The three figures that had entered the bar now joined him at the wrong side of the gap. She had recognised Gerard as he entered, and she saw now the other two were Valanthé and the sidekick; Colin. They were all going to die there.

Gerard didn't seem to think so, and she saw him turn back through the flames the way he had come, disappearing into the smoke. The fire raged on, and a part of the ceiling collapsed down into the spreading inferno. Moments later, Gerard re-emerged from the billowing smoke carrying an enormous wooden beam over one shoulder, as Remy patted down the flames that licked his clothes. The beam was blackened and scorched but looked long enough and sturdy enough to bridge the gap, and he lowered it across.

Valanthé crossed first, taking the precariously balanced beam at a run. Colin tried the same, and nearly fell, but Thessu grabbed him and pulled him clear. Gerard came next, crossing as carefully as the urgent situation would allow, and the balcony creaked as the big man crossed. Epifani saw now that Gerard was injured; he had a vicious wound on his neck, and his hands were bloodied and burnt.

Remy came last, and Epifani offered him a hand as he reached the safety of the far side. With a sour look, he ignored her proffered hand, reaching instead for Thessu to draw him across the last few feet.

They climbed the stairs to the top of the building. The madame and the surviving patrons from the bar had been going room to room, gathering more guests and girls, and there was a big group of them assembled in the attic room at the top of the building when Epifani reached it. Every room she had passed along the way was filled with smoke, and all the balcony rooms were aflame; the Risen must have launched their burning oil flasks onto the balconies of the upper floors as well as through the downstairs windows. The attic room had no such balcony; it was full of smoke, but no flames. The fires hadn't reached it yet.

Thessu and Gerard were eying the solitary window in the room, which was high up in the rafters facing away from the street. It hadn't been smashed; maybe hadn't been seen. They must be planning to escape onto the roof and get to safety along the rooftops.

But Epifani had seen something else in the attic room. Something odd. "Why is there a damn sex swing in here?" she asked between coughs.

CHAPTER 14

They wouldn't all have fit through the tiny window in the roof, so Remy opened a store closet in the eaves opposite the attic room door, and produced a fire axe, which he used to enlarge the roof window. He smashed the glass easily enough, and set to work on the frame. He was at full stretch though, and his swings lacked the power and accuracy to chop into the frame effectively.

"Give it to me, Remy," Gerard said stalwartly. "I can reach it."

Remy eyed him dubiously, concerned about his injuries; especially the nasty bite wound on his neck which was still oozing blood. However, with the smoke getting thicker and the floor feeling hotter, it was clear that the fire had reached the floor below, so Remy reluctantly handed over the axe and the big man took it and started chopping. Blood flowed freely from Gerard's wounds with every swing of the axe, but the frame disintegrated quickly under the heavy blows. It didn't take him long.

Once Gerard was done, he looked dizzy, and Thessu had to steady him, but still they all managed to clamber up and out through the enlarged window, onto the roof to escape the burning building.

Valanthé led the way across the rooftops to the far side of the commercial terrace, staying below the roofline so they couldn't be seen from the street. They all snuck in through the roof window in the attic of a merchant's store, where they paused to rest while Thessu treated Gerard's injuries and Valanthé scouted ahead to check the way down was clear and no assailants were watching the storefront.

"Why in the hell did you bring a kid into a burnin' buildin'?" Remy demanded, sitting down next to Gerard and Thessu.

"We didn't bring him," Gerard replied, sounding a little lethargic. "We told him to stay put and he didn't listen. Ouch!" Thessu had removed the big man's ruined doublet and undershirt, and was doing his best to dress the wound on his neck with the supplies from his satchel.

Gerard winced as Thessu applied a salve. It needed stitches – as did the cut on his hand – but that would have to wait.

Remy rounded on the kid, who was sitting close by, holding Thessu's medical kit. "That true, Colin? I seem to remember havin' a long talk wi' you about you listenin' to instructions in dangerous situations!"

Colin looked sheepish, and answered in a breathless staccato. "I know Remy and I stayed away from the fight like I was told but then Valanthé vomited frogs all over the pirate corpses and it looked like the battle was over and the corpses were just standing around covered in frogs so I went to join Valanthé and Gerard and Valanthé said 'fuck you' to a pirate and she ran into the building with Gerard and then I was just stood there with all the corpses standing around me but then the corpses started moving again so I also said 'fuck you' to the pirate and then I ran in."

Remy understood very little of that, especially whatever that was about frogs. "Pirates?" he queried, turning to Gerard.

Gerard nodded. "Apparently so. Valanthé recognised two captains from the Scarlet Fist. Also the two necromancers who jumped me and the Baron two eves ago were there too; it seems they're working for the Fist."

"Any idea why the Scarlet Fist burned down the saloon?" Remy asked.

"One of the captains told Valanthé that people inside the building were looking for something they shouldn't, and had to die," Gerard replied.

"I don't think they meant your mother's teapot, Remy," Thessu added without looking up from Gerard's wound, and Remy agreed, snorting out a bitter laugh. The pirates must have been on the trail of Thessu and Epifani.

"Joanna Pianna?" Remy asked, and Thessu nodded. "What in the hell is so special about her and her baby?"

"I don't know," Thessu shrugged. "When I find her, I'll ask her."

Remy glanced down the stairwell, but there was no sign of Valanthé returning. Scanning the room, he saw Madame Cass looking distraught. She had lost her home and her livelihood, as had Isabela and the other girls from the Madrigal that had joined them. They were consoling each other. The Madrigal's guests – all men – were looking flighty, like they would rather brave the corpses than the inconsolable women.

Epifani was looking pensive in a corner by herself. Remy considered her coolly. She had made no effort to help anyone except herself. Remy had saved her life twice now, and she was as ungrateful this time as she had been the first time.

She saw him looking at her, and seemed indecisive about something, then she seemed to make up her mind and walked over to him. She didn't apologise – which wasn't surprising – instead, she squatted down next to him, and handed him a little cloth bundle from her pocket, and a book.

"I've bookmarked the page," she said, and she backed away again, looking unsure.

Remy opened the bundle, intrigued. It wrapped the broken bowl and stem of an antique ceramic goblet. Confused, he examined the book. It was something of an antique as well, with flimsy yellowed pages of hand-printed text, bound in cracked old leather. He flipped it open to the page that was bookmarked, and he read. He read the text, and he read the hand-written note written on top of the text. And he slammed the book shut and cast it away in disgust, sliding it back across the floor towards Epifani, and the broken goblet as well.

All thoughts of Joanna Pianna disappeared from Remy's mind. He had been right; the book confirmed that his mother was killed because of her gift. He was wrong about the motive though; she hadn't been tortured into revealing some aspect of the future, she was ritually murdered so her gift of foresight – her ability to see the tapestry of fate – could be stolen from her. His eyes blazed, and he headed down the stairs without a backwards look. It was time to find the culprit and get some redemption for spilling his mother's secret and causing her death.

* * *

Before he did anything, Remy had to get away from the Madrigal; away from Isla Doblé. He took a heavy hooded cloak from the merchant's store, and snuck out the back door. A crowd had formed to watch the fire at the saloon, and he tried to melt into it as best as he could. If the pirates were watching, they didn't stop him, and he made his way through the back-streets and alleys to one of the river docks on the western side of the island, where there was a regular ferry across the channel to Isla Roja. He was in luck; the ferry was in dock.

He paid the ferryman to take him to the other side; two copper deniers. The corpse beckoned him on board with a bony hand, watching him with empty eye sockets from under the tattered grey hood of its oversized robe. The ferry was a rickety flat-bottomed river barge with a low gunwale and no seats. A half dozen passengers – both living and dead – had already boarded before him, and Remy pressed forward to stand at the front, staring fixedly ahead and avoiding eye contact with any of them. The Risen ferryman let a few more passengers board after him, and then pushed off, punting the barge across the channel with long practiced movements of its barge pole making no splash. Isla Roja wasn't far; it wouldn't take long to get there.

Isla Roja wasn't the largest of the islands, but it was certainly the tallest. Where most of La Crosse was built on the silty alluvial islands formed by the forking course of the Poconovo river as it flowed across the delta, Isla Roja was a rock. Millennia ago, the city had been founded there on the most prominent, most permanent island of the delta. Even though the ocean docks and main commercial districts had long since moved to the neighbouring Isla Verdé and the other islands, Isla Roja was still the spiritual and political centre of the city, home to the Corto Dogé – seat of the Dogé and Cabal Court – and the Basilica Grandé; the great Ziggurat. It was also where the noble houses of La Crosse built their grand palazzos. If the murderer truly was one of the powerful men to whom he had told his mother's secret, he would be found there in that enclave of the rich.

Remy stepped off the barge as it pulled alongside the jetty on the north side of Isla Roja, and headed straight for the dimly-lit back-streets. The island sloped up towards the south-west and the narrow cobbled streets followed that incline with sloping stretches between the close-spaced buildings, interspersed by occasional flights of stone steps. He found a quiet back-street and followed it for a time, before ducking through a stone arch into a sheltered unlit courtyard set back from the street. Squatting down in a shadowy corner of the courtyard, he pulled out the candle his father had given him, then secured it in a little brass holder.

What had his father said? Ask it a question while lighting it, and it would lead to the answer? Something like that. He pinched the wick of the candle and focussed his molten core to channel heat to his fingertips. His eyes were blazing; his molten core was broiling with rage and the heat came quickly, but unfocused. The candle deformed in its holder as the wax softened, and the wick smouldered but did not light. Taking a calming breath, he tried again. This time the wick sparked to life, and he spoke clearly, "who killed my mother, Brigitte Du Rosier?"

The little candle flickered in the breath of his words, then settled to a steady yellow flame with a thin trail of smoke. It looked like a normal candle flame. Remy stared at it confusedly; how was this supposed to answer his question? He tried moving the candle, watching the flame closely to see if it pointed in any direction, or flickered differently as he moved around it. It flickered in a normal way as it was moved and disturbed, with no obvious preference for any direction. Frustrated, he almost snuffed it out, but the smoke caught his attention; it pawed at him.

The thin trail of smoke – almost invisible in the shadowy corner of the courtyard – had coiled in the air above the candle. It had coiled into a shape; a smoky outline. The smoky outline of a creature. Four legged with a wide face and a long tail, it hovered silently in place, its movements a blur of smoke wisps and coils. A raccoon. The smoke raccoon was agitated, seeming eager to get moving, and it strained at the limits of the drifting line of vapour that tethered it to its candle like a leash. The smoke raccoon seemed to want to bound out of the courtyard, but was quite unable to leave the vicinity of the candle.

Understanding what it was he had to do now, Remy let the smoke raccoon lead him out of the courtyard, carrying the little candleholder carefully in one hand, while with the other hand he masked the flame from being disturbed by his motion. The smoke raccoon bounded happily through the stone archway like a puppy going for its walkies. It looked back to make sure Remy was following, then it turned to lead him southwards.

As he followed, Remy marvelled at how lifelike it seemed in its appearance and its movements. It struck him that no mortal gift could create such a thing, and he wondered if the smoke racoon hadn't once been a real living creature, imprisoned in the candle by his father's fell magic. The devil kept the full extent of his power a secret even from his son.

The smoke raccoon led him along the street, soon emerging onto a wide well-lit boulevard that Remy knew led past the Ziggurat, and the vast stepped sides of that massive structure loomed high over the buildings ahead, dominating the skyline. He would rather have kept to the back-streets, but the smoke raccoon insisted he follow, resisting his attempts to find a different path to wherever the creature was leading him.

He resigned himself to taking the boulevard, which was busy with carriages and rickshaws and litters. He got hostile looks from the well-to-do people he passed, for he was looking particularly out of place with black soot-stained face and clothes under a rough-spun hooded cloak that barely covered his fiendling horns. Thankfully, nobody looked too closely at the wispy smoke-coil creature he was taking for walkies.

The bigger problem of following the boulevard, was that city deputies often patrolled near the Ziggurat. Sure enough, as the thoroughfare passed the last of the intervening buildings and the vista opened out to reveal the full majesty of the enormous structure, he saw ahead a group of them manning a checkpoint where the boulevard passed the guard post that abutted the lowest step of the massive Ziggurat.

There were six deputies, obvious in their light blue coats and tricorn hats, with polished silver badges of office displayed prominently on their shoulder-belts, and with long-barrelled muskets slung over one shoulder. They were checking all traffic entering the exclusive Corto Dogé district south of the Ziggurat.

The smoke raccoon seemed oblivious to them, and quite determined that Remy should continue along the boulevard right past them. There was no way he could do that without being stopped and questioned at the very least – which he didn't have time for – and it was more than a little likely he would be prevented from going any further since he had no legitimate business south of the Ziggurat.

Despite the silent protestations of his ethereal companion, he turned back, looking for another way south. He followed an alley that seemed to run parallel to the boulevard, but soon found the way blocked by the walled garden of a palazzo that turned the alley into a dead-end. Finding no alternative, he reached up to place the candle on the top of the wall, then climbed over, retrieving the candle once he had dropped down on the far side. Seeming to warm to the new course, the smoke raccoon encouraged him across the garden; which was something of a maze of box hedges and flower beds tended by Risen who clacked their jaws as he passed but made no move to oppose him.

At the far side of the garden, he found the spot where the wall was most in shadow, and climbed up. From the top of the wall he could see the alley on the far side led back to the boulevard, beyond the checkpoint and, leaving the candle on the top to retrieve once he landed, he dropped down into the alleyway.

He landed gracefully, but before he could retrieve the candle, two deputies turned into the alley. Remy shrank back into the shadows between the cobblestone buttresses of the wall, and hoped the men hadn't seen him... and that they wouldn't notice the out-of-place candle on the wall above him. He closed his eyes to mask their flame as the deputies strode closer.

Waiting in the darkness, he took small shallow breaths and listened to the approaching footsteps of the deputies. He got a sudden taste of warm smoke, and knew the smoke raccoon was pawing at him once again trying to get him moving. He almost coughed it out, but managed to hold his breath. He expected any moment to hear the deputies address him, or to feel a hand on his shoulder, but instead he heard their footsteps recede away along the alleyway past him.

He opened his eyes and peered through a thick peal of smoke. The raccoon wasn't pawing at him, it was smothering him; it had flattened itself against him to conceal him from the deputies. It bounded playfully away from him to hover in the middle of the alleyway, and stuck its tongue out at them. Then it started pawing at him to get him moving.

Remy collected the candle and headed on out of the alleyway, the raccoon once again leading the way. Now seeming to understand his need to avoid arrest, it led him on a more circuitous route southwards and he saw no other deputies on the way. They passed the red dome of the Corto Dogé and the Ruby Plaza, passed rows of grand palazzos in prime cliff-top positions overlooking the ocean, passed all of Isla Roja until only one building remained in their path, the palazzo at the southern tip of the island. Palazzo Fandandolin. There was no mistaking the raccoon's intent, it was headed straight to it.

Palazzo Fandandolin was a grand square building of cream-coloured stone, four stories tall, surrounded on all sides on each level by a stacked colonnade of marble pillars. Between every column of every level of every colonnade around the building stood a sentinel; a corpse soldier in burnished bronze armour, which gleamed green and gold in the reflected light of viridian uplighters that shone below each one.

Identical Risen spearmen also stood on each step of the symmetrical marble staircases that led from the street to the grand entrance on the second storey. The corpse guards all had such a stillness that they might have been statues; but Remy knew they were not. Barring one lofty minaret above the far corner, the building was a study in symmetry, a grand palatial fortress. Palazzo Fandandolin was the home of the Dandolo family.

This was the very place where Remy had revealed his mother's secret to Domenico Dandolo and his cadre of rich powerful friends... but only one of them lived here. There was no doubt now, the raccoon had led him to his mother's murderer; had led him to the home of Domenico Dandolo. He was the murderer.

Remy halted, and the smoke raccoon pawed at him once more. It wanted to climb the steps past the sentinels, it wanted to assail the grand entrance. The candle had almost burned out, so the creature's urgency was well-founded – it didn't have long left – but there was no way in that way. No, it had served its purpose, had confirmed who had killed his mother, and he passed his hand through the wisps of smoke as if petting the creature. And it quieted and settled down to rest on his shoulder as the last of the candle sputtered its last coughs of flame and died. And the lingering smoke on his shoulder drifted away into the twilight sky.

Remy stood in shadows opposite the palazzo for a minute, letting the rage seethe over him, letting his eyes blaze with incandescent fury as he remembered the snide, arrogant man who he had tried to impress in that place, remembering the gory details of the ritual he had read in Epifani's book. Remembering what Domenico Dandolo had done to his mother.

As he watched, there was a flurry of motion at the grand entrance to the palazzo. The great doors opened, and four skeleton corpses emerged like the clockwork movement of a timepiece, carrying the forward handles of an ostentatious gilded litter. The noble house of Dandolo coated their skeleton corpses in sapphire blue enamel, and decorated their skulls with six-inch metal spikes through the top.

The litter emerged fully through the doors, revealing four more spiked enamelled skeletons carrying the rear handles. The small retinue of enamelled skeleton corpses turned the litter towards one of the sweeping staircases that led down to the street. As one, the Risen spearmen on the stairs turned to face the same way, joining the retinue in front and behind of the gilded litter. At some unseen signal, the clockwork-seeming movement continued as the litter and its cohort of leading and trailing corpses moved down the stair in unison.

Remy smiled; it could only be Domenico riding in that litter. Fate had delivered him a perfect opportunity for vengeance at the very moment he wanted it most. The corpses would carry the murderer right past him.

Remy was so focussed on the litter, he hadn't heard the men approach from the shadows behind him. By the time he recognised the danger, it was too late, they were on him. He managed to half-turn and grab the basket hilt of his rapier, but they bundled him to the ground before he could draw it and, with his arms grappled as he fell, his face cracked hard onto the cobbles. His head rang from the impact and he tasted blood in his mouth, his senses swimming as his assailants pinned him firmly to the ground. He tried to look up but his head was firmly restrained. He couldn't even see who had accosted him.

He got one last blurry glimpse of the palazzo before he blacked out, and he saw the sapphire corpses carry the litter down the remaining stairs as the Risen spearmen at the front of the column marched right past him without so much as looking at him. "Domenico," he sputtered towards the litter, spraying the cobbles with blood, his voice sounding muffled; disconnected. He wouldn't get his vengeance this eve, but he would get it soon. He would kill Domenico Dandolo. He passed out before the bastard's gilded litter even reached him.

CHAPTER 15

The Baron's consciousness returned suddenly, and he fell off the chaise longue. He yelped in pain as he landed on his injured arm, and looked down at his wounds, surprised to see them dressed and bound. He had only just received the injuries fighting the necromancers at the guild, yet here he was back at the manor, with the injuries bound. He must have blacked out again, and Gerard or Thessu must have brought him home. He felt cold.

Sitting up, he checked his pocket for Belle and found her gone. He looked around for the doll, but couldn't see her. "Belle my dear?" he called anxiously, but she didn't respond. Suddenly there was a crash of noise, and the Baron looked round to see Jeff at the pianoforte; he had started playing a mournful tune.

"Ah, Jeff old boy, have you seen dear Belle anywhere?" The corpse regarded him with eyes cloudy like curdled milk, and shook his head slowly as he continued to play, the remaining fragments of dried skin on his arms crackling and flaking with the movement. Standing shakily, the Baron walked to the parlour door, calling again for Belle. Still no answer. He tried calling for Remy and Valanthé and Colin, but they didn't answer either. He heard the creaking of the house and the whistling of the wind and the lugubrious sound of the pianoforte.

Turning back into the parlour, he saw a courtesy tray had been set on the sideboard by the door with a pitcher and glass and a lidded pot. He walked over, and poured himself a glass of water from the pitcher. It tasted warm and stale, but he downed it all and poured another. Lifting the lid to the pot, he found it filled with dried fruit and nuts and he took a handful and ate them greedily. A folded piece of paper was held down by the pot, and he pulled it out and read it.

It was a note from Valanthé. It confirmed that Gerard had indeed returned him to the islet, but they had all left shortly thereafter to retrieve the deeds from Palazzo Laurentin. The Baron felt a pang of guilt that they had all undertaken the difficult and dangerous task on his behalf, while he had been… where had he been? As always, he remembered nothing of his absence.

"We must thank them my dear," he said to Belle, before remembering that she wasn't in her customary spot in his pocket. A wave of anxiety flooded over him once more; the note didn't mention her at all. Had she gone with Remy and Valanthé to Palazzo Laurentin? Had she even returned from the guild with him and Gerard? He had no way to know. She'd always been smart and capable, but she was so young; she had never been in dangerous situations without him before, what if she got hurt?

He searched the manor, and she definitely wasn't there. He wondered whether he should try the crypt, but decided against it; Belle definitely wouldn't have visited their ancestors without him. Also he didn't want to alarm the spirits by admitting she was missing; at least, not yet. She was their favourite after all.

Instead he headed outside, where he spotted the alligator wallowing in the muddy water that had filled his pit after the recent storm. "Good evening Rufus," he said to the great beast. Rufus startled, seeming embarrassed to have been caught wallowing, and he paddled across the pit towards the near bank, near where the Baron had previously hung a large towel over the cast iron railing of the manor's entrance portico. The alligator paused at the water's edge as if waiting, then snorted impatiently at the Baron when he didn't take the hint.

"Oh of course, do pardon me," the Baron said embarrassedly, turning around to give the alligator some privacy. When he looked back around, the huge beast was lounging on the grassy bank with the muddy towel wrapped around him, his head resting contentedly on a log.

"My, your collection has grown, old bean," the Baron said, marvelling at the impressive assortment of shoes the alligator had assembled on makeshift shelves at the back of his pit. The alligator swelled with pride.

"Did Valanthé give you those fine heeled boots?" At that, the beast's pride-swell seemed to become a guilty deflation, which made the Baron chuckle. "Don't worry, I wont tell her. But have you by any chance seen Belle anywhere?"

Rufus indicated that he had not, and the Baron bade him good evening, and headed down towards the derelict boat house, on the off-chance that his gondola might be there.

"I have been looking everywhere for you!" he exulted, when he found Belle on the seat of the gondola, which was rocking against the jetty outside the boat house. "Oh you poor dear," he said, noting her loose threads and the tufts of matted stuffing that protruded from her ripped seams. She was dirty and bedraggled, and he wondered how exactly she had gotten back to the islet. He flicked away the mud and loose stitching, and gave her an affectionate squeeze, before tucking her back into his pocket, good as new.

He paused to thank the little boat once more and it rocked gently against the jetty in response. Then he headed back along the path to the manor, patting the lifeless doll in his pocket. "You shall have to tell me all about your adventures my dear," he told her. "Perhaps over a nice mug of cocoa?"

***

Valanthé checked on the Baron as soon as she returned to the islet. He wasn't in the parlour where she had left him so she worried for an instant that the guilty look the alligator had given her on her way in, might mean the Baron had been eaten; a fear deepened by the funereal music coming from the pianoforte. She needn't have worried, the Baron appeared in the doorway from the dining room, clutching a steaming mug of what smelled like chocolate.

"Baron, you're okay? Sorry we left you so long," she said.

"Good evening Valanthé," he replied. "Oh goodness, are you alright? You look a state!"

It was true. She was coated in soot and grime from the fire and the crawl along the rooftops, and stank of smoke and vomit. The others were much the same; they were also coated smoke and grime …though perhaps less vomit. Gerard looked the worst though. Colin and Thessu had come in behind Valanthé, each of them supporting one side of the big man as he staggered in through the door. Topless, he looked pale despite the encrusted dirt and grime and had makeshift dressings on his hands and neck, which were dark with seeping blood.

"Into the parlour with him," the Baron said, setting down his drink and rushing past them to lay a blanket over the chaise longue.

"No, there is better," said Thessu, gesturing to one of the parlour footstools with his beaked mask, which he had removed and now carried in one hand. "I need him upright to sew that wound."

The Baron nodded assent, not quite concealing his surprise at Thessu's scaly, shrivelled pallor. Valanthé guessed he hadn't seen the monk without his mask before; his otherworldly appearance had certainly startled her when he'd first removed it! She helped him move the blanket to cover the footstool, which creaked under Gerard's weight as the others lowered him down onto it.

"Are you okay?" the Baron asked him, then turned to ask Valanthé, "what happened?"

"I'm fine," Gerard managed to say, though his eyes were unfocused. "Just feeling a little faint. Colin, give him the deed."

Colin, who was carrying Gerard's things under one arm, rummaged through the bundle, handing the Baron first the fire axe Gerard had brought from the Madrigal, then the ripped and bloody ruin that was his wadded doublet and undershirt. Finally he proffered the folded sheet of parchment. It didn't seem to have fared too badly despite the fire and blood, and the Baron swapped it for the axe and the wadded clothes.

"Thank you Colin my boy." The Baron unfolded the document and read the contents. While he read, Thessu got to work removing the temporary dressing on Gerard's shoulder, and Colin stood awkwardly, like he wasn't sure whether he could put Gerard's bloody clothes down somewhere.

"Thank you, all of you," the Baron said, once he had finished reading. Then he folded the parchment up once more and tucked it into the inside pocket of his jacket. "Now, what happened out there?"

"I'll fill you in on everything in a moment," Valanthé replied. "But first, has Remy returned here?"

"No. Wasn't he with you?" the Baron replied, seeming concerned.

"He was. He was right there with us, and then she..." here Valanthé pointed at Epifani, who was lingering in the hallway, her shadow cast into the room by the bright green glow of the chandelier behind her.

"…she apparently showed him something that spooked him, and he left without a word."

"I already told you," Epifani spat back at her, "it was a private conversation between Remy and myself. And I genuinely don't know where the stupid man went."

Valanthé rolled her eyes at the woman's intransigence. She had been sullen and defensive since they'd snuck away from the Madrigal, and had been needlessly hostile to the leased corpses who rowed them to the islet in Gerard's barge. Valanthé eyed her narrowly, as Epifani helped herself to a handful of dried fruit and nuts from the dish on the sideboard, then sprawled out thoughtlessly on the chaise longue, covering it in soot.

"I will need a bowl of clean water and some clean towels," Thessu said, opening his satchel. He rummaged inside, setting aside a green glass bottle wrapped in twine cord that had been jammed in on top of the other satchel contents, and then retrieved the medical case he needed from beneath it.

"I hope that's to clean the wound?" Valanthé asked, looking dubiously at the bottle, "because I know that stuff can be pretty lethal if you drink it. I'm sure the Baron has something nicer. Brandy maybe?"

"You recognise this?" Thessu asked, rounding on her suddenly. Epifani sat forward intently as well. What was so special about a bottle of bootleg booze?

Valanthé shrugged. "Um, yeah… it's pirate moonshine, right? Theres a floating distillery on Flotsam near where I was quartered, that makes awful concoctions in bottles just like that, using whatever ingredients they can get their hands on."

Epifani and Thessu looked at each other meaningfully. "On Flotsam you say?" Thessu asked, and he and Epifani again shared another meaningful look. Somehow, Valanthé knew she'd given them a clue and they would soon be picking up their search for Joanna Pianna on the floating pirate outpost. Valanthé didn't want to know, and rolled her eyes once again.

"Actually," Gerard said, still sounding somewhat disconnected, "I think I would quite like some brandy."

The Baron directed Colin to take Gerard's ruined clothes to the kitchen midden for disposal and return with the water and towels for

Thessu, and brandy for Gerard. Epifani was asleep and snoring before the boy returned. Valanthé watched Thessu as the monk expertly cleaned and sewed and dressed Gerard's wounds – and incongruously slapped them to make them heal – while she filled the Baron in on everything that had happened since he blacked out.

Thankfully, they had all had a chance to rest and freshen up before the pirates came to Isla Festa. They arrived just after twinbells the following evening, and announced their arrival with cannon-fire.

***

"What the…?" Epifani shrieked, startled awake by the enormous crashing noise. Climbing quickly into her boots, she retrieved her stiletto from under her pillow and tucked it into its hidden sheath by her right heel, then dashed out of the little room and onto the landing.

The Baron had quartered her in an upstairs bedchamber with exposed lath and plaster on the walls and bare floorboards underfoot. The hints of pastel paintwork on the remaining patches of plaster, plus broken, rotten cots piled in one corner all indicated it might once have been a nursery, but as with most of the rooms in the decrepit manor, it was dilapidated and stank of mould and decay.

She had slept fitfully, and the house had done its best to keep her awake by creaking and whistling and dripping at intervals calculated to catch her just as she was dozing off, but none of its premeditated noises had been as obviously destructive as that crash had been.

The others in the manor had reacted just as rapidly, and they were all now rushing out from their own rooms, and piling down the stairs to see what the destructive smashing noise had been. Epifani was first to the stairs and took them at pace, rushing down two steps at a time, with Thessu close behind. She hit the entrance hall at the bottom of the grand staircase, and bolted for the adjacent parlour, but she could already sense what was in there.

"Damn it!" she muttered as she burst through the parlour door. She had been right; the corpse butler was fine, and so was its damned pianoforte. She turned and left the parlour and followed Thessu who had gone straight to the Baron's study on the far side of the hall. She nearly crashed into him as he pulled up at the doorway.

The Baron's study was a ruin. There was a huge hole in the front wall where a window had been, and the antique leather-topped desk that had been under the window was smashed completely in half. All the shelves around the room had collapsed along with their contents and there, half-buried in the debris, was a smoking cannonball. The cannonball had clearly torn through the wall and ripped across the floorboards, tearing them apart before cracking into the wall opposite.

A huge chunk of ceiling plaster above the back wall collapsed into the room then, adding to the debris, and an alligator peered in through the hole in the front wall from outside. It looked like the same one that had snuck into the house and tried to steal her boots yestereve while she napped on the chaise longue.

The Baron joined them at the doorway then; he had been slowest to reach the study. He looked pained. "Good grief, my study!" he exclaimed. "Rufus, old bean, are you alright?"

Epifani had no idea who Rufus was, but the alligator growled menacingly and bolted away, and the Baron nodded curtly as if agreeing with its sentiment. Epifani eyed the departing alligator through narrowed eyes as it left. If it touched her boots again she would have a new pair made from its tanned hide.

The Baron strode to the parlour and threw the door open. "Jeff!" he called.

Seriously? 'Jeff'? Who names their corpses 'Jeff'? Who names their corpses at all?

"Jeff, we're under attack," the Baron continued. "You know what to do!"

The Risen butler accepted the instruction with a curt nod of agreement and stiffly raised its hands high over the pianoforte. Then – after a dramatic pause – it hammered down aggressively on the keyboard, pounding out a familiar tune in a disconcerting minor key. A dolorous battle rally.

The Baron turned back to them then, and Epifani saw he had visibly darkened. The shadows of his face had deepened unnaturally and his jaunty half-smile had gone, his features stretched and contorted into an intimidating snarl. He looked frightening, and Epifani gasped.

The Baron headed for the front door and, collecting his cane and hat and cape, he strode purposefully out of the manor, taking the shadows with him. Epifani followed behind with the rest of his houseguests.

The source of the cannonball was obvious once they'd gone a little way along the path towards the boat house. A galley was anchored two hundred yards offshore, beyond the mangrove-shallows and reed-beds that surrounded the islet, silhouetted against the ever-setting sun. Not a war-galley thankfully, but a smaller coastal vessel which nevertheless still probably had half a dozen deck guns in its broadside. Blinking into the half-light that spilled around the boat, Epifani saw it flew the dark red sails of the Scarlet Fist.

The Baron strode to the end of the jetty beyond the boathouse and, cupping his hands around his mouth, yelled, "you have my attention. What do you want?"

On the deck of the galley, there was a commotion, and then Epifani spotted some familiar faces approach the gunwale and stand between two of the deck guns that were pointed menacingly towards the shore. Two blonde men in the slashed black doublets of the necromancers' guild. They were stood with a fat ginger man in a tricorn hat.

"It's those blonde necromancers who attacked us at the guild," the Baron stated.

"And burned down the saloon," added Thessu.

"And killed the cook," Epifani muttered quietly to herself.

"The man with them is the pirate captain who tried to kill me outside the Pit," added Gerard.

"Wasn't he also one of the pirates who led the attack on the Madrigal?" asked Colin.

"Lugwort," Valanthé spat, nodding contemptuously.

Some more men approached the gunwale of the galley then; two pirate crewmen holding a third individual between them, who seemed to be bound and gagged. It was obvious from his horns who it was.

The shout came back from the galley, "We 'ave yer fiendlin' friend! Send over Valanthé an' we'll send 'im back to ye!"

They all looked at Valanthé, who looked as surprised as any of them. From what Epifani had gathered, the young woman had been unceremoniously fired by the Fist for refusing orders. Why did they want her back so badly?

"I thought you were fired by the Fist," Colin said. "Why do they want you back so badly?"

"Colin my boy," the Baron replied. "I was just wondering the exact same thing."

"I thought they were trying to prevent anyone else looking for Joanna Pianna," Thessu interjected, "I don't know why they aren't asking for Epifani and I?"

Gerard shook his head. "They aren't asking for you two because they don't want you two. Valanthé is the only one they want *alive*. They mean to kill the rest of us, and Remy as well."

Colin gasped. "I hope it wasn't my fault? Maybe I should not have said 'fuck you' to him?"

The Baron's smile returned for an instant, and he placed a fatherly hand on Colin's shoulder. "Don't worry my boy, pirates don't kill people for swearing, they probably liked your attitude."

Colin smiled, reassured. "Maybe I should say it again then?" and before anyone could stop him, he yelled "fuck you" towards the galley at the top of his voice.

Epifani buried her face in her palms; Remy's idiot sidekick was going to get them all killed. She looked at Valanthé. "Think you can convince them to clear off if you go nicely?"

The woman shook her head. "I don't know why they want me, but Gerard's right; once they have me, they'll bombard the island with cannon-fire, and send landing parties to finish us off once the house is a ruin."

"Maybe our best bet is to refuse then, and force them to come and get you without bombarding the Islet first? Find a defensible position and kill them as they land," Epifani suggested.

"No. There's no guarantee they want her that badly," Gerard said. "The only thing that guarantees, is that Remy dies."

"Remy can't die," Epifani blurted out, without thinking. "I won't let him." They all looked at her surprisedly. In fact she'd surprised herself as well. She didn't know why she'd said that.

She glowered back at them, "What? He saved me twice. I owe him!" And she realised then that it was true. She did feel like she owed Remy; owed all of these people. She didn't like that feeling one bit.

"Then we need a way to get him safely off that boat without trading Valanthé away and without giving those pirates an opportunity to kill us all," the Baron said, rubbing his chin in thought. His darkness had returned and he seemed more focused; more determined. More in charge. "Valanthé, you've spent time with the Scarlet Fist; how many crew on that ship, and how many Risen?"

"Probably fifteen or so crew; likely they're all on deck manning those cannons," Valanthé replied. "There'll be twenty, maybe twenty-five galley corpses below deck."

"Plus two necromancers," Thessu added.

The Baron nodded and his eyes shadowed further. "That's a lot."

"You're surely not thinking of attacking the boat?" Epifani asked, trying not to sound as sceptical as she felt.

"Well I for one would rather go down fighting than cowering in a cellar while they bring my house down on top of me," the Baron replied.

"Seconded," Gerard said.

"Thirded," Thessu said.

"Fourth-ded?" Colin added, unsure of the word rather than the sentiment.

"Well you're all mad," Epifani said. "But if you can think of a way to get us there, I can keep the Risen below deck and away from the fray."

"There's no way to get there," Valanthé replied. "They'll see us coming and kill us all with massed gunfire before we get close."

The Baron's dark and snarling face contorted into a malicious smirk. He looked like a man with a plan. "Oh, they aren't going to see us coming. Gerard old boy, I assume you can swim?"

CHAPTER 16

"Ugh! I can't believe I agreed to this," Epifani muttered for the fourth time.

"So you said," Thessu replied, "Four times now. Why don't you try being a little bit more positive?"

Epifani didn't seem very positive. "But this isn't going to work," she retorted, "and I'm going to die smelling like a pit corpse!"

"Purity of purpose demands…" Thessu started, but Epifani cut him off, growling, "if you're about to utter a goddam mantra, I swear I'll shove this goddam oar where the ever-setting sun don't shine!"

"Shh!" Valanthé hissed, and they shushed. It had been amusing at first when the Baron had outlined his plan and told Epifani; who hated the Risen, and Thessu; who had that over-developed sense of smell, that they would need to dress in rags borrowed from Gerard's barge corpses. But Epifani complained constantly, and the small amount of joy it brought Valanthé to see the belligerent woman suffer, was more than outweighed by the constant carping she was forced to endure on the short trip to the galley in Gerard's barge.

Valanthé stood at the tiller of the boat, with Epifani and Thessu sat in front of her rowing in sync with a pair of genuine Risen corpses. Despite Epifani's complaining, she had done what needed to be done, and the two of them had covered themselves in muck and rags, and affixed coins to their foreheads in a passable attempt at corpse disguises. They even managed to row convincingly enough.

Rowing over to the galley was the easy bit though, and she grimaced as the pirate ship loomed ahead. They would all have to rely on each other to play their parts, or they would all be dead. She trusted the Baron, but some aspects of his plan sounded fanciful, and she had been highly dubious that it would work. Remy was the wild card though; he would have to play his part in the plan without anyone having told him that a plan was afoot.

For now though, she could only worry about her part. She steered the barge alongside the bow of the galley, as scarlet goons leered down at them from the deck above. She tossed up a mooring rope, and one of the scarlets secured it. In exchange, a rope ladder was dropped over the side for her; just a short one as the deck wasn't that far above. She checked her sword was nice and loose in its scabbard – she still only had the short sword – then she quickly tied up her hair, which had come loose, and climbed up.

***

Remy knew something was afoot when he saw all his friends go into the islet's derelict boat house, and not all of them had come out again. The Baron, Gerard and Colin had emerged after a short while, hastening back towards the manor, while Valanthé emerged in the stern of the barge that was heading over to the galley. That meant either that Thessu and Epifani were still in the boat house – which is what the pirates seemed to have concluded – or else…

It was subtle, but two of the corpses rowing Valanthé over were not quite moving like the Risen do. Were they… breathing? At one point Valanthé seemed to shush them, which confirmed his suspicion, and Remy smiled beneath his gag at the thought of how much Epifani must be complaining right now. He stifled his mirth. He was a captive; he wasn't supposed to be finding anything funny.

Mostly, he was relieved though. Valanthé had to know that the pirates were going to kill everyone as soon as she was securely aboard, and he had been alarmed to see her heading across to hand herself over to the pirates without a fight. But Thessu and Epifani sneaking aboard meant a fight was likely. And he would be ready.

Valanthé drew the boat up alongside, and Lugwort and four of the pirates waited for her at the top of a rope ladder. The rest of the crew watched her arrive, and seemingly none of them were giving the corpses in her barge a second thought. Good.

The two pirates assigned to watch over him were also distracted by Valanthé, and when she paused to free her long hair with a seductive flick that arched her back – accentuating her lithe figure and her curves

– then teased it back up to tie, Remy wondered whether she had done so deliberately to distract the crew. He took the opportunity whether it was deliberate or not, and channelled heat from his molten core to his hands. Hopefully the pirates were distracted enough not to notice the ropes smoking.

"Welcome home girly," Lugwort said with a malevolent grin as Valanthé crested the gunwale and dropped gracefully onto the deck. She scowled at him, and his smile broadened. "Hand over yer sword now, that's a good lass."

Remy watched her draw the sword, but shake her head. "Not until Remy's ashore and we're underway," she replied. Remy knew that wasn't going to happen. And he knew Valanthé knew it too.

Lugwort pretended to consider it, then started barking orders. To the pirates surrounding Valanthé he yelled, "seize her." Then to the two either side of Remy he yelled, "run him through..." but Remy was already moving.

As the pirate on his left grabbed hold of his shoulders, the one on his right stepped round to face him with sword-arm chambered to thrust his sword through Remy's chest. Remy hadn't waited though, and had pulled his hands apart, tearing them free of the smouldering ropes that had bound them behind his back, even as he increased the heat and lit the rope bindings on fire. The sword thrust forwards but Remy pivoted, slamming his left hand with its flaming rope binding into the groin of the man who held him, while he parried the sword-thrust with the flaming rope bindings of his right forearm.

The sword thrust deflected into the pirate on his left, who screamed as the sword-tip scraped a gash across his chest. Then his groin caught fire where Remy had struck him, and he let go of Remy's shoulders. The pirate facing him chambered another thrust. He wouldn't miss a second time, but Remy was free now, and he dove back away from the man.

Then the man exploded. In fact, the whole back of the ship seemed to explode.

***

Gerard broke the surface of the water as quietly as he could, filling his lungs with a couple of quick breaths before slipping back under. He and the Baron clung to the far side of the pirate ship's waterline under the beam of the hull below the level of the galley ports, where they couldn't be seen from the deck.

Ordinarily, alligators in the water would be an ominous presence that swimmers would do well to avoid, but Gerard was much reassured that Rufus was still lurking nearby, the enormous beast visible under the water as a great black shadow a little way away. Gerard and the Baron had set out from the overgrown north shore of the islet, the Baron in a red and white striped long-sleeve bathing suit and swimming cap, Gerard in undershirt and shorts.

They both had wounds that were only part-healed – despite Thessu's treatment and amazing restorative power – and the monk had pleaded with them to sit this one out, but they were all needed on that ship if they were to stand any chance, and wading through the swamp was easier on their injuries than rowing would be. So they waded through the mangrove-shallows and the reed beds to reach the open river, where the Baron had instructed Rufus to wait.

Rufus had met them there as arranged, and they had held their breath and clung to his back for the stealthy underwater sprint through murky water to the galley; unseen by anyone on the ship.

Gerard was still astonished at how much the alligator had comprehended; surely not all alligators were that intelligent? Had the beast become close to the Baron because he was so clever, or had he become more clever because he was so close to the Baron? The Baron did have an unusual tendency to treat creatures and even inanimate objects as more lifelike than they were, and they often seemed more lifelike as a result. That was something to ponder later; right now he was simply grateful to Rufus for carrying them there and for waiting with them until the right moment to climb up.

Gerard had brought a rope and grapnel, which he would launch at the deck above as soon as the right moment came. Like the Baron, Gerard also carried a weapon slung on his back; the Baron had his sword cane, and Gerard had his axe. The Baron had offered him a spare rapier, but he quite liked the heft of the axe in his hands, and there was a poetic justice to using some part of the Madrigal to kill the men who burned it down.

They didn't have to wait long. They heard the gentle knock on the hull from the shoreward side that must have been Valanthé drawing alongside in the barge, and shortly after that they felt the ship rocked by the impact of heavy grapeshot striking the deck at the stern of the galley, and the pitter-patter of the resulting shower of shrapnel and debris and body-parts. Jeff had fired the manor's big gun. There was a moment of shocked calm before maimed pirates started screaming, but Gerard didn't wait for that.

As soon as he felt the shot impact, he pushed off from the side of the hull and reached for Rufus. The big beast was there ready, treading water so that Gerard could climb onto his back once more; he needed a stable platform to launch the grapnel.

The alligator growled as he accidently kneed him in the snout as he clambered up, but the beast stayed put and Gerard, apologising, was able to rise to his knees on his back. He launched the grapnel high over the gunwale and into the rigging where it latched in place. He tested leaning on the end of the rope with all his weight, and it held. Gerard was again grateful to the alligator. Apparently Rufus liked shoes… he would get some sequined high-heels made for him in thanks.

Having checked his axe was secure, Gerard started up the rope. He quickly reached the gunwale and immediately came face to face with three pirates. They stared at him blankly; not quite grasping who he was or what he was doing there.

He didn't wait for them to work it out and level their muskets at him, instead he launched himself over the railing at them, scattering them like ninepins. One of them was quicker to recover than the others, and levelled the musket at his head. Gerard grabbed the end of the barrel with one hand, angling it away from him, while he retrieved his axe from his back with the other. Still holding the muzzle of the musket, he swung the axe one-handed, chopping deep into the neck of the man. The musket fired as the man slumped, and Gerard yelped, releasing the barrel; surprised but unharmed as the musket ball missed him completely. The other two pirates were recovered now as well, but they were also too close to accurately discharge their weapons, and Gerard laid into them with the axe.

***

Before the grapeshot even struck the ship, Thessu was moving. He reacted as soon as he saw the flash of the big gun firing from the roof door of the manor's south tower. The sound of it firing reached him less than a second later, a loud rumble that echoed across the water like thunder, and Thessu was already two rungs up the rope ladder when he heard it. That was followed by a high-pitched whistling sound a second later, which Thessu heard as he reached the top of the ladder, dropping down from the gunwale behind Valanthé as the grapeshot struck. She had reacted almost as quickly on hearing the big gun fire, and was moving to take cover behind one of the galley's deck guns. He joined her as she crouched down behind the cannon, its cast iron barrel protecting them from the rain of wooden debris and body parts as Jeff's grapeshot cannister shredded the back of the ship. Shrapnel pattered around them, and a pirate's severed foot bounced off the cannon-mount and over the side of the vessel.

Thessu saw that Lugwort had ducked for cover as well; the pirate captain was experienced enough to recognise the sound of incoming cannon-fire, and he moved quickly for such a fat man, ducking behind the mast. The other nearby pirates weren't so experienced, and Thessu saw one of them clobbered by a length of wooden railing, while another was knocked over by a chunk of bloody torso.

As soon as the last piece of shrapnel landed, Thessu was up again. He quickly scanned the deck, and saw astern that Remy had avoided the grapeshot and managed to free himself, but the pirate next to him hadn't been so lucky, and had seemingly caught one of the bunched metal projectiles in the chest, exploding him into pieces and drenching Remy in gore.

Pirates who had kept their footing nearby to where Thessu and Valanthé had taken cover, were now bearing down on them with cutlasses; however that wasn't the only immediate danger. He saw other pirates across the deck were readying muskets, and one of the blonde necromancers was heading towards the deck hatch that led down to the galley deck; presumably to summon the galley corpses. He also saw one of the gun crews towards the bow – those furthest from the impact – were preparing their cannon to fire back at the manor.

But he also saw Epifani climbing up over the gunwale behind him, and saw Gerard's grapnel hook sail over the far side of the deck and lodge in the rigging. He would leave the musketeers on the far side to Gerard and the Baron.

"Epifani, stop that necromancer!" he called over his shoulder.

"On it," she replied.

Valanthé sprang at the nearest two pirates, buying Thessu a moment to deal with the gun crew along the deck. He leapt up onto the cannon mount he had sheltered behind, drawing the three throwing stars he had brought with him from the pocket of the ragged corpse jacket he was wearing.

He steadied himself on the barrel of the cannon, and flung the vicious stars at the pirates one after the other. The first one struck the loader, one of its vicious spikes sticking into the mans chest, and he staggered backwards, but too late as he'd already placed the charge and shot into the end of the barrel. The second star struck the primer in his shoulder, and he also staggered, but yanked out the projectile and went back to pouring powder into the vent hole at the base of the barrel. The third star struck the rammer in the back of the head, and he fell, dropping his ramrod. The fuse-man cursed at Thessu, then lit the powder in the vent hole with his match-cord.

Thessu smiled. The shot wouldn't go anywhere; it hadn't been rammed. He didn't watch the misfire, instead he jumped down to help Valanthé.

***

The Baron followed Gerard up, and peered over the deck just in time to watch the big man launch himself into the shocked pirates, hacking one down with a vicious blow to the neck, and rounding on two more before any of them realised they'd been boarded.

Across the deck, he could see Thessu had boarded as well; he was jumping down from a cannon to join Valanthé, who was being hard pressed by two pirates with cutlasses. Epifani was also on deck, rushing to intercept one of the necromancers. Looking aft, he saw Remy, and sucked in a breath; the fiendling was covered in blood and his arms were on fire. But Remy didn't seem perturbed by either. As the Baron watched, he saw his friend pluck a rapier from the ground, shake off the severed hand that had been holding it, and grip it himself. He was fine.

All in all, the plan seemed to be working, insofar as they had all boarded successfully, and Remy was free and seemingly unharmed and, while the stern of the ship was a mess of splintered wood and body parts, none of the body parts belonged to his friends. He would have to congratulate Jeff on his incredible accuracy. Truth be told, he had wondered if the antique big gun would fire... or if the antique corpse could fire it. Colin must have helped him up the ladder to the mansard roof of the tower as instructed, and helped him load and aim the gun.

Suddenly, he heard the thunderous roar of one of the galley's cannons firing back towards the manor, but the shot sounded wrong, like perhaps it hadn't been loaded properly, and he shortly after heard the splash of the shot landing short of the islet. The pirates didn't have the accuracy of an ancient corpse and a teenage boy!

Still, the fight was just starting and the pirates were now rallying after the initial shock of the assault, and they still had the advantage of numbers and necromancers.

The Baron was on the deck now, and had pulled his cane from his back and, holding the wooden shaft in one hand he clicked down the catch on the silver handle to draw forth the slim foil blade with his other hand. He saw the second blonde necromancer standing behind two pirates, all three of them bathed in the shifting green glow of a viridian lamp swinging loose from the rigging above them. The pirates were armed with muskets and were taking aim at Valanthé and Thessu. He would have to be quick.

He charged across the deck at the pirates, and they reacted by turning their muskets on him. He wasn't going to reach them before they shot... but Remy was. The fiendling slammed a musket aside with his sword just as it fired, blasting its shot into the deck at the Baron's feet as he ran. The second pirate jerked away of his own accord, reacting to the flaming fist that swung towards his face, and sent his shot high into the rigging overhead.

The Baron watched Remy's burning fist continue into the man's cheek as he flinched away, then reeled backwards, giving Remy the moment he needed to drive his sword through the chest of the first pirate. It was a quick flick in and out again with the front third of his blade, likely severing the major arteries of the man's heart. A red stain spread from the wound to quickly saturate the pirate's tunic and he crumpled. He hit the deck, his blood flowing like spilled wine, and he was dead within two heartbeats. Remy rounded on the second pirate, just as the Baron reached them and squared off with the blonde necromancer.

"You got him, Baron?" Remy asked.

"Oh, he's mine," the Baron replied, eying the necromancer furiously.

The two necromancers were identical, so the Baron couldn't be sure if this was the one that had cut him and mortified the flesh on his arm back at the guild, or if it had been his twin. He hoped it was this one. The duel would go very differently this time; he had his sword ready this time.

The necromancer wasn't about to fight fair though. He held the Baron's gaze for a long moment as they faced off, and the Baron realised too late that while the man was standing still, his shadow wasn't just shifting in the rolling light of the lamp that swung overhead, it was moving purposefully of its own accord. His shadow, a syrupy black mass, had flowed over to the body of the pirate Remy had killed, and was seeping into it. The corpse spasmed for a second, writhing as if in agony and then, temporarily raised and under the necromancer's control, it lunged for the Baron's ankles. Good grief, he had raised it without even looking at it!

Instinctively, the Baron flinched back, but the corpse had grabbed his ankle in a tight grip, and the Baron almost fell, barely managing to keep his footing.

The corpse hauled itself forwards, pushing itself up to its knees, grabbing the back of the Barons thigh with its other hand. It was using him to pull itself up. The Baron clubbed its arm away hard with the wooden shaft of his cane, and it faltered, falling to one hand but keeping the other tightly gripped on his ankle.

However, the necromancer wasn't standing idle while the Baron fended off the corpse. He thrust his sword forward with a vicious lunge at the Baron's chest, which he barely parried with his own blade. Unable to step back though, the Baron felt the deflected blade-tip scrape across his trailing shoulder, and he winced with the pain and, more importantly, the humiliation of losing another duel against this bastard.

The necromancer recovered his stance while the corpse continued grasping. The Baron dealt it another blow with the cane, hard across its head, while keeping his eyes – and his sword – levelled at the necromancer. The corpse stumbled, but grabbed the elbow of the Baron's sword arm, drawing him off-balance once more. The necromancer thrust his sword at him again as he stumbled.

Parrying with the cane, the Baron took another deflected cut – thankfully no deeper than the first had been, but across the chest this time – and a plume of blood soaked the front of his striped bathing top just above where Belle was tucked into the breast pocket, the doll dressed in her own miniature red and white striped swimwear.

The Baron recoiled from the cut, but the corpse still had him snagged, and he fell hard to the deck. His sword clattered from his hand as he landed, and the corpse clambered up him to pin him down. Squirming backwards along the deck, he used the cane to fend off the corpse, while the necromancer stalked forward, looming over them both. The necromancer didn't bother avoiding the corpse, he positioned the tip of his sword between its shoulders and leant his weight down through it, intending to impale them together.

The Baron kicked the corpse hard just as the necromancer's sword drove through it, managing to shimmy himself away along the deck underneath it, just as the sword burst through the corpse's chest, pinning it to the deck between the Baron's legs and narrowly avoiding impaling his groin or severing his femoral artery.

The necromancer cursed and pulled his sword back, but the blade was lodged fast into the wooden deck. As he braced to pull it free with two hands, the Baron shimmied the rest of the way out from under the stuck corpse. With a great effort, the necromancer pulled his blade free, but the Baron had quickly collected his own sword and, before the necromancer could bring his freed blade to bear once more, the Baron lunged low across the deck and ran him through from below. It was a rising thrust that took him in the groin and drove up through his torso, the blade bursting out from his belly and scything upwards to his ribcage, emerging with a spurt of blood and a mass of entrails that slopped out wetly. The necromancer dropped his sword and reached for his guts, scrabbling to hold them in.

The Baron withdrew his sword and rose to his feet as the necromancer looked at him pleadingly, then collapsed to his knees on top of the corpse he had raised, still clutching his wound. The Baron eyed him dispassionately, and Belle did likewise, the doll's head lolling expressionlessly against his breast pocket. As they looked on, the corpse spasmed again and the necromancer's missing shadow seeped out of it, oozing back into place beneath the necromancer and reattaching itself to him; a normal shadow once more. The corpse was done… and so was the necromancer.

The Baron grimaced, his nose assailed by the faecal smell of the man's guts, and he looked away, belatedly covering Belle's button eyes with one hand; she was too young to see such a grisly death. He scanned the deck to see which of his friends needed help.

***

The necromancer had already reached the deck hatch before Epifani caught up with him. He quickly lifted the hatch door open, letting it fall aside to reveal a wooden ladder down to the darkness of the galley deck. Epifani had her stiletto knife in hand as she grabbed his sword arm above the wrist with her free hand, restraining him from thrusting his rapier at her or climbing down the ladder.

Pulling him round to face her, she saw from his crooked still-swollen nose, that this was the same one who had killed the cook at the Madrigal. Good. She thrust her stiletto in a wide arc aimed round his flank at his kidney, but the man caught her wrist with his own free hand, and they stood there for a moment, locked together in a grapple, neither of them able to wield their weapons. She sank low onto her haunches as they grappled, feeling the flesh of her wrist starting to sour under his grasp, and he pressed forward, looming over her. She sprung suddenly forwards and up, driving the top of her head into his face. She felt the crunch of his nose breaking once more, and his grip loosened.

She tore her knife hand free of him. Her skin had started to mortify where he had gripped it, though he'd thankfully not held the grip for long enough to cause injury. It was painful though. She ignored the pain, and drove her stiletto into him. He grabbed at her wrist ineffectually, blinded by the mess of blood his face had become, and she stabbed him again. Once... Twice... Three times... Four... She counted out the thrusts as she rapidly stuck him again and again and again, as his free-flowing blood covered them both. By twenty, he had stopped struggling.

She let him drop through the open trapdoor to land in a crumpled bloody heap on the floor of the galley deck below. "That was for the cook," she muttered under her breath.

The galley corpses were already climbing up though, and the first of them quickly reached the top of the ladder, snapping its jaw in a rage. The odious creature was now clambering up onto the deck, even as its odious presence pressed against her mind, beating down her mental barriers with vicious, malevolent intensity. The necromancer must have reached out with his mind and imposed his will on them the instant he opened the door, impelling them to repel boarders; she had been too slow to stop him. Maybe she shouldn't have spent those precious seconds tearing off the vile corpse rags she wore over her clothes before she boarded the galley.

The first Risen corpse lunged at her waist from the mouth of the trapdoor as two more clambered up behind it. She pressed the point of her bloody stiletto into the gap below its ear, between the skull and the jaw, then drove it hard through the gap into its brain stem. She smiled in satisfaction as it disanimated, crumpling against the frame of the trapdoor, and its malevolent presence receded from her mind. The Risen needed finesse, not brute force.

The next two corpses scrambled over the first but, buoyed by her victory, she focussed on their presence in her mind. She was not scared of these Risen, would not cower behind her mental barriers. She was not weak, she was Epifani Pye, slayer of the dead, and she forced her mental landscape to change, forced her perspective to shift. The Risen were not malicious invaders poised to overwhelm her, they had carelessly strayed into the place where she was strongest; they had thrown themselves onto her mercy. And she had none.

With iron will, she embraced these two trespassers on her mind at once. Embraced them both so tightly that they struggled to break free. She tightened her mind's embrace; she didn't just strangle them, she crushed them. Both corpses collapsed, disanimated, and fell back down the hatchway into the mass of angry dead flesh and bones that were flooding up from below.

The effort had drained her though, and she staggered to one knee as more of the corpses forced their way up to the hatch. The next two, she squeezed more carefully, trying to expend less of her energy, but that took longer. By the time they disanimated, they had climbed fully out onto the deck, and she had had to scramble backwards as they emerged, lashing and mauling at her with frenzied vigour. Retreating in the face of them shifted her mental perspective back once more, and she wondered then if she hadn't been overconfident.

The next corpse fully resisted her attempt to smother it, and it emerged triumphant through the trapdoor, looming over her with frothing jaw clacking wildly as she scuttled away further.

Gerard cleaved its head off with an axe.

He grabbed the face of the next one and launched it back down the ladder. Then he did what she should have done in the first place, and slammed the hatch door shut, leaning all his weight on it to hold it closed.

"Care to join me?" he asked, and she scrambled over to him, adding her own weight to hold the door. She had disanimated four corpses – more than she ever had before – but still not nearly enough to complete the task she had set herself. She felt chagrined that she had needed help once again. She would need to keep developing her ability so that she didn't need help next time.

***

Between them, Valanthé and Thessu made short work of the three scarlet goons who had attacked them. The first had fallen for a feint, blocking high as Valanthé slashed low across his belly, opening him up from hip to breast.

Thessu had nonchalantly disarmed and disabled the second, using a simple wooden baton that might have been part of the gunwale railing that he scooped up from the deck. He had blocked a backhand cutlass swing, letting his baton slide over the pirate's forearm before gripping it in both hands in such a way that it crushed the pirate's wrist between his crossed arms and the baton. He then swept backwards, forcing the pirate to drop the cutlass and faceplant into the deck, before repeating the baton manoeuvre on the man's neck, strangling him between crossed wrists and baton until he passed out.

The third had attacked Valanthé with a longsword. Her own longsword, she realised, that she had lost at the Madrigal. It was an elegant weapon, long and straight with a thin double-edged blade, backward-swept guard, and a heavy pommel flying a long red tassel. It was the longer, lighter twin of the short sword in her hand. The pirate hacked with it like a cutlass, and she winced as she parried his clumsy swing. If he had chipped her blade with his woodchopping she would be very upset! She opened his throat with a shallow cut with just the tip of her short sword, and she snatched her longsword from his grip as he fell.

Then Lugwort shot her.

She heard the flintlock pistol fire, and wondered who the fat pirate was shooting at. She took one step towards him, intent on reaching him before he reloaded, but her leg buckled underneath her as her body realised he had been shooting at her, and he had hit. She stumbled to one knee but was determined not to look down, not to feel the pain, not to register that she had been shot at all.

"No butterflies this time girly?" he mocked, "No frog vomit?"

Pushing herself back up, she marched over to him even as her body screamed at her to pay attention to the important wound it had taken. The pirate reloaded quickly but she smacked the gun aside before he could fire a second time. He backed up, stumbling backwards into the mast, and she scissored her swords either side of his neck.

He dropped the pistol, defeated. "Alright girly, I yield. Ye won't kill yer old uncle Lugwort will ye?"

She tightened the scissor and he sucked in a breath as he flinched backwards against the mast, a trickle of blood running down his neck on both sides. He wasn't her uncle. And she had no compunction about killing him. She felt a hand on her shoulder, and glanced back. Remy.

Looking around, she saw the handful of remaining goons on deck had also yielded, dropping their weapons as the Baron and Thessu strode among them triumphant. She looked for Gerard and Epifani and saw them lounging coolly on a trapdoor. It was over; they'd won.

She felt Remy's hand still on her shoulder, and listened then to her body's protests. Lowering her swords, she looked down. He had shot her in the thigh. She hobbled over to a cannon mount, and perched down on it, undoing one of her belts to use as a tourniquet.

"Per'aps I shouldn' ha' shot ye," the pirate offered.

Remy struck him hard in the jaw with the steel pommel of his rapier, and Lugwort winced and spat out a gold tooth.

"Perhaps I shouldn't have hit you," Remy replied. "Valanthé, you want me to shoot this fat fuck?"

She tightened the belt hard around her thigh, and felt faint for a moment with the pain, but she gritted her teeth and held out from fainting. She shook her head. "Not yet. I want to ask him some questions first."

Remy picked up the man's flintlock pistol, which was a fine-looking weapon, and he stood, admiring it. "I like your pistol," he said to Lugwort. "I think maybe I'll keep it." Lugwort shrugged indifferently.

"You should give it to Colin," Valanthé said, teeth gritted through the pain as she tightened the belt around her thigh. "He's terrible at throwing knives, but that grapeshot proves he can at least shoot pretty accurately."

"Colin fired that?" Remy asked, incredulous.

Valanthé nodded. "Colin and Jeff did, yes."

Remy looked simultaneously surprised, afraid and annoyed. "It's a wonder he didn't kill us all!"

The Baron and Thessu had gathered the remaining scarlets together now, and arranged them on their knees facing the gunwale with their hands behind their heads, while Gerard and Epifani had managed to block the trapdoor with a cannon mount. The four of them came over to join Remy and Valanthé, who had secured her tourniquet and hobbled back to the pirate. Thessu looked at her concernedly, but she waved him away. She would let him tend her wound later.

"So what do ye want to know, girly?" the pirate asked.

Valanthé bristled at him. "Remy will you please shoot him in the face if he calls me 'girly' one more time."

"It would be ma pleasure," the fiendling replied.

Lugwort grimaced. "Valanthé. What is it ye want to know?"

Epifani butted in. "I would like to know what's so important about Joanna Pianna that you're willing to kill innocent people to stop us looking for her?"

The pirate looked nonplussed. "Fuck knows," he shrugged. "I gots me orders an' they don't involve me askin' why."

"And where do those orders come from?" Valanthé asked.

"From your ol' pal Crosskeys o'course," Lugwort replied with a snarl. Valanthé had assumed as much, and she frowned. Despite everything that had happened, she still quite liked Captain Crosskeys. Perhaps naïvely, she had hoped she wouldn't have to kill him.

"And where is Joanna Pianna now?" Thessu asked.

"No clue," the pirate replied. "Crosskeys don't tell me what I don't need to know."

"What about an old blind lady with dark skin like mine?" Epifani asked. "You know anyone by that description?"

Again the pirate shrugged.

"You know what, Remy," Valanthé said, "I don't think the captain here is being very informative."

"You want me to shoot him?" Remy offered.

Valanthé considered it, but Gerard intervened. "No, I've got a better idea." He strode forward, reaching down to grab Lugwort by the ankle, then yanked him off his feet so he landed hard on the deck. Gerard dragged him across the deck to the gunwale by his ankle, then lifted him bodily up and over the side like he weighed no more than an infant. He held him there, dangling head-first over the side of the galley.

They all looked down to see Rufus still prowling in the water below, and the enormous alligator snapped viciously at the pirate captain. "Shall we try that again," Gerard said, nodding to Epifani.

Epifani looked impressed. "Tell me where Crosskeys would likely stash Joanna and the blind woman?" she demanded. "We've already guessed they're on Flotsam somewhere."

The pirate hesitated so Gerard lowered him further, towards the giant alligator, who was thrashing and jumping at him. If Rufus was merely play-acting as a vicious hungry predator, he was very convincing in the role.

"Don't take too long answering, you're not getting any lighter…" Gerard said.

"I don't know, could be anywhere," the pirate replied, seeming to decide either that Gerard wouldn't genuinely drop him, or that the Baron's tame alligator wouldn't genuinely hurt him.

Rufus must have sensed Lugwort's scepticism, as he leapt fully ten feet out of the water, leaving only his tail submerged. The pirate waved his hands in front of his face to fend the beast away, and Rufus clamped onto his arm, sinking his massive serrated teeth into the pirate. Gerard stumbled as the alligator dangled off the pirate's arm, unable to hold up both Lugwort and the giant alligator despite his prodigious strength.

Lugwort nearly fell, but Rufus thrashed hard and dropped away first. The pirate screamed. The alligator had ripped his hand off, and he clutched at the bloody mangled stump of his wrist, as blood spurted out and, in the water below, the alligator chomped the pirate's hand in his massive maw, and swallowed it down. He looked like he was preparing to jump again and take another bite.

"Theres a ship," Lugwort blurted out. "A river boat deep in the heart o' Flotsam, surrounded by high-sided junks. It's orf limits to all at Crosskeys' orders. If they's anywhere, they's there." He sounded frantic now; all doubt that it was a bluff had evaporated.

Epifani looked at Valanthé. She didn't know any off-limits river boat, but she knew where the high sided junks were clustered. It was perfectly possible that a river boat was concealed between them. "I think I know where he means," she said.

"Any other questions for him?" Gerard asked.

Valanthé nodded. "I'd like to know why he wanted me back so badly."

"Because of Darkmourn!" the pirate bellowed, holding the bloody stump of his wrist tight against his side with his good hand. "Ye have the same gift he had!"

Valanthé had heard 'Darkmourn' a couple of times now from the pirates whenever her power had burst forth. Was it someone's name? "Who's 'Darkmourn'?"

"Don't ye know anything?" the pirate spat in response, his pain and fear now coloured by anger. "He were only the greatest pirate captain o' the last century! He were me mentor, an' he were mentor to Crosskeys an' all. Before he took charge, we was just a band o' pillagers, raidin' small settlements an' villages up and down the coast, but he turned the Scarlet Fist into a legitimate operation. An' damn your eyes, ye have the same gift for the extraordinary as he had!"

Valanthé looked at the others. None of them seemed to have heard of him either. "Where is he now, this dread pirate, Darkmourn?" she asked.

Lugwort scowled up at her, his eyes murderous. "Gone. He always liked piratin', but it were the sea he loved. He got bored and decided to sail to the edge o' the world, and keep on going. That were five years ago; he never returned. Now pull me up!"

She signalled for Gerard to haul him back in, and Gerard looked relieved. He was extraordinarily strong, but dangling the fat pirate over the side of a boat by his ankles must have taken a tremendous effort.

Gerard dumped him unceremoniously on the deck, saying cheerfully, "maybe if you live, you can get yourself a hook for that stump."

As he landed though, Valanthé caught a glimpse of something gold at the man's neck. She peered closer and saw a battle-scarred and dented medallion. She recognised it; it had her family crest on it. It was her father's medallion, not gold, but brass. She snatched it from Lugwort's neck, snapping the chain it had been attached to.

"Where did you get this?" she demanded.

"Darkmourn giv' me that 'afore he left," the pirate replied. His voice sounded fainter now; blood was still pouring from his mangled stump and his anger ebbed away with his consciousness. "He gave each o' us a share o' his booty that he'd collected over the years from tradin' and raidin'… He tol' me that were one o' his favourites, an' he got it where he got his powers from."

"That's my father's medallion," Valanthé said mechanically. She was also feeling a little faint from blood loss. "He was killed by brigands who attacked my village when I was a child."

"You think Darkmourn killed your father, girly?" the pirate said.

Remy looked at her inquiringly then. She sighed, and nodded, and he shot Lugwort in the face. She had warned him about calling her 'girly'.

They stood around the pirate's body in silence for a long minute as his life drained away across the deck. His face was a shattered, bloody mess, unrecognisable behind his ginger beard. "Remy are we safe here?" the Baron asked. For some reason he covered the button eyes of the doll in his pocket as they watched Lugwort die. "Are more pirates going to come to the islet looking for us?"

The fiendling considered for a moment, then shook his head. "I think we're safe. It were Lugwort's men who followed me to Roja, and who followed y'all here. I don't think they told anyone where they was headin'."

"No they wouldn't have wanted to share the bounty," Valanthé confirmed. "We'll be good for a couple of eves at least, so long as we can get rid of this ship."

"Good," the Baron said. "Then I suggest we regroup in the manor and work out what to do next."

CHAPTER 17

After the battle of yestereve, the Baron had taken charge of disposing of the galley. As much as he'd have liked to have held on to their prize, there was no way to keep it since it belonged to the Scarlet Fist, and no way to scuttle it in the shallow water where it had moored. So he'd cut the anchor chain and rudder chain, and – with Gerard's help – felled the mast, then left the ship to drift downstream of its own accord; another wreck to feed to Flotsam.

The others had debated what to do with the pirates they had captured. Epifani had suggested they feed them all to Rufus, but the Baron had made it clear that killing captives was unconscionable, and also that Rufus was more partial to fish suppers than people, and he had been merely playing along when he attacked the pirate captain.

Just as he'd thought, the captives were of no interest to the alligator – other than that he taxed them their shoes – and so the surviving pirates were ditched on one of the uninhabited islands of the outer swamp where they would no doubt be picked up in a few eves, perhaps a week. Certainly no more than two… unless of course they fancied the swim through alligator-infested waters.

Epifani had also vehemently objected to sending for a corpse collector to take the dead pirates away for raising. For some reason she'd wanted to bury them in the dirt or feed them to Rufus as well. This would have prevented them from paying their lives forward by serving the living and, as Remy pointed out, would have meant forgoing a substantial corpse-geld.

In the end, reason had prevailed when Remy handed her a spade and told her she'd have to dig all the holes herself if she wanted to bury them, and so she'd gone for a long punt in the Baron's gondola while the corpse collector came and went so she didn't have to be present for the handover. While she was gone, Remy reasoned that she probably wouldn't want a share of the corpse-geld since she'd disagreed so vehemently with the practice of buying and selling corpses, so they divided it between the rest of them; five livres and fifteen sols each. Remy also insisted – quite rightly, the Baron thought – on looking after Colin's share, since he'd been so careless as to lose his coin purse the last time he'd been given any money.

After all that, and once the group had rested and freshened up, and once Thessu had tended their wounds, they assembled in the manor's dining room to discuss their situation.

"I hope none of you mind if I start things off," the Baron began, pouring wine into the last of the glasses so they each had one in front of them. "It seems uncanny to me how we all got thrown together by chance, yet our lives are so interconnected that we keep bumping into each other and having to work together. Do any of you think it is just a coincidence?"

He looked around the room. Gerard shook his head, while Thessu and Valanthé looked deep in thought. Epifani downed her glass of wine in one, and reached for the bottle to top it up again. Remy passed it down to her. Only Colin tentatively raised a hand, then pulled it down again when he saw that nobody else had.

"I don't believe in fate if that's what you're getting at," Epifani said as she poured herself more wine. "But yes I agree it's getting ridiculous now."

"How would you explain it then?" Valanthé asked her.

"Well it's not fate; I think someone has been manipulating you all," Epifani replied.

"It's both," Remy said matter-of-factly. "It's fate, an' it's been manipulated. How much do y'all know about the tapestry o' fate?"

"Only what you've told us about your mother," Gerard replied.

Remy nodded. "My mother could see the future. She described readin' fates as like followin' the threads of a tapestry. She could follow the threads an' see where each one led."

"That sounds very similar to how the seer of my order can sample the future." Thessu replied. "Mother Oracle sees the fates as wisps of smoke, and she can enter a dream-like state where she floats along the swirling vapours to see where each one leads."

"Bullshit," Epifani scoffed.

Remy ignored her. "My mother had the ability to change those fates by changin' the pattern o' the weave. If someone's been manipulatin' us, they got the same ability she had."

"Bullshit," Epifani said again.

Remy rounded on her. "Epifani, why don't you tell everyone why you lookin' for Joanna Pianna?"

"Yes I would very much like to hear that," the Baron said, and the others nodded in agreement. Epifani stared daggers at Remy, and drank her wine.

"What Epifani ain't tellin' y'all," Remy continued, "is that she's lookin' for Joanna Pianna because some unknown person tol' her that's how she gets rid o' Risen from the world, ain't that right?"

"Some unknown person?" Gerard queried.

"Unknown to her," Remy confirmed. "But it's the same person that killed my mom an' took her power o' foresight. Same person that used that power to read the tapestry and manipulate Miss Epifani-doesn't-believe-in-fate right here into doin' his biddin'. Well you might like to know, Epifani, that you been doin' the biddin' of Domenico Dandolo."

"Domenico Dandolo?" Colin interjected. "He has no interest in getting rid of the Risen! His family owns more corpses than anyone else in La Crosse!"

"No shit," said Remy, and he snatched the wine bottle back from Epifani, and topped up his own glass, as Epifani glowered at him.

"So why are you looking for Miss Pianna?" the Baron asked Thessu.

"Because of a vision Mother Oracle had," he replied, pulling out a scrap of parchment from a fold in his robes. This he read aloud. *"The southern queen arrived at last, a century deserted. Thessu finds the witch was cast, a doom may be averted."* Finished, he folded it back up and returned it to his pocket.

"Well, that doesn't say anything about getting rid of the Risen," Gerard said.

"No," Thessu agreed. "But I have no idea what 'doom' may be averted by finding her. It's not clear to me that Mother Oracle necessarily wants the same outcome Epifani does."

"So what does she want then?" Epifani asked defensively.

Thessu sighed through his mask. "For hundreds of years, my order has promoted peace and prosperity in the realm of Twilight. Usually that means preserving the status quo and avoiding any upheaval; I can't realistically foresee Mother Oracle welcoming an end to universal undeath. The dead serving the living has been part of our culture for millennia."

"I don't care about preservin' the status quo or getting' rid o' the Risen." Remy interjected. "Domenico Dandolo killed my mother. I will prevent him from achievin' whatever he set out to achieve, an' then I will kill him."

The mood darkened then as it dawned on them all that although their fates may be intertwined, they weren't all necessarily on the same side.

"So where do the rest of us fit in?" Colin asked, after an uncomfortable silence.

"Well, the Baron and I still don't know where we went for a hundred years on the Queen of the South," Gerard said, and the Baron nodded his agreement.

"Or why we keep losing our consciousness," he continued. "But I can't help but think Joanna Pianna is the key to that as well. The only thing that ties her to us is that we were all on that cruise together."

"And for me," Valanthé added, "it seems like the answers I'm seeking are on Flotsam as well."

"Darkmourn and your father and Crosskeys?" Remy guessed.

Valanthé nodded. "The man who killed my father established the Scarlet Fist. And now the Scarlet Fist are killing anyone who looks for Joanna Pianna. It's all related."

"So that leaves me," Colin said dejectedly. "I don't have any relation to Joanna Pianna."

"Colin my boy, you are the glue that holds us together," said the Baron reassuringly.

"An' you got your own mysteries to solve," Remy added. "Like who your real parents are, an' why a Mama D'Ombre gave you to the Du Laurentins. I for one will help you get to the bottom o' that."

The boy didn't look convinced. Remy placed a hand on his shoulder.

"Colin, you part o' this group now. The Fearless Fiendlin's, remember? We goin' help each other out, an' we goin' figure all this out." He smiled encouragingly, and the boy gave a half-smile in return.

"Here I got you somethin'. Consider it a thank you for your part in that rescue yestereve." Remy placed the pirate's flintlock pistol on the table. He had cleaned and polished it. Next to it he placed a powder flask and a pouch of lead shot.

Colin's eyes widened, and his half-smile became a wide grin as he picked up the gun.

"Thank you Remy. Thank you all. Excuse me I have something in my eye," and he dashed out of the room.

"So… Morrow's-eve we go to Flotsam?" Remy asked. They all nodded. It was agreed.

***

They assembled by the boat house the following eve to head to Flotsam. Thessu checked on everyone's injuries while they waited for Remy and Colin, who had yet to arrive. The mortified flesh on the Baron's arm was looking red and angry; which was a significant improvement. His other cuts were also healing nicely, as was Gerard's corpse bite and the burns on his hands. Valanthé's gunshot wound was the biggest concern.

The pistol ball had thankfully missed her bones and arteries and had lodged in the muscle of her thigh about two inches in. Thessu had removed the ball and sterilised and dressed the wound, and used his healing power to advance her recovery as much as he could. He wouldn't sew it; it would need to heal from the inside out and the wound would meanwhile bleed and suppurate. He would need to clean and heal it every eve.

Until it was significantly more healed, she couldn't place her weight on the leg and so required a crutch to walk. She certainly wouldn't be able to fight on it, yet she stubbornly refused to stay behind. He gave her some willow bark extract for the pain.

They continued to wait and, as they waited, Thessu's ears pricked up as he heard the trill of a familiar songbird nearby. He hadn't heard this particular birdsong in months; not since he departed the southern continent aboard the Volant. It sounded like the trill of a red cardinal, a pretty common songbird back home, but very much out of place here on the northern continent.

Looking around to find the source of the call, he saw it was indeed a red cardinal songbird, sat on a high branch of a nearby mangrove tree. It was a pretty bird, bright red with a red beak and a plume of red feathers on its head. It chirruped a couple more times, then cocked its head at him and fluttered down to land on the path near where he stood. Then it chirruped again.

"What an unusual bird," Gerard said. "I've never seen one like it."

"You wouldn't have," Thessu replied. "It's native to the southern continent; they don't usually cross the gulf."

The others looked on with interest as Thessu knelt down to the bird, which hopped forward along the path and allowed him to cup his hands around it and lift it up. It was quite tame. As it should be; it was a messenger from the monastery. The little bird's precious cargo was contained in a tiny hollow dowel which was tied to its leg.

Thessu unpicked the knot and handed the bird carefully to Gerard, who cooed at it. Thessu cracked the dowel in half to retrieve the tightly-rolled slip of paper from within.

It took him a minute to decode the message, which was written in a simple cypher used by his order.

"It's from Brother Superior," Thessu announced. "He's the senior monk of my order."

"Is he the one who made up all those stupid mantras?" Epifani asked. "What does he want?"

Thessu double-checked his decoding, then read the note aloud.

"Brother, we grow concerned. Mother Oracle has had another vision: 'Thessu delivers by his hands, Twilight's death in far-off lands.' You are ordered to take no steps that might endanger the realm. And brother, please do kindly send your report at your earliest convenience."

He read it again to make sure he understood it. Mother Oracle had had a vision in which he delivered the death of Twilight. He would never do such a thing, it was a nonsense! Destroy the world? No, he would give his life to preserve it, as he had vowed. Was Mother Oracle mistaken somehow?

"How the hell did that stupid bird know how to find you?" Epifani asked, interrupting his introspection.

Thessu rolled the note back up and placed it in his pocket. He would write a reply and dispatch the bird with it later once they returned from

Flotsam. He would have more to report once he had found Joanna Pianna.

"I raised this bird from a chick," Thessu said in reply, as he retrieved the cardinal from Gerard. "It knows me and it knows its home. It can find its way between us both."

"It's a pet then?" Gerard asked. "What's its name?"

Thessu shrugged. "Bird number seventeen."

He searched in his satchel for the pouchful of seeds that he kept there, glad he had kept it even though the last of the birds he had brought with him from the monastery had died during his long voyage aboard the Volant.

He took a generous pinch of seeds from the pouch and tried feeding seventeen whilst holding it close. It was exhausted from its long flight across the gulf though, and wouldn't feed, so Thessu lifted his mask and chewed the seeds himself. He spat the seed mulch back into his hand, and this time the bird ate it hungrily. He settled it in his satchel and replaced his mask; he would have to keep the little messenger with him until it was recovered enough to make the return journey.

Remy and Colin arrived then. Remy was sopping wet.

Thessu recoiled. Remy wasn't just wet, he stank. Even with the filter slits of his mask firmly shut, he could smell a foul odour emanating from the fiendling. "What happened to you?" he asked. The others shrank away as well, with differing degrees of politeness.

Remy gave them a look of repressed anger. "Ask him," he said, gesturing at Colin.

They all looked at Colin.

"W…well I wanted to repay Remy for all his kindness, so I thought I would do something nice for him," he stammered, while looking sheepishly at the ground. "So I washed his clothes."

Remy snorted derisively, and pushed past Epifani, who was blocking the path to the boat house. Epifani held her nose, looking at Remy with disgust in her eyes as he passed. "Ugh, Remy, you are repulsive! I'm not sharing the boat with you smelling like that!"

"Bite me, Epifani," the fiendling said, pushing the door open to the boat house. He slammed it again behind him.

"Colin my boy," the Baron began. "How – exactly – did you wash his clothes?"

"Well, I have never washed clothes before. So it was a bit of a process of trial and error. First I filled a bucket with water…"

"What water did you use?" Thessu asked, though he was pretty sure he knew the answer.

"Well I didn't want to waste the filtered water, so I filled up at the shore."

"You… washed his clothes with swamp water?" the Baron sounded incredulous.

Colin nodded, confirming Thessu's guess. "I thought it would be fine once I added soap."

"What soap did you add?" Gerard asked.

"Well I couldn't find any soap but I remembered you telling me that in the wilderness you can make soap from ash and lard… I couldn't find any ash."

"So you used lard?"

The boy nodded, looking even more downcast. "I rubbed the clothes in the lard and soaked them in the water. Then I thought it would be fine after I scrubbed it."

Thessu detected another unpleasant undercurrent to the aroma which wasn't explained by swamp water and lard. "Colin, I'm dreading to ask, what did you scrub his clothes with?"

"Well, again I wasn't sure what to use, but I found a long-handled brush in a holder next to the toilet…"

Valanthé burst out laughing then, while the Baron and Epifani and Gerard stared aghast. The toilet brush explained the faecal notes in Remy's pungent odour.

"Shut up Valanthé," came Remy's muffled reply to the laughter from inside the boat house.

Colin looked perfectly miserable now. "And then nobody told me you had to run the clothes through a mangle to wring them out, or hang them up to dry them."

"So what did you do with them next?" Valanthé asked, wiping tears of laughter from her eyes.

Remy pushed the door open again. "He goddamn folded 'em neatly up and put 'em back in my room drippin' wet wi' shit. Can we go now please?"

Remy turned back into the boat house, still squelching as he walked, and the rest of them trooped in after him, still laughing.

***

It had started raining gently as they set off and, as was often the case in the realm of Twilight, the gentle rain quickly became a downpour. Remy was relieved that the cleansing rain seemed to be washing some of the foulness out of his clothes, and before long, everyone else was just as soaked as he had been.

It was a tight fit in the barge with the seven of them and four corpses. Remy sat in the bow and watched the city pass by as the corpses rowed them south along the forking channels of the delta. The city's viridian glow was made hazy by the rain and shadowed by the gathered clouds that obscured the ever-setting sun, so that all the islands and life of the city melded into a single indistinct green blur against the slate black sky. Time passed slowly as the blur of La Crosse passed by.

As they rowed south past the last of the city blur, the swampy Pocanovo delta gave way to the roiling waters of the Gulf of Mezarcana, and the little boat – more suited to river currents than ocean waves – struggled in the churning waters of the gulf. In the distance ahead was another indistinct green blur, obscured by shadow and rain. The floating pirate island of Flotsam.

After a time, the rain eased a little, such that the indistinct green blur ahead resolved into a haze of individual viridian lights that oscillated with the waves. The corpses rowed on and, as they got closer, the outpost became clearer. It was a ramshackle maritime graveyard of worn-out barges, galleys, ships and all manner of floating detritus lashed together in haphazard fashion. An island built of cast-offs, home to a population of castaways. Remy felt an affinity to the place, though he had never been there before.

There wasn't anywhere obvious to dock, like a jetty or such, but as the boat edged closer to the outpost, Remy saw that many of the outermost ships and boats were still crewed and seaworthy and were merely moored up alongside the floating mass, rather than being a permanent part of it. He got a sense that Flotsam never quite looked the same way twice, as outlying ships came and went, or stayed too long and were consumed by the island, replacing any mass that had sunk or been scuttled for building materials. He saw a lot of furled red sails among the larger ships; the red sails of the Scarlet Fist.

Valanthé was directing Gerard at the tiller, and the boat continued round the outpost for some time, before turning back to pull up alongside a retired river-bus. The river-bus had been stripped of its furnace and paddles, and had been lashed to the island's mass and decked out with hundreds of cages for battery hens under a jerry-rigged canopy of patchwork sailcloth. It was as good a place as any to moor up. It was noisy and smelly, but about as far as it was possible to be from the large red-sailed galleys of the pirate fleet.

Remy jumped out to lash the bow of the boat to the hen bus, while Thessu lashed the stern. They were studiously ignored by the dozen men and women who seemed to live among the cages of the hen bus and were sleeping and cooking and feeding and plucking. Remy followed Valanthé's lead in studiously ignoring them in return. It seemed to be an unspoken rule of the floating island that strangers in close proximity mustn't acknowledge one another, in order to preserve the illusion of personal space. It was the same on the city's slum islands, Remy knew.

"Good evening, how do you do?" Colin said to the people as he disembarked the boat. Of course he did; obviously he had never stepped foot in a slum. "We are just passing through, I hope it is alright if we tie up alongside your bus?"

The people all stopped what they were doing to stare at him greedily. Remy scowled and flashed each of them a glimpse of his sword and Gerard did the same with his axe. The people went back to whatever they were doing.

"Should we bring the corpses with us?" Gerard asked as he helped Valanthé out.

"No, leave them here to mind the boat," she replied.

Gerard nodded, and bade the corpses to wait.

"Let's go. It's this way," Valanthé said, bracing on her crutch as she crossed the deck of the hen bus.

Remy followed with the others, and she led them onto the deck of the next boat, which had the hull of a coastal galley but the tiered upper decks seem to have been assembled from scavenged hulls of other ships, packed together like the densest of island slums. Beyond that, they climbed up a rope ladder to what must once have been the sterncastle of a battle-damaged carrack, and then a rope bridge connected to the foc's'le of a ramshackle caravel beyond.

On they went from one wreck to the next, and Valanthé accepted help from Gerard or Remy whenever she couldn't manage the route on her crutch. Remy was impressed at how easily she navigated the maze of wrecks. Every deck was piled high with multi-tiered shanty cabins and driftwood shacks, and every available space in the floating favela was crammed with people.

The inhabitants of Flotsam all studiously avoided eye contact. They were mostly a scrawny lot of scavengers and scallywags who seemed to know to mind their own business. Remy had the feeling of being watched by every pair of eyes they passed, though he never saw anybody ever look right at them.

Valanthé's route meandered across dozens of boats and ships as it headed deeper into the heart of Flotsam. Eventually the route took them through a door hacked into the side of an old galleon and across its former gun deck, the guns stripped out and replaced by dimly-lit stalls where illicit goods were bought and sold; the galleon was one of Flotsam's notorious black market ships. It was packed with people, and they had to push through the crowd to reach the door at the far side of the gun deck. Remy gave Colin his gun back. The kid had lost it to a pickpocket without realising, and Remy had reclaimed it for him.

The door at the far side of the gun deck opened out onto a gantry, from where they caught their first sight of their destination; the galleon was adjacent to some of the high-sided junks that Lugwort had told them about. Crosskeys' off-limits river boat must be just beyond them.

The gantry ran the length of the galleon on the outside of its hull, and they walked astern to where it abutted the hull of the nearest high-sided junk.

Gerard launched his grapnel high into the rigging of the junk and, when the coast was clear, they climbed up one-by-one to the poop deck of the junk above, led by Thessu. They had to be stealthy, as the junks all seemed to be patrolled by pirates of the Fist; though thankfully the pirates weren't doing a very thorough job of keeping watch. The few pirates they saw mostly seemed to be sheltering from the rain, which had gotten heavier once more.

Remy went last and joined the others atop the junk, where he found them huddled at the aft of the ship looking down on the mysterious river boat at the centre of the cluster, exactly where Lugwort had said it would be. It was an old fashioned paddle steamer and its name was painted on the side of its hull in bold white lettering. *'The Queen of the South'.*

CHAPTER 18

They knew as soon as they saw the paddle steamer that they were in the right place; it was too much of a coincidence. That being said, someone – Crosskeys perhaps – must have gone to a lot of effort to take the Queen of the South from its dockyard and conceal it in the heart of Flotsam, and they all wondered why.

Remy saw the Baron and Gerard exchange a wary look. They had spent a week aboard this vessel, and it had cost them a hundred years. It was understandable why they might be unsure about returning to it.

The Queen of the South was a big vessel for a river cruiser, with a distinctive paddle wheel at the stern and an open foredeck at the bow. Amidships, three passenger decks were stacked one atop the other, each having wraparound galleried balconies, all topped by a pair of steam funnels. In contrast to every other vessel they had seen in Flotsam, the paddle steamer looked deserted. And it looked pristine. There were none of the shanty wood and canvas cabins sprawled on its decks like those that covered every other vessel, and it had suffered no obvious salvaging or pillaging of its fittings like had rendered the rest of Flotsam unseaworthy.

With the rain beating down and the ever-setting sun still obscured by heavy cloud, the vessel was dark and shadowed. None of its deck-lights were lit; in fact most of the ship was unlit, except for the lowest tier of passenger decks amidships, from which emanated the ghostly green glow of viridian lamps.

A pair of pirates were patrolling on the deck of the adjacent junk, so climbing down onto the steamer's open foredeck had to be carefully timed to those brief moments when the pirates weren't looking their way. Valanthé and Thessu were the first down, rappelling onto the deck on ropes lowered over the side of the junk as the two pirates paced away. They then had to duck into the shadows of the steamer's foredeck as the pirates turned and paused, seeming to have an animated discussion. It took several excruciating minutes before the pirates concluded their argument and resumed their pacing, and the rest of the group joined Valanthé and Thessu on the deck of the Queen of the South.

When the coast was clear, they all crossed the foredeck to the double doors of the galleried structure amidships, and stepped inside.

The ship's interior was richly decorated, with luxurious carpet, wood-panelled walls, stained glass windows, red velvet curtains and soft furnishings, and polished brass fixtures throughout. It all seemed highly out-of-place in the midst of Flotsam's 'pirate castaway' aesthetic. The space was filled with tables and chairs in the manner of a comfortable lounge bar, with cosy booths along the side walls. Tables were laid with crockery and cutlery for a dinner service, and each of them lit by a little viridian light. The double doors closed behind them and it felt almost as if they were somewhere else entirely. They could easily be a thousand miles from Flotsam instead of right in the heart of it.

"Why, it hasn't changed at all," Gerard exclaimed, looking around the place, and the Baron nodded his agreement. Remy idly picked up one of the monogrammed ashtrays from the table; like all of the crockery, it was pristine white with a stylised 'QotS' logo.

"I don't mind telling you old boy," the Baron said, examining a printed menu, "I'm finding this a little surreal. Everything is exactly as it was the evening we embarked on our cruise."

A young woman with shoulder-length blonde hair emerged from one of the booths, carefully arranging little occult-looking ornaments and trinkets on the table. She was dressed in a ragged black robe and had a grey wig tucked under one arm. She finished with the trinkets, and climbed awkwardly up onto a chair to hang a string of tiny shrunken skulls across the booth's entrance. Atop the chair, it was obvious she was pregnant. Remy recognised her from when she had stayed at the Madrigal; she had been pregnant then as well.

"Joanna!" Gerard and the Baron exclaimed together.

"Good evenin' gentlemen," she replied without looking at them. "I ain't set up for fortune tellin' jus' yet; if you come back in a good half hour I'll be ready to read your cards for you."

"Joanna, it's us!" Gerard insisted.

The woman turned to regard them then. There was no recognition in her eyes. "Pardon me gentlemen, you have me at a disadvantage, I don' believe I've had the pleasure?"

"Miss Pianna, we met on the voyage to La Crosse last year," the Baron said, then gestured to himself and Gerard. "It's Baron De Ville and Mister Malblanq."

"You're mistaken, sir," she replied confusedly. "I've never been to La Crosse. This will be my first voyage to the city, and I've certainly never met either of you fine gentlemen before either."

Remy walked over to her then, and offered her his hand to help her down from the chair. She took it and climbed down tentatively, a look of mistrust in her eyes. Remy prided himself on being unforgettable; the horns helped with that. But she had no recognition of him either.

"You are Joanna Pianna though, aren't you?" Thessu asked.

She looked very defensive now. "That is my name, yes."

Thessu Pressed on. "And you travelled aboard the Queen of the South for its famous voyage to La Crosse?"

She looked perplexed. "Why no sir, I haven't yet had the pleasure of travellin' anywhere. The Queen hasn't yet set sail for La Crosse. We'll be gettin' underway presently."

"But we are already in La Crosse," Colin said. "Look, we are in Flotsam!" and he threw open the doors to reveal the ship at rest in the heart of Flotsam, tightly enclosed by pirate junks. Remy peeked through the door to check he really was still in Flotsam. He saw the junks as expected, and the rain still beating down.

Joanna looked even more perplexed. "How... how can that be?"

They stood aside as she strode across the lounge to the double doors. She startled when she reached the doorway and looked through at the surrounding junks. She took a tentative step out into the rain... and vanished.

She reappeared where they had first seen her, emerging from one of the booths, busying herself with carefully arranging little occult-looking ornaments and trinkets on the table once more.

She seemed to sense them staring at her, and said, "good evenin' gentlemen, I ain't set up for fortune tellin' jus' yet; if you come back in a good half hour I'll be ready to read your cards for you."

They all looked at each other dumbfounded. "Didn't we jus' do this?" Remy asked quietly. They all nodded at him. "What in the hell is goin' on?"

Joanna seemed to be making an effort to ignore them all, as she climbed awkwardly up onto a chair once more to hang a string of tiny shrunken skulls across the booth's entrance.

"Joanna Pianna?" Thessu asked.

The woman turned to regard them then. There was again no recognition in her eyes. She didn't even seem to remember that they had just had the exact same interaction. "Pardon me gentlemen, you have me at a disadvantage, I don' believe I've had the pleasure?"

Gerard had clearly decided to take a different tack this time. "Miss Pianna, you are in danger. We're here to help you, will you please come with us?"

"Danger? What danger?" She eyed them warily, her eyes lingering on their weapons.

"Please, miss," Remy said, following Gerard's lead. "It is vitally important that you come with us. We'll take you somewhere safe."

"Sir, it is you who be makin' me feel unsafe. I shall have to ask y'all to leave this instant. The lounge is closed to passengers until dinner service."

Remy considered whether to simply grab the woman. From the way Epifani and Gerard edged closer, it looked like they'd also had the same thought. Joanna shrank away from them, clearly frightened. Epifani lunged at her suddenly, grabbing at her wrists, and Joanna pulled away with a shriek. She backed away as Epifani stalked forwards like a cat ready to pounce.

The shadows behind Joanna suddenly moved, striking out at Epifani, knocking her backwards. She slammed into a table which rocked over, spilling its crockery onto the floor where it smashed. Epifani looked up, rage in her eyes, to see what had struck her. There was nothing to see; only shadow. It was a spectre. The Risen shadow hovered in front of Joanna, a formless grey silhouette that wafted and billowed like smoke.

Joanna seemed as dumbfounded as everyone else at the spectre's appearance; clearly she hadn't known it was there. After a moment of stunned surprise, she screamed and turned towards the doors at the far end of the lounge bar. With Epifani knocked back, Gerard was closest to her and he darted quickly forward to grab her.

Another shadow struck out from the adjacent booth, flinging the heavy table across Gerard's path. A second spectre! Batting the table aside without breaking his stride, Gerard dove at Joanna. She screamed again, tripping as she dodged the upturned table and the big man's grasp.

The spectres both moved lightning fast to assist the falling woman, pouring through the air like spilled ink through water. The first one flowed around Gerard before solidifying into a barrier to keep him from reaching Joanna, while the other flowed around her and cushioned her fall, catching her gently in its shadowy embrace. This seemed to frighten her greatly and she screamed again and thrashed at the ebbing shadow.

"Back off!" Remy yelled; not to the spectres – who were clearly there to protect Joanna – but to Gerard and Epifani, who were both now struggling to get past the protective Risen shadows that were blocking their way. Epifani had drawn her stiletto and Gerard his axe. They couldn't harm the shadows with those, Remy knew; they could only endanger the young lady, and that's not why they were there.

Gerard seemed to have listened, and was struggling to extricate himself from the spectre, wrenching the haft of the axe away from its grasp and stepping back. Epifani seemed to have ignored Remy though, and slashed her stiletto at the Risen shadow, the blade passing through it ineffectually. Epifani withdrew and adopted that grimace she sometimes had; the scowl of effort and disgust she got when she was concentrating on snuffing out Risen. Damn her! She was trying to kill Joanna's protectors!

"Epifani, no!" Remy yelled. "Don't do it!"

She snapped a questioning look at him, her face still contorted with the force of will she was exerting on the spectre.

"Let it go, Epifani." Remy said as calmly as he could, pressing between her and the shadow. "Please?"

Epifani relaxed. She looked at Remy with narrowed eyes; she had listened, but she wasn't happy about it.

Joanna extricated herself from the protective grasp of the spectre that had grabbed her, and she inched back away from them all fearfully.

At that moment the double doors at the far end of the lounge bar were thrown open, and standing there in the doorway was an old woman with dark skin wrinkled like old leather, and thin white hair hanging limply past her shoulders. Her eyes were covered by a strip of red cloth which wrapped around her head. The blind woman.

Joanna Pianna saw her and sighed with relief. "Aunt Sundra!" she exclaimed, and ran over to the old woman, who stepped forward to receive her embrace. The old woman turned her blind eyes to Epifani and Remy and Gerard as Joanna cowered behind her. Gerard tensed and hefted his axe, as Epifani readied her stiletto and Valanthé and the Baron stood poised to draw their swords.

"You bunch of crazy damn fools!" the old woman yelled. "Are y'all tryin' to kill us all? Lower your goddamn weapons this instant!"

The spectres both withdrew to the shadows in the corners from whence they'd come. Gerard lowered his axe, and the Baron and Valanthé relaxed their grips on their sword hilts. Epifani still obstinately held her stiletto in an aggressive stance. She stared at the blind woman for a long moment, as the blind woman seemed to stare back at her. Epifani yelped suddenly, and Remy watched as Epifani's stiletto cracked apart in her hand under the old woman's blind gaze, leaving a thin trail of blood where the splinters of broken metal had sliced into her palm. Epifani dropped the broken shards of steel to the floor.

The old woman sagged, resting her weight on the heavy cane she used. "I hate doin' that, it leaves me with the mother of all headaches. Don't make me do it no more!"

Epifani glowered darkly, nursing her hand. Remy tapped her shoulder peaceably, then held up his hands palms open to signify cooperation. He wanted to talk, not fight. He still didn't have an answer to what in the hell was going on. "We've lowered our weapons, ma'am."

The old woman nodded, and the tension eased as she relaxed her shoulders. "Now, what in the hell y'all doin' here? Don't ya know this ship's off limits?"

"We came here to find Joanna Pianna," Remy began.

"We're here to save her from whatever trouble she's in," the Baron said.

"Save her? Ha! She weren't in no danger 'til you crazy sumbitches came in here swingin' weapons and tryin' to grab her! You ain't got the brains you was born with!"

"Madame Sundra, was it?" Remy asked as agreeably as he could muster. "Do you think you could tell us what in the hell is goin' on?"

"You used to call me Aunt Sundra," the woman said, adopting a calmer tone. "Though you was just a lil' boy when I last saw you, so I ain't surprised you don' remember. I were friends with your mother Brigitte for many years."

Remy looked at her sceptically. He did recall his mother being visited by a dark-skinned human woman from time to time. He couldn't say if it was definitely this woman.

The old woman turned her blind gaze to the Baron and Gerard. "You two was on this boat wasn't you?"

The Baron and Gerard nodded. "Yes ma'am," Gerard said.

The old woman sighed. "I guess y'all are owed an explanation. Let's all step outside and I'll explain it all."

She gestured to the double door through which they'd entered from the foredeck, and started shambling towards it. "Joanna sweetheart, your aunt Sundra's a lil' shaky on her feet... you think you can help me?"

"Why of course, Aunt Sundra," the young woman said.

They all stood aside as the old blind woman walked past them towards the door, supported by Joanna, who glared distrustfully at them all as she passed.

The instant Joanna stepped over the threshold, she faded away once again, reappearing back at the booth where they had first found her adjusting her trinkets. The overturned tables and broken crockery were also miraculously restored to their original pristine state. Aunt Sundra kept on walking, and beckoned them all to follow her out of the lounge.

Once they joined her on the foredeck, she turned to them, saying, "I'm guessin' I should start at the beginnin'. Have you heard o' the tapestry o' fate?"

They all nodded. Remy had already explained to the others about his mother's ability.

"If you noddin', I can't see it," Aunt Sundra said. "I'm blind, remember..."

"You saw my knife well enough," Epifani grumbled.

The blind woman rounded on her. "I see your threads, Lady Pye. I see only threads."

"Yes madame Sundra," the Baron said. "Remy has told us of his mother's ability."

"Good. Well I got the same ability; or I did before I got too old to use it properly. What we had, Remy's ma and me, is the means o' seein' the great tapestry and with a great effort, we could fix broken threads and darn holes here and there to stop the tapestry from frayin'. We weren't shapin' the course o' destiny, we were keepin' it on track. It was our great purpose to preserve order in the world and keep fate on course."

"Yes ma'am that's what my mom tol' me as well," Remy said, exasperated. "That still don't help me understand what's happenin' here."

"I was getting' to that Remy. Still impatient I see! A hundred years ago, the weavers of that time – your ancestors and mine – found a malignant thread that would eventually cause the whole tapestry to smoulder and burn away. The thread belonged to an unborn child, whose birth would herald the end of all things. If the child's fate was left to run its course, all the threads in the tapestry would be cut short when he died. What that means is, his death somehow triggers some great cataclysm that ends the world or kills everyone in it."

"Joanna's child?" the Baron asked.

Aunt Sundra nodded. "That poor child's fate is to cause the destruction o' the world. Once he's born, his life is a wax candle burnin' down to the end. When that child dies, the world dies with him."

"What do you mean it dies?" Gerard asked. "What cataclysm?"

"Earthquakes an' landslides an' tidal waves for sure. More than that we don' know," she admitted. "Somethin' apocalyptic. Threads get cut when people die. But when that child dies, all the threads get cut; the whole tapestry! We can't see any future past that; there ain't no tapestry left to read!"

"So why not change the child's fate?" Remy asked.

The woman tutted. "They tried, the weavers back then. They knew they had to change the child's fate before he was born, else he'd be stuck with it. They tried to change his fate so he could live a normal life, but that child's fate was strong. So strong that they struggled to change it in any meanin'ful way."

"Did they manage it?" Thessu asked.

She shook her head. "Nope. They saw they would run out o' time before the child was born, so they bought themselves some more time by loopin' the child's thread, an' the mother's thread, an' the threads of everyone else nearby. They kept them loopin' over the same week over an' over while they worked on weavin' that child a new fate. For a hundred years those threads looped round and round while the rest o' the world moved on without 'em."

"That's where we were for a hundred years?" Gerard gasped. "Stuck in a loop of time? All to prevent Joanna's baby being born?"

She nodded. "I'm afraid so. I'm sorry to say you must ha' relived that same voyage tens o' thousands o' times. Meanwhile generations o' weavers came and went all tryin' to fix the child's fate, till it got to be our turn, Remy's ma an' me. An' we ain't managed it either. He's still destined to cause the destruction o' the world when he dies."

"So you brought Joanna here and stuck her in another loop?" Epifani said.

The old woman shrugged. "That's the best I can do to keep the world safe. If she's stuck in there, she ain't givin' birth, an' the child's fate still ain't sealed. An' we still got hope."

"Is there anyone else who can fix the child's thread?" Remy asked.

She shook her head. "Your sister Elise has the gift, but she ain't been trained. No. Your ma an' I were the last o' the weavers. Someone killed her an' they're comin' for me next. Once I'm gone, there ain't no-one left to keep Joanna's baby safe."

They all looked at each other, stunned by what the old woman had told them. Epifani muttered 'bullshit' under her breath, but Remy could tell that even she was in no real doubt about the truth of Aunt Sundra's words. Joanna was being kept in a timeloop to prevent her child from being born, because the world was fated to be destroyed when the child died. And once he was born that fate was unalterable.

"So that explains where we were for a hundred years," the Baron said. "Is that also why Gerard and I keep blacking out?"

"Blackin' out you say?" she frowned. "That might explain some odd behaviour o' your threads. It look like your two threads are frayed somehow. Like they ain't all there, some part o' them is missin' an' I can't grasp 'em fully. No, that weren't caused by the loop. That's sommat else."

"So what did cause it?" Gerard asked, almost pleadingly. "And how can it be fixed?"

"I'm sorry, I don't know," she replied, to Gerard and the Baron's obvious disappointment. "But I'll take a look an' see if I can figure it out. All your threads sure are interestin'. Wish I'd grasped y'all sooner. Lot o' changes been made by someone!"

"But… wasn't it you that manipulated us all? Didn't you bring us all together?" Colin asked.

Aunt Sundra startled. "Who said that?"

"I did," Colin replied.

She looked around, suddenly seeming like the blind woman she was. "Hmm. I don't see your thread, stranger."

Colin looked downcast. Remy rolled his eyes. He knew he would have to console the kid again later. Tell him yes he was still important even if the old mystic hadn't bothered to unpick his thread from the tapestry.

"No I ain't manipulated any o' your threads," Aunt Sundra said. "I been usin' whatever's left o' my power to keep Joanna safe, I don't got the strength to change any fates while I focus on that. I sure didn't assemble y'all and bring ya here. Which begs the question o' course; of who did? Someone clearly did… an' I don' know anyone else who has the gift."

Remy realised the old woman didn't know about Domenico. "Domenico Dandolo killed my mom," Remy said. "He killed her an' took her gift. He maybe can see the tapestry as well now. And he been lookin' for Joanna."

She gasped, then slumped heavily on her cane. "Dandolo? Then mercy, we all in trouble. I'll look at his thread and see if you right. Joanna needs to be protected no matter what."

"Maybe you should move her somewhere else then?" Valanthé stated. "I don't see how a pirate outpost is the safest place for her to be kept?"

Another voice answered her question. A gruff, masculine voice. "It's safe enough when you're under the protection o' the Fist!"

They all looked up. The voice belonged to a muscular pirate with an eye patch covering a scar that ran across his face. He was stood on the deck of one of the junks overlooking the Queen.

Aunt Sundra reacted first and, moving quicker than she had any right to, she ducked back into the lounge bar, slamming and barring the door behind her.

Valanthé scowled at the pirate and drew her swords. "Crosskeys!"

They all followed suit, but they saw the pirate captain was not alone. There were dozens of pirates swarming over the decks of the surrounding junks above, all pointing muskets and flintlocks down at them. There was another man with Crosskeys, a man in the blue coat of a city deputy. No. In fact that was no deputy, that was the Sherriff of La Crosse himself, the nobleman responsible for order in the city. The Sherriff held up a rolled up scroll.

"Remy Du Rosier, Baron De Ville, Gerard Malblanq, Lady Epifani Pye, Valanthé Luxalim, Thessu of the Order of Mercy. I have a warrant here from the Cabal Court for your arrest. Drop your weapons and lay face down on the deck."

CHAPTER 19

Gerard snapped suddenly back to his body and immediately wished he hadn't. He was aching all over and his head was pounding viciously. Groaning, he set aside his pounding headache to look around as his eyes slowly swam back into focus. He was lying on the floor of a dingy prison cell. He reached up to rub his head, and realised his hands were bound together by thick rope.

"Glad to have you back with us, old boy," came the Baron's voice.

Gerard looked around to find him. The small cell he was laying in had rough-hewn granite walls on three sides, and a door of iron bars on the fourth. He was alone. Through the dim light of a viridian lamp beyond the door, he could see other cells arranged around a circular central chamber. He saw the Baron waving at him from one of the cells opposite.

"How long was I out?" Gerard asked, wincing through the pain of talking out loud. His jaw hurt immensely.

"Hard to tell," the Baron answered. "Two eves at least."

Rising awkwardly, Gerard paused to grit his teeth through the cramps in his legs from the awkward position he'd been laying in. He leant down to rub them, and saw his arms and legs were covered in cuts and bruises. He wore itchy rough-spun woollen undergarments only; there was no sign of his clothes or any of his belongings. It seemed he had been laying in his own waste for some time as well. Two eves. And meanwhile he had been stripped and imprisoned and seemingly beaten.

"I don't suppose Belle is in there with you?" the Baron asked. I haven't seen her since we left Flotsam."

Gerard looked around his cell. The Baron's doll wasn't there. "I'm sorry no," he replied, his voice cracking as he spoke. He was parched. "Is there water?"

The Baron shook his head. "Not for another few hours at least. The guard corpses only bring a cupful twice an eve."

"You can have mine," another voice said. Thessu's voice.

Gerard peered through the bars, trying to see where the voice had come from. Pressing his face right up against the cell door he saw a pair of bound arms emerge from the cell next to his, holding a small ceramic drinking cup. The arms – presumably Thessu's – placed the cup on the ground outside his cell as far as he could reach towards Gerard.

"Thank you," Gerard said, as he stretched his own arms between the bars of his cell door to try and reach the cup. "Did they arrest everyone?"

"Everyone except Colin," Thessu replied.

"And you know he's goin' be pissy about bein' left out again," said another voice on the far side of Thessu; Remy's voice.

Gerard chortled, then winced at his aching jaw. "Did they beat everyone, or just me?"

"They beat Epifani pretty bad when she tried fightin' 'em," Remy replied. "The rest o' us had the sense to come quietly. They didn't beat you, but they wasn't exactly gentle with you when you lost your consciousness. You might ha' been rolled down some stairs to get you here. You blackin' out was bad timin' I guess."

Gerard smiled ruefully. He would have been beaten regardless, he had been just about to try and fight his way free when he blacked out. "Is Epifani here? Is she okay?"

"I'm fine," came her voice from a cell on the other side of him. She sounded angry. Epifani always sounded angry.

Gerard still hadn't retrieved Thessu's cup. No matter how he twisted and stretched his arms, he couldn't quite reach it. The bars were annoyingly close together, so he could only reach his arms through the gap as far as his elbows, but the cells were just that little bit too far apart so that the cup was just beyond his reach. He drew back and tried again.

"Have they said what they plan to do with us?" he grunted through clenched teeth as he stretched for the cup once more.

"They ain't said, but I'm choosin' to be optimistic 'cause we ain't dead yet," Remy answered.

"Enough of us are of noble birth that we should at least get a trial before they kill us," the Baron offered helpfully.

"Perhaps I'm unfamiliar with the legal process here in La Crosse," Thessu said. "Where I come from, people aren't killed just because they're found guilty of a crime; most offences allow a fine to be paid. Is it not the same here?"

"It is," Valanthé said, joining the conversation from her own cell. "But if you can't afford the fine, they take everything you own. What kills you is if you still can't pay the fine, and your corpse is forfeit."

"An' if you ain't done with it yet... too bad," Remy concluded.

"You northerners are barbaric," Thessu muttered.

"Remy, you think your dad will pay our fines?" Epifani asked. Remy didn't answer.

Gerard had now lowered himself right to the cell floor, lying sideways with his face pressed up against the wall and his bound arms forced painfully through the gap between the wall and the first iron bar, blindly grasping for the cup that lay just beyond reach. At full stretch his fingertips brushed the side of it, and he tried to close his hands around it, but instead it slid further away out of reach. Cursing, he forced his arms further through the gap, and felt the rough stone wall tearing at the flesh of his arms. Again he couldn't quite reach the cup and it slid further away, sloshing some of its contents onto the floor as he fingertipped it clumsily.

Angrily, he rose back up to his feet. He just wanted a damn cup of water for his dry throat! He could reach it if his hands weren't bound or if the gaps between bars were just a little wider. Or if he could get the door open. He examined his bindings in the dim green light. Two dozen loops of good thick rope, tightly knotted. Strong as he was, he wasn't going to be able to pull them apart with brute strength, and he couldn't scrape them apart on the rough stone wall without scraping all the skin off his wrists as well.

Next he examined the doorframe. It was formed of a thick band of iron which was well secured to the surrounding stone. The door was another heavy iron frame hinged to the outer frame at one side and bolted closed by a thick padlocked bolt on the other side. He wouldn't be able to force the door without a lever, which he didn't have. The weak point seemed to be the bars, which ran the full height of the door top to bottom. If the door had been constructed with a mid-brace in the middle, he definitely wouldn't be able to pull them apart, but they weren't. So maybe he could.

He grabbed one of the bars and leaned away with all his weight. The door rattled against the frame and the bar flexed a little under the strain – perhaps a half inch – then returned to position when he let go. He would need to apply more force than that.

The cell was just wide enough for him to lie on his side across its width. Placing one foot high on the side wall, he reached to grab one of the bars towards the far side of the cell. His foot slipped and he fell to the floor, which earned him a snort of derision from Epifani.

At the second attempt, he was able to grab one of the bars with both hands as his foot pressed against the wall. Gingerly, he lifted his other foot to join the first, so he was lying sideways at waist-height, holding himself up by bracing his feet on the wall and his hands on one of the bars near the opposite wall of the cell. He wriggled his hands up the bar, as his feet walked higher up the wall until he was at the midpoint of its height. Straightening his legs, he pushed the bar away from the wall with all his might. It flexed a good way towards the next bar this time, but he needed more force to deform it so it wouldn't return to straight when he released. Summoning every ounce of force, he pushed the bar away, and the doorframe creaked as the bar gradually deformed. There was no derisive snort from Epifani this time, instead his friends were all watching with bated breath. None of them made a sound.

He stepped down to the ground, panting, and released his grip on the bar. It had moved four inches off centre, and remained bent out of shape after he let go. Reaching through the gap, he collected the cup with ease and drank deeply of the warm, stale water.

"You think you could bend those enough to squeeze through?" Thessu asked. "And maybe ours as well? I don't think I want to wait around for northern justice to kill me and pawn my corpse."

"Yeah, and I don't want to rely on Remy's dad bailing us out," Epifani added.

"No, you shouldn't," Remy said soberly.

Gerard nodded. The gap was far too narrow to squeeze through. He would catch his breath then stretch the bar again.

On his second attempt, the bar bent another two inches off centre, and the inner frame of the door was deformed at the top and bottom where the bar attached to it. On his third attempt, the bar tore free from the top of the door. It was a simple matter then to heave the loose bar back and forth to snap it free from the bottom of the door as well. The gap still wasn't anything like wide enough to shimmy through between the bars, but now he had a lever.

As the others watched on, he jammed the bar between the door and the frame near the locking bolt. He pulled the bar with all his weight and the door deformed away from the frame, increasing the gap between frame and door. He forced the bar further through the gap and heaved again. This time the door buckled outwards, freeing the locking bolt from its catch, and the door swung open. Gerard strode out with his lever to muted applause, and got to work on Thessu's door.

***

Epifani watched as Gerard freed all the others in turn, leaving her to last. That was fine; she already knew where she stood with them all. She thanked Gerard tersely once he'd jimmied open her cell door.

Remy had seemingly burned away his own bonds and so untied Gerard and Thessu. It was Thessu that untied Epifani's bonds after she walked out of the cell. She joined Valanthé and Remy at the banded wooden door that led out of the cell block. Remy was working on the lock. He seemed to be struggling, no doubt because he didn't have his tools, instead using two thin slivers of metal that had been the clips either side of the handle of a waste pail, bent straight. He also didn't seem to be very good at picking locks.

"Are we sure this is a good idea?" the Baron queried. "Perhaps we would still be better off staying put and arguing our case in court?"

"Stay if you want Baron, it's no skin off my tits," Epifani snapped. "But I for one have no intention of being killed so my corpse can work off a damn court debt."

The Baron frowned. "Maybe I'm missing something; will the charges really be so dire?"

"We burgled a palazzo and set it on fire," said Valanthé flatly.

"To recover my property," the Baron protested. "And the fire was an accident!"

"We captured a pirate ship and killed some of the crew," added Gerard.

The Baron protested again. "That one was self defence! They kidnapped Remy and fired round shot at my house! They burned down the Madrigal!"

Remy looked up from the lock. "Baron, it's cute you think they'll only charge us wi' stuff we actually did. All those scrapes we got into will be needin' a scapegoat. We'll be blamed for the fire at the Madrigal an' a bunch o' other shit we had nothin' to do with."

Fire glinted in Remy's eyes then, burning with a ferocious intensity. "An' even if we somehow able to walk free from court," he continued, "it'll take too long. You heard what the ol' woman said; Domenico Dandolo killed my mom an' now he after her too. We got to stop Domenico Dandolo an' save the world, an' we can't do that while we rottin' here waitin' for our moment in court. No sir, our best bet is to get the hell outta here a' soon as humanly possible."

The Baron nodded and Remy turned his attention back to the lock.

Epifani watched him darkly. She didn't know whether the person who had sent her the goblet and the note in the book of rituals really was Domenico Dandolo as the fiendling insisted. She would stick with Remy and the others and reserve judgement until she confirmed one way or the other whether there really was a way to rid the realm of Risen, and if Joanna really was the key to that.

Right now though, they needed to work together to get out of here. Epifani knew from when they'd been brought in, that they were deep in the dungeons below the Ruby Plaza; the Isla Roja garrison of the city deputies, adjacent to the Corto Dogé. They had passed several guard posts on their route here, so she knew their escape from the dungeon was anything but guaranteed; even if they got out of this cell block.

Remy laboured for some time before the lock finally clicked and the door swung open into the silent, dimly-lit corridor beyond. The corridor stretched off into the distance, periodically branching off towards other cell blocks. Epifani immediately sensed the faint but unmistakeable presence of Risen.

"Corpses," she whispered, indicating down the length of the corridor towards the far end, where it turned a corner into the first of the guard posts they would need to pass through. "Two of them I think, just round that corner."

Remy nodded, replying in equally hushed tones. "Can you take them out?"

Two was do-able. "Yes," she whispered back. "If there's only two of them."

"Could you maybe impel them to leave instead?" the Baron suggested, joining their hushed conversation. "Like how the necromancer mentally impelled those galley corpses to attack us on the pirate ship?"

"Why the hell would I want to do that?" Epifani scowled at him. The very idea was disgusting to her. She wasn't a damn necromancer, and she wasn't authorised to command the guard corpses. She would have to ask the damn things nicely; welcome their hateful presence warmly into her mind and then seduce them. She wouldn't do it.

The Baron sighed and waved the idea away. "Doesn't matter. I just thought if there was a way to do it without adding to the trouble we're in..."

"They're only corpses," she retorted as she started along the corridor, stepping as stealthily as she could. The others followed, Valanthé having to lean on Thessu and hobble along without her crutch.

The noxious presence of the Risen grew as Epifani approached the end of the corridor, and she signalled the others to hold back as she crept the last few feet. She sensed another, fainter presence as well – the living – but quietened somehow... asleep perhaps? They'd have had to have been unconscious to have slept through the racket Gerard made opening those cell doors! Why hadn't the guard come to investigate?

She saw why when she carefully peeked around the corner, peering round at ground level where the shadows were darkest. She saw the two Risen as expected; a pair of armed guard corpses stood to attention in alcoves either side of the little guard post, in which a chubby city deputy sat slumped over a desk, snoring quietly. She smelled alcohol and vomit and... was that mint?

Before she did anything else, she took a step back and, closing her eyes, took a deep breath. Prepared, she lowered her mental barriers and embraced the sinister presence of the two Risen. The stillness of the pair of corpses in their alcoves belied their raging, feral presence in her mind, and they rent and tore at her as she allowed them into herself. She enveloped them both and with her mind she stifled their rage, almost soothing them as she suffocated them. The two guard corpses collapsed to the ground, disanimated.

Epifani spat the foul taste of them out of her mouth and fought the urge to retch. She beckoned the others forward.

"Good work," Remy whispered as he reached her.

He must have sensed how much that took out of her though, as he placed a steadying hand on her shoulder. "I'm fine," she said, brushing his hand away.

Remy narrowed his eyes, not looking convinced, but they turned their attention back to the deputy at the guard post.

Approaching him warily, Epifani saw he was slumped in a pool of his own foul-smelling sick. A familiar-looking bottle lay on its side on the table. It was the mint liqueur bottle they had rescued from the Madrigal; he had drank it all. No wonder he was passed out, that bootleg stuff smelled lethal! However, if he'd been drinking their booze, it meant the rest of their things might be nearby as well.

Remy seemed to have the same thought, and he looked around, then gestured towards a pair of cells along the corridor beyond the guard post. The two cells seemed to be being used as a storeroom of sorts, judging by the racks of shelves she could see through the bars.

"We should get his keys," Remy whispered.

Epifani nodded. "Anything so I don't have to watch you pick another lock with your clumsy ham fists."

They both stepped carefully round the table to get behind the drunk guard, but before they could frisk him, the Baron cleared his throat quietly, drawing their attention back to the corridor.

He was holding up a bunch of keys. Where had he gotten those from? Had he just stumbled into them? He had something else in his hand too. Was that his creepy doll? Where had the doll come from? Had it just been lying in his path with the keys?

Just then the deputy stirred and they all froze. With her mental barriers still down, she felt the man's presence more strongly than she had before. He was waking.

The living had never had much of a presence in her mind; they lacked the angry ferocity of the dead, and she could only sense them at all because she had trained her mind to focus on Risen. It was almost an accidental byproduct of her training that she could also distinguish a living presence from the clamour of the dead. A thought struck her then; perhaps she could soothe him back to sleep as she had soothed the raging corpses… though perhaps without suffocating him to death in the process.

She had never tried to affect a living presence before. It was faint, the man's presence, almost ethereal. She tried to grasp it with her mind but could not. It had felt the same when she had first taught herself to squash the Risen; to grasp them she had needed physical touch. She would try that.

Remy shot her a warning look and shook his head as she reached out to the waking deputy, but she placed her hand gently on his back regardless. She tried again to grasp his presence in her mind. It wasn't exactly solid, but she felt something, like it was water or sand that trickled through her mental grasp. It felt silky; quite unlike the thorny abrasive texture of the Risen. She had no idea what to do with it.

The presence recoiled suddenly from her mental touch and the man startled awake, flailing wildly, his eyes filled with panic and distress. Remy clubbed him hard on the back of the head with the heavy glass liqueur bottle, and the man slumped back to the desk.

"What the hell were you doin'," the fiendling demanded once he'd checked the man was out cold.

Epifani shrugged, concealing her elation from him. She hadn't put the deputy to sleep but something she'd done with her mind had definitely affected him. It was an ability she didn't know she had, but one that she resolved to develop further. Her comrades didn't need to know.

They quickly frisked the unconscious deputy. Remy took the man's pistol, then they tied him up and left him out of sight under the desk. Meanwhile the Baron got the storage cells open, and they all quickly gathered their clothes and belongings and weapons.

Epifani found something unfamiliar among her own belongings. A bundle of sapphire-blue silk, tied with a ribbon. It had a note attached to it.

'Accept this gift to replace the one the blind bitch broke. Thank you for finding Joanna for me. We have a long journey ahead, but with every step we take, we become one step closer to ridding the world of Risen.'

Intrigued, she untied the ribbon and unfurled the bundle, and found inside a sheathed stiletto. Drawing it from its sheath, she saw the blade was exquisite; razor sharp and perfectly balanced, it was far superior to her old one. The hilt felt welcoming in her hand, like it was moulded especially for her. It was an excellent weapon, ideal for slaying the Risen. She tucked it into her boot, along with the note. Regardless who sent it and what they wanted from her, she did need a new dagger and this one was excellent.

"What's that you've got there?" Remy asked.

"Nothing," she shrugged, setting the silk cloth aside.

"Why do you have a silk scarf dyed Dandolo blue?" he asked. Damn. If she had realised the significance of the square of silk, she would have concealed it better.

"It's not mine… it must have been put with my things by mistake." She picked up her own neckerchief from the pile of belongings then, a square of plain grey cotton. "This one's mine."

Remy continued to eye her suspiciously, but she finished gathering her things and brushed past him to join the others.

***

Their escape from the dungeon proved to be surprisingly easy. The Baron didn't know if that was a good thing or not, as he still worried that they should have waited in their cells and made their case in court. A small part of him maybe wanted to be caught and returned to a cell, but Remy had made a valid point about the urgency of getting out quickly. Domenico Dandolo – or whoever it was who had killed Remy's mother and now posed a threat to Joanna and perhaps everyone else in the realm of Twilight – needed to be stopped.

In any case he was in a better disposition now that he had found Belle, and he had returned her to his pocket as soon as he had donned his suit once more. He then led them carefully back along the route they had been brought in, using the keys to unlock the intervening doors along the way.

They passed one more guard post on their way out, which was near the dungeon exit and manned only by Risen corpses, which Epifani was able to neutralise. The process did seem to exhaust her, but she seemed much more adept at it than when the Baron had first seen her do it scant weeks earlier on the Doblé bridge when they had first met.

After the guard post, the passageway diverged, one route heading back the way they'd been brought in, up via the Ruby Plaza, while the other seemed to head in an entirely different direction, though also upwards. Epifani had sensed a full cohort of corpses blocking the passageway that led to the Ruby Plaza, so they instead headed into the other passageway, and followed that instead.

The unfamiliar passageway rose up several flights of stairs, the walls becoming smoother and more finely worked as the passage rose. The six of them stuck to the shadows as best as they could, though the passageway became better lit the higher they climbed. They eventually came to a pair of double doors at the end of the passageway.

"Corpses," Epifani whispered. "A little way past the doors. Maybe four of them."

The Baron grimaced. Four was better than a cohort, so this was still the better route out. He checked one of the doors and found it unlocked, so he tentatively turned the handle and opened it a crack.

Luxurious golden light streamed through from beyond the door; a jarring change from the muted green viridian light of the passageway they had been following. The Baron peered through the crack and saw an elaborate hallway with marble floor and walls and ornate fixtures and fittings in gold leaf and turquoise. Gilded chandeliers cast warm candlelight over the grand portraits of regal-looking men and women which lined the galleried walls of the hallway. The four Risen corpses Epifani had sensed weren't guards, they were ancient skeleton corpses; their bones covered in squares of mineral turquoise mosaic. The turquoise corpses were bustling up and down the hallway; three carrying silver serving trays, the fourth a commode. Further along the hallway, a group of flamboyantly-dressed women with powdered wigs and coiffured poodles stood talking and laughing. The Baron quietly closed the door.

His comrades looked at him expectantly. "It's the Corto Dogé," he said grimly.

"Shit," Remy and Epifani both said together.

"Are you sure?" Gerard asked.

The Baron nodded. The turquoise skeletons had been the giveaway. "Did you see a way out?" Thessu asked.

"No. We'll have to look for one," the Baron replied.

"We should walk through boldly," Epifani said. "Act like we are supposed to be there and nobody will stop us."

"I agree," said Remy, and the others nodded assent as well.

Still dubious, the Baron accepted the group's decision. He straightened his suit and hat and smoothed his moustache. He checked the others were ready, and opened the door wide, walking straight through as confidently as he could.

He immediately walked straight into someone heading the other way, and sent them sprawling to the floor with a loud clatter.

The turquoise skeletons all stopped what they were doing to look at the commotion, as did the group of women along the hallway, their poodles yapping noisily.

The Baron winced, and reached a hand down to help up the person he had clattered into, a slight figure in an elaborate silk courtier's robe and powdered wig, saying, "Pardon me sir, I didn't see you there." The figure took his hand, and smiled broadly as the Baron lifted him up.

"Ah, that was easier than I thought! I was coming to find you!" the figure said.

The Baron took a moment to recognise him. His face was powdered white and the nubs of his horns were covered by his wig. "Colin my boy! What are you doing here?"

The boy dusted himself off and straightened his wig. He looked comically small in the oversized robe and headpiece. "I have come to get you out of here of course! Come with me, I will get you out."

Colin turned to the skeletons and other onlookers then, saying, "I am fine, everything is fine. I am a court official, I am here on official court business to escort these people through the palace." The skeleton corpses seemed unconvinced but went about their business. One of the women said something amusing behind a silk fan and the others laughed and they picked up their conversation again. Only their poodles continued to eye them suspiciously.

"Colin you look ridiculous!" Remy said. "Where did you get that dumb-ass robe an' wig?"

Colin grinned broadly, patting the curled white locks of the wig that fell past his shoulder. "I quite like it actually. Come on, it is this way. We have to hurry."

The Baron set aside his misgivings and gestured for the boy to lead on. Colin led them determinedly along the hallway, past the corpses and courtiers that lined the route, all of whom gave them wary looks as they passed but didn't move to stop them. Then he turned left abruptly and led them along another corridor even grander than the first, and up a flight of steps to a set of grand white and gold double doors, twenty feet high.

The doors were barred by a pair of enormous turquoise-mosaic skeletons holding massive crossed golden spears across the doorway, with six more huge skeleton corpses standing to attention either side of them. Epifani drew back from the corpses, and hissed urgently at the Baron and Colin to find another way out. The Baron ignored her. It was too late now; they had to trust that Colin knew what he was doing.

"I am a son of the noble house of Du Laurentin," the boy said confidently to the door corpses. "I command you open these doors to me," and the pair of skeleton corpses barring the doors duly uncrossed their spears and threw the doors open, filling the doorway with natural twilight that streamed in from beyond the doors, while the other six stepped aside and rapped their own spears on the floor three times, perfectly synchronised. The corpses ushered them all through the doorway and into the twilight beyond.

They walked into a vast galleried auditorium. The light that streamed in came from a grand domed skylight in the ceiling high above, the west-facing half of the dome being clear glass while the east-facing half was mirrored to reflect the light of the ever-setting sun downwards into the vast chamber. This wasn't the exit, and the Baron winced as he realised where he was. The others realised too, and rounded on the hapless youth who'd led them there.

Maybe they shouldn't have trusted the young fiendling to know what he was doing. He'd led them to the Cabal Court chamber at the very heart of the Corto Dogé. The turquoise skeleton corpses slammed the doors shut behind them.

An audience of hundreds of well-dressed people – seemingly half the nobles of the city – sat in tiers of seating facing a raised dais, on which were nine empty thrones. The audience muttered in hushed tones as they entered. Every eye was on them and the Baron again wished he'd stayed in his cell.

The central throne on the dais was the grand gilded throne of the Dogé, flanked by four smaller gilded thrones on each side for his ruling Cabal. At the foot of the raised dais, a cohort of turquoise-mosaic skeleton corpses stood protectively with golden spears, and the Baron saw a dozen more of the ancient Risen standing to attention around the chamber, along with a dozen city deputies.

Colin strode forward, seemingly unperturbed by the assemblage, and took a seat on a low bench in front of the audience, facing the dais. He gestured for the rest of them to take the vacant seats on the bench next to him.

Remy strode over to him, and loomed over the boy. The Baron saw his eyes flaming with suppressed anger as he spoke through gritted teeth. "I thought you were gettin' us out of here?"

"I am!" Colin replied, seeming surprised by Remy's anger. "I'm here to defend you in your trial!"

CHAPTER 20

Remy stared at Colin in disbelief. They all did. How in the hell did he think he could defend them in a trial? Colin had no idea what he was doing; he was just a kid! Remy looked around the court chamber. Two dozen armed and armoured corpses were watching them closely, not to mention all the city deputies and the assembled necromancers, cultists and nobles in the audience. Now they were here, there was no avoiding it; they would be tried for their crimes.

He rounded on the kid once more. "Colin, there ain't no way you defendin' us in trial! I'll take my chances wi' the court myself! You off the damn case!"

Colin reacted angrily. "That's not an option, Remy," he snapped. "The only reason you have been granted a trial is because I am the adopted son of a noble family. Commoners do not get trials, and even nobles need a peer to defend them. There was no-one else willing to stand up for you. Without me to defend you, your lives would already be forfeit, and I would be having this argument with your reanimated corpse! Now sit down!"

There was nothing else to do then, so Remy sat down and the others followed suit. When did Colin get so damn determined?

The low murmur of the audience hushed in anticipation as a court official in a liveried turquoise coat and a powdered wig marched to a lectern at the foot of the dais, accompanied by a flunkey with a long-handled ceremonial mace. The flunkey rapped the pommel of the mace on the ground three times, and the court official spoke in a loud, regal voice, "My Lords and Ladies, prey stand for the ruling Cabal!"

With a bustle of obedience the audience rose to its feet. Colin did the same, as did Remy and the others. Everyone except Epifani, who sat stalwartly disobedient with crossed arms. Was she chewing gum? Where had she gotten gum from? The liveried court official glowered at her, but continued to introduce the Cabal.

"The Guildmaster of Necromancers, Caballier Nero," he announced, and a tall slim figure emerged from a side door onto the dais. He wore a white hooded robe with his face completely obscured by a white porcelain mask shaped like the face of an owl. Nero walked across the dais and took a seat on the throne at the far left.

"Cardinal of the Ziggurat, Caballier Astrakhan," and a smaller figure emerged, also clad in the all-concealing white robe and owl mask of the Cabal.

"Dick," Epifani muttered under her breath as he entered. Astrakhan walked the short distance to the far right-hand throne and sat upon it, his porcelain owl mask turned to look directly at Epifani.

"First Sea Lord, Caballier Crosskeys," the court official continued, and the unmistakable figure of Captain Crosskeys emerged, his white cloak tight over his broad frame and bulging muscles. He seemed to pause to look at Valanthé as he entered, before walking to his seat on the second-from left-most throne.

"The Lords of the Isles, Caballiers Huron, La Plagne, and Giovani," and more masked and hooded figures emerged, taking the next thrones towards the centre. Caballier Giovani – the last of the three Lords of the Isles to enter – adjusted his owl mask as he crossed the dais, and Remy got the briefest look at his face, and he gasped.

Caballier Giovani had one of his father's human faces. In fact the very face he had worn to dinner on Isla Maria Angelou; his kindly middle-aged man face. The devil's eyes seemed to sparkle with mischief as he met Remy's gaze briefly, before he finished fake-adjusting his mask and his face disappeared behind it, and he too took his seat on one of the thrones. Remy let out a long, astonished breath. His father had machinated a seat on the Cabal! That had to be good news, right?

"Lord of Verdé, Caballier Roux," the court official continued, and another figure emerged and took the seat to the left of the Dogé's grand throne.

Then the court official announced the last member of the Cabal, and Remy froze. "Lord of Roja, Caballier Dandolo."

The figure that emerged, fully masked and robed, paused haughtily in the doorway, before walking to the final throne next to the Dogé's. Caballier Dandolo didn't even bother to look at Remy before sitting in the throne and looking disdainfully away.

Remy felt a hand on his shoulder and he turned. He looked back at the Baron's concerned face. Remy hadn't realised he had strode towards the dais, his eyes burning and his fists clenched, smouldering the sleeves of his tunic. The Risen guards at the foot of the dais had lowered their spears towards him as well.

Swallowing the flaming bile that had formed in his throat, Remy let the Baron draw him back to the bench. He relaxed his fists and quelled his fire but continued to stare incandescent rage at the man who killed his mother. Caballier Dandolo never met his gaze. Seething, Remy wondered when Domenico had gotten a seat on the Cabal. He was sure the man hadn't been a Caballier when they'd met at the Fandandolin ball.

Once Remy had cooled, the court official continued. "His excellency the Dogé of La Crosse, Jean Michel Don A'Tellio." There was a long pause before the Dogé appeared. He was a wizened old man, hunched over in a wooden wheelchair. The chair squeaked as it rolled slowly across the dais, pushed by a truly ancient looking skeleton corpse, the turquoise mosaic that enamelled its bones complemented by polished aquamarine gemstones set into its face and flashes of burnished gold projecting from between its ribs.

The Dogé was robed in white like the others, but unmasked; his elaborate porcelain mask lay on his lap, atop the woollen blanket that was draped over his legs. He looked tired. Old and tired.

The skeleton wheeled him over to the grand throne in the centre of the dais, then stepped round and lifted the elderly Dogé and placed him – almost tenderly – onto it, blanket and all. The frail figure of the Dogé was dwarfed by the enormous chair, and if the intention was for him to look imposing, it achieved the opposite. The old man pulled out an ear trumpet which he placed to one of his ears, then gestured for the court official to proceed.

"You may be seated," the official stated, and the audience sat, accompanied by rustling and murmuring.

The mace flunkey rapped the pommel on the floor three more times, and the court official bowed low to the Cabal, then cleared his throat pompously.

"I am Lance-Colonel Lemuel Simms Montrose De Launey the fourth, Comte d'Arnauld," he announced. "I shall be representing the city of La Crosse in these matters this evening. Who is speaking on behalf of the... criminals?"

All eyes turned to Colin who suddenly seemed very small and very young. He stood shakily, the bench scraping noisily on the floor as he rose. "I am Salvatoré Col Haolim Primo Martelaar Delmond Du Laurentin. I shall be speaking on behalf of the criminals."

Remy elbowed him. "Defendants!" he hissed.

"Yes I mean the defendants," Colin corrected, his voice faltering. "I shall be speaking on behalf of the defendants."

There were quiet mutterings from around the court, and Remy heard the words "fiendling" and "devil spawn" muttered all too loudly from the courtiers and audience behind them, and the pompous official – De Launey – curled his lip contemptuously.

"We are here to assess the guilt of these... persons on a list of crimes which speak to a reign of terror inflicted on our fair city. I shall read out the charges." Here, De Launey dramatically unrolled a long scroll, letting it droop onto the floor and roll away for effect.

"The charges are as follows; that you did steal and subsequently destroy an artifact of historical significance from the Basilica Grandé of the Ziggurat. That you did grievously assault four of the Faithful of the Ziggurat. That you did commit arson of the library of the necromancers' guild. That you did commit arson of the Madrigal Saloon. That you did commit burglary of the Palazzo Laurentin, and arson of the same. That you did commit piracy of a privateer galley. That you did murder a commissioned privateer captain and nine of his crew. That you did murder the lighthouse keeper of Ponté Emilia. That you did murder two necromancers of the guild. That you did trespass in a restricted area of the protectorate of Flotsam. That you did disturb the peace, resist arrest, and cause much additional property damage including causing the disanimation of dozens of Risen corpses."

Here a uniformed city deputy walked over to De Launey and discreetly whispered something in his ear. His eyebrows raised, and he continued, obviously relaying what he had just been told. "That you did grievously assault and unlawfully detain a city deputy while escaping from lawful custody. How do you plead?"

Colin stood once more and cleared his throat. "Your excellences," he said. "My clients are definitely not guilty of at least two of those."

Remy groaned. They were all going to die.

***

Over the next two hours, De Launey summoned a series of witnesses who testified to their guilt. One of the death priests they had fought on the Doblé bridge. The first mate of Lugwort's ship, recently rescued from the swamp where he'd been left. A man who claimed to be one of the patrons from the Madrigal the eve it burned down, but who definitely wasn't. The steward of Palazzo Laurentin, who claimed to have seen them rob it, and definitely hadn't. And more besides.

Despite his youth and incompetence, Colin actually didn't do too bad a job at cross-examination, doing enough to expose the false witnesses and shed doubt on the testimony of the real ones. He even had a dig at his adopted father the Marquis Du Laurentin – who of course was in the audience, sat in the centre of the upper gallery – when he pressed the palazzo steward on where his master had been during the burglary. The whole court knew of the Marquis' having turned up at the palace for an orgy with the Dogé; it was the hottest gossip in town. Even the frail old Dogé chuckled at the line of questioning, and the Marquis – a large man in a red silk coat and powdered wig so long it trailed on the floor – turned as red as his coat.

Colin also feigned sleep when Sofokles of Halla delivered a tedious monologue of how he'd been accosted and dunked in the river, which earned the kid more credit with the equally bored audience.

Remy was proud of him.

The case for the defence also benefitted from a key piece of De Launey's evidence – the fragments of the goblet which were found on Epifani when she was arrested – having gone missing. Remy could guess where they had gone; he knew his father was keen to acquire the goblet and when the disappearance of the evidence was relayed to the court, Caballier Giovani moved his mask to scratch his face; subtly showing Remy a mischievous smile that confirmed it. Epifani must have seen it too, and she cackled loudly as De Launey fumed.

In the end, what had seemed like a strong case now hung in the balance, much to the chagrin of De Launey and the Marquis up in the gallery. When De Launey had no more witnesses to call, the flunkey rapped the pommel of the mace on the ground three times. De Launey bowed once more to the Cabal, then turned to the audience, "My Lords and Ladies, prey stand for the verdict."

The audience rose once more, a hush of expectation over the court. Even Epifani stood this time, after some cajoling from Colin. The Cabal rose as well; all except the Dogé.

"What happens now?" Colin whispered.

"Ain't you supposed to know?" Remy rounded on him. "You the one defendin'!"

The Baron thankfully knew the process, and leaned across to answer Colin's query. "Each of them will indicate their verdict by facing us if they believe we are innocent, or turning away if they think we are guilty. It's a majority decision, and the Dogé will only rule if it needs a tie-breaker."

De Launey called then on each of the Cabal in turn to indicate a verdict.

"Caballier Nero?" he asked, and the guildmaster of necromancers turned away. That wasn't unexpected; two of his own had been killed on the pirate galley, and his library had been attacked. He needed some scapegoats.

"Caballier Astrakhan?" The Cardinal turned away, which was also to be expected. The man was head priest of the Ziggurat, and Epifani had been rudely gesticulating at him all through the trial.

"Caballier Crosskeys?" The pirate captain paused when De Launey called upon him, seeming to consider it for a moment. Then he too turned his back. Valanthé visibly sagged; she had clearly hoped her former mentor would rule in her favour, if only to get his hands on her and her powerful gift.

Caballiers Huron and La Plagne also turned away when called upon, and the audience rippled with murmuring. It was over; five of the nine had judged them guilty.

De Launey smiled cruelly as he continued, unable to keep the gloating tone out of his voice as he called on the remaining Caballiers. "Caballier Giovani?" Remy saw his father shrug almost imperceptibly, and then he turned away as well.

Remy shook his head bitterly. He had no doubt that his father had calculated it was better for himself to be seen going along with the majority decision than to register a protest vote against. The devil wouldn't even vote to save his son's life unless it gained him something. Remy wasn't even surprised.

Caballiers Roux and Dandolo also returned a guilty verdict, so it was unanimous. The flunkey rapped the mace three more times, and the Cabal returned to their seats. The elderly Dogé nodded to each of his Caballiers, turning to have a quiet word with the two next to him, Roux and Dandolo. He then scribbled something on a slip of paper, and beckoned De Launey over to hand it to him.

De Launey took the slip and read it, frowned, then called for quiet once more. "My Lords and Ladies, the court has found the defendants guilty. His excellency the Dogé of La Crosse and his most esteemed Cabal have set retribution at ninety thousand livres."

A murmur rippled across the audience. Ninety thousand livres was a vast sum. From De Launey's tone though, Remy knew the pompous asshole had wanted more. It didn't matter; ninety thousand might as well be ninety million. They couldn't pay it.

"If the debt cannot be covered by payment or forfeiture of possessions," De Launey continued, "then your lives will be forfeit so that your corpses can be sold to pay more of the debt."

Colin turned to Remy and the others then, as the court chamber dissolved into chatter. He had disappointment in his face. "I am sorry everyone, I did my best. Let's pay the ninety thousand livres and get out of here. Maybe we could go somewhere for lunch? I'm starving."

They all stared at him dumbstruck. "Colin, do you have ninety thousand livres?" Valanthé asked.

"No of course not," he replied.

"Colin, none of us have ninety thousand livres," Remy clarified. He checked with the others. They all shook their heads mutely; they had nothing close to that.

"Oh," the kid said, slowly realising.

"Oh indeed." Valanthé said.

They all looked at each other for a long moment, then Epifani broke the silence. "Remy why are you smoking?"

Remy looked at her, confused; he sure wanted a cigarette but hadn't lit one yet. Then he yelped in surprise as he felt his chest burning; a sharp sensation just in front of his left armpit. Looking down, he saw his tunic was smouldering; a scorch mark in the shape of a perfect circle had formed out of nowhere. He unbuttoned his tunic and reached inside, finding two slips of paper had appeared in his inside pocket. He looked accusingly towards the dais at Caballier Giovani, who met his gaze from behind his mask.

Remy looked down at the slips. The first was a note, the words etched in ash as if drawn by a tiny burning ember. *'You didn't think I'd let your life be forfeit did you? We can work out how you'll pay me back later.'*

The second slip was a banker's draft for fourteen thousand, nine hundred and seventy three livres, thirteen sols and five deniers. It was an oddly exact amount, and Remy realised it was exactly his share of the ninety thousand, less the cash he had on him; calculated precisely to the denier. Damn him.

In truth he hadn't really doubted his father would bail him out, though he dreaded to think what he would have to do for him to repay such a debt. However that still left his friends forfeit. Looking back at the devil, he shook his head. He couldn't accept. The note in his hand smoked and a new line of text burned into the paper. *'Why not?'*

Remy gestured towards his friends. The note burned again. *'What are they worth to you, Remy?'*

In that moment he knew his father had played him, and had once again gotten exactly what he wanted. The bastard probably set up this whole trial in order to put Remy in his debt. All Remy had to do was nod, and he would be beholden to his father forever. One nod and he could free his friends. And all it would cost him was his own freedom.

De Launey came over then, his grin almost too broad for his fat face. The cohort of corpses from the foot of the dais had stepped forward with him, spears readied. "What will it be ladies and gentlemen? Cash or forfeit?"

Before they could answer him, before Remy could accept his father's ultimatum, the big double doors crashed open and all eyes turned to see who had barged in. It was an old woman with dark skin and white hair, and a red cloth tied across her blind eyes. Aunt Sundra.

"What was that price De Launey?" Aunt Sundra asked loudly. "Ninety thousand? I think you'll find this covers it," and she held up a slip of paper. A banker's draft.

***

Valanthé could have kissed the old woman. She had felt the panic rising, felt her gift bubbling over, and had no idea what was about to happen. If the old woman hadn't come in just then, she was sure she would have lost control. But now it settled back down as Aunt Sundra handed De Launey the draft, and the pompous ass looked ready to bubble over himself, he was so angry.

The court chamber was in uproar as the nobles in attendance all reacted to events by shouting and jostling. Valanthé was pleased to hear some cheering and clapping among the boos; though perhaps they were happy for the entertainment rather than happy that the defendants had been spared.

Amidst the commotion, Remy seemed to have acquired a bankers draft as well, and held it up above his head. Staring coldly at one of the Caballiers, he tore it in half for some reason, and this seemed to make the Caballier – Giovanni, she thought – very cross. Strange.

De Launey nodded tersely having verified the draft, and the cohort of Risen backed away to the foot of the stage once more. Aunt Sundra hobbled over to Valanthé and the others, leaning heavily on her cane, and beckoned them close.

"Thank you ma'am for saving us," the Baron said, relief written clear on his face.

"Can I ask why you did that?" Valanthé asked.

The old woman nodded. "Remember what I said about a malignant thread that would destroy the tapestry o' fate?"

"Yes ma'am," Valanthé said.

"Well after y'all were taken away, I searched the great tapestry to trace all ya threads, and I seen ya fates all be intertwined with that malignant thread in a complicated weave that I'm still tryin' to unpick. But I can see that all ya fates ha' been adjusted many times an' not by me nor Remy's ma. An' not by Domenico Dandolo neither. The adjustments go back at least ten years, maybe fifteen."

"I don't understand," the Baron said. "What does all that mean?"

Aunt Sundra shook her head. "I don' understand it neither. It's subtle, but y'all ha' been woven together by some unknown person, with the express aim o' bringin' ya here an' tyin' ya close to that malignant thread."

Remy looked confused as well. "But I thought you and mom were the last weavers?"

"That's what I thought. But it looks like someone else has been doin' it, and doin' it expertly."

"Are you sure it ain't him?" Remy insisted, pointing at Caballier Dandolo, who was in close discussion with the Dogé.

"Him who?" Sundra asked, perplexed.

"Domenico Dandolo," Remy hissed. "I tol' you he killed my mom an' took her gift. Now he's on the damn Cabal! Lord o' Roja no less!"

"That there ain't Domenico!" the old lady retorted shrilly. "The Lord of Roja is Citrine Don Dandolo, Domenico's mother! An' there ain't no love lost between mother an' son; they hate each other!"

Remy looked taken aback, and Valanthé saw the flames that had been in his eyes since the trial began, suddenly faded away.

"In any case," Aunt Sundra continued, "even if Domenico took your ma's gift, an' learned how to use it already, he still only been able to read the tapestry for the past month. An' like I said, your threads ha' all been manipulated for years. It weren't him that brought y'all together.

"Still, I looked into Domenico's thread after we met, an' I agree he's involved in all this somehow. But he headed out o' town yestereve; gone to his family's plantation inland. An' he'll be stayin' there for the next month. So Joanna should be safe in the meantime."

"I'm sorry ma'am," Valanthé interjected. "That's all very interesting, but you didn't answer my question. Why did you pay our court debt?"

"Well young lady, for good or ill, ya destiny's all tied up with that unborn child and the end o' the world he heralds, and I can't let ya die until I know what part y'all play. I looked at the weave that binds y'all together, an' I'm makin' a educated guess that y'all are here to help keep Joanna an' her unborn baby safe."

They all looked at each other thoughtfully. Valanthé narrowed her eyes at Epifani, and saw Remy doing the same. If someone had manipulated the fates to bring them all together to keep Joanna safe, why bring her? Epifani didn't seem to particularly want to preserve the status quo or protect Joanna from Domenico. Could Sundra be wrong? Had they instead been brought together to kill the child and bring about a great cataclysm? Thessu's Mother Oracle seemed to think that's exactly what he would do.

"So anyway," Aunt Sundra continued, "I'm takin' the risk an I'm trustin' whoever changed the tapestry knows what they doin'."

Here she wagged a finger at each of them in turn. "But no more burnin' down buildin's and causin' mayhem. Y'all workin' for me now. We got to keep Joanna safe."

"Yes Aunt Sundra," Remy muttered, and the rest of them parroted the same.

"Madame Sundra, was my thread included in the weave?" Colin asked tentatively.

The way the old woman looked around blindly, answered the question. She still couldn't see him, so didn't have sight of his thread. The boy realised this as well and looked downcast.

"I don't see another thread in the weave, no. But I'll look again, I'm sure I'll find ya close by."

The hubbub in the chamber was dying down, and the old lady wrapped up their conversation. "Get your affairs in order and I'll meet y'all back at the Queen o' the South, morrow's-eve."

De Launey was calling for hush now, and the audience settled back down into their seats, though many had already left the chamber since the main event was over.

"My Lords and Ladies, that concludes this evening's trial. Is there any other business to be put in front of the Cabal this eve?"

A long moment passed in which no business was raised, and then Valanthé realised the Baron had stepped forward, holding up a folded document. The deed they had taken from Palazzo Laurentin; the one that had granted De Ville manor to the Marquis.

"Your excellences," the Baron began. "I am Baron De Ville. This deed of ownership over De Ville Manor was granted by this court, on the basis that my descendants left no heirs. Since I am not dead, the grant was invalid and the deed needs to be rescinded."

The Baron had reached the foot of the dais, and offered the document up past the skeleton corpses to the Cabal.

The Dogé was already beckoning for his wheelchair, and absently took the deed from the Baron's outstretched grasp as the ancient turquoise skeleton corpse approached with the squeaky chair.

"Thank you your excellency," the Baron continued. "If it please the court to consider my request I would... oh."

The Dogé absently voided the deed with a stroke of his quill, then stamped it with his signet without bothering to read it. He handed it back to the Baron as his Risen assistant lifted him out of the throne and onto the wheelchair. That was that, De Ville manor was legally restored to the Baron.

A man started yelling from the audience gallery, then. A fat man in a red coat with a powdered wig that trailed onto the floor. The Marquis Du Laurentin.

"This is an outrage!" the Marquis shouted. "That is one of the very documents they stole from my palazzo! They robbed me and set fire to my home, and now they are getting away scot free! That manor is mine! It belongs to me!"

The ladies either side of him were restraining the man from causing even more of a scene, but he pushed past them to the front of the gallery tier, where he leaned out over the balustrade, still yelling about the insult to his honour. "I demand satisfaction!" he shouted.

The Baron had the good sense not to goad him further. Valanthé didn't. "If it's satisfaction you want, pal, you're a little late; I hear the orgy was last week!"

This got a titter of laughter from the audience, and Valanthé knew from the look the Baron gave her, that she had messed up. The Marquis quietened. He theatrically removed one of his white gloves and held it up, showing it to the audience, who hushed expectantly. The Marquis balled up the glove, and tossed it down at the Baron.

"I can bear your insults no longer! I demand the right of combat to settle the contested ownership of Isla Festa. I demand you duel me for it, or forfeit your claim!"

All eyes turned to the Baron then. Valanthé winced and looked apologetically at him. He frowned at her, but he walked over to where the glove had landed, and bent down to pick it up. He held the glove up resignedly, and a murmur of delight and anticipation rippled through the crowd.

"Send your seconds to arrange terms morrow's-eve," the Marquis shouted down. Then he narrowed his eyes and pointed right at Valanthé. "And I hope you choose her as one of your seconds."

Court was adjourned after that.

CHAPTER 21

"How's your leg holding up?" Thessu asked.

Valanthé tested her weight on it and grimaced. "Getting better."

He grimaced as well; he could smell the wound. He had examined it yestereve, after they returned to the manor from the Corto Dogé, and again this eve before they set out for Flotsam once more. It was healing well, and he had aged the wound further with healing power, but the fibres of the muscle had still not fully knitted together and it was still oozing pus.

He had advised Valanthé that it was still too soon for her to be walking unaided, but the young woman could be just as stubborn as Epifani when she wanted to be. He watched her closely as she hobbled across the deck of the cargo barge they had moored up against; she was in more pain than she was letting on.

Four of them had travelled once more to the floating pirate outpost of Flotsam, and Valanthé again led the way as they set off across the morass of wrecks towards the Queen of the South, with Colin and Epifani following behind her.

"Are you sure you don't want the crutch?" Thessu called after them.

Valanthé ignored the question. "Come on, it's this way."

Thessu sighed, then turned to follow as well. At least she had admitted that she couldn't fight effectively with such a wound, and therefore couldn't second the Baron for his duel with the Marquis. Remy and Gerard had volunteered instead, and they had dropped the two of them on Isla Verdé on their way to Flotsam. They both had errands to run, then would go to Isla Roja to agree terms with the Marquis' seconds. Meanwhile the Baron stayed behind at the manor to prepare for the duel, and the rest of them went to meet Aunt Sundra as agreed.

Thessu had wanted to report back to his order everything he'd learnt from the old blind woman about the tapestry and the Queen of the South and Joanna Pianna and her unborn child. However, he'd been unable to send any report; the little messenger bird had died in his satchel while he'd been imprisoned. Brother Superior would have to wait for an update. He would be most displeased. Brother Superior was always most displeased.

The junks that surrounded the Queen of the South were better guarded this time round; no doubt because they'd slipped past the pirate's ineffectual cordon the last time they came. They had no need to slip past this time; Sundra had invited them, and the pirates waved them past.

They found the old woman sat in a rocking chair on the balcony above the paddle steamer's lounge bar. She had her puckered mouth pressed around the fat black stub of a cigar, and was dragging on it languidly as she rocked back and forth, its embers glowing furiously as she sucked in its smoke. Thessu waved to her from the deck below.

Sundra breathed the smoke out without removing the cigar from her mouth, and it fumed around the stub, shrouding her in coils of smoke. Thessu could smell it from down below the balcony. Hickory and spice and ash. And tobacco of course.

"If you wavin' I can't see it," she said, as she removed the cigar to absently pick a speck of tobacco leaf off of her tongue. "I'm blind, remember!"

Epifani looked doubtful. "Bullshit," she muttered quietly to Thessu. "That old witch can see fine, I'm sure of it. Her blindness is a ruse!"

Thessu was certain her blindness was no ruse. Despite the cigar smoke, he could still smell the tumour that he'd detected the first time they'd met her. It was fully compressing her optic nerve and her prognosis was a matter of months, maybe less. He wondered if she knew. If her gift was like Remy's mother's, then she couldn't foresee her own future; indeed Thessu himself might be the only one who knew what her future held. Weeks of worsening migraines followed by rapid deterioration and death.

"Come on up," she called down through teeth that gripped the cigar once more. They headed up.

She had clearly known how many of them to expect; four wicker chairs had been arranged around a low table on the balcony where she rocked back and forth. "Have yourselves a sit-down," she said, "I took the liberty of pouring y'all some lemonade."

There was indeed a glass of lemonade for each of them on the table, though her own glass was empty, as was the pitcher in the centre of the table. They sat, and claimed a glass each.

"How's Joanna?" Epifani asked.

"She fine," the old lady said. "It's best we don't disturb her any more than we need to though. Ma strength is wanin' an' I can keep her loopin' better if there ain't no variations."

Sundra looked around then, before frowning. "Is the young man with you?"

Colin drooped, suddenly seeming disappointed. "I'm here." He had been leaning forward in the chair next to hers, seeming eager to be seen by the blind woman. She hadn't seen him.

She stopped rocking and felt blindly for him, finding his arm, and patted down to his hand which was resting on the arm of his chair. She placed her own hand reassuringly on his. "Could you be a dear and pour an ol' lady some more lemonade?" she asked him.

"I would, Madame Sundra," the boy said, "but the jug appears to be empty."

She tutted. "Think you can fetch a fresh one from the galley?" she asked. "Take those steps down two decks and the galley kitchen's on your left. You'll find fresh pitchers in the larder."

"Yes ma'am," he said, rising, and walked sullenly away.

Once he had gone, Sundra took a last puff of the cigar then stubbed it out in a heavy glass ashtray on the table. She beckoned the others in close then, with a conspiratorial wave. "I still ain't found that boy's thread. I'd expected to find it easily, since he been interactin' with y'all. I searched back all your threads lookin' for the interactions, and I can't see anythin' for him at all."

"What does that mean?" Valanthé asked.

"I ain't got a clue," the old woman replied. "I ain't never heard o' anyone who don't got a thread before, but I'm wonderin' if maybe he don't... Or maybe it's jus' hidin' from me? I had to reach out to him jus' now to check he even real at all. Where'd you say you picked him up? What's his story?"

Valanthé and Thessu quickly recapped how the boy had come to be part of their group; attaching himself first to Remy, because of their shared fiendling heritage.

"Wait!" Aunt Sundra interjected. "You tellin' me that boy is a fiendlin'?"

"Well yes; isn't it obvious?" Thessu said.

"Not to me it ain't!" she retorted. "I can't see horns, I'm blind, remember!"

Thessu sighed. The horns were far from the most obvious indicator. Couldn't she smell his unpleasant coal-tar scent? Couldn't anyone?

"Yes he's a fiendling," Valanthé confirmed. "He was adopted as a child by the Marquis Du Laurentin, and the Marquis disinherited him when his horns came through and he turned out not to be entirely human."

"So who his real parents?" Aunt Sundra asked, sounding perplexed.

"Nobody knows," Thessu replied. "Remy said the adoption was arranged by the dumber mummas."

"The Mamas D'Ombre?" queried Sundra.

"Yes that's it." Thessu agreed.

"Dumber mummas! Ha!" Epifani repeated, chortling. "I like that name better."

Thessu ignored her. "Remy wants to go and see his sister and get some answers about the adoption."

"I think I'd like to know those answers as well," Sundra concluded. "I can't help but think that boy's story is tied up wi' all this somehow." Here she gestured around at them and the paddle steamer.

"What makes you think that?" Thessu asked. "Surely if his thread isn't woven with ours he can't be too important a part of what's happening here?"

She shook her head. "No, young man you mistaken. If somethin' wrong wi' his thread; if it's missin' or out o' place so's I can't find it, then he's likely *more* important not less. It means whoever been manipulatin' ya threads took extra care o' his to keep 'im hidden from me. So he might actually be the most important piece o' the puzzle!"

They sat back in their chairs and absorbed that. Colin was important somehow. They'd better not tell him, it would go right to his head.

"Tell Remy to go see Elise wi' ma blessin'," Aunt Sundra said in conclusion. "Also remind him the Dandolo estate ain't too far inland o' there…" The inference was clear, Remy also had her tacit blessing to take his vengeance on Domenico while he was out of town. Thessu saw

Epifani's eyes narrow at the suggestion, but she didn't voice an objection. She looked shifty though. She always looked shifty. He would keep an eye on her.

Colin stomped back up the steps then, carrying a pitcher of lemonade that was sloshing over the sides. He didn't seem to notice the awkward silence as he filled Sundra's glass and placed the pitcher down next to it.

Aunt Sundra broke the silence. "Valanthé, I hope ya don't mind, I invited someone else to join us here. Someone very keen to talk to you."

She gestured down to the deck, and they all turned to peer over the balcony. A pirate was climbing down onto the deck below from the neighbouring junk. Tall and broad with a scar across his face running under a leather eye patch, his hair tinged with grey. A glossy black parrot fluttered down to perch on his shoulder as he landed on the deck.

"Crosskeys!" Valanthé hissed.

***

Remy found his father in the little bistro on Isla Maria Angelou; the same one he had taken him to. The devil was sat in a dimly-lit private booth at the back of the dining area, busy captivating a pretty girl with his charming conversation. Gusteau was wearing his kindly man face; his Caballier Giovani face. The girl – who couldn't have been more than twenty – probably had no idea who he was; no idea what he was. She looked completely smitten.

The devil looked up and smiled warmly as Remy approached, but Remy wasn't fooled. His father didn't much like to be disturbed, and as he strode over he knew he was interrupting a special moment for his father and the girl. The special moment when a predator snags his prey.

"Remy, what an unexpected pleasure," Gusteau said. "But I am indisposed as you can see. Perhaps we could 'ave a conversation a little later?"

Remy picked up the bowl from in front of his father. Soupe à l'oignon. He tipped it into the devil's lap.

The girl squealed, and Gusteau jumped to his feet, his eyes blazing with anger. Remy's eyes blazed angrily as well, and they stood staring fire at each other for a moment. The girl scooted out from the booth, pushing past him towards the washroom as she dabbed at her fitted bodice with a napkin; some of the soup had splattered onto her, and a gelatinous onion dribbled down her bosom.

Remy sat in her seat opposite the devil, and grabbed a hunk of bread from the little basket on the table. "How 'bout now?" he asked, buttering the bread with the girl's knife. "You still indisposed?"

Gusteau brushed the globules of onion soup off of his trousers onto the floor and sat. He reached for the wine bottle that sat on the table and poured himself a big glass of the deep red liquid. Remy, his mouth full of buttered bread, tapped his own glass with the butter knife. Gusteau tutted, and tipped the rest of the bottle into Remy's glass.

"You set that trial up to get me into your debt." Remy said through half-chewed bread. It was a statement, not a question. Gusteau shrugged and took a long gulp of his wine.

"That can only mean you want somethin' from me." Again, it wasn't a question, and Gusteau didn't respond.

"I don't know why you always got to manipulate people, Pop. Why can't you jus' ask me what you want from me. If it's in my power, I'll do it for you. I love you Pop, an' I know you love me too."

That seemed to catch Gusteau off-guard, and he sat back, swirling the wine around his glass, deep in thought. "I wish it were zat simple Remy. I am a devil, I am not capable of love. But I am capable of pride and ambition and desire. I wish to be proud of my son. I wish for you to share my ambitions and my desires. I will tell you what I want but not 'ere. Come, we will go somewhere more private."

The devil stood – his lap completely clean with no sign of the spilled soup – and he waited for Remy to rise. Remy downed the wine and pocketed some more of the delicious bread, then followed his father towards the exit.

"Please send another bottle of ze red, and inform ze young lady zat I will be back shortly," Gusteau said to the waiter as he passed, pressing a silver coin into the man's hand. Then he pushed open the door and they stepped out onto a cobbled alleyway.

Gusteau circled a finger in the air, summoning a fiery porthole to another place. It looked like a dimly-lit wooden cabin. Gusteau stepped through, and beckoned his son to follow. Remy followed warily.

Immediately he lost his balance, and caught it by leaning on a bulkhead. The cabin was aboard a ship; an ocean clipper perhaps. The deck creaked and rolled under him, and rivulets of water sloshed back and forth across the deck with each pitch of the ship.

Gusteau – no longer wearing the face of Giovani – chuckled at him. Remy could barely see him in the darkness of the cabin, his intense black silhouette fading into the shadows between the pitching light of the ever-setting sun that shone through a solitary porthole.

"I am stringing out ze Dogé's life," Gusteau said. "Jean Michel Don A'Tellio is a very frail old man. 'E should have died of 'is illnesses many months ago."

That was an interesting start. He had seen the Dogé in the court, and he did indeed look very frail.

"When ze time is right," Gusteau continued, "I shall let 'im die. Just as soon as I can be sure ze throne will go to Giovani and not to one of ze others."

"You want to be elected Dogé?" Remy asked, bewildered. His father always struck him as a little preposterous. He was a devil; he had the power to seize the throne if he wanted it. Why he wanted to go through the charade of playing Caballier and getting elected, Remy couldn't fathom.

"Caballier Dandolo will support me to be Dogé when ze time comes. But not if zere continues to be bad blood between you and Domenico. Citrine 'ates 'er son, but she won't abide you killing 'im. Instead let 'er make amends to us. Set aside your vengeance and take your place at my side! On my Cabal!"

"That's what you want from me?" Remy was incredulous. "You want me to let him live? He killed Mom!"

"You zink I don't know zat?" Gusteau fumed. "If you kill 'im, you get nothing for 'er death! But if 'e lives, you get ze most powerful family in La Crosse doing everyzing zey can to make it up to you! You get a seat on ze Cabal!"

"Vengeance ain't nothin', Pop. You taught me that! I won't do it!"

Gusteau sighed. "And zat is why I tried to get leverage."

They stared at each other for a long moment more, or rather, Remy felt his father's gaze bore into his own. His face was a mask of shadow.

"If zat is your decision, zen I won't insult you by trying to change your mind," Gusteau said finally. "But now you know what you are giving up to pursue zis path. I wish you good luck Remy."

Gusteau held out a silhouette hand, and Remy shook it. "Thanks Pop."

"You 'ad better be quick, Remy. Domenico is out of town right now, but I doubt 'e will be away from 'is army of guards for much longer."

Remy nodded. "I'll pay him a visit as soon as I've seen Elise."

The devil withdrew his hand and turned away. He circled another flaming porthole in the air at the far side of the cabin, which led back to the alleyway. The devil stepped through, becoming Caballier Giovani once more. Remy went to follow, but Gusteau held up a hand to stop him.

"Zis is for ze soup and ze girl," he said with a mischievous grin, and the flaming porthole vanished.

Cursing, Remy looked around. The ever-setting sun was on the ship's right. Whatever ship his father had ditched him on was sailing south, headed away from La Crosse. Damn him!

***

Valanthé stood warily, fondling the handles of her swords as Crosskeys approached the stairs up to the balcony. She wasn't sure how she felt about her former patron. He had tried to kill her friends at the Madrigal. He had sought her capture, and had handed her over to the sheriff. Then he had judged her guilty at the Corto Dogé. Still, he approached alone, his hands raised. And she had previously quite liked him.

"It's good ter see you lass," the pirate said in his seafarers accent, the salt water dripping off every syllable. "Might you an' I go fer a walk?"

"Aak! Go fer a walk, fatty!" repeated the parrot.

Valanthé was comforted by Thessu and Epifani's presence at her side. They also had good reason to dislike the captain, and stood warily, seeming prepared for trouble. Even Colin was hurriedly loading his pistol. He would need to practice that; he spilled his pouch of shot on the table, and the pistol balls scattered away, dropping onto the balcony floor and rolling across it.

"Aak! He's dropped 'is balls! He's dropped 'is balls!" the parrot clamoured, flapping its wings in excitement.

Valanthé cocked her head, her grip tight on her long sword, and lowered her weight ready to pounce, despite the screaming pain in her leg and the boy scrabbling for balls at her feet. "A walk? That depends," she said as menacingly as she could. "Were you there the eve Darkmourn visited my village? The eve he took my father's gift?"

Crosskeys shook his head sadly. "No lass. He already had his powers before I met him. He never directly said how he came by 'em. But I'll tell ye what I know if ye'll let me?"

Valanthé looked to Thessu and Epifani. Epifani still glared at the pirate, but Thessu placed a reassuring hand on Valanthé's shoulder and nodded his agreement. She loosened her grip and relaxed her posture; the pain in her thigh easing as she shifted her weight onto her good leg.

"We can walk on the deck there," she called down, "but I won't leave my friends' sight."

"Aak! Your friends are losers! He's dropped 'is balls!"

The pirate grinned. "That be acceptable. The foredeck it is."

She eyed him warily as she walked down the stairs to the deck, trying not to show him how much pain she was in.

"If you're here to take my gift, you're going to be disappointed," she told him flatly as she reached him. "I don't intend to give it up."

"Aak! Give it up, sugar tits!"

She gave the parrot a stony glare.

"I'm not here t'relieve you of yer gift, no," Crosskeys stated, his eyes mirthful. He gestured towards the far side of the foredeck, and they strolled in that direction. "Though it's no secret Val, that I'm envious of yer powers. Darkmourn had 'em, an' 'e became a legend."

"Aak! Darkmourn's a legend!"

"The truth is," the pirate continued, "Darkmourn ne'er told me how 'e came by 'is powers. I wouldn't know how ter take 'em from ye."

Valanthé knew how. The Bloode Goblette. Remy had told her how Dandolo had exsanguinated his mother to steal her gift. She wondered if Darkmourn had bled her father the same way. She wondered if Crosskeys would seem so agreeable if the goblet hadn't been smashed.

He seemed to sense her rising anger. He stopped and faced her, his face full of conviction. "He were a great man and a greater pirate, but he always had a darkness in him. An o'erwhelming guilt. It made him bitter and lonely and prone to awful bouts of melancholy. I won't take yer powers, Val," he grinned widely then, "because I'm far too jolly to take on that much darkness."

"Aak! Too jolly fat!"

Valanthé glowered at the pirate. "Tell me what you know about his visit to my village."

His grin faded away. "Darkmourn never spoke about it. All's I know fer certain is, he acquired his gift from some coastal village before I met him. What I pieced together o'er the years o' knowin' him, was that he did something terrible to that village."

That immediately resonated true. She knew that when her father was killed by brigands – which she now knew were pirates of the nascent Scarlet Fist – many people had been killed; many children. Roberos Luxalim – her father – had been the village schoolteacher. He and all the children in his care had been killed.

"Darkmourn weren't evil, Val. He were ashamed o'what he did," Crosskeys continued, "and o' the people he killed there. In fact I got the impression he ne'er meant to kill anyone. The only thing that gave him any solace was writin' to the families o' the people he killed askin' forgiveness, an' the hope that he might get a reply one eve. But he ne'er did. In the end he stopped tryin', and before he left on his last voyage, he gave me his letter-writin' signet. That's when I knew he was leavin' us – us who loved him best, loved him like family – an' he didn't plan on returnin'."

"Aak, he left his family!"

Here Crosskeys pulled out a worn brass signet and held it out to her. She took it and examined it. The ring of the man who killed her father. The design had a crescent shape and a hooded eye motif. It looked familiar somehow, but she couldn't place where she'd seen it.

"He wrote letters?" she asked.

"Aye, expressin' his remorse. They went unanswered."

She wondered if any of the letters had gone to her mother. Perhaps that's where she'd seen the signet design before?

"Did he really sail off the edge of the world?" Valanthé asked, still inspecting the ring; turning it over in her hands.

"Aye he did," Crosskeys nodded sadly. "He took a crew o' hardy souls keen ter explore what lay beyond the sunset sea, an' sailed right into the ever-settin' sun. Nobody's ever even found the edge, ne'er mind sailed beyond it."

"Aak! Found the edge! Sailed beyond it!"

"Did he find the edge?" she asked. She was torn between hoping he died and hoping he didn't; so she could have her reckoning with him.

"I like ter think so, or maybe he's still lookin'," the pirate replied. Then he shrugged. "Or maybe his ship became his coffin."

"Aak! He's in his coffin! He's in his coffin!"

"Come back to the Fist, Val," he asked earnestly, pulling her attention away from the ring suddenly. She looked at him incredulously. How could he think she would even consider it? Darkmourn had killed her father; the Fist had killed her father. She was more inclined to destroy the privateers than join them.

"Ye have Darkmourn's gift an' none o' his darkness," he continued, still sounding earnest, his usual jollity dispensed with. "Ye would be an asset to the Fist, Val. Ye could help me finish what he started; help me modernise and legitimize the fleet. If ye let me train ye, ye could have yer own command in a few years, yer own commission. There's no limit what ye could achieve; ye could even lead the Fist after me. Ye could be the greatest Sea Lord ever, surpassin' even him."

She almost considered it. Then shook her head angrily and thrust the ring back at him.

He took it with a nod, his face sad but understanding. "Well the offer be there if ye change yer mind."

"Aak! Ye change yer mind!" the parrot said.

***

The Baron took the time to clean and press his suit by hand, and starch and iron his shirt. Then he polished and buffed his wingtip shoes to a mirror shine. He shaved carefully, and dabbed cologne under his jawline. He trimmed his eyebrows and oiled and shaped his moustache.

He brushed and oiled his hair into a debonair side parting. Finally he dressed in the pressed black shirt and white cravat and pinstripe suit, the clothes all still warm from the iron.

He adjusted his collar and cuffs as he peered at himself in the looking glass, then plumped Belle up and tucked her into his breast pocket. He donned his shoes and spats and gloves, then top hat, cape and cane. He checked himself again in the glass, adjusting his collar and cuffs once more.

"I know," he replied softly to Belle, imagining the doll had told him to stop worrying.

He just hoped they were presentable enough; they were going to visit their ancestors.

He smiled a jocular half-smile at his reflection, and the anxious man in the mirror smiled back, far less convincingly than the Baron had hoped.

Resignedly, he walked down the stairs to the front door, then picked up the hooded viridian lantern that sat at the threshold, and walked out. Rufus growled at him encouragingly as he emerged.

"Thank you old bean," the Baron said in reply, giving the beast a weak smile. He headed round the perimeter of the manor to the gated stair that led down to the crypt below.

The ornate iron gate swung open for him, squeaking on its rusty hinges. He sparked the lantern on, and it sputtered to life, casting its eerie green glow down onto the bare stone steps lined with twisted iron railings and onto the heavy reinforced black door at the bottom of the stair.

He descended the stair, his steps crunching the dry browning leaves that had settled there, and which billowed away as he passed, disturbed by the ill wind which followed him down. The heavy black door swung open for him as well. It too squeaked on its hinges, announcing his arrival to the ancestors within.

His footsteps rang loudly on the cold stone as he stepped forth into the crypt, and the echoes rumbled back to him in tones of disappointment. The door creaked shut behind him, and only the dismal green glow of his lantern lit the catacomb, its pale green light dimmed by the thick press of disapproving shadow that filled the space between the soot-grey columns and low-vaulted alcoves of his family entombment.

He took a deep breath of stale, bitter air and paced forwards towards the main vault of the crypt, his footsteps continuing to ring on the stone and echo disappointment back to him.

Each shadowy alcove contained the remains of a hallowed ancestor. Not their bones or bodies of course; for once they'd died they had no use for those. The dead served the living, and that was just as true of the De Ville family as of everyone else in the realm of Twilight. No, the alcoves he passed each contained a hewn slate shelf, on which the most treasured belongings of a lifetime's accrual were preserved and enshrined.

The personality of each of his forbears was expressed by the things they had treasured. The most martial of his ancestors left weapons, while those of a more artistic bent left musical instruments or brushes or sculptors tools or other artisanal implements. The most religious left articles of faith, the highest achievers left masks of high office.

Here in the outer vault of the crypt, the shrines were to minor relations; the younger sons and daughters of the line, the subsidiary family branches, the unwed aunts and uncles. The Baron paused at each of the shrines in turn, dipping his head in silent respect. At some of them he stopped to adjust the artifacts where they had been disturbed by time and decay, and he flicked away the dirt and deterioration, restoring the displays to spotless condition. At each he felt the presence of an ancestor.

In the quiet darkness of the crypt they shared their sadness with him. Also their joy. He shared as well in their revulsion, their excitement, their desperation, their indifference, the full gamut of emotions. He heard their music in the vaulted echoes, and their laughter and their tears. Mostly though, he shared in their grief. Disappointment and despair and grief; all for what had become of the family line.

He lingered for a long minute at the shrine of his aunt. The adored older sister of his father the tenth Baron, she had died suddenly in her teenage years. His father had then mourned her for the rest of his life. He straightened her treasures. A silver hairbrush and looking glass. A leather-bound diary that locked with a silver clasp. A dollhouse for knitted dolls. He felt no presence at her shrine; she no longer resided there. He had never known her in life; she had died decades before he was born. But he knew her well now, for Belladonna De Ville was with him always.

He continued on and stepped into the main vault of the crypt, where the Barons De Ville had their shrines. Here the grief and disappointment was most acute, and the echoes hung mute in the air like the absent cry of a stillborn child.

He silently shared in all their emotions as he bowed to each in turn. Despite all the amends he was trying to make, the Barons still blamed him for the family's demise. And as he shared their emotions, he blamed himself. If he hadn't gotten himself stranded on the Queen of the South, his lesser heirs would never have inherited, and the family would not have died out. None of the amends he was making would ever be good enough. He was not good enough. He continued to loathe himself as he cleaned and tidied the shrines of better men.

"Honoured ancestors," he began once the shrines were all spotless. "I come before you seeking guidance."

He felt their annoyance. He didn't deserve their guidance. He should have stayed lost on the Poconovo. He should have called them 'Revered Ancestors' instead of 'Honoured ancestors'. He missed some moss under the Caballier mask of Hector De Ville, the seventh Baron.

He pressed on. "I have recovered the deeds to the islet and the manor, but now it seems I am to fight a duel with the Marquis Du Laurentin, who is a renowned duellist. I do not know how I can beat him."

He felt their dissatisfaction that the deeds had needed recovering in the first place. He shouldn't have taken so long to recover them. He shouldn't have accepted a duel. He should try pistols. He should forfeit. He should focus on more important matters like repairing his grandfather's desk and restoring his study which still had a pirate's round-shot in it.

He turned to the shrine of Hamish De Ville, the eighth Baron and a renowned duellist of his time. His basket-hilted claymore – now patinated with rust – was the centre-piece of his shrine. "Revered ancestor, might I ask you to accompany me to my duel, that I might benefit from your wisdom and experience?"

He felt his great-grandfather's indecision. He felt his contempt. He felt his desire to fight once more. He felt finally, his begrudging acceptance of the request.

Relieved, the Baron stepped forward to his ancestor's shrine. Family legends told of Hamish De Ville having fought with claymores and having won many duels, cutting his opponents to shreds.

He reached out to grasp the heavy sword from the shrine, but felt his hand drawn faintly towards another of his forebear's artifacts instead. Something else that his long-dead spirit wished to inhabit. He closed his hand around the carry-handle of an odd rectangular tin, its lid corroded shut. It was extremely heavy, and rattled like it contained hundreds of nails.

"Are you sure, revered ancestor, that I shouldn't take the claymore?"

He felt his great-grandfather's arrogant mirth. So, perplexed, he took the heavy tin. As he lifted it, he realised time's corrosion had perforated holes in the bottom of its thin outer casing, and a trail of fine powder trickled out. It had a distinctive smell to it. He felt the eighth Baron's annoyance, and he paused to clean the shrine once more. He lifted the tin again and flicked away the worst of the corrosion, careful not to spill any more of his great-grandfather's precious gunpowder.

***

Remy was late. This in itself was not surprising; Remy seemed to be late more often than not, however Remy was extremely late and Gerard frowned, expecting the bell towers of the island to chime elevenbells at any moment. After the others had dropped them off on Isla Verdé, he had returned with Remy to the Casa del Sol Riz, Gerard intending to pack his belongings and check out of his apartments while Remy confronted his father.

The Baron had earlier invited Gerard to stay at De Ville manor with him and the others, and it seemed to make sense that he do so while their fates seemed so intertwined. So he had changed and freshened up, and packed his clothes and belongings into trunks. Liveried porter corpses carried his trunks down to a waiting litter while he settled his account, then he bade the litter corpses to wait while he ran another quick errand.

Isla Verdé was a hive of activity. Carnival season was approaching, and the city was deep in preparation. Homes and businesses were decorated with masks and skulls, and teams of Risen were hanging more skulls and effigies from street lamps. The Piazza Grandé was cleared of corpse pens and filled instead with half-built stages and marquees being erected for the forthcoming festivities. The population of the core islands swelled during carnival season, and Isla Verdé was already noticeably more crowded than usual.

It had taken him two hours, but eventually Gerard found a cobbler willing to refashion some red sequined court shoes so that they might fit an alligator. He had paid the man handsomely, and the man promised to have them delivered to Rufus within a week.

Gerard had hurried through the crowds to get back to the Casa, anxious that he had kept Remy waiting and they had urgent business on Isla Roja; they had to go to Palazzo Laurentin and make arrangements for the Baron's duel.

Remy hadn't been waiting. In fact, Gerard had waited another two hours and still Remy didn't show. He had enquired of the maître d'hôtel as to Remy's whereabouts, and the man claimed not to have seen him at all that evening. Gerard grew increasingly concerned; if they didn't meet whoever was seconding the Marquis' before the eve was out, the Marquis could claim right of forfeit.

The bell towers around the island chimed elevenbells, and Gerard resolved to head to the Palazzo without Remy. Formal duels among the nobility were arranged by the seconds – two supporters of each principal – who met to agree the terms of the duel and also fought in it. He wasn't sure what the implication would be if only one of the Baron's seconds arrived to make arrangements; would the duel still be forfeit? He would have to find out, he could wait for Remy no longer; he had to get to the palazzo before newbells. He left a note for Remy with the maître d', then returned to the litter.

"Palazzo Laurentin, if you please," he said to one of the litter corpses. The corpse clacked its jaw, and Gerard climbed inside. Then the corpse folded the stepladder away, and closed the door behind him.

The Risen hadn't carried him far – perhaps only twenty yards – when there was a frantic knock on the door. Remy, finally! He bade the corpses halt, and threw the door open, but it wasn't Remy, it was

Valanthé. Damn, he had forgotten he had arranged for the others to collect them at tenbells, expecting to be long finished by then.

"What happened with the Marquis?" Valanthé asked, hauling herself aboard.

"I haven't been there yet, I'm on my way there now," Gerard replied, helping her up.

Valanthé frowned. "What do you mean you haven't been there yet? Cutting it a little fine aren't you?" Then she seemed to notice the fiendling's absence. "Where's Remy?"

"Missing," Gerard said concernedly. "He went to see the Don and hasn't returned. I waited as long as I could."

Valanthé seemed worried as well but, ever-practical, she pulled the door closed and rapped the ceiling of the litter for the Risen to get going. "You were right to set off without him, we have to get to the Palazzo before newbells. Remy can catch up with us later. I'll step in as the other second."

Gerard frowned at her. "Your leg isn't up to a duel, Val."

She shook her head. "I know, but it seems there's no choice. If you turn up alone, the Baron will be considered as having forfeit."

"Are you sure?" he queried.

"No," she conceded with a shake of her head. "But you can bet the Marquis would claim it so."

Gerard sighed, she was probably right. A duellist required two seconds. He wondered if perhaps one of the others could take Remy's place instead though, so that Valanthé didn't have to. All of them could fight. "Where are the others?"

"Epifani and Thessu are going to stay on the Queen of the South," she replied. "To better protect Joanna."

From her tone, it didn't sound like Valanthé quite believed that. He raised an eyebrow and she elaborated further. "Well, Epifani said she would stay to protect Joanna, and I think Thessu decided to stay to protect Joanna from Epifani."

Gerard also wasn't convinced her intentions were entirely aligned with theirs. "And what do you think? Is Epifani really going to protect her?"

Valanthé considered for a moment, then shrugged. "I don't think she knows yet. I think mostly she wants to stay there because she's got it into her head that the manor is deliberately screwing with her, leaking on her head and keeping her awake and suchlike."

Gerard chuckled. It was entirely possible that the manor had been screwing with her.

"Still, I'm glad Thessu stayed on the steamer as well," Valanthé concluded.

Gerard felt the same. But that still meant none of them could get there in time to take Remy's place instead of Valanthé. "What about Colin? Surely he didn't stay behind as well?"

"No, he's waiting with the barge. I wasn't sure if I would find you at the Casa."

The litter jostled slightly as the corpses turned them onto a main boulevard that led to one of the three bridges that crossed to Isla Roja. It was busy with traffic and revellers already getting into the carnival spirit a few eves early, and musicians played lively music from the balconies of the bars and bordellos that lined the bridge. The crowds jostled the litter further as they crossed to Isla Roja, but still they made it to Palazzo Laurentin with time to spare.

The litter drew up outside the palazzo gate. The grand entrance to the palazzo was on the western side of the building, where an ornate gatehouse stood astride the high wall that enclosed the palazzo's gardens. Gerard and Valanthé stepped down from the litter and strode to the gatehouse.

A guard corpse in the yellow and red livery of the Du Laurentins stood to immaculate attention in front of the wrought iron gate with halberd held ready.

The guard corpse rapped his halberd butt on the cobbles as Gerard and Valanthé approached. After a moment, another liveried figure stepped into view beyond the gate, visible through the ornate bars; a middle-aged gentleman in a fine red and yellow coat and powdered wig. The gatekeeper.

"Please inform the Marquis that Baron De Ville's seconds are here to agree terms for their duel," Gerard announced to the gatekeeper.

The man nodded curtly. "Of course sir. One moment please sir," and he hurried away to the house, leaving Gerard and Valanthé to wait outside the gate.

While they waited, Valanthé filled Gerard in on everything she'd learned on Flotsam about Colin's likely importance, and about Darkmourn's regret about raiding her village.

"Something's sure not adding up about Colin," Gerard concurred, frowning. "Perhaps we should all go with Remy to speak to the Mamas?"

"That was my thought too," Valanthé nodded. "Once we're done with this duel we should go to his village."

"How about your village as well?" Gerard asked.

That seemed to catch her off guard, and she looked at him quizzically.

"It sounds like you need to find out the truth about what happened the eve Darkmourn came," Gerard continued, "if you're considering becoming Crosskeys' apprentice?"

She looked sceptical, like she hadn't been seriously considering it. But maybe she should. "My mother would know what happened," she said dubiously.

"Then let's take a detour there as well," he concluded.

She didn't look very enamoured of the idea. In fact she looked apprehensive. She never had told him why she'd left her village in the first place.

"You're not keen to return home?" he asked.

She shrugged. "I'm not sure how welcome I'd be."

"Well, first things first, let's secure the manor for the Baron," he said, changing the subject. "We're not going anywhere if we don't win this duel."

Presently they spotted the gatekeeper returning, and behind him were two figures, presumably the Marquis' seconds. One of them he recognised; it was the bombastic court official from their trial – De Launey – dressed in polished steel cuirass over a heavy red coat and carrying under one arm a plumed cavalryman's helmet, while his other hand rested on the hilt of a heavy cavalry sabre. He marched towards them in tall black boots and riding spurs that clinked as he walked.

The other second was a woman, much shorter and slighter than De Launey, but perhaps more imposing, for she wore the black slashed doublet and cape of a necromancer. She had a slender rapier sheathed at her hip and walked with the easy confidence that only came with great skill. As they approached, Gerard saw that she was quite astonishingly beautiful.

Perhaps in her mid thirties, she had warm olive skin and big brown eyes that sparkled in the dusky light of the ever-setting sun. She had high cheekbones, an aquiline nose, and full lips painted ruby red. Her features were framed by two loose strands of hair which fell either side of her face, having escaped the neat plait which tied back the rest of her long black hair.

"Oof," Gerard said, as Valanthé elbowed him in the ribs. He took her hint and stopped staring at the woman in black.

De Launey marched over, with the woman at his side. He reached out a hand towards Gerard. Gerard reached through the bars of the gate to shake his hand. De Launey pulled his hand away, aghast.

"I'm not shaking your hand, you imbecile!" he admonished. "I want that!" He pointed at the Marquis' white glove which Gerard carried on behalf of the Baron. He was supposed to return it to formally accept the duel.

Gerard felt his cheeks flush, and handed the glove to the pompous man, who snatched it away. The woman next to him stepped forward then, her eyes sparkling with amusement as she smiled warmly.

"Bongiorno, Signor," the woman said. "I am Donatella Del Torro Rosso. You may shake my hand-a," and she carefully removed her own black lace glove and reached a delicate hand through the bars. She had a musical voice, and damn if that accent wasn't magical!

Gerard clasped her hand. She had a strong grip and surprisingly, a callused palm. Gerard understood from that, that the rapier was not just for show. "Gerard Malblanq," he said awkwardly, suddenly aware of how squeaky his voice sounded. Valanthé elbowed him again, and he let go. "And may I present Miss Valanthé Luxalim."

"Charmed-a," the woman said, smiling a half smile at Valanthé. "You know of course my colleague-a, Lemuel Simms De Launey, the Comté D'Arnault?"

"Charmed," De Launey said, sounding anything but.

De Launey stuffed the Marquis' glove into his sword belt, and placed his cavalryman's helmet on his head. Either by happenstance or design, the low brow of the helmet forced him to look down his nose at Gerard and Valanthé. "His grace the Marquis Du Laurentin wishes to settle this matter as soon as possible," he said firmly.

"As does his grace the Baron De Ville," Gerard replied, equally firmly. De Launey curled his lip. Perhaps mere Barons didn't warrant a 'his grace'.

Donatella interjected then, saying, "the Marquis has the honour of sponsoring a revel at the Greater Pit arena morrows-eve-a." She turned to Valanthé then, "if morrow's-eve is not too soon-a, he could add you to the schedule at tenbells-a?"

Valanthé and Gerard exchanged a look. The revels were grand entertainments laid on for the cityfolk by the wealthy elite in the run-up to Carnival. The Marquis must have paid a fortune to sponsor the first revel of the season in the Greater Pit. It would be packed with spectators.

"I'm not sure the Baron wishes the duel to be such a public affair," Valanthé countered.

"It will be quite impossible to arrange a duel that isn't public-a," Donatella replied. "Crowds will watch wherever we agree upon-a. The arena has the benefit of keeping spectators at bay-a."

"Fine," Valanthé frowned. "Swords or Pistols?"

"Our side have suggested the time and venue. The choice of weapon is yours," De Launey sneered. "You may bring whatever weapon or weapons you desire."

"Then we shall do precisely that," Gerard replied. "We propose no limitation on weapons or format."

It was De Launey's turn to frown then. Good. Gerard had seen his friends fight; they would do well in a melee. Plus they had plenty of captured pirate muskets and pistols to choose from, back at the manor.

"First blood, death or yield?" the cavalryman replied.

"Yield," Gerard replied, and Valanthé nodded.

"Very well," De Launey stated. "First principal to yield will be declared the loser and will relinquish all claim on Isla Festa to the victor. No weapons prohibited. Morrow's-eve at tenbells at the Greater Pit."

"We'll be there," Gerard said.

"It was a pleasure to meet you, Gerard-a," Donatella said, smiling. "I look forward to seeing you again morrow's eve-a."

"Um yes, I also do look forward to you." Gerard fumbled.

"Ciao Gerard. Valanthé," she said, then turned and walked away without looking back. Gerard watched her go, and earned himself another elbow in the ribs. "What?" he asked.

Valanthé rolled her eyes and beckoned back to the litter. "Come on, let's go tell the Baron."

"One moment," Gerard replied. "Theres something I need to do first."

Before they left, Gerard liberated the halberd from the guard corpse. It was just the thing to use against a cavalry sabre and a rapier.

CHAPTER 22

The Piazza Grandé was just as busy the next eve as it had been the last time Valanthé had been there, though it was an entirely different sort of crowd this time. The corpse markets were closed for carnival season, and so the pens of cadavers and Risen and associated trades were gone, replaced with food stalls and stages and sideshows. The ingrained smell of death was ever-present, but now masked by the mingled scents of charred meats and incense and fireworks.

For the next two weeks, the Pits would be restored to their original purpose, as arenas for games and parades and races and gladiatorial contests and entertainments of all sorts. These revels would be sponsored each eve by a different noble house eager to showcase their wealth and curry favour with the city folk and nobility. With the Dogé in such poor health, the season's revels were expected to be particularly lavish, as potential successors vied for favour.

The revels in the Greater Pit this eve were sponsored by the Marquis Du Laurentin, and Valanthé heard the roar of the appreciative audience from across the plaza. It sounded packed in there. And it sounded like the audience were enjoying the entertainment thus far.

"Make way for the Baron De Ville, come to fight for his honour in the Greater Pit!" yelled Colin, parting the crowds as he led their little group across the piazza. Valanthé and the Baron marched behind him, the Baron carrying a long-barrelled musket and Valanthé a pistol in addition to their usual weaponry. Gerard brought up the rear, loudly rapping the butt of his halberd on the cobbles with each stride. The big man had foregone his usual flamboyant style, instead wearing an understated grey doublet under a polished steel cuirass and pauldrons.

They drew many looks of surprise and disquiet as they crossed the plaza. Colin repeated his call at intervals, quite unnecessarily since the crowd hastened out of their way as soon as they saw them. Several people even screamed at their approach, startled by the sudden appearance in their midst of the duellists… and of the giant alligator that accompanied them.

Valanthé struggled to contain her laughter at the sight of Rufus waddling along at Colin's side, the beast lifting his head pompously – regally even – and quite ignoring the commotion he was causing. A woman with a yappy little dog walked obliviously almost right into him before falling over herself in fright and scrabbling to grab the dog out of danger. The yappy dog shat itself right in her arms, and Valanthé had to mask her face with her hand to keep her composure. She pressed her knuckles firmly into the hollow of the wound in her thigh, letting the jolt of pain wash away her mirth. Composed, she kept on walking and tried not to look at the silly alligator.

By the time they reached the Greater Pit, they were accompanied by a buzz of excitement and a substantial following of people. Stewards met them at the entrance to the arched tunnel that led to the heart of the Pit, while the crowd of followers headed round to public stairs that led straight up to the tiered stands, there to join the audience and, hopefully, to cheer for the Baron.

Valanthé heard the raucous noise of the arena grow louder as she walked through the tunnel, and she saw the vast space had been completely transformed from when she was last here buying galley corpses for Captain Lugwort; the corpse pens had gone, and the tiered stands were filled with thousands of people. Perhaps ten thousand had turned out for the evening's revel in the Greater Pit. She shared an apprehensive look with the others. It was a far larger crowd than she'd been expecting, and she wasn't sure how their duel could possibly entertain such a crowd.

The stewards held them back at the mouth of the tunnel while the previous round of entertainment – a theatrical re-enactment of a famous sea battle – was concluded. The arena floor was filled with wreckage as mock 'ships' – in reality, flimsy wooden replicas that moved on wheels – did choreographed battle against each other with staged cannon-fire.

The last two ships were manoeuvring around the arena, each pushed across the sand by a cohort of Risen corpses half-concealed in their hulls. Above deck, one of the ships was crewed by living sailors – seemingly the heroes of this diorama – and the other by Risen. The Risen fired their broadside of cannonets – all smoke powder and no shot

– and the heroes gamely fell about as if struck by grapeshot, accompanied by boos and jeering from the audience. Valanthé smiled. She had recently seen first-hand what real grapeshot could do.

The captain of the heroic vessel staggered to his feet theatrically, accompanied by cheers from the audience, and raised his sword up high as the other heroic sailors did likewise. The captain lowered his sword and the heroic ship fired back with a boom that echoed around the arena, and Valanthé realised then that their own cannonets had been properly loaded with shot. The cannonets were small calibre, and likely the powder was spiked to reduce the blast and the danger to the audience, but still the flimsy corpse ship was torn apart by the close-range barrage.

Wood and other debris pattered around the vessel, and the corpses on deck of the unfortunate ship were definitely not acting when they fell, mangled, off its shattered deck. The audience cheered and the heroic captain and crew of the victorious vessel lapped up the adulation as they rolled away, out of the arena through the tunnel at the far side, bowing and waving as they went.

The Risen that had survived the encounter then picked themselves up from the wrecks around the arena and cleared away the debris, wheeling their broken wrecks out through the tunnel, then returning to pile wood and mangled corpses onto handcarts.

The heroic crew came back out on foot to take a bow, and the audience showed their appreciation with long applause. The nobles in their exclusive pavilion in the centre of the north stand showed their own appreciation by tossing down purses of coins, which the heroic crew greedily scurried over to collect.

Valanthé had rarely been as nervous as she was then, having to follow such a spectacular show and fight in front of such a huge crowd. What was she thinking? She couldn't fight with her leg only half-healed; she would make a fool out of herself. Where in the hell was Remy? Why hadn't he returned? She felt the panic rising; felt her wild power surging. Gerard must have sensed the danger, and he grabbed her shoulders with gauntleted hands and held her firm.

"Save it!" he urged. "Save it for when you need it!"

She nodded and swallowed hard, and Gerard released her. The Baron handed her a cup of water and she downed it gratefully.

"What are you doing you silly reptile?" Colin said.

Valanthé looked around to see the boy admonishing the alligator. Rufus had found a discarded tricorn hat on the ground just outside the tunnel, and seemed to be trying to wriggle it onto his head.

Laughing, Valanthé knelt down to help him, her panic subsiding for now. She positioned the hat between his ears and the alligator snorted out a puff of breath. "You're welcome," she told him.

***

A man, liveried in the yellow and red of Du Laurentin, strode out into the centre of the arena floor and the crowd hushed expectantly as he gestured for quiet. The man – the arena announcer – raised a speaking cone to his mouth and bellowed loudly and clearly through it, and his words echoed round the hushed arena.

"Boy, do I have a treat for you next!" He paused for the smattering of applause to die down, before continuing. "Your gracious host this evening, his grace the Marquis du Laurentin…"

Colin booed loudly as his adopted father's name was announced. Rufus joined him with a loud rumbling growl. Gerard wanted to hear what the man was saying though, so turned to shush the two of them.

The announcer had continued regardless, "…will be settling a score with the nefarious Baron De Ville and his dangerous posse of thieves, arsonists and murderers!"

He paused then for the crowd to jeer, encouraging a louder response from the crowd by beckoning for more boos. Once it died down again, he continued through the speaking cone. "The seconds met yestereve and agreed an unlimited melee! No weapons prohibited!" Here he paused again as the crowd cheered loudly. They seemed to welcome the prospect of a melee rather than a staid formal duel with swords or pistols.

"Before the duellists enter, I have a request from Baron De Ville's seconds," and here he unfurled a scroll and read from it. "*'Kindly instruct the crowd not to boo the Baron as the sound makes his bowels loose, and he might have a trouser accident'*… What do you all have to say about that?"

The crowd booed and jeered loudly.

"Why would you send that note?" Colin asked incredulously. "They will boo louder now!"

"We didn't, of course!" Gerard growled back angrily. "He's trying to turn the crowd against us!"

Colin sucked in a breath. "Why, are we the bad guys? Don't the bad guys always lose?"

Gerard scowled at the youth, and saw Valanthé doing the same. Colin really was quite infuriatingly naïve. The Baron seemed to be ignoring the crowd and was loading his musket as he stared intently across the arena to the opposite tunnel, where the Marquis would be emerging. He wasn't visible yet.

"My Lords and Ladies, I give you Baron De Ville and his cronies!" The announcer gestured towards them, and the stewards hustled them forwards into the arena.

"Good luck," Colin said, a look of worry on his face as he hunkered down to sit with Rufus. They would watch the duel from the tunnel.

"Thanks," Gerard said, and marched out with his halberd raised, he and Valanthé on either side of the Baron.

As they stepped out of the tunnel and into the acid green light that shone down onto the arena floor, the crowd booed and jeered as loudly as they could, joined and encouraged by the announcer. When the jeering started to die down, the announcer faked a bathroom noise through the speaking cone, while pointing incriminatingly at the Baron, and the jeers continued anew, along with laughter.

They made their way to the centre of the arena, doing their best to ignore the hostility of the crowd. The announcer stalked back away from them in mock fear, and Gerard was tempted to smack him, or at least give him a reason to be fearful, but knew that would just reinforce their status as the heels, so he swallowed down his anger and checked on Valanthé.

She looked spooked. Not afraid – or at least not afraid of the fight to come – but she looked like she had looked outside the Madrigal, when he had seen her gift explode as a wild surge of toads. She looked like she was struggling to contain it once more. He gave her a reassuring smile, which she returned half-heartedly.

When it became clear to the announcer that they weren't going to rise to his bait and chase him around the arena, he introduced their opponents. "Please put your hands together and welcome your gracious host for this evening's revel, the Marquis Du Laurentin!"

He stretched out the last syllable of the Marquis' introduction for a full ten seconds, as the crowd erupted in applause, and the stewards by the far tunnel stepped aside. There was a thunderous noise of hoofbeats, and suddenly a bone-white war chariot emerged at full pelt, drawn by three corpse horses.

The Marquis, clad in a powder-white helm and matching cuirass over a white surcoat, drove the Risen horses with one hand on the reins as he waved to the crowd with the other. Not normally a popular man, he had laid on a fine show for the crowd this evening, and they showed their gratitude with loud applause.

The chariot thundered around the perimeter of the arena, as Gerard and the others watched with narrowed eyes. "Show-off," Valanthé muttered.

Not done, the announcer continued. "And please welcome as well the Marquis' seconds, Donatella Del Torro Rosso, and Lemuel Simms De Launey, the Comte D'Arnault!"

Two more bone-white war chariots emerged then, both identical to the Marquis'. Donatella and De Launey wore matching white surcoats and cuirasses, De Launey wearing his plumed cavalry helmet, also powdered white. Donatella had foregone her necromancer's robes for the duel, and had also left her long hair loose; it trailed behind her as she rode like a black pennant in the wind. She was a vision of grace and beauty and carefree abandon. A raven-haired Siren.

"Ouch!" Gerard said; Valanthé had elbowed him again.

The three corpse chariots continued to race around the perimeter of the arena floor. Gerard wondered how many more laps they'd do before they reined in and got off their stupid chariots; he was ready for the duel to start already. He looked around for the announcer so he could tell him to get on with it, but couldn't see the man; he must have withdrawn already.

It dawned on Gerard then that the Marquis and his seconds had no intention of getting off their chariots for the duel. He cursed under his breath. *'No weapons prohibited'*. They had been played.

"Any chance Jeff is in the stands with the manor's big gun?" Gerard asked.

The Baron shook his head grimly. "I'm afraid not, old boy."

He heard the muffled sounds of the island's bell towers ringing tenbells over the din of the crowd. Then a gunshot rang out. It had begun.

CHAPTER 23

The Marquis had fired the opening shot. He held a smoking flintlock pistol in one hand, and the chariot's reins in the other as he raced across the arena. Whoever he had been shooting at, he had missed. Gerard saw the Baron level his musket to fire back, while he and Valanthé also reacted quickly once the duel had started, jogging to intercept the nearest chariot. Gerard led the way with Valanthé just behind him, slowed by her injury.

The nearest chariot was De Launey's. The cavalryman was driving the chariot down the long straight of the arena floor's perimeter, and Gerard jogged towards its path, ready to attack him with his halberd as he drove past. De Launey instead jerked the reins aside, steering the chariot directly at him, intending to ride him down.

Seeing the danger but unable to halt his momentum, Gerard instead increased his speed to cross the redirected chariot's path just in front of it, intending now to attack De Launey from the far side. With horror though, he realised Valanthé was too slow to do the same, she was still in the chariot's way.

He spun as he reached the far side of the chariot, already swinging the halberd in a downward arc at it as it raced past him.

His halberd scythed down between the back of the corpse horses and the front of the cart, the halberd shaft striking the draught pole that connected the cart to the yoke. De Launey nearly dropped the reins as they too were snagged by the halberd, but he kept hold and grinned cruelly at Gerard as the cart continued past him, still aimed straight at Valanthé.

Gerard – his momentum still carrying him towards the perimeter of the arena floor – wrenched the halberd with him, pulling with all his strength. Its blade hooked the draught pole and yanked the chariot back towards the perimeter and away from Valanthé.

The chariot careened right past her, forcibly steered towards the perimeter instead. Horses and cart both scraped along the wall of the perimeter, accompanied by shrieks of delight from the baying crowd and curses from De Launey. Valanthé was unharmed, but it had come at a cost; Gerard's halberd had been wrenched out of his grip and dragged away, still snagged by the chariot.

Valanthé joined him by the perimeter wall, but another chariot was now headed down the straight, following close behind De Launey's. Donatella's.

Her chariot's path would narrowly pass them by, but as it approached, the necromancer raised her hand towards them. Black flames lanced forth from her outstretched hand. Balefire! Donatella must be a very powerful necromancer indeed!

The black flames engulfed Gerard, and his back slammed into the perimeter wall as the balefire flooded over him like an onrushing ocean wave. This too earned shrieks of delight from the crowd. Blinded by the searing pain, he pushed off from the wall, lashing out blindly with a bare fist at the passing chariot.

He felt his punch impact flesh, and the crunch of bones breaking beneath, as the chariot blazed past them in a thunder of hooves and a whoosh of displaced air. He blinked away tears as the necromancer's balefire subsided, leaving him scorched and smoking. He looked round for the chariot, which he saw was now careening wildly, Donatella struggling to control it.

"Did I get her?" Gerard asked, patting down the burning embers from his doublet.

"You punched a horse," Valanthé replied. "I'm useless here," she continued bitterly. "Can you get me onto that chariot?"

Donatella's chariot hadn't gone far; it had lost much of its speed as the corpse horse had foundered and she'd had to wrestle back control. "I can try."

Valanthé was already hastening after the chariot. Gerard raced after it as well, grabbing her outstretched arm as he passed her. He took two more big paces towards the chariot, then hauled Valanthé forwards, launching her towards it with all his might. She flew forwards as he stumbled and fell, landing hard on the arena floor.

Spitting the sand out of his mouth, he saw with relief that she'd made it onto the back of the chariot. He also saw his halberd lying on the ground a little farther ahead.

***

The Marquis' second shot whizzed past the Baron's shoulder. That was much closer than his first shot had been, and he hoped the Marquis had no more loaded pistols. The Baron still had his musket loaded and levelled at him, tracking his target as the Marquis drove the chariot down the long straight of the arena floor. He pulled the trigger and the flint struck down the steel, sparking the powder in the chamber.

The gun fired with a bang and a plume of smoke, and the shot slammed into the wooden side of the Marquis' chariot. The panel splintered, but the shot didn't penetrate. He had missed. The Baron narrowed his eyes, feeling annoyance at his own incompetence. Wetting his lips, he reloaded the musket. His annoyance wasn't his own; it was his great-grandfather's. He had brought it with him.

Without taking his eyes off his target, he poured powder and rammed a wadded ball down the muzzle, then primed and cocked the flint and steel once more.

The Marquis had turned the chariot back round, but instead of aiming down the back straight, The Baron saw that he was lining the chariot up to drive straight at him. He saw him flick the reins to encourage the Risen horses to another charge. The unrelenting corpses knew no exhaustion, no fear; they knew only obedience. Lining up as directed to run him down, they barrelled forwards towards him.

The Baron waited until the last moment, then squeezed the trigger and the bullet blasted out of the barrel towards its target, and he knew this time his aim was true. He dove clear as the horses thundered past, landing hard on the arena floor, where he rolled and looked back to watch the Marquis' fall from his chariot.

But he didn't fall. The bullet had dinged off the man's helm; a glancing shot that scraped a gouge out of its white powder coating. The Marquis jolted back, then recovered, urging his chariot forward once more.

Ignoring the self-loathing that wasn't his own, the Baron reached again for his musket. The back of the chariot was open. If he wanted to win, he should hold his shot next time as the Marquis approached, and shoot him in the back after he passed. It was a cynical notion, but his cynicism also wasn't his own. He would do as his great-grandfather bade.

As he reloaded, he looked to his friends. He saw Valanthé struggling with the necromancer on the back of her chariot. He saw Gerard collect his halberd from the sand then turn and race towards him. The Baron then looked round to find the third chariot; and dove out of its way; De Launey was driving it directly at him.

He landed just wide of the chariot's path, but looked back with surging horror – his great-grandfather's as well as his own – Belle had fallen from his pocket and the nearest corpse horse's hooves were about to trample her into the sand. He reached out and grabbed at her urgently. His hand closed around her, then he rolled away across the sand as the horses thundered past just inches away from him.

De Launey leaned out over the side of the chariot cart as it passed, swinging a vicious scything cut at him with his cavalry sabre as he lay prone. He kept rolling, and felt the crunch of the sabre striking the heavy tin that was slung across his back. He felt his great-grandfather's indignation mixed with his own relief; the heirloom might have just saved his life. Hopefully the sabre hadn't rent its casing too badly.

Picking himself up from the ground, he tucked Belle securely back into his breast pocket. The crowd had cheered De Launey's sabre strike, but the Baron also registered some applause as he rose unharmed. The booing certainly seemed to have reduced.

He saw De Launey looking back at him from the chariot as it continued past; levelling his sabre directly at him in an unspoken promise. However, the man hadn't seen Gerard approach to intercept him. Gerard swung his halberd down in an arcing cut at the chariot.

De Launey must have spotted him at the last second as he pulled back hard on the reins; but too late. Gerard's halberd sliced down, chopping into the back of the near-side corpse horse just behind its lank rotten mane. The strike cleaved the horse near in half. The disanimated horse collapsed to the arena ground, dragging the others down with it.

The cart's momentum carried it forward over the crumpled horses, the draught-pole breaking in half as the cart flipped up and over, landing hard on its top-side with De Launey thrown clear. He hit the ground hard and lay still. The crowd screamed a mix of horror and elation at the destruction.

The Baron needed to finish reloading. He looked for the ramrod he had dropped when he dove clear of the second chariot, and winced as he found it in the sand. The ramrod was bent almost double – the chariot must have rolled right over it – and he felt the pang of borrowed self-loathing even more acutely. He discarded the useless musket and reached for his sword cane, looking round to see where the Marquis was. As usual, he would have to do things the hard way.

***

Valanthé had surprised Donatella when she'd appeared on the back of her chariot. She had almost buckled as she landed due to the pain in her thigh, but she grabbed the rail and hauled herself upright. Donatella had to grab the rail with both hands as well, as the cart rocked wildly with the impact of Valanthé's arrival.

Despite the pain, Valanthé recovered first, and lunged forward to grab the necromancer and pull her free of the rail. She had seen the horrific necrotic wounds that the Baron and Epifani had sustained when they had fought with necromancers, so she knew to avoid skin-on-skin contact with Donatella. Valanthé instead wrapped her fingers through the bitch's hair and yanked it back. Donatella yelped, but clung on to rail and reins with one hand, turning to reach back at Valanthé's face with her other hand. Valanthé flinched away as the necromancer grabbed at her, fighting to prevent the woman from scouring the flesh from her face.

The chariot raced onwards around the arena as the women struggled, the cart rocking wildly under their shifting weight and Valanthé could barely hear the crowd over the thundering hooves and onrushing wind. She struck the necromancer's grasping arm aside finally, and gathered it under her own arm, pinning it in place even as it spewed black shadow flames that lapped up her back. She pulled herself closer to the woman, relaxing the tension in the hair she'd grabbed. She wrapped her loosened fistful of Donatella's hair around the bitch's neck, then yanked it hard. Donatella yelped, and let go of the rail and reins to claw at the hair that tightened on her throat.

Valanthé felt the heat of the balefire scorching up her back. She pulled the hair tighter across Donatella's throat, but with neither of them now holding the rail, they both staggered backwards and teetered on the edge of falling from the chariot.

Panic suddenly surged in Valanthé; if they fell now, she would land hard on the ground with Donatella on top of her. She would take the brunt of the impact. Letting go of Donatella's pinned arm, she reached instead for the side rail, but Donatella must have realised the same thing, for she placed a foot on the front rail and pushed them both backwards off the back of the chariot.

The panic bubbled over in that instant between falling and landing. The ground rushed up to hit her hard, and she braced for the impact.

Her landing was cushioned by hay bales that had appeared beneath her. Her wild surging panic had gifted her hay bales.

Donatella landed on top of her nevertheless, forcing all the breath out of her lungs. They both lay motionless for a moment, Donatella cradled in her arms almost tenderly, and the breath that Valanthé sucked in contained the sweet jasmine scent of the older woman's perfume. Then the balefire that had been lapping up her back ignited the hay, and all Valanthé could smell was acrid smoke.

Donatella reacted quickest, jumping up to her feet and drawing her rapier as she gracefully turned into a fencing stance in one smooth movement. Valanthé leapt up after her, and immediately buckled. She had asked too much of her half-healed leg, and it gave way under her weight. She staggered but stayed upright, managing to hobble clear of the hay bales. Checking over her shoulder she saw the flames had spread quickly and the bales burned furiously, but her combat leathers merely smoked; thankfully her back was not aflame.

She returned her focus to Donatella, who still stood in fencing stance in front of her. She narrowed her eyes at the necromancer and tossed down the clump of black hair she still held in her hand. Donatella's face contorted into a scowl as she reached up to her scalp and found the bare patch behind her right temple. The bitch spat an angry curse. Valanthé drew her swords.

***

Gerard wrenched his halberd free of the wreck and stalked over to where De Launey lay. The man looked bloodied and dazed, but otherwise unharmed. He kicked the man's sabre away from him and held the blade of his halberd over his neck.

"Do you yield?" Gerard asked.

The man winced and looked away. Gerard lowered the blade to rest across the top of his chest where the powder-white cuirass had pulled away. Blood welled up under the blade and trickled down the line of his collarbone, soaking into his stark white surcoat.

"Do you yield?" Gerard repeated, more forcefully.

The man grimaced and nodded. "I yield," he said, in barely a whisper.

Gerard shouldered his halberd and reached out a hand to help the man up. The man looked at Gerard's hand in disgust and refused to take it, pushing himself up without help. Gerard shrugged and left him.

When he looked up, he saw Valanthé and Donatella both fall from the chariot at the far side of the arena, Valanthé wreathed in black flame. They landed on something flammable – hay maybe? – and both leapt up as the balefire sparked it to ignite.

He also saw the empty chariot from which they'd fallen, careening wildly across the arena, the corpse horses still galloping but uncontrolled. They seemed to be following the Marquis' chariot, which was reaching the end of the straight. It looked like the Marquis was trying to reload his pistols. The unmanned chariot slowed at the end of the straight, the corpse horses struggling to coordinate a turn. Then he saw a figure grab hold of the empty cart and haul themself aboard. Gerard smiled; it was the Baron.

That answered his unspoken question of which of his friends to help; he would leave the Marquis to the Baron. Valanthé needed him more. The crowd – seeming much more appreciative of the three of them than they'd been when the duel started – urged him across the arena and cheered the Baron up onto the chariot.

Gerard had crossed two thirds of the way to Valanthé when he heard the rumble of hooves behind him. Surprised, he turned just in time to fend off a cavalry sabre. He parried it with the shaft of his halberd, and staggered backwards. De Launey had yielded, yet the jackass had reclaimed his sword and mounted one of the surviving corpse horses from his wrecked chariot!

The crowd seemed to think it unfair too, and they booed the cheat loudly.

De Launey reined the corpse horse round for another pass, and Gerard set his halberd to meet the charge. As the horse galloped towards him, he braced to impale the beast on the spike of his halberd, but De Launey was too wily a horseman to ride onto a spike, and he veered past, slashing a vicious swipe that skidded across the back of Gerard's cuirass and pauldron as he ducked aside. The tip of the blade just scored his arm at the end of its swing, and Gerard's doublet reddened just below his pauldron.

De Launey wheeled the galloping horse round again, but Gerard wasn't going to wait for that. As the horse turned at speed, it exposed its entire flank to Gerard, and he wasn't going to pass up such a target.

He hefted the halberd to his shoulder and launched it like a javelin. It was a heavy polearm, unbalanced and completely unsuitable for throwing, but Gerard put enough force into it that it didn't matter. The spiked tip of the halberd took the corpse horse through the base of its neck, and it stumbled and collapsed.

Without saddle or stirrups, De Launey was again thrown clear, and he landed hard a second time. Gerard was far more angry this time he wrenched his halberd free. The Risen horse was struggling to rise, its jaw grotesquely broken and dangling loose after its fall, so Gerard forced its head back down and rammed the steel-shod butt of the halberd into its skull, hard. It disanimated. Then he stalked over to De Launey and stood over him, gelatinous gobbets of horse brain dribbling down the shaft of the halberd as he held it poised to crush the cavalryman's skull as well.

"I yield, I yield!" the man called out, far more believably this second time. He seemed in great pain, but Gerard wouldn't trust him to stay down a second time. He needed to be sure he would not interfere again; needed to be sure he could not. He strode back to the unfortunate corpse horse and, setting his halberd aside for a moment, he grabbed it by its hind legs. He dragged it across the sand to De Launey, who had pushed himself up to one elbow.

"Please?" the man said, holding out a hand for Gerard, but Gerard ignored it. He bent down and, with great effort, picked up the horse and dumped it on the man, crushing him back down to the sand. He was going nowhere. He heard the crack of bones breaking, and didn't care. The crowd cheered uproariously.

***

The Baron had never driven a chariot before, and as he flicked the reins to spur the horses, they took off at such a speed that he almost fell backwards off it. He kept his footing, and drove the horses in pursuit of the Marquis, whose chariot was half a straight ahead of him.

The Marquis kept his chariot racing around the perimeter and wheeled his horses into the turn at the end of the south straight, behind the burning hay bales where Donatella and Valanthé were furiously duelling. The Baron wrenched the reins; he would turn his chariot across the arena floor on the near side of the burning bales, and intercept the Marquis' chariot on the north straight.

The horses turned sharply – too sharply – and the inside wheel of the cart lifted off the sand. The Baron – who was familiar with sailing if not charioteering – threw his weight over the rising wheel to counterbalance the turn. The chariot righted itself, but a part of him derided himself on his sloppy charioteering. He saw Donatella pegging Valanthé back towards the burning bales as he passed, and he worried for his friend. He hoped she had the sense to yield if she lost.

He completed the turn and, as he had hoped, his chariot entered the north straight alongside the Marquis. The Marquis levelled a pistol at him as the chariots drew level, and the Baron veered his horses closer, lunging with his cane to strike the muzzle of the pistol aside. The pistol fired in the same instant, and the Baron flinched away as he felt the powder burn scorch his cheek.

The two carts pulled apart and the Baron lost ground on the Marquis, whose chariot was pulling ahead. Patting down his burning moustache, the Baron watched the Marquis holster his pistol and draw out another. He levelled the gun, and the Baron ducked behind the rail of his chariot cart. The Marquis never got a clear shot, and withdrew the pistol to focus on turning the chariot as they both approached the end of the north straight. He wheeled it again around the perimeter of the turn, while the Baron wheeled his around on his inside. The two chariots emerged onto the south straight neck and neck again, and the Marquis levelled the pistol once more.

The Baron yanked his reins, and the carts slammed together, the impact causing the Marquis to drop the pistol. It flew out of his hand to the sand below, and the Marquis flinched back to the far side of his cart, clumsily drawing his sword as the two chariots thundered down the straight.

Drawing his own foil blade from his cane, the Baron leant out from his chariot over the railing of the Marquis' and flicked his blade at the man's face. The Marquis, still struggling to free his sword, recoiled from the blade, the tip of which skittered across both cheeks of his helm, scoring a cut across the bridge of the man's nose. As both their weight shifted towards the far side of the Marquis' chariot, the chariots veered into the perimeter wall, and the outside horse bucked as it scraped along it.

The Marquis finally freed his sword and lunged back at the Baron with his longer, heavier blade, advancing as he slashed and forcing the Baron back. Their shifting weight veered the chariots back towards the arena centre, and they both looked ahead to see they were aimed directly at De Launey's wrecked chariot. They both yanked their reins aside to steer their chariots either side of the wreck, but neither shifted; the carts had locked together in the impact. They shared a look of anger; there was no avoiding the wreck.

Then the Baron blacked out.

**

Valanthé saw Gerard unhorse De Launey, and she saw the Baron race past on the chariot in pursuit of the Marquis. Donatella pressed again, flicking her rapier high, then low. Valanthé parried clumsily, her movement restricted by the half-healed wound in her thigh and the bonfire of burning hay behind her.

She heard Colin call from the nearby tunnel entrance, "you've got this Valanthé, I believe in you!" She then heard a supportive rumble from the alligator in the hat.

She smiled ruefully; she didn't got this. Donatella was good. Not as good as her, but good enough. Valanthé knew the best she could do now was to keep her opponent occupied as long as she could to buy the Baron and Gerard time to beat the Marquis. Her leg was numb; wooden. It no longer did what she demanded of it. She wouldn't be helping defeat the Marquis, she was no longer mobile.

Donatella was stuck there too, and Valanthé saw in her face that she knew it. The necromancer couldn't leave her unbeaten; she still had her loaded pistol tucked into her belt and they both knew that Valanthé would shoot her given half a chance. Getting increasingly impatient, the necromancer feinted a high slash before slashing low instead. Valanthé ignored the feint and blocked low with her heavy short sword, thrusting a riposte with her long sword. Donatella flinched back, knowing Valanthé couldn't press the attack. Their eyes met and they both smiled grimly. They were locked in a stalemate. Good.

In the corner of her eye, Valanthé saw Gerard across the arena, dropping a dead horse onto De Launey. Donatella heard the crowd cheer and glanced back to see it too, and Valanthé spotted the woman let out a little gasp at Gerard's display of strength. Then they locked eyes again, and there was a glint of desperation in the necromancer's eyes. They both knew Donatella was almost out of time.

Donatella redoubled her attack, circling round as she flicked the rapier ferociously at Valanthé's arms. Valanthé parried with the long sword, but her leg disobeyed her once more as she tried to turn, and her sword swung clumsily away from the parry as she stumbled. She felt the tip of Donatella's rapier rake across the back of her hand, the cut slicing through her leather cuff. The long sword flew from her grip as she recoiled, and she struck out with the short sword to fend Donatella away.

The necromancer never stopped moving though, she whirled as she dodged the short sword and swung her rapier back towards Valanthé, a look of triumph on her face. Valanthé threw herself forwards inside the swing of the rapier, desperately lunging to grab hold of the woman with her free hand, now slick with blood. Not to be denied her victory though, Donatella skipped back, redirecting her swing down at Valanthés lunging hand. The rapier skidded down her leather sleeve as Valanthé grasped nothing but air. Unable to step forward to regain her balance, Valanthé fell to the sand.

Donatella struck the short sword from her other hand as she landed, and rested the tip of the rapier on the back of Valanthé's neck, to the sound of cheering from the crowd.

"I yield," Valanthé heard herself say. It was a bitter pill to swallow; she knew she would have easily bested the woman if she'd had full use of her leg.

The sword tip withdrew and Valanthé looked up. Gerard was barrelling towards them and Donatella had already raced off to meet him. Behind them, Valanthé saw the two chariots of the Baron and the Marquis locked together, aiming straight at the wreck of De Launey's.

She saw the two men unable to steer clear, and watched the Marquis leap off the back of his chariot, stumbling to the ground and rolling into a heap. The Baron seemed oddly stationary, and she silently urged him to jump.

"Jump, Baron!" Colin urged from the tunnel.

The Baron was unmoving. He stood as still as a statue as the chariots bore down on the wreck.

At the last moment, she saw him move. His upper body completely rigid, he turned and stepped three paces mechanically off the back of the chariot, placing his foot onto the sand, just as the corpse horses jumped the wreck that lay in their path.

The Baron fell backwards onto the sand, falling into a sitting position, his upper body still rigid, and he skidded across the sand in that rigid seated position. The strange metal canister he carried must have snagged on something; it tore loose from his back and landed a little way away from where he came to rest. The horses cleared the wreck but the chariot carts both smashed into it, both of them destroyed in the crunch of wood and debris.

Valanthé stared at the Baron, who was still sat unmoving on the ground as wooden debris peppered the sand around him, not even flinching as a length of railing clubbed into his back. Had he lost his consciousness? How had he taken those steps if he had? Amazingly, his knitted doll – Belle – was still perched on the top of his head. Why would he have put it there of all places?

***

Gerard was too late to help Valanthé; Donatella had already forced her to yield. He skidded to a halt as the beautiful necromancer raced towards him, her rapier in hand. He reluctantly raised his halberd to fight her.

Then he heard the crash behind him, and turned to see the two chariots had collided with the wreck, and splintered wood was flung in all directions. Both sets of corpse horses stumbled as their momentum was checked by the crash, but they kept on racing, dragging their broken yokes and draught poles behind them.

Gerard looked for the Baron and the Marquis. He saw both; the Baron nearest, sat up looking stunned, and the Marquis further back, prone on the ground and groaning. He looked back to Donatella and the necromancer grinned wolfishly at him as they locked eyes for an instant. She wasn't slowing her approach, but she also wasn't headed towards him. She was running to the Baron.

Gerard realised then that he and Donatella were in a race; which of them could force their opposing primary to yield first. He lowered his halberd and ran towards the Marquis. It would be a close call which of them would reach their target first, but he had faith that the Baron would at least not be first to yield.

He sprinted as fast as he could towards the Marquis' prone form. The man looked like he had broken his leg in the leap from the chariot. The Marquis edged away across the sand, a look of fear on his face, which contorted into a look of triumph as the man looked past Gerard to Donatella.

Glancing back, Gerard saw Donatella had reached the Baron, and was stood a few feet from him, demanding he yield. Something was wrong though; the Baron was still sat rigid as Donatella approached, and Gerard realised his friend had lost his consciousness. He couldn't yield, he could only die.

No time for idle threats, he stomped on the Marquis' broken leg. The man contorted in agony and Gerard chambered his foot and stomped down again. The ragged end of the man's tibia bone burst through his skin with an eruption of blood.

"Stop! I yield!" the Marquis screamed, tears streaming from his face.

Gerard looked back at Donatella and the Baron. He was wreathed in balefire which was projecting from her outstretched hand. Realising she had lost, she lowered her hand. The black flames licked around the Baron's rigid form for a moment more before subsiding, leaving him burnt and smoking but blessedly he was not aflame, except for some glowing orange embers around his blackened hair and clothing. She conceded to Gerard with a smile and a tilt of her head, then she applauded him daintily, and he grinned at her.

The crowd erupted in cheering and applause and Gerard raised his halberd high above his head in triumph.

Barely noticed, a curious trickle of orange flame – started by the embers of balefire – sputtered across the sand from the Baron towards where his odd rectangular canister had landed, right where Donatella stood. The curious flame was following a trail of gunpowder spilt from the canister, and Gerard watched with horror as the flame reached the end of the trail, and the canister exploded.

Flames leapt up out of the canister, and Donatella screamed. Her blood sprayed everywhere, as she was shredded by the forest of metal spikes that exploded from the canister, and she disappeared behind the peal of smoke and spray of blood.

Gerard raced to help her. He made it three steps before he too lost his consciousness, and blacked out.

Chapter 24

After the duel had concluded, Valanthé had been the last combatant able to walk unaided, and she'd only managed that by leaning on the Baron's musket as a makeshift crutch. Nevertheless, the Baron had been declared the winner and the crowd had applauded long and loud for that well-deserved outcome. The nobles in their exclusive pavilion in the centre of the north stand had thrown down fat purses of coins, which Valanthé had collected as she hobbled round with Rufus on her victory lap.

She had needed some assistance from Colin and the arena stewards to carry Gerard and the Baron out, though only she was injured; Gerard and the Baron had merely lost their consciousness. Bad timing, sure, but it would have been infinitely worse if they had blacked out before the duel started.

The Marquis' team had been far worse off. Surgeons had rushed out as soon as the explosion ended the duel, and worked on all three of them, right there on the sand of the arena.

It had taken five stewards to remove the dead horse from on top of De Launey. From the bloody bubbles that frothed out of his mouth as he breathed, Valanthé guessed his broken ribs had punctured his lung. The Marquis had an open fracture of his tibia bone just above his ankle. The surgeons had worked quickly to reduce the fracture, and Valanthé had never heard a scream quite like how the Marquis had screamed when they'd pulled his foot and knee apart to relocate the broken bone.

Donatella's injuries had been the worst. One medic had doggedly tried to staunch the stream of blood from her catastrophic wounds but he may as well have tried damming the Poconovo by hand. All the other surgeons had instead gravitated towards the casualties that could be saved. Of their three adversaries, Donatella had least deserved to die, and Valanthé left before she had to watch her do so.

It took an age to get back to Isla Festa, and Gerard and the Baron still showed no sign of waking. Valanthé and Colin managed to get the Baron up to his bed, but there was no way they could have carried Gerard up the stairs, so they laid the big man on the chaise longue in the parlour. Exhausted, Valanthé then retired to her own room to peel off her combat leathers and clean and dress her wounds. The boy offered to help of course, but she declined, unable to shake the thought that he was more interested in removing her leathers than in providing medical care.

She winced in pain as she peeled back the old dressing on her thigh. As she'd feared, she had reopened the gunshot wound, and thin watery blood had saturated the bandage. She applied the healing balm the way Thessu had shown her, but she lacked his gift for healing and, as she mopped away the tears of pain, she wished he was there to help. He and Epifani were still on Flotsam protecting Joanna.

She wished any of her friends were there to help her. Gerard and the Baron were hollow shells until they came around again, and Remy was still missing. She allowed herself a pang of worry for him; despite having told herself his absence was an inconvenience only, she grew more and more concerned for the rakish fiendling. Where the blazes was he?

She almost swallowed her pride and asked Colin to help after all. Almost. Before she could, the manor reverberated with an urgent banging on the front door, that rippled through the creaking walls of the old building. She heard Colin run downstairs to answer it. A few moments later, she heard Remy's voice in the hallway and, as the relief washed over her, she threw open her door to yell at him.

***

It took Remy more than two full eves to get back to the manor. Damn his father and his little jest! What had been the point of him telling Remy to act quickly on Domenico's absence, only to strand him uselessly on a tea clipper heading south?

He had made his presence known to the captain of the ship he was on – the Manatee – who as ill luck would have it, was a one-time paramour of Remy's. The man had soured at the sight of him on his ship and seemed as likely to throw Remy overboard as turn around and take him back to the city.

The man also had no desire to take Remy on a cruise to the trade ports of the southern continent though, and so the Manatee signalled the next north-bound ship they crossed paths with to arrange his cross-decking; near a full eve later when they sighted the steam hulk 'Jubilee Garden', carrying coal and Risen to La Crosse. The steam hulk was big and slow and, having no passenger cabins and no love of fiendlings or stowaways, the captain confined him to the hold, where he had spent the eve-long voyage in the suffocating darkness, surrounded by coal and corpses.

**

"Where the blazes were you?" Valanthé fumed. Remy was a state; he looked filthy and bedraggled, and smelled worse. Almost as bad as that time Colin had washed his clothes in swamp water and lard.

"Don't ask," Remy said wearily, turning to look at her. He gasped and looked politely away. Colin did no such gentlemanly thing at the sight of her in her doorway in her underwear, and she pulled the door back across herself angrily.

"Are y'alright Val?" Remy said concernedly, still averting his eyes. "Your leg is bleedin', An' your hand too."

"Don't change the subject, where the blazes were you? You were supposed to second the Baron in his duel! I had to fight in your place!"

The fiendling sagged, eyes closed. "I'm sorry, Val. If you give me a moment to get fixed up, I'll come an' explain."

He looked so sorry for himself, that Valanthé relented. "Fine."

He returned a half hour later; he and the boy were lugging something heavy along the hallway. She opened the door a crack and peered out. The boys were wrestling the old copper tub from the Baron's room. She gave Remy a quizzical look.

He smiled that smile he thought was winsome. "From the look of you, you need this even more than me," he said. "Might we bring it in for you?" Maybe his smile was a little bit winsome. A soak in warm water would be most welcome after the exertions of the duel. She opened the door wider to admit them, and they placed the tub down at the end of her bed, then they trooped out to fetch water.

It took them eight trips up and down the stairs with pails before the two of them had filled the tub with warm water from the kitchen, made fragrant with oil of lavender, and Colin never once stole a look at her though she remained in her underwear throughout. Presumably Remy had had a word with him about staring.

She thanked them once it was done. Colin lingered for a moment, but Remy dragged him out before he could do anything to ruin their kind gesture, like offer to help her undress or something creepy like that.

While she bathed, Remy sat in the hallway on the other side of the door, and told her about his interesting conversation with his father. In exchange, she first checked Colin wasn't listening – he wasn't – and told Remy what they'd learned from Aunt Sundra about the boy's likely importance, and the old woman's desire for them to find out more about him. She also told him about Sundra's tacit approval of Remy visiting his vengeance upon Domenico while he was out of town, and what Crosskeys had told her about Darkmourn. It turned out they had both been given very interesting offers.

She learned that Remy had been offered a seat on the Cabal once his father became Dogé, if he abandoned his vengeance and let Domenico live. Valanthé had similarly been offered the chance at a privateer commission and could perhaps rise to be Sea Lord in future, if she forgave Darkmourn and the Scarlet Fist for the murder of her father and became Crosskeys' apprentice.

"You're still going to kill Domenico, aren't you?" Valanthé asked.

"Yes," Remy replied without pause. "Devils have their schemin' and humans make a virtue out o' forgiveness. But I'm a fiendlin' and fiendlin's value vengeance. Besides, even if he hadn't killed my mom, he needs to die to save Aunt Sundra, an' keep Joanna an' her baby safe."

He was right of course. Whatever Domenico was planning, it involved Joanna Pianna, and had required Remy's mother's death. He needed to be stopped.

"How 'bout you?" Remy asked. "Can you forgive the Fist?"

"No," Valanthé replied, though with less surety than Remy had managed. "Not until I've read the letters Darkmourn sent. Not until I've made sense of what happened when he killed my father."

"Well, sounds like we need to take ourselves a lil' trip. You ever been to a fiendlin' village? First thing morrow's eve, how 'bout we take the kid and go visit my lil' sister and the Mamas and find out where in the hell he came from. Your village is west along the coast, right? That means it's sort o' on the way to the Dandolo plantation. We can take a lil' detour and drop in on your mom and you can read the letters, then we visit Domenico and save the world."

Valanthé pondered for a moment, unsure. She knew Gerard was keen to go as well, and had also suggested tacking on a detour to her village. She sighed. She would have to get over her reluctance to return if she wanted to find out what happened to her father, and she knew they couldn't wait for the big man to regain his consciousness. She would go with Remy.

"Sounds good," she said finally, "apart from one thing..."

"Yes we have to bring Colin," Remy shot back straight away, correctly guessing what she was going to suggest.

After that he told her about the devil having stranded him on a tea clipper, and the ordeal he'd been through to get back, and she told him everything about the duel.

Once they had caught each other up on everything, the bath was cold so she rose and wrapped herself in a towel, then asked him if he wouldn't mind coming in to help her dress her wounds, which he did. His hands were much warmer than Thessu's, and he had a very comforting bedside manner. She was glad he was back safe.

***

There was no sign of either the Baron or Gerard rousing the next eve. So at fourbells they fed and watered them both, left them each a note and a comfort tray, and packed for the swamp.

Remy had slept fitfully; this would be his first homecoming in more than a year, and the first since his mother had died as a consequence of his spilling her secret. As he had told Valanthé yestereve, forgiveness was not a fiendling virtue. He had warned her that they might get an icy reception; he wasn't even sure that his sister Elise would see him.

He was on the boat house jetty, loading the barge, deep in thought and worry when Colin approached.

"My soul cries at your betrayal Remy," the kid said angrily. "But I have decided to forgive you."

"Um, thanks," Remy replied. "That's mighty kind of you Colin. What are you forgivin' me for, exactly."

"You know what, backstabber," he snapped back.

Mystified, Remy shook his head. "I really don't."

"You know how I feel about Valanthé, and you told me you weren't interested in her, and still you had sex with her anyway. I saw you sneak out of her room yestereve. Now corpses tend the fields where my sadness grows."

Remy rolled his eyes at the teenage nonsense. "Really? Corpses?" He had no idea where Colin's supposed feelings for Valanthé had come from. Probably from him having seen her in her brassiere.

Colin struck a lovelorn pose, slumping back against the wall of the derelict boathouse, which shuddered out a creak in response. It almost sounded like laughter.

"Not that it's any o' your business," Remy said curtly, "but I was in her room to dress her wounds an' nothin' more."

"Oh really?" the kid snapped back bitterly, "just tending her wounds were you?"

"Yes," Remy insisted.

"Well I could have done that for her so you're still a backstabber," Colin fumed.

"Well then it's a good job you just forgave me then, ain't it?"

Valanthé walked up to the jetty then, hobbling on her crutch. Colin pushed past Remy to be the first to offer her assistance. "Can I carry that for you?" he asked.

"My crutch?" she replied, confused. "No, I sort of need it Colin."

She continued along the jetty and reached out a hand to Remy as she reached the barge, and he helped her down into the seat facing the tiller, then climbed down into the seat opposite her.

Colin fumed from the jetty. "Remy may I sit in the stern seat please?" he asked.

"Sorry kid, only one seat at the tiller, an' you don't know the way. You goin' need to sit at the front to even the load."

Colin stared angrily for a moment, then sulked off to the seat at the bow, at the far side of the four corpse rowers. Valanthé gave Remy a quizzical look, and he waved it away, exasperated.

"I left a note for Epifani and Thessu in case they return to the manor," she said, changing the subject, "but I was wondering if we shouldn't just swing by Flotsam instead and let Sundra know that we're heading inland, and see if Epifani and Thessu want to come along?"

Remy shook his head. "I thought about that as well, and I figure we shouldn't. I don't entirely trust Epifani not to try an' stop me killin' Domenico if she comes along, and I don't entirely trust her not to harm Joanna if Thessu comes along an' leaves her behind."

Valanthé seemed to consider that, and nodded agreement. "Alright. Let's get going then."

Rufus swam out to see them off as the corpses paddled them away from the jetty and out of the mooring shallows. He swam alongside them for a time as they set off from the islet, before turning back soon after with a farewell flick of his tail. They continued upstream at a steady pace, passing some of the outer islands of La Crosse as they headed north-west along the branching course of the Poconovo Delta, headed for the river proper.

After two hours of slow paddling upstream against the current, they crossed the deepest part of the river at the farthest boundary of the city and the swamp. The lights of the city immediately disappeared from view behind the thick vegetation as their route then headed away from the river towards the west, across the swollen floodplain of the swamp.

Away from the river course, where no clearing or dredging had made the route navigable, the current dropped away and their route followed a meandering path across reedbeds and stagnant pools separated by dense groves of mangrove trees. Little twilight filtered through the dark canopy of foliage, and they relied instead on the eerie green glow of the little viridian lamp at the prow of the barge to guide their way.

The swamp quietened as they passed; the clicking and cawing and croaking always seemed to be at a distance and they never caught sight of cricket or bird or toad. They saw eyes though; reflected emerald in the lamp-light, the ever-watchful eyes and long sinuous snouts of massive alligators that watched their passage intently. Silent assassins that begrudged the barge people that had invaded their domain and quietened their prey.

An hour into the swamp, Colin broke the silence. "Remy, will you tell me when we reach the swamp?"

Remy blinked at the incongruous question. But of course, the kid had never been to the swamp before; He'd never left the city before. At least he wasn't still sounding pissy about the seating arrangements.

"This is it Colin," he replied matter-of-factly. "This is the swamp."

"Oh," Colin said, sounding disappointed and looking around. "I'd always been told it was a nightmarish place," he continued. "My wet-nurse used to tell me to be good because naughty boys got sent to the swamp... but this isn't a bad place at all. It's kind of quiet."

"Well I sure don't think it's a bad place," Remy agreed. "I grew up here. Quiet is a good word for it I guess. It has a certain timeless tranquillity to it."

Colin considered for a long moment. "I quite like it," he concluded.

Valanthé didn't seem to be appreciating the swamp as much as Colin was; she had seemed tense and uncomfortable since they left the river. The mosquitos were probably part of the cause of that; the bloodsuckers seemed to like her, though neither Remy nor Colin had been troubled by them at all. Despite being covered head to toe in her patched-up combat leathers, she had still been bitten relentlessly.

"I can't believe you like it here," she said, turning to Colin as she swatted away another mosquito. "Didn't you grow up in a palazzo? Don't you find this enclosing and oppressive?"

"I did, and no," he said. "But didn't you grow up in a forest? Aren't you used to that feeling?"

"I did, and no," she returned.

They continued west through the swamp for another two hours, until the deep pools of stagnant water suddenly thinned out, and even the shallow draft of the barge scraped across concealed hazards in places.

They were close now, and the knot in Remy's stomach tightened as he saw the familiar landmarks that demarcated the boundary of his tribal home, and the pangs of guilt and shame he'd been trying to suppress returned anew. Valanthé must have sensed his trepidation, as she smiled weakly at him in a way that must have been intended to be reassuring, though she looked like she would also rather be anywhere else than here.

Deciding it would be best to arrive discreetly rather than paddle right into the heart of the village, he steered the barge a little way around the village boundary before turning in towards it. He turned them into a familiar reedbed and, after a dozen more strokes of the oars, the barge scraped up the bank of a shallow sandbar on the far side of the reeds, and he bade the corpses to halt. The Risen pulled in their oars, and Remy took a deep calming breath, then strode the length of the barge to the bow. He directed Colin to help him, and they both stepped out into the knee-deep water of the reed bed and hauled the barge up the bank to the treeline beyond.

Colin hastened back to be first to help Valanthé out of the barge, and Valanthé accepted his help with a curt "thank you."

Her crutch sank into the wet sand as she hobbled up the bank, and she leaned on Colin for assistance, which made him beam. "Is it far?" she asked once she'd joined him by the treeline. "I had assumed we'd be able to reach it directly by boat?"

"It's just over this rise," he replied, gesturing up the tree-lined embankment. "The village has plenty of landin' jetties, but I wanted to avoid makin' a grand entrance in case we ain't welcome. This way is more discreet."

"Lead on then," she said, and so he did.

***

The embankment was steeper than it had looked, but Valanthé made it to the top with a little help from Remy and Colin. Colin was being especially attentive, which she found a little disconcerting, but she was glad of the help. Her thigh actually didn't hurt too badly in truth; she could probably have managed without the assistance and without the crutch, but she didn't want to push herself too hard and set her healing back again.

From the top of the rise she saw the twilight sky through the canopy of leaves above, stained green by the chartreuse glow of viridian lights ahead. Remy was right, the village was close.

They pressed on through the thick growth of trees at the top of the embankment, and her breath caught in her throat as they emerged from the undergrowth and she finally saw the fiendling village beyond.

The embankment on which they stood formed part of a roughly circular raised barrier that sloped down to enclose a wide reed-filled lagoon perhaps half a mile across, ringed by a sandbar at the base of the enclosing embankment.

Open to the twilight sky above, the lagoon was filled with tens of dozens of ramshackle stilt-houses that sat above the reeds, joined by interconnecting wooden piers and rope bridges, all lit by the yellow-green lights of the village.

It was a charming jumble; a hodgepodge of rustic wooden stilt-huts that rose on wooden piles from the swamp, hemmed in by a barricade of overgrown sandbars. What was it Remy had said about the swamp? That it had a 'timeless tranquillity'? She hadn't thought so, but the village certainly fit that description. It was exactly as she had imagined it.

"Is that it?" Colin asked, frowning, "It's nothing like how I imagined it!"

"How did you imagine it?" Valanthé asked, genuinely curious.

"Something more like palazzos. Something recognisable," the boy replied plaintively. "Are those houses? They look like wooden huts! Remy why do the villagers here choose to live in such tiny little huts?"

That brought Remy out of his quiet reverie, and he looked at Colin with incredulity. "Because they poor, Colin! Regular folk don't live in palazzos!"

"Oh," the boy said, seeming deflated.

"I don't see any people," Valanthé noted. "Where is everyone?"

The village wasn't exactly deserted; there were plenty of working corpses around, hanging washing on lines or punting small watercraft between the jetties of the stilt-huts, or sat on the banks of the sandbar mending fishing nets. Smoke rose from chimneys and cook fires around the village, and there were other signs of life as well. Just no people.

"I'm not sure," Remy answered after a moment, a note of concern in his voice. "We should probably go see."

"Remy, the Risen!" Colin exclaimed in alarm. "The Risen are all fiendlings!"

Valanthé looked and saw it was true, she hadn't noticed before but yes, all the Risen around the village had a pair of fiendling horns sprouting from their foreheads.

"O' course," Remy replied. "This a fiendlin' village! Who'd you think would be servin' the livin' here? Come on, it's this way."

Remy guided them down the far side of the embankment, towards where the nearest stilt hut was built; partly over the lagoon and partly overhanging the sand at the base of the embankment.

They climbed the rope ladder that led up from the sand to the hut's veranda, and peered in through the window. It was a one-room shack, and Valanthé saw a cooking pot hung over a fire in the hearth, and a rough wooden table was laid as if for a meal. But nobody was home. It was a little eerie.

Remy shrugged and beckoned them cautiously forward to the rickety rope bridge that connected the hut to another one, closer to the centre of the village.

They passed one of the village Risen on the bridge. Remy tipped his hat to the corpse, and the corpse returned the gesture. "Where is everyone, friend?" Remy asked. The corpse clacked its jaw and gestured in the direction they had been heading, towards the centre of the village.

Remy pressed on, and Colin and Valanthé both mimicked the same gesture Remy had made as they passed the corpse, and the corpse returned it to them both, and continued on its way.

They crossed the rope-bridge, and headed straight to the next one, then Remy stopped them half way across it. Valanthé heard a muffled noise floating across the lagoon. The faint sound of singing.

"Shit," Remy said. "I know where everyone is."

"Where?" Valanthé asked.

He looked pained. "It's the Sabbath," he said. "Everyone's at church."

"What's Sabbath?" Colin asked. "And what's church?"

Remy buried his face in his hands, then rubbed them back across his scalp. "I tol' you fiendlin's were god-fearin' people. They believe in a god, and once a week on the eve o'Sabbath, they go to a community buildin' called a church and praise an' worship their god."

"'Their' god?" Valanthé queried. "Not you? You don't believe in a god?"

He shook his head wearily. "Growin' up with a devil for a father ain't exactly conducive to religious observance. Him disparagin' their beliefs is one o' the reasons he ain't welcome here no more."

Like most people, Valanthé adhered to no religion, though she was aware some people did believe in one or more gods. She knew a little about the beliefs of the Crosse Cult, the death-revering religion of the Ziggurat; enough to know that joyful singing played no part of it. In contrast, she knew nothing about the fiendlings' monotheistic religion or beliefs, but was interested to see what was going on in the village church, and what everyone was so joyous about.

"I guess my sister would be at church as well, probably leadin' prayer with the other Mamas D'Ombre," Remy said after a moment of consideration. "We should wait by the boat an' head back when prayer be finished."

"Hell no!" Valanthé replied with a grin. "I want to see this church!"

She headed past Remy, who looked mournfully at her, but she wasn't going to pass up this chance to pay him back for dragging her through that mosquito-infested quagmire. Colin followed her with a shrug and Remy resignedly trooped after them.

The church turned out to be a large building at the very centre of the village. Round and squat and clad in shiplap wooden planks, it was rustic and somewhat dilapidated but was nevertheless taller and grander than any of the other buildings Valanthé had seen in the village. It had a shingle roof pierced in the centre by a short wooden spire. Like all the other buildings, it was raised above the lagoon on thick wooden piles and was surrounded by a covered wooden veranda. The sound of many people singing and clapping was coming from within.

As they approached, Valanthé saw a group of fiendling men lingering by the veranda, surreptitiously smoking cigarettes. The men eyed them warily.

"Remy Du Rosier, that you?" one of the men called out; a short, wiry fiendling in his late twenties or early thirties perhaps, with red hair under a straw hat and skin a much paler copper than Remy's. He had a thick bayou accent – thicker even than Remy's – and a gravelly voice no doubt earned from a lifetime of smoking cigarettes outside of places. He stepped forward to block their way, giving Valanthé and Colin a cursory look before levelling his gaze at Remy.

"How comes you don' go to church n'more?" the man asked.

"I could say the same to you, Caleb," Remy replied, "I see you lingerin' outside as usual. But I'm headin' there now ain't I?... if you'll step aside?"

The man – Caleb – took a long drag of his cigarette as he locked eyes with Remy, then tapped the ash off over the rail of the veranda and exhaled the smoke out the corner of his mouth in one long puff. Then he stood aside, and gestured them towards the door. Remy tipped his hat, and the men all returned the gesture. None of them took their eyes off Remy as the three of them walked past the men to reach the door to the church.

"Friend of yours?" Valanthé asked in a low voice.

"My cousin," Remy said matter-of-factly, then he took a deep breath and pushed the door open, and they stepped through into the church.

***

It had been many years since Remy had been to church. As a young child, he'd gone with his mother every week as was expected, and had actually quite enjoyed it. It was only later, once he started to understand that it wasn't just singing and dancing – that there was a religiosity to it – that he started to question it.

His parents had wildly different opinions on the matter; she being a pious woman and community leader, and he a devil. In fact they had wildly different opinions on a great many things, and they had managed to make their relationship work mostly by avoiding those differences. When Remy began to question his faith, his parents had radically different advice for him, and he was caught in the middle of many arguments. To maintain the status quo, he continued to go to church.

His father eventually left anyway. Remy continued going every week for several years after that, but his doubts gnawed at him, and he eventually stopped. The first time Remy skipped church, he was a teenager. He stayed at home during prayer, and cried. Skipping church meant cutting himself off from the beating heart of the community, and though he didn't leave the village for the city until many years later, he took his first step away from the community that eve in his room.

The church was thronged with people, and was stifling hot; just as he remembered it. Prayer hadn't changed since his youth, the praise was led by a choir of adulants in sequined robes, who stood on the little platform at the centre of the chamber, belting out a jubilant song filled with hallelujahs. The choir were accompanied by the surrounding congregation who were all dancing and swaying and clapping along, and chorusing sing-song responses on cue.

Remy knew everyone in there, and everyone knew him. He immediately regretted not insisting they wait outside, as many eyes bore down on him and his two unfamiliar companions. A murmur of consternation spread through the congregation, though the jubilant singing of praise continued regardless.

Remy tried to edge back towards the door, but Colin and Valanthé were both pressing forward through the throng. Colin was clapping along enthusiastically, and getting some encouraging smiles and gestures from the nearby villagers. He seemed to have caught the eye of a gaggle of teenage girls near the front, and was not-so-subtly headed their way. Valanthé seemed to be joining in as well, though he sensed from the wicked grin she gave him, that she was doing so ironically.

The crowd parted to let them pass, and Remy saw through the gap three Mamas D'Ombre at the front of the congregation, obvious from their dun brown robes and veils. One of them must be Elise, but he couldn't tell which because of the veils. One of the three was tall and broad however, while the other two were very much alike each other in height and build, both being short and slender. She must be one of those two, he reasoned. One of them pointed him out to the other, and there was no backing out now, Elise definitely knew he was there.

Thankfully it was nearly over. The jubilant song reached a crescendo of 'Praised be the Lord!' repeated over and over by the congregation and adulant choir to the rhythm of clapping and the jingle of a tambour. Then people from the congregation started shouting out things they were grateful for in the gaps between praise.

"He gave us the bountiful river," one shouted out.

"Praised be the Lord!" the crowd sang in reply.

"He blessed me with a healthy baby daughter," shouted another. "Praised be the Lord!"

"He cured my husband's fever," shouted another. "Praised be the Lord!"

And so it went on, until finally one of the petite Mamas who might be Elise stepped forward and raised her veil. It was her!

"He brought my brother back to me this evenin'," she said tentatively, a tremble in her voice that might be anger. Remy saw she had been crying.

"Praised be the Lord!" the crowd responded with unexpected enthusiasm, and repeated it over and over. All eyes were on the two of them now.

The crowd parted further as she walked across to him. Her eyes were puffy from crying, and she looked far older and more weary than when he'd last seen her, as if the intervening months had weighed heavily on her. He shouldn't have stayed away so long.

Remy tensed as she strode closer, overwhelmed by guilt and remorse. He'd caused their mother's death. He'd caused Elise's tears, and the sadness she hid behind her veil. He'd selfishly skipped the memorial service to avoid her anger. He hated himself every bit as much as she must hate him; as much as they all must hate him.

Elise hurled herself at him, and he braced for her rage. She flung her arms around him and... embraced him. Prayer ended then with tumultuous applause as the church erupted into cheering and clapping. Remy pulled away, startled, to look at her. She was smiling. Could she be... happy to see him?

She pulled him close once again, and he held her tightly. The congregation filed past boisterously, many of them patting him on the back and welcoming him back home as they left the church. There was no anger from anyone.

Eventually, Elise pulled back, and – still smiling – dabbed the tears from her eyes.

"Elise I'm so sorry 'bout Mom," Remy said.

"Don't be silly Rem, you ain't got nothin' to apologise for. Pop said you blamed yourself for Momma, but nothin' that happened to her was your fault."

"I should ha' come sooner," he said forlornly.

"Yep, you should ha'," she scolded, "But I knew you wouldn't. I knew you'd come this very eve, in fact. I had the date circled in my diary for weeks now."

He looked at her quizzically. "How did you know?"

She laughed. "'Cause I got Momma's gift o'course! I been learnin' to use it!" She reached up and pinched the ruffle at the neckline of his doublet then. "Now, what in the hell you wearin'? you look like a prize-winnin' turkey-fowl in that get-up!"

He smiled, and brushed a loose fold of her veil behind her ear. "I could say the same to you! How come you took vows?"

"Because it was my fate," she shrugged. "An' because the Mamas been guidin' me through a turbulent time." Here she looked back at the other two veiled community leaders, who were both in animated discussion with some of the congregants. The taller of the two waved a hand in acknowledgement at him and Elise, then continued his conversation.

"Mostly though, I took vows 'cause I found comfort in my faith," Elise continued. "Remy, how come you don't come to church no more?"

His mother used to ask him exactly the same thing, and the argument that followed usually made her sad and him angry. He looked at her uncomfortably, then realised she was teasing him. "Oh don't start on that!"

She laughed loudly then, and it warmed his heart. Damn but it was good to see her. He'd been such a fool, staying away to punish himself. His kid sister – barely sixteen years old – had suddenly gotten so grown up.

"Ain't you goin' introduce me to your friends?" Elise asked, looking over at Valanthé – who was waiting discreetly out of the way, and Colin – who was getting acquainted with a trio of giggly village girls.

"You must be Valanthé?" Elise said warmly, holding her hand out for Valanthé to shake. "Is your leg healin' up good from the gunshot?"

Valanthé paused and looked quizzically at Remy.

"It seem like she got my Mom's gift for readin' the tapestry," he said.

"I'm still learnin'," added Elise, as Valanthé shook her hand. "I ain't near as good as Momma was yet."

Elise looked over at Colin then, saying, "is that him?"

"Him who?" Remy and Valanthé both said.

"The fiendlin' you found, o'course," she replied. "Salvatoré?"

Colin looked over then, and excused himself from the girls he had been impressing, giving them a low bow and flourish of his hat in parting, which made them all giggle excitedly. He walked over and introduced himself to Elise.

"A pleasure to make your acquaintance," he said, sweeping another low bow in her direction, "I am Salvatoré Col Haolim Primo Martelaar Delmond Du Laurentin." His full name was – as always – a rapid-fire mouthful of syllables. "And you must be Remy's sister Elise. He never told me you were so beautiful."

Remy threw him an angry look, while Valanthé laughed into her hands.

"Oh my, so polite!" Elise said, her cheeks flushing pink. "Um, Hi. Yes. Welcome Salvatoré."

"Colin. My friends call me Colin," he replied, affecting a charming smile. "And I would like very much to be your friend."

Elise looked flustered. "Colin. Um. Do you like... bread, Colin? Damn I'm sorry I don't know why I asked that, I don't have any bread right now. Golly you're tall. Um... what village are you from, Colin?"

Remy intervened then, filling the space between the two of them and throwing an arm across Colin's shoulders to subtly angle him away from his little sister. "That's one o' the reasons we here," he said. "We gotta try an' figure that out. Colin was adopted into a noble family in La Crosse, an' he didn't know anythin' about his heritage until I found him."

Colin nodded along in agreement. "Remy has become something of a mentor to me, and has been teaching me some ancient fiendling customs. We have been getting into fights and burgling houses and setting fire to buildings and feeding people to alligators."

Elise looked at him mutely for a second, and Remy could have strangled the kid then, but then she burst out laughing at his jest.

The tall Mama D'Ombre came over to join them then, and Elise wiped the tears of laughter from her eyes and made introductions. "Mama Cristophe, you remember my brother Remy? Remy this is Mama Cristophe, he the one taken over as chapter head after Momma died."

Mama Cristophe lifted his veil and Remy saw he was a weathered old man with a bald, liver-spotted head and white mutton-chop whiskers. Remy thought maybe he remembered meeting him before; as a child he hadn't known men could become Mamas D'Ombre until he met one; perhaps that had been Cristophe. There sure weren't many men who'd taken vows.

"Good t'see y'again, Remy," Cristophe said in a vibrant, lively voice that belied his years. "My condolences on your mother Brigitte's passin'."

"And this is Valanthé and Colin," Elise added, gesturing to the others. "Colin here was adopted by city folk, he's come to try and learn some more about his heritage."

"Really, I'm trying to find out who my birth parents are," Colin said. "We were hoping you might be able to point us in the right direction, since the Mamas D'Ombre arranged my adoption. Perhaps you might know if there might be some records somewhere?"

Cristophe frowned. "A Mama D'Ombre arranged your adoption? To city folk?"

"Human city folk," Remy clarified. "I have the adoption certificate here. Colin was adopted into the noble house of Du Laurentin, an' it's stamped wi' the seal of a Mama D'Ombre."

Remy pulled the adoption certificate out of his doublet, and handed it to Mama Cristophe. Cristophe looked at it dubiously, then pulled out a little glass lens on a chain from under his robe. He placed the lens – the monocle – over one eye and squinted at the document.

"I'm real sorry to break it to you," he concluded after a long pause, "but I think this is a fake."

"How do you figure?" Remy asked.

"Look here," Cristophe said, pointing to the certificate. "See it's dated fourteen years ago, an' it sure looks like it's fourteen years old; paper is worn an' creased an' ink is faded an' all, an' it's got that musty smell paper starts to get when it's aged a lil'."

"So what makes you think it is a fake?" Colin urged.

"On account o' the stamp. It don't match the date. See those runes around the edge o' the stamp? Those change every year. This stamp don't got the right runes from fourteen years ago." He looked up at them, locking eyes with Remy. "This stamp got this year's runes."

"What does that mean?" Colin asked, a look of anguish on his face.

"If I had to guess," Cristophe continued, "I'd say whoever stamped this wanted you to think a Mama D'Ombre arranged the adoption for some reason, and got hold o' one of our signets somehow, without realisin' the signet changed each year. It's the only explanation that adds up."

"Could they have done it fourteen years ago?" Valanthé asked.

Cristophe shook his head. "No. The runes for each year ain't known in advance. They're based on the omens seen in the last bells o' year's end. If it's stamped wi' this year's seal, it must ha' been stamped this year."

"The same sigil was used in a necromantic ritual," Valanthé added, remembering how she'd met Gerard in the Pit. "One of our friends was mistakenly struck with a Risen's marque of ownership along with a batch of other corpses, and the marque bore that same sigil."

"Your friend and the other corpses were human?" Cristophe asked. Valanthé nodded. "Then I'm afraid that was likely fake as well. Mamas D'Ombre only tend to fiendlin's. Theres no good reason why a Mama would ever raise a batch o' human corpses. It'd be against our teachin's."

Valanthé and Remy shared a resigned look. They were back to square one; there was no explanation to be found here for Colin's past.

Colin slumped, looking downcast, and Remy – who still had one arm around him – held him tightly.

"I'm sorry we couldn't shed more light on this for you young man," Cristophe said, handing the certificate back. "You remain a mystery."

"I was hoping to solve the mystery," Colin said despondently, looking like he was a whisker away from crying. "I want to know who my parents are and why I was adopted. I was hoping to learn that I belong somewhere."

Remy was about to reassure the kid, but Elise beat him to it.

"O' course you belong somewhere, Colin! You belong here," and she tapped Remy on his chest above his heart. "An' if you belong there then you belong here as well," and she tapped her own heart.

She embraced them both then, and Colin started blubbing.

After a long moment, they pulled apart. "You're stayin' for the evenin'," she said to Remy. It wasn't a question. "I had the guest hut made up for y'all, and I been marinadin' some gator steaks the way you like. I know you got some other places to be before you head back to La Crosse, so morrow's-eve, once you've fed an' rested, I've asked cousin Caleb to guide your boat through the swamp for you. He'll see you safe to your next destination."

Remy marvelled at his sister once more. Truly, when did she grow up so much. When did she become the older sibling?

CHAPTER 25

It was nice seeing Remy relax; he had been so tense on the journey to the swamp. In fact he'd been tense since Valanthé had met him, but once it was clear Elise didn't blame him for their mother's death, it was like a weight was lifted off him.

He was warmer and more open without his guilt, and she liked him far better. Elise was delightful, of course, and everyone in the village had been kind and welcoming. Despite not having learnt anything about Colin's past, she was glad they came. Valanthé only hoped her own homecoming would be as revitalising.

Mama Cristophe hosted them for supper after prayer, at the priory hut behind the church where the three Mamas each had a room. Only Elise and Cristophe joined them for supper though; the other Mama they'd seen at church had gone to minister to outlying hamlets.

True to her word, Elise had prepared alligator steak. She had marinated it in small chunks in a sticky sweet sauce, which she blackened in a hot pan with ground spices. Apparently it was a fiendling delicacy and it was nice enough, Valanthé thought, but too spicy for her palette and for Colin's as well. Remy seemed to like it very much.

They stayed up past newbells – or at least she guessed it was past newbells – eating and drinking and sharing tales of their adventures. Valanthé enjoyed the evening very much indeed, in fact she hadn't laughed so much in years. Colin even stopped acting weird around her; instead the boy seemed to be trying to charm Elise, and Elise didn't seem to mind. Remy minded though, which added greatly to Valanthé's amusement.

At the end of the evening, they bade Elise and Cristophe good evening and farewell, then retired to the guest hut, which was perfectly comfortable if a little damp.

It must have been fivebells when they woke the next eve, though the village didn't seem to ring bells on the hour, so how the villagers kept time was a mystery to Valanthé. Nevertheless, Elise had told her that cousin Caleb would collect them at fivebells, so fivebells it must be as there came a loud knock on the door of the hut, and Valanthé opened it to the ginger-haired fiendling from outside the church yestereve. He wore the same straw hat, and was chewing a toothpick.

"You must be Remy's cousin Caleb," Valanthé said conversationally. "We haven't been introduced, I'm Valanthé."

"Yep," he said.

After an awkward pause, Valanthé tried again, "I want to thank you for guiding us Caleb, do you know where we're headed?"

"Yep," he said.

Another awkward pause. Valanthé closed the door and roused Remy and Colin.

***

Remy's cousin Caleb was clearly a man of few words, and said little else to any of them before they departed. He was especially rude to Remy. He was apparently an expert navigator though and, according to Elise, he knew the swamp better than anyone else. After a couple of hours of following his little one-man canoe through the swamp, Valanthé begrudgingly conceded that maybe that was right.

Caleb led their corpse barge ever westwards, guiding them through even the densest and most impenetrable thickets of foliage. Despite the water getting ever shallower and more boggy the further from the river they went, Caleb always managed to find a navigable channel through even the shallowest of the stagnant pools and reed beds, and their Risen paddled ever after his little canoe.

Caleb's route carefully avoided all the hidden sandbars that they would otherwise have bottomed-out on, and all the clumps of impassable mangrove that would have necessitated getting out and carrying their boats.

Eventually, the swamp thinned out and they followed Caleb as he paddled his canoe into the neck of a slender tributary of the Poconovo, a nameless little creek that took them past the last of the mangroves and finally out of the swamp. They paddled upstream on the little creek for a couple more hours, until it ceased to be navigable. Caleb beached his canoe on the shallow bank of the creek, then leapt out and hauled it further up the bank, mooring up against a tree stump.

Remy and Colin moored the barge next to Caleb's, and Valanthé climbed out to join them. She noted with relief that her leg seemed strong enough now that she was able to climb out of the barge without any help. She decided to leave her crutch in the boat; for the next leg of the journey they would be on horseback.

"Where's these horses then Caleb?" Remy asked his cousin.

Caleb spat out his chewed up toothpick and took a rolled-up cigarette from behind his ear, lighting it with a pinch of heat between finger and thumb the same way Remy did.

"Follow the levee a half mile an' you'll come to a farmstead," he said finally, after puffing out the first few breaths to get the cigarette going. "Farmer there'll have horses."

"You're not coming with us?" Colin said.

"Nope," Caleb replied. Then after a pause he added, "I don't like horses."

That was the first time Valanthé had heard him volunteer something more to the conversation than the barest minimum. "You prefer boats?" Valanthé asked.

"Not 'specially," he replied, turning to snap a dead branch off the tree stump. Pulling a hook and line from his pack, he sat on the bank and cast off with his makeshift rod. They left him there to fish and turned to follow his directions along the levee.

"Keep your headin' a hand's width to the left of the ever-settin' sun on the horizon," he called out as they walked away, "and you'll hit the track to her village in 'bout four hours."

"Thank you Caleb," Colin called out. Cousin Caleb didn't respond.

***

It was a pleasant change to be out of the swamp again and away from the damn mosquitos. It had been a long time since Valanthé had seen open countryside like there was here, beyond the western edge of the swamp. It must have been forested once, she thought, as evidenced by the ancient tree stumps that sprouted all along the levee.

The land beyond the bank of the levee had long been cleared of stumps and turned into arable farm land, and they walked past fields of knee-high crops that might next year be wheat and maize.

"Why do the crops look so stunted?" Colin asked, sounding perplexed.

"What do you mean?" Valanthé asked. They looked like perfectly normal year-old growth to her.

"The crops there; they're so small."

Remy and Valanthé shared a look. Obviously the boy knew nothing about farming. Valanthé gestured that it was Remy's turn to educate him, though in truth it was always Remy's turn; Colin was his sidekick not hers.

"They're small... because they ain't finished growin' yet," Remy said patiently.

"How long do crops take to grow?" he asked.

"About two years, maybe two an' half," Remy shrugged. "Those look like they got another year or so before harvest."

Colin continued looking perplexed. "But I'm sure my adopted father's plantations are harvested every year?"

Remy turned and gestured across the fields with a sweep of an arm. "Can you see Risen in these fields, Colin?"

"Um. No," Colin said tentatively.

"That's the difference," Remy replied. "The ever-settin' sun is too weak for crops to grow quick. They don't get enough light. But if Risen tend the fields, the crops grow twice as fast an' twice as high."

"The Risen tend them how?" he asked.

"I don't know Colin, I ain't no farmer. I guess they light them, water them, prune them, pest them, fertilise them. They make a huge difference, an' that's why universal undeath was first adopted thousands o' years ago. Without Risen tendin' crops; without the dead servin' the livin', us city folk would all starve."

"So why don't the farmers here have Risen?" Colin asked.

"Because they poor, Colin," Remy replied. "Workin' corpses are expensive. Necromancers are expensive."

Valanthé found herself marvelling at her friend's remarkable patience. That's why it was always his job to educate the boy.

Colin paused for a long moment, deep in thought. He looked like he was on the verge of understanding a deep truth about the world.

"But if poor farmers can't afford to grow crops efficiently and rich farmers can," he said tentatively, "don't the poor just get poorer and the rich get richer?"

Remy clapped him on the back then as Valanthé applauded. Colin had reasoned out the dire consequences of inequality all by himself. Not bad for a spoilt rich kid, Valanthé thought.

They saw a green glow of artificial light along the levee, which led them to the farmstead about half a mile away as promised. Outside the farmstead on a scratchy patch of bare ground, were four Risen horses tethered to a post. Remy haggled a price with the farmer to hire three of them, and soon they headed off on horseback, just to the left of due west as Caleb had instructed.

The corpse horses were scrawny and well past their best; they had a ripe smell to them, and Valanthé's had a slight limp and pulled to the right, which Remy had joked was fitting, since she did as well.

"Good job Epifani didn't come," Valanthé commented as they trotted out of sight of the farmstead. "I don't think she'd have been very comfortable on a Risen horse."

"No she would not!" Remy chuckled.

"Why do you never see living horses?" Colin asked.

"Lots o' reasons," Remy answered. "Mostly on account o' them bein' skittish around the Risen. But also livin' horses need feedin' an' restin' where Risen horses don't."

"I have never seen a living horse," Colin said forlornly.

"Neither have I," Remy admitted.

"I have," Valanthé said. "There's a stud farm on the far side of the forest where my village is. When I was younger I liked to go and watch the young foals frolicking. There was one foal in particular that used to trot over to me and eat carrots from my hand. She had the sweetest temperament and the most adorable white marking on her head in the shape of a heart."

"What happened to her," Colin asked.

Valanthé saddened at the memory. "As soon as she was fully grown, she was killed and shipped off to the Pits to be raised and sold. Like Remy said, horses need feeding and corpse horses don't."

"That's sad," Colin said.

"That's life," Valanthé replied with a shrug, and they continued on in silence. She'd already scanned the heads of these horses, as she did with every Risen horse she came across. None of them had heart-shaped markings under their copper marque of ownership.

***

They reached the track that led to the forest after four hours of riding across country – exactly as Caleb had said – and took the opportunity to rest and stretch their legs before tackling the last leg of the journey. Remy opened the little cloth bundle of smoked fish that Elise had given him for the trip, and held it out for Valanthé to take some.

"I'm hopin' you know where y'are now?" he asked.

Valanthé nodded, taking some of the thin flaky strips of catfish from the bundle. "Yes," she replied. "We'll reach the forest in an hour. We'll be at my village in another two."

She looked anxious at the prospect and he gave her a reassuring smile; their situations the reverse of yestereve in the swamp. "I'm sure your kinfolk will be jus' as welcomin' as mine were," he told her.

She looked doubtful, and chewed thoughtfully on a strip of fish.

"Why did you leave your village?" Colin asked, before balking at the smell of the catfish bundle when Remy thrust it towards him.

Valanthé sighed and leant back, reclining against a boulder at the edge of the track as she chewed. It didn't look like she was going to answer him, until after a long pause she closed her eyes and looked away, saying, "I spent years trying to control my gift and hold it back from overflowing wildly. I never did get the hang of it."

"An' the village folk didn't understand?" Remy guessed.

She shook her head sadly. "My mother never said anything, nobody in the village did." She took another bite of the fish before continuing. "But I could tell they were scared of me, of what might happen near me.

My grandfather taught me to fight, in the hope some martial discipline might help me control the surges."

"It didn't work?" Remy asked.

She looked up and locked eyes with him for a long moment, before answering. "It worked until he got ill and died. I got upset and my gift opened a sinkhole that swallowed his house. I packed my things and left after that, and I haven't been back since. It's been more than a year."

"I'm so sorry, Val," Remy said.

"Wow, how big was the sinkhole," Colin said, seeming impressed. Then his face fell as a realisation seemed to dawn on him. "Or are the houses in your village as small as in Remy's? Are there no palazzos there either?"

They both gave him a withering look.

"It's a little village Colin," Valanthé said. "It has little houses."

"Don't you believe it Colin," Remy interjected with a wink, "I'll bet she grew up in a palazzo, same as you."

"Yeah right," she snorted. "Palazzo Luxalim!" she added sarcastically. "I'm sure my mother will have luxury suites made up in the guest wing for each of us!"

They set off once more, and the track continued gently uphill for an hour, before rising steeply to crest a ridge of low hills. From the top of the ridge, they looked down into a dark green valley of ancient woodland that stretched off into the distance, all the way to the sea beyond. The dusky light of the ever-setting sun glinted off the tree tops of the valley, giving the forest canopy a silver lining that lent it the appearance of a stormcloud. It was at once beautiful and ominous.

They continued down the track from the ridge, and on into the forest below. Remy lit the little viridian lamp he'd brought from the barge, and they passed from the dim twilight of the ridge into the darkness of the forest.

Remy found the feel of the forest was surprisingly similar to that of the swamp. Very little light penetrated the dense canopy above and, like the swamp, the temperature dropped and the humidity rose the deeper they went. It had the same timelessness and tranquillity to it that the swamp had.

The track continued through the forest, slowly descending along the valley as it wound towards the coast. After an hour, they saw twilight filtering through the darkness of the trees ahead, and heard the sound of crashing waves amidst the rustling leaves and smelt the salt of the sea intermingled with the wet earthy smell of the woods. Soon after, the woodland vista opened out to a wide horizon as the track abruptly ended at a cliff-edge.

Remy doused the lamp as they adjusted to the light once more, and peered down to the breakwater fifty feet below, where the inky waters of the Gulf of Mezarcana were lapping at the rocks at the base of the cliffs.

"It's this way," Valanthé said, turning her corpse horse and leading them along the cliff edge on a wide, grassy path that skirted the edge of the forest along the cliff-top.

The cliff-top path continued along the forest fringe until it opened out to a wide grassy meadow, with the forest on one side and the cliff edge on the other. In the centre of the meadow, Remy saw the broken remains of a circle of standing stones, fallen to ruin. It must once have been a monument of some sort, but now the stones lay broken and ruined and grown over with vines and ivy.

He heard the sounds of village life close by – cockerels clucking and children playing – coming from within the forest near where it bordered the meadow, and saw the tell-tale glow of viridian lamps shine out from between the trunks of the forest fringe.

Valanthé climbed down from her horse, and Remy and Colin did the same. They followed her as she led her corpse horse across the meadow – giving the ruined henge a wide berth, Remy noticed – and into the forest, heading towards the diffuse green glow of habitation.

A hundred yards into the forest, they reached her village. It was smaller than his own village; perhaps four dozen small single-storey wooden houses arranged around a circular clearing, all enclosed by a low earthen rampart topped with a wooden palisade. As a defensive fortification, the palisade seemed to Remy to be in quite a poor state of repair, and was probably only good for keeping wolves out and chickens in; and maybe that was sufficient.

The entrance – a wide wooden gate that closed off an opening in the palisade wall – was unguarded, but there were plenty of villagers visible inside, all of whom eyed them warily as they pushed the gate open and stepped through. The children they had heard playing all now hushed and joined the staring, and Remy saw a look of immense discomfort on Valanthé's face as she led her horse to a hobbling post just inside the gate. Even the chickens quietened their scratching and clucking to add to the uncomfortable silence as they hobbled their horses.

Colin broke the silence. "You there," he called out to a group of gawping children a few years younger than himself. "Go and tell the mistress of Palazzo Luxalim that her daughter Valanthé has returned, and brought guests. Have her set a fire in three of her guest suites and draw warm baths."

Remy thought – as he had done many times in the past few weeks – about whether he shouldn't rather have dragged the kid into the river and held him under, that eve they met on Isla Doblé. Colin's ridiculous demand did nothing to alleviate the uncomfortable staring of the villagers, and Valanthé reddened visibly. She looked panicked. Remy turned to her and clasped her hands.

"Look at me," he said. "It's goin' be okay." He channelled a gentle warmth through his hands into hers, which he hoped she found reassuring.

"Thank you," she whispered, squeezing his hands in response. "Sometimes I want to drown that damn kid," she added, and Remy nodded sympathetically. He knew exactly how she felt.

"Val!" called a woman's voice from across the clearing.

Looking up, Remy saw a short, plump woman with greying hair tied in a bun, hasten across the clearing, pushing past other onlookers. The woman had a full face with cheeks flushed red from the exertion of jogging over, but she had the same intense almond eyes that Valanthé had. The woman looked like she might embrace Valanthé, but stopped short a few yards away, seeming like she had thought twice about it.

"Hello mother," Valanthé said.

The woman hesitated – conflicting emotions rolling across her face – then she crossed the remaining few yards and gathered Valanthé into a hug. She pulled away a few moments later, saying, "and where the blazes have you been? I have been worried sick about you!"

"I've been in La Crosse, mum," Valanthé replied. "Like I told you I would be."

A man walked up beside the woman then, a short stocky man with balding head and face as flushed as hers had been. He placed a hand possessively on the woman's back, and turned to the rest of the villagers, saying, "you don't have to hover like a swarm of wasps! Come say hello to our wayward daughter, or go on about your business now."

The villagers dispersed amidst audible muttering and consternation, and the children went back to their game; though kept stealing glances in their direction. The chickens obediently resumed their scratching and clucking.

Remy saw Valanthé eye the man curiously. "Hello Bryn," she said, looking askance at his hand which still rested on her mother's back. He pulled the hand back, and reached out instead to shake hands with Remy.

"Welcome to the village," he said amiably. "We don't see fiendlings here very often. Oh my, you have warm hands!"

"Mother, this is my friend Remy Du Rosier, and this is Colin. Remy, Colin, this is my mother Shavyre Luxalim."

"Shavyre *Calazar*," the man – Bryn – corrected. "Your mother and I were married earlier this year."

This was obviously a surprise to Valanthé, and Shavyre looked at him annoyedly for having blurted it out, then back to her daughter, a worried look in her eyes. She was clearly concerned how Valanthé would react. No, Remy realised; she was scared Valanthé might overreact and accidentally destroy something.

Remy understood then that Valanthé had been right, her mother and the other villagers here were scared of her. They would definitely not be getting the same warm welcome they had received in the swamp.

"It's a pleasure to meet you Mrs Calazar," Remy said, breaking the tension. "Bryn, was it? it's a pleasure to meet you as well, congratulations on your nuptuals."

"Yes, yes. Let's get you all inside and away from these people gawping at us all," Shavyre said uncomfortably. "It's this way." She gestured across the clearing towards a nondescript little house half in the shadow of the forest and half in the twilight glow of the sun. The house looked like a two-room shack, very similar to the swamp huts he was used to, just without the stilt piles. As they crossed towards it, the woman glared an angry look at the handful of remaining villagers who stopped to stare at them.

"You still okay?" Remy asked Valanthé quietly as they followed her mother and her new stepfather, then lowered his voice further, saying, "Who is this guy Bryn?"

"I'm okay. A little shocked. Bryn is the tanner, and also works as the village healer. He was always kind to my mother and me after my father died, and tried to help me control my gift. I had no idea they'd gotten together."

He reached out and gave her shoulder a comforting squeeze, and she smiled at him gratefully.

"That… is the smallest palazzo I have ever seen!" Colin announced bitterly and they both chuckled.

***

Valanthé had managed to swallow down the surge of wildness that had threatened to burst forth when they arrived in the village, and again when Bryn had announced his marriage to her mother. She didn't dislike Bryn; he was a kind man and probably a good match for her mother, but it had still been a shock.

Walking into her childhood home, to find everything different and cluttered with his belongings, was another shock.

Bryn bustled in first and started clearing things away and moving furniture so that everyone could be seated around a low table, all the while keeping up a constant patter of cheery small-talk with Remy and Colin, while her mother stood by and watched from the doorway, her face a mask of disquiet.

Valanthé sat on a familiar wooden armchair – one of the few items of furniture in the house that she recognised – uncomfortably aware of her mother's glare. Valanthé was very appreciative of Remy in that moment, as the fiendling absorbed all of Bryn's nervous energy, leaving her to gather her thoughts in silence while her mother did the same.

She looked up after a moment when she realised someone had asked her a question; Bryn was looking at her expectantly.

"Tea?" Remy repeated. "Bryn would like to know if you'd like some tea?"

She nodded, and Bryn bustled off to the fireplace, where a lidded kettle pan was suspended over the embers of a smouldering fire. He moved the pan down to sit lower over the heat, and fetched a ceramic teapot and five small handled bowls from a sideboard cabinet. He placed some dried tea leaves from a container into the pot and when the pan started steaming, he ladled some of the hot water in to steep.

Her mother eventually joined her at the table, and they sat in uncomfortable silence for a time.

"You've changed," she finally said. "You look... different. More grown-up, I'd say. I'm not sure I like this black leather get-up you're wearing; and it's torn, look." She leaned in closer to look at the patched-up sleeve of Valanthé's combat leathers and the bandaged wound on the back of her hand beneath, where Donatella had cut her during the duel.

"Oh but you're hurt," she exclaimed, then frowned disapprovingly. "Valanthé Luxalim have you been fighting? You know how I feel about you fighting."

"It's fine mum," she replied. "It's nothing to worry about." She resolved not to tell her about the gunshot wound in her thigh.

Her mother sighed. "I guess you'd better tell me everything you've been doing in La Crosse then."

She did. Or at least, she gave her the abridged version without all of the fighting and without the trial in the Cabal Court or any of the events that led to it. Bryn served the tea as she explained that she was working with some privateers for a time, and then met Remy and Colin and some other new friends after taking a job working for the Baron instead.

When she was done, her mother shook her head disapprovingly. "Well I can't say I approve, Valanthé. I don't know why a nice girl would be getting messed up with privateers and fiendlings and the like and getting involved in duels." She leaned in closer then, saying, "I assume you and the fiendling here are... um... together? I saw him holding your hand earlier. I can't say I approve of that either."

"His name is Remy, mum, and no we aren't together, he's just a friend who's kind enough to care about me."

Her mother looked dubious, so Valanthé turned the question back on her. "And what about you and Bryn? when did that happen?"

"Well, you know Bryn and I were growing closer before you left, Val," she replied. "He wasn't just coming here to see you, don't you know! I kept him at arms length for your sake, but after you left there was no need for that. He told me to put myself first for a change, so that's exactly what I've been doing."

"I'm happy for you mum," Valanthé said.

Her mother nodded, looking like she might say 'thank you', but instead blurted out, "Why are you here, Val? Why did you come back?"

The conversation between Bryn and Colin and Remy paused then, interrupted by the aggressive tone of her mother's question. Remy and Bryn both looked at each other, and Bryn voiced their unspoken mutual thought. "Remy would you and Colin like a quick tour of the village?"

"I was just about to suggest somethin' similar," Remy replied. "I'd be mighty keen to see the tannin' hut you been tellin' me so much about. You say you got wolf pelts dryin' there?"

"I'll stay here," Colin said.

"No I think you should come see the tannery as well, Colin," said Remy, throwing an arm around the boy and guiding him towards the door regardless.

Once they were alone, Valanthé reached into her pocket and pulled out the medallion she'd taken from Lugwort. Her father's medallion.

Her mother gasped. "Where did you get that? You can't possibly have that!"

"I took it from a pirate," she said matter-of-factly. "He got it from someone called Darkmourn."

She was watching her mother closely and saw the flinch of recognition in her eyes when she said that name.

"He was the one who killed father wasn't he?" Valanthé asked.

Her mother sighed. "Your father's gone, Val. My heart broke that eve. I spent years being angry and sad about it, and later I was angry with myself because I stopped being sad about it. I'm past all that now, I've moved on. We all have. So why dredge it all up again?"

Valanthé persisted. "I just want to know why father died! He was like me, wasn't he? He had the same gift I have?"

Her mother snorted. "It's no gift Val, but yes he was cursed with the same affliction you have."

"And Darkmourn and the pirates killed him for it?" Valanthé asked. Her mother made no answer. Again though, she was watching her reactions closely. Her mother was hiding something, and the answer to her question wasn't a simple 'yes'.

"Mother?" she pressed.

"The fecking pirates took your father from us Val, and that's all there is to it!" she shot back angrily. "Why must you be dredging up the past all of a sudden? You know I think I have a migraine coming on."

"Mother!" Valanthé insisted. "Please, I know Darkmourn wrote you letters."

She again caught the flinch in her mother's eyes. She had looked for an instant… at the sideboard. Valanthé stood and strode over to it. She knew exactly where the letters were.

Her mother tried to block her way, but Valanthé got there first.

"Don't read them Val, please," her mother said plaintively as Valanthé threw open the door to the bottom cabinet. Paying her mother no heed, she rooted around in the cabinet until she found what she was looking for; a lidded wooden box that she'd last seen as a child. She had asked her mother about it once and been unfairly berated for going through her things, and told never to touch it again. It was sealed with a simple locking clasp. She could prise it open easily enough with her dagger.

"He's not dead, Val," her mother blurted out.

Valanthé stopped. "What?"

"Your father isn't dead. The eve the brigands came – the pirates – they didn't kill him and the children, he did that himself," her mother said.

Valanthé repeated, "what?" once more.

"His affliction frightened me but he assured me he had it under control. And so he did. Until he didn't," her mother continued. She led Valanthé back to where they'd been sitting, and they both sat back in their chairs, Valanthé still clutching the box tightly.

"Your father was teaching some of the older children of the village up at the henge when the brigands came, looking for their protection money. Roberos never agreed with paying them off to leave the village alone, and thought he could frighten them off with a little surge of wild magic instead. He lost control and exploded. He exploded, Val! A blast of fire erupted out of him, destroying the henge and killing all the children in his class. He was completely unharmed."

Valanthé's head was swimming. All her life she'd believed a very different version of that story. That her father had been the village schoolteacher and had died protecting some children from brigands, and it was the brigands who'd destroyed the henge and killed everyone.

"You're telling me he lived?" Valanthé pressed. "So where is he?"

"He felt so guilty and ashamed that he asked the brigands – the pirates – if he could leave with them," she replied.

"What?" she said again. It made no sense. "Why did you lie to me?"

Her mother sighed again. "It wasn't a lie at first. The brigands were blamed for the explosion of course and it was assumed he'd died there too. The henge was such a mess of broken stones and ruined bodies that nobody looked too closely at the remains.

"The first I knew that he hadn't died was when a letter arrived from this 'Darkmourn' wherein he told me what he'd done. He'd changed his name and joined the pirate gang. For your sake, I kept up the pretence that he was killed in the raid and I never opened another letter from that coward... though I couldn't bring myself to burn them like I wanted to. Eventually he stopped writing. I think the rest of the village never quite believed the story, and knew his affliction had something to do with what had happened. And that's why they all got wary of you when you started exhibiting the same dangerous affliction."

It was all too much. She tried to swallow down the wild surge that bubbled up once more, but could not. She and her mother were both dumped onto the floor as the chairs they were sat on suddenly disintegrated into splinters and sawdust. The table also collapsed into a mound of sawdust, and their two tea cups spilled down the mound, both landing upside-down half-immersed in the splinters.

"Valanthé!" her mother yelled at her, but the surge wasn't finished, and both cups shook violently, before disgorging a steady stream of startled kittens. The little furballs tumbled out of the cups down onto the floor, then bolted off to the far corners of the house in fright.

"Are you quite finished?" her mother asked, sitting up amidst the destruction of her chair as a pair of ginger tabbies scurried across her lap.

"Sorry," Valanthé said miserably, though in truth she knew she might not be finished; it depended if her mother had any more surprises for her. Or if the letters did. She rose quickly and picked up the two cups, both still spouting kittens, and dashed them against the floor. With the cups broken, the torrent of cats subsided. She looked around. About fifty agitated kittens had overrun the house.

"I'll read these outside," she said, and headed for the door with the wooden box of letters before her mother could stop her.

'My darling Shay…' the first one began.

***

Half an hour later, she was sat on a fallen tree trunk just outside the village gate, eyes red from crying. She had read them all. The letters were from her father. There was no doubt about it, Darkmourn *was* her father. The letters talked about his love for her mother Shavyre and for her, and begged for a reply so that his exile might be made a little more bearable.

The letters detailed his increasing involvement with the privateers and eventual elevation to leader of the newly-formed Scarlet Fist. His guilt drove him to make a success of things, make a name for himself, but all the while he was craving her mother's forgiveness. The letters grew more desperate for an answer; the absence of any response from her increasingly condemned him, and he grew increasingly despondent.

In his last letter, he begged a final time for news of his beloved daughter and pleaded for just a tiny sign that he wasn't worthless, else he would give up on this world and head to the next. And that's exactly what he'd evidently done. Her mother hadn't even read the letters.

When Remy found her and sat down next to her, she slumped onto his shoulder and started crying once more. Once she had composed herself, she wiped her eyes and blew her nose on the handkerchief he gave her.

"You ain't goin' explode are you?" Remy asked, looking dubiously at the handkerchief. She shook her head and filled him in on the contents of the letters. He was just as surprised as she had been to learn the truth about Darkmourn. Having survived the raid she thought had killed him, he had run away and become leader of the Scarlet Fist, only to kill himself out of grief five years ago.

"No, you don't know he's dead," Remy insisted.

"He sailed off the edge of the world and never came back," she said.

Remy smiled. "That don't mean he's dead. That only mean he ain't returned yet. Maybe he will, an' when he does you goin' be waitin' for him. You goin' give him the forgiveness he always craved. An' he goin' be so proud o' you."

"Proud of me? Why?" she asked.

"Because you amazin'!" he replied, lifting her chin to lock eyes with her. She felt the soothing warmth in his hands once more. Did he really think that?

"An' if that ain't enough," he continued, "he'll be proud when you follow in his footsteps an' take ol' Captain Crosskeys up on his offer to be his apprentice."

She hadn't considered that, but of course he was right. She could accept Crosskeys' offer now she knew Darkmourn didn't kill her father.

"Thank you Remy," she said, and they sat in silence for a long moment. It was nice.

"Now, how in the hell did your momma's house get filled wi' cats an' sawdust?" he asked, and they both chuckled. Then she collected up all the letters and returned them to the box. That was hers now, she decided.

They returned to the house to find all the sawdust and splinters swept up, and the kittens rounded up and secured in a pair of large baskets too big for them to climb out of. Colin and Bryn were sat by the baskets, cheerfully naming the cats and feeding each of them in turn from leather skins filled with milk. Her mother was preparing broth in the pan over the hearth.

"Broth will be ready soon," she said without looking up. "But I don't have enough bowls now, and I've no table to serve it on any more, so I guess we'll all have to make do."

Valanthé walked over to stand beside her mother and silently helped chop the vegetables to make the broth.

"You'll have to bed down with the kittens this evening," her mother continued, "Because I have kittens now and no furniture. I'm sure the three of you can make do on the floor for one evening."

Valanthé knew the unspoken part of that statement was that her mother wanted them to leave as soon as they woke morrow's-eve. That was fine. She didn't want to stay there one moment longer than they had to. And she didn't intend to ever come back again. She carried on wordlessly chopping vegetables while her mother angrily pretended everything was fine.

CHAPTER 26

The path northwards through the valley stuck close to the bank of the stream that flowed through the forest, too narrow for the three of them to ride side-by-side, so they proceeded one after the other, their corpse horses trotting along the muddy trail in silence.

Valanthé had said an awkward farewell to her mother and Bryn at the gate of the village in the drizzling rain and, after riding her Risen horse out through the gate, she had turned to take one last look at the place she grew up, not knowing when or if she would ever return. It was a small place. Far too small for her now.

The rain persisted as they rode north alongside the streambed; a thin, saturating rain that soaked through their clothes and dampened their spirits. Not that their spirits could be much more dampened; Colin's mood was reflective of theirs, and Valanthé was subdued by the events of yestereve and the knowledge that she had very much outgrown her old life. And as for Remy...

She glanced back at the fiendling on his horse behind her and frowned. It was like a candle had been snuffed out. Yestereve, he had been warm and sage and full of empathy, but now he had the tension of a loaded flintlock. The reason was obvious; they were headed now towards the Dandolo plantation. Towards his vengeance for his mother's death. They were headed to a murder.

The track soon veered away from the stream, and left the woodland behind as it climbed out of the valley and wound its way instead past bocage fields of subsistence farms and smallholdings and the stunted crops that grew there.

They passed row upon barren row of muddy furrows, or fields of stunted cotton or cereal crops tended by subsistence farmers eking out a living as best as they could in the thin light of the ever-setting sun.

Here and there they passed cohorts of Risen tending the crops; working slowly up and down the rows weeding, watering, pruning, or just lighting the crops with handheld viridian lamps. It looked like slow, painstaking labour, but it was easy to see which farmers could afford the necessary corpse labourers; their crops looked almost healthy.

Valanthé thought about what they'd discussed with Colin yestereve; about why the dead serve the living. Risen were necessary because farming – like so many other industries – was labour-intensive, and if the living did the labouring, then those labouring would consume more than they could produce.

She thought as well about Epifani. The stubborn woman had insisted that the world would be a better place without any Risen, but seeing these farms made the case for corpse labour quite starkly; there was no getting rid of the Risen until farmers could grow crops just as efficiently without them.

The track eventually straightened out and widened as it reached the flatter, more fertile plains further north, where the meagre smallholdings gave way to the vast, well-tended plantations of the rich nobles of La Crosse.

Cresting a low rise, they saw before them a wide vista of regimented fields of maize and wheat and cotton, of apples and sugar and tobacco and much more besides, all tended by a veritable army of Risen and all bathed in the chartreuse glow of overhead viridian lamps that up-lit the twilight sky.

These bountiful green-lit fields of healthy-looking crops – with their thousands of attendant corpse labourers – stretched to the horizon, the landscape dotted here and there with the plantation-houses of the landed nobility; imposing white stucco mansions in grand classical style.

The rain worsened as they rode on, the rainwater pooling in irrigation ditches either side of the track; which thankfully prevented the track itself from becoming too muddy. At a crossroads, Valanthé asked for directions to the Dandolo plantation from a pair of bedraggled Risen that were clearing the mud from a blocked irrigation channel. They were a particularly pitiful pair of corpses, and the one that answered her was missing its jawbone so could only point and bob its head, though she could see the muscles of its face move under its taut skin, still trying to clack its missing mandible.

They rode on, and by following further directions from working corpses, eventually came in sight of the Dandolo plantation. It was the largest plantation they had yet seen, filled with the healthiest-looking crops and tended by the biggest army of Risen.

Ahead, a group of armoured guard corpses stood to rigid attention at the spot where a gravel path forked off the track they were following, snaking through the fields towards a distant plantation house that overlooked a lake in the centre of the plantation. Even at this distance, she could see that the plantation house was enormously grand; all white stucco colonnades and wraparound verandas flanking a domed central portico.

Valanthé looked back at Remy and saw his eyes were aflame. He nodded slowly. This was it.

***

There was no doubt in Remy's mind that they were at the right place. And that Domenico was here. The Risen spearmen standing guard were armoured in the same burnished bronze armour he had seen on the guard corpses at Palazzo Fandandolin. Setting armoured Risen to guard a muddy track through a field was a folly; they could simply ride past and cut across the fields to avoid them. That is what they did.

Remy took the lead and rode past the Risen guards, who eyed them warily. Wordlessly, he led Colin and Valanthé along the track another mile to where it curved around an apple orchard. There they dismounted and hobbled their corpse horses out of sight amidst the trees.

From there, they stole across the orchard – ignoring the Risen labourers they passed and being ignored in return – and on through a field of grape vines and a field of sunflowers which led finally to a walled garden in the shadow of the plantation house. They hunkered down behind the wall, staying out of sight as a patrolling cohort of armoured guard corpses marched past.

When the coast was clear, Remy peered round at the house. A veranda ran around the ground floor of the building, and here on the shadowed eastern façade, it looked like kitchens and service areas lay beyond the veranda. Above the veranda were galleried balconies, all in darkness except for one balcony on the top floor which was lit by the faint green glow of a dimmed light within.

"Any idea which rooms are his?" Valanthé whispered from behind his shoulder.

He shook his head. "It wont be any of the rooms on this side. The master suite will be on the sunward side on the top floor. I'll climb up to one of the darkened rooms on that floor and get in from there. You two wait here."

"No. You're not doing this alone Remy! I didn't come all this way to hold your cape for you!" Valanthé snapped back. "I'm coming with you."

"Me too!" Colin insisted. "We are a team, remember!"

Remy shook his head. "Your leg ain't up to climbin'," he told her. "And you," he said to Colin, "ain't never climbed shit before."

"My leg hasn't bothered me all evening," she shot back. "And you don't get to tell me what I can and cannot do. I am coming with you."

"Me too!" Colin insisted once more.

Remy started to object, then saw the look of determination on both their faces and acquiesced. "Well fine then. Follow close."

He loped forward quietly towards the house, ducking down behind the railing of the veranda. Colin and Valanthé joined him there a moment later. Risking a look into the house, he saw a handful of kitchen staff cooking unhurriedly. There weren't many of them, which Remy thought must be good news; it meant Domenico didn't have much of an entourage with him. He signalled to the others to follow him up, then climbed up onto the rail and pulled himself up to the darkened balcony above.

Colin followed up clumsily, and Remy reached down a hand to help the kid up. He made it up with a little help, joining Remy atop the railing of the balcony above. He peered down to Valanthé, and couldn't see her. He heard a 'psst' and looked up; she was on the balcony above them already. He marvelled at her again; the woman was like a cat!

They joined her on the top floor balcony and hunkered down in the shadow outside the unlit rooms. Remy gestured for quiet and slunk along the balcony to peek through the glazed doors of the one room that was lit, checking for any occupants.

Looking in, he saw a luxuriously appointed room, with white panelled walls painted with gorgeous fresco paintings, ornate white furniture with tastefully gilded accents and, in the centre of the room, a grand white and gold four-poster bed, draped with heavy sapphire cloth. All was untidy though, with discarded clothing and the detritus of a party scattered around the room.

Three figures were in the bed – asleep by the look of it – their naked forms lying prostrate, tangled in bedsheets. Three men. He stopped dead, and was overcome with rage. One of the men was unmistakeably Domenico Dandolo. Remy seethed. His mother's murderer was right there, unguarded and unaware.

He felt a hand on his shoulder, and whirled angrily. It was Valanthé. She recoiled from his rage; no doubt his eyes reflected the blazing inferno of his anger. He drew her to the side of the doors, out of sight of the occupants, and growled "Domenico" in a low whisper.

"I thought you said he'd be on the sunward side," she queried, "in the master suite?"

"Well he ain't," he replied.

Colin joined them then. "Dandolo is in there," Valanthé whispered to him. He wordlessly nodded and drew his pistol, and Remy and Valanthé both drew their weapons as well.

Remy tested the handles of the glazed doors and was mildly surprised when they clicked open. It was all so easy! Gesturing for the others to follow quietly, he carefully eased the door open, and stepped into the room. Into Domenico Dandolo's bedchamber. The bedchamber of the man who killed his mother.

He stalked forward towards the bed, stepping gingerly between discarded clothes and shoes and scattered oyster shells and half-eaten canapes and empty liquor bottles. It must have been some party, Remy mused.

Dandolo was flanked by the two men, both attractive young men in their early twenties, with square jaws and hairless chests of chiselled muscles. Domenico – sprawled on the bed between the two men – was a few years older, flabby and flaccid, with long dank locks surrounding a shiny bald pate, and wiry black body hair stark against his milk-pale skin.

Remy levelled the point of his rapier at the man's neck.

One of the men in the bed with him woke first, and let out a startled yelp which woke the others. Domenico's eyes opened groggily, and he rubbed them into focus before opening them wide in alarm at the sight of Remy's blade. Shimmying away, he backed further into his pillows as he stared at the sword, then his eyes travelled up the blade to the hand that wielded it. Then his eyes widened further.

"Remy?" he said incredulously, "Remy du Rosier? Is it truly you?"

Remy was dimly aware of Valanthé and Colin levelling their weapons at the other two men in the bed, but his blazing anger was focused on Domenico. Remy's eyes narrowed as he saw Domenico smile, and he rested the tip of the blade in the notch at the base of the man's throat. The smile faded as he shied away.

"I'm sorry Remy," he squealed. "Please! They mean nothing to me, I swear! I don't even know their names!"

What was he talking about? Did he mean the two men?

"I ain't here for them, Domenico," Remy replied as levelly as he could. "I'm here for you and you alone."

"You heard him! Get the hell out!" Valanthé barked at one of the other two naked men. "And you as well," she snapped at the other.

The two men exchanged a look and hurriedly got out of the bed. One of them reached for some clothes heaped at the base of a bed post; a pair of pantaloons with the legs pulled inside out. Valanthé rapped his hand smartly with the flat of her blade, and he withdrew it. "I didn't say grab your clothes, I just said go!" she yelled. The two men side-stepped around the bed fearfully, then bolted for the door naked. One of them lingered in the doorway, and Colin levelled his pistol at the man's head. He left with a squeal, closing the door behind him.

Domenico squirmed further away from Remy's blade, shimmying back until he was pressed up against the headboard. He reached for a pair of spectacles on the bedside table, and Remy allowed him to put them on.

"Remy! it is you!" the fucker said, even daring to smile again. "I'm so glad you're here Remy, I missed you so much!"

Astonished that the weasel would even try that shit with him, Remy pressed his blade further and drew a drop of blood that trickled down, lost in the man's chest hair.

"Don't you be tryin' that shit wi' me, Domenico!" Remy spat.

Domenico squealed, and started jabbering breathlessly. "Please Remy, I haven't stopped thinking about that eve after the masked ball, when we got drunk on cognac and we told each other our deepest secrets and at small-bells we fell asleep in each others arms… I felt so safe and so comfortable, you made all the world's troubles disappear… Remy it was the best eve of my life! But when I woke and you were gone, I was crushed! I kept thinking you'd come back and we could… I don't know, grab a coffee maybe or go dancing? But you disappeared, and nobody knew where… I cried, Remy! I mourned for you! …Where have you been, Remy? How come you don't come to parties any more?"

Remy wavered. He hadn't expected Domenico to act so pathetically when faced with death. He lowered his blade a fraction, then steeled himself. This man had killed his mother. Remy had told him about her gift and he had killed her for it. Any doubt he had had about Domenico's guilt had been erased when he'd asked the smoke raccoon who killed her, and the creature had led him to this man's house.

He pressed the sword back to the man's neck once more, resolved to ignore his pathetic excuses. "You ain't goin' to weasel out of this Domenico," he yelled at him, "I'm goin' to kill you!"

Domenico started crying then. "Remy, no please," he blubbed. "I told you those men didn't mean anything, I'm sorry you had to see them here with me."

"You think… you think I'm goin' kill you out of jealousy?" Remy said, astonished.

Domenico nodded. "I know you have that fiery temper Remy, your tremendous passion is one of the things I love about you! I hoped you'd come and you did, you came all this way to rescue me, and I blew it! I'm so sorry Remy!"

Remy lowered his sword, the fire in his eyes fading. "Rescue you? Rescue you from what?"

"From my mother of course!" Domenico replied, pulling a sheet up to cover his nakedness and smoothing his dishevelled hair down embarrassedly.

Remy blinked. Domenico's mother was one of the Caballiers from their trial. What was her name again? "Your mother… Citrine?"

"Yes that's right," he answered. "My mother, Citrine Don Dandolo. She rules the house with an iron fist; she's been keeping me imprisoned here, her damn corpse guards wont let me leave!" He reached out a hand to rest on Remy's own, saying plaintively, "Remy, you know how much I love carnival! That monster is making me miss carnival!"

Remy looked over at Valanthé and Colin. Colin looked perplexed – he always looked perplexed – but Valanthé seemed to be grasping the same realisation that he was. It had been Citrine all along. He turned back to Domenico to confirm. "Domenico, I'm goin' ask you some simple questions an' I'd appreciate some straight answers. Did you kill my mother?"

Domenico looked aghast. "No of course not Remy, I would never do…"

"Next question," Remy interrupted. "Did you tell anyone the secrets I shared wi' you?"

"No…" he answered tentatively. "But I wrote about that evening in my dream journal… and I think my mother Citrine may have… read it," he trailed off anxiously.

"Domenico, this one's real important. Why did she send you here?"

He waved his hand dismissively. "I don't know. She's completely obsessed with death and dark magic. She was spouting some nonsense about a magic tapestry, and pulling some threads out of the way of a pattern she was weaving."

Remy cursed and sheathed his sword, then turned to the balcony. "Time to go," he said to Valanthé and Colin. Valanthé was already at the balcony door, yanking it back open. "I mean now, Colin!" he yelled at the kid, and Colin holstered his gun and hastened after them.

"Remy, wait!" Domenico called in a shrill voice from the bed. "I'm… I'm not ready, I… I need to shower and shave and… and pack a few trunks of clothes! Could we maybe go after breakfast?" Remy ignored him and followed Valanthé and Colin through the door.

"Remy! You can't go without me Remy! What sort of rescue is this?" Remy closed the door behind him, Domenico's muffled protests diminishing as the three of them hastened away.

"I don't understand, Remy; what does all this mean?" Colin puffed as they ran across the fields back the way they'd come.

"It means it were Citrine Don Dandolo that killed my mother and took her gift." Remy replied, slowing so the kid could catch up with them. "It means we been played! It means she put Domenico here to lure us away from the city so she can make her move against Sundra and Joanna, and we fell for it. It means we gotta get back to La Crosse as fast as humanly possible an' hope we ain't too late!"

"But they're protected," Colin protested. "By Epifani and Thessu and two unkillable spectres!"

He still wasn't getting it. Remy stopped and caught hold of Colin, grasping him firmly by the shoulders. "Epifani can kill the spectres," he said. "She may be the only one who can... Don't you see that must be why Citrine has been manipulatin' her with that bullshit about gettin' rid o' the Risen? She needs her to take out the girl's protectors!"

"But she wouldn't..." he replied uncertainly.

"Really? What you think Epifani's goin' do when Citrine shows up and feeds her more o' her Risen bullshit and tells her she just needs to kill two shadow corpses an' all her wishes will come true? You think Epifani even needs much encouragin' to kill corpses?"

"Oh," the kid said.

"Oh indeed," Remy replied. And they resumed running towards their horses.

CHAPTER 27

CHAPTER 27

A cold grey mist swirled around an unfamiliar landscape. The man's feet pounded down onto soft and sodden grass as he ran blindly through the fog, looking back over his shoulder in alarm. He heard the sound of ragged breathing. It was his. His lungs burned with the effort of his blind run. Other shapes were nearby, blurry outlines of other people hurrying with him through the fog. A muffled scream on his left drew his attention; one of the blurry figures nearby had been caught, and the fog around them stained red for an instant as they fell, sundered by the whirling blades of one of the demons.

The man's attention snapped back to his own escape, as he stumbled on some unseen hazard, and fought to keep his staggering feet beneath him. He could not, and he tumbled down onto the sodden grass. He pushed himself back up but he was too weak and too slow; he felt searing pain as a snarling beast clamped its jaws on his shoulder, and dragged him back down to the ground, wrenching him over onto his back. From out of the fog came the horned silhouettes of the beast's demonic masters. The man could only watch as they approached and loomed over him, jabbering in their angry guttural language, their blades at his neck.

At that instant, Gerard's consciousness returned. He blinked for a second, unsure where he was. He had just been in two different places seemingly at once, and neither of them was the courtyard of the manor, where he now found himself.

"Donatella!" he called out, for the tragic end to the duel had been the last thing he'd seen. Before he blacked out, he had been in the arena watching in horror as Donatella was caught in an explosion. He had been there just moments ago, yet somehow he had also just been running through the fog in some alien place he didn't recognise.

Was it a dream? Had he dreamt he was running through the fog chased by demons? Had he dreamt he had fallen on sodden ground and a vicious beast had sunk its teeth into his shoulder?

He focussed on his surroundings. He was lying on the bare ground of the courtyard behind the kitchen of De Ville manor. He was lying in a puddle of some sort. Still groggy, he pushed himself up onto one elbow and wiped the wetness off his clothes, and his hand came away covered in blood. Pain hit him then, and he looked at the source of it. Rows of ragged puncture wounds in his shoulder that had shredded his doublet and the flesh beneath.

He looked through the dense black smoke that filled the courtyard like a pall and saw a trail of bloody drag-marks leading from the kitchen door to his position here. Someone had dragged his comatose body out of the fire. The fire! All around him, the structures surrounding the courtyard were ablaze. Thick orange flames engulfed the ground floor of the manor and lapped up the walls to the upper floors.

Rufus the alligator was next to him. His sequinned red cape was blackened and scorched, and his teeth were dripping with blood. Gerard's own blood, he realised. The puncture wounds from the alligator's teeth were painful, but superficial; it was a small price to pay for the alligator having dragged him clear of the fire.

It must have been a dream, he thought, that place of fog and demons. A vivid dream conjured by the smoke and the alligator that dragged him out of it. It had seemed very real. He hoped the other memory – of Donatella being ripped apart by an explosion – was a dream as well; but he knew it was not. He put it out of his mind.

"Thank you Rufus," he said to the alligator as he scrambled to his feet. "You saved my life." The alligator didn't look too sure; he was rumbling plaintively and looking around at their unfortunate predicament.

The small courtyard they were in was fully enclosed by the kitchen, the scullery and the dining room. All of those were burning ferociously. What in darnation had happened here? Why was the manor on fire? And where was everybody else?

"What happened here?" he asked the alligator, without even thinking how the creature might answer him; if he could even understand him.

Rufus did understand him. The alligator turned and grabbed something in his great maw and dropped it at Gerard's feet. It was the leg of a skeleton corpse. Arson then. Risen had obviously attacked the manor and Rufus had fought to defend it, and had ripped at least one Risen corpse apart. Good for him!

Something about the corpse's leg also answered Gerard's next question before he asked it. The bones glinted a warm blue in the firelight; it was enamelled in sapphire blue enamel. The skeleton belonged to the noble house of Dandolo. Maybe Domenico wasn't out of town after all; or maybe he'd come back?

Gerard kicked the leg away in disgust, and looked for a way out of the courtyard. He blinked the smoke out of his eyes and hunkered down low to the ground where it wasn't so thick. There was no way through the kitchen or the scullery, but the dining room might have a path through it; from what he could see through the smoke-stained glass of the double doors, the flames didn't look too bad in there.

He took one tentative step in that direction then, just as the blackened glass of the doors shattered outwards, the shards of broken glass exploding out into the courtyard. Gerard shielded his eyes, and when he looked back, the blaze in that room – which had seemed less fierce than elsewhere in the manor – had doubled in ferocity as the air from the courtyard flowed in and fed the flames. The room was instantly an impassable inferno.

A figure burst out through the broken doors, just ahead of the leaping flames. Gerard forced his weeping eyes to see who it was. Wretchedly thin and blackened by smoke, he didn't immediately recognise the figure. Then he realised it was the corpse butler, Jeff.

Its threadbare suit had been burned off it – as had much of its threadbare skin – and its exposed, blackened bones smoked as the ashes of its remaining flesh still smouldered. The ancient Risen corpse – more skeleton than corpse now – shuffled backwards out of the flames, dragging a heavy shape out of the fire. Gerard rushed to help, frantic to see which of his friends the corpse had rescued, and what state they were in. It was none of his friends. The corpse had rescued its pianoforte. Blackened and burnt, the instrument was a ruin. It would never play another note, but still the corpse had tried to save it, and Gerard helped it drag the remains out into the courtyard.

"Is anyone else still inside?" he yelled at the corpse, barely audible over the roar of the inferno, then succumbed to a fit of coughing as the smoke burned his throat. Jeff clacked its blackened jaw excitedly and, dropping the wreck of its pianoforte, gestured frantically up to the floor above.

"The Baron?" Gerard asked through coughs, and the corpse nodded.

"Just him?" He asked and it nodded its head again.

Gerard looked up through the roiling smoke to the balcony above the dining room. The Baron's balcony. He could see rippling flames had completely engulfed the Baron's bedchamber, flowing up the walls and across the ceiling of that room and burning ferociously. Nobody was alive in there.

He looked away sadly, shaking his head, but Jeff continued gesticulating insistently at the upper floor. Resigned, Gerard hunkered down once more, shielding his eyes from the heat and bright glare of the blaze and scanned the upper floor again where the corpse was indicating. Indicating not at the Baron's bedchamber, he realised, but at a little window on the floor above. The third floor window of the north tower, which rose adjacent to the dining room and the Baron's bedroom above.

He squinted through watering eyes and obscuring smoke. Could it be? Yes! A figure was stood at the window of the third floor of the tower, silhouetted by the glow of flames behind them. The Baron! He seemed to be slowly rapping on the window. There was something odd about the way he was standing so still, striking the glass almost mechanically. Why didn't he just break the window and climb down?

The interior of the tower was ablaze on the floors below where the Baron was standing, and hot smoke poured out from gaps in the smouldering shiplap wood that covered the exterior and the dense growth of ivy that climbed up the side of it. Gerard grabbed a thick bough of the ivy and tested it with his weight. It was dry and brittle and smouldering, but it didn't come away.

Tentatively, Gerard pulled himself up and reached for the next handhold, ignoring the uncomfortable heat from the fire just beyond the wall, and the sharp pain of the puncture wounds in his shoulder. He couldn't ignore the stinging smoke though, and had to clamp his eyes shut tightly to keep the smoke out, feeling blindly for every handhold after the first.

Twice his grasping hands pulled away clumps of ivy and he almost slipped, and both times the tower groaned in response, its beams and walls creaking as the fire ate it from the inside out. Both times he managed to cling on and blindly find a sturdy branch to grasp, the ivy matching his determination to cling on to the tower.

It couldn't have taken much time, but it felt like an age before he reached up and grasped the sill of the third floor window. He pulled himself up level with the sill and, opening his stinging eyes, he peered in. It was indeed the Baron. His friend was striking at the glass mechanically with one hand, and the glass reverberated with each strike, the noise drowned by the deafening roar of the fire. The Baron was seemingly trying to break the glass, but his blows were too feeble.

Gerard yelled at his friend to stand back. The Baron didn't react. Gerard struck the window with an elbow, and it shattered. He knocked away the larger fragments of broken glass that remained attached to the frame.

"Can you climb down?" Gerard yelled. The Baron didn't answer. In fact he showed no reaction to Gerard's arrival or the window breaking at all, except that he stopped uselessly rapping at the window pane.

Gerard blinked away the acrid smoke once more and looked closely at his friend. The Baron's eyes were completely vacant and unseeing; he was completely absent. Belle was perched on his head for some reason. How had the doll not fallen off? Gerard didn't have time to ponder how the Baron had been able to get to the window and strike the glass whilst blacked out, instead he pulled himself up to the sill and threw one leg in. He grabbed Belle from the Baron's head, and stuffed her securely inside his bloody doublet. Then, planting one foot on the floor, he reached in and grabbed the Baron bodily and hauled him across his shoulders. He was lighter than he looked.

Climbing up had been difficult and precarious, but climbing down with the Baron across his shoulders was far more so. The fire was now licking through the gaps it had burnt in the shiplap, and the ivy was starting to burn. Gerard didn't climb down so much as slip down, and he landed hard at the bottom of the tower, and stumbled backwards into Jeff. The ancient corpse braced him and kept him from falling.

As soon as he landed and stepped back, the tower groaned – sounding almost like a sigh of relief – and the wall ignited with a pent-up fury. A ball of liquid flame rolled up the wall from the base, completely consuming the shiplap and the ivy. Gerard found himself silently thanking the tower for holding the flames back until he was down.

That still left him trapped in the courtyard with a comatose man, an ancient Risen corpse and a cross-dressing alligator, while the surrounding buildings burned furiously.

Gerard looked around for a way out and saw only fire and smoke. There was only one thing for it; the Baron had told him explicitly never to go there but there was no choice now. At the far side of the courtyard at the side of the burning scullery was a raised metal grille in the ground; a vent for the catacombs below. The only way out of the courtyard now, was through the crypt.

***

Heat. A dry, scorching, all-encompassing heat; the very air burned the man's throat as he breathed through the tattered veil that covered his mouth. His hands shielded his eyes from a violent barrage of fine red-hot sand; a storm of heated particles powered by a rageful torrent of deafening wind that blasted into his face. He forced his eyes open and saw a searing white light through the translucent gaps between the fingers of his hands.

Turning away from the jet of blasting fury, he hurried across the burning, roiling sand. The hot wind lashed at his back, billowing round him to claw viciously at his face. Where was she? He looked around anxiously, risking another glance towards the raging furnace. He couldn't see her. He couldn't see anything. He felt panic rising. She had been with him a moment ago – guiding him, helping him – for he was useless without her. He didn't belong in this hellscape but she had lived her whole life here; she knew its dangers well. He would surely have died here without her.

A hand reached out and grabbed him. It was her! He felt a warmth that had nothing to do with the furious heat of the hell he was in. She pulled him close and embraced him as the burning sand whipped around them both with an elemental fury.

At that instant, the Baron's consciousness returned. A moment earlier he had been in the arena driving a corpse chariot. He was no longer in the arena; he must have blacked out. He was no longer in that other place either; that hell of blasting heat and burning sand. What was that other place, and who was that woman who had embraced him? he had loved her, he thought… had it been a dream? It had seemed so real!

His senses ebbed back into focus, and he struggled to see. There was heat in this place too; the heat of fire. There was smoke too, so thick he couldn't see. His throat was cloyed with the acrid fumes and he was immediately overcome with a fit of coughing. His chest was constrained; someone had a burly arm around him, they were hauling him up a flight of stone steps as flames lapped around them. Whoever it was, was coughing too.

That other place was surely a dream. His unconscious must have invented it to make sense of what was really happening; he wasn't being embraced lovingly in hell, he was being dragged out of a burning building in La Crosse.

He pulled away, his legs flailing for purchase on the steps, and the person – the man – released him and he turned to see it was his friend Gerard. A length of burning wood dropped down into the stairwell from above, narrowly missing them and showering them with burning ash. Gerard grabbed him by the shoulder and guided him up the rest of the steps as more burning debris dropped down to join the piles of it that already lay around the scorched ground.

They ran clear of the burning building, and the Baron finally realised where he was when his feet crunched on the gravel of the path, and he turned to see his family home completely engulfed in flame. He stopped, aghast. What the devil was happening? Gerard pulled him further away, and they were joined by Jeff and Rufus – who had followed them up the stairs and away from the burning house – and they all halted finally by the derelict boathouse.

"What happened?" the Baron asked plaintively. "Is everyone okay? Where are the others?" then he checked his breast pocket in a panic. "Where is Belle?"

"I didn't see what happened, I was blacked out as well. I came to a few minutes before you did," Gerard answered. He was black from the smoke – they all were – but the big man was also slick with blood from a wound on his shoulder. "But Rufus had destroyed a sapphire blue skeleton corpse."

"Dandolo!" the Baron exclaimed. "I thought Domenico was out of town?"

"So did I," Gerard replied grimly. "I don't know where the others are," he continued, "I don't think they were here. The four of us are fine. I have Belle here."

Gerard reached into his ruined doublet and retrieved the knitted doll; she too was black with smoke. Relieved that she at least was safe, the Baron took her gratefully and settled her in his pocket where she belonged.

His house though! And all his ancestors! As he watched, the burning south tower collapsed into the structure with a crunch of splintering wood and a burst of flame that rolled out across the rest of the burning manor, sending up a plume of smoke and debris.

"I'm so sorry Baron," Gerard said, placing a hand on his shoulder supportively. Rufus nuzzled up next to him as well, and Jeff looked on mournfully.

"I brought you out through the crypt," Gerard said. "I know you told me never to go there, but it was the only way."

The Baron had told him not to go there because his ancestors would have been angry. That didn't matter now. Without their shrines – without the artifacts of their lives that anchored them here – they would be gone forever. The burning building would collapse into the crypt below and the fires would destroy the last remnants of the De Villes.

"I grabbed these on my way through the crypt," Gerard said, setting a shoulder bag down on the ground. The Baron startled as he recognised the bag. It had been his grandmother's knitting bag.

"I don't know why," Gerard continued, "but something seemed to urge me to grab this and fill it with as many of the trinkets from the alcoves as I could."

The Baron watched as the big man tipped out the bag onto the ground, and dozens of his ancestor's treasures tumbled out. Medals and signets and books and cameos and all sorts. The fifth Baron's spectacles.

The sixth Baron's flute. His father's pocket watch. And so much more besides.

"I'm sorry," Gerard said. "It was dark and smoky and we were hurrying so I didn't know what things to rescue, I just grabbed handfuls of things and stuffed them into the bag. I hope I did the right thing in saving them?"

The Baron embraced his friend in a back-slapping hug. "You did the right thing, old boy. Thank you. Truly."

He released Gerard and stooped to pack all the things back into the bag. As he did so he felt his ancestors with him. It was faint, but they were still there.

They watched the house burn sombrely for a long moment, and the Baron felt the anger building. He turned to his friend. "Domenico Dandolo burned down my house." It was more a statement than a question.

"Yes," Gerard said simply.

The Baron dusted himself down. He knew what he had to do, and watching the house burn wasn't it. "Come on. We have to get to Flotsam."

Gerard nodded. "I know. I… I was just giving you a minute."

"We don't have a minute." The Baron said curtly. "We need to get to Flotsam before they attack Joanna and Sundra. Hopefully Epifani and Thessu will still be there, and maybe the others as well. They'll need our help."

The Baron turned and jogged towards the landing jetty, Gerard joining him a pace behind. They reached the end of the jetty where the two-man gondola was moored, and they caught a look across the delta towards the city. The core islands were aglow with multi-coloured lights, the sky above lit with fireworks. Carnival had started.

To the south of the core islands though, a distinctive amber glow lit the sky above the gulf. Not the glow of carnival lights, instead the glow of fire. There was fire on the floating island of Flotsam.

"I think we might be too late," Gerard said grimly.

"No, there might still be time," the Baron replied, hurrying to untie the gondola. "I don't think they've got to Joanna yet,"

"How can you tell?" Gerard asked.

"No earthquakes," he said matter-of-factly. "The world hasn't ended yet."

***

Thessu smelled trouble long before the alarm bells were rung. Fire was always the biggest danger onboard a ship, and that danger was magnified here on Flotsam where tens of thousands of people lived cheek-by-jowl upon the wrecks of many ships. Thessu smelled the tell-tale scent of burning pitch from his passenger cabin on the Queen of the South, and bolted out the door. He ran up the stairs to the foredeck, and on up two more flights to the observation deck at the top of the ship.

Epifani was already there, sat sharpening her stiletto. She was often sharpening her stiletto. She had picked up a new one from somewhere, and spent a quite unnecessary amount of time honing and polishing it. Epifani looked up at him quizzically as he emerged onto the deck. "Fire," Thessu said breathlessly.

"Again?" Epifani answered with a dismissive wave of her knife. "Theres always a damn fire." She returned to her work, making slow precise passes of the blade across a leather strop. "Some drunken pirate probably fell asleep with a lit cigarette again."

Thessu strode to the gunwale and scanned the floating island around them. The high-sided junks that surrounded the paddle steamer blocked much of the view, but he could see the tell-tale coil of smoke rising from the far side of the outpost to the east. He opened the filter slits of his mask and took a good sniff. It didn't seem too serious; perhaps Epifani was right. Carnival was underway, and many of the pirates – indeed many of the inhabitants of the city – would have gone to the core islands to join the festivities. Most of them would be returning drunk.

Alarm bells rang out soon after, calling muster for the pump crews, and Thessu was reassured that the fire would soon be brought under control. He watched the smoke rise for a minute, unable to really see what was happening, then turned to Epifani. "Any word from the others?"

"Nope," she answered without looking up.

Thessu frowned. The others had been gone for several eves, and had left him and Epifani to guard the girl and the old woman. Not that they needed much guarding; not with two spectres and a cordon of Scarlet Fist pirates already watching over them. Mostly they avoided disturbing Joanna and stayed out of Aunt Sundra's way, and took turns sitting up here supposedly watching out for trouble. It was very boring. 'Peace is born of vigilance,' he thought.

He turned back to the rising smoke in time to see the explosion. It began with a flare of stark white light, far brighter than the ever-setting sun behind him. He flinched away from the light.

When he looked back, the light had gone, replaced by a rising column of flame. Then he felt the blast a moment before he heard it. The shockwave ripped across the water and up through the structure of the ship – of all the ships in Flotsam – tearing away loose planks and smashing windows as it expanded outwards. The sound was deafening despite his covered ears, and echoes rumbled round the island. The column of flame roared upwards through its own halo of smoke, forming a burning cloud in the shape of an umbrella.

Epifani joined him at the gunwale. "What happened?" she yelled, and Thessu barely heard her, the sound muffled by the reverberations from the blast and the continuing ringing in his ears.

"The fire must have breached the magazine of one of the warships," Thessu yelled in response. He could barely hear his own voice. "I doubt it was a drunk with a cigarette," he continued. "Not even pirates are stupid enough to smoke in the powder magazine!"

"Or maybe you don't grasp how stupid pirates are!" Epifani retorted.

The umbrella of fire and smoke billowed up into the sky, leaving a rich amber glow behind and several wide plumes of thick smoke; the explosion must have started many fires.

The noise of the blast quickly subsided, but the ringing persisted. Alarm bells were ringing all across Flotsam, calling all crews to muster. Every able seaman on the outpost was being summoned to assist the pump crews. Thessu knew they would have their work cut out for them, no doubt the warship and the ships surrounding it would be beyond help, and the fire marshals would be ordering crews to douse or scuttle ships further from the fires to halt their spread.

Thessu was torn whether or not to go and help with the wounded. There would be dozens – maybe hundreds – of casualties from the explosion and the fires. He only wished he fully trusted Epifani enough to leave Joanna and Sundra in her care. Perhaps if some of the Scarlet Fist crews that maintained the cordon on the surrounding junks came aboard to take his place, he could go and be useful.

"The pirates are leaving," Epifani announced, gesturing at the junks that surrounded the paddle steamer. Thessu looked at their decks and saw she was right, the pirates on board those ships were scurrying away. Those crews were supposedly exempt from general muster; they had orders to stay and guard the Queen of the South no matter what. They were hastening away to help regardless; or possibly, the pirates were just hastening away. They were pirates after all. Damn.

"We should check on Joanna," Epifani said. "And the old woman, if she's awake?"

"I ain't goin' sleep through that racket!" Aunt Sundra said. They both turned to see her climbing the last of the steps to the observation deck. Thessu was glad to see the old woman up and about, then frowned. His filter slits were still open; he could smell her tumour from across the deck. They hadn't seen much of her the past couple of eves; her condition had worsened, and she suffered constant migraines. She looked drawn and frail.

"Was that a explosion?" the old woman asked, leaning heavily on her stick as she hobbled over to join them by the gunwale.

"Yes, my guess is the magazine of one of the warships exploded," Epifani answered. "It's a shame nobody knew it was going to happen," she continued dryly. "If only we could see the future we could have warned them."

Aunt Sundra gave the woman a sour look. Epifani had baited her similarly several times over the past few eves. It was a familiar conversation. "You know I only see things if I'm lookin' for 'em. An' I been too tired to look at much."

"The pirates are mustering to help," Thessu said.

"Yes. You should go too," she replied. "There's goin' be a lot o' people needin' doctorin'."

Thessu frowned. "I don't want to leave you unguarded. Especially with the pirates leaving their posts."

Sundra smiled and patted his hand reassuringly. "I ain't unguarded. I got ma shadows, an' I got Epifani here."

Thessu's frown deepened. The old woman knew his reservations about Epifani; they'd had their own repeated conversations over the past few eves, and she'd dismissed his concerns. For some reason the old woman trusted her.

"Are you sure?" he asked.

"I am," she replied. "Go put that gift o' yours to use. Epifani, will you kindly join me in the lounge? We should probably sit wi' Joanna since it's jus' the two of us now."

Thessu gave Epifani a last searching look. She looked shifty as usual. He sighed and checked his medical bag, then hurried off towards the fires.

***

"Good evenin' Aunt Sundra," Joanna said as the old lady stepped through into the lounge bar alongside Epifani. Joanna was dressed as always as a fortune-teller, a heavy black witch's robe covering her baby bump, and was decorating her booth with arcane-seeming bric-a-brac as she always did at the start of her loop.

"Good evenin' Joanna," the old lady replied. "I hope you don't mind if I rest my old bones in one of these booths?"

"Of course I don't mind, just so long as you know…" Joanna started.

"…That the bar ain't open yet and guests ain't supposed to be here until dinner service?" Aunt Sundra completed.

Joanna laughed. "Why, you always know exactly what I'm goin' say!"

Epifani snorted. Even she knew everything the girl was going to say. She paid Joanna no heed, instead she glowered at the shadows in the booths behind where the young woman was setting up, where she knew two spectres were lurking.

She had become more accustomed to their malevolent presence over the past few eves, though not to the extent that she could tolerate them; if anything the opposite was the case. Instead, familiarity only meant she was more aware of them. When she'd first encountered them they had almost eluded her, so subtle was their presence, but since then, she had learnt to distinguish them from the background clamour of Risen that dwelt in Flotsam. She was confident now that she would never again be surprised by a Risen shadow, and that she could suffocate one just as easily as a regular corpse.

Aunt Sundra lowered herself into a comfortable armchair in one of the booths near the door, and Epifani sat opposite, taking the seat that afforded the best view of Joanna, and of the shadows behind her where the spectres lurked. Epifani and Sundra sat in silence for a time, as Joanna bustled about, lighting her candles and hanging her strings of bones and shrunken skulls.

"I've got something for you, Epifani," Sundra said suddenly, interrupting the silence.

Epifani regarded her coolly. "Oh yes? What's that?"

The old woman reached into her handbag and pulled out a slender bundle; something wrapped in a square of undyed cotton. She placed it on the table between them. It looked to Epifani a lot like the wrapped-up stiletto she had received from Dandolo.

Curiously, Epifani reached out to the bundle and unfolded the cotton wrap. Inside was indeed another stiletto. It had none of the quality that the one from Dandolo had; it was a purely functional item, with a hammered steel blade and a cord leather grip. It was a pale imitation of the exquisite one in her boot.

"Thanks, but I've already got one," Epifani said, flipping the loose corner of cotton back over the knife and sitting back in her chair, arms folded.

Sundra seemed to consider a long moment before asking, "Epifani, how do you think fate weavers affect the tapestry?"

Epifani shrugged, not sure what that had to do with the stiletto and not sure that she believed all the nonsense about tapestries in any case. "I dunno, you tell me?"

"Well we talk about weavin' fates and unpickin' knots, an' I'm sure it sounds like a load o' mystical hocus-pocus," Sundra said. Epifani smirked at that. That was exactly what it sounded like.

"The truth is that most of it ain't magic," the woman continued. "At the most basic level, changing the course o' destiny means ensurin' different choices are made, ones with a more desirable outcome. A lot o' the time, the wrong choices get made simply because people don't know they got a choice at all. Ensurin' the right choice gets made and the right outcome results, is often as simple as presentin' a choice to someone who didn't know they had one."

Sundra pushed the flap of cotton aside again, once more revealing the simple blade on the table. "I know you already got a replacement dagger, an' I know who gave it to you. Would you kindly put it on the table next to this one please?"

Intrigued, Epifani reached down and withdrew the elegant stiletto from the concealed sheath in her boot. She debated whether she trusted the old woman not to shatter it like she had her last one. She placed it cautiously on the table, watching the woman like a hawk, her hands resting either side of the two blades.

"There now," Sundra continued. "Two stilettos. One from Dandolo an' one from me. One o' them an exquisite work of art, no doubt a pleasure to wield, the other purely functional. It'll do the same job, but maybe wont feel so comfortable. It might seem like the choice of which one to use is obvious... an' maybe it is."

Here the old woman reached out and placed her hands on Epifani's. Her hands were cold, her skin delicate like fine silk. "But I want you to know you have a choice, Epifani. And when the time comes to choose, I want you to make that choice consciously, in full awareness that there were other options you could o' picked and you didn't. An' I'll have to trust that you goin' make the right choice."

Epifani looked dubiously at the two blades. It really wasn't much of a choice, she knew exactly which one she preferred. The Dandolo blade was lighter, sharper, more fine in every way. What point was the old woman trying to make? She was uncomfortable with Sundra's hands on hers, and so pulled away. "Um. Sure. I'll try and choose the right knife."

"She's not talking about knives Epifani," said an unfamiliar voice. "She's trying to sow doubt in your mind about your greater purpose; ridding the world of Risen."

Epifani startled and leapt to her feet, her eyes on the doors behind her. She hadn't heard anyone enter. Stood in the doorway was a woman Epifani didn't recognise, a tall middle-aged woman with fine features and close-cropped grey hair, wearing a gown of sapphire silk.

Joanna screamed; not at the woman, instead at the two spectres who leapt out of the shadows to shield her from the sapphire woman. Epifani felt their presence flare in her mind like a smouldering fire doused with oil. She flinched away involuntarily, repulsed by them.

Aunt Sundra stood and concentrated on the sapphire woman. Then she gasped. "Citrine! It was you all along? I been keepin' tabs on the wrong Dandolo!"

The woman – Citrine Don Dandolo – smiled triumphantly. "This charade is over, Sundra. It's time for Joanna's child to be born and fulfil his destiny."

"You're crazy!" Sundra said, shaking with anger. "That boy's destiny is to end the world, you damn fool!"

Citrine laughed and shook her head pityingly, then walked slowly forward. The spectres tensed and pressed close around Joanna as she approached, and Joanna screamed once more.

"That boy's destiny is so much more interesting than that," Citrine said dismissively. "But you and your coven are too narrow-minded to see the bigger picture. You think the destruction of the tapestry means the destruction of the world; I assure you it does not."

"Tell me how killing Joanna gets rid of the Risen," Epifani demanded.

"I'm not going to kill her," Citrine replied evenly. "Only her child has to die. Come with me Epifani, we will take the girl from here and I will explain everything."

"No!" Sundra yelled, stepping in front of Epifani to face the intruder. The old woman leant heavily on her stick and seemed to focus her blind gaze on Citrine in the same way she had done when she had caused Epifani's old stiletto to shatter. Citrine winced and took a step backwards, and then she too seemed to focus her gaze. The air between them crackled and fizzed, Citrine appearing blurred through the rapidly vibrating haze.

Tables and chairs within the volume of crackling air suddenly cracked and broke apart in an orgy of violent destruction. The wood of the furniture splintered and sundered, the glassware, crockery and lamps on the tables shattered and the tablecloths ripped apart. Even the carpet underfoot pulled apart in great swathes of ripped material and the deck-boards beneath burst away from their joists.

Then Sundra's walking stick exploded into matchstick-sized shards of wood, and the old lady crumpled. Epifani caught her as she fell, and saw a trickle of blood seeping out from beneath her blindfold. She opened her mouth to talk, and Epifani saw it too was full of blood, which stained her teeth red and seeped out from the corners, running down her chin.

"Joanna's not goin' anywhere, Citrine," Sundra said falteringly. Once she crosses that threshold the loop'll reset!"

"Only while you're alive, my dear," Citrine replied, wiping the blood that had trickled from her own mouth and nose. She focussed again and the air between her and Sundra crackled once more. The deck-boards underfoot tore up by Citrine's feet, then a wave of destruction ripped across the gap between them, shredding carpet and deck-boards and everything in its path. The riptide reached Sundra before she or Epifani could react, and the old woman – still slumped in Epifani's arms – convulsed as the force tore apart the front of her tunic, shredding clothing and flesh and bone. Joanna screamed once more as Aunt Sundra coughed out a torrent of blood.

Epifani felt the old woman's heart booming in her chest like a drum. One boom. Two booms. Three booms. There wasn't a fourth, and she slumped lifeless in Epifani's arms. Her frail body had been shredded like her walking stick.

Citrine staggered, catching her balance on what was left of the doorframe. She looked exhausted by the exertion, and the trickle of blood from her nose had become a flood. She caught the blood in a silk handkerchief, which she wadded to her nose.

"Now we just have those irksome shadows to deal with," she said sternly. "This is your moment Epifani. I know you can feel their odious presence, I know you long to snuff them out. If you're ready to join me, kill them, and we can take the next step on our journey together."

Epifani laid the old woman on the floor carefully and stood back up. This then was the real choice the old woman had meant with her stiletto metaphor. She looked grimly at the two hateful spectres that were restraining Joanna, then swept her gaze between the old woman lying dead on the floor and the sapphire woman who had killed her. The woman who had bailed her out and the woman who had condemned her. The woman who had trusted her and the woman who wanted her to betray that trust. The woman who had tried to protect the world and the woman who promised to usher in a new one without the Risen. Epifani knew what choice to make. Damn them both!

She reached back to the knives on the table, and winced as the repercussions of her choice sank in. She took a deep breath and closed her hand around the hilt of the stiletto resignedly. Around the hilt of the simple stiletto Sundra had given her. In that moment, she just couldn't betray Remy and the others.

CHAPTER 28

Thessu returned to the Queen of the South as quickly as he could.

The cause of the explosion on the far side of the outpost had been pretty much as he had guessed; a fire had ignited the powder magazine of a Scarlet Fist warship. What he hadn't guessed though, was that the fire had been started deliberately.

The duty warden at the muster point had told him that an unknown galley had drawn up alongside the warship, and spilled forth a cohort of Risen that had boarded the ship and overwhelmed the dock crew, before lighting fires around the sealed magazine.

Thessu immediately recognised the description of the Risen. According to the duty warden, among the cohort were skeleton corpses with blue enamelled bones and spikes adorning their skulls. Skeleton corpses of the house of Dandolo. The explosion – the fires – were nothing more than a distraction; he knew Joanna was the target.

There were many casualties. Scores were dead and hundreds more were badly burned or injured in the blast. Many more would likely die in the resulting fire, which the pump crews were struggling to contain. He wanted to stay; more lives would be lost because he didn't. He would repay Domenico Dandolo for that.

When he reached the Queen of the South, it was devastated. The doors to the lounge bar were torn apart and hanging off the heavily damaged frame. Inside, the room was a wreck of broken furniture and furnishings, and of disanimated corpses.

He found Sundra's body first, and her injuries made no sense. She had been ripped apart as if by an explosion, but there were no signs of burns or shrapnel as an explosion might produce. Her blindfold had slipped off and her dead eyes stared vacantly. They were milk-white with cataracts; she had been blind long before her tumour appeared. He hadn't known that about her.

He followed Epifani's scent and found her buried under the wreckage of Joanna's booth. She was alive, but unconscious. She had taken a blow to her head and was likely concussed, but otherwise had no significant injuries. He moved the debris off of her, and passed a tiny vial of ammonia under her nose to wake her.

"Where's Joanna?" she asked when she came round.

"I was going to ask you that," Thessu replied, placing the foul smelling salt back in his medical kit. "She's not here. Easy, don't try and get up. Take a moment."

"No, we don't have a moment," Epifani said urgently, attempting to rise. "Citrine killed Sundra and took Joanna. We have to go after her."

"Citrine? Citrine Don Dandolo?" Thessu asked, perplexed. Why would Caballier Dandolo have killed Sundra and taken Joanna, wasn't it her son that had posed the danger? And didn't they supposedly hate each other?

Epifani rose groggily. "Yes it was her all along. Domenico wasn't involved."

Thessu helped her up, and they scanned the wreckage of the lounge bar. "Did you kill all these Risen," Thessu asked, impressed by the number of disanimated corpses buried in the debris. There were at least twenty that he could see.

Epifani shook her head. "I got three or four, the two spectres killed most of them. Citrine ripped the lounge apart with her mind, trying to find their copper marques. She destroyed them but it cost her most of her Risen and most of her strength. Still I couldn't stop her taking the girl once the spectres were dead. Where is Crosskeys?"

"Crosskeys the pirate?" Thessu queried. "He was here as well?"

"He came in just after Citrine left. I told him to follow her. Then I must have blacked out. How long was I out?"

"About ten minutes," Thessu estimated.

Epifani cursed and pushed past Thessu towards the door. "Come on, we've got to catch them up."

Thessu studied her for a moment before following. Epifani had fought to protect Joanna. Maybe he'd been wrong to mistrust her?

***

"Look there, old boy," the Baron said to Gerard. "That galley is going at quite a clip!"

Gerard looked up from his position at the back of the little two-man gondola, where he was paddling furiously to get them to Flotsam. The galley the Baron had indicated was indeed racing away from the outpost at a very fast rate, heading northwards towards the core islands. With the dense smoke of the raging fires on Flotsam clinging heavily to the ocean's surface, they wouldn't have seen the ship at all as it raced through the darkness with no lamps lit, if it hadn't passed to the west of them, directly in front of the ever-setting sun.

"I see it." Gerard replied.

"They're mad to be going that quickly in this mire with no lights on," the Baron continued. "Especially with so many other boats in the water."

Gerard agreed. The stretch of water between Flotsam and the core islands of the city was always busy, but the strait was especially full of boats during carnival, ferrying revellers to and from the festivities. This evening though, there was a good deal of added congestion from boats abandoning Flotsam to escape the fire, and the waters around the outpost were a miasma of dim green lights haloed by the veiling smoke.

Hundreds of small craft – all that were seaworthy plus many that weren't – had peeled away from the floating island to hold at a safe distance. Gerard and the Baron had already had to steer their gondola around several rickety boats and rafts that they had happened upon, those craft appearing suddenly from the smoke as they drifted haphazardly away from the outpost.

"Look, there's another one!" the Baron announced, pointing through the smoke to another brooding shadow; a second galley that raced recklessly after the first. The second galley was far bigger and seemingly faster, with the sense to have viridian lamps lit. From its outline, it was a sleek wargalley.

Gerard ignored the pair of galleys to the west of them as he focused on paddling the gondola south, putting all his effort into getting the two of them to Flotsam as quickly as possible.

Suddenly an enormous boom echoed across the water, followed by several more in quick succession. Gerard turned to see that the first galley – close to having been caught by the second – had come about to turn its flank to face its pursuer, and had fired its broadside cannons. The darkened galley was suddenly lit with the glow of a dozen cannon blasts that volleyed fire towards the larger ship that pursued it, each blast of the cannons illuminating for an instant the deck of the lead galley, and the dozens of indistinct figures that were crewing it.

Gerard couldn't tell through the smoke what damage the cannon fire had done, only that the pursuing ship had been struck, and the sound of cannon balls ripping through wood and screaming crew reverberated across the water.

Even as the cannon fire ripped into it, the pursuing ship maintained its course and speed, propelled by dozens of oars pulling powerfully in unison. If anything, the speed of the pursuing ship increased, and it turned to point directly at the flank of its prey.

"By golly old boy, I think she's going to ram her!" the Baron announced, standing up in the prow of the gondola to get a better look at the unfolding battle. "What the devil is going on? Why are those ships battling each other?"

"Baron, I get the distinct impression that whatever happened on Flotsam, we missed it," Gerard said. He nodded at the two ships. "That's where we need to be headed."

"Yes, I think you're right," the Baron said gravely. "Can you get us there?"

"Let's see," Gerard replied. He turned the gondola towards the west, and started paddling with renewed vigour, the prow of the gondola lifting out of the water with each violent thrust of the paddle. The Baron stumbled backwards, almost falling overboard as the gondola suddenly changed direction and accelerated.

"Gerard," the Baron said, scrambling back to his seat. "Please try and get us there in one piece. I don't want to have to swim there on the back of an alligator!"

Gerard smirked as he paddled. The last time they'd boarded a ship, that's exactly what they'd done. Sadly, they hadn't brought an alligator with them this time.

***

The big man got them to the wargalley surprisingly quickly, yet they had still missed much of the battle, and it wasn't until they got aboard that the Baron worked out what was going on.

They were still approaching the wargalley when it slammed into the smaller ship it had been chasing. The wargalley was built for such manoeuvres, having as it did a steel-capped ram protruding from the front of its hull below the waterline. They were close enough now that the Baron recognised the wargalley. It was the flagship of the Scarlet Fist – the Triton – and the huge carved wooden figurehead of a fearsome sea warrior with trident and conch shell adorned the prow of the ship just below the bowsprit.

The smaller galley had jinked desperately to avoid presenting its flank perpendicular to the Triton's ram, and the galley corpses of that unknown ship had used their oars to try and fend the approaching wargalley away.

The Triton was too heavy and travelling too quickly to be halted by such tactics however, and the oars of the smaller vessel crumpled and snapped as Crosskeys' flagship powered through them, its ram striking the unfortunate galley just aft of amidships. The smaller vessel shuddered and rocked as the Triton's momentum carried it forward to imbed deeply in its flank, locking the two ships together.

The deck of the Triton was several feet above that of the smaller vessel it had rammed, and the Baron watched the crew of the bigger ship – the pirate crew – clambering down onto the other ship's deck, where a pitched battle began.

The hulls of the ships loomed overhead as Gerard paddled them closer, and they lost sight of the fighting above them.

"Which ship?" Gerard asked urgently, the big man sounding puffed out from his formidable effort.

"The smaller," the Baron replied, thinking that the battle was happening mostly on the deck of that ship, and also that it would be easier to climb.

Gerard grunted agreement, and turned the gondola towards the unknown galley that had been rammed. As they approached, they got a good look at the damage inflicted by the ram; the smaller vessel was holed below the waterline, and only the Triton's continuing presence plugging that hole was preventing the catastrophic flooding of that unfortunate vessel.

Pulling alongside the unknown galley, Gerard lined the gondola up below where a broken spar was hanging down over the side of that vessel, dangling loose from severed rigging lines. Gerard checked his axe was securely slung across his back, then reached up to grab the spar, testing it would hold his weight. It held, and he started hauling himself up. The Baron once again marvelled at his friend's strength and indefatigability. The man had just escaped a burning building, then had rowed them here at a sprint, and he didn't even pause for breath before climbing a rope into a battle.

The Baron followed him up, and soon pulled himself up over the galley's gunwale. He had seen the battle only from a distance through swirling smoke; he hadn't recognised the combatants except to infer that one side were pirates. He hadn't been certain that he had a stake in this battle, or which side he was on. But he saw now that his inference was correct about the pirates, and also that the crew of the unknown galley were mostly Risen.

The Risen crew were a mixture of armoured corpse warriors in burnished bronze armour, and a handful of unarmoured skeleton corpses, their bones lacquered blue. The Scarlet Fist pirates of the Triton were battling against Risen of the house of Dandolo. These were the same Risen that had burned down De Ville manor, and the Baron had no doubt now which side he was on. He sided with the pirates.

The cohort of bronze-armoured Risen had formed a defensive formation of interlocked shields and spearpoints surrounding the smaller group of skeleton corpses, and what looked like a middle-aged woman in a sapphire gown. The cohort might have been formidable on land, but it was clear the corpses were not trained in marine warfare, and the tight confines of the cluttered deck made the formation impractical.

Nimble pirates attacked while ducking in and out from behind the masts and rigging and deck guns, drawing the armoured corpses out of formation before darting in between the jabbing spearpoints. Once close in, they attacked the vulnerable gaps between armour plates with sword and point-blank pistol fire. Risen of course could not easily be killed by such wounds, and so a stalemate of sorts had quickly formed where neither side could get an advantage. The sapphire woman at the centre of the Risen formation – the Baron thought he ought to know who she was, but he didn't – got increasingly frustrated as her corpses were repeatedly drawn out of position and whittled down by the greater numbers of the pirates. Perhaps she was their necromancer?

Gerard seemed to have no interest in a slow attritional stalemate however, and while the Baron was still taking stock of the situation and clambering over the gunwale, the big man thundered across the deck towards the Risen cohort.

The Baron watched as Gerard struck into the formation, swatting a spearpoint aside as he shouldered all his weight into an armoured corpse, launching it six feet up into the air; up and over the heads of the corpses behind, and on over the side of the ship. Not done, he powered into the gap he had made, laying into the corpses left and right with a huge sweeping swing of his axe that decapitated one corpse's head and continued in an arc that swung down and round, cleaving clean through the leg of another, armour and all.

The Baron hastened forward to help his friend, but before he got halfway across the deck, the ship rocked as something huge dropped down onto the deck behind him. The Baron turned and gasped in shock; the huge figurehead of the Triton – the carved wooden statue of the sea warrior with trident and conch – had ripped free of the prow of the pirate ship and dropped down onto the deck of the smaller galley below. Somehow the inanimate statue had been imbued with the simulacrum of life.

The wooden figurehead slowly rose on its scaled piscine tail to its full height – twice the height of a man – and then hurled its conch across the deck, bowling pirates down like ninepins. It then started laying into the pirates with its carved wooden trident, swung in big two-handed swings like a massive club. One pirate, too shocked to move or duck, took the heavy bludgeoning swing full force to the side of his head, and his skull caved in under the force of the blow; he skittered twenty feet across the deck and was dead before his body landed. Another pirate ducked under the swing just in time, but his skull was caved in just as thoroughly as the figurehead's heavy wooden tail lashed around in a trailing arc that followed in the wake of the trident swing.

A rattle of gunfire rang out from above as a group of quick-thinking pirates still aboard the Triton fired a volley of muskets at the monstrous creature. The shots pattered into the figurehead, denting and splintering off small chunks of its hardwood body. The wooden warrior ignored the superficial damage, and swung its trident through the group, crushing rib-cages and sweeping four of the pirates over the side of their ship.

The Baron stumbled backwards away from the figurehead as it continued lashing wildly at pirates. He considered the creature, and considered the slender blade of his cane sword. He knew he couldn't harm it with that. The pirates had realised the same about their own weapons and were also retreating away from it. The thing was unstoppable! If he had had time, the Baron would have marvelled at it; he had never seen such magic before, but a scream of pain behind him returned his focus to the battle. One of the nearby pirates had been impaled by a corpse's spearpoint. Without realising, the Baron had backed up almost into the formation of Risen.

The pirates had been gaining the upper hand; Gerard's attack had driven a wedge through the ranks of the armoured Risen, and crewmen from the Triton had immediately poured into the gap, but the appearance of the figurehead behind them had thwarted the attack. The Risen closed ranks around Gerard and a handful of others, who were now surrounded by the corpse soldiers.

A shout came from across the deck of the galley then, over the din of battle. "Scarlets! Rally to me, me hearties! A hundred livres for whoever cuts down that bitch!"

The Baron looked and saw it was Crosskeys; the one-eyed pirate captain was in the thick of the fighting on the far side of the armoured formation from Gerard's group. Between them, in the centre of the formation, the sapphire woman was barely visible. Her face was gritted in concentration as she stared right past the Baron to the wooden warrior, and her unblinking eyes were weeping blood. Whoever she was, Crosskeys wanted her dead.

She was no mere necromancer, the Baron realised, as it dawned on him that it was she who had animated the monstrous figurehead. The Baron knew what the thing was now, it was a golem. He had never thought to see such magic in his lifetime; that woman had rare gifts indeed if she could create a golem!

Crosskeys was right; he had surely figured it out as well, that the best way to defeat the golem was to kill the woman!

The formation of armoured Risen that protected her were stretched in two directions by Crosskeys and Gerard. The ranks were thinnest directly in front of the Baron; only two ranks of armoured Risen stood between him and the woman. Gritting his teeth, he turned his back to the golem and pressed forwards towards the bristling ranks of spearmen.

The corpse soldiers in the front rank held their ground in the face of the Baron and the pirates at his side; the two corpses nearest him jabbing their spears toward him as he closed. The Baron rapped both speartips aside with his cane sword, then moved swiftly forward into the gap between the shafts. The spearman in the second rank had its spear poking through into that same gap, and the Baron twisted to catch that spear under his trailing arm as it jabbed at him, clamping his free hand onto the shaft.

He pulled hard on that spear shaft to off-balance the second rank spearman and launch himself forward towards it. As his body struck the shield of the left-hand spearman in the front rank, he thrust his cane sword through the gap and into the head of the second-rank spearman whose spear he had grabbed.

The Baron's sword struck the corpse soldier between the cheeks of its open-face helm, catching it under its top lip. The sword tip continued on, clumsily raking across its left cheek, ripping a flap of skin away from its face before catching in its cheekbone just below its left eye. The slender blade flexed as his momentum carried him towards the corpse, but he had missed his mark and failed to penetrate its facial bones. The ugly wound he had caused would not trouble the corpse.

The front rank spearman whose shield the Baron had struck, braced and slammed the shield back into him. Winded, the Baron released his grip on the spear shaft and dodged back again, parrying the two speartips of the front-rank spearmen once more as he withdrew. The disciplined corpse soldiers stayed in formation, their unruffled demeanour daring him to try again.

He didn't have to. The two spearmen in the front rank, and the one behind suddenly crumpled and collapsed, disanimated, to the deck.

"Go Baron! Now!" called a voice from behind him. Epifani's voice. He didn't hesitate, he leapt forward into the gap before the armoured

Risen could close ranks, and burst through the formation towards the sapphire woman.

The woman's face was still seeping from every orifice and the front of her gown was slick with blood. One of the sapphire skeleton corpses threw itself in the Baron's way, but too late to prevent him driving his cane sword at her heart. His aim was true, and the slender foil blade pierced the woman's chest between two ribs and drove through her body almost to the hilt, the blade erupting from her back with a spurt of blood.

Blood welled at the site of the wound, and as the sapphire skeleton tackled the Baron aside, he withdrew the blade, and more blood spurted out as it came free.

The sapphire skeleton corpse tried to wrestle the Baron to the deck, but skeletons only became skeletons by wasting away; they retained their strength but lacked the weight and bulk of a living person or a corpse. The Baron knocked the skeleton aside, and tossed it clear over the side of the ship, and for a moment imagined how Gerard must feel after performing a prodigious feat of strength.

He looked back at the woman, expecting to see her collapsing dead to the deck, instead she remained standing, her face still clenched in concentration. His aim had been true, his sword had run her through where her heart should be; blood should be gouting forth in pulsating bursts with each pump of her dying heart. It was not. Thick, viscous blood simply seeped out slowly from the wound in a gradually widening stain on her gown. She turned her gaze on him, and he felt a cold dread as she smiled malevolently.

He instinctually leapt aside as an enormous cudgel slammed down into the deck where he had been standing, hard enough to shatter the deck boards. He looked up to see the monstrous figurehead looming over him. The golem wrenched its trident free of the deck and whirled it round in a vicious arc aimed at the Baron's head. There would be no avoiding the deadly swing and he threw his hands up ineffectually to cover his head as he flinched away.

There was an almighty crack of breaking wood and something big and heavy missed his head by mere inches as it flew off over the side of the ship. He opened his eyes to see Gerard stood before him, his feet braced and his axe recoiling from having struck the trident mid-swing.

The big man had cleaved a path through the formation of Risen to reach him, and had chopped through the shaft of the trident and one of the figurehead's hands in one great swing of his axe. Two-thirds of the trident shaft had flown overboard, along with one of the hands that held it.

The enormous figurehead tossed aside the butt of the broken trident and reared up to its full impressive height once more, dwarfing Gerard. Then it exploded. The Baron flinched away again as huge chunks of wood cleaved off the creature. Then he looked across the deck to see what had happened.

Two crazy pirates had fired one of the galley's deck guns at point-blank range. They had taken out the creature and a pair of Risen in a single cannon shot. By some miracle, neither Gerard nor the Baron had been killed by the shot or the shrapnel, and nor had any of the pirates.

The shot had struck the figurehead in the back at the base of its torso. The cannonball had ripped a huge chunk of its flank clean off it, and it staggered, holding onto one of the galley's masts to keep itself upright.

The muzzle-smoke cleared and the Baron saw the two crazy pirates weren't pirates at all; it was Thessu and Epifani. The Baron would chastise them for their recklessness later. The figurehead was still moving; still dangerous. Someone still had to kill the sapphire woman.

The Baron turned his attention back towards her to see her grimacing as she fought to keep the golem animated. All around her, corpses were being felled by the pirates who now pressed their advantage. The battle was all but won. The Baron stalked forward and drove his sword through her chest once more, again to little effect. Why wouldn't she die?

Gerard struck her with his axe. He chopped down at her neck, cleaving through collarbone and ribs, hacking her open from shoulder to sternum. The side of her body flopped away limply, and she gasped and collapsed to her knees, her opposite arm reaching across to hold herself together. As she fell, so did the figurehead. It hardened in that last pose it had held, leaning on a mast, then fell face-first to the deck where it crushed two more of the Risen underneath it.

The pirates cheered and, led by Captain Crosskeys, redoubled their efforts to mop up the last of the Dandolo corpses.

Thessu and Epifani jogged over to join the Baron and Gerard by the sapphire woman. "Is she dead?" Thessu asked.

She wasn't. The woman not only wasn't dead, she somehow managed to talk, despite her devastating wounds and the fact her lungs had been cleaved open by an axe.

"You'll come to regret your choice Epifani," she said, not even sounding hoarse. "When you do, you can always change your mind. The option will always be there, I'll make sure of it."

Then she did another impossible thing. She stood back up again.

They were all too dumbstruck to react. The woman still wasn't finished doing the impossible. She didn't just stand, she walked. She walked the few paces to the side of the ship, swung her legs up and over the gunwale, and dropped down over the side.

"What the fuck?" Gerard exclaimed.

The four of them rushed to the gunwale and looked down. There was no sign of her.

"Does anybody know who that was?" the Baron asked, certain they hadn't seen the last of her.

"That was Citrine Don Dandolo." Thessu said matter-of-factly. "She killed Sundra and took Joanna."

"She took her? Where?" the Baron asked.

"She must be somewhere on this ship," Epifani replied, looking around. "We have to get her somewhere safe. Where is she?"

"Below deck maybe?" Gerard guessed, looking around. "Or in the sterncastle?"

"No," Thessu said. "She's there." He was pointing out across the gulf to the north, where, almost out of sight in the distance through smoke and dim light, a small rowboat – one of the galley's tenders – was sculling furiously away from the battle, headed towards the ocean dock of Isla Verdé. The little boat had almost reached it. Once her captors had taken Joanna ashore, they would disappear into the carnival crowds.

There was no way to get there in time. Joanna was lost to them.

CHAPTER 29

"Oh look, they're celebrating the carnival on Flotsam as well," Colin said cheerily as the outpost finally came into view. "There's some sort of regatta of little boats, and they've lit pretty beacon lights."

Remy turned wearily around to look upon the floating island, still far to the south, out in the gulf beyond the delta. In truth he was dreading that first look at their destination; they had spent the past fourteen unbroken hours in a race to get back and he feared that once he looked, he would see that their efforts had all been in vain.

First on horseback, they had ridden their corpse horses to destruction to get back to the little creek where they had left cousin Caleb. He'd been reclining on the riverbank in almost the exact same pose as when they had left him, except he'd built a rudimentary shelter from leaves and sticks, and a dozen little fish were grilling over a little campfire. The Risen horses had collapsed as soon as they dismounted, completely spent.

They had abandoned the rotten, disanimated carcasses of the horses by the levee, along with a small pouch of gold livres as apology, hoping the farmer from whom they'd hired the beasts would find them. Remy had explained their urgency to cousin Caleb, and he'd wordlessly abandoned his shelter and his lunch and his canoe, and taken the tiller of their barge to better pilot them in haste. From there, they'd paddled down the creek and across the swamp, then on down the mighty Poconovo. To preserve their barge corpses, Remy and Valanthé and Colin had been taking shifts on the oars. Still the barge corpses were showing their exhaustion, and so were the three of them.

The last leg of the journey had been across the Poconovo Delta, navigating the many branching channels of the river that threaded between the islands of La Crosse. And now, as they rounded the southern tip of isla Vecta – a small island famous for its glass blowing, which lay just to the east of Isla Verdé – they finally caught sight of their destination.

"Colin, those ain't beacons," Remy said with a frustrated sigh. "They fires. Flotsam is on fire! And that ain't no regatta, that's a sea battle!"

Smoke hung heavy across the gulf from the fires, and whatever the battle had been about, it looked like they had missed it. A large wargalley had rammed and boarded a smaller vessel, and the two ships were now locked together, the smaller galley devastated by a pitched battle on its deck that had seemingly just concluded. They were too far away to make out who the combatants had been, but the bigger of the galleys looked like a pirate vessel.

"Remy, look!" Valanthé said urgently.

Remy turned to look where she was indicating. Valanthé was pointing the other direction, towards Isla Verdé, where a big crowd had gathered on the dockside to watch the dramatic scenes unfolding in the gulf. The docks would have been busy anyway, Remy reasoned, due to the carnival crowds arriving on the core islands for the festivities. "What am I looking at, Valanthé?"

She redirected his gaze towards a little rowboat that was racing towards a small pontoon at the near side of the dock where the crowds were much lighter. The rowboat was dangerously overloaded and travelling dangerously fast without a light, propelled at the oars by six corpse soldiers in heavy armour while three passengers sat squashed together at the stern. It was peculiar, but Remy still didn't grasp the significance, and he looked back at Valanthé quizzically. What had he missed?

She rolled her eyes exasperatedly. "The passengers, Remy! Look close!"

He stood up in the boat to take a closer look. He couldn't tell anything about the three figures sat at the stern of the little rowboat at this distance; they had their backs to him. Then he realised what he was missing.

"Skeleton corpses," he scowled. "With spikes on the top of their skulls. I know those corpses!"

In the dim light, their colours were muted grey, but he knew close-up they would be blue. The noble house of Dandolo enamelled their skeleton corpses sapphire blue, and adorned their skulls with metal spikes.

Valanthé nodded. "I think the other passenger isn't a willing one," she frowned. "In fact, I think it's Joanna!"

Remy couldn't tell anything about the third passenger, but on the off-chance she was right, they had to check.

"Caleb, follow that boat," Remy instructed.

"A'ight." Caleb said, and swung the tiller round, redirecting the barge towards the northwest, directly towards the little pontoon where the rowboat was headed.

As they rowed closer, they saw the rowboat pull alongside the pontoon, and the armoured corpses quickly disembarked, before two of them reached back and grabbed the third passenger from the boat while the slender skeleton corpses scrambled out. As they did that, their captive tried to pull away, distressed, and let out a muffled scream. She was gagged and her hands were tied. Remy didn't get a look at her face – which was covered by the hood of her cloak – but he did see she had a noticeable baby bump. He was sure it was Joanna.

By the time Caleb had the barge drawn up behind the rowboat, the corpses had already dragged the girl – Joanna – to the end of the pontoon where three sapphire-blue corpse buggies were waiting; small four-wheeled open-top carriages each drawn by two Risen horses, driven by a corpse driver.

The Dandolo corpses piled into the three buggies, dragging Joanna with them and pushing her down into one of the footwells. They sped off along the docking pier towards the esplanade and the maritime district of Isla Verdé beyond, as Remy and Valanthé and Colin leapt off the barge.

"Wait here, Caleb," Remy called back.

"A'ight," his cousin replied, nonplussed.

Remy's legs were aching from the punishing journey, but their effort hadn't been wasted; they were not yet too late! If only they could catch those buggies they could recover Joanna and it would all have been worth it!

They raced along the docking pier and vaulted the steps up to the busy esplanade, which was gaudily decorated with festive bunting and banners and brightly-coloured lanterns and strings of plaster skulls. The speedy buggies were already in the distance, turning north onto one of the side streets that ran parallel to the main thoroughfare through the maritime district. They were headed towards the commercial centre of the island, the Piazza Grandé, and the three bridges entertainment district. Where were they taking her?

They lost sight of the buggies, and were soon caught up in the crowd of people on the esplanade. All those who had been watching the naval engagement from the dockside were slowly drifting back towards the festivities now that the battle had concluded.

Remy felt a pang of regret to be missing the revels; this had previously been his favourite time of year. Every noble house in La Crosse would be demonstrating their largesse over the carnival season and, while not every house could afford to sponsor a spectacular revel in the Pits, there would be hundreds of other events and entertainments all over the core islands. The festivities drew huge crowds, and kept them in the party mood with liberal free food and drink.

Remy led the three of them into the street the corpse buggies had taken, and they glimpsed the buggies again, far ahead through the thronging crowd, turning into another side street and out of sight once more.

They lost and regained sight of the buggies twice more as they pressed through the crowds after them. The way northwards got ever more crowded the further they went, as the maritime district gave way to commercial streets lined with bars and bordellos. Every street was a riot of colour and noise; every establishment was hosting a lively party with food and drink and entertainment, and every street was more busy and more noisy and more gaudily decorated than the last. Every galleried balcony was packed with musicians and revellers and dancers, and the many bands and musicians on the streets and balconies vied for dominance among the cacophony.

"Pardon me… excuse me miss… make way there please…" Remy said to the people as he pressed past, leading the way through the throngs for the three of them. He was getting increasingly irate at the crowds. Most were either unable or unwilling to move aside with any urgency, and some of the revellers were making their pursuit of the buggies especially hard.

One woman – topless bar the strings of beads and flowers around her neck that draped over her chest immodestly – grabbed Remy's face with both hands as he passed, and drunkenly planted a big, wet kiss on him.

"Remy we don't have time for that!" Valanthé admonished.

"I know," Remy answered through gritted teeth as he pulled away from the woman. He grabbed her shoulders and steered her aside, then stepped past and put his hand out to prevent her drunken friends from accosting him as well. He felt something drop lightly over his head, and reached up to find one of the woman's flower necklaces draped half over his head and half tangled in his horns. His payment for the kiss, he knew. The women screeched with laughter. Damn he missed carnival!

Colin had fallen behind, and Remy reached back to grab him and pull him forward through the crowd. The kid's eyes were wide as saucers; he didn't seem to know where to look, so overwhelming were the sights and sounds and smells of the raucous carnival streets. Mostly he was looking at boobs.

"Remy, please can we come back here later," he asked plaintively as Remy pulled him away from the gaggle of topless women. "Once we've done whatever it is we're supposed to be doing?"

"Sure, kid," Remy replied dismissively. "Once we're done savin' the world."

They pressed on to the next junction, which opened out to the Piazza Grandé, and Remy caught a glimpse of one of the corpse buggies on the west side of the piazza, heading towards the nearest of the three bridges to Isla Roja. They jogged across a rare gap in the crowds before getting waylaid again; a bare-chested man – his body stained purple and yellow by coloured powder dye – jovially attempted to place a string of beads over Valanthé's head, while leaning in for a kiss. She slapped his hands aside and kneed him in the crotch, then jogged away. That was one way to deal with unwanted attention, Remy thought wryly.

"They're headed for the three bridges," Valanthé called out.

"Yes, I see one there, headed for the first bridge," Remy replied, pointing at the retreating buggy.

"No! Look," she said, gesturing across the piazza to the north-west. "They've split up. They're headed to all three of the bridges! Which buggy has Joanna in?"

"Shit," he said. He had no idea which one was carrying Joanna. They would have to split up and take one each.

***

The Piazza Grandé was more busy than Valanthé had ever seen it; revels had clearly just finished in both Pits, and crowds were emptying out of both the arenas and filling the plaza between. The crowds were enjoying music and entertainments from several bandstands and stages around the plaza, and refreshments bought from the many food and drink stalls and market barrows that trundled through the crowds with different wares for sale. The scent of death that usually lingered in the plaza was masked by the smell of the crowd; the smell of warm sweat and stale beer.

As well as food and drink, and the ubiquitous strings of beads and feathers and flowers, the barrow corpses were also selling paper bags filled with powder dye, and a high-spirited dye fight was in progress, a huge free-for-all where participants gaily pelted each other with multi-coloured powders.

The quickest way to the farthest bridge was through the middle of the ruck, so Valanthé dipped her head and charged through, nimbly avoiding several powder bags before she was hit; a package struck her in the side of her torso and exploded red powder all over her chest. Then another clipped her thigh, painting the left side of her combat leathers blue. The raucous crowd cheered both strikes, and she narrowly avoided more striking her back as she pressed on towards the bridge road.

The crowd was denser as she approached the northernmost bridge. Besides being major thoroughfares and traffic bottlenecks, the three bridges that connected Isla Verdé to Isla Roja were destinations in and of themselves, and were famous for the bars and casinos that lined them. During carnival they were completely rammed with people. She saw the corpse buggy ahead, not quite halfway across the bridge. It was bogged down in crowds as well, and was making very little headway.

She tried pushing through the crowd and found it impassable. She looked up instead to the galleried balconies of the bars and casinos that enclosed the bridge-top all along its span. Those too were full of revellers, but they didn't seem quite so packed as the bridge was at street level.

She forced her way through the crowd to the veranda of the nearest building, a busy saloon bar, and scrambled up onto the railing and up to the balcony above, where a three-piece band were enthusiastically playing upbeat music for the crowd. She clambered past them, pushing a cornet angrily aside as the irate musician tried to blast it in her face.

She climbed over the railing and stepped gingerly across the gap onto the balcony of the next building, where she barged past a troupe of dancing girls, and on to the next balcony where a well-to-do couple were sedately drinking wine and soaking up the carnival atmosphere, while their son was furtively watching the dancing girls next door.

She pressed on across several more balconies, finally gaining ground on the corpse buggy which seemed to be stuck in the crowd below. The seventh balcony was level with the buggy, and as she reached it, she looked down into its open carriage. As well as the corpse driver and two Risen spearmen in burnished bronze armour, she saw a cloaked and hooded figure bundled in the footwell. Joanna!

Valanthé shimmied down to street level once more, drawing her short sword as she pushed through the crowd towards the buggy. The Risen driver was lashing the horses to get them moving, but the backs of the corpse horses were already shredded by lash-marks; there was nowhere for them to go, the crowd ahead was too dense. The buggy inched forwards a couple of feet at most before Valanthé was upon it.

She leapt up onto the back of the buggy behind one of the seated corpse soldiers, and reached over the top of its head to grab the brow of its open-face helm. Yanking back on the helm, she pulled it free of the corpse's head, leaving its padded coif behind. It turned to face her, clacking its jaw angrily as it reached back for its helm. Valanthé swung her leg into the buggy behind the corpse as it stretched, planting her foot on the seat, and swiftly pressed the tip of her blade into the gap at the top of its armoured gorget at the back of its neck.

She plunged the blade down behind its gorget and levered down with both hands to expose the top of its bony spine. It writhed and grabbed at her, but she held the sword in place perpendicular to its neck with one hand, and hammered on the pommel with the other. That drove the sword-tip between the base of its skull and the top of its spine like a wedge, severing its spinal cord. It slumped forward on the seat, disanimated.

The other Risen soldier had gotten to its feet and chambered its spear, and she barely had time to wrench her sword free and leap clear to avoid its thrust. She dropped down into the crowd once more, and ducked under the buggy as the other corpse soldier peered over the back of it, looking for her. Scrambling between the rear wheels on hands and knees, she headed for the buggy's left side nearest to where she had seen the head of the cloaked figure in the footwell.

She popped up at the side, and jumped back in. Bracing herself on the frame of the buggy, she planted her boot on the side of the second corpse soldier and pushed as hard as she could. It staggered, and held itself from falling only by grabbing hold of the frame as it teetered on the far side. She hacked her sword down at its hand hard enough to crush the gauntlet onto its fingers, possibly severing some of them. It fell backwards off the buggy into the crowd, buying her a few seconds. Maybe enough to get Joanna out.

Ignoring the corpse driver, which obviously didn't have martial orders, she pushed aside the body of the first armoured corpse that was slumped on the seat, then reached down to the cloaked figure in the footwell. Joanna was wriggling under her hooded cloak, perhaps trying to free her hands; or maybe just clutching her baby bump protectively.

Hurriedly, Valanthé pulled the hood of Joanna's cloak aside. The hood caught on something, and she yanked it harder. It ripped away, and Valanthé gasped. The figure was not Joanna; the hood had been caught on its skull spike. The blue-enamelled skeleton in the footwell – a decoy, she realised – turned to face Valanthé then, its sapphire jaw clacking like laughter. It had no baby bump; instead it was holding a small keg like as might contain gunpowder. And in its other hand, a lit match-cord. Before she could stop it, it yanked the cork plug out of the keg and shoved the match-cord into the plug-hole.

"Shit," she managed to say, before it exploded.

***

The crowds on the central bridge of the three were the thickest Remy had yet seen. Fireworks were launching from the roof of one of the buildings that lined the bridge about halfway across its span, and revellers had packed the bridge at street level to watch the show and enjoy free food and drink sponsored by one of the minor noble houses of the city.

Remy had had to force his way through the crowd to even reach the bridge, but with it already so busy and with more people pressing into the narrow defile between the close-packed buildings to watch the fireworks, it had become almost impassable. At least the corpse buggy was also struggling to get through the bottle-neck; he saw it a mere fifty yards ahead through the crowd, stopped completely still by the press of people.

He redoubled his effort to reach the buggy, forcefully shoving people aside to create space, which earned him angry reactions from those people he shoved. A drink was tipped over him, and he ignored it. A little further on, someone struck him in the back, and he ignored that too.

He finally reached the corpse buggy and found it overrun by the crowd. Dozens of people had clambered onto it to gain a better vantage point to see the fireworks, or just to escape the press. The crowd of people standing on its seats and running board and rims and clinging on to its sides or sat astride the corpse horses that drew it, were every bit as densely packed as the surrounding throngs, and the corpse driver clacked its jaw at them impotently.

There was no sign of the other Dandolo corpses that had boarded at the dock. He yanked a youth off the back of the buggy out of his way, and climbed up to get a look ahead, to try and spot the distinctive armoured Risen or sapphire skeletons; or better yet, to try and spot Joanna.

Fireworks had been shooting overhead, intermittently illuminating the crowd with shifting light in a variety of colours. A red light bloomed as another one exploded spectacularly overhead, and he saw the light reflected in the upturned faces of the roiling crowd ahead, and from the burnished bronze armour of the two corpse soldiers in their midst. They were pushing through the crowd, dragging a cloaked and hooded figure along with them. That must be Joanna!

Remy barged his way across the open top of the buggy, and dropped down beside one of the corpse horses. He lost sight of the armoured corpses as the glow of the firework faded, so forced his way forward to where he'd last seen them, shoving people aside to get past.

An armoured fist lashed out from the crowd ahead of him and struck him in the face. He saw it late, but still flinched back away from the blow just in time to save himself a broken nose. He reeled back, pain flaring from the bloody welt in his cheek, and caught himself on the press of people around him. It wouldn't do to fall prone here if he could avoid it; the crowd was such that he would likely get crushed. The Risen corpse pushed forward towards him, the nearby revellers doing their best to step back out of its way.

It swung another gauntleted fist towards his face, and Remy stepped to the side, blocking the swing clumsily as he struggled to regain his balance. He clung to its arm and it stumbled forwards, encumbered by his grip and the press of people, and losing its own balance. He glared into its rotten decrepit face for an instant as they both teetered, then both fell heavily to the ground, landing side-by-side.

Reacting quickest, Remy yanked the corpse's arm from under it to stop it pushing itself up, then he twisted, shifting his weight to slam the corpse onto its back, then threw a leg across it to sit astride it. It struggled, flailing angrily with its arms but unable to rise with Remy's weight pressing it down. He didn't have time for a prolonged fight; he had lost sight of the other Risen spearman and of Joanna, so he gritted his teeth and reached through the open face of its helm with both hands.

His thumbs found the corpse's copper marque hammered into its forehead beneath the brow of its helm. Remy's eyes flared angry flames and he channelled heat from his core through his hands and into the small metal disc. The disc heated rapidly, blackening and deforming, and the corpse's skin scorched and caught fire in a halo around it. Still Remy clung on, ignoring the frantic blows of its arms trying to dislodge him. It must only have been a few seconds, but seemed like an age before the disc finally softened and then melted, the molten copper dribbling down the burning ruin of its face, and the corpse disanimated.

Remy stood, patting down his sleeves where they had been singed by the bonfire that the corpse's head had become, and shoved the shocked crowd aside to press on towards Joanna.

He didn't have to go very far. The other corpse soldier was only a little way ahead; it had a long knife drawn and was half-dragging, half carrying the bundled figure that must be Joanna alongside it through the crowd.

Remy drew his rapier and with his other hand, grabbed the corpse's arm that was wrapped around the slender hooded figure, wrenching it away from across cloaked shoulders. The figure stumbled, dropping to both knees, hands protectively holding something beneath the cloak; something with the outline of a baby bump.

The armoured corpse whirled to face him, and Remy parried its knife aside then stepped defensively between it and the kneeling figure it had been hauling through the crowd. He only barely parried a second knife slash; the press of the crowd and the need to defend Joanna was giving him no room to move.

He shouldered forwards before the corpse could swing again, and white-hot pain lanced through his shoulder as he slammed into its breastplate. It stumbled back, flailing its arms as it struck the packed crowd behind it, creating the space he needed to kill it. Remy thrust his rapier up through the exposed gap under its raised chin, above the top of its armoured gorget.

The blade drove up through its throat, piercing the soft palette at the top of its mouth, and on into its brain, flexing as it caught on the roof of its skull beyond. He wrenched his sword free as the corpse collapsed, disanimated, in the arms of the alarmed people of the crowd behind it. A man screamed, and pushed the body of the corpse to the ground, disgusted.

Remy turned to the cloaked and hooded figure, still kneeling on the ground clutching what he assumed was a baby bump under the cloak. He reached out a hand and tore back the hood.

***

The Risen spearman saved Valanthé's life. Not on purpose, of course, in fact it had very little say in the matter; it was already disanimated. With no time for her panic to well up and bubble over in the brief instant before the skeleton corpse blew itself up, Valanthé lunged across the cab of the buggy to the body of the first corpse she had killed, which was still slumped dead in its seat. With a super-human effort born of necessity, she yanked it bodily from the seat and turned to hold it as a shield between her and the exploding powder keg.

The blast slammed into the body of the armoured corpse like a wall of angry flame that all but engulfed her impromptu meat-shield. The flames exploded with such force that it threw them both backwards, clear out of the buggy, and into the arms of the other corpse soldier who had been rising to its feet. They all landed heavily, Valanthé momentarily stunned and winded by the impact, her ears ringing and her eyes blinded.

"Get up!" she told herself through gritted teeth as her senses swam back into focus. She shoved the armoured body of the first Risen corpse aside from where it had landed on top of her, and looked urgently to the second, which was lying next to her on the ground. It was covered in burning wooden debris and had a scorched, blue-enamelled femur embedded in its face; it wasn't going to get up.

She wriggled fully out from under the first corpse, and saw that it too had been blasted with shrapnel. More burning debris lay on that corpse, and it had a length of twisted, blackened iron – a band from the powder keg perhaps – lodged in its shoulder, it having sliced clean through a bronze pauldron. A Dandolo skull spike also protruded from its breastplate, the top of the sapphire skeleton's skull still attached. She checked herself over. She was singed but not burnt. Bruised but not broken. She had the disanimated corpse to thank for that.

The buggy was a bonfire. The intense heat of the conflagration and the thick acrid smoke urged her to get moving. She laboured to her feet and sheathed her sword, then someone shoved her hard in the back, and she almost fell prone once more. Another shove from the other direction kept her upright. Someone stumbled over the corpses and fell. Several someones. They tried to rise, but more people kept pressing all around, adding to the crush.

Muffled background noises resolved into terrified screaming all around her. The densely-packed crowds were panicking, and as she forced her way away from the bonfire, she was caught up in the tide of panicked people. People were going to be trampled to death, she realised. She felt the rising panic herself and swallowed it down hard. A surge of wild magic now could only make things worse. Much worse.

A youth next to her stumbled and fell, dragging another down with him. Valanthé quickly reached out and hauled the nearer one back up to his feet but the crowd had already carried her away from the other. She didn't see him get back up, and there was no way to fight through the crowd of people and go back; no way to go anywhere other than where the tide was carrying her.

The tide carried her towards the buildings. She tripped on something and nearly fell. Not something; someone. She caught a glimpse of blonde hair and pale skin as she stumbled over it, and then the crowd surged and it was gone. People on the balconies were reaching down into the crowd, hauling people up to safety, and she could do nothing more than reach up and hope. She reached up. And hoped.

Hands clasped around hers, and she scrambled up the people around her as she was dragged up to the balcony. She grabbed hold of the bars of the railing and hauled herself up and over. The balcony was crowded with people; she had no idea which one of them had rescued her.

Valanthé looked down and gasped at the scene. She hadn't travelled very far from the buggy, perhaps only twenty yards along the bridge back towards Isla Verdé. The buggy was still burning furiously, and she saw now that burning debris had been thrown in a wide ring around it, and there were several smaller fires burning. Pyres, she realised; most of the smaller fires were burning bodies. A further trail of flaming destruction headed west across the bridge towards Isla Roja; the two burning corpse horses from the buggy had clearly blazed a path through the crowd before the fires consumed them.

Everywhere was a crush of people; all those revellers in the packed bars and casinos had joined the crowds on the street, panicked at the thought of the fires spreading to the wooden buildings that lined the bridge. The blast had killed many people; Valanthé dreaded to think how many more would be killed by the crush, their bodies laying hidden until the street could be cleared.

She did what she could to help; she hauled people up onto the balcony. A topless woman, her strings of beads lost to the crush. Two little boys, held up above their father's head. A man. A woman. Another man. Endless people.

Someone pulled her away from the railing, someone bigger and stronger with a longer reach. Numbly, she wiped the tears from her eyes and headed in to join the other rescuees inside the building.

She remembered Remy and Colin were chasing buggies on the other two bridges. One of them would hopefully have found Joanna, but the other would likely have found a decoy much like this one. There was a good chance one of them was dead; killed by an explosion or the resulting crush.

"Damn you Citrine!" she cursed angrily as she made her way up the stairs towards the top floor of the building. From there she would make her way back to Isla Verdé across the rooftops; she had to find out which of her friends had been killed.

***

Joanna was bloody and bruised under the hood, and her panicked expression showed no recognition in her eyes. Remy sheathed his rapier and squatted down next to her, but still she shied away.

"Miss Pianna, my name is Remy Du Rosier. I'm a friend of Aunt Sundra, I'd like to get you somewhere safe away from these corpses if that's alright?"

He stood and reached down a hand to help her up. "Please miss, it ain't safe here."

Her eyes flitted to the body of the corpse soldier Remy had killed, then back to him. She nodded agreement and reached up to take his hand, then suddenly winced like she was in pain. It seemed to pass after a moment and she rose. "Thank you Mister Du Rosier, I don't really know what's happenin' but I would very much like to go somewhere safe away from these corpses."

As she stood, Remy realised what had momentarily caused her pain before easing. Her hands were on her belly. Her baby was coming.

Chapter 30

"Fiendling horns!" Gerard announced, "I think it's Remy!"

"It's about time," Epifani grumbled, though she was secretly relieved if he was safe. "Has he got Joanna with him?"

"Maybe. I can't tell," Gerard replied. "He's with someone... maybe two people. One of them looks injured."

Epifani climbed up next to the big man on the wall of the esplanade and peered across the crowds of people. It sure looked like Remy's horns, she thought, but they'd previously mistaken other people in the crowd for their fiendling companion or his sidekick. Those people turned out to be wearing carnival masks with plaster horns.

She turned to Thessu, who had also climbed up. "Can you smell if it's him?"

He shook his head, and the stupid leather beak of his mask swung side to side. "No, there's too many people, I can't pick out a single scent from the crowd. It looks like he might be coming this way though, so we'll know soon enough."

"More waiting then," Epifani grumbled, and climbed back down to resume pacing back and forth along the pontoon.

In the aftermath of the battle, they had watched impotently from the gunwale of the galley as the tender with Joanna aboard had rowed towards Isla Verdé, before disappearing out of sight among the many ships and barges and other watercraft of the busy dock.

They had all piled into the Baron's gondola and the little rowboat that Epifani and Thessu had stolen from Flotsam, and powered across the strait after Joanna, in the full knowledge that she would surely have disappeared by the time they reached Isla Verdé. After a thorough search of the piers and jetties that might have been suitable for a small boat like the one Joanna had been seen on, they spotted it and, to their great surprise, Gerard had recognised his own barge moored up behind it.

Within it, they found his four leased corpses looking very worse for wear.

Epifani had taken an instant dislike to the fiendling they had discovered lounging in Gerard's barge. He had had his feet up with a wide-brimmed hat covering his face and a stubby fishing pole resting on his boot, its line trailing limply over the side of the barge. She'd guessed he must be a friend of Remy's.

"You there," she had said to him, "where's Remy?"

"Gone," the fiendling drawled in reply without looking up or lifting his hat.

She had waited for further explanation, but none had seemed to be coming. "Will he be coming back?"

"Yup," the fiendling replied from under his hat, again offering nothing further. Damned yokel!

"Pardon me old chap," the Baron had tried, "Do you know where he might be headed?"

"Nope," came the reply.

"How's the fishing?" Gerard had asked congenially, trying a different approach.

The fiendling had lifted his hat for that one, glanced at his line, and pulled the brim down again. "It's shit."

They had eventually managed to drag out of him in one- or two-word answers that Joanna had been taken away in a carriage, and Remy and Valanthé and Colin had gone after her. And that he was waiting for them to come back like Remy had told him. And so there had been nothing else for them to do except wait with the laconic fiendling for Remy and Valanthé to return, and hope they brought Joanna with them.

They had soon learned from revellers leaving the island, that there had been a deadly crush in the Three Bridges district, and many people had been trampled. Epifani had hoped Remy and Joanna weren't caught up in it.

"It is Remy!" Gerard exulted. "And Valanthé and one other as well!"

Epifani hastened back to the esplanade, hoping the other was Joanna and not Remy's annoying sidekick.

She was in luck; it was Joanna! Remy and Valanthé were either side of her, helping her walk. All three of them looked terrible. Remy had a bloody welt on his cheek and a black eye, and Valanthé was covered in cuts and bruises and scorch marks. Joanna was also badly bruised, and hobbling awkwardly like she was in great pain. She looked exhausted.

"The baby is coming," Thessu announced, sniffing the air through his mask. "She's dilated an inch and a half."

"Ugh, how do you know that?" Epifani replied disgustedly, and stepped onto the esplanade to go and help carry Joanna.

Remy seemed surprised to see her, and gave her a wary look. "Is Colin with you?" he asked.

"Good to see you too Remy," she said bitterly. "No, a cretin in a straw hat told us the kid was with you."

"Ah, you met my cousin Caleb," Remy said, smiling wryly. "Colin was with us, yes, but we got separated, an' Valanthé got herself blown up by a decoy. We think Colin might ha' been caught by another."

"So he's dead then?" Epifani asked bluntly. Remy and Valanthé gave her a frosty look.

"We don't know," Valanthé said. "We'll have to wait and hope he comes soon."

The thought of waiting longer made Epifani groan; perhaps too loudly, as it earned her another frosty look from the others.

They carried Joanna back to the barge, where the fiendling – Remy's cousin Caleb – begrudgingly moved aside so she could sit as comfortably as possible, which meant leaning back in the bow seat, resting her back on her wadded-up cloak. She balked at the sight of Thessu, but Remy assured her he was a trained physician, and she begrudgingly let him examine her belly. He prodded the sides of her belly bump with gloved fingers.

"How far apart are the contractions?" he asked.

"The what?" she answered.

"The pain that comes and goes. How often is it coming on?"

She considered for a moment. "About every five minutes, sommat like that?" she replied.

Thessu nodded, and his stupid mask wobbled up and down. "I'm going to get you something for the pain, okay?"

He stepped back onto the pontoon, gesturing for Remy and Valanthé to join him for a quiet word. Remy – who had been holding Joanna's hand – gave it a squeeze and followed after Thessu. Epifani leant in close to join the huddle, and Gerard and the Baron came over as well.

"We don't have long before this baby is coming out," Thessu said matter-of-factly.

"How long?" Epifani asked.

Thessu shrugged. "Maybe an hour. Maybe several hours. The process has started and it will take as long as it takes. We've got to get her somewhere clean and safe."

"Back to the manor?" Valanthé suggested.

Gerard and the Baron exchanged a look. "The manor is gone," Gerard said grimly. "Citrine Don Dandolo burned it down."

Remy looked away and shook his head angrily while Valanthé gasped. "I'm so sorry Baron," she said.

"I'm guessin' Sundra's dead?" Remy asked, "and the Queen o' the South ain't an option?"

"She's dead," Epifani confirmed. Remy's eyes narrowed at her suspiciously and she looked away guiltily, wishing she had done more to save the old woman.

"Surely there are midwives here on Isla Verdé?" the Baron queried. "There must be somewhere nearby we can take her?"

"Nowhere nearby is safe from Citrine," Thessu replied. "We need to take Joanna out of her reach."

"To my sister then," Remy said. "The swamp gotta be out o' Citrine's reach."

Epifani balked. "That's your plan? Thessu said to take her somewhere safe and clean, and you suggest the sodding swamp?"

"That's right," he replied, staring at her coldly. "If we can get Joanna to Elise before the baby comes, maybe she can still do somethin' to prevent the baby bein' born."

"Nothing can medically stop this baby being born or dying in the attempt," Thessu replied.

"Well I didn't mean anything medical," Remy continued. "Elise got the same gift Sundra and my mom had, to see the tapestry. Maybe she can weave a loop o' time like the weavers did."

"And if not?" Thessu asked dubiously.

"Then she's also a Mama D'Ombre now. The Mamas are trained as midwives. Does everyone agree?"

Epifani was reluctant to leave the city and head into the swamp, but she didn't have a better idea. She nodded her agreement as all the others concurred.

"Good. Let's go," Remy said, turning back towards the barge.

"I thought you wanted to wait for Colin?" Epifani said.

Remy shook his head sadly without looking back at her. "No, he was on the nearest o' the three bridges, and he wouldn't ha' been slowed down by bringin' a pregnant lady through the crowd like we was." He paused, then added bitterly, "since he weren't back here before us, he's probably dead."

The others all hung their heads in sad agreement, and Epifani let out a long breath, more annoyed than sad. She didn't know why they'd ever let the idiot kid tag along into dangerous situations with them in the first place.

Valanthé placed a comforting hand on Remy's back, and he half-turned to her as she leant in to him. Their foreheads rested together and she wrapped her other arm around him as well. After a moment, Gerard joined the embrace, wrapping his big arms around both of them, and the Baron patted Remy's shoulder comfortingly.

"I'm sorry he's dead," Epifani said, feeling more left-out than sorry.

"Who's dead?" a voice called from the esplanade at the head of the pontoon. They all turned to see Colin, strolling unhurriedly towards them.

"You're dead, you lil' shit!" Remy roared at him, pushing clear of the embrace. "Where in the hell you been?"

"I'm sorry Remy," the kid said sheepishly. "It's possible I got a little distracted and didn't reach the buggy." Shirtless, he had a dozen strings of beads and flowers and feathers round his neck, and green and purple powder in his hair and over his body.

"Dammit Colin! You an' I are goin' have a lil' talk about priorities!" Remy yelled, looking like he might pitch the kid off the side of the pontoon. Instead he turned abruptly back to the barge, wiping hurriedly at his eyes with a sleeve.

"We goin' somewhere, Rem?" the other fiendling – his cousin Caleb – asked.

Remy nodded. "Home, Caleb. An' don't spare the corpses."

***

After four hours of hard rowing, the corpses were spent. They had powered the overladen barge upstream against the current of the Poconovo, then maintained their punishing pace through mangrove pools and reed beds, as Caleb charted the fastest possible course to Remy's home village.

Thessu had never seen Risen disanimate from exhaustion before. He knew that was the fate that awaited them all at the end of their service – once damage and decay made it uneconomical to maintain them – but it was unusual for it to happen to well-preserved corpses in their prime service years like these four had been.

They had gotten gradually weaker and more jerky in their movements until, one by one, they drew back a last stroke of their paddles and – with a final shudder and clacking of their jaws in apology – they crumpled into lifeless heaps on their seats. Gerard had pitched the first one's body over the side, and taken its place, and Remy had done the same for the second. Valanthé and the Baron replaced the last two Risen when they too disanimated.

Thessu felt a pang of regret over the four tireless corpses who had destroyed themselves to get the barge to its destination at a sprint. He knew his regret was misplaced; the sprint was necessary, for Joanna and the baby were not doing well, and they might both die if they didn't get there quickly.

Her contractions had gotten stronger and closer together, but it was clear her cervix wasn't getting any more dilated. Her water hadn't yet broken – which was actually a good thing, given the unsanitary conditions of the barge – but her body was trying to expel the baby regardless, and there was nowhere for him to go. Thessu also worried about her blood pressure, which was dangerously high.

Joanna gritted her teeth and breathed through another contraction, and Thessu urged her not to push. He had removed his mask completely as she remained stubbornly apprehensive of it, and he was suffering through the overwhelming stench of the swamp and the mingled scents of corpses and childbirth, but still she hadn't warmed to him.

She seemed to have warmed to Colin though; the young fiendling had taken over hand-holding duty from Remy, and was babbling away happily to her about their recent exploits, and she seemed to find it calming to listen to his prattle.

"Let's count out the breaths together," Colin said soothingly, "and then I'll tell you about how I single-handedly rescued Remy from a spectre. One, two, three..."

"How's she doin' Thessu?" Remy asked breathlessly between strokes of the paddle.

"She's doing great," Thessu lied. "How much further is it?"

"Not far," the fiendling lied in reply.

The barge eventually turned into a narrow channel between impassable groves of mangroves and, as they entered the channel, Thessu saw the glow of viridian lamps ahead. The channel carved a snaking path between two overgrown islets and, as they continued along it, the swamp ahead seemed to thin out and the canopy of foliage overhead seemed to open up.

Thessu soon realised that the islets either side of the channel were actually both part of a circular barrier island enclosing a lagoon perhaps half a mile across. A secret lagoon in the heart of the swamp; a lagoon filled with interconnected wooden houses raised above the water's surface on wooden piles.

Remy's village, Thessu presumed. They had paddled right into the heart of it without him realising. The village was alive with people everywhere – fiendlings and the Risen corpses of fiendlings – the smell was suddenly overwhelming.

"Welcome to my home," Remy announced grandly.

"Don't expect any palazzos though," Colin added quietly for Joanna's benefit. "The people here actually live in those shabby little stilt huts, if you can believe it!"

Joanna smiled weakly. "I think it's perfectly charmin'."

Caleb brought them alongside a little jetty, where two figures in brown robes and veils seemed to be waiting for them.

"Welcome back Remy," the smaller of the figures – a young fiendling woman – said. "The priory hut has been set up for child-birthin'."

"Thank you Elise," Remy replied as he and the Baron jumped out and tied up the barge. "I should ha' known you'd be expectin' us."

The woman – clearly Remy's sister Elise – embraced him while the others clambered out and Thessu and Colin helped Joanna to her feet. The other figure in brown on the jetty – a fiendling man of advanced years – reached out a hand to help her out. "Miss Joanna is it? My name is Mama Cristophe, and this is my colleague Mama Elise. We got everythin' set up inside for you to have your baby."

He turned to the rest of them then, saying, "I'll be delighted to make the acquaintance o' the rest o' y'all once the young lady is settled. You must be tired an' hungry, so we got a guest hut set up where y'all can rest an' eat an' freshen up. Remy, will you kindly show your friends to the guest hut? Caleb – there's food an' drink for you as well o' course."

"Is there shrimp?" Caleb asked.

The man sighed. "Yes Caleb, there's shrimp."

"I don't like shrimp," Caleb replied, then lounged back in the barge with his feet up, and started rolling a cigarette.

***

Remy drew Elise aside, out of earshot of Joanna and Cristophe. "Elise I sure am glad you knew we was comin', but I was hopin' you might have a way to prevent this baby bein' born. Aunt Sundra seemed to think…"

"I know what she thought, Remy," Elise interrupted. "An' as far as I can tell she was right. When that child is born his fate will be sealed. An' when he dies, all the threads o' the tapestry will be cut short. His is a malignant thread, an' his death will destroy the whole tapestry. Aunt Sundra's dead, ain't she?"

Remy nodded. "She were killed by Citrine Don Dandolo. It were also Citrine that killed Mom."

He paused for that to sink in, but she didn't look surprised. "You knew?"

She looked down sadly. "I didn' learn about it until after you left here, and by then it were too late. You ain't gonna like to hear it Rem, but bad things gotta be allowed to happen sometimes to prevent worse things happenin'."

He smiled ruefully. That had been something their mother always used to say when disaster struck. It was exasperating.

"Elise I need to ask if you can put Joanna into a loop of time, like Sundra did?" Remy continued.

She shook her head. "No, I can't. But I know my own fate. It will be my life's work to protect that child from Citrine until he's old enough to take the fight to her."

"There's no stopping the birth?" he checked.

"There's no stopping the birth," she confirmed. She looked away sadly then. "Remy, as soon as that child is born I will be leavin' an' takin' him with me. I will hide him somewhere safe where Citrine will never find him."

Remy was lost for words. Leaving? How could she be leaving?

Elise threw herself against him in another embrace, then pulled away. "Get your friends to the guest hut Remy; I'll say goodbye before I go."

Remy stood mutely. He didn't have the words to tell her he needed her to stay. She patted his cheek tenderly, then strode back to Joanna and Cristophe.

The others thanked the two Mamas, and wished Joanna best of luck, then Elise and Cristophe led Joanna away, accompanied by Thessu. Remy took the others to the guest house; they were all of them exhausted.

***

Thessu waited just inside the door of the priory hut, allowing the two Mamas to take the lead with Joanna, and watched their efforts with interest. Mama Cristophe in particular seemed to be an experienced midwife and Elise an excellent apprentice; if they needed to call upon Thessu's medical assistance, then things with Joanna were dire indeed.

The communal chamber of the priory hut was cramped and equipment was rudimentary, but an effort had been made to clean the room beforehand, and a bed had been made up with fresh linen. A pile of clean towels had been stacked beside a basin of warm water on a side table. Doors to the other rooms in the hut had been closed, except for one which was left ajar.

Thessu saw a third Mama D'Ombre in that room; a fiendling woman of about thirty, Thessu thought, though she remained in the room and didn't remove her veil like Elise and Cristophe had done. She was sat cross-legged on the bare floor surrounded by a circle of candles. "Prayin' for the baby," Cristophe had said in explanation.

The pile of clean towels on the side table had been quickly depleted when Cristophe broke Joanna's membranes with a bone needle to release her waters, in order to encourage her cervix to open. Thessu could immediately smell blood in the fluid and Cristophe seemed concerned about that as well. He also encouraged Joanna out of the bed and had her moving around the room and rocking in a chair, supposedly also to encourage dilation.

Several hours later, it was clear it wasn't working. Joanna's blood pressure was still dangerously high and her contractions were so close together that she barely got any respite. Her body wanted to expel the baby, but there was still nowhere for him to go. Joanna was getting weaker, and so was the baby. Thessu had stood aside long enough; it was time for him to step in and help.

Thessu caught Mama Cristophe's eye, and the elderly fiendling finished mopping Joanna's brow, handing the damp cloth to Elise, and came over.

"The baby's head is obstructed," Cristophe said, confirming Thessu's assessment. "Baby is in a good position but the birth canal is too tight, and he's showin' signs o' distress. I can cut him out and save the baby, but the mother won't survive that. If I don't, then we'll likely lose them both."

Thessu nodded. The fact the man was willing to attempt abdominal surgery to save the baby was a testament to his expertise, but that sort of surgery was simply not survivable for the mother. "I may have another way. May I take a look?"

Cristophe nodded curtly, so Thessu washed his hands and examined Joanna. As Cristophe had said, the baby was clearly obstructed and distressed. He straightened up and wiped his hands. "Joanna?"

She looked at him exhaustedly. He explained the situation to her, as Cristophe had already done, and she nodded.

"I know what comes next," she said. "You want to cut him out o' me. Do it, doc. Save the baby."

"I don't think we're there yet," Thessu replied. "I'd like to try something else first, that may save you as well. I'm going to cut through the cartilage that holds your pelvic bones together, to open up your pelvis. Hopefully that'll give the baby enough room to come out. It's going to be extremely painful, Joanna, but if it works, there's a good chance you'll both live."

"An' if it don't work?" she asked.

"Then we still have the option to cut him out of you."

She considered for a moment as she grimaced through another painful contraction, then nodded. "Do it, doc."

There was no time to lose. Thessu opened up his medical bag and withdrew his scalpel, forceps and bone shears. "Mama Elise, we're going to need the strongest alcohol you have. And tell your friend over there to pray harder."

It worked.

With the pelvis opened up, the baby's head was able to engage in the birth canal and the cervix dilated quickly. Half an hour after he sheared Joanna's pelvic bones apart, Thessu delivered a healthy baby boy. With a little help, the child slipped out wetly into Thessu's waiting hands, accompanied by a syrup of blood and shit, and he wailed plaintively as Thessu held him up for Cristophe to tie and cut his cord.

Joanna was able to hold him briefly, before she died.

The blood that flowed out with the baby continued to flow, not stopping with the afterbirth. Thessu and Cristophe both tried to locate the bleed, but could not, and the end came quickly.

As her life drained out of her onto the bed, Joanna smiled at the perfect baby who clamped to her breast and slept, his bright pink skin stark against the bloodless pallor of her own.

"What was the name of that nice boy in the boat?" she asked weakly through cracked white lips. "The one who kept me company wi' tall tales?"

"You mean Colin?" Thessu asked.

"That was it; Colin. That's a good strong name for a boy."

She stroked the soft new skin of her son as he slept on her chest. And then she slowly drifted off and was gone. Thessu reached down and closed her eyelids once the blood stopped flowing, and it was clear she had died.

He slumped against the wall in silent contemplation, and a thought suddenly struck him. He had delivered a baby. What had Mother Oracle's prophecy been? The one in the note from Brother Superior? He dug it out of his satchel and re-read it.

'Thessu delivers by his hands, Twilight's death in far-off lands.'

***

Remy slept fitfully in the guest hut. He was certainly exhausted after many eves of travel, but the fate of Joanna and the baby were weighing on his mind. So he rose and dressed in clothes still damp from the washing line that hung on the sunward side of the veranda, and made his way to the priory hut to join the group of people waiting there.

Valanthé was there already, sat on a gently-rocking bench swing, which was suspended from the veranda roof by thick ropes. Her hair was loose, and it tumbled carelessly over her shoulders. She wore a loose fiendling shift that had been laid out in the hut for their use – he had seen her combat leathers drying on the line – and was wrapped in a patchwork knitted quilt. She saw him and smiled, and lifted one side of the quilt up for him to join her under it, draping her arm and the quilt across his shoulders when he sat close beside her.

"Did I miss anythin'?" he asked.

"Lots of screaming about half an hour ago," she replied. "Then we thought we heard a baby wailing, but since then it's been quiet."

"A baby wailin'?" he asked. That had to be good news.

"Maybe. I hope so," she answered.

"I hope so too," he said, and she squeezed his shoulder under the quilt reassuringly.

"Ugh, you two are sickening," Epifani said, a look of disgust on her face. She had been pacing back and forth along the deck, scowling at the fiendlings who lingered nearby, waiting for the Mamas to emerge.

"You want to join us under here, Epifani?" Remy asked, lifting the corner of the quilt invitingly. "There's room on the bench for three…"

She looked at him disparagingly. "I'd rather mount a corpse horse. What is your fascination with swings anyway?"

Remy wasn't sure what she meant by that, but realised Valanthé was suppressing a laugh. Then he remembered they'd both seen the attic room of the Madrigal where he'd been staying before it burnt down. "That was a very different sort o' swing," he protested. "An' it weren't mine, it jus' came wi' the room!"

"If you say so Remy." Epifani replied sniffily. "But I've seen your sex den, so it's a polite 'no thanks' to joining you on anything that swings," and she strode away to resume her pacing. Valanthé gave up trying to suppress her mirth.

Colin walked over then. "What is going on?"

"We jus' waitin' for news," Remy answered, glad to talk about anything else. "Valanthé thought she heard a baby wailin' a lil' while ago, but we ain't heard anythin' since."

"Then I shall wait with you," he said, and sat down on the bench on the far side of Valanthé. "Oh wow, this whole bench swings!" and he rocked the bench vigorously back and forth and Valanthé laughed again while Remy feigned indifference.

The door to the priory hut opened shortly after, and everyone turned to see Elise emerge, veiled once more, holding a little bundle of blankets. A swaddled baby. Remy leapt up off of the bench and hurried over to her, with the others close behind.

"Everyone, I'd like you to meet baby Colin."

"What!" Remy and Epifani and Valanthé all shrieked at once. "She named him Colin?" Remy asked, astonished.

"Yes, she wanted to name him after the nice boy who kept her company in the boat," Elise replied, and there was a touch of sadness in her voice. "It were her last wish, before she died."

Valanthé gasped.

"She died?" Epifani asked.

Elise nodded. "Yes, I'm afraid Joanna didn' make it. Master Thessu did everythin' he could to save her life."

"But the boy is healthy?" Epifani queried. "He's going to be okay?"

"It seems so yes," Elise replied.

Remy peered down at the little pink thing asleep in his sister's arms. Human infants weren't so very different from fiendling infants. He looked so small and vulnerable. Remy wanted to hold him, protect him, keep him safe.

"She named him after me?" Colin asked mournfully, peering down at his namesake. "I barely knew her."

"Would you like to hold him?" Elise asked.

Remy and Valanthé exchanged a nervous look, but Colin nodded eagerly and Elise carefully placed the baby in his arms, careful to ensure the baby's head was well supported. The kid had probably never held a baby before.

"He's so tiny," Colin said in wonder. "He's amazing!"

"Shame he's got such a shit name," Epifani quipped.

"Can we see Joanna?" Valanthé asked.

"Yes. Come in," she replied, turning back through the door. Remy followed with the others close behind.

The communal room of the priory hut was a mess of bloody sheets and towels which Cristophe was busy collecting, while Thessu was stood to one side, washing his medical tools in a bloody basin. Joanna lay on the bed in the centre of the room, a fresh sheet laid over her to her shoulders, though the red stain of blood seeped through it from below.

Remy approached the bed where she lay, and stood quietly with her for a time. Her face was grey and drawn, her eyelids closed. She looked peaceful.

"I'm sorry Joanna," he said quietly, overcome by remorse. The poor girl had been terribly mistreated by generations of well-meaning weavers, who had looped her thread to prevent her baby's birth. And it was all for nought, because in the end his birth couldn't be prevented, and now she was dead. It all made him so angry; all her friends and family lived a hundred years ago, and she died here in the company of strangers. Citrine had killed a lot of people to break her out of that loop, but perhaps she should never have been there in the first place.

He felt a gentle hand on his shoulder, and turned to see Elise. She lifted her veil, and her cheeks were red and puffy and her eyes streaming with tears. She had reclaimed the baby from Colin, and had donned a travelling cloak and slung a travel bag over her shoulder.

"It's time for me to go, Remy," she said.

He looked at her forlornly. "Go? Go where?"

"I can't tell you that Rem," she replied. "If I tell you, you'll try an' stop me, and you mustn't. I'm goin' somewhere this child will be safe. Somewhere he'll be hidden from Citrine. I'm goin' hide his thread from her."

Remy felt tears welling in his eyes. He knew from the look of her that her mind was made up, and he had to trust that she was doing the right thing. She could read the tapestry; there was no point trying to argue that she was wrong. He searched her eyes for some shred of doubt that he could latch upon to insist she stay. There was none. "When will I see you again?" he asked finally.

She embraced him with one arm, still holding the baby protectively with her other. "You'll see me real soon, I promise."

"It's time to go Elise," someone said. Remy turned to see it was the third Mama D'Ombre – the one he hadn't met yet – who had been sat praying in a circle of candles in a back room. She now stood in the doorway of that room. There was a strange shimmering light in the room behind her, and Remy recognised it was the ember glow of a smoke porthole like the ones his father used, but different somehow; hazy and ethereal. It hovered in the air above the prayer circle, its frame fed by the wafting smoke of the candles.

Remy had never known anyone to be able to conjure such portholes except his father. The other Mama clearly had that gift; that must be what she'd been doing in that prayer circle. Remy couldn't see where it led.

"Goodbye Remy," Elise said. "I love you, big brother."

"I love you too, lil' sister," he replied miserably. "You look after that baby now."

She smiled sadly, and walked away. She stopped to embrace Cristophe and Colin and finally the other Mama D'Ombre, then she stepped through the porthole without looking back and, just like that, she and the baby were gone. The porthole disappeared behind them.

A long moment passed in silence, then the other Mama walked over to Remy. She lifted her veil, and Remy gasped. It was Elise.

"I told you you'd see me real soon," she said. She looked like she had aged about fifteen years.

CHAPTER 31

"Elise?" Remy exclaimed, astonished. "What in the hell is goin' on?"

"It's like I told you, Rem," she replied, the corners of her eyes wrinkling as she smiled. "I took that baby somewhere safe. Somewhere Citrine couldn't find him."

Remy didn't understand. "Where in all the hells did you take him? And what in all the hells happened to you?" he yelled angrily.

Elise – the older Elise – clasped his hands in hers. "Why I took him to the past o' course. Fourteen and a half years into the past."

"You... can do that?" Remy asked, even more astonished.

"Only once. It cost me most o' my power to open that porthole to the past. I just sacrificed everything to send my younger self into the past with baby Colin."

"With baby... Colin?" Valanthé asked meaningfully.

Elise nodded slowly at her and she gasped, covering her mouth with a hand. Remy looked at her quizzically. Whatever realisation Valanthé had arrived at, it eluded Remy.

"Ask her what became of the baby," Valanthé urged. "Ask her who raised him."

Then it dawned on Remy what she meant.

"Who raised the baby, Elise?" he asked. He suspected he already knew the answer.

She looked at him levelly and confirmed his suspicion. "I had him adopted into a wealthy human family. The Du Laurentins."

Everyone turned to look at Colin.

"No," he said dully. "I would have known if they had adopted another baby."

"The baby is you, dumbass!" Epifani said in an exasperated tone.

The slow dawning of realisation grew on Colin's face. He looked anguishedly at each of them, and finally rested his gaze on Joanna. The woman who was lying dead in front of them… was his mother. He turned and fled out of the hut.

***

"What's the matter Colin my boy?" the Baron asked, as the young fiendling rushed towards him and Gerard. The two of them had risen to find everyone else gone from the guest hut, so had dressed and headed towards the priory house to find them. They met Colin coming the other way as they crossed the last rope bridge along the way. He looked distraught.

Colin tried to push past them, but the rope bridge was narrow, and Gerard wrapped his big arms around the boy to hold him up.

"Whoa, calm your corpses there, lad," the big man said. "What's the matter?"

Colin tried futilely to escape his grasp, beating his hands against Gerard's chest, then slumped into his embrace, his body heaving with sobs as his tears flowed forth.

"Is it something with Miss Pianna and the baby?" the Baron asked. "What's happened?"

"I'm the baby," he wailed between sobs, his face buried in Gerard's shoulder.

The Baron and Gerard exchanged a confused look. The Baron offered Colin a handkerchief. "What do you mean my boy?"

"I'm not your boy Baron!" he spat back, pushing himself away from Gerard and snatching the handkerchief. "It seems I'm Joanna's boy!"

They waited a moment while Colin blew his nose and composed himself. After wiping his eyes he turned his head to the sky and recounted what had happened. "Joanna had the baby and called him Colin and then she died. Elise took the baby through a magic doorway to the past and gave him to the Marquis fourteen years ago. I'm Joanna's baby."

"Oh my goodness!" the Baron exclaimed.

"Elise is gone?" Gerard said. "Is that not her there?"

The Baron looked to where Gerard was pointing. A fiendling woman who looked very much like Elise had just stepped out of the priory house. She did look older though.

"That's the Elise who took me to the past," Colin replied. "She's fourteen years older now as well."

"Where were you rushing to, my boy?" the Baron asked.

Colin shrugged. "I don't know."

"Why don't we go hear what she has to say," Gerard suggested.

"That sounds like a good idea," the Baron agreed. Reluctantly, Colin nodded and the three of them headed to the veranda outside the priory house, where the woman who looked like Elise had sat on a rocking bench. The others emerged from the priory house as well, and joined them on the veranda.

"Miss Du Rosier I presume?" the Baron said. "Can you tell us what happened."

The woman – Elise – greeted them warmly and confirmed what Colin had said. Joanna was dead and he was her son.

"I took Colin to the past to keep him safe," Elise recounted. "Fourteen years ago was long before Citrine got her powers o' foresight, so I knew I had plenty o' time to learn to weave the tapestry. I couldn't change his fate – nobody can – but I was able to conceal his thread so even those with the gift o' foresight couldn't see him."

She paused to let that sink in. That explained why Aunt Sundra couldn't see Colin.

"An' while he enjoyed a normal, happy childhood free of any interference…"

"A normal happy childhood?" Remy interrupted scornfully. "You knew he was a fiendlin' and you took him away from his people and gave him to a human couple!"

"A wealthy human couple, yes, who gave him everythin' he needed, includin' the kick he needed to meet y'all. An' don't berate me Remy, remember you my lil' brother now."

"Oh, do not start with that 'lil' brother' shit!" Remy snapped. "I am your big brother, an' I always will be!"

"Wait, Joanna was human," Valanthé interjected. "How come Colin is a fiendling?"

"That I do not know," Elise replied, frowning. "Colin, it's possible your father was a fiendlin'."

"Or a devil," the boy said matter-of-factly.

"That also may be possible," Elise conceded. "Might even be the most likely case, given the diabolical fate you're stuck with."

She again paused for effect, before adding, "Joanna never said who the father was, but she were pregnant for a hundred years. I'm sorry Colin, that means if your father were a fiendlin', he's certainly long dead by now."

Colin looked crestfallen once more. The kid had only just learnt that his birth mother was dead, and now understood that his real father was likely dead as well. Dead or a devil. The Baron was closest to him, and pulled him into a tight embrace. He felt Belle in his breast pocket, pressed between them, and imagined her hugging the boy as well.

"So you're the one who manipulated us all to bring us together?" Epifani asked.

Elise nodded. "Yes. For fourteen years, I worked to re-weave all your threads to make sure y'all met an' took Colin under your wing, an' worked together to keep him safe." She smiled wryly. "I been mighty busy the past few months tyin' all your threads together."

Gerard's hand went to the scars on his forehead. "You're the one who raised the batch of corpses I was part of!"

"Yes," she replied unapologetically.

"What else did you do?" Epifani growled.

"Hundreds o' things!" she exclaimed. "For you Epifani, what's goin' piss you off most, is that it were me who told the zealots about your safehouse. It were tricky timin' on that one to make sure you was out when they came knockin', an' that you'd be able to catch the river bus to Isla Doble."

"But it couldn't all have been you? Not even Mom was that good! Surely it was pure chance that we even met Colin!" Remy insisted.

"Was it Rem?" she grinned. "My future self told me exactly what changes to make, an' I had fourteen years to prepare. Hundreds o' things had to line up to get y'all in the right place at the right time, but when everythin' else was in place, I jus' had to hang some posters an' sit on a bench in the path of a runaway barrel."

They all angrily spoke over each other then, demanding more answers from her about what else she'd done to manipulate them all. The Baron cut through them all. He wasn't interested in recriminations about what brought them together. He had another pressing concern.

"Silence!" he called, and his voice reverberated through the wood of the veranda, shaking the walls and rattling the lattice windows of the priory house and echoing back from the surrounding buildings, rumbling away to nothing like the aftermath of a thunderclap. They all quietened down and looked at him, surprised at his sudden menace.

He relaxed his tension and released the shadows he had wreathed himself in. He restored his jaunty smile and asked Elise, "why do Gerard and I keep blacking out?"

Her own smile faded. "That I do not know. I been tryin' to understand that myself. The best I can tell you is that you ain't blackin' out at all."

"It sure seems like we are," Gerard replied.

"No. Aunt Sundra told you your threads were frayed? That's only part o' the story. Some strand o' your threads has gone somewhere else, an' don't ask me how or where or why, 'cause I don't know, an' it ain't supposed to be possible. Somehow a part o' your threads are somewhere else an' I can't find them anywhere in the tapestry, and I looked everywhere.

"When it seems like you blackin' out, I suspect your consciousness is transferrin' to your lost strands. I think there's a good chance some part o' you both is livin' another life somewhere else, an' when you fall asleep or black out in one place, you wake up in the other. I have no idea where it is you both go."

It sounded crazy, but somehow seemed to ring true. The Baron remembered the vivid dream he had had the last time he blacked out. "Is it possible I could remember the last instant of one life when I wake in the other?"

Elise shrugged. "I have no idea. Do you remember anythin'?"

"Only a snatch of a memory," the Baron replied. "A place of scalding heat where the very air burned to breathe it."

"I had a vivid instant of somewhere else when I last blacked out as well," Gerard added. "It wasn't hot though, it was a place of dense fog; I was being chased through the fog by demonic creatures."

Elise looked at them with alarm. "I'm so sorry. It sounds like you both in Hell."

***

As next of kin, Colin could have arranged for Joanna's body to be taken for sale in the city as was expected, but instead he donated it to the village and Cristophe performed the ritual to raise it for service. Fiendling communities owned all their Risen jointly, and so her corpse was put to work dredging the waterways.

First though, Thessu wanted to understand why Joanna had died, and whether it had been anything to do with the operation he performed, so he asked if he could dissect the corpse before it was put to work. Cristophe was hesitant, since vivisection of Risen corpses was apparently not common practice among fiendling communities; which maybe explained why their medicine was so relatively primitive. "Knowledge is won by attrition," he told the elderly fiendling.

Cristophe eventually agreed to the procedure, since he too had been curious as to what caused the corpse's death. Thessu dissected its abdomen, and learned that its womb had ruptured when the afterbirth came away. His surgery to widen its pelvis had not been at fault, and nothing he could have done could have prevented its death. Satisfied, he sewed the corpse back up and thanked it, before sending it on its way. It clacked its jaw at him in response. Then he cleaned his surgical implements once again.

Thessu emerged from the priory house to find the others were still lingering, asking Elise more questions. He frowned at her as she rocked gently on the bench swing. He should have known from their scent that the two fiendling women in the priory hut for the birth were one and the same, and he thought ruefully that he shouldn't have tried so hard to ignore their unpleasant coal-tar smell. He should have tolerated it in order to learn something. "Purity of purpose demands sacrifices," he muttered under his breath.

"Thessu old boy," the Baron called, beckoning him over. "We were just discussing our next move."

"We're goin' kill the bitch that murdered my mom, an' burned down the Baron's house, an' tried to kill Joanna an' end the world, an kill us all." Remy said. "Citrine Don Dandolo goin' die."

Thessu looked at each of them disapprovingly. "You're all agreed?"

One by one they all nodded. Even Epifani.

"How 'bout you Thessu? You in?" Remy asked.

Thessu considered. "Well, she didn't burn down my house or kill my mom. And Joanna died without any help from Citrine. But I just delivered that baby," here he pointed at Colin, "and I'm not going to let her kill him. All right. I'll see this through to the end. I'm in."

Colin came over and hugged him awkwardly. "Thank you Thessu. And also, I never said thank you for delivering me."

"You're welcome, Colin. I'm happy to assist any time you need help being born."

The boy beamed. "I appreciate that. If I can ever do the same for you, just let me know."

"So now we've agreed a course of action," Gerard mused, "we just need a plan to break into the most heavily-guarded palazzo in the city, and kill a woman who can see the future and wouldn't die even when I chopped her near in half. Anyone got any ideas about that?"

"Let's start at the beginning old chap," the Baron replied. "What do we know about the palazzo? Elise my dear, can you tell us anything?"

"I can tell you what little I know about Citrine," Elise offered. "But I can't help with the palazzo. Remy's been there though…"

They all looked to Remy, who looked suddenly very uncomfortable. Nevertheless he shared what little he knew about Palazzo Fandandolin. His recollection of the layout was patchy at best and he had scant information about security. It was all very discouraging.

Meanwhile, Remy's cousin Caleb approached the priory house and lingered nearby. Thessu watched the fiendling lean against a railing and start to roll a cigarette. He'd clearly been hunting, as he leaned a long thin skewer against the railing next to him, which dripped blood onto the wooden decking from the dozen or so small creatures threaded onto it. It looked like bats and rodents mostly.

Cousin Caleb caught Remy's eye, and Remy's woeful description of the palazzo petered out.

"What is it Caleb," Remy asked.

Caleb spat over the side of the railing. "Someone comed lookin' for you Rem. He a city slicker... like you. He seems like a prick..."

Remy seemed intrigued. "Someone lookin' for me huh? He give a name?"

"Nope," Caleb replied.

Remy looked at him with raised eyebrows, and he eventually sighed and offered more. "I found him stuck in the mud while I was out checkin' my traps. I thought he were lost, but he's asked for you by name. He's demandin' porters to fetch his bags an' for someone to clean his boots an' draw him a bath. You got porters an' a bathtub, Remy?"

"No Caleb, I don' got porters an' a bathtub."

Caleb finished rolling his cigarette and placed one end of it in his mouth. He ought to smoke less, Thessu thought; cousin Caleb had early stage emphysema.

"That's what I thought," the fiendling said, his cigarette dangling limply from his lip as he drawled. "So I brought him here. I don't like him."

He gestured languidly down over the railing to the swampy lagoon below.

Curious, they all headed to the railing to look down at who had come to see Remy. It was a paunchy man wearing fine silk clothes and an ermine cloak, all of which were splattered with mud. There was a big wet patch of mud on his backside, and his finely braided hair was matted and dishevelled.

The man was climbing tentatively out of a little canoe which was drawn up to rest on the muddy sediment that had accumulated below, at the base of the wooden piles that supported the nearby church building. He looked very precarious and, as they watched, the man started whining loudly at how horrible everything was.

"Ugh what is this?" the man shouted disgustedly. "More mud? Ugh I hate this horrid swamp! How can anyone live like this? I hate this! I want a bath! Remy, where are you?"

Thessu looked to the others. Valanthé was stifling a laugh with both hands while Remy looked mortified.

"Remy do you know that loser?" Epifani asked him, her voice dripping with contempt. "Who is he?"

"Domenico Dandolo," Remy replied quietly, shrinking away from the railing. His embarrassment was highly amusing. The others seemed to think so too, Gerard and the Baron both stifled laughter as well.

"Greetings Domenico Dandolo!" Thessu shouted down, while Gerard and the Baron waved. "Remy is right here!"

"Goddammit I will kill you all," Remy muttered humourlessly through clenched teeth as the man – Domenico – looked up at them, tried to wave back, then fell on his backside in foot-deep muddy water. He just sat there sobbing pathetically, slapping the water in disgust.

"City slickers," Caleb said disparagingly, hoisting the bloody skewer of swamp-kill onto his shoulder and turning to leave. "I don't like city slickers."

As Caleb strode away, Thessu saw something on the fiendling's skewer that caught his eye. Something that had no business being skewered by a fiendling in a northern continent swamp. It was one of the songbirds his order used as messengers; a red cardinal.

"Excuse me Caleb, I think you have one of my birds on your skewer," Thessu said.

The fiendling turned, holding his stick of macabre trophies defensively. "Nope. All these critters are mine."

Thessu tilted his head to examine the stick more closely. It was definitely a red cardinal, the bright red plumage of its crest was clearly visible, pressed between a fruit bat and a toad. The tiny songbird had been speared right through its thorax.

"That red bird is a messenger bird," Thessu said. "I think it might have a message for me."

Caleb peered at the bird, then lifted the skewer up and turned it so the cardinal was by the side of his head. He craned his neck to mimic listening to it with one ear.

"Nope. It don't got a message," the fiendling said flatly.

With the skewer turned, Thessu could see that it did. Its little leg was stuck out at an odd angle, and it had a tiny wooden dowel tied to it. "You can keep the bird, Caleb, I just need that little dowel on its leg."

Caleb eyed him suspiciously, then peered once more at the bird on the skewer and saw what Thessu was pointing at. He took a long drag of his cigarette, and tipped the ash onto the deck at Thessu's feet. Then he replaced the cigarette on his lip, and took a grip of the poor bird's leg between finger and thumb. He twisted the leg clean off the bird and handed it to Thessu, message and all. Then turned once more and walked away.

Thessu sighed and unpicked the bloody dowel from the bird's leg, then snapped it open to reveal the tightly-coiled roll of paper inside. He unfurled it, and his brow furrowed as he deciphered the code. It was another missive from Brother Superior.

'Brother, I have arrived in La Crosse with the crusader cadre, and the apocalypse is still imminent and you are nowhere to be found! Present yourself to me at once, at the east pier of Isla Manxa. I expect a full update on the nature of the apocalypse, and your role in it.'

"What does it say," Epifani asked.

Thessu frowned. "It says I'm in trouble."

***

"Don't look at me Remy, I'm disgusting!"

Remy sighed. "Get out o' the mud, Domenico!" He had thrown down a rope ladder used for accessing the undercroft of wooden piles beneath the church, but Domenico just sat forlornly in the mud, wailing so loudly that he had attracted quite an audience; half the village seemed to be watching from the wooden walkways and rope bridges nearby.

"Goddammit Domenico, you're embarrassin' me!" Remy yelled down, when it became clear the man wasn't going to get up of his own accord. Remy climbed down the ladder himself and, standing on the lowest rung, reached out a hand. "Take my hand, goddammit."

"Don't yell at me Remy," he wailed back loudly, the scene attracting more and more of the villagers to come and watch. "Can't you see I'm already upset! I loved you and you threw away our love and left me all alone! I died, Remy, when you left me in that big bed all alone! You hollowed me out! I'm hollow, Remy!" and he burst into tears again, the tears carving a furrow down his heavily powdered cheeks.

Remy screwed his eyes shut as a ripple of mocking laughter murmured through the crowd of villagers. This cannot be happening, Remy thought, completely mortified. Surely this must be a dream. He opened his eyes tentatively, hoping not to see the ridiculous nobleman in his village any more. No such luck; there he still was.

Domenico – still ignoring Remy's hand – pulled a sodden brown handkerchief out of his breast pocket and wrung it out, then blew his nose into it loudly. At that moment the heavens opened and a heavy downpour of rain started falling and Domenico wailed despondently.

Remy swallowed his anger down and tried again. "Domenico?" no answer. " 'Meni? Please take my hand and I'll help you up out o' the mud."

Domenico nodded and grabbed his hand. Remy hauled him up out of the mud and helped him up the ladder to the walkway above. He sniffled the whole time, and slipped irritatingly on every rung, grunting exaggeratedly at the effort of climbing, like he had never had to exert himself ever before.

"Go on now," Remy said to the crowd. "Show's over. You can all go 'bout your business now."

Most of the crowd slowly drifted away into the rain, but some lingered on, hoping for an encore. "Shame on you Remy, abandonin' a nice young man like that," said an old spinster as she hobbled past him with a stick in one hand and an umbrella in the other.

"Evenin' Miss Amanda," Remy muttered in reply. "Nice weather, ain't it?"

Once the crowd had thinned sufficiently, he pulled Domenico aside. "What the hell you doin' here 'Meni?"

"I ran away Remy! With just the clothes on my back and a few dozen other outfits. We can still be together," he pleaded. "We can live in a modest little palazzo somewhere with just a handful of servants and some peacocks, and I can get a job to support us both; maybe as a baker or something. I don't mind baking; I made toast once."

Remy sighed again. Domenico looked so pathetic with his clothes all sodden with mud and with fat rivulets of raindrops running down his cheeks, washing away the remainder of his powder-white face mask. Remy gazed into his piggy eyes with wonder; him coming here and throwing himself at Remy like he had, was perfectly absurd.

Remy considered what to say to the perfectly absurd man who claimed to love him. He placed his hands on Domenico's shoulders, and leaned in close, saying, "'Meni... get the fuck out o' my village and get the fuck out o' my life!"

Domenico jolted backwards in surprise, his lip quivering and his eyes welling. Then he turned and ran recklessly away along the walkway – now slippery with rainwater – and slipped, catching himself on the railing, while wailing despondently once again.

"I'm glad you let him down gently!" Valanthé said from under cover of the nearby veranda, her voice dripping with amusement.

"It's the best way," Remy shrugged, watching the ridiculous man struggle to keep his footing on the slick wooden decking.

"Is it?" she asked. "We were just discussing how to break into Palazzo Fandandolin; maybe he had some information we could use? It is his house after all."

Remy looked at her with alarm. "You want me to...?"

"Pump him for information, yes," she interjected, a wicked grin on her face. "Come on, Remy, the poor man is hollow. He needs you to fill him in!"

The others chuckled, but Remy was unamused, and he glared acidly at Valanthé.

"Go on," she urged, shooing him towards where Domenico was still stumbling blindly through the rain. "Go find out the best way into that palazzo."

Remy sighed. Goddammit she was right. Could this evening get any worse? "'Meni, come back," he called. "I'm sorry I lost my temper." He swallowed the bile that was rising in his throat and walked sullenly through the rain towards the nobleman, ignoring the sniggering from Valanthé and the others. "Come on 'Meni, how 'bout I draw you that bath you wanted?"

***

Isla Manxa was one of the smaller islands of the Poconovo Delta, situated just a short distance to the north-east of Isla Verdé, and best known for its tanneries and for the production of saltpetre for gunpowder. Despite its relatively central location near the core of the city, the island was sparsely populated and infrequently visited; both its landmark industries relied heavily on excrement in the production process, a fact which led to the island's unofficial name, the Cabal's Colon.

Thessu's eyes watered as they rowed towards it. It was typical of Brother Superior to base himself there; the man's favourite mantras were all the ones about hardship. In the Order of Mercy, the weakest disciples were taught by the strongest masters, and Thessu had been privileged to be thought the very worst of the orphan intake the year he was born, and so had been raised by Brother Superior himself. He had endured worse hardships at the man's hands than bad smells.

"Ugh, I can smell it already," Epifani complained as they approached the island, pulling up her neckerchief as the faecal aroma wafted across the delta from the island ahead. The others wrinkled their noses as well.

The east pier extended far into the river, allowing boats to dock at the island without getting too close to the stink. As their barge approached from the north, they saw two cargo barges were already docked there. One appeared to be delivering materials – barrels of piss, judging by the smell – while the other seemed to be loading up with finished goods. Porter corpses walked the length of the pier with wooden handcarts, loading and unloading the two boats.

Gerard and the Baron paddled their barge towards the end of the pier, giving Thessu a good look at the two moored vessels. Neither looked like they had anything to do with his monastic order. However, as they passed them, Thessu caught sight of a third vessel, unlit and moored at the base of the pier in the shadow of the island. That third vessel had an unusual high-sided hull with no galley ports, and a trio of short masts with steeply-angled top-spars. Its sails were furled, but they almost certainly had a battened fan-shape; those clam shell sails were the distinguishing feature of ships from the southern tip of the southern continent where Thessu was from. Where that ship was from. He pointed it out to the others.

"Shall we moor up next to it?" Remy asked from the tiller.

"No thanks," Epifani replied, "I have no desire to get any closer to that shit-smelling island!"

"Maybe if you'd taken a turn on the oars, you'd have earnt yourself a say," Remy admonished her. "I was askin' Thessu."

"Moor up halfway along the pier," Thessu directed. "I'll check it out on foot."

Remy acknowledged, and steered them into a vacant berth halfway between the fan-sailed ship and the two cargo barges. The Risen porters that were heading back and forth along the pier gave them an unwelcoming gaze upon seeing they had brought no cargo to unload, but did nothing to prevent them mooring alongside the pier.

Thessu jumped out onto the creaky wooden decking of the pier, still slick from the earlier rain that had only recently stopped. He took a moment to steel himself, before walking towards the increasing stink of the island. Towards the fan-sailed ship.

There was no sign of anyone aboard the ship, but Thessu had no doubt he was being watched. As he approached, a figure stepped into his path from out of the shadows that clung to the hull of the ship. Fully covered by a heavy cloak and hood, and silhouetted by the viridian lights of the island behind him, the shapeless figure stood blocking his path.

Thessu stopped ten paces from the figure and bowed low. From his scent, Thessu could tell the figure was a man despite the foul masking stench of tanning and saltpetre production. A man of the southern continent. The figure returned the greeting then turned towards the island, and as he turned, Thessu saw on his face the silhouette of a beaked leather mask much like his own. The man also had a pair of curved swords sheathed across his back.

Thessu followed ten paces behind the man, walking past the fan-sailed ship towards the island, the deck-boards of the pier creaking with each footstep.

"Brother Thessu," a husky voice hissed from behind him.

Thessu whirled. He hadn't heard anyone behind him, hadn't smelled them. A man stood in the centre of the pier, his long green robe tied with a red sash. The man lifted his beaked mask to reveal a weather-worn face with bushy grey eyebrows over stern red eyes and pale, wrinkled skin tinged green in the reflected light of Isla Manxa. Brother Superior of the Order of Mercy. He was flanked by six other monks of the order, all of whom had also dropped down noiselessly from the deck of the fan-sailed ship above.

Thessu glanced back over his shoulder at the monk he had been following. That man was now also flanked by half a dozen other brothers, all well armed. The monks of the Crusader Cadre, Thessu knew; the elite warriors who were the order's ultimate instrument of peace. They weren't a combat force, they were an assassination squad. They didn't fight wars, they ended them.

"I had hoped you were dead," Brother Superior hissed menacingly.

"Hi Dad," Thessu replied.

"None of that insolence!" the senior monk scolded angrily. Thessu chuckled to himself; the man who raised him really did hate being called 'Dad'. Thessu thought about doubling down by tossing out one of the mantras – the twenty-ninth seemed appropriate; 'anger fuels the flames that burn the innocent' – but instead he sighed and greeted the Brother Superior with a stiff bow.

Brother Superior collected himself and returned the bow – never breaking eye contact – before starting to prowl around Thessu in a slow circle. "Give me your report, brother Thessu. Start by telling me what has prevented you from replying to my birds; clearly you have forgotten your mantras or you would have remembered the fifth; 'there is no excuse but death'."

Thessu hadn't forgotten his mantras; that too was one of the Brother Superior's favourites. Every mantra had its trial, and none of the trials had been as difficult as the fifth had been.

Thessu quickly recounted the events of the past several weeks, turning to maintain eye contact with the senior monk as he circled round him. He focussed his retelling on the important details that related to Mother Oracle's apocalyptic prophecies, as confirmed by the other women with foresight that he had met.

He told Brother Superior about Joanna Pianna and the terrible fate that awaited her child, and about the loop of time in which the Queen of the South had been kept, the purpose of which was to delay that fate as long as possible. And he told him about Citrine Don Dandolo, and that she had killed those women with foresight, in order to tear Joanna from the loop, bring about the child's birth, and fulfil his catastrophic fate that would bring destruction to the world. And he told him about Joanna's death and the child's birth, and how a young fiendling woman had sacrificed herself to take the child to safety.

He kept some unnecessary details back of course; trivial details that would be of no interest to the Brother Superior. Trivial details like that Thessu had been arrested and tried for assault, murder, theft and arson. He also didn't tell him that Colin was Joanna's baby. He and the others had promised to keep that a secret in order to protect the boy, and he wouldn't break that promise unless Brother Superior demanded it. He had simply said that Elise had taken the baby into hiding and she could use her gift to ensure Citrine couldn't track him.

Once Brother Superior had heard enough, he stopped circling and held up a hand for silence. Then he backed away past the other monks, and along the pier towards the island, well out of earshot. Thessu watched with interest as his mentor pulled out an ornate silver looking-glass from inside his robe, and held it up as if to look at it. He averted his eyes from the glass as if in deference, never making eye contact with it, while seeming to have a conversation with it. Finally he bowed to the looking-glass, and put it away inside his robe once more.

"Mother Oracle does not think the danger has subsided," he said, returning to Thessu and the other monks. "The path is unclear, but for now you get the benefit of the doubt, brother Thessu."

At an unseen command from Brother Superior, the other monks immediately relaxed and stepped back. Until they stepped back, Thessu hadn't even realised how delicately poised the assassins had been to draw their weapons and strike him down if Brother Superior hadn't liked his report. Thessu felt chastened. He hadn't realised quite how alarmed the order had been over his failure to reply or his appearance in Mother Oracle's latest apocalyptic prophecies. They had clearly assumed he'd gone rogue.

Thessu met the eyes of the man who had raised him. Would Brother Superior really have killed him? Yes, he realised, seeing the man's eyes were no longer so stern now that the decision had been made to spare him. Now his eyes had a far more familiar aspect; the familiar aspect of disapproval and disappointment that Thessu knew so well.

He sighed and looked back along the pier to his friends, who were all waiting close by. He beckoned them along the pier now that the danger had passed. They had a job to do; they hadn't come to Isla Manxa for monks. Thessu saw that Gerard had already acquired a hand cart from somewhere. Good. That would make loading the cargo much easier.

"What is your plan to kill the witch Citrine?" Brother Superior asked.

"We have a way in," Thessu replied, "and perhaps a way to kill her, despite her apparent invulnerability. But she has the gift of foresight; whatever we do, she will know we are coming. We will have to be clever."

"A sharpened mind is worth a thousand swords," Brother Superior replied grimly.

CHAPTER 32

CHAPTER 32

Getting into Palazzo Fandandolin would be the first challenge. Domenico had given Remy a wealth of information about the palazzo, including a possible way in that was unguarded. However, there was a high degree of uncertainty to the information Domenico relayed; it relied on his memories of his early childhood.

He'd told Remy that as a small boy, he had mostly been kept confined in the nursery suite with only his wet-nurses and governess for company. But he'd been an inquisitive child, and had occasionally managed to creep out to explore the palazzo. On one such occasion, he'd gone exploring during some renovations to his mother's suite. He had snuck past the construction workers and found a long-forgotten door, chained shut with a thick iron chain. Curious, he had been able to squeeze through the gap under the chain, and found that the door led to a narrow shaft heading down below the palazzo. He'd climbed down a long way in near-total darkness and had emerged in a magical fairy cave of sparkling gemstones and crystal-clear water.

He'd lost track of time exploring the magical cavern, and when he returned to the palazzo above, he had been soundly caned. The renovations were soon completed, and Domenico never found the door or the cave again.

When he was a little older, he'd learned more about the Palazzo's history, and this too he relayed to Remy. The southern tip of Isla Roja, where the palazzo was located, was a rocky outcrop that rose high above the surface of the river delta with steep-sided cliffs on either side. That rocky outcrop was apparently peppered with natural caves, and one corner of Palazzo Fandandolin was sited directly above one such cave.

When the palazzo was first built hundreds of years ago, the cave entrance had been bricked up to seal it off from the river, and the roof had been reinforced with brick columns to provide a strong foundation to the palazzo above. The original architects left an access shaft from the palazzo down into the cave so that the foundations could be periodically inspected and maintained. Over the centuries though, the palazzo above was extended and reconfigured, and the access shaft sealed off and forgotten, and it was that access shaft that Domenico had discovered. The cave and the access shaft still lay there somewhere, and that secret entrance now led straight up to Citrine's apartments.

Following Domenico's vague directions, they had paddled their barge to the southern cape of Isla Roja, to the base of the cliffs below the grounds of Palazzo Fandandolin. Somewhere in the rock face there was a bricked-up cave entrance.

Remy steered as close to the rocks as he dared, wary of unseen hazards underwater and of the treacherous currents that swirled unpredictably here at the convergence of two river channels.

"What exactly are we looking for Remy?" Epifani asked. "Is it a big crack, or more of a little tunnel?"

"I already told you, I don't know," Remy snapped back angrily. "Why you keep askin' me?"

Epifani chuckled slyly. "Because you're the expert on Dandolo's entrances, Remy."

Remy gritted his teeth and ignored her. They'd slowly traversed along the base of the cliffs on both sides of the cape and not seen anything that might be a sealed cave. Remy was worried that lingering at the base of the cliffs – like they were doing – would start to look suspicious if they stayed much longer, but they didn't have a lot of choice.

Remy pulled the tiller, steering the boat in a tight circle to head back again. "I'm goin' turn around, we can go again the other way."

"Isn't that what you said to Domenico?" Gerard asked, struggling to suppress his mirth.

Remy gave him a cold stare. "Really? You as well Gerard?"

Gerard waved a hand apologetically, laughter rendering him unable to talk. The others were laughing too.

"Does anyone else have any other witty innuendos they want to share?" Remy growled. "How 'bout you Colin? You got anythin' you want to get off your chest?"

"Um. Nipples?" Colin said uncertainly, and more laughter ensued.

"I can see Domenico's crack," the Baron said. Remy turned to glare at him as well, but saw the Baron was pointing up at the cliff. Remy looked up to where the Baron was indicating.

Here on the eastern side of Isla Roja's southern cape, the cliffs were all fully in shadow, so it was hard to see much definition in the rocks at all. But there did indeed seem to be an unusually deep shadow between two steep crags, a cleft in the rock face stretching approximately forty feet in height, sited a mere ten feet above the rocks at the base of the cliff at its lowest point.

Remy swung the barge towards the rocks. Someone would need to climb out to check whether that shadow was indeed the sealed entrance to the cave, and Remy volunteered Gerard and Epifani for that task. Epifani climbed out onto the rocks, grumbling about having to do everything, while Gerard hefted the pick and sledge and other tools they had brought with from the village as well as the viridian lamp from the bow of the boat. The two of them scrambled up the rocks to the shadowy cliff face while Remy and the others watched from the boat.

The shadows swam away from the chartreuse light of Gerard's lamp, and it was clear they were in the right place; the narrow cleft did indeed seem to be an opening in the cliff face, and the lamplight further revealed that it had been blocked up by a course of square-hewn stone blocks just a little way inside the opening, forming a shallow alcove that was just wide enough for someone to stand in.

Remy watched with amusement as Gerard lifted Epifani up by her waist so she could peer into the alcove formed by the bricked-up cave entrance, and an angry seagull pecked and flapped and screeched at her, and Gerard almost dropped her as they both cowered and fled from the angry bird.

They eventually shooed the bird away, and cleared the nests and scree and detritus from the base of the cleft sufficiently so that Gerard could climb up into the alcove. There he got to work on removing one of the massive stone blocks from the seal, breaking it apart piece by piece with hammer and chisel. Remy winced at the sound of the hammer-strikes, which reverberated loudly through the rock and echoed across the channel to Isla Verdé and back again, but thankfully the channel was not too busy, and the few boats that passed by on close approach all showed no interest in what they were doing.

"He's done," Remy announced, seeing Gerard shove the last broken fragment of the stone block aside then beckon them over. The barge had drifted away from the rocks in the meantime, so Valanthé and the Baron paddled them back and they all clambered out and carefully unloaded their cargo; five kegs of gunpowder they'd acquired from the Isla Manxa powder mills.

The Baron took a moment to thank their barge. It wouldn't do to leave it moored at the base of the cliffs; someone might see it and investigate what it was doing there, and possibly chance upon the broken blockwork and realise the palazzo was being infiltrated from below. So they had little choice but to abandon their trusty barge. It rocked gently against the rocks in reply to the Baron, then turned in the swirling current and floated away. It would drift downstream, out of the city and into the Gulf of Mezarcana, where it would likely be absorbed by the floating island of Flotsam. Gerard would definitely not be getting his deposit back, if that was even at question since the four leased corpses had already been destroyed.

"Remy, you get to be first into Domenico's back passage," Epifani said, gesturing at the narrow gap through the wall that Gerard had made. Remy glowered at her and climbed up to the alcove. Through the gap, he saw only a yawning darkness. He smelled cold, stale air and heard the reverberating echoes of silence resonating from a vast empty chasm. He clambered through and reached back for the lantern.

With the lantern in hand, Remy carefully headed deeper into the narrow cleft in the rock face as it sloped down and to the left, before the opening widened into a natural cavern, and Remy gasped. The dim lantern-light twinkled in reflection from countless tiny crystals of quartz that sparkled from the walls of the cavern like sequins. The cavern was vast; far taller and deeper than it was wide, and the twinkling walls either side disappeared into shadow at the furthest limits of the lantern's reach.

The base of the cavern was a pool of crystal-clear water so still and so clear that the sequin sparkle of the quartz rocks shone from beneath the surface just as brightly as above, and Remy didn't even realise there was water there until his boot scuffed a loose stone into it, and the surface rippled. The cavern was just as Domenico had described. It was beautiful.

Across the water where the cavern disappeared into shadow, Remy saw tall patches of darkness where no faint glimmer of crystal reflection could be seen. Silhouettes, he realised, of huge brickwork columns rising from the cavern floor. Man-made structures built to support the roof of the cavern far above. Those columns must be the lowest foundations of the palazzo.

Noises behind him told him the others were climbing through the gap into the cavern. Valanthé came through first and gasped in wonder at the twinkling reflections. Gerard and Colin seemed similarly awed.

"What are those twinkling lights?" the kid asked, and his voice echoed round the cavern like the low rumble of distant thunder.

"Reflections from the quartz crystals in the rock, I think," the big man replied in a reverential whisper.

Colin wasn't listening to the answer. "Echo!" he called loudly, and smiled smugly when the cave called it back at him.

"Isn't it wonderful my dear," the Baron said quietly to Belle as they came through next, and Remy wasn't the only one to eye the doll suspiciously. She dangled limply in the Baron's pocket and gave him no reply.

Epifani clambered through the gap in the wall last. "Ugh you didn't tell me Dandolo's passage was so tight Remy."

Remy wondered if Epifani might accidentally fall into the crystal water and drown.

"I think I can see the foundations over there," Remy said, indicating the silhouetted columns. "I think there's a way round to the left that avoids the water."

"What water?" Epifani replied, then splashed into the pool, and water sloshed up her legs. "Ah shit it's cold, you could have warned me!"

Good enough, Remy thought.

They skirted the pool to the left and found a route past as he had thought. As they approached closer, the lantern revealed that the silhouettes were indeed huge brickwork columns, all interconnected by soaring brick arches high above. When planning their infiltration, They had briefly entertained the idea of demolishing the foundations to bring down the palazzo above, but Remy now realised that wouldn't be possible. The enormous edifices would take a vast amount of explosives to bring down; far more than could be carried in by the six of them.

Instead they explored the columns, looking for the way up. If Domenico was right, there would be an access shaft somewhere that led up to the palazzo above.

"Here," Gerard called, and the cavern echoed it back. He beckoned everyone over to one of the columns.

Remy approached, bringing the lantern, and saw what Gerard had seen; a narrow arched opening at the bottom of the column. Remy shone the lantern in through the opening, revealing a slender hollow running up the inside of the column for its entire height. There were metal rungs hammered into the inside of the column, providing ladder access upwards. Peering up, Remy saw the ladder shaft disappeared into the darkness high above, beyond the reach of the feeble lantern light. The hollow was tight and claustrophobic, and the darkness ominous.

"Who wants to go first?" Remy asked.

"First to climb Dandolo's shaft?" Epifani quipped. "That's you, that is Remy."

"I'll go first," Valanthé offered, giving Remy an apologetic look.

She should be apologetic, Remy thought. Convincing Domenico to tell him about this place had been her idea. Remy had spent four hours bathing that idiot, holding his hand, braiding his hair, massaging his back and …other things. The act itself had been worth it so far, the information Domenico provided had been sound. But being teased by Epifani was definitely not worth it.

"Go right ahead," Remy replied, and gestured for Valanthé to take the lead. She took Gerard's proffered rope and tied it around herself.

***

To Gerard's great relief, Valanthé reached the top with rope to spare. He secured the trailing end of the rope around the girth of the first keg, and tapped the wall of the hollow column to indicate to Valanthé they were ready.

The heavy keg lifted jerkily off the ground as Valanthé hauled it up. The Baron followed it up, climbing the ladder behind the barrel to ensure it didn't snag or crack against the walls. The trailing end of the rope was tossed back down once the keg was up safely, and Gerard secured the next one. In that way, all five kegs were hauled to the top of the shaft. Gerard accompanied the last of the five, bringing with him their viridian lamp.

The ladder shaft in the hollow of the huge brickwork column was a tight fit for the big man. As he climbed the rough-cast iron rungs, he was surprised to find that there were arched openings in the column wall at regular intervals – inspection windows, he guessed – which gave views of the interconnecting spans of brick arches that connected the columns, and of the twinkling cavern beyond. The last such window looked out on the stalactites that filled the roof of the cavern, and Gerard realised that the shaft rose past the highest extent of the cave; which made sense if it accessed the palazzo above.

The top of the shaft was in sight above, and Gerard could see by the light of the lamp clipped at his waist, the faces of Epifani and the Baron peering down at him. Colin was there too, taking a turn hauling up the last keg.

Reaching the top of the shaft, Gerard pulled himself up over the lip of a narrow stone ledge. A haze of disturbed dust billowed around him as he clambered up onto the ledge and straightened up.

"Took you long enough," Epifani grumbled.

Gerard ignored her. Valanthé was holding her hand out for the lamp, and Gerard unclipped it and handed it to her. "Where next?" he asked.

"Through there," she replied, taking the lamp and shining it on a pair of ancient double doors that seemed to be chained closed from the other side. Remy was crouched down at the narrow gap where the doors pressed open slightly against the restraint of the chain.

"You can open it, Remy?" Gerard asked.

Epifani replied for him, with another tedious and predictable comment about opening Domenico's back door. Gerard ignored her; the innuendos were beyond tiresome now.

"We've worked the padlock round to the gap," Remy said, ignoring Epifani as well. "But I needed the light to open it."

"We should have brought more lamps," Colin opined, and nobody disagreed.

Remy quickly had the padlock removed, and the chain swung free with a clang. The doors opened creakily on rusted hinges, onto a dark musty corridor filled with piles of unwanted clutter. Gerard saw a broken statue, discarded washbasins, leftover plaster mouldings and the like, all covered in a thick layer of dust. It gave the impression of being detritus that had not been disposed of properly after a bathroom remodelling, and looked like it had lain undisturbed for decades. This was indeed a forgotten corner of the palazzo.

"Which way?" Valanthé asked, shining the lantern to left and right along the corridor.

"Left," Remy replied, then turned to Colin. "Colin, this is where we leave you. Stay out o' trouble and we'll see you later."

The kid looked frightened – having no desire to be left in the darkness of the abandoned corridor with the dust and the mice – but to his credit, he nodded curtly and stepped back. The plan always called for leaving Colin somewhere safe before the coming fight. He was too important.

Valanthé – still holding the lamp – led the rest of them along the corridor to the left, where their footsteps were probably the first to disturb the inch-thick layer of dust since Domenico Dandolo had gone exploring as a child. It soon became clear why; the corridor ended in a dead end, the doorway that presumably led on to the rest of the palazzo had been bricked up. Valanthé looked to Epifani.

"I sense Risen," Epifani said quietly, suddenly taking things more seriously. "Not in the chamber beyond that wall, but close by for sure."

Valanthé beckoned Gerard forward. "You're up."

Setting down the pair of kegs he was holding, Gerard unslung the pick and heavy sledge from across his back. He scraped one tip of the pick gently across a line of mortar that stood proud of the brickwork. The mortar crumbled away readily, dropping into the dust at the base of the wall. Satisfied that the brickwork was weak, he set the pick aside and hefted the sledge.

"Everyone get ready," he whispered. "This won't take long, but it will be loud. Everything's going to happen quickly once I break through this wall."

"Do it." Epifani said, placing her own keg to one side of Gerard's, and drawing her stiletto. "I'm ready."

"Same," Valanthé said. Remy and the Baron likewise drew weapons in preparation and nodded their readiness.

Gerard set his weight and lifted the heavy sledge hammer over his head. They were about to see how good Citrine's power of foresight was, and if their plan to overcome it was any good.

He brought the sledge crashing down into the wall with an immense crack of breaking masonry. The effect was immediate, half a dozen bricks were dislodged from the centre of the wall, and whatever had lined the facing side of the bricks on the far side of the wall had shattered away from it, exposing a jagged hole about a foot wide. Bright green artificial light streamed through from beyond the wall, bringing with it a haze of warm humid air.

Gerard struck the wall again twice more. Three times. Four. The hole widened considerably with each blow of the hammer, until the hammer blows had forged an opening into the chamber beyond. It was a bathroom.

They quickly climbed through the gap into a vast and lavishly decorated bathing chamber, with white marble walls lined by pilasters and a dozen oversized white marble statues, all surrounding a circular sunken bathing pool perhaps thirty feet across, with a domed ceiling high above. It was steaming with hot, sweet-scented water; which they'd now ruined by smashing through the wall and contaminating the pool with brick dust and broken marble.

The Risen that Epifani had sensed then stepped into the chamber from a grand doorway in the opposite wall. Two child-sized skeleton corpses enamelled in sapphire blue enamel. Both stood rigidly by the door, waiting with bath towels and toiletries on silver trays.

Ignoring the corpse attendants, Gerard instead looked to the marble statues that lined the room; sculptures of beautiful nude women and men holding amphorae. The smallest was ten feet tall, and the largest more than twenty; a giant statue of a man with the physique of a demigod, naked except for a high-crested helmet gilded in gold leaf. Gerard eyed them suspiciously. He had seen Citrine animate the figurehead of the Scarlet Fist's flagship to fight for her, and so he hefted his sledge and stepped towards the nearest of the statues. If he could smash them, he reasoned, he could deny Citrine the opportunity of animating these to defend her.

He was too late. Citrine's gift of foresight was at least as good as they'd expected. She had already animated the statues, and as Gerard swung the big hammer hard at the legs of one of them – a sculpture of a nude young woman seductively dangling a bunch of grapes into her mouth – it came alive. It slammed its carved marble grapes down hard onto Gerard's head, while side-stepping to the back of its pedestal, away from his hammer blow.

Gerard flinched as the carved stone fruit broke hard against his brow, leaving a deep gouge. The bunch broke off at the stem, and the jagged splinter of the stem scraped down the side of his face, cutting a further gash in his cheek. At the same moment, Gerard's hammer chipped a small chunk of stone from the statue's knee, and continued swinging past.

Staggering off-balance and with blood trickling down his face, Gerard continued the swing almost blindly, bringing the hammer behind his head and back round to strike where he expected his marble adversary to be. The hammer unexpectedly slammed into something well before the climax of the swing, the impact jarring up his arms and he almost dropped it. Blinking blood out of his eyes, he saw the statue had blocked his swing with one long-limbed arm against the haft of the hammer, taking most of the momentum out of the swing. Its arm broke at the point of impact, and fell to shatter on the floor, but its other arm was swinging down to club him over the head.

Still stunned from the first blow and jarred from the second, he barely managed to flinch aside, and the statue's swinging forearm scraped down his back, catching on his trusty axe which was still slung there. The blow continued downwards, pulling the axe down, and yanking Gerard down with it. With a yelp of surprise, he released his sledge hammer and threw down a hand to stop from falling, and the hammer skittered away across the mosaic floor.

He heard then the sounds of shouting and masonry breaking around the chamber; other statues must have animated as well. The statue of the nude woman – now one-armed – loomed over him, chambering its leg to stomp down on him as he sprawled awkwardly beneath it. Pushing himself up to his feet, he dove closer, driving his shoulder upwards to lift into the statue's crotch. Caught off balance, it tried to put its raised foot back down on the pedestal but Gerard caught its thigh over his other shoulder and, bracing, he lifted with all his strength. He picked the heavy statue up off the pedestal with its thighs on his shoulders and its crotch in his face, its anatomically-correct marble labia scraping painfully across his mouth and nose.

Staggering under the immense weight, he heard Epifani's muffled yelling, "Gerard! Now is not the time for that!" and he reddened despite himself.

The statue squeezed its thighs together and Gerard felt his head be crushed as if in a vice. Turning back to face the room, he threw his weight forward. The statue fell with him, and its back cracked across the lip of the bath. It broke into several large chunks of marble; its torso falling into the steaming water with a huge splash. It flapped vainly with its remaining arm to try and stay afloat, but that wasn't going to happen; it was made of stone. It sank straight to the bottom.

He wriggled free of its disanimated legs and crotch, and looked around the chamber. Six other statues had come to life, including the twenty-foot tall demigod. Two each had cornered Remy and Epifani and the Baron, and there was much destruction as those three evaded clumsy blows from heavy marble limbs.

They'd known Citrine could animate statues – golems, the Baron had called them – so the sculptures coming to life hadn't been unexpected. Now it was up to the Baron and Valanthé to deal with them.

***

The Baron dove to the side as a huge chunk of masonry slammed into the floor where he had been stood. The trick seemed to be to keep moving, as the big marble golems were slow and clumsy. He'd drawn two of them away from the others and was leading them a merry chase around the far side of the sunken bath from where he'd entered, and they'd followed him, smashing the walls and pilasters and floor with their arms and legs as clubs, trying to get him.

One of them – the smaller of the two – had broken its own arm off by striking a marble pedestal as the Baron had ducked behind it, and had picked up its own broken forearm in its other hand, and swung it at the Baron like a club. The other golem – the big one with the exaggerated musculature and the gilded helmet – had taken to flinging heavy chunks of masonry at him instead. The Baron narrowly avoided a heavy marble basin in the shape of a clamshell that smashed into the floor after having been wrenched off a wall and launched at him from across the pool.

He needed to try and keep them busy a little longer. As he ducked and dove, he was trying to concentrate on the magic that animated them, trying to understand how Citrine had done it.

Whilst making their plans earlier, the others – led by Gerard – had asked if the Baron could also animate golems the same way Citrine did, since they had all seen how things gained more of a semblance of life in his presence. They listed Belle and Rufus and Jeff and even De Ville manor as things that seemed more alive in his presence than they ought to be.

He had told them they were partly right, but that animating golems the amazing way Citrine could, was not his gift. One of his ancestors had been blessed with that rare ability, but whatever small affinity or vestigial gift he had inherited for that sort of thing, it didn't seem to be enough. Nevertheless, he concentrated on the magic in the hope that he too could replicate it.

"Anything, Baron?" Remy yelled anxiously.

"No Remy," he answered, disappointed but unsurprised by his failure. "Like I told you, that's not my gift."

"Time to get out of here then!" Remy replied. He too was hard-pressed by two golems, as was Epifani.

The Baron looked for Valanthé. He couldn't see her by the wall breach where they'd entered. Hopefully that meant she was ready; they'd bought her as much time as they could. He saw Epifani running towards the breach. She slipped on water at the edge of the pool and fell hard to the floor. Gerard grabbed her as he raced past, also heading back the way they'd come. Gerard tossed her bodily through the breach and then jumped through himself. Remy was almost there as well.

The Baron was furthest, but golems blocked both sides of the pool. "Well my dear, it looks like we are taking an early bath," he said to Belle and, quickly brushing his hat off his head and tossing his cane and musket aside, he dove into the warm soapy water, now murky and gritty with rubble.

The momentum of his dive carried him through the water, clear across the pool, well past the golems either side. One launched a huge chunk of broken masonry in his path, and it broke the surface right in front of him, but he was able to nimbly steer past it as it sank to the bottom. As he arrived at the far side and glided up towards the surface however, he felt a hand close around his ankle. Alarmed, he looked down through the cloudy water to see the pale white marble torso of a statue, lying face-up on the bottom of the pool with an expressionless face. It was the one Gerard had smashed. It had grasped his foot with its one remaining arm, and now yanked him down.

The Baron kicked and fought to escape, managing to reach up and grab the lip of the pool with one hand to try and pull against the golem's grasp, but it held fast and he was trapped below the surface. Someone grabbed his hand and pulled. Remy! The Baron kicked hard with his free leg against the golem's grasp, and finally came free, though the golem retained his left shoe and white cotton spat. A small price to pay, he thought, as Remy hauled him out. The two of them ran pell-mell for the gap in the wall where they'd entered the chamber, and they dove through the breach just in front of the nearest two statues.

"Keep going," Remy called as they stumbled to the dusty floor. The Baron saw the joggling green light of the lamp along the corridor; the others were all ahead of them and hastening further away. Behind them in the chamber, the golems set to work smashing the wall, trying to enlarge the gap Gerard had made, to make room for them to get through. It would only take them a few moments; moments which the Baron and Remy used to race away from the breach. Away from the five kegs of gunpowder that Valanthé had rigged to explode, just inside the chamber.

"Now, Valanthé!" Remy called as they raced past her, and she lit the end of a thin trail of gunpowder that she had poured along the corridor. It sputtered to life in a burst of fizzing orange sparks, and shot off along the corridor towards the broken wall and the six animated statues, while she and the others all ducked into alcoves and behind brickwork.

The trail of sparks sputtered out before it reached its destination. "What the…" Valanthé said.

"It's you, you idiots," Epifani said accusingly at the Baron and Remy. "You must have disturbed the powder trail when you blundered through the wall!"

The Baron winced, thinking actually that he had maybe gotten it wet; he was soaked and dripping from the pool. He looked back towards the breach. The golems were almost through. There was no way to escape them in the narrow corridor and nowhere else to go.

"Back down the shaft!" Remy called.

"No!" the Baron urged, looking around at the broken basins and other sanitaryware that lined the corridor. "There's no escape down the shaft, they'll just drop this junk on our heads as we climb down!"

"He's right," Valanthé added urgently. "I don't want to be crushed to death by Citrine's discarded toilet!"

"Fuck this," Epifani said, and snatched the viridian lamp from Valanthé. She ran a short distance back along the corridor towards the bathroom, and launched the lamp straight at it. It struck the wall and shattered on impact. Burning acid-green vitriol splattered out to cover the brickwork and the marble golems and... boom.

CHAPTER 33

CHAPTER 33

The bathing chamber was a ruin. They picked their way across the rubble at the end of the corridor and carefully across the huge void that had opened up in the floor just inside the chamber. The void exposed broken and twisted lead pipes and steam ducts that had lain below the floor, and below those the dingy brick cellar that might have been the boiler room, now flooded with dirty water from the bathing pool which had cracked in two, its filthy water largely drained.

Valanthé surveyed the destruction with satisfaction. When they'd formulated their plan, she had wondered whether five kegs of gunpowder would be sufficient for dealing with the statues that Domenico had described, knowing that Citrine would foresee their coming and guessing she would animate them. They had guessed correctly. And five kegs had indeed been enough. Among the shattered columns and broken masonry of the chamber, were mingled the remains of the animated statues; broken white marble body parts were scattered around the chamber, buried in rubble. One elegant arm was embedded in a wall, having been blasted clear across the chamber.

"I don't see the big one," Gerard said, scanning the debris. "The demigod with the golden helm."

Valanthé was looking down at it. "Over here," she called, and Gerard and the Baron picked their way across the rubble to join her at the edge of the sunken pool.

The big statue was laying in the puddle of dirty water that remained at the bottom of the broken pool. Badly chipped and pitted and scorched black with powder burns, it had a huge chunk missing from the side of its head, but it was otherwise largely intact. It had lost a leg though; severed half-way down its muscular marble thigh, leaving a jagged stump. It was still moving, but pitiful jerky movements.

"Think it can climb out with one leg?" Valanthé asked, concerned.

The Baron's brow furrowed as he considered. "I think we'll be fine."

Epifani joined them at the edge of the broken pool. She too was blackened and scorched, the dark mahogany skin of her face weeping blood from several powder burns. She spat black phlegm down at the statue, then strode away towards the door.

Remy was already heading in the same direction, and the rest of them followed. The Baron stopped to pick up his hat and cane and musket from the rubble at the far side of the pool. Valanthé watched him flick away the scuff marks and the dust and grime as he had already done for his sodden clothing, leaving them once again pristine. He looked ready for a formal dinner as always. She smiled at the incongruity of his one bare foot though; he hadn't managed to find his missing shoe.

Valanthé stopped at the doorway to take a clean towel from one of the two little corpse attendants that were still stood there offering a tray of them. She wiped the masonry dust off her face, and handed the soiled towel back to the skeletal child, which curtsied and clacked its enamelled jaw in response.

Valanthé took a second towel and handed it to Epifani. Epifani glowered at the two Risen but took the towel and wiped some of the soot and blood off her face, tossing the towel deliberately away from the attendants once she was done, then she marched haughtily away. Sighing, Valanthé followed her out of the bathroom. At least the woman had stopped teasing Remy.

The hallway beyond the chamber was likewise clad in white marble, lined with tall fluted pilasters. Following the directions Remy had gotten from Domenico, they walked the length of the hallway and up a short flight of stone steps to emerge at one end of a grand galleried audience chamber.

Two colonnades of fluted white marble columns ran the length of the long chamber, the columns supporting a high mezzanine balcony either side of a central aisle, and an airy vaulted roof above. Elaborate stained-glass windows high on the west-facing wall refracted a patchwork of multicolour twilight down into the long central aisle of the chamber.

At the far side of the chamber was a grand pair of double doors. From Domenico's directions, they knew these led to Citrine's private apartments. High above the doors, looking down on the central aisle of the audience chamber, was an elegant balcony shaped like an open clamshell.

Their footsteps rang loudly on the marble floor, resonating round the hushed expanse of the chamber in a way that invited more care to being quiet.

"Good evening to you all," a woman said, her refined voice startling them to a halt as it echoed loudly down the galleried chamber.

Tensing, Valanthé gripped her swords tighter as she looked around for the source of the voice. A flicker of sapphire movement drew her eyes to the far side of the chamber beyond the pooling light of the stained glass windows. There she saw a middle-aged woman in a fine sapphire gown was looking down on them all from deep in the shadows at the back of the clamshell balcony.

"Citrine!" Remy growled. He'd spotted her too.

The woman on the balcony – Citrine – glanced at a pocket-watch. "You're right on time Remy, here exactly when I expected you," she leered, her voice dripping with veiled menace. "I do so appreciate when my guests are punctual."

Valanthé saw fires burning in her friend's eyes. "We ain't your guests Citrine," he replied. "We here to kill you."

Citrine tutted. "Straight to business, Remy? No foreplay? How very disappointing. I'd hoped you'd have inherited some subtlety from your father, but it seems you just don't have his gift for getting what you want."

"I want you dead," Remy said matter-of-factly.

"Yes and I want to know where your bitch sister took the baby!" Citrine snapped back. "Only one of us is going to get what we want this evening and I'm afraid it isn't you!"

"You sure 'bout that?" he asked, then lifted his flintlock pistol and fired.

The shadows at the back of the balcony leapt in front of her, wrapping her in a curtain of darkness. The shot struck the wreathing shadows and tinkled harmlessly to the floor below the balcony.

***

"Spectres!" Epifani growled. She had sensed something, just at the periphery of her mind. When they solidified in front of Citrine, their presence became far more pronounced. There were two of the Risen shadows. She could suffocate them, she thought, but she would need to be closer for that. A lot closer.

A second shot rang out, louder than the first, and Epifani turned to see the Baron had fired his antique musket at the woman. That too was intercepted by the shadows that enveloped Citrine, and the musket ball fell harmlessly to the floor.

Epifani glowered at the Baron; he had wasted his shot foolishly. And he looked ridiculous in his finery with one bare foot. At least he no longer had the creepy doll with him, he had thankfully dropped that thing in the bathing pool.

Next, something bigger flew through the air at Citrine; Gerard had wastefully launched his axe two-handed at her in an overhead throw. It whistled as it spun through the air towards her. She stood unflinching as it sailed her way, the axe looking like it might just skim her shoulder before slamming into the wall behind her, but Epifani knew it would not, and indeed it too seemed to strike one of the Risen shadows harmlessly, then it too fell to the floor below with a loud clatter.

Citrine sighed. "Like I said Remy, you have no subtlety. The way you all blundered in here blowing things up and making a racket, I didn't need your mother's foresight to hear you coming from a mile away!"

Epifani saw a glimmer of movement disturbing the beams of light from the high windows.

"Well it's a good job we jus' the distraction then, ain't it?" Remy replied.

Right on cue, the windows shattered.

***

The greatest purpose of the Order of Mercy was to prevent unnecessary suffering. As primarily a medical order, adherents knew that all medicine was a mercy, but the order had been named for the final duty a medic must perform for a patient when all else had failed; granting the mercy of death. Brothers of the order were trained to be exceptional killers. When circumstances arose where death could prevent suffering, they would be on hand to see it done. Sometimes many people had to die to prevent the suffering of many more, and brothers could be merciless in pursuit of their primary purpose. None more so than the Crusader Cadre.

Killing Risen had been no issue, but Thessu balked when called upon to kill the living.

He had scaled the cliffs of Isla Roja with his brother monks, being among the first to reach the summit. He had looked down in triumph at the members of the Cadre still below, then seen Brother Superior's disapproving gaze. Of course the senior monk had been the very first to reach the top of the cliffs – that was typical of him – and had swiftly and silently dispatched the Risen sentry that was there without the need for any look of triumph.

Next they had crossed the palazzo grounds; an ornamental garden of low hedgerows and flower beds, and Thessu had used a sai – a three-pronged knife – to dispatch the next Risen corpse they had come across. He had been just as swift and silent as Brother Superior had been when dispatching the first. Thessu had then looked to Brother Superior for approval, and had seen the man silently disarm and dispatch another corpse. With a groan, Thessu realised the corpse that his mentor had dispatched had been about to shoot him.

In one swift motion, the senior monk had smothered the musket's firing mechanism just as the trigger had been pulled, his hand catching the hammer in the webbing between index finger and thumb, noiselessly blocking the flint from striking the steel and firing loudly at Thessu. At the same time, Brother Superior had grabbed the corpse's face with his other hand and kicked its legs out from under it. They had disappeared from view behind a low hedge as the corpse fell and, a moment later, Brother Superior had reappeared and had calmly tossed aside the dismantled parts of the gun's firing mechanism, all without even a glance in Thessu's direction.

Next, the monks had noiselessly scaled the walls of the palazzo itself. The palazzo had none of the bronze-armoured Risen spearmen that Remy had described as being stationed on the galleried balconies; Citrine's cohorts seemed much diminished since her foray to Flotsam.

Thessu had let Brother Superior and the Cadre ascend first, and the monks climbed swiftly up from one galleried balcony to the next, heading towards the roof. As last man up, Thessu had been closest when a liveried valet of the palazzo had walked out onto one of the lower balconies, and happened to glance up.

Thessu had reacted swiftly, and had swung down to land beside him, quickly grabbing the man and covering his mouth before he could scream. He had tried to scream anyway, and his muffled yelp was cut short, descending into a bout of coughing when Thessu struck him hard in the solar plexus, causing his diaphragm to spasm. Thessu had looked around for a means of restraining the man, and had seen one of the Crusaders was climbing back down to assist.

The elite warrior monk had dropped down silently next to Thessu, and replaced Thessu's hand on the valet's mouth with his own. Thessu had released the valet, and reached for the length of knotted cord he had earlier used to tie up his sleeves, intending to tie the man up with it. Before he could, the Crusader had broken the man's neck in one swift brutal movement.

Maintaining his silence had been hard. Thessu had looked angrily at his brother monk and the Crusader had looked back solemnly from behind his beaked mask. Thessu saw unflinching duty in his eyes, but the gravity of what he had done was not lost on him; there was sadness as well. There was also an unspoken accusation in his eyes – that Thessu should have done the deed himself – for they needed to maintain the element of surprise to stand any chance of succeeding. Instead he had balked.

'Purity of purpose demands sacrifices,' he thought bitterly. The tenth mantra was swiftly becoming his least favourite. Swallowing down his unseemly anger, he resumed climbing alongside the Crusader.

Thessu felt the explosion rock the palazzo just as his hand grasped the edge of the roof. The blast meant the others had encountered animated statues – golems – and he paused his climb for the briefest of moments while the reverberations settled and a flock of rock pigeons hastened noisily away overhead. Brother Superior peered down at him from the roof and offered him a hand. He didn't need a hand. He finished the climb without assistance, vaulting over the side to land with a flourish, and endured another look of disapproval.

The monks crossed the rooftops of the palazzo in a stealthy run, staying in the shadows low to the ridges and chimneys of the roofscape, heading to the south-west corner of the building where Citrine's apartments were known to be. Thessu pulled up beside one of the crusaders, crouching low to one side of a large stained-glass window; one of a dozen mullioned glazed arches in the vaulted flank of the roof in this corner of the building.

Peeking past the frame of the window, Thessu saw the large open chamber within. He could see five figures on the floor of the chamber. His friends. Good, they were in the right place. A pistol shot rang out, followed by the report of a musket firing, and Thessu craned to see whom they had fired at. He saw her at the far side of the chamber; the woman they had come to kill. She had wrapped herself in shadow; she was protected by spectres, Thessu knew.

That had been expected, but massed fire of many missiles at once stood at least a chance of overwhelming them. If they surprised her, perhaps they could shoot her before the spectres could react… and just maybe, if they caught her unawares, perhaps they might test her invulnerability.

He looked to Brother Superior – who was poised by the next window along – and signalled to confirm the woman on the balcony was indeed Citrine Don Dandolo. Each pair of monks repositioned themselves for the strike; one in each pair made ready to smash the windows, while the other lined up a shot with a crossbow, all ready to fire in unison.

Brother Superior gave the command, and all at once the windows on both sides of the chamber broke and the massed crossbows all loosed their bolts at Citrine. Thessu held his breath, hoping this would work and they wouldn't have to rely on their backup plan.

***

The Baron regretted wasting his musket shot. He should have fired at the same time the monks shot their crossbows from the high windows, to increase the chance that one of the missiles would evade Citrine's spectres. He looked to Gerard, and saw the big man was also regretting his haste in having hurled his axe too soon as well.

The instant the glass broke, a flock of crossbow bolts took flight towards the woman on the balcony. The shadows around Citrine reacted quickly, wrapping around her like a warm winter blanket. Before a single fragment of the broken glass had landed on the galleries or floor below, the bolts had struck their target. They all disappeared into the writhing shadows, and the Baron sucked in a breath, hoping beyond hope that at least one had gotten through. He heard the drum beat of his heart booming in the silence as he watched the crossbow bolts fall to the floor as if in slow motion, the hollow patter of their landing lost among the discord of glass finally striking the marble after an eternity of falling.

Citrine smiled from the shadows. All of the bolts had been deflected. She looked neither surprised nor perturbed by the cadre of warrior monks at her roof.

The monks – their attack stymied – moved quickly, securing ropes to the frames of the windows, then they rappelled down onto the mezzanine galleries below the high windows on both sides of the chamber. As one, they drew weapons and rushed along the galleries towards the far end of the chamber, where they would be a mere leap from Citrine's clamshell balcony. Thessu was among them.

"Risen!" Epifani yelled, but her warning was unnecessary. Doors at the far end of the mezzanine galleries burst open, and bronze-armoured corpses marched out, blocking the monks from reaching Citrine. The double doors beneath her clamshell balcony likewise burst open, and more of the Risen soldiers marched forth, quickly forming a shield wall below her balcony.

The monks clashed their swords against the shields and spears of the corpses on the galleries, but the narrow walkways were impassable; a dozen heavy spearmen on each was more than enough to bar them both. There was no way for them to reach Citrine from there.

Below, in the central aisle of the chamber, the ranks of Risen pouring through the double doors swelled to more than thirty. The Baron looked to his friends. The five of them couldn't get past so many. Nevertheless, he knelt and reloaded his musket.

"Is this it? Your big plan to kill me?" Citrine called down, her voice full of scorn. "Did you forget I can read the tapestry, you imbeciles! Did you really think I wasn't following all your threads? Did you think you could bring a team of fucking assassins and I wouldn't notice?"

Gerard hefted the heavy sledge hammer, while Epifani gritted her teeth and clutched her stiletto and Valanthé took a ready stance with her swords. The Baron stood, his musket ready once more, and he nodded to Remy, who returned the gesture. It was time for the backup plan.

"We didn' forget about your stolen gift Citrine, we know you can read the tapestry an' we figured you'd be watchin' all our threads," Remy called back, shouting loudly to be heard over the slow crunch of armoured boots on marble as the shield wall of the Risen paced towards them, while swords clashed on shields on the galleries above.

"But I tol' you we was a distraction," Remy continued. "An' they's a distraction also. But you ain't watchin' all our threads; we know for a fact there's some you can't see."

Remy turned to the Baron then. "Baron, you ready?"

The Baron nodded, and with finger and thumb in his mouth, he blew a loud whistle.

Behind them, down the steps and along the hallway, footsteps rang out. Heavy clicking, thumping footsteps. Click-thump. Click-thump. Click-thump. The heavy click of metal and the heavy thump of marble.

Citrine peered down from her balcony, curious at the odd noise of what was approaching. "No!" she gasped when she saw it.

The Baron smiled at the approaching golem. "Hello my dear!"

The broken statue of the demigod with golden helm was limping along the hallway towards them. One-eyed and one-legged, it carried a massive length of lead pipe wrenched from under the floor of the bathing chamber, which it used as a crutch to support its huge frame. Belle was sat lifeless on its head, propped up by the crest of the golem's golden helm.

The doll was – had always been – the physical manifestation of the Baron's dead aunt. Belladonna De Ville had died young, but in life she had liked to play with dolls. She had liked to bring them to life and have them play families in her dollhouse. The Baron couldn't raise a golem to fight Citrine, but Belle could. She was the most gifted prodigy that the De Villes had ever produced, and the ancestors were right to favour her over him.

Chapter 34

Epifani watched in astonishment as the golem approached. When the Baron had told them about the true nature of his doll, she had scoffed at his ludicrous claim, but here it was riding the huge animated marble statue from the bathing chamber. The hallway was double-height, yet the monstrous figure of the golem had to crouch awkwardly as it hobbled towards them on its makeshift crutch.

"Out of her way," the Baron urged, pulling Epifani aside as the golem reached up from the bottom of the short flight of steps that led to the audience chamber, taking a grip of one of the pilasters that framed the chamber's entrance at the top of the steps. Epifani joined the others in stepping back out of its path, as the golem slammed its crutch down on the middle step and ducked its head into the chamber. The crutch bowed as the golem scaled the steps in one huge stride, but it did not buckle. The statue straightened up inside the chamber, its head looming above the height of the galleries either side of the central aisle.

Meanwhile, the Risen soldiers of Citrine's shield wall had continued their pacing forward, and now stood halfway along the central aisle of the long chamber in a phalanx ten wide and three deep, with shields set and spears couched in a defensive stance. The golem stepped inexorably forward towards them, passing Epifani and the Baron on one side, and Remy, Gerard and Valanthé on the other.

In five limping strides, it was upon the phalanx of corpse soldiers. The hapless Risen jabbed at its leg and crotch with spears, but their spear tips scraped harmlessly off its pitted marble hide with barely a scratch. The formation broke apart as corpses next tried to bodily restrain it and, as it lifted its crutch for another step, three armoured Risen dangled from the end of the thick lead pipe. One fell off in mid air to crash down amidst its fellows, the other two clinging on as the crutch slammed down past the phalanx.

The golem dragged its leg forward through the formation, smashing four of the Risen aside and dragging four more along, one of which was crushed underfoot as the golem slammed its leg back down beyond the phalanx. It wobbled, off balance, and thrust out a hand to grasp the lip of the gallery to steady itself.

Epifani looked to Citrine up on the balcony at the far side of the chamber, and saw the woman deep in concentration. Her eyes wept blood, as she had seen them do once before on the deck of the galley when she had raised the figurehead of the pirate vessel to defend her. Was she trying to take back control of the golem?

It seemed like that was exactly what she was trying. The golem lurched, then clung to the lip of the gallery with both hands, dislodging chunks of masonry from the marble balustrade there. Its crutch fell away, and armoured Risen moved smartly out of the way of the falling length of lead pipe. It struck the floor with a crash, bouncing once before settling. The golem wobbled on its one leg, and the Risen clamoured around it, bludgeoning at the marble limb with their shields. The monks on the gallery where it was leaning were being forced back by the armoured corpses there, and Risen were soon bludgeoning the golem's hands and arms as well.

A shot rang out, and Epifani looked to see the Baron had fired at Citrine again; an attempt to break her concentration perhaps. The shot struck the shadows as before, and Citrine never even flinched.

With jerky movements a testament to the ongoing contest for control of the golem, it lunged joltingly with outstretched hand at the armoured Risen on the gallery. Unable to dodge away in the press, one of the corpses was snatched up in its great marble fist. With a creak of metal and crunch of bones, it crushed the corpse in its vice-like grip, its own fingers cracking and fracturing as it squeezed. The golem shuddered away from the gallery momentarily, and launched the corpse at the clamshell balcony. The crushed and twisted mass of bronze and bone slammed into the wall behind where Citrine had been standing. It had missed her, but Citrine's shadows hadn't blocked it, instead they'd pulled Citrine aside, and that at least had broken her concentration.

Momentarily free of Citrine's influence, the golem snatched another corpse from the gallery and launched that at Citrine as well, and the shadows moved her aside once more. The golem shuffled further along the gallery's edge as the remaining Risen there backed away. Below, Risen continued bludgeoning at its leg. The marble of its knee was now badly cracked; the Risen might yet bring the golem down.

Epifani hurried over to assist it, with the others close behind. She reached out with her mind to grasp the odious presence of the nearest Risen. She felt it prickle against her, a writhing black coil of rage. Before she could wrap her mind around it, it vanished. Gerard had smashed its skull in with his sledge hammer.

"Dammit, Gerard that one was mine!" she scolded.

He didn't answer, he had moved on to the next one. She grabbed another one instead, calming her annoyance and reaching with her mind to envelop the noxious presence. That one too vanished. Valanthé had impaled it with her long sword.

"For fuck's sake, get your own ones!" she shouted to nobody in particular.

This time she grabbed one from the gallery. That one disappeared from under her grasp as well; one of the monks up there had broken its neck. She looked up angrily at the monk, who must have sensed her anger because he peered down at her and waved cheerily. It was Thessu.

The other monks were withdrawing, Epifani realised. With no way to reach Citrine from the gallery, they were clambering down to join the melee at floor level. Thessu was one of the last ones down, and soon joined her and the others in combat against the Risen there, which were still in disarray from the golem having smashed through their phalanx.

Most of the Risen that had been bludgeoning the golem's leg now turned to face the new threat posed by the monks, and the golem was able to inch its way towards the end of the gallery. Citrine was again concentrating hard though, and blood trickled freely down her face to pool on the collar of her gown in a slowly widening stain. It was working; the golem's movements were jerky and mal-coordinated once more. Unable to do anything about Citrine, Epifani suffocated the last two corpses that were still attacking the golem's leg, and just in time; the golem's knee was fractured almost clean through, and marble fragments tumbled from the crack with each of its jerky movements.

At last though, it reached the end of the gallery, and steadied itself to lunge across to Citrine's clamshell balcony. No doubt when it got there, it would crush the woman the same way it had crushed the armoured corpses, whether spectres were there or not. It planted its leg halfway between the gallery and the balcony, then pushed off to pivot its weight across the gap. But with a crack, its leg finally broke.

The golem tumbled, throwing up its hands towards the clamshell balcony to stop itself from crashing face-first to the floor. Somehow it managed to grasp the lip of the balcony, and hold on, but the Baron's doll tumbled from its head, falling to the marble floor below.

"Mine!" Citrine exulted, having finally wrested control of the golem from the doll. But her exultation was short-lived. The doll had done enough.

The golem's body swung beneath the clamshell balcony, its great weight still clamped onto the balcony's lip. With a crack of breaking masonry, the whole edifice tore from the wall and fell twenty feet to the floor below, where it shattered with a great plume of powdered masonry dust and scattered debris. The golem was crushed beneath it.

Citrine was thrown clear by the heavy impact, landing a short distance away amidst a pile of broken marble chunks in the central aisle of the chamber. She rose, a lot bloodier than she had been before she fell, and with her head twisted unnaturally to one side so she was looking back behind one shoulder. Her neck was broken. Epifani marvelled; how was that not fatal?

The remaining armoured Risen tried to rally to her, attempting to form a defensive circle around their mistress. The spectres – which had dissipated at the moment of impact – also rallied, returning to wrap themselves around her once more.

Wreathed in shadow once again, Citrine took her head in her hands and, with a sickening crunch, she wrenched it back to face the front. Blood spluttered from her mouth as she let out a faint gasp, then she smiled wickedly. One of the monks had gotten past the cordon of Risen and was bearing down on her with levelled sword.

With a flick of her eyes, she directed the spectres, and one of the liquid shadows lunged to scoop a big chunk of broken marble from the rubble at her feet, and in the same fluid movement, used it to smash the leaping monk aside. The chunk of masonry struck the unfortunate warrior in the side of his head with an audible crunch of breaking bone and a spray of blood, and the force of the blow sent his dead body spinning sideways to slam into one of the marble columns.

Epifani pressed forward. She was close enough to the spectres now to do something about them, and she reached out with her mind to them. Much like the spectres Aunt Sundra had employed to protect Joanna, these two were elusive, their presence as ethereal as their physical manifestation was. She needed them to go rigid.

"Remy, shoot that bitch," she called.

"With pleasure," the fiendling replied.

He levelled his pistol and took aim through a gap in the half-formed phalanx of Risen that surrounded her. He fired, and Epifani sensed the spectres become more corporeal as they reacted to block the shot. She grasped them both with the ruthless embrace of her mind. Grasped them and squeezed them. They fought to escape, but having blocked the shot, they went ethereal once more. She almost had them – but not quite – and she felt them slip through the fingers of her mind.

"Again!" Epifani roared. But nobody had a gun loaded and ready. Instead Gerard struck an armoured corpse in the front rank of the nascent shield wall, a vicious uppercut swing with his hammer. The corpse flew up and over the second rank of corpses, its legs swinging up over its head as it tumbled through the air, heading straight for Citrine.

The spectres tensed to protect her, and Epifani crushed them in an instant. They disanimated and disappeared from her mind. The flying corpse continued its arc, clattering down on Citrine unobstructed, crushing her back down onto the pile of rubble once more.

***

Remy watched the warrior monks fight with admiration. They were lightning fast and deadly, and their nimble footwork and martial prowess was what chiefly won the fight. The remaining corpse soldiers – scattered and in disarray – struggled to form a cohesive shield wall after Citrine fell, and they were quickly picked off and defeated.

Remy had assisted as well of course, though his contributions were overshadowed by Gerard, whose hammer smashed the lines of Risen before they formed; and Epifani, whose mind disanimated the corpses that Gerard missed.

Remy surveyed the pile of rubble and bodies as he loaded his pistol once more. Most of the bodies were the disanimated corpses of the Risen, their burnished bronze armour now dented and dulled. Some warrior monks lay among them, and some others had retreated, wounded, but the fight was won and Citrine was beaten.

A last armoured corpse that was still fighting, finally fell with one of Thessu's odd three-pronged weapons through the copper marque on its forehead. Remy saw Thessu look around in triumph towards his mentor, who was not watching. Brother Superior was selflessly tending to the wounded monks.

The remaining Risen disengaged and backed away to Citrine, one of them having dragged her back to her feet. Just two Risen corpses still stood. That last pair flanked Citrine protectively, and she seemed to tense, focussing intently on something with eyes tightly closed.

Suddenly the air around her crackled, and blood sprayed from her eyes as they opened and she threw back her head and unclenched her fists as if releasing a pent up force.

Masonry debris from the pile around her suddenly exploded away from her, catapulted indiscriminately towards Remy and the others in a wavefront of destructive force set to bludgeon them all.

"Val!" Remy yelled urgently. They'd expected a final trick like that from Citrine; they knew what she was capable of. Valanthé had insisted that her gift was unreliable, and she wasn't sure if it would kick in when it was needed so they shouldn't rely on it. In the split second before they were all struck by heavy blocks, he knew they had no choice; either her gift would save them or they were likely dead.

Remy shielded his face uselessly as a huge hunk of masonry rocketed straight at his head. Then it struck him, and knocked him down. Only, it wasn't masonry when it struck him, it was snow.

He sat up and brushed the clumps of hard-packed snow off of his face. Damn it was cold! Remy had never seen snow before of course; snow didn't fall in the coastal lowlands and swamps, only ever on the eastern flanks of high hills and mountains where no sun ever shone. He looked around to see Valanthé grinning sheepishly; she and the others were also picking themselves up and brushing themselves off, marvelling at their amazing fortune.

Remy looked to Citrine. It was still just her and the last two Risen corpses left, and it was clear she was spent; she had no more tricks to play. She looked astonished that anyone had survived the explosion of masonry to oppose her.

"It's over, Citrine," Remy announced.

"You haven't beaten me; this is a stalemate is all," she spat back. "I'm afraid you still won't be getting what you came here for, Remy. You must know I cannot be killed!"

Remy finished loading his pistol, tucked the ramrod in its holder, then pulled the hammer back to cock it. He levelled it at her, and fired. The two corpses threw up their shields to cover her, but the shot struck her regardless. Another ragged hole appeared in her torn and bloody gown, just above her left breast, and more blood seeped out from the ragged hole in her chest beneath.

Citrine didn't flinch. "You see Remy? No matter what you do to me, I will live on. And I will find Joanna's child. And I will sacrifice him."

Remy thought about shooting her again. He thought about testing her claim. He thought about scouring the flesh from her bones with fire, then grinding what was left of her into bonemeal. He weighed up the pleasure he would get from torturing the woman who killed his mother, against the impotence of knowing she would survive it unharmed. With a sigh, he lowered his pistol. Following his lead, the others lowered their own weapons as well. She was right; they couldn't kill her with those.

Citrine threw back her head and laughed a foul maniacal cackle of triumph. The bones of her neck jutted grotesquely to one side as she did so, the skin blue and bulbous with welled-up blood below the surface. She turned to walk away, pushing defiantly past two of the monks who had circled round behind her. Then she happened to look up to where her clamshell balcony had been sited, and she froze.

Above the jagged fragments that outlined where the broken structure had attached to the wall was a door; the door to her private apartments. The door was open. A figure stood in the doorway.

"You found it then, Colin?" Remy called up to the kid.

"I think so," he replied, and he held up a silver strongbox, sealed with a padlock shaped like a skull.

Citrine gasped. "How...?"

Before she could finish her sentence, Valanthé and Thessu both grabbed her and slammed her face-down onto the floor. At the same instant, Gerard swung his hammer hard into the head of one of the remaining Risen, and the Baron fired his musket through the eye of the other.

Remy beckoned for the strongbox and Colin tossed it down. Remy made no attempt to catch it. It struck the floor with a clang and Citrine screamed, writhing as if in agony. Smiling, Remy stepped over to where the strongbox lay and picked it up. He looked over at Citrine, still restrained face-down on the floor by Thessu and Valanthé. She lifted her head, her eyes wide in pain and panic and her breathing raspy and forced.

"Who is that boy? How did he get hold of my casket?" she wheezed. "I scoured the tapestry and did not see it happen! It should not be possible!"

Remy smirked and gave the kid a thumbs up, which he returned. Elise had spent fourteen years hiding his thread from view; Citrine couldn't see his thread any more than Aunt Sundra could. While Remy and the others had been distracting her, Colin had snuck into Citrine's sanctuary unseen and found the key to killing her. Elise had told him what to look for.

"I'll be the one asking questions," Remy said, placing the strongbox down on a chunk of masonry and squatting down by Citrine's head. "Let's start with a simple one. What's in the box?"

Citrine looked at him with wrath in her eyes. "Fuck you."

Remy shook his head ruefully. He stood, then kicked her hard in the face. Citrine spat out a gobbet of blood and a broken tooth. Remy turned to the strongbox and lifted the clasp to examine the padlock, which looked ornamental and not especially sturdy. He repositioned the flimsy padlock to lie flat on the masonry, and struck it with the pommel of his rapier. It took a couple of strikes, then the clasp snapped off.

Lifting the lid, he looked inside to find the box was padded with dark blue velvet, protecting an odd egg-shaped object. Made of glazed white porcelain, the object was clearly fragile and likely hollow. Lifting it out of the padding and turning it round in his hands, he saw it had a woman's face etched on one side, and little stumpy arms and legs. It was obviously an effigy of some sort, and the face was Citrine's. He shook it gently, and determined that it was definitely hollow, and had something sealed inside. He lifted it to his ear, and the sound told him exactly what it was.

Remy smiled broadly and sat down on the large chunk of masonry, holding Citrine's porcelain effigy in his lap. Citrine still glared hatefully at him.

"Why don't we try another question," Remy asked. "Why you tryin' to sacrifice Joanna's baby an' end the world?"

Citrine replied through bloody, gritted teeth. "I'm not trying to end the world, I'm trying to save it!"

"Bullshit," Gerard scoffed.

Remy nodded. "Yup, it sure does sound like bullshit. You can see the tapestry Citrine, you know full well it ends when that boy dies!"

Citrine ran her tongue over her jagged teeth and spat out another gobbet of blood. "Remy do you like this place?"

Remy looked around at the ruined chamber, filled with rubble and bodies. "It's a lil' run down for my likin'. Why? You thinkin' o' sellin'?"

Her eyes narrowed. "No you idiot! Not the room. Do you like the realm of Twilight? Would you not like to feel the warmth of the sun full on your face? Or look up at the night sky and see all the stars of heaven up above you?"

She twisted awkwardly to look at Epifani then. "And you Epifani, would you not like to live in a world where the dead do not have to serve the living? A world where the dead can rest?"

Remy raised a sceptical eyebrow. What was she talking about? Why would stars be in the sky, and why would the ever-setting sun feel warm? And why would the dead ever need to rest?

"We live in the realm of Twilight," Citrine continued, a hint of pleading in her voice now. "But this is not the only realm. Our world is separated into four realms. They are not supposed to be separate; the world was created wrong! The sun is not supposed to hang low in the sky for ever, it is supposed to rise and fall; to move across the sky and give us a cycle of day and night. The baby's fate isn't to end the world; he will unite it!"

***

"You really expect us to believe that?" Remy asked with incredulity in his voice. Epifani shared his incredulity, but she wanted to hear more about the Risen. She strode over to stand next to Remy, and looked down at Citrine.

"Are there no Risen in these other realms?" she asked her.

"No, only here," Citrine replied. "Think about it Epifani; the Risen are only needed here because the light of the ever-setting sun is too weak to grow crops without help. If the sun rose and fell, crops would grow faster, and the dead wouldn't need to toil in the fields! If the sun rose and fell, the dead wouldn't need to serve the living at all!"

Epifani let out a long whistling breath. She'd always hated universal undeath and believed the abhorrent practice was unnatural, but she'd only ever thought of it as a moral dilemma. Of course it never was; it had always been an issue of economics. Citrine was right; if there was a way to make the sun shine brighter, then Risen could be made redundant.

She smiled to Remy, lost in the possibilities offered by Citrine's rising and falling sun. Remy wasn't seeming so convinced though. In fact he looked decidedly uneasy as he met her gaze.

"Are the other realms like Twilight at all?" Valanthé asked.

"No," Citrine replied, her head twisting on her broken neck to look straight at the woman who was pinning down her shoulder. "They do not have an ever-setting sun like we do, it is elsewhere in the sky for them. One of the four sees no sun at all; you cannot imagine the hardships that the people there endure! If you knew how much they suffer – how much the people of all the other realms suffer – you would weep for them as I do! I want to end their suffering! I want to save them!"

"How?" Epifani asked.

"The realms want to be united, but a powerful force keeps them apart. That force is channelled along hidden lay lines that converge at a single location in each realm; a focal nexus. Every few hundred years, a baby may be born in one of the realms with the rarest of gifts; a soul infused with the same force that divides the realms.

"If such a child were to die at a realm's focal nexus, their soul would release its pent-up force at the moment of death, disrupting the lay lines that converge there and weakening the force that holds the realms apart for a time."

"You're talking about Joanna's baby?" Epifani asked.

Citrine nodded. "Yes, he is one such martyr."

"I've heard enough," Remy announced, standing up and lifting Citrine's porcelain effigy high above his head, ready to dash it onto the floor.

"Wait Remy," Epifani said, placing a hand on his arm. "Please, I want to hear what she has to say."

"Yes, let her finish," Gerard added, and Valanthé and the Baron nodded also.

"I would like to hear this as well," Colin called down from the ruined balcony above. They all looked up at him. Unknown to Citrine, he was Joanna's baby. Her words affected him more than anyone.

Remy fumed and lowered the effigy, but Epifani knew she didn't have long. "Where are these focal points you mentioned? The nexuses?"

Citrine replied quickly, her words urgent; she also must have realised she didn't have much time. "People are unwittingly drawn towards the convergence of the lay lines. Great cities form around them, and at their centre, people build great structures without ever understanding the compulsion. Impressive monoliths of engineering; pyramids and towers and… a Ziggurat."

Epifani looked up at Colin, and considered the youth carefully, and considered where they stood; near the southern tip of Isla Roja… a stone's throw from the Ziggurat. Then she turned back to Citrine. "So if Joanna's baby were to die at the Ziggurat, the realms would reunite?"

"Epifani, I'm warnin' you…" Remy interjected, a note of menace loud in his voice.

Citrine ignored the fiendling. "That would be the first step. It would disrupt the Twilight nexus for a time – perhaps a year or two – but the other three would compensate. No, all four power centres must be disrupted for the realms to reunite. We have a narrow window of opportunity because for the first time in many thousands of years, there is one such martyr alive in each of the four realms. Four lives can end the separation and the suffering! Just four sacrifices and the realms will unite and the heavens will start to turn through night and day as they are supposed to. Epifani! The world is broken! Someone has to fix it!"

***

Remy could listen to no more of this. His eyes ablaze with all the fire of his core, he dashed Citrine's Effigy to the floor. It impacted with a dull wet crump, the broken fragments of white porcelain held close by gelatinous globs of blood so dark it might have been black. Citrine screamed in agony.

"I know I am not virtuous," Remy said, ignoring the screaming from Citrine and the irate look from Epifani. "But I have been thinking a lot about virtue recently."

He tapped the broken shell of the effigy aside with his foot, and it skittered away in a trail of oozing ichor to reveal a big hunk of black throbbing meat that pulsated arrhythmically. The beating heart of Citrine Don Dandolo.

Remy blazed his eyes even hotter, and smoke coiled up around his horns. Even Epifani took a step back from the blazing manifestation of his anger. "There is one virtue that fiendlin's hold especially dear," he continued, "and I know in that regard that I surely am a virtuous man. Fiendlin's value vengeance."

He speared the heart with his rapier, and channelled all his fury down the blade. The heart burst into flames. In an instant, it was charred and blackened ashes.

And Citrine died.

CHAPTER 35

With her last breath, Citrine let out a whimper. She lay prostrate on her front, her head still twisted awkwardly to one side. At the end she hadn't been defiant, hadn't been monstrous; instead she had looked sad. Gerard had watched a solitary tear creep down her cheek, cleaning a furrow through the dried blood and grime of her face.

In the silence that followed, Epifani stalked away broodily while Valanthé accompanied Remy as he paced back and forth to calm his fury. The Baron retrieved Belle and dusted her off, tucking her away in his breast pocket once more, while Thessu checked on some of the wounded monks, finding that Brother Superior had that task well in hand.

Gerard rooted around in the rubble below the balcony, finally finding the trusty axe that he had foolishly thrown at Citrine at the start of the fight. The sledge hammer had been great, but he and the axe had history, and right now he needed it. He returned to where Citrine lay, and with a leisurely swing, buried the blade of the axe in her back.

"For fuck's sake!" Epifani yelled. "She's dead already!"

Gerard shrugged. "Just making sure."

"You're hurt," Thessu noted.

Gerard nodded. One of the last corpses had landed a lucky blow with a spear that slipped under his left pauldron, and blood saturated his doublet. He had other wounds as well, but that was the most pressing. Thessu sat him down on a big hunk of masonry and unbuckled his pauldron strap to reveal the deep cut, and he started to clean and patch it up.

"Thank you Thessu. And thank you, Belle," Gerard said as the Baron walked over with the doll in his pocket. "You were amazing this evening, we couldn't have done it without you." The doll lolled mutely against the Baron's lapel as she always did, with no sign of recognition or response, and Gerard felt a little silly gushing with praise towards her.

Colin – who had come down from the balcony – joined them then. He looked a little stunned, which was understandable. "What's that you've got there?" Gerard asked.

Colin looked down at the thing he was holding. It looked like a bundle of twigs wrapped in white cloth. "Oh, I found this in Citrine's sanctuary as well," he said, holding it up. "It was wrapped in a tight coil of Risen entrails. I had to cut it out; the entrails tried to attack me!"

Gerard eyed it dubiously. It didn't look like anything much. "Wrapped in entrails you say?"

Colin nodded, and handed it to him with a shrug. "There were lots of creepy things in there, but this was sort of the focal point of the room… the arrangement made it seem important."

Gerard examined the bundle, turning it over in his hands. It was indeed made of twigs and cloth, bound together by loops of thin twine. The twigs had been arranged in the shape of a man, with a bundle of twigs for a body and smaller stubby pairs of twigs arranged as arms and legs, with a thicker knot of wood for a head. The twine, Gerard realised was partly made of human hair; white wisps of brittle hair so fine as to seem almost translucent were threaded through the twine and the twigs. The twig doll was dressed in an entrail-stained white overall and its face was painted white.

"Here, what do you make of that?" Gerard said, handing it to the Baron. It was similar to a doll after all; maybe he would have some insight into it?

He didn't. The Baron examined it just as uncertainly as Gerard had done. "Maybe there's some significance to the white robe and face?" he offered.

Gerard frowned. "Don't the Cabal wear white robes and masks?"

"What's that?" Remy asked, as he and Valanthé joined them.

"A twig doll," Gerard replied, and the Baron handed it to him. "Colin found it in Citrine's sanctuary, tightly bound in Risen entrails. It's dressed like a Cabal member."

Remy winced at the doll and shook his head. "It's the Dogé."

Gerard looked at him questioningly. "How could the Dogé be a doll?"

"I mean it's a representation of him," Remy clarified. "I heard o' that sort o' necromancy before, an' my father tol' me the ol' Dogé was gravely ill. My father was schemin' with Citrine to keep the ol' man alive until they was ready to take his place. That doll was tightly bound you said? …I wonder if that's the real reason the Dogé were gravely ill in the first place?"

Gerard let out a long breath. He had also heard of that rare sort of magic before. "Citrine really was a witch wasn't she?"

Remy nodded. "Can you believe that bullshit she was spoutin' though?" he scoffed. "Realms an' lay lines an' martyrs?"

Gerard exchanged a look with the others. Of course it had sounded absurd, but no more so than what he'd already accepted about a magic tapestry and the end of the world. Citrine's yarn at least gave some explanation for why Colin's death was so important, and some reasoning why Citrine had tried to kill him.

Remy seemed to catch on then that he was the only one who fully doubted what Citrine had said. "You can't be serious? She's manipulatin' y'all! She made all that shit up to try an' weasel out o' this with her life!"

"No Remy," Colin replied, and his tone brooked no argument. "She was telling the truth, I am certain of it." Gerard had never heard him so earnest; the boy sounded haunted.

"Well I don't buy it," Remy said; though he sounded less sure than he had a moment before. "It's all a lil' too convenient, ain't it? The whole world is broken, an' Citrine's the only one who can fix it?"

"Actually it sounded decidedly inconvenient," Thessu replied, without lifting his focus from sewing the wound in Gerard's shoulder. "To fix the other realms you have to go there, but nobody ever has or we'd have heard of it before. So how is one supposed to go to these other places if a magic barrier keeps them separate?"

"It's obvious, isn't it?" Valanthé replied with a faraway look. "You sail off the edge of the world… Like my father did."

Gerard's jaw dropped open. Her father, the pirate Darkmourn, had indeed sailed off the edge of the world. Had he gone to one of the other realms?

"Your father never came back, Val!" Remy retorted.

Valanthé locked eyes with him. "That doesn't mean he didn't make it there! I think he showed us the way!"

Epifani, who had been hovering at the edge of the conversation, joined in then; though she seemed unable to make eye contact with any of them. "Also, Citrine never said she was the only one who could fix the world." She seemed to swallow hard before continuing. "I think we should do it. Unite the realms."

They all turned on Epifani. Gerard angrily voiced how they all felt then. "Epifani, you are not sacrificing Colin!"

Thessu looked at him with alarm, a reaction which Gerard didn't immediately understand.

Then another voice cut in. "What do you mean 'Colin'?" It was Brother Superior, and then Gerard realised his mistake; he'd let slip the secret of where Joanna's baby was. Her baby was stood right there between Remy and Valanthé, and Brother Superior was sizing him up.

***

Thessu looked from Gerard to Brother Superior. The senior monk was staring at Colin. Thessu tensed, recognising the same inscrutable expression that he'd observed on his mentor's face when he'd gone to meet him on Isla Manxa, and he'd held Thessu's life in his hands while weighing up his report. He was right now weighing up whether the Order of Mercy – indeed the entire realm of Twilight – would be better served by killing the boy or saving him.

Thessu rose from tending Gerard's shoulder and edged closer to Brother Superior, who raised a finger to stop him without ever taking his eyes off of Colin. Remy and Valanthé both stepped forward protectively between the senior monk and the boy. The Crusader Cadre were wordlessly rising to their feet as well, the deadly assassins roused by the sudden unspoken tension in the chamber.

With all eyes on him, Brother Superior reached inside his robe and withdrew once more the ornate silver looking-glass that Thessu had seen him speak with on the east pier of Isla Manxa. He was closer this time, so Thessu heard the conversation. And he saw with whom his mentor was speaking.

As before, Brother Superior averted his eyes from the glass in deference, holding it to one side of his unhalting gaze towards Colin.

"Sacred Mother Oracle; with humility I supplicate to thee." Brother Superior began, with an inclination of his head. "Thou'st heard the witchen's words?"

After a delay of a few seconds, the looking-glass glowed with an unnatural light, and Thessu watched it slowly resolve to an image in the glass. The wispy tendrils of light coalesced to form the outline of a giant snake, and Thessu fought the urge to look away as well; in his culture it was forbidden to look upon a Naja.

Long held to be sacred in the southern continent, Naja hatched from the eggs of the giant cobras they resembled, but that resemblance ended soon after they hatched, for Naja were no mere snakes. Far bigger and far more intelligent than any giant cobra, and bestowed with long life and powerful gifts to match the rarest that humans ever received, the Naja were held to be sacred for good reason. Mother Oracle, the seer who founded his order, was an ancient and powerful Naja.

The wispy light writhed in the glass as Mother Oracle flicked out her forked tongue and slowly nodded her great flat head. There was again a delay of a few seconds, then she spoke, her words a rasping hiss.

"The boy wouldst ssspin the heavens but dessstruction is the price of such upheaval. The outcome isss... uncertain, but the price isss not. The desssruction that was heralded mussst not occur. The realms mussst not unite. The sssun mussst not ssset on Twilight."

Thessu relaxed a little; at least Mother Oracle was not about to order Colin's death upon the Ziggurat. Thessu had delivered that baby boy, he was not about to allow him to be murdered. Then he tensed again when he realised what might be coming next.

"I humbly concur," Brother Superior replied. "Dost thou wish the boy protected?"

There would be another delay of a few seconds before Mother Oracle's reply reached through the glass to them, and Thessu took that brief moment to prepare himself for what he must do if he didn't like the answer. In that instant, he finally understood the meaning of the tenth mantra, and what exactly he would have to sacrifice to maintain the purity of his purpose. In that instant he finally understood his purpose.

"No…" Mother Oracle began, and Thessu didn't wait for her to finish.

He covered the rubble-strewn ground in a flash, reaching Brother Superior before the senior monk could react. Thessu struck him, and immediately felt his momentum redirected as Brother Superior spun expertly out of the way, drawing him forwards with one arm across the back of his shoulders and the other wrapping over his leading arm. As Thessu stumbled forwards, Brother Superior pivoted, releasing his grip from Thessu's leading arm as he changed direction, slamming his now outstretched arm back into Thessu's onrushing face, crushing the beak of his mask and propelling his head backwards.

With his lower half still travelling forwards and his upper half slammed back, Thessu's body back-flipped, his legs flying up over his head. The top of his head hit the ground hard, and his body – still spinning – slammed down behind it, dropping him onto his face. His leather beak mask crumpled; it had split open all down its length.

He looked up through cracked and broken goggles to watch the silver looking-glass still sailing through the air; Thessu had knocked it out of the senior monk's hand exactly as he had intended. The looking-glass struck a pillar and shattered, spraying broken fragments of glass in all directions. His mentor had floored him easily, but Thessu had achieved his objective. They would not get to hear the rest of Mother Oracle's judgement.

Thessu released the tension he had been holding in one long breath. He had been confident that Mother Oracle would oppose Citrine; that she would want to preserve order in the world and reject the chaos and destruction that would come from Citrine's plan to free the sun to move across the sky. But Thessu had realised that was only part of it.

Mother Oracle also had another choice to make. She would either act to protect Colin so he couldn't be killed at the Ziggurat, or she would act to *ensure* he couldn't be killed there; by ordering him taken out of the city and killed as far from the Ziggurat as possible. As soon as she'd said 'No' to the question of whether to protect him, Thessu knew she meant to order the boy taken away and killed.

He had dashed the looking-glass out of Brother Superior's hands so he couldn't receive that order. Thessu's purpose, he realised, was to protect the boy he had delivered; and that purpose demanded he sacrifice his vows to the Order of Mercy. His sacrifice had bought them time.

Brother Superior watched the looking-glass shatter as well. "You think that will distract me from my duty?" he raged. "We both know what the reverend Mother was about to say!" He dropped his body weight onto Thessu's back, pressing him down into the rubble.

"Yes... she was about to remind you that the rich and beautiful are also worthy of love," Thessu replied facetiously, quoting one of the mantras.

"Insolence!" the senior monk fumed. "She was going to insist the boy be taken from La Crosse and killed far from the Ziggurat!"

All the others bristled at that; Remy and Valanthé still flanked Colin protectively, while the Baron and Gerard – and yes even Epifani – pressed forwards threateningly with weapons held ready. Gerard's wound was still only half-sewn; the needle and thread dangled absurdly from the big man's shoulder. Thessu raised one hand to halt them, and with his other he pulled his crushed and broken mask aside so he could better address Brother Superior.

"Are you certain?" Thessu asked his mentor. "The boy's fate seems pretty important, should you not double-check that really is her will before you do something that might endanger the realm?"

Brother Superior sighed ruefully. "Only a fool is certain," he muttered, then he stood, lifting his weight off of Thessu, and helped him to his feet. Their eyes met and Thessu saw something new in his mentor's gaze. Or rather, he saw the absence of something old. Brother Superior was no longer disappointed. He was cross though. That hadn't changed.

Wordlessly, the senior monk circled a finger in the air, and the Crusaders gathered their weapons and their wounded and quickly left the way they had entered, scaling ropes up to the galleries and on up to the roof through the broken windows. Brother Superior was the last to leave, his gaze lingering on Thessu. Then he too turned and left. In the end, Thessu had proved him right; he was not cut out to deliver the mercy that the Order demanded, and they both knew it.

"Goodbye Dad," Thessu said under his breath as he watched the man who raised him leave the chamber. When next they met, they would surely be enemies.

***

"We should go as well," Valanthé urged. "There are plenty more Dandolo corpses in the palazzo, and no doubt the household has summoned sheriff's deputies." In fact she was surprised they weren't there already; Citrine must have warned her retainers to avoid this wing of the palazzo and ignore sounds of combat. Even the most dedicated retainers had their limits though; the combat had been exceptionally loud and destructive, and Citrine had been killed.

"We didn't decide what to do with the martyr," Epifani insisted.

Valanthé had never liked Epifani, but even she was surprised at how quickly the woman had turned on their young companion. Was Colin now just a martyr to be sacrificed? Just a means to an end for her?

"He ain't no martyr!" Remy retorted before Valanthé could voice her own disapproval at Epifani's use of the term. "An' we ain't goin' let you kill him!"

"But you must see that uniting the realms is the right thing to do?" Epifani pleaded.

"Can we maybe discuss this later?" Valanthé suggested, keen to get away from the palazzo.

"No, we're discussin' this now," Remy replied firmly. "An' the answer is no, Epifani. We ain't goin' listen to the last words of a crazy old witch, an' we ain't goin' kill Colin, an' we ain't goin' traipse the world searchin' for far-off fantasy lands that probably don't exist! Our job now is the same as it was before; to protect that child from the people who want to kill him. An' if that means I got to protect him from you, then I'll cut you down right now with a happy song in my heart."

"As will I," Gerard said, hefting his axe once more and stepping towards Epifani.

"My dear lady, you must see reason," the Baron said, stepping between them and Epifani. "We didn't save him from Citrine's evil scheme to then enact her evil scheme ourselves!"

Epifani narrowed her eyes at him. "It's not evil!" she spat. "Universal undeath is evil! Citrine has found a way to end that practice!" She turned to Thessu then. "What was that stupid mantra you're always quoting? Purity of purpose requires sacrifices or something like that? Surely at least you agree with me that uniting the realms is worth a little sacrifice?"

Thessu unbuckled the strap of his broken mask, and removed it. His features, still ringed by the indent where it had been tightly sealed to his face, were pale and puzzled with wrinkles. He took a long last look at his broken mask, then discarded it without hesitation. "No," he replied. "I won't kill him to prevent the realms uniting, and I won't kill him to unite the realms. In short, I won't kill him."

Epifani looked to Valanthé then. "And I suppose you're against me as well?"

Valanthé considered for a moment. She was intrigued by the idea of exploring beyond the edge of the world and maybe finding her father. But she didn't agree with sacrificing anyone.

Before she could answer, Colin spoke up. "Surely I get a say? I think maybe we should consider uniting the realms."

Remy rounded on him incredulously. "Colin! you know that means you got to die, right?"

Colin nodded tentatively. "I can't explain it, but it feels at least possible that it might be the right thing to do?"

"Exactly!" Epifani exulted. "You heard him; it's the right thing to do! Come on Colin, let's get you to the Ziggurat before those damn monks come back!"

"Absolutely not!" the Baron said, blocking Epifani from reaching towards Colin.

"But you heard him," Epifani protested, "He wants to die to save the world!"

"He is fourteen years old!" Gerard roared. "He doesn't get to make that decision!"

"Please, let me finish," Colin said meekly. "I don't want to die yet and I haven't made any decision. But nobody said I had to be the first to be sacrificed..."

Valanthé smiled broadly, understanding what the kid was suggesting. She placed a calming hand on Remy's shoulder and another on Gerard's. "He's right, we can go to these other realms first and see for ourselves if Citrine was telling the truth."

"Exactly!" Colin exclaimed. "I want to see the world before I die to save it!"

CHAPTER 36

The extent of the fire damage was visible before they even arrived at Isla Festa. The mangrove trees that surrounded the manor were all burned back to blackened stumps while the manor itself – usually visible through the trees – was conspicuous by its absence.

The Baron didn't feel the familiar weight of his ancestors as he walked up to the ruin from the old boat house, his boots squelching in the mud as he walked through the light drizzle that was falling from an ashen Twilight sky.

When the remains of the manor came into view, he stopped dead, shocked by the scale of the destruction. The outline of the house was marked by a skeletal framework of charred and broken beam stumps, which jutted out from the pile of masonry rubble the house had become. All of it was shrouded in a thick black coating of cold wet ashes.

The Baron clasped his grandmother's knitting bag and its precious contents – the few heirlooms of his ancestors that Gerard had rescued – and held it close.

"Maybe you can rebuild?" Valanthé suggested. She and the others had walked up behind him.

The Baron shook his head, looking towards the exposed entrance to the crypt. It was obvious that the manor had collapsed into the catacombs below, and it was unlikely that anything had survived the cave-in. "No, dear lady," he replied sadly. "My ancestors are no longer there. And besides, I don't have the livres for rebuilding."

The Baron turned to face his comrades then, knowing what he had to do, and gulped down the lump in his throat. "No, I will sell the islet and we can put the funds towards our expedition."

"Are you sure, Baron?" Valanthé asked, surprised.

The Baron was sure. With no wife and no heirs and with only remnants of his ancestors remaining, he really would be the last De Ville, and he now carried his father's pocket watch and his crushing disappointment everywhere he went in a canvas knitting bag. He knew he would never be worthy of his family's approval but maybe he could still achieve something of renown with his life. And just maybe he could find a way to restore Belladonna and appease his father's fury.

"Yes," he replied determinedly. "We are going to need a ship and a crew and provisions for a lengthy voyage if we're going to find these other realms and go there."

"If these other realms even exist," Remy grumbled. "An' if it's even possible to go there."

"Well, we're going to need plenty of funds regardless if we're going to look," the Baron replied.

"Will it be enough?" Colin asked.

The Baron shrugged. "I have no idea my dear boy. I have never mounted an expedition before, this will be the first time for any of us. I'm sure it will be quite an adventure!"

"Does she really have to come with?" Gerard asked, indicating Epifani, who was lingering back with a sour expression.

Epifani, overhearing, shot him an icy glare. "You're not leaving me behind; I'm not letting that kid out of my sight!"

The Baron ignored the bickering. They had already had this argument more than once since they left Palazzo Fandandolin. Epifani had begrudgingly agreed with Colin's proposal that they seek out the other realms and learn the truth of Citrine's claims, before any decision was made about uniting the realms and freeing the sun. Epifani seemed to have already made up her mind that Colin should be sacrificed, but away from the city she would protect him with her life. He was no good to her if he died anywhere other than the Ziggurat.

Pacing away from the others through the saturating drizzle, the Baron slowly worked his way around the fringes of the rubble pile, picking up and discarding fragments of charred wood and stone from the shroud of muddy black ashes that surrounded the ruined house. None of it was recognisable. Then he turned a corner past the ruin of the kitchen, and he saw Jeff and Rufus.

They were in a small cleared area that was probably where the kitchen courtyard had been, surrounded by high piles of rubble and debris. They each sat sullenly on a small heap of wreckage; Jeff the ancient corpse butler atop the blackened fragments of the pianoforte,

Rufus the alligator nestled amidst a small collection of broken and ruined shoes.

The alligator saw the Baron first, and grunted with pleasure at the sight of him, his huge leathery tail swaying side-to-side in great sweeps. He rumbled forwards, and the Baron petted him gently as the great beast nuzzled at his hands. "I'm happy to see you too," the Baron said, and indeed he was; a tear was trickling down his cheek among the raindrops.

The alligator mournfully gestured its head towards the sad pile of burned and broken shoes – the few treasures he had managed to salvage from the wreckage – and the Baron sympathised with just how wretched the beast felt.

Jeff rose then from his own sad heap with a crack of stiff and rigid joints, and the Baron saw the corpse's charred left arm now ended at the wrist. Clearly, after the Baron had left him with the fire still raging, he had returned to the blaze to salvage more of his precious instrument. His hand was gone and all the skin above that joint had flayed off to leave bare blackened bone beneath, and the fire had scorched more of him besides. He looked as pitiful as the broken fragments of the pianoforte he had been sat on, and the neatly arranged row of broken black and white piano keys laid out beside it.

The Baron considered the two of them. Apart from Belle, the corpse and the beast had been his closest companions since he first returned from his hundred-year sojourn on the Queen of the South. For more than a year, they had been at his side. They were family. But there was nothing for them here now that the manor was destroyed, and there was no place for them on the expedition he would be embarking on. He embraced them both tightly. It was time to say farewell.

He caressed the butler's decrepit face, gently brushing aside his last lank lock of hair in much the same way he had done when they had first met. Then, with the blade of a pocket knife, he prised the tarnished copper marque from Jeff's forehead. Loosened by fire and years of decay, it came away easily. "It is my great pleasure to have been your friend, my dear Jeff," the Baron said sadly. "Corpse J, I release you from your bondage."

The corpse opened its jaw once, as if to speak, then the taut muscles of its face pulled its lips into what might have been a smile. And then it was gone. What remained of its skin flaked and broke apart like dry leaves as the Baron lowered its disanimated bones back down onto the sodden heap that was once a pianoforte.

Rufus moaned forlornly and the Baron pulled him close, his arms wrapping round the great beast's neck for one last embrace. "It is my great pleasure to have been your friend also, my dear Rufus." The Baron's words caught in his throat, and he continued in barely a whisper. "I release you as well."

The wild alligator immediately bucked and pulled away sharply. It snapped at him in fear and anger, then bolted away, headed for the swamp and for the familiar company of its own kind, trampling across the pile of shoes – its former treasures – in its haste to escape. The Baron watched it disappear into the reeds without it giving him a backwards glance.

He picked up one of the discarded piano keys and one of the sequined shoes and placed them in the canvas knitting bag amongst the other heirlooms of his family. Then he sat down and wept, and imagined the inanimate doll in his pocket embracing him and weeping as well.

***

"Valanthé Luxalim!" a voice called out loudly. Valanthé turned to see three men approaching from the boat house jetty. The one who had spoken – a well-dressed man in a dark turquoise tabard – was reading from a scroll. The two men who flanked him wore the light blue coats and tricorn hats of city deputies, and had muskets readied.

"Remy Du Rosier, Baron De Ville, Gerard Malblanq," the man in turquoise continued, squinting at the scroll which was no doubt getting soaked by the driving rain.

"Oh shit," Remy said, alarmed. "Are we bein' arrested again?"

Valanthé reached for the hilt of her longsword. She hadn't much liked getting arrested the first time. Perhaps they would need to leave La Crosse far sooner than she thought.

"Lady Epifani Pye, Thessu of the Order of Mercy and Salvatoré Du Laurentin also known as Colin," the man concluded, rolling up his scroll. "His excellency the Dogé of La Crosse, Jean Michel Don

A'Tellio, requests the pleasure of your company at the Corto Dogé for coffee and a conversation at your earliest convenience."

"Oh shit," Remy said, even more alarmed. "That can't be good!"

"We're not under arrest?" Colin queried.

"Not yet," Valanthé replied warily, her hand still resting on the hilt of her sword. "I think that probably depends on what the Dogé thinks about the death of one of his Caballiers."

The man in turquoise – the livery of the Corto Dogé, Valanthé realised – wore a forced smile. "Will you all please come with me?" he urged. "I have a barge waiting to take you all to the Dogé now."

"But he said we could come when it was convenient," Colin replied, sounding affronted. "Right now is not terribly convenient, but perhaps we could fit him in… maybe next month?"

The man from the Corto Dogé looked at him askance and Remy sighed. "No, Colin. When the Dogé says 'at your convenience' he means 'right goddamn now'."

Valanthé loosened the grip on her sword and followed after Remy who had started towards the men. "Come on, Remy's right; let's get it over with. The next summons probably won't be so polite."

"Where's the Baron?" Gerard asked, looking around.

"He's coming," Thessu replied, sniffing the air. "And he's stopped crying, which is good."

The Baron joined them as they passed the boat house. His eyes did indeed look puffy like he might have been crying, which wasn't too surprising given the destruction of his house. Valanthé thought about consoling him, but he wore his jaunty smile like a mask, so clearly didn't want to talk about it. She would catch him later when the others weren't around, and she would keep an eye on him in case his jaunty smile ever slipped.

The man from the Corto Dogé led them to his boat. Not just any boat; he'd come in an enormous river barge with a glossy white hull and a gilded golden roof, manned by a team of skeleton corpses, their bones enamelled in turquoise mosaic. It was considerably larger and more luxurious even than the one they had taken from Palazzo Fandandolin. A pair of trumpeters either side of the gangplank played a fanfare as they boarded.

"Any idea what the Dogé wants wi' us," Remy asked the courtier as he stepped aboard.

The man broadened his fake smile and gestured for them all to take seats under the gilded canopy. "I'm sure his excellency will make all that clear once you are brought before him."

Valanthé was pleased to be out of the drizzle at least, and pushed in front of Epifani to prevent her from taking the driest seat for herself. Valanthé smiled as Epifani glowered at her. She considered it was probably a good sign that they were sat under cover at all; the men from the court took their places on the open deck in front of the canopied section.

The trumpeters played another fanfare and the turquoise skeleton corpses pushed off from the jetty, turning the barge to face west. Ahead, the core islands were obscured by the rain but the hazy green glow of the city still lit the way across the delta. Behind the dirty green glow of La Crosse, the ever-setting sun was just now peeking out between the slate-grey clouds on the western horizon, silhouetting the city and silvering the wave-tips of the surrounding water.

The ever-setting sun, Valanthé thought. She couldn't imagine it ever being anywhere else in the sky, and she had so many questions. If the sun moved across the sky, wouldn't trees and plants grow in a spiral as the light drew them in different directions? wouldn't a rising and falling sun make temperatures fluctuate wildly? And how could ships travel in open water without a fixed beacon to navigate by? She yearned to find out the unfathomable answers to those questions and many more.

The gilded barge skirted to the south of Isla Verdé and on past the cliffs of Isla Roja that they had so recently left. Valanthé craned her neck to catch sight of Palazzo Fandandolin high above, but the palazzo was concealed by the rim of the cliffs. The barge continued northwards along the coastline on the far side of the island, where it approached a covered wharf. The Dogé's private wharf, Valanthé guessed. The Corto Dogé really was exceedingly close to the palazzo of the house of Dandolo.

"We should have come straight here and saved ourselves the detour back and forth," Epifani grumbled.

The barge glid up to a berth alongside the covered wharf amidst further fanfare from the trumpeters aboard the barge, and a return fanfare from a second pair on the dockside. Sheriff's deputies stood to attention with shouldered muskets at intervals all along the wharf, while liveried Risen footmen of the court stood ready with guide ropes and boarding planks and long lantern poles and silver trays of refreshments. Refreshments were another good sign, Valanthé thought, and she helped herself to a goblet of hot wine and a sweet pastry as she disembarked.

"Ugh! you get away from me!" Epifani squealed, as one of the corpses attempted to hand her a goblet. Valanthé watched her push the goblet aside, and the warm red liquid sloshed out onto the deck of the wharf. The corpse clacked its jaw in apology and Valanthé smirked as it and two more corpses then bustled over to wipe at Epifani with handkerchiefs where some droplets of wine had splattered on her clothes. Epifani squealed again, completely aghast at being manhandled by three corpses. Then Thessu stumbled past uncharacteristically clumsily, and another goblet somehow tipped over to splash on her as well.

Once they extricated themselves from the press of apologetic corpses, the Risen footmen led them along the wharf to the base of the cliffs, where a switchback flight of stairs rose up the side of the cliff to the Corto Dogé high above. They were in good humour as they climbed the stairs; Epifani provided endless entertainment when Risen were nearby. The rain had worsened and she refused the services of an umbrella corpse, so by the time they reached the top, she was soaked.

At the top of the cliff, the stairs arrived at a cloistered courtyard of translucent white marble. They crossed the courtyard to a grand entrance of the main Corto Dogé building, in the shadow of the great ruby dome. The liveried Risen footmen passed them over to a cadre of turquoise-mosaic skeleton corpses, these more prestigious chaperones led by a clearly ancient turquoise skeleton corpse with aquamarine gemstones set into its face and odd golden tubes protruding from between its ribs. Valanthé had seen such a corpse pushing the Dogé's wheelchair at their trial. Could it be the same one? The Dogé's chief corpse steward perhaps?

Epifani balked again as the turquoise skeletons made to form an honour guard around them.

"Oh, that's okay," Remy told them good-naturedly, "she jus' a lil' embarrassed 'cause she so wet. Could you maybe get some towels and towel her down a lil' some?"

"Don't you goddamn dare!" Epifani countered. "I swear I'll disanimate the next goddamn stiff that tries to touch me!"

The ancient aquamarine skeleton gave them an unamused glare – a look that was unnaturally lifelike for a corpse – instantly sobering their jovial mood. Then it spoke.

Its jaw opened unnaturally wide to reveal a concertina of folded leather with the appearance of an accordion. The mechanism sucked air down to its chest, where it whistled out from the tubes that projected from between its ribs; not gold but brass. The skeleton dextrously covered five of the tubes in sequence with its bony fingers as air pumped through, and the tubes produced five sounds – phonemes – which melded together to form an artificial facsimile of speech; hollow and guttural and grating. It sounded like death.

FOLLOW, it said.

They looked at each other, astonished. The skeleton and its mechanical voicebox were quite remarkable. Epifani looked like she was about to explode with anger and revulsion. Gerard and Remy restrained her from attacking the Doge's chief corpse steward.

The corpse led them along a long marble hallway with a colonnade of gilded columns either side, and on to a grand antechamber with some over-sized uncomfortable-looking white marble benches.

WAIT, it said, gesturing at the chairs. Then it left.

The bench was indeed uncomfortable. Did palazzo architects not consider comfort at all when designing their masterpieces? The décor here was much like it had been in Palazzo Fandandolin – the rich of La Crosse really did like white marble and gold, Valanthé mused – but here it was even grander and more austere. She could never picture herself living in a place like this.

The aquamarine skeleton quickly returned, and indicated that they should follow it once more. They were led through another long marble hallway and up a flight of marble stairs to a grand double door, with two enormous turquoise-mosaic skeleton corpses standing guard either side, holding long golden halberds. The corpses snapped to attention as the aquamarine skeleton threw the doors open.

ENTER, it said, gesturing them through. Valanthé shuddered. Even she had to admit the corpse was creepy.

Beyond the doors was a surprisingly modest sitting room; not exactly cramped but on a far more normal scale than everything else Valanthé had seen of the palace. It was nicely decorated for comfort, with brightly-coloured soft furnishings and upholstery. Eight comfortable-looking armchairs surrounded a low coffee table, and an old man sat in one of the armchairs. Valanthé recognised him as Jean-Michel Don A'Tellio, the Dogé of La Crosse.

***

When Remy last saw the Dogé, he had looked frail and unwell, and had needed an ear trumpet and a wheelchair. He still looked old, but no longer frail. He looked hale and hearty.

"Ah, greetings!" the Dogé said, with unexpected warmth. "It is a pleasure to welcome you to my home!"

Then the Dogé stood and walked gingerly over to greet them, holding out a hand, which Remy shook, surprised to find the man had a firm grip. His health seemed quite remarkably improved. The aquamarine skeleton bowed and departed, closing the doors behind it, as the Dogé greeted the others and then gestured towards the armchairs. "Please, do take a seat."

"Your excellency," Remy said, holding the Dogé's chair out for him. "Might I enquire about your health? You seem quite remarkably improved since we last saw you!"

"Ah yes, it's the strangest thing," the Dogé replied as he took his seat. The others – apart from Epifani of course – all waited for the Dogé to sit before they joined him around the low table.

"For months my health has been deteriorating," the Dogé continued, "like the life was being suffocated out of me somehow… and then all of a sudden I woke up this evening, and felt fine! Like I'd broken free of a crushing death grip. My doctors can't explain it!"

Remy exchanged a knowing look with Gerard and the Baron. The Dogé no longer felt suffocated by a crushing death grip; he probably hadn't felt so since they freed his effigy from the binding of Risen entrails. The old man looked to a side door which opened then. "Ah, here comes the coffee!"

A man entered the room from the side door, carrying a tray with a black coffee pot and eight little cups. A man with a kindly face, which Remy recognised. It was one of his father's human faces; the face the devil wore to sit on the Cabal. Caballier Giovani.

Giovani – his father – looked chagrined at having to fetch coffee, and irritatedly placed the tray on the table, then seemed to notice that there were not enough chairs for him to join the group, so he narrowed his eyes at Remy, willing him to give up his chair so the devil could sit. Remy sat back in the chair, crossing his legs defiantly. The devil – fuming – stood awkwardly to one side.

"Will you not pour it, Giovani," the Dogé asked. "Or do you expect our honoured guests to have to serve themselves?"

Remy watched with amusement as the devil poured coffee for each of them in turn.

Epifani – either not realising that Giovani was a human face of Don Gusteau, or not caring – demanded cream and sugar, and the devil fetched her cream and sugar.

"Now the cake, Giovani," the Dogé urged, and Giovani irritatedly served everyone a slice of cinnamon cake.

"Pardon me your excellency, but might I enquire why you asked us here this evening?" the Baron enquired as he took his slice from Giovani.

The old man dabbed at his mouth with a napkin before answering. "Well I've been following your exploits for a few weeks now, ever since my dear friend Sundra took you under her wing. Some of my advisors suggested that my ill health meant I shouldn't bother myself with such trivial matters, but if the end of the world is a trivial matter then I need better advisors," and here the Dogé looked pointedly at Giovani. "So the child is safe now?" he asked, looking back to the Baron.

Jean-Michel Don A'Tellio was clearly very well informed. "Yes your excellency," the Baron replied with a curt nod.

"Very safe," Remy added with a knowing smile. "That baby will never be seen again, I guarantee it…"

"No, no, don't give me details," the Dogé interjected, waving his hand airily. "I don't need to know where the child is, and I know these walls have ears." Here he again looked pointedly at Giovani for a moment.

"I was very upset to learn that one of my Caballiers was intriguing to harm that child, and I was relieved to hear that they were not successful. No, that child is safest if as few people as possible know his whereabouts, there are still many who want to see him harmed... and many more who wish to use him for their own ends. Indeed, I'm afraid to say my recent bout of ill health has encouraged far too much intriguing from certain members of my Cabal. I'll be putting a stop to that. Oh dear, my fork!"

The Dogé's cake fork innocuously fell to the floor, bouncing under his chair, and he gestured with his eyebrow for Giovani to pick it up. Remy stifled his mirth as his father bent down and retrieved it, glaring daggers at him the whole time while Remy smirked. "No, no! I don't want it back! ...fetch me a new one!" and Giovani skulked off to do that. The devil left the room and Remy suddenly felt a sharp pain in his leg. He startled, looking down to see the fork had appeared there and jabbed him in his thigh. Remy quickly plucked it out of the air with a chuckle. His father really didn't like being made the fool.

"What are your plans now?" the Dogé asked, ignoring Remy's startled yelp. "Will you be staying in La Crosse?" Remy got the distinct impression that the old man knew exactly what was going on, and he knew exactly what their plans were.

"No your excellency," Valanthé answered, "Indeed we plan to mount an expedition to the edge of the world and beyond."

"Oh how exciting!" the Dogé exulted. "You must tell me all about it! ...unless, you know, it concerns Joanna's baby, in which case you must not."

"It does concern him yes," Valanthé replied tentatively.

"Well in which case you must allow me to furnish you with a ship to take you wherever you wish to go," the old man said excitedly.

"That ...would be amazing," Valanthé replied enthusiastically, and Remy shared in her surprise and gratitude.

"Wonderful," the Dogé continued. "I will instruct our faithful Sea Lord to have a ship and crew prepared for a long voyage and placed at your disposal."

"Thank you your Excellency, that is most generous!" the Baron blurted out, and Remy sensed his relief. He then realised just how much his friend had been prepared to sacrifice; he would have sold off everything he had left of his family's home to fund this crazy excursion.

"You don't need to sell the manor now, Baron!" Colin exclaimed.

"Oh, my dear Baron, you were going to sell?" the Dogé interjected.

"I'm afraid so, your excellency. My home was burned down in the recent... conflict with Caballier Dandolo, and I lack the funds to rebuild."

"Burned down, you say? How dreadful!" the old man replied, with a sly smile as the devil returned with a clean cake fork. "You hear that Giovani? the Baron's house burned down."

"Very sad, your excellency," Giovani replied disinterestedly.

"I say Giovani, as Lord of the Isles, don't you have discretionary funds for municipal works on the outer isles?" the Dogé continued.

Giovani was no longer disinterested. "I... do, your excellency, 'owever ze funds are all allocated of course."

"Well I'm sure a small sum can be found to rebuild De Ville Manor, it is after all an important historical monument," the Dogé insisted, and the old man stared down the devil.

The devil flinched first. "But of course, your excellency, I shall see it done."

"Wonderful," the Dogé said.

"Ninety thousand livres ought to do it," Remy interjected slyly.

"Ninety... thousand...!" Giovani stammered.

"Why not make it a nice round hundred?" the Dogé concluded, then he picked up a little silver bell from the table, and rang it. After a moment, the double doors reopened and the aquamarine skeleton corpse stood in the doorway. "Call for the treasurer. Caballier Giovani will be making a pledge of funds," the old man said. "And I require a scribe, I have a message to send to Sea Lord Crosskeys."

YES, the skeleton said, then inclined its head and closed the doors once more.

The old man smiled broadly. "He's a good man, Crosskeys, very loyal. I like him very much. In fact I feel he'd make a fine Dogé when I'm gone."

They made small talk while they finished their coffee and cake, then the Dogé rose, indicating their audience was over. He held out a hand to shake each of their hands once more. "It was a pleasure to meet you all."

Remy shook his hand gratefully. Jean-Michel Don A'Tellio was a remarkably astute old man, and he was very glad to have met him. He risked a last glance at his father, and saw the devil still seething with rage behind his false smile and his false face. Good. Remy let the cake fork drop carelessly onto the floor before he left.

***

"That can't be it can it?" Colin grumbled, nodding towards the little open-decked caravel at the quayside.

It wasn't. He was looking at the wrong ship. Gerard grabbed his shoulders and turned him to face the right direction. The ship they had come to see, was the sleek black wargalley at the end of the quay.

"Oh that's better," he said, brightening.

The ship was moored in a deep-water berth of the ocean docks on the southern side of Isla Verdé, undergoing repairs of some kind. It had a wide beam and three tall masts jutting up from the open deck between fo'c'stle and sterncastle. Below was a galley deck of forty pairs of oars and a gun deck of twenty gun broadside. Bright red sails of the Scarlet Fist were furled on the yard arms of the masts. If this really was the boat that Crosskeys was preparing for them, then both he and the Dogé had been especially generous. Seagulls screeched overhead as they walked curiously along the quay towards the wargalley.

"Why does it look so familiar?" Epifani asked.

Gerard thought it was familiar as well, but he also couldn't place it.

"Isn't it obvious?" Thessu asked. "Look at the bowsprit. The figurehead is missing…"

Gerard followed his gaze and sure enough, the figurehead of the ship was conspicuous by its absence. He puzzled for a moment and then snapped his fingers in recognition. "The Triton!" he announced. "This was the ship that rammed Citrine's galley!"

Remy gasped. "Crosskeys is givin' us his flagship?"

"It looks like it," Valanthé replied, sounding just as surprised.

Gerard took off his hat and rubbed the back of his neck. He hoped the old pirate was giving them a capable crew as well; the Triton was a lot of ship for a group of people with limited experience of sailing. He pulled out the message they had received from Crosskeys and re-read it. He'd told them to come and see the ship he was providing for them and meet its captain. The Baron had blacked out again, but the rest of them had come. The Triton was moored in the berth that Crosskeys had indicated.

"Arr, she's a beauty, ain't she?"

Gerard turned to see Captain Crosskeys approaching along the quay behind them. His parrot was circling overhead, and swooped down to land on his bicorn hat.

"Aak, I'm a beauty," the bird mimicked, hopping down onto the pirate's shoulder.

"You're giving us your flagship?" Gerard asked.

"No, lad," the Sea Lord replied with a chuckle. "I'm *loanin'* ye me flagship. That be an important distinction! I'll be gettin' it back, won't I?"

"Aak, won't be getting it back!"

"That ain't what I said, feathers!" Crosskeys growled at the bird, which was now preening itself disinterestedly.

"It's undergoing repairs?" Valanthé queried, indicating towards the ship's bow where a work crew were suspended over the side of the vessel in a cradle, replacing hull planks below the bowsprit.

"Just superficial damage from the battle," the pirate replied dismissively. "And she needs a new figurehead o' course. She'll be patched up good as new before ye depart."

"But it'll be ready to depart soon?" Valanthé queried.

"Aye, in a couple of weeks."

Gerard exchanged a concerned look with the others. Was the damage worse than Crosskeys implied? They had hoped to depart much sooner than that; they needed to leave the city before the monks returned for Colin.

The pirate held up his hands reassuringly. "Don't worry lads and lasses, the repairs won't delay ye. A two week turnaround gives us a chance to properly prepare the ship for a long voyage. I promise ye, in two weeks ye'll have a fully crewed and provisioned wargalley. Do ye know where yer headin'?"

"West," Valanthé stated determinedly.

Crosskeys raised an eyebrow. "West, eh? Toward the ever-setting sun?"

"Aak! Darkmourn's gone west," the parrot interjected.

Crosskeys chuckled. "Aye, feathers. That 'e did." He grinned broadly, a twinkle in his eye for Valanthé. "So then, shall we go see yer ship, and meet yer captain?"

They walked along the quay towards the ship, and Gerard saw that there were other repairs in progress; crew were replacing blocks and lines and rigging, but none of the damage looked serious to his inexpert eyes.

"Who's the captain?" Colin asked. "Do we know him?"

"Her," Crosskeys corrected, striding forward purposefully. "Her name is Kiki …but I recommend ye don't call her that. Cap'n K is what she prefers."

"Aak! Don't call her Kiki," the parrot added.

"An' don't be fooled by her small stature," Crosskeys urged, grasping the rung of the ladder up to the ship's deck. "Cap'n K is the saltiest pirate in me fleet, an' the strongest an' bravest also."

Gerard followed the old pirate up the ladder. As they stepped over the gunwale, the shout went up, "Admiral on deck!" and the crew on deck all stood to attention.

"As you were, lads," Crosskeys replied.

"Aak! back to work you lazy swab rats."

"Ah, and here comes Cap'n K…" Crosskeys indicated across the deck. Gerard looked, but couldn't see anyone approaching. Remy and Colin, who had just joined them on deck, also craned their necks to get a first glimpse of their new captain.

Then Gerard saw something fluttering in the air. Was that a bird? No; it was leaving a trail of silver sparkles… it was a fairy! Kiki was a fairy!

They all looked stunned towards their tiny captain. She was the first fairy that Gerard – in fact that any of them – had ever seen.

"I told you the Scarlet Fist had a fairy in its ranks," Valanthé said, boarding the ship with a big grin on her face.

"An' we thought you was jus' windin' Colin up!" Remy countered, voicing their shared surprise and wonder.

A normally secretive and insular people, it was remarkable to see a fairy outside of their woodland home; in fact it would be remarkable enough to see one inside their woodland home, so small and reclusive were their kind.

Small enough to fit in Gerard's hand, she nevertheless looked the part of a pirate captain, her tiny form dressed in black combat leathers that were a miniature of Valanthé's, topped with a black tricorn hat. The pale skin of her tiny face was offset by heavy black eye shadow, and as she hovered in place, Gerard saw her delicate wings were patinated with angry silver and black swirls that spilled silver sparkles as they rapidly beat the air. The sparkles glowed faintly as they fell, and then vanished like chaff from fireworks.

Kiki did a crisp salute with a tiny hand, which Crosskeys returned. She then turned to the rest of them and greeted them in a surprisingly loud and assured voice. "Welcome aboard the Twiton," she said, her accent coarse with just the cutest hint of a lisp. "We're on schedule for departure in two weeks. Pwovisions are ordered and I'll be gettin' 'em stowed over the next few eves and buyin' more stiffs. Most of the cwew are signed on alweady, and I'll be pwessgangin' the west and cwackin' heads to get 'em shipshape before we set sail."

They all stood, jaws wide in amazement, as Crosskeys and Valanthé grinned broadly.

"Excuse me," Kiki said, seeming to have spotted something out of place on deck.

"She's adorable," Colin gushed as the fairy flittered away.

Crosskeys threw him a warning look. "I wouldn't say that to 'er either," he replied in a whisper. "Don't call her Kiki and don't call her adorable."

Kiki hovered over to two crewmen who were squeezing past a cannon that was blocking their way, and she yelled at an impossibly loud volume, "If the fuckin' cannon is blockin' the gangway, fuckin' move it, you cwetins!"

As if the yelling and the cursing wasn't incongruous enough, she then effortlessly shoved the heavy cannon aside, and hauled it to its proper location on the deck. She was remarkably strong, and Gerard was impressed. The crewmen, seemingly used to such displays from their captain, saluted her and replied in unison, "Aye, Aye, Cap'n K!"

Kiki returned from admonishing her crew, still leaving a trail of sparkles in her wake, just as Epifani clambered over the gunwale from the quayside to join them.

"Where's this Kiki then?" Epifani asked.

Kiki squared up to her, flitting right up into the woman's face. "That one you get for fwee. But no second chances. Call me Captain K."

Epifani's eyes widened in surprise at the tiny pirate. "Kiki," she exclaimed. "You're a fairy! You're adorable!"

Kiki shoved her, and Epifani went sailing back over the side of the gunwale with arms spinning, to land with a splash in the dirty water of the dock.

"Aak! Don't call her Kiki," the parrot said.

Kiki turned angrily towards the bird. "Cwosskeys, I am not going to miss your wotten pawwot!"

Crosskeys grimaced. "Actually, about that," he said, turning to Valanthé. "This daft bird belonged to Darkmourn. He gave me 'im when he left, now I'm givin' 'im to you. I hope ye find your Da." He plucked the parrot off his shoulder and placed it on Valanthé's. She and the parrot looked very unsurely at each other.

"Here, take 'is treats," Crosskeys added, untying a small pouch from his belt. "But don't give him too many or he'll get fat."

"Aak, walk the plank, fatty!"

Kiki looked aghast at the unwelcome bird, and Crosskeys smiled. "Sorry, K!"

Kiki rolled her eyes, and then grinned. She checked none of her crew could see her, then gave the old pirate a kiss on his bearded cheek.

"Begone with ye, ye'll make an old man blush!" Crosskeys insisted. "Ladies; I'll leave ye to yer ship. I'll be seein yer orf afore ye sail." He accepted another salute, and then clambered down over the gunwale.

Gerard scanned the ship, grinning broadly at their great turn of fortune. It was a good ship; far better even than he'd hoped for. Then he saw her on the deck of the sterncastle; a vision in black. In the black slashed doublet and cape of the guild, she had a patchy growth of new hair on her head where her flowing locks had burned away, and a black half-mask covering the right side of her face where she'd been terribly scarred and lost an eye to the explosion. She had also lost her right arm below the elbow. She had a sadness too, which was by far the biggest difference since he'd last seen her.

"I believe you know our ship's necwomancer?" Kiki said. "She's new to the ship as well; she only joined us yestereve. Donatella Del Towwo Wosso."

Gerard's grin broadened. Donatella! This was going to be an enjoyable voyage...

**

Epifani glowered up from the quayside at the others on the deck of the ship above. She could already tell that this voyage would be intolerable, and wondered why she had let herself be convinced to take the martyr out of the city. She should have taken him to the Ziggurat and done what needed to be done. It was so clear to her that the realms needed to be united, and delaying Colin's sacrifice had been a mistake.

She flicked her hair back, running her hands back through it to squeeze the nasty dock water out. Then she knelt and checked the stiletto in the ankle sheath of her right boot. The simple blade – the gift from Aunt Sundra – was still there. Aunt Sundra had tried to convince her that she always had a choice, and had offered her the blade as a metaphor, to remind her she could choose to ignore Citrine if she wanted.

She looked up at her comrades once more – at their smug faces all laughing at her expense – and questioned her choice, wondering if she shouldn't rather have done more to help Citrine instead of thwarting her.

Surreptitiously, she then checked the other sheath in her left boot. The exquisite stiletto Citrine had given her was still there. Aunt Sundra had been right; she had a choice. But Citrine had been right as well; she could always change her mind.

It was time for her to change her mind. She lifted Aunt Sundra's stiletto out of her right boot and let it drop over the side of the dock, where it disappeared into the murky water.

"Bide your time Epifani," the intruder whispered at the periphery of her mind. "You are on the right path to unite the realms and rid the world of Risen. Stay the course and we will both get what we want."

"I know," Epifani growled through gritted teeth, quelling for now the sinister intruder that spoke into her mind with the voice of Citrine Don Dandolo.

EPILOGUE

EPILOGUE

The air burned the man's throat with every breath he took through the light linen veil that obscured the stark white light beyond. Something moved underneath him. A beast. He was riding a huge beast of some sort, and the overpowering smell of it was at once unpleasant and familiar.

The beast took off suddenly at pace, and the man clung on, taking a panicked grip of a thick tuft of its coarse mane as the beast bucked. The beast lashed its hind legs, and the man felt himself falling. He landed hard on the parched ground and lay stunned for a moment, flat on his back, staring up at the light. He wasn't hurt; merely embarrassed. He was still so useless in this place! The sound of laughter filled his ears and someone loomed over him. It was her. She was a dark silhouette against the bright light of the full sun which shone down from high overhead, but he was sure she was smiling. He loved her smile.

At that instant, the Baron's consciousness returned, and he remembered that snatch of the other life he'd been living in that place where the full face of the sun shone down from above. He knew then that he hadn't been in hell. That alien place with its sun high overhead must be one of the realms that lay beyond the edge of the world; beyond the ever-setting sun.

The story continues in book two:

BEYOND THE EVER-SETTING SUN

ABOUT THE AUTHOR

Matt Phillips is the author of the Ever-Setting Sun series. He is a single parent of three children and one grown-up, all of whom are incredibly supportive of his writing… so long as they don't have to read any of it. When not writing fantasy novels, he can be found doing woodwork or glass fusing or jewellery-making in the log cabin he built in his garden, or working a day job as a software engineer in London. He also snowboards, teaches jujitsu and plays Dungeons & Dragons… and DM'd the campaign upon which these novels are based.

Follow him on socials for details of new releases and for insights and updates and artwork from the realm of Twilight and beyond.

    www.tiktok.com/@matthew.phillips.author

    www.instagram.com/matthew.phillips.author

    www.goodreads.com/author/show/56674927.Matthew_Phillips

    eversettingsun.wordpress.com

ABOUT THE AUTHOR

9 781068 497803